READER'S DIGEST
SELECT EDITIONS

The condensations in this volume
are published with the consent of the authors
and the publishers © 2007 Reader's Digest.

www.readersdigest.co.uk

The Reader's Digest Association Limited
11 Westferry Circus Canary Wharf London E14 4HE

For information as to ownership of
copyright in the material of this book,
and acknowledgments, see last page.

Printed in Germany
ISBN 978 0 276 44226 1

SELECTED AND CONDENSED
BY READER'S DIGEST

THE READER'S DIGEST ASSOCIATION LIMITED, LONDON

CONTENTS

Ex-Marine Joe Pike is as tough as steel, a man of few words and a consummate professional who handles tricky situations without the slightest flicker of emotion. But when he's hired to protect the spoilt daughter of a rich, LA businessman, he not only has to stay on watch around the clock and outmanoeuvre an unidentified enemy, he's also up against the charms of the feisty Larkin Conner Barkley.

THE WATCHMAN
ROBERT CRAIS
9

'Never let the customer get the upper hand,' is rule number one for GP Dr Fingal O'Reilly, and he's quick to pass on the advice to newly trained Barry Laverty when the lad joins his medical practice. O'Reilly's motto may not always work, but Laverty learns more about life, love and what really matters from his older mentor than he ever did at medical school. A delightful glimpse of a rural Ireland in the 1960s.

AN IRISH COUNTRY DOCTOR
PATRICK TAYLOR
147

Wealthy Louisiana residents who want to avoid the expense and emotional trauma of a protracted divorce are being offered a solution by an evil partnership: a greedy lawyer, and a scientist who's developed an undetectable means of murder. Alex Morse of the FBI is on their tails in this new blockbuster from one of the best thriller writers to come out of America's steamy Deep South.

TRUE EVIL
GREG ILES
279

Always expect the unexpected when you open a new collection of Select Editions. While you can rest assured that you'll regularly find your favourite authors, plus a generous share of the best sellers that are grabbing everyone's attention, we like

ONE NIGHT AT THE CALL CENTRE

CHETAN BHAGAT

457

to slip in the occasional surprise. Such as Chetan Bhagat's delightfully entertaining and sparky new novel, *One Night at the Call Centre*. While it's a simple tale that can be devoured in one sitting, it lingers in the memory and packs a big, positive message. So we thought it worth sharing with our Select Editions readers. You may be interested to know that in India, where it was first published, it went straight to the top of the country's best-seller lists.

The cast in the story is very ordinary: six young Indian friends who spend their nights fixing other people's problems down the phone lines of a Delhi call centre. The irony is that they have their own nagging dilemmas, which are always at the heart of their lively nocturnal discussions, and these seem unsoluble until they get a very special call from a most unexpected quarter. To find out more, you'll have to start reading.

When you've had the chance to dip into your latest Select Editions, let us know what you think of Chetan Bhagat's book and the others in the volume. We'd love to hear from you at select_editions@readersdigest.co.uk.

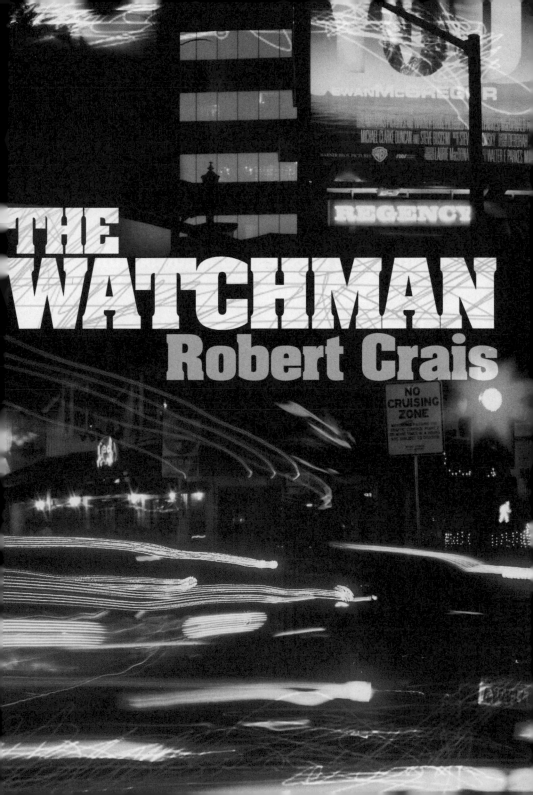

People sometimes stumble
into big trouble unexpectedly,
as Larkin Conner Barkley does
when she crashes her Aston Martin
in the early hours. . .
Her father reacts by putting her
under the 24-hour protection of
Joe Pike. But why does she require
the 'watchman's' services? And
who is out to get her?

PROLOGUE

City of Angels

The city was hers for a single hour, just the one magic hour, only hers. The morning of the accident, between three and four when the streets were empty and the angels watched, she flew east on Wilshire Boulevard at eighty miles per hour, never once slowing for the red lights along that stretch called the Miracle Mile, red after red, blowing through lights without even slowing; glittering blue streaks of mascara on her cheeks.

She would later tell the police she was at a club on Yucca in Hollywood, one of those clubs *du jour* with paparazzi clotted by the door. She had spent an hour seeing her friends (trustfund Westsiders and A-list young Hollywood; actors, agents and musicians she had no problem naming for the police), all taking cellphone pictures of each other and posing with rainbow drinks. The police sergeant who interviewed her would raise his eyebrows when she told him she had not been drinking, but the breathalyser confirmed her story.

Three was her witching hour. She gave a hundred to the valet for her Aston Martin, and red-lined away. Five blocks later—alone—she stopped in the middle of Hollywood Boulevard, shut the engine and enjoyed a cashmere breeze. Jasmine and the scent of rosemary came from the hills. The stillness of the city at this hour was breathtaking.

She gazed up at the buildings, and imagined angels perched on the edge of the roofs watching her as if in an eternal dream: we give you the city. Set yourself free.

Her name was Larkin Conner Barkley. She was twenty-two years old. She lived in a hip loft downtown in an area catering to emerging painters and musicians, not far from the Los Angeles River.

Larkin pushed the accelerator and felt the wind lift her hair. She bore south on Vine, then east on Wilshire again, laughing as light poles flicked past; red or green, she didn't care. Honking horns were lost in the rush. Her long hair, the colour of pennies, whipped and lashed. She closed her eyes, held them closed, then popped them wide and laughed that she still flew straight and true—a $200,000 Tuxedo Black convertible blur, running wild and free across the city. She flashed over the arch at MacArthur Park, then slowed, just barely enough, as she flew over the freeway into the tangle of one-way downtown streets. She ran hard for the river; slowing more, finally, inevitably, as everything rippled and blurred . . .

She told herself it was the dry night wind and lashing hair, the way her eyes filled when her lonely race finished, but it was always the same. For those few minutes running across the city, she could be herself, purely and truly, only to lose herself once more when she slowed . . .

Larkin lurched across Alameda, her speed draining like a wound.

She turned north on an industrial street parallel with the river. Her building was only blocks away when the air bag exploded. The Aston Martin spun sideways, then stopped.

Larkin released her belt and stumbled from the car. A silver Mercedes sedan was on the sidewalk, its rear fender broken and bent. A man and woman were in the front seat, the man behind the wheel. A second man was in the rear. The driver was helping the woman, whose face was bleeding; the man in the back was trying to pull himself up, but unable to rise.

Larkin slapped the driver's side window. 'Are you all right? Can I help?'

The driver stared at her blankly before truly seeing her, then opened his door. He was cut above his left eye.

Larkin said, 'Ohmigod. I'm sorry. I'll call 911. I'll get an ambulance.'

The driver was in his fifties, well-dressed and tanned, with a large gold ring on his right hand and a beautiful watch on his left. The woman stared dumbly at blood on her hands. The back-seat passenger spilled out of the rear door, fell to his knees, then used the side of the car to climb to his feet.

He said, 'We're OK. It's nothing.'

Larkin had to get help for these people. 'Please sit down. I'll call—'

'No. Let me see about you.'

The man from the back seat took a step towards her but sank to a knee. Larkin saw him clearly, lit by the headlights from her car. His eyes were large, and so dark they looked black in the fractured light.

Larkin hurried to her car. She found her cellphone, and was dialling 911 when the Mercedes backed off the sidewalk, its rear fender dragging.

'Hey wait—!'

Larkin called after them again, but they didn't slow. She was memorising their licence plate when she heard the man from the back seat running away hard up the middle of the street.

A tinny voice cut through her confusion. 'Emergency operator, hello?'

'I had a wreck, an auto accident—'

'Was anyone injured?'

'They drove away. This man, I don't know—'

Larkin closed her eyes and recited the licence number. She was scared she would forget it so she pulled out her lip gloss—Cherry Pink Ice—and wrote the number on her arm.

'Ma'am, do you need help?'

Larkin felt wobbly. The earth tilted and she sat in the street.

'Ma'am, tell me where you are.'

Larkin lay back on the cool, hard street. Dark buildings huddled over her like priests in black frocks. She searched their roofs for angels.

The first patrol car arrived in seven minutes; the paramedics three minutes later. Larkin thought it would end that night when the police finished their questions, but her nightmare had only begun.

1

The girl was moody getting out of the car, making a sour face to let him know she hated the shabby house and sun-scorched street. He searched the surrounding houses for threats as he waited for her, clearing the area the way another man might clear his throat. He felt obvious wearing the long-sleeved shirt. The Los Angeles sun was too hot for the sleeves, but he had to hide what was under the shirt.

She said, 'I can't stay here.'

'Lower your voice.'

'I haven't eaten all day and now this smell is making me feel strange.'

'We'll eat when we're safe.'

The house opened and the woman Bud had told him to expect appeared, a squat woman with large white teeth and friendly eyes. Mrs Imelda Arcano managed several rentals in Eagle Rock, and Bud's office had dealt with her before. He hoped she wouldn't notice the four neat holes that had been punched into their left rear fender the night before.

He turned to the girl. 'The attitude makes you memorable. Lose it. You want to be invisible.'

'Why don't I wait in the car?'

Leaving her was unthinkable.

'Don't say anything. Avoid eye contact. Let me handle her.'

The girl laughed. 'I want to see that, you *handling* her. I want to see you *charm* her.'

He took the girl's arm and headed towards the house. To her credit, she fell in beside him without making a scene. Even with her wearing the over-sized sunglasses, he wanted her out of sight as quickly as possible.

Mrs Arcano smiled wider as they reached the front door, welcoming them. 'Mr Johnson?'

'Yes.'

'It's so hot today, isn't it? I'm Imelda Arcano.'

After the nightmare in Malibu, Bud's office had arranged the new house, dropped the cash, and told Mrs Arcano whatever she needed to hear, which probably wasn't much. This would be easy money, low-profile tenants who would be gone in a week. They were to meet Mrs Arcano only so she could give them the keys.

Imelda Arcano beckoned them inside. The man hesitated to glance back at the street. It was narrow and treeless, which was good. He could see well in both directions, though the small homes were set close together, which was bad. The narrow alleys would fill with shadows at dusk.

He wanted Mrs Arcano out of the way as quickly as possible, but she latched on to the girl—one of those female to female things—and gave them the tour, leading them through the two tiny bedrooms and bathroom, the microscopic living room and kitchen, the grassless back yard. He glanced out of the back door at the rusty chainlink fence that separated this house from the one behind it. A white pit bull was chained to a post in the neighbouring yard. It lay with its chin on its paws but it was not sleeping.

The girl said, 'Does the TV work?'

'Oh, yes, you have cable. But there is no telephone. There really is no point in having the phone company create a line for such a short stay.'

He had told the girl not to get into conversation. He cut it off. 'We have our cells. You can hand over the keys and be on your way.'

Mrs Arcano stiffened, peeled two keys from her keyring, then left.

For the first time that day he left the girl alone because he wanted to bring their gear into the house. He wanted to call Bud, to find out what in hell happened back there, but mostly he wanted to make sure the girl was safe. He brought his and the girl's duffles into the house, along with the bag they had grabbed at the Rite-Aid store.

The television was on, the girl hopping through the local stations.

When he walked in, she laughed, then mimicked him. '"*Hand over the keys and be on your way*." Oh, that charmed her. That certainly made you forgettable.'

He turned off the television and held out the Rite-Aid bag.

'Do your hair. We'll get something to eat when you're finished.'

'I wanted to see if we're on the news.'

'Can't hear with the TV. We want to hear. Maybe later.'

'I can turn off the sound.'

'Do the hair.'

He peeled off his shirt. He was wearing a Kimber .45 semi-automatic pushed into the waist of his pants. He opened his duffle and took out a clip holster for the Kimber and a second gun, already holstered, a Colt Python .357 Magnum. He clipped the Kimber onto the front of his pants and the Python on his right side.

He took a roll of duct tape from his bag and went to the kitchen. He made sure the back door was locked, then moved to the tiny back bedroom, locked the windows and pulled the shades. He tore off strips of duct tape and sealed the shades over the windows. If anyone managed to raise a window they would make noise tearing the shade from the wall and he would hear. He took out his Randall knife and made a three-inch vertical slit in each shade, just enough for him to finger open so he could cover the approaches to the house. He heard her go into the bathroom. Finally cooperating. He knew she was scared, so he was surprised she had been trying as hard as she had.

On his way to the front bedroom he passed the bathroom. She was in front of the mirror, cutting away her rich copper hair with the cheap Rite-Aid scissors, leaving two inches of jagged spikes. Boxes of Clairol hair colour lined the sink. She saw him in the mirror and glared.

'I hate this. I'm going to look so bad.'

She had peeled down to her bra, but left the door open. He guessed she wanted him to see. The $500 jeans rode low on her hips below a smiling dolphin jumping between the dimples on the small of her back. Her bra was light blue and sheer, and the perfect colour against her olive skin. Looking at him, she played with her hair. She fluffed the spikes, shaped them, then considered them.

She said, 'What about white? I could go white. That make you happy?'

'Dark. Nondescript.'

'I could go blue. Blue might be fun.' She turned to pose her body. 'Would you love it? Retropunk?'

He continued on to the front bedroom without answering. She hadn't bought blue. She probably thought he hadn't been paying attention, but he paid attention to everything. He locked and taped the front bedroom windows, then returned to the bathroom. The water was running, and she was leaning over the sink, wearing clear plastic gloves, massaging colour into her hair. He took out his cellphone, calling Bud Flynn as he watched.

He said, 'We're in place. What happened last night?'

'I'm still trying to find out. I got no idea. Is the new house OK?'

'They had our location, Bud. I want to know how.'

'I'm working on it. Do you need anything?'

'I need to know how.'

He closed the phone as she stood, water running down the trough of her spine to the dolphin until she wrapped her hair in a towel. Only then did she find him in the mirror again, and smiled.

'You're looking at my ass.'

The pit bull barked.

He did not hesitate. He drew the Python and ran to the back bedroom. He fingered open a slit in the shade as the girl hurried up behind him.

She said, 'What is it?'

'Shh.'

The pit was trying to see something to their left, the flat top of its head furrowed and its nubby ears perked, no longer barking as it tested the air.

Pike watched through the slit, listening hard as the pit was listening.

The girl whispered, 'What?'

The pit exploded with frenzied barking as it jumped against its chain.

Pike spoke fast over his shoulder even as the first man came round the end of the garage. It was happening again.

'Front of the house, but don't open the door. Go. Fast.'

The towel fell from her hair as he pushed her ahead. He hooked their duffles over his shoulder, guiding her to the door. He checked the front window shade. A single man was walking up the drive as another moved across the yard towards the house.

He cupped her face and forced her to see him. She had to see past her fear, and hear him. Her eyes met his and he knew they were together.

'Watch me. Don't look at them or anything else. Watch me until I motion for you, then run for the car as fast as you can.'

He jerked open the door, set up fast on the man in the drive and fired the Colt twice. He reset on the man coming across the yard. The four shots sounded like two—baboombaboom—then he ran to the centre of the front yard. He saw no more men, so he waved out the girl.

'*Go.*'

She ran as hard as she could, he had to hand it to her. Pike fell in behind her, running backwards, staying close to shield her body with his, because the pit bull was still barking. More men were coming.

A third man came round the corner of the house into the drive, saw Pike, then dived backwards. Pike fired his last two shots. Wood and stucco exploded from the edge of the house, but the man had made cover and the Python was dry. The third man popped back and fired three shots, missing Pike, but hitting his Jeep. Pike didn't have time to holster the Python. He dropped it to jerk free the Kimber, pounded out two more shots, then ran for the car. The girl had the driver's door open, but was just standing there.

Pike shouted, 'Get in. *In.*'

Another man appeared at the edge of the house, snapping out shots as fast as he could. Pike fired, but the man had already taken cover.

Pike pushed the girl across the console, jammed the key into the ignition and gunned his Jeep to the corner. He four-wheeled the turn, buried the accelerator, then glanced at the girl.

'You good? Are you hurt?'

She stared straight ahead, her eyes wet. 'Those men are dead.'

Pike placed his hand on her thigh. 'Larkin, look at me.'

She clenched her eyes and kneaded her hands. 'Three men just died. Three more men.'

He made his deep voice soft. 'I won't let anything happen to you. Do you hear me?'

She nodded.

Pike swerved through an intersection, then accelerated onto the freeway. They had been at the house in Eagle Rock for twenty-eight minutes, and now they were running. Again.

BLASTING NORTH on the 101. Pike gave no warning before cutting across four lanes of traffic to the exit ramp. Larkin screamed. They hit the bottom of the ramp sideways, Pike turning hard across oncoming lanes. Horns and tyres shrieked as he turned again up the opposite on-ramp, back the way they had come. The girl was hugging her legs, like they tell you to do when an airplane is going to crash. Pike pushed the Jeep to the next exit, then pegged the brakes at the last moment and fell off again, checking the rearview even as they fell.

The girl moaned. 'Stop it. Stop—Jesus, you're going to get us killed.'

They came out by USC, busy with afternoon traffic. Pike cut in to the Chevron station at the bottom of the ramp, then jammed to a stop. They sat, engine running, Pike pushing bullets into the Kimber's magazine as he studied the passengers in each car coming down the ramp. None acted like killers on the hunt.

He said, 'Did you recognise the men at the house? The one in the front yard, you passed him. Have you seen him before?'

'I couldn't—God, it happened—no.'

She hadn't seen the two he killed earlier, either; just dark smudges falling. Pike himself had barely seen them; coarse men in their twenties or thirties; black T-shirts and pistols.

Pike's cellphone vibrated, but he ignored it. He backed from the end of the building, then turned away from the freeway, picking up speed as he grew confident they weren't being followed.

Ten blocks later, Pike eased into a strip mall, one of those places where the stores went out of business every two months. He turned past the end of the mall into a narrow alley, and saw nothing but dumpsters and potholes. He shut the engine, got out and opened her door.

'Get out.'

She didn't move fast enough, so he pulled her out.

'Hey! What—*stop it*!'

'Did you call someone?'

'*No.*'

He pinned her against the Jeep with his hip as he searched her pockets for a cellphone. She tried to push him away, but he ignored her.

'Stop that—how could I call? I was with you. Stop—'

He snatched her floppy Prada bag from the floorboard and dumped the contents onto the seat.

'You *freak*! I don't have a phone. You took it!'

He searched the pockets, then stared at her, thinking.

'They found us.'

'*I don't know how they found us!*'

'Let me see your shoes.'

He pushed her backwards into the Jeep and pulled off her shoes. This time, she didn't resist. She sank back onto the seat as he lifted her feet.

Pike wondered if they had placed a transponder on her. He checked the heels of her shoes, then looked at her belt and the metal buttons that held her jeans. She drew a deep breath as he pulled off her belt.

She said, 'Like that?'

Pike ignored her smile. It was nasty and perfect.

'Want me to take off my pants?'

He pulled her duffle from the back seat and she laughed.

'You are such a freak. My things haven't been out of my sight since I went with the marshals, you freak! Why don't you *say something*? Why don't you *talk to me*?'

Pike didn't believe he would find anything but he had to check, so he did, ignoring her. He had learned this with the Marines—the one time a man didn't clean his rifle, that's when it jammed.

'Are we just going to stay here? Is it even *safe* here? I want to go home.'

'They almost killed you at home.'

'They've almost killed me *twice* with you. *I want to go home.*'

Pike took out his cellphone and checked his messages. There were three incoming calls from Bud Flynn. He hit his 'send' button to return the calls, and wondered if they were being tracked by his own cellphone. Maybe they knew his number.

Bud answered immediately. 'You scared the hell out of me. I thought you were done when you didn't answer.'

'They found us again.'

'Get outta here. Where are you?'

'Listen. She wants to come home.'

Pike was watching the girl when he said it, and she was staring back.

Bud didn't answer right away, but when he did his voice was soft. 'Now let's take it easy. Let's everybody calm down. Is she safe?'

'Yes.'

'I want to make sure I understand—are you talking about the Malibu house or the house I just sent you to, the one in Eagle Rock?'

Bud had sent them to a safe house in Malibu the night before, then put them onto the Eagle Rock house when shooters hit Malibu.

'Eagle Rock. You gave me two bad houses, Bud.'

'Not possible. They could *not* have known about this house.'

'Three more men died. Do the feds have me covered on this or not?'

Bud already knew about the two in Malibu. The feds had screamed, but promised to cover for Pike and the girl with the locals.

Now Bud didn't sound confident. 'I'll talk to them.'

'Talk fast. I lost one of my guns, the .357. When the police run the numbers, they'll have my name.'

Bud made a soft hiss that sounded more tired than angry. 'OK, put her on.'

Pike held out the phone. The girl put it to her ear, but now she seemed uncertain. She listened for several minutes, and then she spoke once. 'I'm really scared. Can't I come home?'

Pike knew the answer even before she gave back the phone. Here they were in an alley in southeast Los Angeles, the kind of place she flew over in her family's private Gulfstream, all for being in the wrong place at the wrong time.

Pike took back the phone.

Bud said, 'OK, listen—she's good to stay with you. I think that's best and so does her father. I'll line up another house—'

'Your houses are bad. I'll get us a house.'

'Joe—you can't cut me out like this. How will I know—'

'You gave her to me, Bud. She's mine.'

Pike shut off his phone. The girl was watching him.

'If you want to go home, I'll take you home.'

He thought she was thinking about it, but then she shrugged.

'I'll stay.'

'Get in.'

Pike helped her into his Jeep, then studied both ends of the alley. If a witness had his licence plate, the police might already be looking for a red Jeep Cherokee. He wanted to avoid the police, but he couldn't just sit. When you weren't moving you were nothing but someone's target.

The alley was clear. Right now, Pike and the girl were invisible. If he could keep it that way, the girl would survive.

PIKE TURNED INTO the Bristol Farms on Sunset at Fairfax, and parked as far from the intersection as possible, hiding their Jeep.

'I have to call someone. Get out.'

She said, 'Why don't you call from the car?'

'I don't trust my cell. Get out.'

'Can't I wait here?'

'No.'

Pike was concerned she might change her mind about staying with him, take off running and get herself killed.

Larkin hurried round the Jeep to catch up.

'Who are you calling?'

'We need new wheels and a place to stay. If the police are after us, it changes our moves.'

'What do you mean, moves? What are we going to do?'

Pike was tired of talking, so he didn't. He led her to a bank of payphones at the front of the market and pushed quarters into one.

Larkin glanced into the market. 'I want to get something to eat.'

'Later.'

Pike owned a small gun shop in Culver City. He had five employees; three were former police officers.

A man named Ronnie answered on the second ring. 'Gun shop.'

Pike said, 'I'm calling in two.' He hung up.

Larkin squeezed his arm. 'Who was that?'

'He works for me.'

'Is he a bodyguard, too?'

Pike ignored her, watching the second hand circle his Rolex. Ronnie would be walking next door to the laundromat for Pike's call.

While he waited, two men in their late twenties passed on their way out of the market. One of them looked Larkin up and down, and grinned, and the other stared at her face. She looked back at them. Pike tried to read if the second man recognised her. Out in the parking lot they goosed each other before climbing into a black Toyota, so he decided they hadn't.

Pike said, 'Don't do that again.'

'What?'

'Make eye contact like you did with those guys. Don't do it.'

Pike thought she was going to say something, but instead she pressed her lips together and stared into the market.

'I could have gotten something to eat by now.'

At the two-minute mark, Pike made his call and Ronnie picked up. Pike sketched the situation, then told Ronnie to close the shop and send everyone home. The men who wanted Larkin dead would try to find her by finding him, and the people in his life.

Ronnie said, 'I hear you. What do you need?'

'A car and a cellphone. Get one of those prepaid phones.'

'Okey-doke. You can use my old green Lexus, if you want. That OK?'

Ronnie's Lexus was twelve years old. His wife had handed it down to their daughter, who was away at law school, so mostly it sat parked.

Pike told Ronnie to leave the Lexus at an Albertson's they both knew in thirty-five minutes, just leave it and walk away. Thirty-five minutes would give Pike time to hit his condo before ditching the Jeep.

He hung up, and walked the girl back to his Jeep. He felt the passing minutes like a race he was losing. Speed was everything. Speed was life.

She pulled at his arm. 'You're walking too fast.'

'We have a lot to do.'

'Where are we going?'

'My place.'

'Is that where we're going to stay?'

'No. The shooters are going there, too.'

Pike lived in a condominium complex in Culver City. A stucco wall surrounded the grounds, with gates that required a magnetic key. The condos were arranged in four-unit pods laid out around two tennis courts and a pool. Pike's unit was set in a far back corner, shielded from the others.

Pike drove directly to his complex, but didn't enter the property. He circled the wall, looking for anyone who might be watching the gates or watching out for his Jeep, then turned into the rear drive.

Larkin looked around at the buildings. 'This isn't so bad. How much money do bodyguards make?'

Pike said, 'Get on the floor under the dash.'

'Can I get something to eat at your place?'

'You won't be getting out of the car.'

Pike knew she rolled her eyes even without seeing it, but she slithered down under the dash.

'When men ask me to go down like this, it's usually for something else.'

Pike glanced at her. 'Funny.'

'Then why don't you smile? Don't bodyguards ever smile?'

'I'm not a bodyguard.'

Pike drove to the small lot where he normally parked. Only three cars were in the lot, and he recognised all three. He stopped, but did not shut the engine. The grounds were landscaped with palm trees, hibiscus and sleek birds-of-paradise and cement walks wound between the palms. Pike studied the play of greens and browns and colours against the stucco walls. He saw nothing out of the ordinary, so he shut the engine.

'I'll be thirty seconds. Stay here. Don't move.'

Pike slipped out of the Jeep before she could answer and trotted up the walk to his door. He checked the two deadbolt locks and found no sign of tampering. He let himself in and went to a touch pad in the wall. Pike had installed a video-surveillance system which covered the entrance to his home, the ground floor windows and the parking lot. Each of the six cameras made a digital capture every eight seconds.

Pike armed the alarm, let himself out and trotted back to the Jeep.

Larkin was still under the dash. 'What did you do?'

'I don't know anything about these people. If they come here, we'll get their picture and I'll have something to work with.'

'Can I get up?'

'Sure.'

When they passed through the gate, Pike turned towards the Albertson's.

Larkin climbed out from under the dash and fastened her seat belt. She looked calmer now. Better. Pike felt better, too.

She said, 'What are we going to do now?'

'Get the new car, then a safe place to stay. We still have a lot to do.'

'If you're not a bodyguard, what are you? Bud told my father you used to be a policeman.'

'That was a long time ago.'

'What do you do now? When someone asks, say you're at a party or a bar, and you're talking to a woman you like, what do you tell her?'

'Businessman.'

Larkin laughed, but it was high-pitched and strained.

'I grew up with businessmen. You're no businessman.'

Pike wanted her to stop talking, but he knew the fear she had been carrying was heating the way coals heat when you blow on them. This was a quiet time, and the quiet times in combat were the worst. You might be fine when hell was raining down, but in those moments when you had time to think, that's when you shook like a wet dog in the wind. Pike sensed she was feeling like the dog.

'Whatever I am, I won't hurt you, and I won't let anyone else hurt you.'

'You promise?'

'Way it is.' He smoothed the spiky hair still coarse with fresh colour.

She didn't say anything more for a while, and Pike was thankful for the silence.

THE GREEN LEXUS was waiting in the parking lot, just another car in a sea of anonymous vehicles. Pike parked the Jeep in the nearest available space. He fished under the dash, pulled out a holstered .40-calibre Smith & Wesson and dropped it into Larkin's lap.

'Put this in your purse.'

'I'm not touching it. I hate guns.'

He reached under the passenger-side dash, and came out with a .380 Beretta pocket gun and a plastic box containing loaded magazines. He dropped them into her lap, too.

She said, 'Ohmigod, what kind of freak are you?'

He went back under the dash a last time for a sealed plastic bag containing two thousand dollars and credit cards and a driver's licence showing his face in the name of Fred C. Howe. He put the bag into her lap with the guns.

Pike got out and carried their bags to the Lexus, then went to the left front tyre where Ronnie had hidden the key. He loaded their bags into the Lexus, then locked the Jeep and left the key in the same place under the tyre. Ronnie would return for the Jeep later.

Larkin watched Pike with her arms crossed.

'What are we going to do now?'

'First step, get in the car.'

Pike wedged the Kimber under his right thigh, butt out, ready to go. Ronnie had left the phone and a note on the driver's side floorboard. Along with the phone was a charger and an earpiece for hands-free calling.

Larkin said, 'I am *so* starving. Could we *please* get something to eat?'

Pike studied the phone to figure it out, then fired up the Lexus and backed out, already thumbing in the number of a real-estate agent he knew.

'Not yet.'

Larkin coloured with irritation. 'This is *absurd*! I'm so hungry my stomach is eating itself.'

Pike had to get them a place to hide. He had considered a motel, but a motel would increase their contact with people and contact was bad. They needed privacy in a neighbourhood where no one was likely to recognise the girl. They needed immediate occupancy with no questions asked, which meant Pike could not do business with strangers. He had once helped the real-estate agent deal with an abusive ex-husband, and had since bought and sold several properties through her.

When Pike had her on the line he described what he needed. Larkin was slumped against the door on her side of the car, arms crossed and sullen.

She said, 'Help! Help! He's raping me! Help!'

The real-estate agent said, 'Who's that?'

'I'm baby-sitting.'

Larkin leaned closer to the phone. 'And now he won't feed me! *I'm starving to death!*'

Pike cupped the phone so he could continue. 'Can you find me a house?'

'I think I have something that will work. I'll have to get back to you.'

Pike ended the call, then glanced at the girl. She was glaring at him through her dark glasses as if she was waiting to see what he would do. Testing him, maybe. Everything Pike knew about this girl had been told to him by Bud Flynn and the girl's father, and now he knew that Bud's information could not be trusted.

'What's your name?'

She took off her glasses and frowned at him as if he was retarded. 'What are you talking about? Is this some kind of game?'

'What's your name?'

Her face flattened in frustration. 'LARKIN CONNER BARKLEY!'

'Your father?'

'CONNER BARKLEY! MY MOTHER IS DEAD! HER NAME WAS JANICE! I'M AN ONLY CHILD! FUCK *YOU*!'

Pike pointed at her purse. 'Licence and credit cards.'

She didn't object. She snatched up her purse, dug out her wallet and threw it at him. 'Use the cards to buy me some lunch.'

Pike fingered open the wallet and thumbed out her driver's licence. It showed a picture of her with the name Larkin Conner Barkley. Her address showed as a high-rise in Century City, but Bud and her father had described a home in Beverly Hills.

Pike said, 'You live in Century City?'

'That's our corporate office. Everything goes to that address.'

'Where do you live?'

'I got a great loft downtown. We own the building.'

'That where they came for you the first time they tried to kill you?'

'No. I was with my father. In Beverly Hills.'

'Who is Alex Meesh?'

She wilted like a doll melting in the sun. She sank back with her angry confidence gone. 'The man who's trying to kill me.'

Pike had already heard it from her father and Bud, but now he wanted it from her. 'Why does he want you dead?'

She stared out of the windshield at oncoming nothingness. 'I don't know. Because I saw him that night with the Kings. When I had my accident. I'm cooperating with the Justice Department.'

Pike fingered through her credit cards, reading their faces between glances at the road. The cards had all been issued to Larkin Barkley, sometimes with the middle name and sometimes not. Pike pulled out an American Express card and a Visa. The AmEx was one of the special black cards, which indicated she charged at least $150,000 every year. He tossed her wallet back onto the floorboard at her feet.

Pike knew what Bud and her father had told him, but now he wanted to identify the players and find out for himself what was true. He would need help to find out those things, so he dialled another number.

Larkin made a weak smile. 'I hope you're calling for reservations.'

'I'm calling someone who can help us.'

A man answered. 'Elvis Cole Detective Agency.'

'It's me. I'm coming up.'

Pike closed the phone and turned towards the mountains.

2

Thirty-two hours earlier, on the morning it began, Ocean Avenue was lit with smoky gold light from the street lamps and apartment buildings that lined Santa Monica at the edge of the sea. Joe Pike ran along the centre of the street with a coyote pacing him in the shadows on the bluff. It was 3.52 a.m. The Pacific was hidden by night and the earth ended at the crumbling edge of the bluff, swallowed by a black emptiness. Pike enjoyed the peace during that quiet time, running on the crown of the empty street.

He glanced again into the shadows. The coyote loped between the palm trees. It was an old male, its mask white and scarred, come down from the canyons to forage. Every time Pike glanced over, the coyote was watching him, even as it ran. Coyotes had rules for living among men, which was how they flourished in Los Angeles. One of their rules was that they only came out at night. Coyotes probably believed the night belonged to wild things. This coyote probably thought Pike was breaking the rules.

Joe Pike ran this route often: west on Washington from his condo, north on Ocean to San Vicente, then east to Fourth Street where steep concrete steps dropped down the bluff like jagged teeth. One hundred and eighty-nine steps, interrupted four times by small pads built to catch people who fell. This morning, Pike was wearing a rucksack loaded with four ten-pound bags of flour. He would run the steps twenty times, down and up, before turning for home.

He had known the call would come, eventually, but that morning he was lost in the safe, ready feel of sweat and effort when his cellphone vibrated. Pike heeled to a stop and answered.

The man said, 'Bet you don't know who this is.'

Pike had not heard the man's voice since an eight-year-old boy named Ben Chenier was kidnapped. Pike and his friend Elvis Cole had searched for the boy, but they had needed help from the man on the phone to find the kidnapper. The man's price was simple—one day, the man would call with a job for Pike and Pike would have to say yes. The job might be anything and might be the kind of job Pike no longer wanted or did, but that was the price for helping to save Ben Chenier, so Pike had paid it.

Pike said, 'Jon Stone.'

Stone laughed. 'Well. You remember. I told you I would call and this is the call. Now we find out if you're good as your word.'

Pike glanced at his watch. 'It's four a.m.'

'I've been trying to get your number since last night, my man. If I woke you, I'm sorry, but if you stiff me I have to find somebody else.'

'What is it?'

'A package needs looking after, and it's already hot.'

Package meant person. The heat meant attempts had already been made on the target's life.

'Why is the package at risk?'

'I don't know and all I care about is you keeping your word. I gotta tell these people whether you're in or not.'

Grey shapes floated between the palms like ghosts. Two coyotes joined with the first. Their heads hung low, but their eyes caught the gold light. Pike wondered how it would be to run with them, hearing and seeing what they heard and saw, both here in the city and up in the canyons.

Stone was talking, his voice growing strained. 'This guy who called, he said he knew you. Bud Flynn?'

Pike came back from the canyons. 'Yes.'

'Yeah, Flynn's the guy. He has some kinda bodyguard thing with people who have so much dough they shit green. I want some of that green, Pike. You owe me. Are you going to do this thing or not?'

Pike said, 'Yes.'

'That's my boy. I'll call back later with the meet.'

Pike closed his phone. Brake lights flared a quarter of a mile away where San Vicente joined with Ocean. Pike watched the red lights until they disappeared, then hitched his ruck again and continued with his run. Eight or ten coyotes now waited at the edge of light. The city was theirs until sunrise.

FIFTEEN HOURS LATER, Pike arrived at the remains of a church in the high desert, thirty miles north of Los Angeles.

Years of brittle winds, sun and the absence of human care had left the broken stucco walls the colour of dust. It was a lonely place, all the more desolate with the lowering sun at the end of the day.

A black limousine with dark windows and an equally black Hummer were parked nearby, as out of place as gleaming black jewels.

Pike braked his Jeep facing the two vehicles. Blacker shapes moved behind the tinted Hummer glass, but he saw nothing within the limo. He was settling in to wait when Bud Flynn and another man appeared in the church door. The second man appeared nervous, and went back inside as Bud, smiling, came out, stepping into the dwindling sun across twenty years and two lifetimes.

Pike had not seen Bud since the day in the Shortstop Lounge when Pike resigned from the LAPD and wanted Bud to hear it man to man, them being as close as they were. Bud had asked if Pike had another job lined up, and Pike told him that he'd signed on with a professional military corporation out of London. Bud had not approved. He reacted like a disappointed father angered by his son's choice, and that had been that.

Now Pike felt the warm touch of earlier, better memories, and climbed out of the Jeep. Bud was older now, but still looked fit and good to go.

Bud put out his hand. 'Good to see you, Officer Pike. Been a long time. Too long.'

Pike pulled Bud close and hugged him.

'I'm in corporate investigations now, Joe. Fourteen years; fifteen this March. Sometimes the investigation part leads to security work. A friend gave me Stone's name, said he has ex-Secret Service agents on tap—people experienced with high-risk clients. I was looking for someone like that when he floated your name.'

Pike glanced at the Hummer. 'The girl in there?'

Jon Stone had explained the bare bones of it. A young woman from a well-to-do family had survived three murder attempts and Bud Flynn had been hired to protect her. Period. It was enough for Stone to know the girl was rich. A person with Pike's CV could command top dollar, and Stone would bleed these people for every cent he could get.

Flynn turned towards the church. 'Let's go inside. You can meet her father and I'll explain what's going on.'

THE CHURCH smelled of sage and urine. Beer cans and magazines dotted the concrete floor, filthy from the sand blown through the broken walls. Pike guessed the urine smell was left by animals. The second man from the door was standing with a third man. The second man was overweight, with a face like a block and lank hair he pushed from his eyes. His friend was lean and older, maybe in his early fifties, with the intelligent eyes of a businessman and a mouth cut into a permanent frown. A cordovan briefcase sat on the ground by the door.

Bud nodded towards the man with the lank hair.

'Joe, this is Conner Barkley. Mr Barkley, Joe Pike.

Barkley squeezed out an uncomfortable smile. 'Hello.'

He was wearing a silk short-sleeved shirt that showed his belt bulge. The frowning man was tieless in an expensive charcoal sports coat. Pike was wearing a sleeveless grey sweatshirt, jeans and running shoes.

The frowning man took folded papers and a pen from his coat.

'Mr Pike, my name is Gordon Kline. I'm Mr Barkley's attorney. This is a confidentiality agreement, specifying that you may not repeat, relate or in any way disclose anything about the Barkleys said today or while you are in the Barkleys' employ. You'll have to sign this.'

Kline held out the papers and pen, but Pike made no move to take them.

Pike watched Conner Barkley staring at the blocky red arrows inked across his deltoids. He was used to people staring. The arrows had been scribed into his arms before his first combat tour. They pointed forward.

Barkley looked up from the tattoos, his eyes worried. 'This is the man you want to hire?'

'He's the best in the business, Mr Barkley. He'll keep Larkin alive.'

Kline pushed out the papers. 'If you'll just sign here, please.'

Pike said, 'No.'

Barkley's eyebrows bunched liked nervous caterpillars. 'I think we're all right here, Gordon. I think we can press on. Don't you, Bud?'

Kline's frown deepened, but he put away the papers, and Bud continued.

'OK, here's what we have: Mr Barkley's daughter is a federal witness. She's set to offer testimony before the federal grand jury in two weeks. There have been three attempts on her life in the past ten days. All three were close. I have no choice but to think outside the box.'

The desert had filled with red light from the setting sun. Pike felt the temperature dropping.

'Why isn't she in a protection programme?'

Barkley spoke up. 'She was. They almost got her killed.'

Gordon Kline crossed his arms as if the entire United States government was a waste of taxpayers' money. 'Incompetents.'

Bud said, 'Larkin was in a traffic accident eleven days ago—three a.m., she T-boned a Mercedes. There were three people on board: a married couple, George and Elaine King—it was their car—with a male passenger in the rear. You know the name, George King?'

Pike shook his head, so Bud explained. 'A real-estate developer. George was bleeding, so Larkin got out to help. The second man was hurt, too, but he left the scene on foot. Then George pulled himself together enough to drive away, but Larkin got their plate. Next day, the Kings told the police a different story—they say they were alone. A couple of days later, agents from the Justice Department contacted Larkin with a sketch artist. A couple of hundred pictures later, Larkin IDed the missing man as one Alexander Liman Meesh, an indicted murderer the feds believed to be living in Bogotá, Colombia. I have an NCIC file on him I can give you.'

'How did a traffic accident become a federal investigation?'

Kline no longer seemed upset that Pike hadn't signed the papers. Pike would have described him as intent, focused and all business. 'The red flag was King. The DOJ told us they've been investigating him for laundering cash through his real-estate company. They believe Meesh returned to the States with cartel money to invest with King.' Kline darkened, then glanced at the girl's father. 'The government needs Larkin to link King with a known criminal. With her testimony, they believe they can get an indictment and force him to open his books. Her father and I have been against her involvement since the beginning, and look at this mess.'

'So King wants her dead?'

Bud said, 'King is a money man. He has no criminal background, no history of violence. The Justice people think Meesh is trying to protect the cash he's invested in King's projects. If King is indicted, his projects will be frozen along with his assets. King might not even know that Meesh is after the girl. King might not even know where the money actually comes from.'

'Anyone asked the Kings?'

'They've fled. Their office says they're away on a scheduled vacation, but no one at Justice believes it.'

Barkley raked at his hair. 'It's a nightmare. This entire mess is—'

Bud interrupted him. 'Conner—would you give me a minute with Joe? We'll meet you at the car. Gordon, please—'

Barkley frowned like he didn't understand he was being asked to leave, but Kline touched his arm and they left.

When they had gone Pike said, 'I'm not a bodyguard.'

'Joe, listen, the first time they came for her, the kid was at home. That place they have, the Barkleys, it's a fortress—four acres in Beverly Hills north of Sunset, full-on security, a staff. These people are rich.' Bud opened the cordovan briefcase and took out several grainy pictures. The pictures showed three hazy figures in dark clothes moving past a swimming pool at night, then in a courtyard, then outside a set of French doors. 'These were taken by their security cams. You can make out the faces in this one and this one, but we haven't been able to identify them yet. They grabbed a housekeeper, trying to find Larkin. They beat her bad—choked her out and broke three of her teeth and her nose.'

'How close did they get?'

'They made a clean break when the police showed. Then she went into Federal protection. The marshals brought her to a safe house outside San Francisco that evening—that was six days ago. The next night, they came for her again. At the safe house. One US marshal was killed and another wounded. Those boys hit hard.'

Pike heard a car door slam and shifted to the window. Larkin Conner had gotten out of the limo to meet her father and Kline. She had a heart-shaped face with a narrow nose that bent to the left. Bright red hair swirled round her head like coiling snakes. She was wearing tight shorts and a green T-shirt, and had a small dog slung in a pink designer bag under her arm. It was one of those micro-dogs with swollen eyes that shivered when it was nervous. Pike knew it would bark at the wrong time and get her killed.

He turned away from the window. 'The same men?'

'No way to know. Larkin called her parents and was back in Beverly Hills by sunrise. They were done with Federal protection. Mr Barkley hired me and I moved her into a hotel. They hit us again in a matter of hours.'

'So they knew her location all three times.'

'Yes.'

'Your feds have a leak.'

Bud clenched his jaw, like that's what he was thinking though he didn't want to say it. 'I have a house in Malibu. I want you to take her there tonight—just you.'

'How do the feds feel about that?'

'I cut them out. Pitman, he's the boss over there, he thinks I'm making a mistake, but this is the way the Barkleys want it.'

Pike looked back at Bud Flynn. 'Did Stone tell you our set-up?'

Bud stared at him, not understanding. 'What set-up?'

'I don't do contract work any more. I owe him a job. This is his payoff.'

'You're costing a fortune.'

'I'm not taking it. That's not the way I want it or why I'm doing it.'

'If your heart isn't in it, I don't want you to—'

Pike said, 'Officer Flynn—'

Bud stopped. 'Let's meet the girl.'

WHEN PIKE AND FLYNN stepped from the church Gordon Kline stopped talking with Barkley and watched them approach.

'We're good to go,' Flynn said, then he turned to the girl.

'Larkin, this is Joe Pike. You'll be going with him.'

'What if he rapes me?'

Kline said, 'Stop it, Larkin. This is what's best.'

Larkin took off her sunglasses, making a drama of measuring Pike before saying, 'He's kinda cute, I guess. Are you buying him for me, Daddy?'

Barkley glanced at Kline, as if he wanted his lawyer to answer his daughter. He seemed afraid of her.

She turned back to Pike. 'You think you can protect me?'

Pike studied her. She was pretty and used to it, and the clothes indicated she liked being the centre of attention, which would be a problem.

Larkin frowned. 'How come he isn't saying anything? Is he stoned?'

Pike made up his mind. 'Yes.'

Larkin laughed. 'You're stoned?'

'Yes, I can protect you.'

Larkin's grin fell away, and now she considered him with uncertainty shadowed in her eyes. As if all of it was suddenly real.

She said, 'I want to see your eyes. Take off your glasses.'

Pike tipped his head towards the Hummer, where two men in Savile Row suits were unloading suitcases. 'That your stuff?'

'Yeah.'

'One bag, one purse, that's it. No cellphone. No electronics. No iPod.'

Larkin stiffened. 'But I need those things. Daddy, tell him.'

The little dog snarled from its pouch under her arm.

Pike said, 'Get rid of the dog.'

Barkley raked at his hair again, and Kline frowned even more deeply.

A bad hour later, Pike and the girl were on their way.

'JOE—?'

Cole realised Pike had hung up. That was the kind of call you got from Joe Pike. You'd answer the phone, he'd grunt something, and that was it. Polite communication had never been one of Pike's strong points.

Cole went back to waxing his car—a yellow 1966 Sting Ray convertible. He was wearing gym shorts and a T-shirt. The grey shirt was black with sweat, but he wore it to cover his scars. Cole lived in a small A-frame house perched on the edge of a canyon in the Hollywood Hills. It was woody and quiet, and his neighbours often walked their dogs past his house. Cole figured they didn't need to see the liver-coloured stitching that made him look like a lab accident.

Cole hated waxing his car, but he thought maybe waxing would be good therapy. Thirteen weeks earlier, a man named David Reinnike had shot him in the back with a 12-gauge shotgun. The pellets had shattered five ribs, broke his left humerus and collapsed his left lung, and now he moved like a robot with rusty joints. But twice a day every day he pushed past the pain, working himself back into shape.

Cole was still working on the car when a dark green Lexus stopped across his drive. He watched as Pike and a young woman with ragged hair and big sunglasses got out. The woman looked wary, and Pike was wearing a long-sleeved shirt with the sleeves down. Pike never wore long shirts.

Cole limped out to meet them. 'Joseph. You should have told me we had guests. I would have cleaned up.' Cole smiled at the girl, spreading his hands to show off his gym shorts, bare feet and T-shirt. Mr Personable, making a joke of his sweat-soaked appearance. 'I'm Elvis.'

The girl painted him with a smile that was smart and sharp, and jerked a thumb at Pike. 'Thank God you have a personality. Riding around with him is like riding with a corpse.'

'Only until you get to know him. Then you can't shut him up.'

Cole glanced at the Lexus, already sensing this wasn't a social visit. 'What happened to the Jeep?'

Cole noticed how Pike touched her back without familiarity, moving her into the carport. 'Let's go in the house.'

Cole led them into his living room where glass doors opened onto his deck. The girl looked out at the view of the canyon.

She said, 'This isn't so bad.'

'Thanks. I think.'

The money vibe came off her like heat—the $500 Rock & Republic jeans, the Kitson's top, the Oliver Peoples shades. Cole was good at reading people, and had learned—over time—that he was almost always right. The trouble vibe came off her, too. She looked familiar, but he couldn't place her.

Pike said, 'This is Larkin Barkley. She's a witness in a federal investigation. She was in a programme, but that didn't work out. We could use something to eat, maybe a shower, and I'll tell you what's up.'

Cole sensed Pike didn't want to talk in front of the girl, so he smiled and said, 'Why don't you use the shower while I make something to eat?'

Larkin glanced back at him, and Cole read a new vibe. She gave him the same crooked smile she had made in the drive, only now she was telling him he could say nothing that would surprise her, affect her or impress her. Like a challenge, Cole thought.

She said, 'Why don't I eat first? The Pikester won't feed me. He only wants sex.'

Cole said, 'He's like that with me, too, but we've learned to adjust.'

Larkin blinked once, then burst out laughing.

Cole said, 'One point, me; zero, you. Take the shower or wait on the deck. Either way, we don't want you around while we talk.'

She chose the shower.

Pike brought in her bag and showed her to the guest bathroom while Cole went to work in the kitchen. He sliced zucchini, summer squash and eggplant the long way, then drizzled them with olive oil and salt, and put on a grill pan to heat. Pike joined him, but neither of them spoke until they heard the water running. Then Pike dealt out a driver's licence and two credit cards. The AmEx card was black. Money.

'I met her for the first time yesterday, but I don't know anything about her. I need you to help me with that.' Pike followed the credit cards with what appeared to be a text-only criminal-history file from the FBI's National Crime Information Center. 'This is the man who's trying to kill her. His name is Alex Meesh, from Colorado by way of Colombia.'

Cole glanced over the cover page. Alexander Meesh. Wanted for murder.

'South America?'

'Yeah. Went down to flee the murder warrants. The feds gave Bud his record here, but I didn't see much that would help. Maybe you'll see something different.'

Cole listened as Pike described how the girl had found herself in a Justice Department investigation and how her agreement to testify had led to the attempts on her life. Cole listened without comment until Pike described the shootings in Malibu and Eagle Rock.

'Wait. You shot someone?'

'Five. Two last night, three this morning.' Pike, standing there in his kitchen without expression, saying it like anyone else would say their car needed gas.

'Joe. Jesus, *Joe*—are the police after you?'

'I don't know. But if not now, then soon—I lost a gun in Eagle Rock.'

Cole stared at his friend.

'This was self-defence, right? You were defending your life and the life of a federal witness. The feds are with you on that.'

'I don't know. But either way, we have a bigger problem than the police. The shooters knew our location at both safe houses. You see how it is?'

Now Cole understood why Pike wouldn't talk in front of the girl. 'Someone on her side is giving her up.'

'I took her. I cut Bud and the feds out of the loop. I figure as long as no one knows where she is, I can protect her.'

'What are you going to do?'

'Find Meesh.'

'He might be back in Colombia.'

'He's tried to kill this girl five times. You don't want someone dead that badly, then go away and hope it gets done—you make sure it happens.'

Pike went to the pad and pen Cole kept by his phone, and scribbled something. 'I got a new phone. This is the number.'

'You have any idea who's giving her up?'

'Bud is working on it, but who can I trust? Might be one of his people. Might even be one of the feds.'

Cole put the number aside. He turned back to the pan and laid in the vegetables. He loved the smell when they hit the hot steel.

Cole and Pike had been through a lot. They had been friends a long time. When Cole woke from his coma, Joe Pike had been holding his hand.

Cole put down the fork and turned. 'I'll see what I can find out about Meesh. We'll start with Larkin when she's done with the shower. Maybe she knows more than she thinks.'

Pike shifted. 'We can't hang here, Elvis. If these people know who I am, they might try to find me through you. I'm sorry.'

Cole understood. 'Then you talk to her. But one more thing. When I'm looking into Meesh, I'm going to check out your friend Bud Flynn, too.'

Pike's mouth twitched, and Cole wondered if Larkin had noticed that Pike never laughed or smiled. As if the part of a man who could feel that free was dead in Pike, or buried so deep that only a twitch could escape.

Pike said, 'Whatever.'

Cole was building the sandwiches when Pike's cellphone rang, and he took the phone out to the deck.

A few minutes later, the girl came down the hall.

The girl said, 'That smells incredible.'

'Would you like a glass of milk or water?'

'Please. The milk.'

Her eyes were red, and Cole wondered if she had been crying. She caught him looking, and flashed the crooked smile. It was smart and inviting, and could never be made by someone who had just been crying, but there it was. Cole thought this kid had had plenty of practice hiding herself.

She opened the sandwich, and made a little squeal. 'This is perfect! I didn't want to be a pain before, but I'm a vegetarian. How did you know?'

'Didn't. I made these for Joe. He's a vegetarian, too.'

'*Him?*' She glanced out at Pike, and Cole thought her smile straightened.

'Red meat makes him aggressive.'

She laughed, and Cole found himself liking her. She took a tremendous bite of the sandwich. She watched Pike on the deck as she chewed.

'He doesn't say much.'

'He's into telepathy. He can also walk through walls.'

She smiled again, then took another bite, though this one not so large. Her smile was gone and her eyes seemed thoughtful.

'He shot a man right in front of me. I saw the blood.'

'A man who was trying to kill you.'

'It was so loud. Not like in the movies. You can feel it.'

'I know.'

'They keep finding me.'

Cole didn't answer, then Pike stepped in from the deck.

'We have a place. Let's go.'

She glanced at her sandwich. 'I haven't finished. You haven't eaten.'

'We'll eat in the car.'

Cole followed them out, said his goodbyes, and watched them drive away. He did not ask Pike where they were going, and Pike didn't say. He knew Pike would call him when they were safe.

They met back when Pike was still riding a patrol car and Cole was working as an apprentice to old George Feider and still piling up the three thousands hours of experience he needed to be licensed as a private investigator. A few years later when Cole had the hours and Pike was off the job, George retired, so Cole and Pike pooled their money to buy Feider's business. It was agreed that only Cole's name would be on the door. Pike had other businesses by then and only wanted to help Cole part-time, saying that without him covering Cole's back, Cole would probably get himself killed. Cole hadn't known whether or not Pike had been joking, but that was part of Pike's charm.

If they know who I am they might try to find me through you.

Cole took a deep breath. He thought, Let 'em bring it—I got your back, too, brother.

He went to work.

PIKE CRUISED EAST on Sunset Boulevard into the purpling sky, invisible in the anonymous car. When they passed Echo Lake, he turned north into the low hills of Echo Park. The twisting residential streets to the north were narrow and the homes were clapboard shotguns. Prewar street lamps were flickering on in the twilight when they reached the address.

Pike said, 'This is it.'

A narrow grey house with a steep roof sat off the street, with a covered front porch guarding the door and a one-car garage filling the back yard. Pike's real-estate friend had left a key under a potted plant near the door.

Larkin looked warily at the house. 'Who lives here?'

'It's a rental. The owners live in Las Vegas, and they're between tenants.

When you get out, go directly to the front door.'

A sunset breeze out of Chavez Ravine stirred the warm air. Families were outside on their porches, some listening to the radio and others just talking. Most of the neighbours appeared to be Eastern Europeans. Across the street, five young men who sounded Armenian were standing round a late-model BMW, laughing together.

Pike carried her bags. He found the key, then let them into a small living room. A door to their right branched into a bathroom and a front and back bedroom. The little house was clean and neat, but the furniture was worn.

Larkin said, 'I've been thinking. No one knows where we are now, right? We have my credit cards. We have my ATM. We can go wherever we want.'

Pike dropped her bags. 'Take whichever bedroom you want.'

He continued on through both bedrooms and the bathroom and kitchen, checking the windows and pulling the shades. Larkin didn't pick a bedroom. She followed him.

'Just listen. We can take the Gulfstream. My father won't care. We have a fabulous apartment in Sidney. Have you ever been to Oz?'

'You'll be recognised. Someone at the airport, "There's Larkin Barkley in her jet."'

Pike opened the fridge. Two grocery bags, a case of bottled water and a six pack of Corona were waiting. 'My friend left this. Help yourself.'

'OK—we have a house on Avenue George V a block from the Champs-Elysées. I'll pay our way on a commercial flight. It's not a problem.'

'Credit cards leave a trail. Airplanes file flight plans.'

Pike headed back into the living room, and Larkin caught up.

'I'll take cash from the ATM. It's really no problem.'

A single window air conditioner hummed in the living room, left on by Pike's friend. The air blowing from the vents roared like a windstorm with a faraway metallic vibration. Pike turned it off. The silence was filled by barking dogs, and the laughter of the men across the street.

Larkin looked horrified. 'Why did you turn off the air?'

'I couldn't hear.'

'But it's hot. It's going to be an oven in here.'

She had crossed her arms, and her fingers had dug into her flesh. Pike knew this wasn't about Paris or Sidney. It was about being scared.

He touched her arm. 'I know this isn't what you're used to, but we have what we need. Right now—this is a safe place.'

'I'm sorry. I didn't mean to be a bitch.'

THE WATCHMAN | 37

'I'm going to get my things from the car. You OK for a few minutes?'
Larkin made a tired smile. 'Of course. I'll be fine.'
Pike turned off the lamps so he wouldn't be framed in the door, then let himself out. He climbed into the Lexus, then used his new phone to check the messages left on his old phone. Five messages were waiting for him. Bud had left three in a row, all pretty much the same—*'Call me, dammit! You can't just disappear with this girl! She's a federal witness, for Chrissakes! They'll have the FBI looking for you!'*

He had also left a fourth message about an hour later. Pike noted Bud was calmer. *'Here's what I have so far—the stiffs from Malibu weren't identified. I'll find out about Eagle Rock tomorrow. LAPD and the Sheriffs haven't connected you with the shootings. I spoke with Don Pitman—the DOJ agent. He'll do what he can to take care of you with the locals, but he absolutely must talk to you. You gotta call me, man. I don't know what to tell her father. Joe, if you're still alive—call.'*

A dry male voice had left the last message. *'This is Special Agent Don Pitman with the Justice Department. 202-555-6241. Call me, Mr Pike.'*

Pike ended the call, then sat listening to the neighbourhood. He wondered what Bud meant, saying the stiffs in Malibu weren't identified. Pike had thought the shooters would be identified as soon as they reached the coroner, which would give him a lead to find Meesh.

It was full-on dark now, and Pike enjoyed the darkness. Darkness, rain, snow, a storm—anything that hid you was good. He circled the house to check the windows, then slipped back onto the porch and let himself in.

Larkin was no longer in the living room, but he heard her in the kitchen. He took off the long-sleeved shirt, then sat in one of the wing chairs to wait. He heard the rattle of the refrigerator as she wrestled a bottle of water from its plastic wrapping. She came out of the kitchen and was halfway into the living room before she saw him, and was so startled a geyser of water squirted into the air.

'You scared the shit out of me.'
'Sorry.'
She was gasping the way people do, but she made an embarrassed laugh. 'Jesus, say something next time. I didn't hear you come back.'
'Maybe you should put something on.'
She had taken off her clothes except for a sheer bra and a lime-green thong. A gold stud glinted in her navel. She straightened to face him full on. 'I got hot. I told you it would be hot without the air.' She went to the couch,

sat, and put her bare feet up on the coffee table, staring at him. 'Are you sure you don't want to go to Paris? It's cooler in Paris.'

She stared at him with the crooked smile slashing her face as if she and only she had discovered that everything in the world was about sex.

Pike said, 'Who's Don Pitman?'

Her crooked smile vanished. 'I don't want to talk about this right now.'

'I need to know who these people are. He called me.'

Her feet dropped from the table. 'He's one of the people from the government. It was Pitman and another one—Blanchette. Kevin Blanchette is a lawyer from the Attorney General.'

She leaned forward to put the bottle on the table, and her breasts showed round and full in her bra in the dim ochre light. 'I have a tattoo on my ass. Did you see it this morning? I wanted you to see it.'

Pike stared at her.

'It's a dolphin. I think dolphins are beautiful. You see them racing through the water. They look so happy, going fast. I want to be like that.' She came round the table and walked over to Pike and stopped in front of him.

Pike shook his head. 'Don't.'

She knelt and placed her hand on his shoulder, covering his tattoo. 'Why did you have arrows? Tell me why. I need to know that about you.'

Pike moved just enough to lift her hand away. He took her arms and gently pushed her back. 'Please don't do this again.'

She stared at some point between them for a time, then returned to the couch. Pike studied her face. Her eyes glistened in the light from the window.

He said, 'It's going to be all right. You're safe.'

'I don't know you. I don't know these government people or Meesh or the Kings or about laundering money. I only wanted to help. I don't know what happened to my life.' The glisten spread to her cheeks. 'I'm really scared.'

Pike knew it was a mistake even as he went to the couch. He put his arm round her, trying to comfort her the way he had comforted people when he was an officer, a mother whose son had been shot, a child who had been in a traffic accident. She snuggled into him, her hand going to his chest, then lower.

Pike whispered, 'No.'

Larkin ran into the front bedroom, bare feet slapping. The door closed.

Pike sat on the couch in the dark, quiet house. He had been awake for thirty-five hours, but he knew if sleep came it would not last more than an hour or two. He took off his sweatshirt, then floated soundlessly through the house, going to each room, listening to the night beyond the windows, then moving on. When he reached Larkin's door, he heard her crying.

Pike touched the door. 'Larkin.'

The crying stopped, so he knew she was listening.

'The arrows. What they mean is, you control who you are by moving forwards; never back; you move forwards. That's what we're going to do.'

Pike waited, but the girl made no sound. He felt embarrassed and wished he hadn't tried to explain.

He turned away and shut every light in the house. He returned to the living room. He stood in the dark, listening, then fell forwards and silently did pushups, one after another, alone, waiting for the night to pass.

3

The windows grew light by five-thirty the following morning, filling the Echo Park house with the brown gloom of a freshwater pond. Pike had already washed and dressed by then. He was standing in the living room. From his position, he could see the length of the house from the front door through the kitchen to the back door, and the three doorways branching off the tiny hall to both bedrooms and the bathroom. He had been standing in this spot for almost one hour.

Throughout the night, Pike had dozed a few minutes at a time on the couch, but had never been fully asleep. Every hour or so he moved through the house, listening. Houses were living things. When all was well, the noises they made sounded right. Pike listened for rightness.

At five-forty, the girl staggered out of her room and into the bathroom without seeing him. The bathroom light came on, the door closed.

Pike never moved.

The toilet flushed and the door opened. She shuffled out of the bathroom, and in that moment she saw him. She was groggy with sleep.

She said, 'Why are you wearing sunglasses in the dark?'

Pike said nothing.

'What are you doing?'

'Standing.'

'You're strange.'

She shuffled back to her room. The house was once again silent.

At 6.02, his new cellphone vibrated. Pike saw it was Ronnie.

'Yes.'

'The alarm at your condo went off twelve minutes ago.'

Pike had arranged for his security company to call Ronnie's number if they received an alarm. He had also told them not to notify the police.

Pike said, 'What did you tell them?'

'Everything's cool and they should reset the alarm, just like you said. You want me to roll over there?'

'No. I'll take care of it.'

Pike put away the phone. He had figured it was only a matter of time, and now it had come. They had gotten his name, found his address, and now were trying to find him. This told him much—the only people who knew his name were the girl's people, Jon Stone and Bud Flynn. Someone was still selling her out. Pike was right to cut them out of the loop. They would likely return to his condo later. However they handled it would tell him a lot about the size of their operation and their skills. It was important to know your enemy.

But, for now, he had to stay with the girl. The night had passed. She was still alive. He had done his job, but still had much to do.

ANOTHER IN THE long line of classic Pike phone conversations. Cole, out on his deck sweating through some asanas when the phone rings. Six a.m., who else would it be?

'Hello?'

Pike says, 'Be advised. They just hit my condo.'

No heyhowareya? No whaddayadoing? Classic.

Cole showered, then pulled an old .38 from his gun safe and made a cup of coffee. He brought the gun, the coffee, and material on George King and Alexander Meesh out to his deck.

It was a lovely morning, hinting at a brutally hot day.

Cole squinted into the milky haze that filled his canyon, and noticed a redtail hawk circling overhead, searching for field mice and snakes.

The day after Cole came home from the hospital, he went out onto his deck at dawn and struggled through twelve sun salutations from the hatha yoga (just as he had every morning since), then sat on the edge of his deck to watch the hawk. The hawk returned every morning, but Cole never saw it catch anything. He admired its spirit.

Cole reread the material he'd pulled off the Internet on George King. King was a real-estate developer from Orange County who began his career by building a single house using money borrowed from his wife's parents. It was the classic by-his-bootstraps success story: King sold that first house for a profit, built three more, and the houses led to a couple of tiny strip malls. The strip malls led to a real-estate concern that now developed shopping centres, residential tract housing and high-rise commercial office space throughout California, Arizona and Nevada. None of the articles hinted at impropriety or illegal activity.

Cole had found nothing about Alexander Meesh on the Internet. The last entry in the NCIC report Pike had given him said Meesh was currently believed to be living in Bogotá, Colombia. That was dated six years ago.

Reading the NCIC brief was like reading the TV-guide version of a twenty-year criminal career. Meesh had been indicted on two counts of first-degree murder, seven counts of conspiracy to commit murder and sixteen counts of racketeering, all in Colorado. Meesh had murdered a truck driver and his wife in Colorado Springs, Colorado. Meesh believed the driver had double-crossed him by laying off a load of flat-screen TVs to a rival hijacking crew. He poured hot cooking grease on the driver's wife during a twenty-four-hour torture session. Then he went to work on the driver. Meesh clearly wanted the other crews in the area to know he owned the roads.

Nothing explained how a home-grown criminal from Denver had become a financial player for a group of South American drug lords, but Cole didn't care. He wanted to find Meesh, and Meesh was in LA. All criminal histories listed people with whom the subject was known to associate, including friends, family members and gang affiliates. Cole had hoped to find a known associate in LA, but the names were all based in Denver. Now he would try to find out if any of those people had connections in Los Angeles.

A flick of grey dropped from the sky. Cole glanced up, smiling. He wanted to see what the hawk had caught, but that's when his doorbell rang. He limped to the front door with his pistol, and peered through the peephole.

Two men stared back at him, their faces distorted by the fish-eye lens. The man in front had a golfer's tan and short brown hair. The man behind him was taller and black, wearing a blue seersucker coat and sunglasses.

Cole parked the gun in his waistband behind his back, pulled his T-shirt over it, then opened the door.

The man in front said, 'Elvis Cole?'

'He moved to Austria. Can I take a message?'

The man in front held up a black leather badge case showing a federal ID. 'Special Agent Donald Pitman. We'd like a few words.'

They didn't wait for Cole to invite them in.

OUTSIDE THE Echo Park house, the neighbourhood woke with the slowly rising sun. Finches and sparrows chirped. Cars started, then backed out of drives or pulled away from the kerb. The brittle shades that covered the windows brightened until the house was filled with a dim golden light.

Pike poured ground coffee into a small pot, filled the pot with water, then set it on the range. He had been making coffee this way for years. He would bring it to a boil, then pour it through a paper towel or maybe he wouldn't bother with the towel. The coffee would be fine either way.

Pike had just poured some coffee into a Styrofoam cup when his cellphone vibrated.

Cole said, 'Can you talk?'

Pike could see the girl's door from the table. It was closed.

'Yes.'

'Two agents from the Department of Justice came by this morning, Donald Pitman and Kevin Blanchette. They brought your gun. They didn't ask if I knew what was going on or if I had seen you. They just gave me the gun and told me to tell you they were taking care of it.'

'You probably shouldn't call me from your house any more.'

'I walked next door.'

'OK.'

'Pitman said if I heard from you I should tell you to call. He said to tell you the gun was a sign of good faith, but if you didn't call, the good faith would stop.'

'I understand.'

'Couple more things. Nothing in the record connects Meesh to LA, or gives us anything to work with, so the bodies are our best shot. We get them IDed, we might be able to work backwards to Meesh.'

'I'll talk to Bud. Did you check out the girl?'

Cole hesitated, and Pike read a difference in his tone. 'She's in all the magazines. She's rich. She's famous for being rich. I didn't place her with the short hair. She's always in the tabloids—going wild in clubs, making a big scene, that kind of thing. You've seen her.'

'Don't read tabloids.'

'Her father inherited an empire. They own hotel chains in Europe, a couple of airlines, oil fields in Canada. She has to be worth five or six billion.'

'Huh.'

'Keep an eye on her. She's the classic LA wild child.'

'She seems all right.'

'Just so you know.'

Pike wondered why two federal agents would show up at Cole's house with the gun, but mostly he didn't care. He wanted to find Meesh.

He said, 'Can you get Bud Flynn's home address?'

'Am I not the World's Greatest Detective?'

'Something I have to do later. I can't take the girl and I don't want to leave her alone. Could you stay with her?'

'Baby-sit a hot, young, rich chick? I think I can manage.'

Pike ended the call, then punched in Bud Flynn's cell number. Flynn answered on the third ring, sounding hoarse and sleepy. It was only seven-forty. Bud had probably been up pretty late.

Pike said, 'You sound sleepy. Did I wake you?'

As he said it, the girl's door opened and Larkin stepped out. She still wore only the bra and the tiny green thong. She didn't look so wild. She blinked sleepily at him, then went into the bathroom.

Bud said, 'You're killing me, Joe. Jesus, where are you?'

'We're good. Why is everyone so upset?' Pike, having fun.

'You dropped off the world, is why! You can't just disappear. The feds—'

Pike interrupted. 'How many people know I have her? Someone hit my home this morning, Bud, so your leak is still leaking. Trust is in short supply.'

Larkin came out of the bathroom and into the living room. Pike held up his coffee to show her that coffee was available, then pointed the cup towards the kitchen. She didn't seem self-conscious about her lack of clothes. She went into the kitchen.

Bud still had the uncertain voice. 'I understand what you're saying, but we have five bodies to deal with and—'

Pike cut him off again. 'Larkin and I will meet you. Don't tell her father or those feds. Come by yourself, and we'll figure this out.'

'Where?'

'The subway stop in Universal City at noon. What will you be driving?'

'A silver Beemer.'

'Park in the north lot. Wait in your car until I call.'

Pike turned off his phone. Larkin came out of the kitchen waving the pot.

'What is this?'

'Coffee.'

'It's sludge. There's stuff in it.'

Pike finished his cup, then pulled on the long-sleeved shirt. 'Pack your things. We're going to see Bud.'

She lowered the pot, suddenly looking afraid. 'I thought we were safe here.'

'We are. But if something happens, we'll want our things. Get dressed. We have to hurry.'

'But you told him noon. Universal is only twenty minutes away.'

'Let's go. We have to hurry.'

She stomped back into the kitchen and threw the pot into the sink. 'Your coffee *sucks*!'

She didn't seem so wild, even when she threw things.

PIKE DIDN'T TAKE HER to Universal, and didn't wait until noon. Cole had phoned through Bud's home address before they were out of the door.

Bud Flynn lived in an upscale neighbourhood set on the rolling land south of the Hillcrest Country Club in mid-town Los Angeles. Bud's home was a small split-level with a gently sloping drive and a front lawn that struggled against the brutal summer heat. A brace of jacaranda trees coloured the driveway with purple snow.

Larkin swivelled her head as they drove past the house, alert and excited. 'What are we going to do?'

'You're going to stay in the car. I'm going to talk to him.'

Pike parked across the mouth of Bud's drive so Larkin would be clearly visible in the car, then got out and went to the front door. He stood to one side of the door, positioning himself so he could not be seen from the windows. He called Bud's cell.

Bud said, 'Gotta be you, Joe. The incoming call says restricted.'

'Look in your driveway.'

Pike heard movement over the phone, then the front door opened. Bud stepped out. He stared at the girl, but didn't yet see Pike. He looked tired.

Pike said, 'Bud.'

Bud showed no surprise. 'What did you think I would do, have Universal surrounded?' he said, scowling.

Pike made a rolling gesture so Larkin would roll down her window.

'Say hi to Bud.'

Larkin waved, and called back from the car. 'Hi, Bud!'

Pike turned back to Bud, but Bud was still scowling.

'What do you think you're doing? Do you know how much shit I'm in?'

'I'm showing you she's alive and well. You can tell her father she's fine.'

Bud's scowl grew irritated. 'Now waitaminute, goddammit—this isn't only about the girl. You dropped five bodies in two days. You think, what, Pitman can tell LAPD, "Hey, it's all right, our civilian killed those dudes to protect our witness," and Northeast Homicide will let it go?'

Pike didn't care if they let it go or not so long as the girl was still in danger. He wondered whether Bud knew that Pitman had returned his gun, and, if not, why Pitman hadn't told him.

'Pitman says if you don't come in he'll issue a warrant for kidnapping.'

The corner of Pike's mouth twitched, and Bud reddened.

'I know it's bullshit, but you're out here running around and nobody knows what's happening. The feds think the problem is me, and that's what they're telling her father. He's this close to firing me.'

'So tell me, Bud—is she safer with you now or me?'

'I turned over my personal records to the DOJ. I gave them my guys' cell records, expenses, everything. Her father, he gave Pitman an open door on his staff, their emails and phones—all of it. We'll plug the leak.'

'Who's checking Pitman?'

Bud blinked, and finally shook his head. His eyes were hard stones hidden by flesh weakened with age. 'Joe. What are you doing?'

'I'm looking for Meesh.'

'You aren't just looking. I don't want to be involved with this.'

'I only have two leads back to Meesh—the men in the morgue and the Kings. If the Kings were in business with him, then they probably knew where he was staying and how to reach him.'

'They're still missing. Pitman has their home and office under twenty-four-hour surveillance. If those people fart, the feds will be on them.'

'Then the men I killed are my last door back to him. What do you know?'

Bud darkened. 'I gotta get my keys. That OK?'

Bud stepped into his house to fish his keys from a blue bowl inside the door. Pike followed him to his car. Bud opened the trunk, and Pike saw the same cordovan briefcase he had seen in the desert. Bud took out three pictures, security stills taken when the Barkleys' home was invaded.

Bud handed them to Pike, and tapped the top picture. 'This man was the only one of the five you shot who was also one of the original home invaders. And this man'—Bud shuffled the pictures to point out a man with prominent cheekbones and a scarred lip— 'he beat the housekeeper. You recognise any of these other guys from Malibu or Eagle Rock?'

'Who are they?'

'Don't know. We haven't been able to identify any of the five people you put in the morgue. They weren't in the system.'

Pike stared at the pictures. It didn't make sense. The type of man you could hire to do murder almost always had a criminal record. The LiveScan system digitised fingerprints, then instantly compared them with computerised records stored by the California Department of Justice and the NCIC files. If a person had ever been arrested anywhere in the country or served in the military, their fingerprints were in those files.

Pike said, 'That doesn't sound right. No IDs or wallets?'

'Not one damn thing of a personal nature. You arrested a lot of people, Joe. How many shitbirds were smart enough to clean up before they did crime?'

Pike shook his head.

'Right. So here we are.' Bud slammed his trunk, then stared at the girl. 'You could just give her back to Pitman. It's your choice, playing it this way.' Then he turned, and with the new angle of light he looked as hard as ever. He said, 'I'm trusting you won't let this little girl down.'

Pike watched Bud walk away, then returned to the Lexus and immediately drove away.

Larkin said, 'He seems like a nice man.'

'He was a good officer.'

'That's what he told my dad about you, that you were a good policeman. What he said was, you were the best young officer he ever worked with.'

4

Pike and Charlie Grissom were seated on the front row in the roll-call room of the Rampart Division Police Station, this being their first official day on the job after having graduated from the Los Angeles Police Academy. Today, they would begin their careers as probationary police officers, known within the department as 'boots'.

They would spend the next year becoming 'street certified' by experienced senior officers known as P-IIIs—Pee Threes—who would be their teachers, their protectors and their gods. At this first roll call, they would introduce themselves to the veterans, which Pike dreaded. Pike wasn't much for talking, and talked about himself least of all.

Sergeant Kelly Levendorf, who was the evening watch commander, rolled through everything from suspected criminal activity to officer birthdays. When he finished he looked up.

'OK, we have some new officers aboard, so we'll let 'em introduce themselves. Officer Grissom, you have one minute, one second.'

Pike thought, here it comes.

Grissom surged to his feet, all gung-ho enthusiasm. He was a short, chunky kid with delicate blond hair, who always seemed anxious to please.

'My name is Charlie Grissom. I graduated from San Diego State with a degree in history. My dad was an officer in San Diego, where I was born. I like to surf, fish and scuba dive. I'm always looking for dive buddies, so look me up if you're interested. I've been dating the same girl for about a year. Being a police officer is all I've ever wanted. My dad wanted me to go on the San Diego PD, but I wanted to be with the best—so I'm here.'

This brought a roar of approval as Grissom returned to his seat.

Levendorf calmed the crowd, then looked at Pike.

'Officer Pike—one minute, one second.'

Pike hadn't gone to college and wouldn't talk about his family. He couldn't see that it mattered anyway. Pike figured, all that mattered was what a man did in the moment at hand, and whether or not he did right.

Pike stood. The officers assembled were all colours and ages. Many were smiling and loose; others looked stern and a lot of them looked bored. Pike noted those officers with two stripes on their sleeves. These were the P-IIIs.

'My name is Joe Pike. I'm not married. I pulled two combat tours in the Marines—' The shift broke into wild applause and cheers. LAPD had a high percentage of Marine Corps veterans. 'I want to be a police officer because the motto says "to protect and to serve". That's what I want to do.'

Pike took his seat to scattered applause, but someone in the back laughed.

'Got us a regular Clint Eastwood. A man of few words.'

Levendorf said, 'Officer Pike, we call this part of the programme "one minute, one second"—so I figure you got about forty seconds to go. Perhaps you'd offer a bit more, self-illumination-wise?'

Pike stood again. 'I qualified as a scout/sniper and served in Force Recon, mostly on long-range reconnaissance teams, hunter/killer teams and priority target missions. I'm black-belt qualified in tae kwon do, kung fu, wing chun and judo. I like to run and work out. I like to read.'

Pike stopped. The shift stared at him. No one applauded.

Finally, an older black P-III with salt-and-pepper hair said, 'Thank God he likes to read—I thought we had us a sissy.'

The shift broke into laughter.

Levendorf ended the roll call, and everyone herded towards the exits. The new guys stayed behind to meet the P-IIIs they were assigned to.

Two senior officers bucked the departing crowd to make their way forward. The burly black officer who made the crack about Pike being a reader went to Grissom. The second P-III was shorter than Pike, with close brown hair, a rusty tan and a thin, no-nonsense mouth. Pike guessed he was in his late-thirties. He came directly to Pike and put out his hand.

'Good to meet you, Officer Pike. I'm Bud Flynn. I'll be your training officer for your first two deployment periods.'

'Yes, sir.'

'You can call me Officer Flynn or sir until I say otherwise, and I will call you Officer Pike, Pike or boot. We clear on that?'

'Yes, sir.'

'Grab your gear and let's go.'

Pike hooked the gear bag over his shoulder and followed Flynn out to the parking lot and a dinged and battered Caprice. Flynn pointed at it.

'This is our shop. Its name is two-adam-forty-four, which will also be your name after I teach you to use the radio. It has so much wrong with it that it would be down-checked on any other police force in America. But our cheap-ass city council won't give us the money to maintain the proper equipment. But do you know what the good news is, Officer Pike?'

'No, sir.'

'The good news is that we are Los Angeles police officers. Which means we will use this piece of shit anyway, and still provide the finest police service available in any major American city.'

Pike liked Flynn's manner, and Flynn's obvious pride in his profession.

Flynn put his gear on the ground at the back of the car, then faced Pike.

'Before we get going I want to make sure we're on the same page. I respect your service, but I don't give a rat's ass about it. Half this police force was in the Marines and the other half are tired of hearing about it. This is a city in the United States of America. It isn't a war zone.'

'Yes, sir. I understand.'

'That piss you off, me saying that?'

'No, sir.'

Flynn studied Pike as if he suspected he was lying. 'Well, if you are, you hide it well, which is good. Because out here, you will not show your true feelings to anyone. Whatever you feel about the low lifes, degenerates and citizens we deal with—be they victim or criminal—you will keep your personal opinions to yourself. We clear?'

'Yes, sir.'

Flynn popped the trunk. Pike stowed his gear as Flynn went on. 'The academy taught you statutes and procedure, but I am going to teach you the two most important lessons you receive. The first is this: You will see people at their creative, industrious worst—and I am going to teach you how to read them. You are going to learn how to tell a lie from the truth and how to figure out what's right even when everyone is wrong. From this, you will learn how to dispense justice in a fair and even-handed way, which is what the people of our city deserve. Clear?'

'Yes, sir.'

'Any questions?'

'What's the other thing?'

Flynn's eyebrows arched as if he was about to dispense the wisdom of the ages. 'You will learn how not to hate them. You'll see some sorry bastards out here, Officer Pike, but people aren't so bad. I'm going to teach you how not to lose sight of that, because hating them's the first step towards hating yourself. We can't have that, can we?'

'No, sir.'

Flynn closed the trunk then turned back to Pike again. 'Now I have a question. When you said why you became an officer, you quoted the LAPD motto, "to protect and to serve". Which is it?'

'Some people can't protect themselves. They need help.'

'And that would be you, Officer Pike, with all that karate and stuff?'

Pike nodded.

'You like to fight?'

'I don't like it or not like it. If I have to, I can.'

Flynn nodded, but the way he sucked at his lips told Pike he was still being read. 'Our job isn't to get in fights, Officer Pike. We don't always have a choice, but you get in enough fights, you'll get your ass kicked for sure. You ever had your ass kicked?'

'Yes, sir.'

Pike would not mention his father.

Flynn still sucked at his lips. 'We get in a fight, we've failed. We pull the trigger, it means we've failed. Do you believe that, Officer Pike?'

'No, sir.'

'I do. What do you think it means?'

'We had no other way.'

Flynn grunted, but Pike couldn't tell if his grunt was approving or not. 'So why is it you want to protect people, Officer Pike?'

Pike knew Flynn was testing him. He met Flynn's gaze with empty blue eyes. 'I don't like bullies.'

'Making you the guy who kicks the bully's ass.'

'Yes.'

'Just so long as we stay within the rule of law.' Then Flynn's calm eyes crinkled gently at the corners. 'Me being your training officer, I read your file, son. I think you have what it takes to make a fine police officer.'

Pike nodded.

'You don't say much, do you?'

'No, sir.'

'Good. I'll do enough talking for both of us. Now let's go protect people.'

FLYNN STARTED OFF by giving Pike a tour of the entire division. During this time, Flynn reviewed radio procedures, let Pike practise exchanges with the dispatchers, and pointed out well-known dirtbag gathering points.

Then Flynn told the dispatchers to begin pitching them calls. Over the next two hours, Pike took a stolen-car report from a sobbing teenage girl, took a shoplifting report from the manager of a convenience store, took a report from a man who had returned home to find his house burgled. At every criminal call they answered, the suspect or perpetrator was long gone or never present, though Pike dutifully and under Flynn's direction logged the complainant's statement and filled out the necessary form.

They were proceeding eastbound on Beverly Boulevard when the dispatcher said, 'Two-adam-forty-four, domestic disturbance at 2721 Harell, woman reported crying for help. You up for that?'

Flynn picked up the mike. 'Two-adam-forty-four inbound.'

Domestic calls were the worst. Pike had heard it again and again at the academy, and Flynn had already mentioned it. When you rolled on a domestic call, you were rolling into the jagged eye of an emotional hurricane.

Flynn said, 'Evening watch is prime time for domestics. We'll probably get three or four tonight. More on a Friday.'

Pike didn't say anything. He knew about domestic violence first-hand. His father had never waited until Friday. Any night would do.

Flynn said, 'When we get there, I'll do the talking. You watch how I handle them, and learn. But keep your eyes open. You never know what's what when you answer one of these things.'

They rolled to a small apartment building near the centre of Rampart. The dispatcher had filled them in: call was placed by one Mrs Esther Villalobos, complaining that male and female neighbours had been arguing all afternoon and had escalated into what Mrs Villalobos described as loud crashing, whereupon the female neighbour, a young Caucasian female named Candace Stanik, shouted 'stop it' several times, then screamed for help. Mrs Villalobos had stated that an unemployed Caucasian male she knew only as 'Dave' sometimes lived at the residence.

When Pike and Flynn arrived at the scene, Pike followed Flynn towards Candace Stanik's apartment. They stopped outside Stanik's door. The windows were lit. They heard no voices, but hacking sobs were distinct.

Flynn looked at Pike and whispered. 'Stand here out of the way. When I go in, you come in right behind me, and take your cue from me. Maybe the guy's already gone. Maybe they've made up and are in there all lovey-dovey. Don't draw your gun unless you see me draw mine. We don't want to escalate the situation. We want to cool it. Understand?'

Pike nodded.

Flynn rapped at the door three times and announced them. 'Police officer. Please open the door.'

The crying stopped and Pike heard movement. Then a young woman spoke from the other side of the door. 'I'm OK. I don't need anything.'

Flynn rapped again. 'Open up, miss. We can't leave until we see you.'

The door opened, and Candace Stanik peered through a thin crack. Pike saw that her nose was broken and her right eye was purple with the mottled skin tight over a swelling lump. Pike had had plenty of eyes like that. Mostly as a kid. Mostly from his father.

Flynn placed his hand on the door. 'Step away, hon. Let me take a look.'

'He's gone. He went to his girlfriend.'

Flynn's voice was gentle, but firm. 'Let us in now, hon.'

Flynn pushed gently on the door until she backed away. Pike shadowed inside, then quickly stepped to the side so they weren't bunched together. Together, they would make a single large target; apart, two targets more difficult to kill.

They were in a cramped living room. Pike noted an entry closet to the left and, across the living room, a tiny kitchen and dining area. A short hall branched off the dining area. The coffee table was turned on its side and the floor was spattered with blood. Candace Stanik was pregnant. Pike guessed seven or eight months. Her T-shirt was streaked with blood and more blood spattered her legs and bare feet. Her lips were split in two places and her nose was broken and she held her belly as if she was cramping.

Flynn spoke softly over his shoulder to Pike. 'Paramedics and additional units.'

Pike keyed his rover, sending a request to the dispatcher.

'I want you to get him! He went to his slut girlfriend—' The girl was growing more agitated and Flynn was working to calm her, lowering his voice, sharing his calm.

'Let's take care of that baby first, all right, hon? Nothing's more important than your baby.' Flynn was everything he had to be—a strong, comforting father figure. You would be safe if you trusted him. Flynn slipped his arm round her shoulders, murmuring, 'You have to sit down first, hon. I'm going to take care of you.' Flynn motioned at Pike. 'I'm OK here. You good with getting the back?'

Pike nodded. He glanced in the kitchen, then stepped into the hall. The bathroom door was open, showing a sink, a tiny tub and a toilet. Pike turned to the bedroom. The door was half open and the light was on. He remembered Flynn's caution about drawing his weapon, but he drew it anyway, then pushed the door wider. The bedroom was a minefield of shopping bags, dirty clothes and boxes. The double bed was dingy with rumpled grey sheets. A closet door hung open on the far side of the bed.

Pike moved quickly and silently. He dropped to a knee, then jerked the tumbled sheets up and glanced under the bed. Nothing.

Pike didn't believe anyone would be in the closet, but he had to check. The closet door was open about six inches. He stood as far to the side as possible, then jerked open the door, letting light flood the dark space behind. Nothing.

In that moment a loud crash came from the living room, riding on top of the thuds of men moving hard, and a voice grunted—'Kill 'em.'

Pike moved fast into the hall. The closet door off the entry had been thrown open. Candace Stanik's boyfriend, who would later be identified as one David Lee Elish, had one arm hooked round Flynn's neck and was holding Flynn's gun arm to prevent Flynn from drawing his weapon. A second man, who would later be identified as George Fabrocini, was stabbing Flynn repeatedly in the chest with a hunting knife. Candace Stanik was curled on the floor.

Over and over, Elish was grunting, 'Kill 'em.'

Pike brought his 9mm up without hesitation and shot Fabrocini in the head. He would have shot Elish too, but the angle was bad. Then he drove hard into Flynn, knocking both men to the floor. He kept driving, digging hard with his legs. He shoved past Flynn and hit Elish hard in the face with his pistol. Elish, trying to rise, had eyes that were wild and frenzied. Pike hit him a second time, and then Elish grew still. Pike turned him over, pinned him to the floor with a knee, and twisted Elish's arms behind his back for the handcuffs.

Only after Elish and the knife were secure did Pike turn back to Flynn, scared the man was bleeding to death. 'Officer Flynn—'

Flynn looked up, fingers laced through the tears in his shirt, his eyes wide and glistening, and his face white. 'Fucking vest stopped the knife.'

THREE HOURS LATER, they were released to leave. A shooting team had come out, along with the evening-shift commander and two use-of-force detectives. Pike and Flynn had been questioned but now they were back in their car.

Pike knew Flynn was shaken, but he figured it was up to Flynn whether or not he wanted to talk about it.

Flynn finally looked over and said, 'You OK?'

'Yes, sir.'

'Listen, what happened in there—you saved me. Thank you for that.'

'You don't have to thank me.'

'I know, but I want you to know I appreciate what you did. You made a fast call. I'm not saying you did anything wrong. I just want you to think about what you did. Sometimes we have to kill people, but our job out here isn't to kill people.'

'Yes, sir. I know that.'

'What happened in there was my fault, not clearing that closet. I saw that damned door. Your first day on the job, and you sure as hell saved my butt. Flynn suddenly reached out and covered Pike's hand. 'You're calm as a stone. Me, I'm shaking like a leaf—'

Pike felt it in Bud Flynn's hand—a faint humming like bees trying to escape a hive. Bud suddenly pulled back his hand as if he was embarrassed. Officer-involved shootings were rare, but gunfights had been part of Pike's life since he left home, and home had been worse—his father's rage; fists and belts and steel-toed work boots falling like rain; his mother, screaming; Pike, screaming. Combat was nothing. Pike remembered a kind of intellectual acceptance that he had to kill other men so they couldn't kill him. Like when he finally grew big enough to choke out his father. Once his father feared him, he stopped beating him and his mother. Simple. Pike's only concerns now were in following the rules of the Los Angeles Police Department. He had. Bud was alive. Pike was alive. Simple.

Pike touched Bud's hand. He wanted to help. 'We're OK.'

Bud's eyes returned to Pike. 'I'm looking at you, and it's like nothing happened. You just killed a man, and there's nothing in your eyes.'

Pike felt embarrassed and took back his hand.

Flynn forced out a laugh. 'You ready to go? We got a hellacious amount of paperwork. That's the worst part about shooting someone.'

Pike took out his sunglasses and put them on, covering his eyes.

Flynn laughed again. 'It's pitch black. You going to wear those things at night?'

Pike said, 'Yes.'

'Well, whatever. That business with you calling me Officer Flynn and me calling you Officer Pike? We're past that. My name is Bud.'

Pike nodded, but Bud was still trembling and the phoney smile made him looked pained. Pike felt sick, thinking he had disappointed his training officer. He vowed to try harder. He wanted to be a good and right man, and he wanted to serve and protect.

5

Pike was driving hard towards Glendale and the LAPD's Scientific Investigation Division when his cellphone buzzed. It was Ronnie. 'They hit your store fourteen minutes ago. In broad daylight.'

Larkin, beside him, said, 'Who is it?'

Pike held up his finger, telling her to wait. 'Did the security guys roll?'

'Code three, lights and sirens, and they called in LAPD. Denny and I are rolling over right now.'

'File a report with the police. If we have any physical damage, have an insurance adjuster come out. If anything needs to be repaired, call out the repairmen today.'

'I get it. You want noise.'

'Loud.'

Pike put down the phone, and Larkin punched him in the arm.

'I hate how you just ignore me. I asked you a question.'

Pike said, 'We're going to see someone in Glendale, then we're going to meet Elvis where you had your accident.'

She slumped back in the seat, sullen.

They climbed up through the Sepulveda Pass, then down into the San Fernando Valley. The valley was always much hotter, and Pike could feel the increasing heat even with the air conditioning.

Larkin was quiet for exactly nine minutes.

Then she said, 'Doesn't anything shock you?'

Pike didn't respond, though he wondered why she would ask such a thing. He glanced at her, then continued driving. 'Day I got to Central Africa, I watched a woman. Her family had been murdered that morning, just two hours before we rolled in. She cut the fingers off her left hand, one by one, one each for her husband and her four children. She started with the thumb.' Pike glanced over again. 'That was how she mourned.'

Larkin folded her hands in her lap. She stared at him. 'What did you do?'

'Found the men who did it.'

Larkin turned to the window. The silence was good.

They drove through the valley heat.

DESPERATION BRED innovation, and John Chen was a desperate man. That same desperation also bred lies, deception and masterful acting, all of which John had employed with convincing brilliance because—well, face it—he was the smartest senior criminalist employed by LAPD's Scientific Investigations Division. In the past few years, John had broken more cases (necessary for career advancement—read money), amassed more face time on the local news (mandatory for hitting on chicks—at six-two and one twenty-seven he needed all the help he could get) and garnered more merit pay raises (essential for leasing a Porsche) than any other rat in the lab. And how had he been rewarded?

More work. Less time to enjoy the fruits of his labours.

Namely, poontang—sex.

John Chen was all about the 'tang. He was a man obsessed; hungry to make up the poontang shortfall which had been his lifelong burden; convinced that every single straight male in California had enjoyed a veritable all-you-can-eat smorgasbord of the stuff since puberty. Except him.

But now John Chen had scored a girlfriend. Well, OK, she wasn't *really* his girlfriend. Ronda Milbank was a married secretary with two kids from Atwater Village he'd met in a bar last night. He bought her a drink, and then another, and then he asked if maybe he could, you know, kinda see her sometime. And Ronda said, sure, tomorrow between eleven and noon.

SCORE!!!!

But then came the problem. Los Angeles is a city of twelve million civilians; untold criminals, all of whom were out doing crime; an unending tsunami of evidence, every item of which had to be documented and analysed by LAPD's understaffed Scientific Investigations Division.

So John knew the answer even without asking. I mean, *what*? 'Oh, sure, John, you need a 'tang break midway through the morning, be my guest.'

Here's how John Chen innovated his departure: that morning during the coffee break, John made a point of walking past his supervisor, Marion, just as he took a bite of his Ralph's Market raspberry-swirl muffin, and screamed—'AHHHHHH!!!' John jumped sideways, grabbing his jaw. Then he shouted—'SONOFABITCH!!! I BROKE MY TOOTH! I GOTTA SEE MY DENTIST!'

'Maybe you just chipped it,' Marion said. 'Here. Let me see.'

John covered his mouth, backing away. 'JESUS, MARION! IT'S KILLING ME. THE NERVE IS EXPOSED!'

Marion would let him die rather than fall farther behind their case load. 'John, please. The pain will fade. In a few minutes you won't even feel it.'

You see how she was?

'It's a broken tooth, Marion—shattered, ruined! I gotta see a dentist. Look, if I leave right now, I'll probably be back by one-thirty or so.'

Marion finally relented. 'All right, but take a van. I might send you straight to a crime scene from the dentist.'

He snatched his keys and evidence kit, and ran for the exit. No way was he gonna tool up to Ronda's house in a clunky SID van. He had washed the Boxster before work and intended to roll up to Ronda's in style! As soon as he reached the first line of parked cars, John Chen punched the air. He was going to get laid.

He turned to run for his car when someone who hadn't been there a moment ago blocked his path.

He startled so bad he screamed again: 'AHHH!' and lurched backwards, falling, until hands hard as vice grips caught him, and held.

Chen hated it when Pike did that—appearing from nowhere and scaring people, and Chen had been afraid of Pike since they first met. He had taken one look at the guy and known Pike was one of those vicious, double-Y chromosome, beer-commercial slope-brows who loved showing up other people. True, Pike had also given him the tips that led to Chen's first break-through case and the acquisition of the 'tangmobile, but Pike still made him nervous.

Chen said, 'You scared the shit out of me. Where'd you come from?'

Pike tipped his head towards a green Lexus parked on the next row.

Chen immediately stood taller. A smokin' hot babe with spiky black hair was in the front seat. She gave him a little wave.

Chen said, 'Man, that chick is hot. Does she put out?'

'I need a favour, John.'

Chen remembered Ronda, and started to edge away. 'Sure, yeah, but I gotta get going. I have an appointment—'

'It can't wait.'

Chen froze in his tracks. 'But—'

Pike said, 'Big case, John. You could make the papers again.'

Ronda vanished like a popping bubble. Another headline case, and he might even be able to spear a gig with a private lab. Move up to a Carrera.

Pike said, 'You know about the two men who were shot in Malibu?'

'That's the sheriffs. Their lab handles all that.'

'The three men who were killed in Eagle Rock?'

'Yeah, sure. We got that one, but it isn't mine. What do you want?'

'The identities of the dead men. LiveScan came back empty. None of the five were in the system.'

'Then what can I do?'

'Run their guns, John. Run the casings.'

Chen knew what Pike was asking and didn't like it. The police covering both crime scenes would have recovered any weapons and spent shell casings found with the bodies, but SID employed only two firearms analysis specialists, and the backlog of guns waiting to be analysed numbered in the thousands.

'I dunno, dude, that backlog is brutal.'

'You came through before. Call Elvis when you know. I won't be around.'

Chen eyed the girl again and figured he knew exactly where Pike would be. 'What's in this for me?'

'The bullets from the Malibu bodies will match the bullets from Eagle Rock. Same shooter, John. LA and the sheriffs have not yet made the connection. Neither has the press.'

Chen's heart began pounding. With the bullets in two different labs, unless the police had some other connecting evidence, it might take months to connect the two shootings—until and unless a superstar criminalist made a miraculous breakthrough.

If Chen played his cards right, he might end up on the national news. Maybe even *60 Minutes*! All thoughts of Ronda were gone.

Pike drifted away towards the Lexus. 'Check it out, John. Call Elvis.' Pike slipped into the car like he was made of hot butter, then drove away.

Chen turned back to the lab, scowling. Marion would wonder why he never left the parking lot. But then Chen realised she had already given him an out—she had told him the pain might pass, and he would tell her it had. Everyone liked being told they were right.

John ran back to the lab. Ronda would get over it.

PIKE KNEW THE GIRL was uneasy about returning to her neighbourhood. This was where her nightmare began. But this was exactly why she had to return. Animals left trails where they passed, and so did men. Meesh and the Kings might have left a trail. Pike intended to drop off the girl with Cole, then head for home. The men who entered his home had left a trail, too.

Cole was waiting on the block where the accident occurred, only three blocks from the girl's building, standing in a nearby doorway. The street was lined with warehouses and other buildings that housed shipping centres, storage units or minimum-wage immigrants building cabinetry and decorative metalwork. Everything about the area was industrial.

When Larkin saw him, she said, 'What's he doing here?'

'Working. He came down to establish the scene at the time of the accident.'

'I don't think it's safe. What if they're waiting for me?'

'Elvis would wave us away.'

'How does *he* know?'

Pike didn't bother answering. He was already missing the silence.

He found a spot to park half a block past the alley. Cole crossed the street to join them. He was wearing olive green cargo shorts, a floral short-sleeved shirt and a faded Dodgers cap.

Cole grinned at the girl. 'Nice neighbourhood. Reminds me of Fallujah.'

'Nice clothes. Reminds me of a twelve-year-old.'

Cole turned towards Pike. 'I love it when she talks that way.'

They were at the exact spot where the girl had ploughed into the Mercedes, where a thin alley opened onto the street. The alley was a dirty fissure between two dingy warehouses. Dozens of shirtless men milled outside, ordering up bottles of soda from a catering van at the kerb.

Pike said, 'OK.' He wanted Cole's report.

'Nada. I talked to every business for two blocks in each direction, and none of these people carry a night watchman except for a shipping company down there'— Cole tipped his head towards the block behind them— 'but he didn't see anything. Says he didn't even know an accident happened until the feds came round. I asked about security cams, too, but nobody runs a camera showing the street, only inside.'

Pike said, 'Did you get the accident report?'

'Yeah—' Cole pulled folded papers from his cargo shorts. 'The accident occurred here at the mouth of the alley. Ms Barkley was proceeding up the street towards us—heading for home, which is three blocks farther down.' Cole then opened the papers to show a sketch drawn by the accident investigator. A rectangle showed the position of Larkin's car, along with lines illustrating the relevant skid marks, and measurements.

'The building here on the right is abandoned. Doors on the front, back and sides are chained, and you can tell they haven't been opened in years. The other building here is set up as a factory. They make ceramic knick-knacks and souvenirs. It's a pretty good bet the Kings weren't down here for a sex party.'

Larkin said, 'I told you. They were backing out.'

Cole raised his eyebrows at her. 'Yeah, but why here and why then?'

The girl said, 'I don't know.'

Pike studied the position of the cars in the sketch. The girl's Aston Martin had slammed into the Mercedes on the driver's side behind the rear wheel as it backed into the street. The force of the impact kicked the Mercedes a quarter turn counterclockwise, and her car had spun to a rest, pointing towards the Mercedes, one headlight smashed but the other illuminating the scene. The police sketch matched everything the girl had described.

Pike said, 'Which way did Meesh go?'

The girl pointed up the street. 'That way. He ran up the middle of the street. The Mercedes went the other way.'

Cole stepped into the street for a better look. 'Did you see him turn off?'

'I wasn't looking. I had nine-one-one on the phone. The Mercedes was gone. I was writing their licence number on my arm, and talking.'

Cole shrugged at Pike. 'There's nothing down here, man. I walked eight blocks in each direction. It's nothing but commercial space and construction sites except for three or four loft conversions like Larkin's.'

Pike grunted, but something was bothering him. He looked back at the crowd of workers and the catering van, then at the cars lining the street.

'Was the Mercedes backing out when you hit it or was it stopped?'

The girl shook her head. 'I don't know. Why does it matter?'

Cole said, 'If they were parked, then what were they doing? Were they looking at something or someone in the alley? Had they just gotten into the car or were they getting out? You see how one thing leads to another?'

Pike glanced back at the street and realised what was bothering him. 'That time of night, all these cars would be gone. With the street empty, your sight line was clear. You hit them, which means they were in front of you. Seems like you would have seen them.'

'I'm not lying.'

The skid marks bore out her version of the accident, but Pike wondered why she hadn't been able to avoid the collision. He thought she had probably been drunk or high, so he flipped to that page in the report. Nope. The tests had come back clean.

'Not saying that. Just trying to figure it out.'

'Well, maybe they backed out really fast. How much longer are we going to stay here? I'm scared.'

Pike glanced at Cole and Cole shrugged.

'I have everything I need from here. I can take her back.'

Pike said, 'He'll stay with you until I get back.'

He started back to the Lexus, but the girl followed him.

'I don't want to stay with him. He'll rape me as soon as you're gone.'

Cole said, 'In your dreams.'

She ignored him, staying with Pike. 'Listen, you're being paid to protect me. My father won't like you dumping me off with the B-team.'

Cole spread his arms. 'B-team?'

Pike got into the Lexus, but Larkin stepped inside the door so he couldn't close it. Pike thought how she didn't seem so much angry as betrayed. He gentled his voice. 'I'm sorry if I should have discussed it with you. I didn't think it would be an issue.'

She stood in the door, breathing.

'You can't come with me, Larkin. I'll see you this evening.'

Pike tugged at the door, nudging her. She didn't move.

Cole said, 'You want me to knock her out?'

The girl stepped back, uttering a final word as Pike pulled the door. 'Asshole.'

Pike drove away without looking back, heading for Culver City.

TWENTY-FIVE MINUTES later, Pike stopped under a sycamore tree on a residential street six blocks from his condo.

He got out of the car, then went to the trunk. He looked through the things Ronnie had left, drank half a bottle of Arrowhead water, then collected his SOG fighting knife, a pair of Zeiss binoculars, the little Beretta and a box of bullets for the .45.

He then drove to a Mobil station located on the other side of the wall outside his complex. He parked behind the station next to the wall. Pike bought gas there often and knew the staff, so they didn't mind. Before he left his car, he fitted the Beretta to his right ankle and the SOG to his left. He made sure the Kimber was loaded, then clipped it behind his back.

Pike moved quickly. He dropped into the condo grounds behind a flat building which faced an enormous communal swimming pool. A lush curtain of banana trees, birds-of-paradise and canna plants hid a sound wall baffling the pool equipment, and continued round the pool and walkways. Pike slipped behind the greenery and made his way across the grounds.

He worked his way from pod to pod and round three parking areas, and finally to his own pod. He did not try to enter, but took a position behind the rice-paper plants at the corner of his building, and settled down to watch. It was a good spot, with a clean view between the leaves of the parking lot and buildings that faced his own.

Pike never moved, and for the first time that day did not feel the passing of time. He simply *was*; safe in his green world, observing. Two hours later, he was finally satisfied no one was watching, but he still didn't move.

He saw the world grow golden, then burnish to a deep copper, then deepen with purple into a murky haze. Cars came and left. People banged through their gates, some wearing flip-flops on their way to the pool. Pike watched until it was full-on dark and then he finally moved. He crept along the side of his condo, checking each window, and found that the second window had been jimmied. Raising it had tripped the alarm.

Pike peered in, but saw only shadows. Nothing moved, and no sounds came from within. He slowly raised the window and lifted himself inside.

The room was dark, but the doorway opening into his living room was bright. Pike had left on the lamp. He drew the Kimber, crept into the living room. The only movement came from the fountain in the corner—a bowl with water burbling quietly over stones. The only sounds were the water and the whisper of the air conditioner.

Pike found no one. They had tried to be careful so he wouldn't know, but an address book was missing from the kitchen, and the phone in his bedroom was in a place Pike never left it.

He returned to the living room. A security camera he had installed himself fed into a hard drive. Pike turned on his television and watched the recording. Single-frame captures at eight-second intervals appeared as a jerky slide show. A man with a pistol entered. He wasn't wearing a mask or gloves, just a dark T-shirt and jeans and running shoes. His hair was longish, and straight, and dark. He was Anglo or Latin, but Pike couldn't tell which. The pictures showed his path in sharp jumps—first as he entered, then across the room, then at the stairs. Then a second man entered. This man was smaller than the first man, and wore a dark button shirt with his shirt tail out over jeans. His hair was also longish and dark, but his skin was darker, and Pike decided this man was Latin.

In the next picture, the first man had returned to the kitchen, and the second man was kneeling at the door. A small black case appeared on the floor, and the second man seemed to be holding the doorknob with both hands. Pike realised he was making keys. The first man returned from searching the house as the keymaker tested the keys.

Pike froze the picture. It was the best view yet of the first man's face. He took out the pictures Bud had given him, and compared them. The keymaker wasn't among them, but the first man was one of the three men who invaded Larkin's home.

Pike backed up the images until he found the best angle on the keymaker, pressed a button, and a laser printer hummed. He tucked the new pictures away. The remaining captures showed the two men leaving through the front door.

Pike turned off the television and called Ronnie.

'I need you on the house. Two men, twenties to thirties, dark hair straight and on the long side, five-eight to five-ten, the shorter guy probably Latin.'

'They at your place now?'

'No, but they'll be back. They made keys.'

'Ah. You want 'em field-dressed?'

'Just let me know.'

Pike reset the alarms, reset the surveillance camera, then went to his fridge. He opened two bottles of Corona, poured the beer down the sink, then placed the empty bottles on the counter. When the men returned, they would see that Pike had been home. They would tell themselves if he came home once he'd come home again, and they might decide to wait.

Pike wanted them to wait.

6

Larkin Conner Barkley stared down the street as if Pike's car had been a shimmering mirage. 'I can't believe he left me like this.'

Cole said, 'The nerve of him. That cad.'

'Fuck you.'

'That's the second time you've hinted at sex, but I still have to refuse.'

Larkin crossed the street without waiting for him and went directly to Cole's car. Some people didn't appreciate humour.

Cole decided to give her some space, so they drove back in silence. He still had questions, but the answers would keep until later.

On the way back, he stopped at a small grocery store in Thai Town, figuring the odds were better she wouldn't be recognised at a small ethnic market. He expected her to give him an argument when he asked her to come in with him, but she didn't. He filled two bags with food, milk, a drawing pad, a plastic ruler and two bottles of plum wine.

When they got back to the house, she took a bath. Cole put away the groceries, then brought the pad and his notes to the table. His notes described in detail every building and business in Larkin Barkley's neighbourhood. Cole set to work drawing a map, building it block by block, and listing the names and addresses of any businesses he had observed, as well as their phone numbers.

After a while, Larkin emerged from the bathroom wrapped in a towel and went into her bedroom. Cole completed his map of her street, then set to work charting the surrounding streets. He was convinced that Meesh and the Kings had been in the area for a purpose. He was also convinced the feds believed the same; twelve of the sixteen people Cole interviewed had also been questioned by agents of the US Department of Justice about the accident.

Then Cole discovered a discrepancy.

Larkin came out of the bedroom wearing fresh five-hundred-dollar jeans, a tight black Ramones T-shirt and an iPod. Her feet were bare. She stretched out on the couch with her feet hanging over the arm, closed her eyes, her right foot moving with the beat.

Cole said, 'Hey.'

Her eyes opened and she looked at him.

Cole said, 'The feds didn't know Meesh was Meesh until you identified him?'

'No. They got all excited when we finally had his name.'

Cole returned to the time line he had built. The twelve people had all been questioned by the feds the day after the accident. All stated the feds had showed them pictures of two men, and all had described the same two pictures. It was as if Pitman knew or suspected Meesh was the missing man even before he met with the girl, and had lied about what he knew.

Twenty minutes later, Larkin rolled off the couch, went to the window. The day was dimming, and soon they would have to pull the shades.

Cole said, 'If you're getting hungry I'll make dinner.'

She didn't hear him. Cole wadded up a piece of paper and bounced it off her back. She turned and took off the headset.

'Did you say something?' she said.

'If you're hungry I'll make dinner.'

'Shouldn't we wait for him?'

'He might be late.'

'I'm OK.'

She went back to the couch and Cole went on with his work.

'Was he really in Africa?'

Cole glanced up. She was looking at him. He was surprised Pike had told her about Africa. Pike rarely spoke of those days.

'What did he tell you?'

'He watched a woman cut off her own fingers. What a gross thing to say. Like I'm supposed to be impressed by that. What a gross and disgusting thing, trying to scare me.' She wrapped her arms across her breasts and stared at the ceiling. 'Is he married?'

'No.'

'I asked him, but he didn't answer. He does that. I'll say something and I know he hears, but he ignores me. I don't like being ignored. It's rude.'

'Yes, it is.'

'Then why does he do it?'

'I asked him once, but he ignored me.'

Larkin didn't find it funny. 'What about the courtesy of polite conversation? Here I am stuck with a man who won't talk. He never laughs. He won't smile. He has absolutely no expression on his face.'

'You're probably used to people trying to impress you—they're trying to get your attention or make you like them. Don't confuse that with being interesting. It isn't. Pike is one of the most interesting men you'll meet. He just doesn't want to entertain you, so he doesn't.'

'It's still boring. You talk a lot. Does that mean you're trying to entertain me?

'It means I'm trying to entertain myself. You're kinda dull.'

Larkin crossed her legs. 'Shouldn't he be back by now?'

'It's still early.'

'Well, is it true? Was he in Africa?'

'He's been to Africa many times. He's been all over the world.'

'Why would he be a mercenary? I think it's sick, getting paid to play soldiers. Anyone who enjoys that kind of thing is insane.'

'I guess that depends on what you do and why you do it. That story he told you about the woman, did he tell you why he was there?'

'Of course not. He never answers when I ask him something.'

He told her. 'A group called the Lord's Resistance Army was running around Central Africa, mostly in Uganda. They kidnapped girls. What they would do was, they'd blow into a village out in the middle of nowhere, shoot up everything with machine guns, loot the place and grab the teenage girls. They've kidnapped hundreds of girls. They take them as slaves, rape them, do whatever.

'The people in those villages, they're farmers, maybe have a few cattle, they didn't have police; but sometimes these villages would get together and pool their money. They figured they needed professionals to stop the kidnappings, so Joe made the trip. The morning of the day Joe and his guys arrived, a raiding party shot up another village and stole more girls. That woman's husband and her sons were murdered. That's the first thing Joe saw when they rolled in, this poor woman mutilating herself.'

Larkin stared at him. 'What did he do?'

Cole knew, but decided to keep it simple. 'Joe did his job. The raids stopped.'

Larkin glanced towards the front windows, but it was darker now, and the light in the room made it impossible to see. 'He did that a lot?'

'He's been all over the world.'

'Why?'

'He's an idealist.'

She finally looked back at him. 'I still think it's creepy. He wouldn't do that kind of thing if he didn't enjoy it.'

'No, probably not. But he probably doesn't enjoy it the way you mean. C'mon, let's make dinner.'

She turned back to the window. 'I'm going to wait.'

Cole went to the kitchen, but didn't begin their dinner. He thought about Pitman. Pitman had told Larkin and her family a version of events that no longer fitted with the facts, and probably never had. Cole had caught Pitman in a lie, and now he wondered if Pitman had lied about anything else.

THE FIREARMS ANALYSIS UNIT was called the Gun Room. You went in there, all you saw were hundreds of guns from the floor to the ceiling, each gun with a tag to identify its make, model and case number; each gun confiscated, used or believed to have been used in a crime.

John Chen eyeballed the hall outside the Gun Room, as he made sure no one was coming. Chen hated hanging round so late, but the firearms analysts were so overworked that the slave-driving bitch Harriet Munson was constantly on their ass, which meant Chen had to wait until Harriet had gone home. Today she had haunted the Gun Room like the Ghost of Christmas Future, and Chen had lived in an absolute agony of nerves all day, knowing Pike was almost certainly out there somewhere right now, waiting, impatient. Pike was a cold-blooded killer, and would probably snap Chen's neck like a pencil.

Chen had come prepared.

The duty analyst that day was a tall, thin woman with close-set eyes named Christine LaMolla. Chen was convinced she was a lesbian.

John crept down the hall, made sure no one was coming, then pressed the buzzer. He heard the lock click, pushed open the door and entered.

LaMolla turned from her computer, smileless. Lesbians never smiled.

Chen held out the cup. He had raced out to the nearest Starbucks and bought their largest mocha. He gave her his toothiest smile.

'For you. I know you guys work late. I thought you might need it.'

LaMolla glanced at the cup again as if she thought it was laced it with acid. John had once asked her out, and she had turned him down flat. Lesbian.

Now she eyeballed Chen with equal suspicion. 'What do you want?'

'You know the shootings we had in Eagle Rock? I need to see the guns.' Mr Nonchalant. Mr Just Another Day at the Office.

Her eyes narrowed. 'You didn't cover the Eagle Rock case.'

'Nah, but something came up in one of my old Inglewood cases. I think they might be connected.'

LaMolla peered at him even harder, then took the coffee. She went to the door, locked it, then leaned with her back to the door, blocking it.

John got the unexpected, more-than-a-little-hopeful notion that maybe she wasn't a lesbian after all; that maybe his luck was about to change for the good—but then she dropped the mocha into a trash can. She crossed her arms. 'What's going on?'

Chen didn't know what to say, and wasn't even sure what she meant. He felt himself squirm. He did his best to look innocent.

'Hey, all I wanna do is see the guns. What's going on?'

'That's what I want to know.'

'Whattaya mean? Jesus, you gonna let me see the guns or not?'

She slowly shook her head. 'The feds took them.'

Chen blinked. 'The feds?'

'Mm. They took one two days ago—a Colt Python, .357. But then they came back yesterday morning for the semis.'

Chen saw his chances for a Carrera upgrade circling the drain. But mostly he imagined Joe Pike beating his ass.

'But that was LAPD evidence! The feds can't just take our stuff.'

'They can when Parker tells us to let them have it. Sixth floor.'

'Parker Centre gave them permission?' The sixth floor of Parker Centre was the power floor—the realm of the Assistant Chiefs.

LaMolla slowly nodded, still watching him with tiny eyes.

John had grown frantic. His mind was racing for some angle or explanation that might appease Joe Pike when a desperate idea came to him.

'What about the shell casings? Did they take the casings?'

Christine shook her head. 'They took everything. Even the casings.' She sighed. 'And you know what was really weird? They wouldn't sign an evidence receipt.'

Anytime evidence was transferred or moved between departments or agencies, a receipt and acceptance of possession had to be signed. It was standard operating procedure. This ensured the chain of evidence remained intact. This prevented evidence tampering.

Chen said, 'But they *had* to.'

LaMolla simply stared at him. 'And now here you come, wanting those same guns. And the casings. What's going on?'

'I don't know.'

Now it looked like the feds and Parker Centre were doing things that no legitimate police agency would ever do, John Chen grew afraid. No Carrera was worth this, or even the smokin' hot 'tang that would follow.

John Chen suddenly felt caught in a claustrophobic nightmare between Pike, the federal government and the shadowy powers within Parker Centre, none of whom could be trusted, and any of which might snuff his life and career without hesitation. His mouth was dry.

'Chris, you're not going to tell—well, I mean, Harriet doesn't need to—'

LaMolla, still considering him with her calm, predatory eyes, uncrossed her arms and spread her hands wide like Moses parting the waters. 'This Gun Room is mine. This is *my* evidence. I don't like someone taking it. I don't like *you* knowing something about it that I don't.' She lowered her arms and stepped away from the door. 'Get out of here, John. Don't come back without something to tell me.'

Chen stepped quickly past her and fled down the hall. He ran directly to his car, jumped in and locked the doors. He started the engine, but sat with his hands clenched in his lap, shaking and terrified.

He fished his cellphone from his pocket. The shaking made it difficult to scroll through the numbers, but Pike had told him to call Elvis Cole when he had something. Cole was Pike's friend. Cole could convince Pike not to kill him. Everyone knew Pike was a monster.

IN THE QUIET of the later night Pike eased up to the Echo Park house. The air was warmer than the evening before, but the same five men still clustered at the car beneath the street light, and families still sat on their porches. Pike parked in the drive and crossed the yard to the porch. The five men glanced over, but not in a threatening way.

Cole opened the door as Pike reached it, and stepped out onto the porch. Pike smelled mint and curry, and wondered why Cole had come out.

Cole spoke low, hiding his voice from the men. 'How'd it go?'

Pike described the two men who searched his home, and unfolded their pictures. Cole cracked open the door long enough to light the pictures. Pike glimpsed the girl, standing in the kitchen. She was wearing an iPod. He had made her get rid of her iPod in the desert.

Pike said, 'Where'd she get the iPod?'

'It's mine. I made Thai, if you want something to eat. That's what we had.'

Pike put away the pictures. The Thai sounded good.

Then Cole lowered his voice even more. 'I got a call from John Chen this evening. The feds confiscated everything from Eagle Rock. The guns, the casings, all of it.'

'Pitman?'

'All Chen knew was the feds.'

'John run the guns before they were taken?'

'They moved in too fast. Here's what's really wild—they took the stuff without papers. Said Parker told them to let it go, no questions asked.'

Pike raised his eyebrows.

'Those D-3s at Homicide Special wouldn't roll over just because Pitman's a fed, not with five unidentified stiffs on the plate. Someone must have—no pun intended—put a gun to their heads.'

Pike agreed. 'He's scared. Only reason to take those guns is he doesn't want LAPD anywhere round this.'

'That, or he's hiding more than this case he's building against the Kings.'

'Like what?' Even with the darkness and deep shadows, Pike could see Cole was troubled.

'I don't know. But I know he hasn't been straight with the girl or her family. Remember they told her they didn't know Meesh was the missing man until she identified him? That morning they had already worked her street, asking about Meesh. They already knew he was in the car.'

Pike realised Cole had come outside so they could talk about this without the girl hearing. 'How do you know that?'

'I heard it from half a dozen people today. Agents from the Department of Justice, showing pictures of two men. I had them describe the pictures, and I'm pretty sure one was King and the other was Meesh.'

Pike took a breath, wondering why Pitman and Blanchette had misled the girl. Pike didn't like it, but none of this affected his mission. Find Meesh. Eliminate the threat. He could deal with Pitman and Blanchette later.

'Let's go back to her neighbourhood tomorrow. I was hoping we'd pick up Meesh's trail, but maybe Pitman's trail is more important.'

'She's not going to like it. She wasn't happy when you left.'

Pike said, 'That food smells pretty good. That curry?'

Cole smiled, and they went into the house. The girl was stretched out on the couch with the headset fixed to her ears. Her eyes were closed, but she looked up when they entered.

Pike said, 'How's it going?'

She raised a hand in a kind of a wave, then closed her eyes again. Her foot bounced with the beat. Pike figured she was still pissed off.

Cole left a few minutes later, and Pike went into the kitchen. Cole had made vegetable curry and rice. Pike stood in the kitchen, eating from the pot. He ate it cold. When he finished eating, he drank a bottle of water. The girl came to the door. 'I'm going to bed.'

Pike nodded. He wanted to say something, but he was still wondering why Pitman had put the girl in this position. Meesh was a murderer, but his prosecution would be handled by the Colorado courts. For Pitman, Meesh was nothing more than a way to bag the Kings for money-laundering. Paper. He had put this girl's life in jeopardy for paper, and he had somehow gotten LAPD to go along. Pike wondered if Bud knew.

The girl went into her bedroom and closed the door.

Pike went to the bathroom, then checked the windows and doors, shut the lights and stretched out on the couch in the dark. The couch was still warm from her, and the impression left by her body was soft.

LARKIN EMERGED from her dream and pulled the headset from her ears. She lay in the darkness, awake, then realised she had to pee.

The house was dark, so she figured he was sleeping somewhere and went directly into the bathroom. She closed the door before she turned on the light. When she finished, she turned out the light, opened the door, and that's when she heard him. Soft, frantic grunts came from the living room. She hesitated, then crept in.

He was asleep on the couch, the pistol on the floor beside him. His body was clenched; his arms rigid at his sides as he jerked and trembled. Even in the poor light, she saw the sweat on his face as his head snapped from side to side. Ohmigod. He was having a nightmare. She wondered if she should wake him.

Larkin moved closer, trying to decide what to do. His hands flexed like claws, then shook and fluttered, and his eyes rolled wildly beneath the lids.

Larkin thought, Man, this must be one monster of a nightmare.

Then he spoke. *Duh* . . . *dah* . . . It sounded like 'daddy'.

She strained closer to make out what he was saying, but all she heard were mumbles and slurs. Then, little by little, he relaxed.

Larkin was very close then, over him, when he mumbled again.

She waited to hear it again, but he fell quiet, and she was probably wrong. A man like him might have nightmares, but not about his daddy.

She watched him, wanted to touch him. She wanted to reach out the way you always want to reach through the bars at a zoo to touch the big animals.

Larkin stood with him for a moment longer, then crept back to her room.

7

The next morning, Pike was cleaning his pistol at the dining table when the girl came out of her room. It was ten minutes after eight. Today she wasn't naked. She wore an over-sized T-shirt draped to her thighs. She wrinkled her nose. 'Ugh. You get high, breathing that stuff?'

Pike had broken down the pistol into its components and was swabbing the barrel with a powder solvent that had the odour of overripe peaches.

He said, 'There's coffee.'

Pike's phone was on the table. He was waiting for Cole so they could hook up at the girl's loft.

The girl said, 'You were dreaming last night. You had a nightmare.'

'Don't remember.'

'It was bad. I didn't know if I should wake you.'

'That's OK.' Pike never remembered his dreams. 'I'm going back to your neighbourhood to see some people Elvis found. Then I'm going to see Bud.'

The girl didn't say anything. She went into the kitchen.

Pike finished cleaning the frame. He saturated the swab with fresh solvent, then went to work on the slide.

The girl returned with a cup of coffee. She sat at the table across from him, watching him. She looked serious.

'We have to talk,' she said.

'OK.'

'I didn't like the way you left me yesterday. If you had told me what you were doing, it would have been fine, but you didn't tell me. You don't even talk to me. OK, I know you're not a talker. I get that. But I'm an adult. These people are trying to kill *me*. I don't need a baby sitter, and I don't like being treated like a child. We've been here two days and they haven't found me, so I guess it's safe. OK, good, thank you. I don't want to go see Bud, and I don't want to sit in the car all day while you talk to people. It's boring, and I'm tired of it. I would rather stay here, and I can stay here by myself.'

Pike put down the barrel. He looked at her. 'Yes.'

'Yes, I can stay here?'

'I said *I* was going to see Bud. I didn't say we. I'm sorry about yesterday. I should have been more considerate.'

The girl's mouth opened, but she didn't say anything. She sipped the coffee, holding the cup with both hands.

Pike slipped the barrel into the slide, dropped the recoil spring guide into place beneath the barrel, then fed the recoil spring onto the guide. He reassembled the gun in seconds. He could put it together blindfolded. Talking to the girl was difficult.

The girl finally spoke. 'OK. Thanks. That's cool.'

His cell vibrated, making a loud buzz on the table. Pike read the screen, thinking it would be Cole, but it wasn't. He placed the phone to his ear.

Ronnie said, 'You have company.'

Pike showed nothing, He said, 'How many?'

'One guy, this time. He's under six, I'd say; hair's kinda long and dark. He just let himself in, walked right in like he owned the place. You want me to introduce myself?'

The girl was watching him. If she knew what he intended to do she would be worried or ask questions, and Pike had used up his talking allowance.

'No, I'll come over and have a word. If he leaves, you have my phone.'

Pike put down the phone, pushed the magazine into the gun, then jacked the slide and set the safety. If he could ever know bliss, it filled him now, but he showed nothing. He had them. He had a line that might bring him to Meesh, and then he would clear the field. All these bastards trying to kill this girl, this one girl, it filled him with a beautiful sorrow. He would clear the field, but not for justice. It would be punishment.

'Who was that?'

'Ronnie. He found someone who might be able to help, so I'm going to meet them. You're going to be OK?'

'Uh-huh. How long will you be?'

Pike stood, holstered the Kimber and clipped it to his waist. He pulled on the long-sleeved shirt to cover his tattoos and the gun. 'Most of the day, maybe. You want me to pick up something?'

'Maybe some fruit. Strawberries. Maybe bananas.'

'OK, then. I'll see you later.'

Pike had mixed feelings about leaving her, but he had convinced himself there was more to protecting her than just keeping her alive. He didn't want her to feel abandoned again. If she needed to feel trusted, then he would trust her.

PIKE WORKED HIS WAY south to the Santa Monica Freeway in the sluggish morning traffic. He didn't hurry. If the man in his condo left, Ronnie would follow him. He filled in Cole from the car. Cole asked if Pike wanted help, but Pike declined, saying Cole's time would be better spent on Pitman as they had planned. Pike still wanted to see Bud, but that could wait. He told Cole about the girl.

Cole said, 'You want me to watch her?'

'Not watch her, but maybe you could stop by.'

'OK. I'll swing by later. I'll drop off some food.'

'She wants strawberries. Maybe bananas.'

'Sure. Whatever.'

'See she's all right, then let me know.'

'Right.'

Pike hadn't heard from Ronnie again by the time he left the freeway, so he called. 'I'm five out. Is he still in my house?'

'Nope. He only stayed inside a few minutes. He's hiding in the bushes behind the dumpsters at the back of your parking lot. He can see your front door from there. Been there about twenty minutes now.'

Pike turned towards his complex. Since the man had taken a position by Pike's condo, Pike could drive through the main gate and park on the grounds. This would allow him easy access to his car.

Pike said, 'What's he wearing?'

'A short-sleeved green shirt with the tail out. And jeans.'

'Call you when I'm in.'

Pike drove through the main gate to a parking lot set behind a group of adjoining pods. He left the Lexus and made his way forward. When he reached the last of the adjoining pods, he stepped behind a large plumeria and disappeared into a world of green. Pike moved along the wall to the end of the building, then turned the corner. The dumpsters were directly in front of him. He studied the thick wall of oleander bushes behind them. The man had picked a good place to hide. Pike couldn't see him through the heavy lace of leaves. He watched the oleanders for almost twenty minutes, and then a bar of light moved behind the leaves.

Pike called Ronnie, cupping his hand over the phone. 'Got him. Thanks.'

'We going to take him?'

Ronnie lived for this stuff, but Pike didn't want him around for the rest of it. Better for Ronnie if Ronnie was gone. 'Goodbye, Ron.'

Pike didn't see Ronnie leave, but didn't expect to. Pike sat on the hard soil without moving, and watched the play of light and colour in the changing face of the oleanders until, finally, a shadow moved within, revealing a glimpse of green that did not fit with its surroundings: the man within the leaves. A branch swayed, telling Pike the man was antsy and bored. Pike read his lack of discipline as weakness. He waited.

Three hours and twelve minutes after Pike took his position, the man peered out from between the branches to make sure no one was looking, then duck-walked out from behind the dumpsters towards the main gate.

Pike hurried back to his car. He drove fast through the rear gate, then circled the complex, pushing hard towards the front entrance. He pulled to the kerb two blocks from the main gate just as the man stepped through a pedestrian gate built into the wall.

The man was now wearing sunglasses, but Pike could see he wasn't one of the men he had seen before. He was dark, with hard shoulders and a lean face, almost certainly Latin. When he moved, his shirt pulled in a way that showed a gun in the waist of his pants. He stopped at a dusty brown Toyota Camry. A moment later, the Camry pulled away.

Pike stayed between three and four cars behind, only tightening up when the Camry beat him through an intersection and traffic began to slow.

They climbed onto the I-10 at Centinela, and dropped off the freeway at Fairfax. The Camry stopped for gas, then continued north up through the city. When they reached Santa Monica Boulevard, the Camry turned west, skirting the bottom of West Hollywood, then Hollywood, then turned into the parking lot of a two-storey motel called the Tropical Shores Motor Hotel.

Pike jerked into a red zone, then trotted back to the drive. The motel was shaped like an L, with an open staircase where the legs of the L joined. The motorcourt was empty except for the Camry and two other cars.

Pike reached the office as the man in the green shirt got out of the Camry. He didn't bother locking his car. He went to a soft-drinks machine against the wall, bought a soda, then walked to a ground-floor room. He stood at the door with his back to the parking lot as he searched for his key.

Pike approached the man from behind. He shifted left or right just enough to stay in the man's blind spot, moving quickly across the lot, watching the key go in the lock, seeing the door open . . .

Pike hooked his left arm under the man's chin, and lifted. He closed his arm on the man's throat, and squeezed as hard as he could, shoving him into the room as he brought out the Kimber, using the man as a shield.

Pike expected more men, but the room was empty.

He toed the door closed. The drapes were open, so Pike could see no one was in the parking lot and no one had stirred from the office.

The man kicked and thrashed, but Pike held him up and off-balance with a knee. The man punched backwards and clawed at Pike's arm. He was strong and in very good shape. His nails cut into Pike's skin.

Pike slipped his free arm across the back of the man's neck, and pushed the man's throat into the crook of his elbow, squeezed, pushed and held it.

The thrashing slowed. The man stopped kicking. His body went limp.

THE CHOKE-HOLD cuts off blood to a man's brain, putting him to sleep like a laptop when its battery is low. While he waited for the man to wake, Pike searched the room.

The dresser and desk drawers were empty, but Pike found four travel bags heaped in the closet. Each contained men's clothing, cigarettes and toiletry items. He found an envelope in the backpack containing $2,600. Tucked in beside the envelope, he found a page from a spiral notebook with handwritten notes and a photograph of Larkin Conner Barkley. It was tight on her face, showing her smile.

Hidden among the clothes in each bag were US passports and round-trip airline tickets between Quito, Ecuador and Los Angeles. The passports showed four men, one of whom was in the chair. His name on the passport was Rulon Martinez, but Pike doubted this was real. Two of the men in the other passports were among the crew that invaded the Barkleys' home. One was the man with the scarred lip who had beaten the Barkleys' housekeeper. The passport showed his name as Jesus Leone. The other was Walter Kleinst. The remaining man, who Pike had never seen, was Ramon Alteiri. The passports claimed all four men were residents of Los Angeles and United States citizens. Pike studied the passports. If they were fakes, they were good fakes.

As Pike shook the clothes and toiletries out of the backpack, the man's eyelids fluttered and his head came up. He stiffened when he realised he could not move. Pike had duct-taped him to a chair. His ankles, thighs, body and arms were bound.

Pike stood directly in front of the man, holding an old Browning 9mm pistol he had been carrying.

He said, 'I can speak Spanish, but English would be better. OK with you?'

The man made a nasty grin like he didn't give a shit one way or the other. 'You better run. You doan know what you messin' with.'

Pike dug his index finger into the soft tissue beneath the man's collarbone where twenty-six individual nerves joined into one bundle. When Pike crushed the bundle hard into the bone, the nerve fired a pain signal not unlike a root canal without Novocain.

The man made a high-pitched buzzing moan. He tried to tear free of the tape and throw over the chair, but Pike pinned his foot with a toe. Tears streamed over his face, and he begged Pike to stop, this time in Spanish.

When Pike finally released the pressure, he knew the pain would burn on, so he touched another spot, this one on the man's neck, which reduced the pain. The man sagged, and his face paled to the colour of meat left in water.

Pike said, 'This is *dim mak*. That's Chinese. It means death touch.' *Dim mak* was the dark side of acupuncture; in one, pressure points used to heal; in the other, to damage. 'I want Alex Meesh.'

The man shook his head violently. 'No no no! I doan know!'

He seemed too scared to be lying, but Pike wanted to see. He held up the man's passport.

'What's your real name?'

The man answered without hesitation. 'Jorge Petrada.'

'Why were you watching my house?'

'For de girl.'

He didn't even blink, saying it. Pike decided he was telling the truth.

'Who told you to find her?'

'Luis. Luis say.'

'Who's Luis?'

Jorge glanced at the passports, so Pike held up the man with the scarred lip.

'*Sí*. Luis.'

Pike checked his watch, then went over to the window—time was passing, and one or more of the other men would likely return. Pike had pulled the drapes, but they were the sheer kind through which you could see. A man with a bulging belly was outside the office, smoking.

'How did you know where to find the girl?'

'Luis. He say your address.'

'You tried to kill her in Eagle Rock and Malibu. You tried up north in the Bay. Who told you where to find her?'

'No no no. I just got here, man. I been here only two days. I doan know nothin' about dat.'

Pike took the airline tickets from the bag, and checked the flight dates. Jorge was telling the truth again. He had flown in with Alteiri only two days ago. Kleinst arrived twelve days ago. Luis had been here for sixteen days.

Pike was returning the tickets to the bag when his cellphone vibrated. It was Cole. 'Yes?'

Cole said, 'Just left her. She's doing fine. I dropped off some food and magazines, stuff like that. I brought a coffee maker so she doesn't have to drink that stuff you make. Everything good on your end?'

'Good.'

'OK. You need anything, call.'

Pike closed his phone. He was staring at Jorge, and Jorge was scared.

'Who does Luis work for?'

The man looked surprised that Pike didn't know. 'Esteban Barone. We all of us work for Barone. This is why you have made a mistake, my friend. You will know fear if you know Barone.'

'What is he? A gangster? A businessman?'

'You know de word, cartel?'

'*Sí*.'

A coarse smile split the man's face, as if he took pride in being part of this thing. 'Barone, he have many soldiers. How many have you?'

Pike took the pictures of the five dead men from his pocket. He held them up one by one. 'I'm evening the odds.'

The man's face darkened and he muttered something in Spanish that Pike did not understand.

Pike went to the window again. The manager was gone.

'How many of you are left?'

The man spit.

Pike dug his thumb into a *dim mak* point between the man's ribs, beneath his pectoral muscle, and held it until the man sobbed.

'Seven!'

Pike released the pressure. 'Four of you sleep here. Where do the other three sleep?'

'I doan know nothin' about dat. Carlos, he put us here from de airport He bring us to Luis, an' Luis say dis where we stay. I not even see dem!'

A new player had entered the game. 'Who's Carlos?'

'Norteamericano. He meet us at de airport. He bring us here.'

'What's his last name?'

'All I know, Carlos. He give us things. De phone, de guns.'

'All right. Where are the others right now?'

'I doan know. I hab my job, they hab theirs.' The man wet his lips. He was growing more nervous, and glanced at the window. Pike wondered if he had seen something.

'They coming back now, Jorge?' Pike drew his pistol.

'No. No, they not comin' back. Tonight they come.'

A shadow crossed the drape, then three fast explosions shattered the glass. Pike was already on the floor. The door crashed open, Luis with a gun, shooting even as Pike fired back, his shots punching Luis into the wall. Then the room was silent. Luis slid down the wall, leaving a red smear.

Pike stayed on the floor, but no more men appeared. He glanced at Jorge, but Jorge's head now sagged, and most of his forehead was missing. He went to the door, irritated that he had failed to control the situation. Luis had probably heard Jorge shrieking or was tipped off by the drapes, but either way the man who was likely his best source of information was dead. Now, the overweight man had come out of his office. Pike pulled Luis out of the way and closed the shattered door.

Pike holstered his gun, then went through Luis's pockets. He found a cellphone, keys, twenty-four dollars and a torn scrap of newspaper with a phone number in the margin. He'd already been through Jorge's pockets and taken his cellphone. Pike put all of it into the backpack, then went back to the drapes. The overweight man had returned to his office. He would be calling the police.

Pike hurried into the bathroom. The housekeeper had left two glasses wrapped in plastic on the lavatory. He brought them to the bodies. He removed a glass from its plastic, folded Jorge's fingers onto the glass, then placed the glass back in its wrapper. He did the same with Luis, and that's when he saw the watch, a platinum Patek Philippe that was as out of place on this man as a diamond on a pile of dung. Pike took off the watch and turned it over. The back of the watch was engraved: *For my lovely George*.

He put the watch and the glasses into the backpack, wiped the surfaces he had touched, and trotted into the bathroom as he heard the approaching sirens. He broke the bathroom window with his pistol, hoisted himself through and dropped into an alley. He hooked the backpack over his shoulder and ran round the side of the building. He slowed when he reached the street, and walked past the motel office as the first patrol car arrived. People on both sides of the street were hiding behind cars and in doorways. Pike walked to his car. He drove away as the second police car arrived.

PIKE PULLED INTO a shopping centre near Griffith Park. A high-pitched whine hummed in his ears from the gunshots, and his shoulders ached. The shooting lived in him and kept him on edge, and that was good.

Nothing about the crime scene would point to him, until—and if—the bullets were matched, and that would take weeks. Jorge and Luis would be two more unidentified bodies in the City of Angels; an open homicide with questions but no answers.

Pike reloaded his pistol, then looked through the things he had taken. The phones might give him a connection to Alexander Meesh.

He studied Jorge's phone first, then used the menu to bring up Jorge's calling history. Jorge had made only three calls, all to the same number. Pike guessed it was probably Luis's number—the new guys got into town, Luis would tell them, here, this is how you reach me. Pike pressed the send button to redial the number. Luis's phone rang.

Luis had made many calls. Pike scrolled through a lengthy list that included at least a dozen calls to Ecuador. Each entry showed the number called, the date and the time of the call. Pike found Luis had called this same number five or six times every day.

He pressed the send button to redial the number. The person at the other end would see the number and think Luis was calling.

A man answered after four rings. 'Did you get the sonofabitch?' The man had a deep, resonant voice, but did not sound like a gangster from Denver or Ecuador. His voice was cultured, and held a trace of something Pike thought might be French.

Pike said, 'Alex Meesh.'

'Wrong number.' The man hung up.

Pike pressed the send button again.

'Luis?'

'Luis and Jorge are dead.'

This time when the man spoke, his voice was wary. 'Who is this?'

'The sonofabitch.'

The man hesitated again. 'What do you want?'

'You.'

Pike turned off the phone.

8

John Chen was terrified after Pike called. He hadn't even waited for an answer, just growled out, '*Meet me outside in an hour.*'

One hour later Chen made his way to the lobby and peered through the glass doors into the parking lot. He was convinced Pike would blame him for losing the guns, and beat him to death in full view of everyone. He saw his 'tangmobile, but he did not see Pike, or Pike's red Cherokee or the green Lexus.

Chen wasn't sure what to do. Maybe Pike had already come and gone. Maybe Pike had not yet arrived, and Chen could still get away! He sprinted for the 'tangmobile, stoked on adrenaline. He jabbed the key-lock button and threw open that beautiful German-built door when—

—Pike spoke behind him. 'John.'

'*Ahh!*' Chen jumped sideways, but Pike caught him and held the door.

'Get in.'

Pike was carrying a black backpack. Chen was certain it contained a gun. Chen latched on to the door like a cat clinging to a sofa.

Chen said, 'Please don't kill me.'

Pike pointed inside. 'Don't be stupid. Get in.' Pike pushed him in, then went round to the passenger side.

Chen couldn't take his eyes off the backpack. 'The feds took the guns. I would have run them, honest to God. I didn't have anything to do with—'

One moment Chen was talking, the next, Pike's hand clamped his mouth like a vice. 'You're my friend, John. You don't have to be afraid. Can I let go now?'

Chen nodded. His friend?

Pike let go. He opened the bag, then held it out.

Chen slowly peeked into the bag, 'What is this?'

'Guns the feds don't know about and two sets of fingerprints.'

Chen saw two small glasses in plastic sleeves, and what appeared to be two 9mm pistols, both beat to hell. He knew right away from the shabby condition that they were street guns; guns that had been stolen, then passed from scumbag to scumbag.

'Where did you get this stuff?'

Pike ignored his question. 'The feds who confiscated the guns—did you get their names?'

'Pitman. Pitman and something else.'

'Blanchette?'

'I don't know. Maybe.'

Chen glanced back at the backpack. He began to feel afraid again, but not afraid Pike would beat him to death; afraid of something deeper. He found Pike watching him. In a weird way, he grew calm. Here was Pike, calm, and his calmness spread to Chen.

John settled back. 'Are there more bodies to go with these guns?'

'Two.'

'Are they connected with Eagle Rock and Malibu?'

'Yes. LAPD is on the scene now. Shots were fired, so they'll know guns are missing, but they won't know who has them. Bullets will be recovered, and those bullets will match one of these guns—the Taurus.'

Chen nodded, taking it in. 'If the feds knew we had these guns, would they take them?'

'Yes, but they won't know. Only you and I know, John. You're going to have to make a choice. Least case, you could be looking at obstructing a federal investigation. Worst case, accessory to homicide. Tell me you want no part, I'll walk away.'

Chen was stunned. He was *flabbergasted*.

'You're giving me a choice?'

'Of course, it's your choice. What did you think?'

Chen stared at Pike, and wondered how he could be so calm. His impassive face; his even voice.

Chen said, 'What's going on?'

'I'm trying to find out. I think the feds confiscated your evidence to hide something. If they knew about these guns, they would confiscate them, too.'

'I can't just walk in, here's two guns. I need a case number.'

'Make up something, John. It's important.'

He looked into the bag again. 'What are the glasses, the fingerprints? Or you want me to print the guns?'

'The men who used these guns will end up with the coroner, but the coroner won't be able to identify them. You will.'

Chen shook his head. 'I can lift the prints and run them, but it's all the same database. If the coroner didn't pull a hit, neither will I.'

'These people aren't in the database. They came from Ecuador.'

Chen glanced at the glasses again. An international search required a special request, and even then you pretty much had to request each search by country. 'This is something big, isn't it?'

'Yes. Big, and getting bigger.'

Chen chewed at his upper lip as he thought through what he would have to do, both for the guns and the prints. He was pretty sure he could get LaMolla to run the guns; she was still furious that the feds took her toys and wouldn't tell her why. 'I'll take care of it.'

Pike got out and walked away.

Chen stared after him, thinking Pike wasn't so bad when you got to know him. *You're my friend, John.*

He smiled. The coroner had five unidentified stiffs, and now he would have two more. Everyone would be wondering who in hell these guys were, but they wouldn't know—until John Chen told them. Chen stuffed the guns under his seat and hurried inside with the glasses. He wanted to identify these guys, not only for himself and what he would get from it, but because he did not want to let down his friend, Joe Pike.

PIKE STOPPED for take-out from an Indian restaurant in Silver Lake. He was starving. A queasy hunger had grown in him as the stress burned from his system.

The sun was long down by the time he arrived at their house and turned into the drive. Everything looked fine. The door was closed and the shades glowed from light within the house. Pike would tell the girl he had made progress, and thought that might make her feel better about things.

He remembered how his silent appearances frightened her, so this time he announced himself. He knocked twice, then opened the door.

'It's me.'

Pike felt the silence as he stepped inside. Cole's iPod was on the coffee table beside an open bottle of water. Her magazines were on the floor. Pike concentrated, listening, thinking she might be playing with him because she hated the way he always surprised her, but he knew it was wrong. The silence of an empty house is like no other silence.

Pike lowered the bag of food on the floor. He drew the Kimber. 'Larkin?'

He moved, checking the bedrooms, the bathroom and the kitchen. The rooms showed no sign of a struggle. The windows and doors had not been jimmied.

He looked for a note. No note. Her purse and other bags were still in her bedroom.

Pike let himself out of the front door and stood in the darkness on the tiny porch. He listened, feeling the neighbourhood—the streetlight above its pool of silver, the neighbours on their porches. Life was normal. Men with guns had not come here. Larkin had likely walked away.

Pike went to the street, trying to decide which way she would go, and why. He decided she had probably walked down to Sunset Boulevard to find a phone, but then a woman on the porch across the street laughed. They were an older couple, and had been on their porch every night, listening to their radio.

He stepped between the cars through the pool of silver light.

He said, 'Excuse me.'

Their porch was lit only by the light coming from within their house. The red tips of their cigarettes floated in the dark like fireflies.

The man drew on his cigarette, and lowered the volume on the radio. 'Good evening.' He spoke in a formal manner with a Russian accent.

Pike said, 'I'm from across the street.'

The woman waved her cigarette. 'We know this. We see you and the young lady.'

'Did you see the young lady today? I think she went for a walk. Did you see which way she went?'

The old man grunted, but with a spin that gave it meaning.

The woman said, 'This is your wife?'

Pike read the weight in her question and took sex off of the table. 'My sister.'

The old man said, 'Ah.'

Something played on the woman's face that suggested she didn't believe him, and she seemed to be thinking about how to answer. She finally decided. 'She go with the boys.'

The old man said, 'Armenians.'

The woman nodded, as if that said it all. 'She talk with them, the way they stand there all the time, them and their car. They are all cousins they say, cousins and brothers, and she go with them. They all drive away.'

Pike said, 'When was this?'

'Not so long ago. We had just come out with the tea.'

An hour ago. No more than an hour.

'You hear them say where they were going?'

The woman tipped her chair back and craned her head towards the open window. 'Rolo! Rolo, come here!'

A boy wearing a Lakers jersey pushed through screen door. He was tall and skinny, and Pike figured him for fourteen or fifteen. 'Yes, gramma?'

'The Armenians, what is that place where they go? That club where you must never go.' The old woman cocked a brow at Pike. 'He knows. He talks with those Armenian boys. They have this club.'

Rolo looked embarrassed, but described what sounded like a dance club not far away in Los Feliz. Rolo didn't remember the name, but described it well enough—an older building north of Sunset that had been freshly whitewashed. Rolo thought it was called something with a Y.

Pike found the building twenty minutes later, wedged between a bookstore and a Vietnamese–French bakery. The sign across the top of the building read *Club Yerevan*. Beneath it, a red leather door was wedged open. Three heavy men stood on the sidewalk outside the door, talking and smoking. A smaller sign above the door read *PARKING IN REAR*.

Pike didn't waste time with the parking lot. He turned into the alley behind the storefronts and pulled over behind the bakery. As he got out of his car the valet saw him and hurried across.

'You cannot park there. Parking there is not allowed.'

Pike ignored him and pushed through the crowd. He shoved past young women with brown cigarettes and smiling men whose eyes never left the women. He stepped into a long, narrow hall where more people lined the walls, shouting at each other over a booming hip-hop dance mix. He shoved open the women's room. The people around him laughed or stared, but Pike moved on without paying attention. He threaded between the sweating bodies and the music grew louder with a throbbing bass beat. The people were chanting, their palms overhead, pushing with the beat as they raised the roof, chanting *GO baybee, GO baybee, GO baybee, GO!*

Larkin was up on the bar, peeled to her bra, playing the crowd like a stripper as she rocked her ass with the chant. She made a slow turn, running her hands from her hair to her crotch, making the nasty smile, and all Pike saw was the dolphin, screaming to be recognised.

The girl saw him as he reached the bar, and stopped dancing abruptly. She straightened, and stared down at him, looking guilty and scared. Pike stopped at her feet, and in that moment they were the only two people not raising the roof.

Pike shouted over the pounding bass. 'Get down!'

She didn't move. Her face was sad in a way he found confusing. He wasn't sure she had heard him.

Larkin did not resist when he pulled her off the bar.

Pike turned away with the girl, and the crowd did not know what to make of it, some laughing, others booing, but then the two oldest cousins and a thick man with a large belly fronted him, the oldest cousin stepping close to block Pike's way as the thick man grabbed his arm. Pike caught the man's thumb even as it touched him, peeling away his hand, rolling it like water turned by a rock, snapping the man face-first into the floor.

The people around them pulled back and he led the girl out.

SHE GOT IN the car without a word. Pike was angry, but anger would only get in the way. His job was to keep her alive. He backed out of the alley fast, then jammed it for Sunset. He didn't speak until they were two blocks away.

'Did you tell them who you are?'

'No.'

'What did you tell them?'

'They had to call me something. I told them Mona.'

Pike kept watch in the mirror, seeing if they were being followed.

'Did anyone recognise you?'

'I don't—how would I know?'

'The way someone looked at you. Someone might have said something.'

'No. They just asked if I dance. They asked what movies I like. Stuff.'

Pike pulled to the kerb outside a liquor store. He cupped her jaw in his hand and tipped her face towards the oncoming headlights. 'Are you drunk?'

'I told you. I don't drink.'

'High?'

'No.'

He studied the play of light in her eyes and decided she was telling the truth. He let go, but she grabbed his hand and kept it to her face.

She said, 'Take off those stupid glasses. Do you know how creepy this is, you with the glasses? Nobody wears sunglasses at night. Let me see. You looked at my eyes, let me see yours.'

She had wanted to see his eyes up in the desert when they met. She had been all attitude then, but now she was angry and frightened.

Pike said, 'They're just eyes.' He opened her fingers and took back his hand. Gently, so he would not hurt her. 'What you did could get us both killed. Do you want to die? Is that what you want? You want to go home, I'll take you home. If you want to die, go home, *then* die, because I will not allow it.'

'I didn't—'

Pike clamped both her hands in his. 'I will sell my life dear, but not for a suicide. I will not waste my life.'

She stared for a moment as if she was confused. 'I'm not asking you to—'

Pike cut her off again. 'If you want to go home, let's go.'

Maybe he squeezed too hard. Her eyes filled with tears. 'All I was doing was driving my car!'

Pike slapped the steering wheel. 'Do you want to live or go dancing? I can have you home in twenty minutes.'

'You don't know what it's like being me!'

'You don't know what it's like being me.'

Headlights and taillights played on her, moving the way light plays in water; yellow and green and blue lights on the shops and signs around them painted her with a confusion of colour. She didn't seem able to speak.

Pike softened his voice. 'Tell me you want to live.'

'I want to live.'

'Say it again.'

'*I want to live!*'

Pike let go of her hands. He straightened behind the wheel. 'We're not so different.'

The girl burst out laughing. 'Ohmigod! Oh my God—*dude*! Maybe *you're* high!'

Pike put the car in gear. Their sameness seemed obvious to him. 'You want to be seen; me, I want to be invisible. It's all the same.'

She fell silent the way people are silent when they think. They drove back to the house in that silence, but once, just the once, she reached out and squeezed his arm, and once, just the once, he patted her hand.

LATER, when the rhythm of her breathing suggested the girl had fallen asleep there on the couch, Pike turned off the final lamp. He would go out later, and wanted no light when he opened the door.

Pike sat quietly, watching her. They had eaten the Indian food, speaking little, her mostly, making fun of the music on Cole's iPod, and now, still wearing the headphones, she had fallen asleep.

The girl seemed even younger in sleep, and smaller, as if some part of her had vanished into the couch.

After a few minutes, Pike moved to the dining table, broke down his pistol and set about cleaning it for the second time that day. Pike had no trouble working in the dark. He had no intention of sleeping. He had to decide whether or not they would abandon the house, and much would depend on the Armenians. Pike was waiting for them.

He was brushing the barrel when he heard them. He went to the front window and saw the five cousins getting out of their BMW.

Pike slipped through the front door. They didn't see him until he reached the sidewalk, and then the youngest said something and they turned as Pike stepped into the street.

It was quiet, this late, there in the peaceful neighbourhood. The porches were empty. Cars were parked and the streets were empty except for Pike and the five cousins, there in the cone of blue light.

Pike stopped a few feet away, looking at each of them until he settled on the oldest, the one who had tried to front him in the bar.

'I figure she didn't tell you we're married, which is why you took her out. I figure now that you know, we won't have this problem again.'

The oldest cousin raised his palms, showing he regretted the misunderstanding. 'No problems, my friend. She said you shared the house, that's all.'

'Hey, we were just chillin' out here, dude. She came out and started talkin' with us.' The youngest had become so Americanised he spoke hip hop with an Armenian accent.

Pike nodded. 'I understand. So we don't have a problem between us.'

'No, man, we are cool.'

Pike read their expressions and body language, to see if they had recognised her. He decided they neither knew nor suspected. Larkin was just another out-of-her-mind chick to these guys, another girl gone wild.

Pike said, 'Mona has done this before and it's caused problems. There's a man, he's been stalking her. If you guys see anyone, will you let me know?'

The oldest said, 'Of course, man. No problem.'

Pike put out his hand, and the oldest shook.

'I am sorry you suffer this, my friend. You must love her very much.'

Pike returned to the house. Larkin was still sleeping. He brought the spread from her bedroom, covered her, then resumed cleaning the pistol.

He watched the sleeping girl while he waited for the following day.

9

Pike slept only a few minutes that night, falling into listless naps that left him more anxious than rested. The hunt was picking up speed, and now he wanted to push harder. The harder he pushed, the faster Meesh would have to react. Meesh would get angry, and Pike would push faster and harder. This was called stressing the enemy, and when Meesh felt enough stress, he would realise he was no longer the hunter: he was the prey. Then he would make a mistake.

At sunrise, Pike went into the bathroom so he wouldn't disturb the girl. He phoned Cole and told him about the motel. Cole said he'd head over.

When Pike left the bathroom the girl was up. She glanced away as if she was still embarrassed about the night before.

She said, 'You make coffee?'

'Didn't want to wake you.'

'I'll do it.'

She started for the kitchen, but he stopped her.

'I have some things here. Come look.'

He took her to the table where he had the passports and papers waiting for Cole. He held up Luis's passport, open to the picture. She studied it for a moment, then shook her head.

'Jesus Leone. Who is he?'

'One of the men who invaded your home. His real name was Luis. I don't know his last name.'

Pike showed her the other passports, but she recognised none of the men.

'Where did you get these?'

Pike ignored the question. He hadn't told her about the motel. 'Have you heard the name Barone?'

'No.'

'How about someone named Carlos?'

She shook her head, then picked up Luis's passport again. She studied the picture, but Pike knew she wasn't thinking about Luis.

'Does it bother you when, you know, you—?'

'No.'

She dropped the passport back with the others. 'Good.'

When Cole arrived, he brought a small television. Pike had not asked for it, and neither had the girl, but Cole brought a thirteen-inch Sony.

'It was just sitting in the guest room,' he said.

They had no cable, but the set came with rabbit-ear antennas. They put it on a table in the living room and turned it on. They couldn't get any of the cable channels, but it showed the local LA stations.

Larkin had been subdued all morning. She parked herself on the couch with a cup of coffee. She stared at one of the local morning shows, but whenever Pike glanced over, she didn't seem to be paying attention. Like she was thinking about other things.

Pike showed Cole the passports. Cole angled the pages to catch the light.

'These are good fakes. Excellent fakes. A dozen of these guys came up?'

'What the man said. Now there are five.'

Pike showed Cole the maps, the airline tickets and a spiral notebook page he took from Luis's travel bag. Indecipherable notes covered the front and back at all angles. Luis had probably taken notes while he was driving, likely with a phone wedged under his ear and one hand on the wheel. Pike guessed they were names and directions. The numbers were clearly phone numbers.

Cole frowned. 'Guess they don't teach penmanship in thug school.' Cole then examined the watch. His eyebrows went up when he read the inscription. 'George as in George King?'

'It's a sixty-thousand-dollar watch.'

'I can run the serial numbers.'

Cole then turned to the phones. Pike had made a list of the outgoing and incoming numbers in each phone's call history. Jorge had made only three calls, all to Luis's number. Luis had made forty-seven calls to nineteen different numbers. Cole glanced at the list, then turned on the phones.

'Too bad we don't know the passwords. We could hear the messages. If they have messages.'

'Leave them on. Maybe someone will call.'

'Maybe you calling that guy wasn't the world's greatest idea. He'll probably dump the phone and buy another.'

'I wanted to stress him.'

Cole glanced at the girl to make sure she wasn't listening, and lowered his voice. 'But you don't think the guy you spoke with was Meesh?'

'There was the accent. It was slight, but I could hear it. French, maybe. Or Spanish. Yesterday I thought he couldn't be Meesh, but now I'm not sure. His file didn't mention an accent, but those briefs leave out a lot.'

Cole skimmed the numbers again. 'OK, I might be able to do something with this. These nineteen numbers mean he called nineteen phones. Not all are going to be throwaways. I'll talk to my friend at the phone company. Maybe she can get call records from the other service providers. Sooner or later we'll hit real phones listed to people with real names.'

Pike caught the girl watching him. 'How're you doing?'

'I'm real good.' She turned back to the television.

Cole was making notes. Neither the maps, nor the tickets, nor the little scraps of paper contained a breakthrough clue, something like a hotel receipt signed by Alexander Meesh, but sooner or later something would pay off and Pike would be closer to him. The chase was about gaining a single step. Then you gained another. Pretty soon you had the guy in your cross hairs. It was all about gaining the one single step.

Pike left Cole to check the front windows. The street and the houses were normal. No new cars had appeared, and no strangers lurked in the bushes. Even though it was still early, Pike felt the day warming and saw what the heat would bring. A light haze hung in a fading sky. By noon, the air would be rich with hydrocarbons and ozone.

He turned from the window. The girl was staring at the television, but had been watching him again.

He said, 'We'll turn on the AC today.'

'That's great. Thanks.'

Pike wondered why she wouldn't look at him. She didn't seem angry and wasn't giving him attitude. He checked to see Cole was still working, then went to the girl. He stood so close she had no choice but look up at him.

She said, 'What?'

'Don't worry about it.'

'What?'

'Last night. Forget it. We're OK, you and me.'

'I know.'

She made a smile as Cole called from the table.

'I found something.' Cole was holding up the spiral notebook page. 'Not the words, but I got most of the numbers. Look—'

Pike went over, and this time the girl came with him. Cole smoothed the page on the table and pointed out one of the numbers: 18187.

'It's an address.' Cole put one of his handmade maps over the spiral page, then looked at Larkin. 'This is your street. The number jumped out because I've been making my notes by address.'

Larkin said, 'I'm at 17922.'

'The numbers get larger as you go south. This is where you had the accident'— Cole touched a place where he had made a small 'X', then tapped the building next to it— 'and this is 18187, right on the alley they were backing out of when you nailed them.'

Cole had written each building's address in a small block as numbers. 18187 was the abandoned warehouse at the mouth of the alley.

Pike said, 'When did Luis arrive in the country?'

Cole checked the dates on the airline ticket. 'Not until four days after the accident. The feds had already been all over the area. Larkin was back with her father in Beverly Hills. If they were lining up on Larkin, they would want her loft and her home in Beverly Hills, but why would they care where the wreck happened?'

Pike knew Cole was right. 'Maybe he went to the building.'

'We should take another look.'

Pike went for a long-sleeved shirt as Cole gathered his work. When he was buttoning the shirt, he caught the girl watching him again.

'You can stay here if you want. You don't have to come sit in the car.'

The girl looked surprised, then glanced away again as if the weight of his eyes was painful. The Larkin he had seen dancing on the bar hadn't been awkward or uncomfortable, but this was a different Larkin. Pike sensed she wanted to say something, but hadn't made peace with what.

She said, 'I'd like to come. If that's OK.'

Not telling or demanding. Asking.

Pike said, 'Whatever you want.'

PIKE AND LARKIN followed Cole down from the hills, cruising silently along streets that were unnaturally clear. He watched the girl from the corner of his eye, and twice she seemed about to speak, but, both times, she turned away. They were crossing Sunset Boulevard when John Chen called.

'I couldn't call before now.'

Chen was whispering so softly Pike had trouble hearing him. Other people were probably around.

'What do you have?'

'You were spot on about those prints.'

'Get an ID?'

'Two out of two through the South American database at Interpol. 'Jorge Manuel Petrada and one Luis Alva Mendoza, Petrada showing arrests all over Colombia, Venezuela and Ecuador. Mendoza managed to spread around his career, too. Both subjects are currently wanted on multiple counts of murder.'

'Who do they work for?'

'Says they're known associates of someone named Esteban Barone, part of the Quito Cartel out of Ecuador, one of the groups who took up the slack after the Medellín and Cali cartels in Colombia were broken.'

'Do they have associates or family here in the US?'

'Not listed here. They were soldiers for this guy, Barone. Nothing suggests they've been here before.'

Chen had confirmed what Pike learned from Jorge, but Pike wasn't hearing anything that would bring him closer to Meesh.

'Did you run the guns?'

'Not yet, but listen—the feds confiscated the Malibu guns, too. Rolled into the Sheriff's lab like they did with us and cleaned them out—guns, casings, everything. Those stiffs from Malibu and Eagle Rock, are they part of this Quito group, too?'

'Yes.'

'Here's what I think—I think the feds already know who they are. I think they just want us out of the picture.'

'You're probably right, John.'

'I don't get it. So they're drug dealers. Why would the feds care if we ID some assholes from Ecuador?'

Pike was wondering the same. The energy the feds were burning to cover their case against the Kings made less sense by the hour. Pike believed Pitman was covering something else, but he didn't know what.

'I don't know everything yet. I know some, but not all. I'll tell you more when I know.'

Chen grunted, the grunt saying he was OK with gambling on an even bigger payoff down the line.

Pike closed his phone, then glanced at the girl.

'The men trying to kill you work for Esteban Barone.'

'I thought they worked for Meesh.'

'He's in business with Meesh. That's what Pitman claimed—that Meesh was up here investing South American money.'

She was staring at him in the same thoughtful way she had all morning.

She said, 'I need to ask you something—what you said last night, that I want to be seen. Why did you say that?'

Pike thought it was obvious. 'You feel invisible. If no one sees you, you don't exist, so you find ways to be seen.'

A soft line appeared between her eyebrows, but she didn't seem angry or insulted. Pike thought she looked sad.

'Jesus, am I that obvious?'

'Yes.'

'How? Because I was dancing on the bar? Go see what they do at Mardi Gras.'

Pike thought about it to give her an example. 'In the desert. How you looked at your father. Looking to see if he was paying attention. He was focused on Bud and his lawyer and me, so you would say something outrageous. You needed to have him see you.'

She glanced out of the window. 'I don't care if he sees me or not.'

'Not now, maybe, but once. You wouldn't need it so badly if you didn't care.'

She looked back at him, and now the line between her brows had softened. 'And how is it you see so clearly?'

Pike never talked about himself, and didn't care much for people who did, but he figured the girl had a right to ask.

'My folks and I would be watching TV, me and my mom and dad, or we'd be eating, and something would set him off. My old man would knock the hell out of me. Or her. I learned to watch for the signs. How his shoulders bunched, how much booze he poured. Half an inch more in the glass, he was ready to go. Little things tell you. You see them, you're OK. You miss them, you go to the hospital. You learn to watch.'

When Pike glanced over her face was sad. 'I'm sorry.'

'Point is, I saw the play between you and your father. You needed something from him you weren't getting, and probably never had.'

She said, 'Thanks for seeing me.'

Pike nodded.

'Bud told Gordon and my father you would protect me. My father, he just looked at Gordon. Gordon, he just wanted to know how much. But Bud told him you were the one. I guess you are.'

'Bud say anything else?'

'Just that we could trust you to get the job done. He guaranteed it.'

Pike took that in without comment or expression, hiding his sadness from the girl as he hid everything else.

THE SHORTSTOP was an LAPD tradition. Located on Sunset Boulevard in Echo Park, the Shortstop Lounge was convenient to Rampart Station and the academy. Birthdays were celebrated as were retirements, promotions and the supercharged moments when an officer survived a shoot-out.

At 0720 hours on Pike's day off, the Shortstop was filled with night-watch officers anxious to burn off the street before heading home. Pike sat at a small table, alone, ignoring the glances. He had expected worse, but he was good with it. He had chosen this place to see Bud Flynn.

Pike now had three years on the job. Of his academy classmates, Pike was the first to kill another human being in the line of duty, a distinction about which he held mixed feelings. Five weeks ago, he had become the first to kill a second man. This second shooting occurred at the Islander Palms Motel, where, by his own admission before an LAPD Board of Review, Joe Pike caused the death of a decorated, twenty-two-year LAPD veteran named Abel Wozniak while defending a paedophile named Leonard DeVille. Abel Wozniak had been Pike's partner.

Bud had the grim look of a gunfighter when he entered the bar, his jaw tight, and his mouth a hard, lipless crevice. He squinted round the room, searching the crowd until Pike raised a hand. They hadn't seen each other in weeks. Since before it happened.

When they made eye contact, Bud stared across the room, then spoke so loud every cop in the place turned to look.

He said, 'There's the best damned man I ever trained, Officer Joe Pike.'

An anonymous voice said, 'Fuck him, and you, too.'

A few of them laughed.

Bud walked directly to Pike's table and mounted a stool. If Bud heard the comments, he did not react. Neither did Pike.

Pike said, 'Thanks for coming.'

'Take off those goddamned sunglasses. They look silly in here.'

Just like Pike was still a boot, and Bud his training officer. Pike didn't take them off.

'I'm leaving the job. I didn't want you to hear it from someone else.'

Bud stared at him like Pike owed him money, then scowled at the men lining the bar. A division robbery detective met Bud's eye.

Bud, maintaining the contact, said, 'What?'

The detective returned to his drink, and Bud turned back to Pike.

'Assholes. Don't let these bastards beat you. Just ride it out.'

Pike spread his hands, taking in the bar and everyone in it. 'We're at the Shortstop. Somebody has something to say, they can say it to my face.'

Bud made a ragged smile then, but it was pained. 'Yeah. I guess that's you. Asking me here instead of someplace else.'

'I'm turning in the papers today. I wanted to tell you, man to man.'

Pike thought Bud Flynn looked disappointed, and was sorry for that.

Bud said, 'Listen. Don't do this. Put in for Metro. That Metro is an elite unit, the best of the best. After Metro, you could do whatever you want.'

'It's done, Bud. I'm out.'

'Goddamn it, you're too good to be out. You're a police officer.'

Pike tried to think of something to say, but couldn't.

Bud suddenly leaned towards him again and lowered his voice. 'What happened in there?' The Islander Palms Motel.

Pike leaned back, and immediately cursed himself for it. Bud would read his move as being evasive. All through Pike's boot year, Bud had taught him to read people—the nuance of body language, expression and action. Pike tried to cover himself by leaning forward again.

'You know what happened. Everyone knows. I told the review board.'

'Struggle for the gun, my ass. I knew Woz, and I sure as hell know you. If you wanted that gun he would've been on his ass before he could fart.'

Pike simply shook his head, trying to be empty. 'That's what happened.'

Bud studied him, then lowered his voice still more. 'I heard the medical examiner said the angle of entry was consistent with a self-inflicted wound.'

Never looking away, Pike repeated what he told the review board. 'Wozniak pointed his weapon at DeVille. I grabbed it, and we struggled. Instead of turning the weapon away from Wozniak, I turned it towards him. The gun discharged during the struggle.'

Bud stared at him so hard it felt as if he was seeing inside Pike's head.

'So what happened in there, it has nothing to do with Wozniak's family.'

Like Bud knew. Like he could read Pike's mind that Wozniak was being investigated for theft and criminal conspiracy, that Pike had been trying to make him resign for the sake of his family.

'No.'

'Nothing to do with his benefits. That if he committed suicide, they would get nothing, but if he died fighting, they still get the cheques.'

Like everything Pike ever thought or felt was written on his face.

'Let it go, Bud. That's what happened.'

Bud finally settled back, and Pike loved and respected him all the more. Bud seemed satisfied with what he had seen. 'What are you going to do?'

'Africa.'

Bud frowned deeper, like why would any sane man give up being a cop to go over there? 'What's over there, the Peace Corps?'

Pike hadn't wanted to get into all this, but now he didn't know how to avoid it.

'It's contract work. They need people with combat experience.'

Bud stiffened, and he was clearly upset. 'You mean a mercenary? Jesus. If you want to play soldier, go back in the goddamn marines. Why in hell do you want to go get yourself killed in a shithole like Africa?'

Pike had taken a contract job with a professional military corporation in London. It was work he understood and at which he excelled, with the clarity of a clearly defined objective. And right now Pike wanted clarity. He would be away from Wozniak's ghost. And from Wozniak's wife.

He said, 'I've got to get going. I wanted to tell you I'm glad you were my TO. I wanted to thank you.'

Pike put out his hand, but Bud did not take it.

'Don't do this.'

'It's done.'

Pike left out his hand, but Bud still did not take it.

Bud slid off the stool, then said, 'Day we met, you wanted to protect and to serve. I guess that's over.'

Pike finally lowered his hand.

'I'm disappointed, son. I thought you were better than this.'

Bud Flynn walked out of the Shortstop, and they would not speak again until they met in the high desert.

THE SAME ROACH COACH sat at the mouth of the alley, only this time of the morning, the thinning crowd of sweatshop workers lingered on the sidewalk with breakfast burritos and plastic containers of orange juice.

Pike studied the warehouse until he found the address, faded and peeling but still readable: 18187. Damn, Cole was good.

Pike glanced at Larkin. 'You sure you're OK with this?'

'I want to be here. I'm OK.'

Cole got out of his car first. He scanned the surrounding roofs and windows like a secret-service agent clearing the way for the president. Then he meandered round to the passenger side. He hefted a long green duffle from behind the seat and slung it over his shoulder. Pike saw him wince.

Cole walked to the girl's side of the Lexus. 'Let's go see what we see.'

Larkin said, 'Are we going to break in?'

Cole laughed. 'It's been known to happen.'

They walked past the catering truck, then down the alley with the abandoned warehouse on their right and the sweatshop on their left. The huge loading doors were still chained, but Cole continued past them down the alley to the next street. At the corner, there was a small parking lot with a second loading dock cut into the building. A metal door was set at ground level on the adjoining wall. A realty sign was wired to the gate, advertising the building for sale or lease.

Cole peered through the fence. 'Yep. They were here.'

He pointed at the corner of the roof. A pale blue alarm panel was mounted near the end of the building, the cover missing. Old wires had been cut, and new wires had been clipped to bypass the old. Whoever jumped the alarms hadn't bothered to replace the cover.

Cole pulled a three-foot bolt cutter from the duffle, snapped the padlock, and Pike pushed open the gate. Cole went directly to the door, and Pike followed with the girl, lagging behind to cover their rear.

The staff door was secured by three industrial-strength deadbolt locks. Cole busted them out of the door with a steel chisel and a ten-pound maul. Pike was proud of the girl. She didn't ask questions or run her mouth. She stood to the side and watched.

When the door swung open, Cole passed a flashlight to Pike and kept one for himself. He also gave them disposable vinyl gloves.

Pike went in first, stepping into a gloomy office suite that had long since been stripped of furniture. A heavy layer of dust and rat droppings covered the floor, and the air was sharp with the smell of urine. Pike snapped on his flashlight and saw a confusion of fresh footprints pressed into the dust. Pike squatted to examine the footprints.

Larkin said, 'Ugh. It stinks in here.'

Cole said, 'What do you think?'

Pike stood. 'Three people. A week or so ago. Maybe ten days.'

He traced his light along a trail of footprints to a second room. A door and a window were set into the wall so the manager could keep an eye on things in the warehouse. An enormous empty space lay beyond the glass, murky with a dim glow from skylights cut into the roof. Pike shone his flashlight through the glass. The empty darkness swallowed the beam, but he saw more footprints beyond.

Cole and the girl came up on either side of him.

Pike said, 'They came here. They looked around, and haven't been back.'

The girl cupped her eyes to the glass. 'What were they looking for? Why would this place have anything to do with me?'

Cole went to the door. 'That's what we want to find out.'

When Cole opened the door, a fresh spike of ammonia burned at Pike's nose, but a stronger smell was behind it; something earthy and organic.

Larkin covered her mouth. 'Ugh.'

Pike followed Cole into the warehouse, with the girl behind him. Their lights swung through the murk like sabres.

The girl saw it first. 'Ohmigod! That's the car I hit!'

A black Mercedes sedan was parked behind them, near the loading dock. The fender behind the left rear wheel was crumpled and bent.

The girl walked over to the car, looked inside, then clutched her belly and heaved.

Cole caught up to her and turned her away as Pike shone his light through the glass. A dead man in the passenger seat was slumped across the centre console. A dead woman was curled on her side in the back seat. Both were naked, with their ankles and knees and wrists bound by cord. Each had been shot in the back of the head. Pike turned to the girl.

Pike said, 'I think it's the Kings, but I don't know. Can you see?'

Larkin was breathing through her mouth. Her face had gone grey, but she came closer to peer into the car.

'That's him. That's George King. Ohmigod.'

Pike glanced at Cole, and Cole nodded.

Pike said, 'Go with Elvis. I'll only be a few minutes.'

'No. I can stay. I'm all right.'

Her face hardened, and Pike liked how she was pulling herself together.

'Cover your mouth and nose. With a handkerchief. If you don't have a handkerchief, use your shirt.'

She pulled up her shirt and pressed it hard with both hands over her mouth and nose, but now she backed away. Cole backed away, too.

The keys were still in the ignition, which meant the car wouldn't be locked. Pike opened the driver's side door. The smell rolled over him. Pike had smelled these things before in Africa; corpses left for days in buildings or along the sides of roads. Nothing smelled worse than the death of another human being. It was the smell of what hid in the future, waiting for you.

Pike checked the man's body. George King had been shot behind the right ear. The bullet exited his left temple, taking a piece of his head the size of a lime with it. Pike found no other wounds. The lack of blood splatter in the car suggested he had been shot outside the vehicle, then placed within it.

A California Vehicle Registration slip and a card offering proof of insurance were clipped to the sun visor, issued in the name of George King.

The woman had also been shot in the back of the head, but she had been shot twice, as if the first bullet hadn't killed her. Most of her right eye and cheek were missing. She was curled on her right side, but her left arm and left hip were mottled deep purple where her blood settled after she died. This suggested they had been killed at a location other than the warehouse.

Pike closed the car, then joined Cole and the girl, standing as far from the car as they could get. He was halfway to them before he took a deep breath. The smell was so bad his eyes were burning.

Cole pointed his light at the ceiling, then along the tyre tracks on the dusty floor. 'They came through the skylight, opened the door from the inside and drove right up the ramp.'

The girl said, 'I think I'm going to throw up again.'

'Let's go. Let's get out of here.'

Outside, they stripped off the latex gloves and breathed deep. Pike squinted at the girl through the brighter light. She saw him watching.

'I'm OK now. It was the smell.'

Cole said, 'When Pitman and Blanchette first approached you, they came to your house?'

'Yeah.'

'When you met them downtown, where did you meet?'

'The Roybal Building. That's where they have federal offices.'

'Was it just Pitman and Blanchette, or were other agents present?'

'What difference does it make?'

Pike said, 'He's trying to decide whether Pitman is really a federal agent. Everything else Pitman told you is turning into a lie. Way Pitman explained it, Meesh wants you dead so you can't testify against the Kings.'

Larkin saw it and shook her head. 'But the Kings are dead.'

'Yeah, and it was Meesh's people who put them here. Meesh knows they're dead.'

Larkin flickered with a growing desperation, as if she was being forced deeper into an already dark and dangerous corner. 'Maybe someone else killed them. Maybe it wasn't Meesh.'

Pike said, 'Luis was wearing George King's watch. It was Meesh.'

'Then why is he still trying to kill me?'

'I don't know.'

Cole turned back to the warehouse. 'Wonder why his people put their bodies back here where you had the accident.'

Pike said, 'Tell her what else.'

Cole turned back. 'The day after your accident—two days before they saw you, Pitman and Blanchette questioned people here. They flashed pictures of two men. One of those pictures matched your description of Meesh. Pitman knew or suspected Meesh was in the car even before they talked to you. They lied to you about what they knew.'

Larkin pressed her palms to her head. Her chin quivered and her nose flared as she fought to control herself. 'Please tell me it can't get worse.'

Pike said, 'We'll figure it out.' Pike pulled her close and held her. He held her for what seemed like a long time, but wasn't really.

10

The building and the bodies within it bothered Cole. Someone had taken an enormous risk by placing their bodies in that location. The killer left them in this particular building to send a message. What Cole didn't yet get was who was sending the message, and who was supposed to receive it.

He dropped off the freeway at Santa Monica Boulevard, then headed to his office on the western edge of Hollywood, four flights up.

Cole liked his office. He had an adjoining room for Joe Pike, though Pike's office had never been used. Two director's chairs faced his desk for those rare occasions when more than one client vied for his attention. Beyond the chairs, French doors opened onto a small balcony. On a clear day, he could step out onto his balcony and see all the way down Santa Monica Boulevard to the Channel Islands.

Cole opened the French doors for the air, then went to his desk. First he phoned a woman in Florida named Marla Hendricks who could track down the warehouse's ownership history. Cole had used her services for years. She was a three-hundred-pound wheelchair-bound grandmother in Jupiter, Florida, who made her living by searching online databases. She did not have access to military, medical or law enforcement sources which were sealed by law, but she could pretty much access anything else.

When Cole finished with Marla, he called his friend at the phone company.

He said, 'I have a list of phone numbers I need to identify.'

'No problemo.'

'Let me warn you. Most of these numbers are probably registered to disposable phones, and four of the numbers are international.'

'I might have a problem with the international numbers if they're unlisted.'

'They're likely to be in Ecuador.'

'They could be in Siberia, it wouldn't matter; foreign providers are reluctant to cooperate unless we go through official channels, which I can't. The disposables—well, if the phones were cash buys, I can't find out who owns them. That information won't exist.'

'Could you get the call records for a particular number? Sooner or later these phones called real phones, and those phones have names. Maybe we can come at it backwards.'

She said, 'I'll try. It depends on the provider. Some of these little companies, well—give me the numbers. I'll see what I can do.'

Cole copied her fax number, sent the list, then put on a pot of coffee. He returned to his desk and reread the NCIC brief on Alexander Meesh. He wanted to see if he had missed anything that would explain the accent Pike reported, or connect Meesh to Esteban Barone or someone named 'Carlos'. He hadn't. Only a single line connected Meesh to South America: '*currently believed to be residing in Bogotá, Colombia.*'

The investigating agents must have developed evidence that placed Meesh in Bogotá, else they would not have entered the statement into the record. Cole noted the investigator's name—Special Agent Daryl Willis with the Colorado State Justice Department. A phone number was listed. It was six years old, but Cole dialled it anyway.

A woman answered. 'Investigations.'

'Daryl Willis, please.'

She put him on hold for almost five minutes.

'This is Willis.'

'Sir, this is Hugh Farnham. I'm a D-2 here at Devonshire Homicide with the Los Angeles Police Department. I'm calling about a homicide you worked a few years ago, a fugitive named Alexander Meesh.' Cole made up a badge number. He doubted Willis would actually copy it.

'Oh, yeah, sure. What do you need?'

'We pulled his brief off NCIC, and you have this alert here saying he fled to Colombia—'

'That's right. He was tied in with a boy down there about the time of the murders. He wanted to bring in drugs, so he worked out something with a boy named Gonzalo Lehder. When we put the indictments on him, that's where he went.'

'Lehder was a supplier?'

'One of the fellas who popped up when the Cali and Medellín cartels fell. Little operations popped up all over down there; maybe thirty or forty of 'em. Some of 'em aren't so little any more.'

'Was Meesh hooked up with someone named Esteban Barone?'

'Sorry. I couldn't tell you. All I knew was Lehder.'

Six years was a long time. Meesh probably started with Lehder, then branched out to Barone and the other cartels. One hundred and twenty million dollars was a lot of investment capital.

Cole said, 'All right, then. Let's get back to Meesh. Did he have any dealings here in LA?'

'Can't say that rings a bell. Sorry. Can I ask what this is regarding?'

'Meesh is in Los Angeles. We believe he's involved in a multiple homicide.'

Willis said, 'This is Alexander Meesh you're talking about?'

'That's right.'

A pause. 'Meesh isn't in Los Angeles, partner. Alex Meesh is dead.'

Cole wasn't sure what to say, but Willis sounded absolutely certain.

Cole said, 'We have a confirmed identification from the Department of Justice. You telling me they're wrong?'

'The Colombians and the DEA were after Lehder in a big way. That's how we know Meesh went down. The Colombian National Police called the DEA, and the DEA called me. Meesh had been setting up a drug deal between Lehder and some Venezuelans, only Lehder turned on him. Killed him.'

'If Meesh is dead, why haven't you closed the warrant for his arrest?'

'The DEA. We knew Meesh was down there through undercover agents in Lehder's operation. If we tagged the file with a note about Meesh's death, those agents would be compromised. Also, you can't affirm a death without a death certificate, and we're not likely to get one.'

'Why is that?'

'Lehder found out Meesh was lying to him about how much dope the Venezuelans were going to sell, so he could steal the difference for himself. Lehder played like he didn't know and sent Meesh up to Venezuela to pick up the dope along with three or four of his boys. Only Lehder's boys shot Meesh in the jungle. His remains were never recovered.'

'Then how can you be sure he's dead? Maybe he escaped?'

'DEA and Colombian UC agents were present when Lehder's boys got back. They brought Meesh's head so Lehder could see. So whoever you got there in LA, he's not Alexander Meesh.'

Cole felt hollow, with a faraway buzz in his head like he had gone too long without eating. 'Can I ask one more question, Mr Willis? Did Meesh have a speech impediment, or maybe speak with an accent?'

Willis laughed. 'Why would he have a damned accent?'

'Thanks, Mr Willis. I appreciate your time.'

Cole put his feet up, leaned back. The call to Willis should have been simple. Cole went into it hoping to learn something about Meesh's connection to Barone, and Barone's connections to Los Angeles—but not this.

PIKE DROVE SLOWLY when they left the warehouse. He rolled the windows down so the air would wash them, and took a long, meandering route through Chinatown, picking up Chinese for later. They drove for more than an hour. Pike hoped the drive and air would help her leave the bodies, but when they got to the house she said, 'I can still smell them. They're in my hair. They're all over me.'

'Take a shower and brush your teeth. Put on fresh clothes.'

Pike phoned Bud while she was in the shower, but he didn't answer. Pike considered leaving a message, but a message might be discovered by someone else, so he decided to call again later.

When the girl returned in fresh clothes and wet hair, Pike took care of himself. He scrubbed hard, massaging the soap in deep, then rinsed and washed again.

He dressed in clean clothes, then stepped out of the bathroom to find

Cole in the living room with Larkin. Cole was holding a manilla envelope. Pike knew something was wrong. The tension in his body was obvious.

Pike said, 'What's up?'

'Got something here to show Larkin. Let's take a look.'

Pike followed them to the table, where Cole opened the envelope. He put two grainy photographs that looked as if they had been run through a fax machine on the table. They showed a dark-haired man with a round face, pocks on his nose and small eyes.

'What do you think? Ever seen this guy?' Conversational with a 'no big deal' nonchalance. Would you like fries with that, ma'am?

'Uh-uh. Who is he?' she said.

'Alexander Meesh.'

Larkin shook her head. 'No, this isn't Meesh.'

'It's Meesh. He was murdered in Colombia five years ago. These are his booking photos faxed from the Denver Police Department. The man you saw with the Kings wasn't Meesh.'

'Then who was he?'

'I don't know.'

'Why would they tell me he was *this* guy?'

Pike said, 'Same reason they lied about everything else.'

Cole looked at Pike.

'Better talk to your friend, Bud. See what else they've been lying about.'

Larkin suddenly stiffened. 'Ohmigod, we have to tell my father.'

Pike hesitated. Whatever Pitman was doing, they had an advantage so long as Pitman didn't know they were onto him. Pike didn't trust Conner Barkley and his lawyers not to give them away.

'We can't tell your father. Not yet.'

Larkin went rigid and flushed. 'I can't not tell him! These people have lied about everything. They're lying to him, too, and he still believes them! He's my father. If you won't tell him, I'll tell him myself!'

Pike studied her, seeing both fear and hope in her eyes. She wanted to protect her father. And maybe, by protecting him, he might finally see her.

Pike took out his phone and punched in Bud's number. This time, he answered. Pike said they needed to see him and the girl's father as soon as possible. It was serious, Pike told him. Pike set the location, then ended the call before Bud could ask questions. When he lowered the phone, he looked at the girl.

'Get your stuff. Let's go.'

THE WAR IN CALIFORNIA between Mexico and the United States had ended in Universal City. The treaty to end hostilities was signed in a small adobe mission known as Campo de Cahuenga at the top of the Cahuenga Pass. The mission now stood unnoticed across the street from Universal Studios, hidden by freeway ramps, parking lots and the entrance to a subway station. It was a good place to meet.

Pike and the girl were waiting with the engine running when the black Hummer turned in. The doors opened the moment it stopped, and Bud, Conner Barkley and Barkley's lawyer, Gordon Kline, stepped out.

Pike wasn't pleased to see Kline. He said, 'Let's do it.' They got out as Bud and the others came to meet them.

Her father said, 'Larkin, it's about time—we've been worried sick about you. Let's get you out of here.'

Larkin didn't move.

'I'm not going anywhere. We came here to warn you.'

Her father seemed flustered. 'But we were so worried.' He looked at Kline. 'Tell her to stop this, Gordon.'

Pike faced Bud and spoke only for him. 'Pitman hasn't been straight. The man he named as Alexander Meesh is not Meesh. Meesh died five years ago.'

Gordon Kline threw up his hands, 'We're not going to listen to this. I will have you prosecuted for kidnapping. I knew you were a lunatic the moment I laid eyes on you.'

Larkin raised her voice, and now it had a hard, angry edge. '*Shut up!*' She grabbed her father's arm. 'Will you please just *listen to me*? We came here to *warn* you.'

Barkley looked pained. 'Don't be like that, Larkin. Everyone's worried.'

Pike took the faxed booking photo from his pocket and gave it to Bud. 'This is Meesh, not the man in the pictures Pitman showed Larkin.'

Kline and Barkley both peered over Flynn's shoulder to see.

Larkin focused on her father. 'They lied to us, Daddy.'

Daddy. It didn't seem like a word she would use. Pike liked her for it, but her using it left him sad.

Kline took a breath. 'We all saw those pictures, and I agree with you— the man in those pictures was not this man. But you make it sound as if they misled us. Two people can have the same name.'

Bud glanced through the attached pages. 'Same name, maybe, but not identical arrest records. This record matches what Pitman gave me when I came on board.'

Gordon raised his eyebrows. 'Really? Then we need to cut Pike loose. He has to go. We need to get Larkin home and then we can ask Mr Pitman. *Believe* me—if I don't like the answers, he'll regret the day he was born.'

'I'm not going home.'

Kline spoke in a tired voice as if he couldn't believe the trouble she was causing. 'Flynn. Would you please put her in the car?'

'No, sir. Not unless it's voluntary.'

Pike said, 'She isn't safe at home, Kline. Don't you get that?'

Gordon Kline gazed up at Pike from under the bushy eyebrows, and his voice was still carefully soft. 'Are you sleeping with her?'

Pike's mouth twitched, but he watched Conner Barkley. Barkley did not react, and Pike felt even more sad for the girl.

Larkin said, 'Fuck you, Gordon.'

'This is obstructing justice. This man, Pike, he's putting you in dangerous situations—and alienating the people trying to help you. All I'm suggesting is maybe Pitman has a good reason for doing what he's doing. We'll ask him, and he'd damn well better explain.'

Pike said, 'Ask him why he pretended he didn't know who was with the Kings the night Larkin hit them.'

'Are you saying he knew?'

'He was flashing pictures of the man the day after the accident—two days before he approached Larkin. You can also ask him why the man he claims to be Meesh is still trying to kill Larkin even though the Kings are dead.'

Kline shook his head. 'I spoke with Agent Pitman this morning. He said they were still looking for the Kings.'

'They've been dead more than a week. We found them yesterday.'

'I don't understand.'

Larkin said, 'Someone put their bodies exactly where I had my accident, Gordon. 18187. I think it was a message. That I'm going to join them.'

Bud stared at Pike. 'How?'

'Executed in another location, then brought to the warehouse in the Mercedes.'

Kline said, 'So what's your point here? Do you believe Pitman is behind the attempts on Larkin's life?'

'I don't know. It would explain the leaks, but all we know for sure is everything he's told you is a lie.'

Larkin said, 'You have to be careful, Daddy. You can't trust him.'

Kline focused on Pike. 'The man who isn't Meesh—do you have any idea who he is?'

'We might have his fingerprints. We might be able to identify him.'

'As an attorney, I am telling you that if you withhold any evidence from the police, you can and probably will be charged with obstruction of justice and possibly as an accessory to the crime. I want you to know that.'

Pike said, 'I'll take my chances.'

Kline nodded. 'Just so you understand. You're fired. Is that clear, Bud? This man is no longer in our employ.'

Larkin shouted over him. 'What is *wrong* with you? Haven't you paid attention?'

Her father said, 'Larkin, honey, he's breaking the law. We can't have that.'

'We came here to *warn* you, Daddy!'

Kline interrupted. 'Conner, I have work. Let's get out of here.' He walked back to the Hummer.

Conner Barkley frowned at his daughter. 'This puts me in jeopardy with the government, Larkin. Think of the exposure with the IRS. Think of the SEC. They could punish me, Larkin.'

It wasn't about Larkin's safety. It was about her father. The exposure.

Pike said, 'Bud, for Mr Barkley's record—I am not in your employ, nor his, and never have been.' Pike glanced at Larkin. 'I'm helping a friend.'

Larkin ran to the Lexus, and Pike followed after her.

'Officer Pike—' Pike glanced back to see Bud make a tight smile. Kline and Barkley were already at the Hummer. 'Call if you need me.'

Pike drove away fast. He knew they had lost the element of surprise. Gordon Kline was probably already on the phone with Pitman. They had to move fast.

Larkin said, 'What are we going to do?'

'Keep going.'

She touched his shoulder. 'We won't back up.'

'We never back up.'

Pike turned into a Safeway parking lot in Burbank, and went into the trunk. Everything he had taken from Jorge and Luis was in it along with their other things. Pike found Larkin's picture. He closed the trunk, then climbed in behind the wheel and pulled back into traffic.

She said, 'What's that?'

'Your picture. The guy who's after you, he gave it to Luis, so we might have his fingerprints.'

Pike took out his phone. He was dialling when Larkin spoke again.

She said, 'You know what's fucked up? I love him.'

'Yeah. I loved mine, too.'

Pike had never said those words to anyone. Not even Elvis Cole.

SO HERE HE WAS, after-hours yet again, working against the rules, flying low in a 100 per cent free-fire danger zone that would get his ass canned if that rotten bitch, Marion, found out, but John Chen absolutely LOVED it! Maybe even better than the 'tang.

OK, well, let's not get carried away. Nothing was better than 'tang.

Chen giggled, a kind of snurfling yuck-yuck-yuck. The other kids always had made fun of his laugh (along with everything else about him), but Chen no longer cared because—as of twenty minutes ago—John Chen was THE MAN!

Chen had this epiphany when Joe Pike called, asking him to drop everything and run a fingerprint check. His personal friend, Joe Pike—who *needed* John Chen—who *valued* Chen's knowledge and skill.

Marion said, 'John! Why are you still here?'

Snuck up right behind him, that bitch.

Caught by surprise, John ducked his head and cringed like he had so many thousands of times before—but then John Chen thought, no—THE MAN does not cringe.

Chen straightened, turned and gave her his most confident smile.

'Finishing some work from yesterday. Don't sweat it, Marion. I punched out an hour ago.'

Chen had already reached his overtime limit of the week.

Marion peered past him into the glue box, an air-tight Plexiglas chamber where Superglue and other toxic chemicals were boiled to enhance fingerprints. Currently John had a photograph of Pike's girlfriend soaking in poisonous fumes.

Marion eyed the picture suspiciously. 'She looks familiar.'

'Yeah, she has one of those faces.'

'What case?'

'The Drano murder. The detectives think a third person might have been at the scene.' John had never felt such confidence in his lies. As if they were coming from a core of absolute truth.

Marion eyed the photograph a moment longer, then stepped away, and John turned back to the box. White smudges were appearing on the front and back surfaces of the photograph. After the water evaporated, an organic residue was left. The fumes from the Superglue reacted with the organics to form a white goo, but growing the goo took time. John figured he still had another ten or fifteen minutes before the prints would be usable.

A reflection moved in the glass, and Chen saw LaMolla at the other side of the lab. She had edged to the door, hiding from Marion. LaMolla waved him over, gestured towards the gun room, then disappeared.

Chen made sure Marion was gone, then hurried out of the lab. LaMolla was waiting at the gun room, holding the door.

She said, 'Get in here. I don't want anyone to see us together.'

Chen said, 'You get anything?'

LaMolla led him to her work bench. 'The Browning was shit; it was stolen in 1982 from a Houston police officer named David Thompson. The BIN showed zip besides the Thompson hit, and nothing rang a bell.'

The National Integrated Ballistic Information Network—the BIN—logged data on firearms, bullets and cartridge casings that had been recovered at crime scenes or otherwise entered into the system.

'But the Taurus was different. Look at this—'

She brought him to her computer. On the screen was a magnified picture of the base of a cartridge casing. The brass casing was a ring surrounding a round silver primer. A shadowed indentation in the centre of the primer showed where the firing pin had struck the primer.

'See here at the top where the pin strike's kinda pointy? I saw that, I thought, gee, I know that pin.'

The indentation looked perfectly round to John, but this was why firearms analysts were wizards.

LaMolla said, 'Last couple of years the Taurus was used in a couple of drive-bys and a robbery–homicide in Exposition Park. No arrests were made, but the suspects were all members of the same gang. MS-13, *Mara Salvatrucha*. It's a pass-around, John.'

A pass-around was a street gun, usually not owned by one person, but passed from user to user within the same gang.

LaMolla shook her head. 'Sorry, man—wish I could give you something more specific, but that's it.'

'It's more than we had.'

Chen hurried back to the glue chamber. The latent prints had developed nicely. He removed the girl's picture using a pair of forceps, and examined it under a magnifying glass. Smudged circular patterns were heaviest on the sides of the picture where people had held it with their thumbs, but more smudges were randomly scattered over the picture's glossy front. He saw several prints he thought would be usable.

Chen clipped the picture to a small metal frame, then gently brushed a fine blue powder over it. He used a can of pressurised air to blow off the excess powder, revealing clusters of dark blue smudges, then examined each of the singular prints.

Chen was pleased. He had twelve separate and singular prints, each showing defined typica. Typica were the characteristic points by which fingerprints could be identified—the loops and swirls and bifurcations that make up a fingerprint.

Chen lifted each print off the picture with a piece of clear tape, then pressed the tape onto a clear plastic backing. One by one, he set them on to a high-resolution digital scanner and photographed them. He fed the pictures into his computer, then used a special program to identify and chart the characteristic points. The FBI's National Crime Information System compared a numerical list of identifying characteristic points. After you had the numbers, everything else was easy. Chen's computer churned out the numbers for each of the twelve prints, and then Chen punched them into the system, making the special request for an international database search.

John checked his watch again. Pike and the girl were sweating out in the parking lot, and he didn't want Pike to lose faith in him.

Chen need not have worried. The NCIC/Interpol logo flashed on his screen and he read the results. He had got positive matches on all twelve prints, identifying seven separate male individuals, two of whom Chen had earlier identified—Jorge Petrada and Luis Mendoza. Four of the remaining men were thugs from South America associated with Esteban Barone, but the seventh man was not.

Chen realised his mouth was dry when he had trouble swallowing.

He knew why the Department of Justice was involved.

He knew why Parker Centre rolled.

John printed the seven files, then cleared his computer so no one would see the downloads. He collected the fingerprint slides and the picture of the girl, and sealed them in an envelope. He took the envelope and the files, and walked out of the lab.

The sun was low in the western sky, searing it with fire. The Verdugo Mountains were purple turning to black. Chen went directly to Pike's car, and he didn't give a damn if Marion saw him because he knew this was bigger than anything he had ever worked on, and, maybe, ever would. He gave Pike the files. 'Read it.'

The girl saw the picture on the cover page, and said, 'That's him! That's the man in the pictures.'

The girl scooted close to Pike, and they read it together. Chen didn't think about how hot she was, or how her hand rested on Pike's thigh as she read. He only thought about what they were reading.

The fingerprint belonged to a man named Khali Vahnich, a forty-two-year-old former investment banker from the Czech Republic who had been convicted of drug trafficking. His activities since that time included additional drug trafficking, illegal arms sales and known associations with terrorist organisations in Europe and the Middle East. A large black alert warning appeared in the centre of the page.

ALERT: THIS MAN IS ON THE TERRORIST WATCH LIST. NOTIFY THE FBI IF YOU BELIEVE HIM TO BE IN YOUR AREA. APPREHEND BY ANY MEANS.

Pike looked up at John when he finished, and Chen would always remember his expression. Pike's face showed nothing, but the gleaming black lenses smouldered with the fire in the sky. Chen felt so proud of Pike then, so terribly, awfully proud that this man had included him.

Pike said, 'Thank you, John.'

Pike put out his hand, and Chen took it, and wanted never to let go, because John Chen felt he had something now, something that made him better than he had ever been; something he wanted to keep forever.

Chen said, 'Good luck, my brother.'

11

Later that night, they ate the Chinese food while Larkin watched television. Pike phoned Cole, filled him in, and they made a plan for the next day.

When the show she was watching ended, Larkin went to her room, but she returned a few minutes later wearing shorts and a different top. She curled up on her end of the couch and flipped through a magazine. Her bare feet were close to Pike. He wanted to rest his hand on her foot, but didn't. He moved to the chair.

Pike didn't care about Pitman or his investigation or why he had lied except for how it affected the girl. He didn't care if Pitman was a good cop or a bad cop, or in business with Vahnich and the Kings. He had been hunting a man named Meesh, but now he was hunting a man named Vahnich. If Pitman was trying to hurt the girl, Pike would hunt Pitman. Pike's interest was the girl.

Pike watched her reading. She caught him watching, and smiled, not the nasty crazy–curved smile, but something softer. With just a touch of the other.

She said, 'You never smile.'

Pike touched his jaw. 'This is me, smiling.'

Larkin laughed and went back to the magazine.

Pike checked his watch. He decided they had waited long enough, so he picked up the phone. 'Here we go.'

Larkin closed her magazine on a finger, and watched with serious eyes.

Pike still had Pitman's number from when Pitman left the message, and now Pitman answered.

'This is Pike.'

'You're something, man.'

'Heard from Kline?'

'Kline, Barkley, Flynn. What in hell do you think you're doing?'

'How about Khali Vahnich? You hear from him?'

Pitman hesitated. 'You have to stop this, Pike.'

'Vahnich changes everything. Larkin wants to come back.'

Pitman hesitated for the second time. 'OK, that's good. That's the smart thing to do here. This is all about keeping her safe.'

Pike said, 'Yes. I'm keeping her safe.'

The girl smiled again as Pike made the arrangements.

At 6.57 a.m. the next morning, Pike watched a blue Ford sedan turn into the Union Station parking lot. The sedan slowed for the hundreds of commuters emerging from the station, then crept to the far end of the lot.

Donald Pitman was driving with Kevin Blanchette as a passenger. Cole had described them well. Both were clean-shaven, nice-looking men in their late thirties. Pitman had a narrow face with a sharp nose; Blanchette was larger, with chubby cheeks and a balding crown.

Neither they nor the other seven federal agents who were concealed in a perimeter round the station saw Pike. They had moved into position ninety minutes earlier. Pike had been in position since 3 a.m.

Pike watched them through his Zeiss binoculars from the second-floor pantry of an Olvera Street Mexican restaurant owned by his friend, Frank Garcia. The ground floor was being remodelled, so the kitchen was closed. Pitman was expecting Pike and Larkin to arrive at 7 a.m., but this did not happen. Larkin and Cole were having breakfast about now and Pike was in the pantry.

At 7.22, Pitman and Blanchette got out of the car. They studied the passing traffic and the commuters coming from the station. Pike knew they were worried. At 7.30, they got back into their car. It wouldn't be much longer until they accepted they had been stood up.

At 7.51, the seven agents watching the area emerged from their hiding places and gathered at the north corner of the parking lot. Pike left the restaurant and trotted to Cole's car, which was parked at the end of Olvera Street. Cole had swapped for the Lexus.

Pike followed the blue sedan south on Alameda Street towards the Roybal Building—the federal offices. The rush-hour stop-and-go was brutal, with only a few cars at a time spurting forward between grudging light changes, but Pike counted on this working for him.

The blue sedan was three cars ahead when the yellow went red, and Pitman was trapped. Pike manoeuvred Cole's car into a loading zone and got out. When the crossing light signalled the lights were about to change, he trotted forward, picking up speed.

Pike closed on the sedan like a shark tracking a blood trail. Neither man saw him, and neither was expecting his assault. Pike reached Blanchette's side of the sedan just as the light turned green, and shattered his window with his pistol.

Pike jerked the door open and pushed his gun into Blanchette's side, screaming, 'Your belt. Pop your belt—'

Pike stripped Blanchette's gun, dragged him from the car and proned him on the street, keeping his gun on Pitman. 'Hands on the wheel! On the wheel or I'll kill you.'

The cars ahead of them were gone. Horns behind them shrieked as Pike slid into the car.

Pitman said, 'Pike?'

Pike stripped Pitman's weapon and tossed it into the back.

'Drive!'

Pitman's eyes flickered with anger. 'I'm a federal agent. You can't—'

Pike hit him hard in the forehead with his pistol, grabbed the wheel and powered through the light.

THEY WERE UNDER the First Street bridge when Pitman woke, parked at the edge of the Los Angeles River channel. Abandoned vehicles collected and impounded by the city were parked in rows there in the dead space beneath the bridge. They were less than eight blocks from Cole's car.

Pitman jerked upright, trying to get away, but Pike had tied his wrists to the wheel with plastic restraints.

'What in hell do you think you're doing, Pike? Let me go!'

Pitman's forehead was split where Pike hit him, leaking a crusty red mask over his face. Pike watched him, holding the pistol loosely in his lap.

Pitman said, 'You assaulted a federal officer. You *kidnapped* me! You are in deep shit. You are breaking major federal laws here!'

Pike said, 'Khali Vahnich. A known terrorist.'

'I'm not discussing this!'

Pike lifted the Kimber just enough to point it. 'We're talking about whether or not you die.'

'*I'm a federal officer! You would be killing a federal officer!*'

Pike nodded, quiet and calm. 'If that's what it takes.'

'Jesus Christ!'

Pike held up Pitman's badge. He had gone through his pockets.

'This was never about the Kings, Pitman. This is about Vahnich. You put a target on her to bag the terrorist. Or protect him.'

'That's insane. I'm not trying to protect him.'

'You told her Khali Vahnich was Alex Meesh.'

'We had to protect the case.'

'You told her he was trying to kill her to protect his investment with the Kings, but the Kings were dead. There was no one to protect.'

'We didn't know they were dead until yesterday, Pike! We didn't know! We thought he was helping them—'

'So why would Vahnich want to kill her? I think you killed the Kings and sold out the girl to help Vahnich.'

Pike raised his pistol again, and Pitman jerked hard against the plastic, his eyes showing the wild fear of a rabbit caught in a snare.

'*We didn't know!* That's God's honest truth! We knew they were in business, Vahnich and the Kings, but we didn't know Vahnich was in LA until just before the accident. Look in the trunk—my briefcase is in the trunk. I'm telling the truth—'

Pike studied Pitman, getting the read, then took the keys and found an oversized briefcase in the trunk. The briefcase was locked. He brought it back to the front seat. He slit open the case with his knife. Letters, memos and files bearing Department of Justice and Homeland Security letterheads were jammed together in no particular order.

Pike said, 'You aren't with Organised Crime.'

'Homeland Security. Look at my notes—'

'Shut up, Pitman.'

Pike saw memos about financial transactions and surveillances on the Kings, and other memos connecting Vahnich with Barone and numerous named and unnamed third parties in South America.

Pike read until he understood, then glanced up at Pitman. 'Vahnich makes money for terrorists.'

Pitman nodded. 'That's the short version. The single biggest source of funding for organised terror outside of state-sponsored contributions in the Middle East is dope. They buy it, sell it, invest in it—and take the profit. These fuckers are rich, Pike. Not the lunatics blowing themselves up, but the organisations. Like every other war machine on the planet, they eat money, and they want more. That's what Vahnich does. He's an investment banker for these fuckers. Invests their funds, turns a profit, then feeds it back to the machine.'

'Through the Kings?'

'You limit your risk by diversification. The Kings are golden in real estate, and Vahnich put a hundred and twenty million into play with the Kings—sixty from the cartels, but sixty was straight out of the war zone. My job is to isolate and capture that money. We don't want it going back to train suicide bombers.'

'Where is it?'

'I don't know. The Kings accepted the transfer into a foreign account, but the money was moved that same day and we don't know where it went. Maybe that's why Vahnich killed them. Maybe he wanted the money back.'

'So all of this is about real estate?'

Pitman laughed, but it was cynical and dry.

'Everything happening in the world today is about real estate, Pike.'

Pike stared at Pitman, thinking about Larkin in the Echo Park house, cut off from her friends and her life, with a man like Vahnich wanting her dead.

'Why is Vahnich trying to kill her?'

'I don't know. I thought I knew. I believed it was about the Kings. I didn't know Vahnich would try to kill her. How could I know that?'

'You should have told those people who they were dealing with.'

Pitman seemed as if he didn't understand what Pike was saying, then shook his head. 'I told them. They knew it was Vahnich. The girl didn't, but her father did. He advised us not to tell her. We had meetings about it, Pike—her father, his attorneys, our people. You don't want to alienate a cooperative witness, but we needed discretion. Barkley said she wouldn't be able to deliver on that. They advised us not to identify Vahnich until just before the testimony.'

'They advised you? Her father lied to her?'

'She isn't the most stable person. She would have used it to draw attention to herself.'

Pike felt cool even in the morning's warmth. He flashed on the girl from the night before, desperate to warn her father. Demanding it.

Pitman said, 'She's a freak, man. You gotta know that by now.'

Pike looked at Pitman's badge again. He thought of his own badge. He had given it up to help Wozniak's family. He had loved that badge and everything it represented, but he had loved Wozniak's family more. Families needed to be protected.

Pike said, 'She just wanted to do the right thing.' He put away his gun. 'We're finished here.'

Pitman tugged at his restraints. 'Cut these things off. Bring her back, Pike. We can protect her, and you might even be able to help us find Vahnich.'

Pike opened the door. 'You're tied to a steering wheel. You can't even protect yourself.'

He got out with the keys and the badge.

Pitman realised Pike was leaving and jerked harder at the wheel. 'What're you doing?'

Pike threw Pitman's badge into the river channel.

'Not my badge! Pike—'

He threw the keys after it.

'Pike!'

Pike left without looking back.

COLE STOPPED by his office to pick up the calling logs before heading on to stay with the girl. His friend at the phone company had faxed twenty-six pages of outgoing and incoming phone numbers, some of which were identified. Cole would have to go through the numbers one by one, but the girl would probably help. He liked the girl. She was funny, and smart, and laughed at his jokes. All the major food groups.

When he let himself in, she was stretched out on the couch, watching TV with the iPod plugged in her ears.

Cole said, 'How can you watch TV and listen to that at the same time?'

She wiggled his iPod. 'Did they stop making music in 1980?'

'I want you to help me with something.'

She sat up, interested. 'What?'

'Phone numbers. We have to build a phone tree tracing the calls to and from the phones Pike found. We'll trace the calls from phone to phone until we identify someone who can help us find Vahnich. It's like join-the-dots.'

He set her up at the table with the list of numbers, and identified which numbers belonged to Jorge, Luis and the man they believed was Khali Vahnich. He showed her what to do, then went to the couch with his phone. That morning he had found a message from Marla Hendricks, informing him that 18187 was owned by the Tanner Family Trust, which also owned several other large commercial properties in downtown LA, all of which were for sale. 18187 had been purchased by Dr William Tanner in 1968 and placed in trust in 1975. The executor of the trust was Tanner's oldest daughter, Ms Elizabeth Little, who was overseeing the sale of the properties. Marla had included Elizabeth Little's Brentwood phone numbers.

Cole scored on the first try.

'Yes, this is Elizabeth Little.'

'My name is Elvis Cole. I'm calling about a property you have for sale. I represent an interested buyer.'

'Which property?'

'A warehouse space downtown—18187.'

'Oh, sure. That's my Dad's. We're dissolving the trust. I'll try to answer your questions, but you should speak with our broker about the terms.'

She sounded normal. Not like someone who would bag away a couple of bodies, or know a person who would.

'You're working with a buyer?'

'That's right.'

'Then you should know this up-front. We'll consider offers, but any offer we accept will be in a back-up position. We have an option arrangement with a buyer for all seven of our properties. I don't think your buyer needs to worry about it, though. The option is about to expire.'

'Someone is buying all seven properties?'

'The upside potential here is enormous with the way downtown real estate is booming. Would your buyer be interested in all seven?'

'What are we talking about, price-wise?'

'Two hundred million. Options are common in deals of this size. People need time to raise the money. Sometimes the deals happen, sometimes they don't. This one looks like it isn't. If that's the case, we'll sell the properties individually.'

'I'll pass that along. How long was the option period?'

'In this case, four months. I think it lapses in, oh, let me think, another four days.'

'One more question, you mind naming the buyer?'

'Not at all. Stentorum Real Holdings. Since Stentorum haven't been able to raise the money, maybe your buyer could help and leverage a partial position. We'd love to have this deal go through.'

Cole copied the name onto his pad. He hung up as Pike walked in.

The girl chirped up. 'Hey, man!'

Cole said, 'Yo.'

Pike stopped inside the door. He didn't move or speak. Pike always looked strange, but now he looked even more strange. Cole wondered what was wrong.

Pike walked out of the living room and into the bathroom. Strange.

Cole picked up his phone again and dialled the information operator. 'I need a listing for Stentorum Real Holdings, please. That's in Los Angeles.'

Larkin looked up. 'That's one of my father's companies.'

The information computer came on with the number. Cole copied it, but never looked away from the girl. When he finished, he went to the table.

'Your father owns Stentorum Real Holdings?'

'I own it, too, technically. It's part of our family holdings.'

Pike stepped from the bathroom. He was shirtless, and scrubbed, as if he had needed to wash away wherever he had been. A spider's web of old scars draped his chest where he had been shot. He pulled on his sweatshirt.

Cole said, 'We need you.'

Pike joined them. 'What?'

'Larkin's father owns something called Stentorum Real Holdings.

Stentorum is trying to buy 18187, along with six other buildings from the same owner. They optioned the right to buy four months ago.'

Cole stared at Pike, letting Pike make the call, what to tell Larkin, what not.

Larkin shook her head. 'What does that mean? My father is buying that building? Where we found the bodies?'

Pike reached across the table, offered his hand. Larkin placed her fingers on his. Pike squeezed. He said, 'Stay with me, OK? Harden up, because it's about to get worse.'

Larkin glanced at Cole, then looked back at Pike. She nodded with a grim resolve. 'Bring it. Both barrels.'

'Your father and Gordon Kline both knew Meesh was Khali Vahnich. They worked out a deal with Pitman to keep you in the dark. Pitman said it was your dad's idea.'

Her fingers tightened until the tendons stood out, but nothing showed on her face. 'Why would they do that?'

'Don't know.'

'Were they in business together, these disgusting people and my father?'

Cole said, 'We're just guessing. We'll ask.'

'I grew up with this! I know a business dispute when I see it! They couldn't close the deal, so somebody has to eat the deposit. Vahnich killed the Kings. Now he wants me and my—' She suddenly stopped. 'Was it my father?'

Cole didn't understand what she was asking, but Pike seemed to know.

'I'll find out.'

Her tanned face mottled as it paled, her eyes showing the kind of pain you'd feel if you were being crushed, as if the last bit of love were being wrung from your heart.

'I don't want to find out. Please don't find out. Please do not tell me.'

Then Cole realised what she had asked of Pike—was her father the person telling Vahnich where to find her?

Cole said, 'We're guessing too much. Let's go be detectives.'

He went to the door. Pike lingered for a moment, then followed him out.

LARKIN WATCHED PIKE leaving, and in the moment he stepped outside, he was framed in the open door. A big man, but not a giant. More average in size than not. With the sleeves covering his arms, and his face turned away, he seemed heartbreakingly normal, which made her love him even more. A superman risked nothing, but an average man risked everything.

When he glanced back before he pulled the door, she saw the emptiness in his face, then the door closed and she was alone.

'Make it right. Please make it right,' she said to the empty room.

She was more frightened now than even those times when the men from Ecuador were shooting. If her father had abandoned her, then she was more alone than she had ever believed could be possible. Larkin felt outside her own body. Except for the fear, she felt nothing. She thought she should be angry or resentful, but a switch had been thrown and now she was empty.

Larkin went into the bathroom and looked at herself in the mirror. She wanted to see if the emptiness showed on her face the way she saw it on Pike. She couldn't tell.

She said, 'I don't care.'

She didn't care what he had done. He was her father. If Pike could carry his father, she could carry hers.

Larkin went back to the table and studied the lists of phone numbers. She found Khali Vahnich's number, then searched for it through each of the twenty-six single-spaced pages. Each time she found it, she marked it. When she finished, she went back to the beginning and picked out the numbers Vahnich had called.

She found it near the bottom of the second page. She recognised the number because it was so familiar. Vahnich had called her company's corporate headquarters. The Barkley Company.

Her vision blurred, so she knew she was crying, but she didn't sob; it was as if someone else was crying, and she was watching from the outside.

Pike and Cole were right. Her father was connected with these people, and now they were both in trouble. Vahnich was trying to use her to get something from her father or punish him, and, either way, he was fucking it up.

12

The Barkley Company occupied the top three floors of a black glass fortress in Century City with enough armed guards, security stations and metal detectors to secure an international airport. Pike called Bud to arrange the meet. Pike did not explain why they wanted to see him, except that it was about Larkin.

Bud said, 'No guns, Joe. I can't let you be armed.'

Pike said, 'Sure.'

When Pike and Cole arrived, attendants took their names and asked for identification, and guards with mirrors examined the bottom of Cole's car.

Cole said, 'If we have to get out of this place fast, we're screwed.'

Pike didn't play off Cole's bait for a joke. He was thinking about the girl. He wanted to hurt the people who were hurting her. He kept reading the pain in her eyes, a pain no one could share and from which she would never escape. And each time he saw it in her he saw it in himself, and wanted to hurt them until they crawled under a table like a shivering dog, crying and pleading with him to stop.

Cole said, 'You're awfully quiet. Even for you.'

'I'm good.'

Bud was waiting in the lobby with two visitor passes they had to wear round their necks. Bud had already signed them in.

He said, 'You want to tell me what this is about before we go up?'

'No.'

They boarded a special elevator that went directly to the top floor.

As they rode up, Bud said, 'How's she doing?'

'Not so good.'

'Just keep her safe. I think there's a lot these bastards aren't telling us.'

When the doors opened, Bud led them into a reception area where an older woman with curly blonde hair sat at a desk. She recognised Bud.

'He's back there somewhere. They're having some kind of problem.'

Cole nudged Pike and whispered. 'Already? We just arrived.'

They followed Bud down a long hall that looked like an art gallery, then found Conner Barkley outside his office with a small group of well-dressed men and women. Barkley looked as if he had just rolled out of bed. His hair was sticking out at odd angles and his eyes were nervous and red. When he saw them approaching, he frowned at Bud.

'I didn't know you were bringing these people.'

Pike grabbed Barkley by the throat and pushed him backwards into his office.

Bud was caught off guard.

'Joe! Are you crazy?'

Chaos exploded like incoming mortars, but Pike ignored it. The well-dressed people were shocked and shouting. Pike pushed Barkley into the wall as Cole and Bud surged into the office behind him and slammed the door, Bud trying to pull him off Barkley.

Pike squeezed Barkley's throat. 'Stentorum Real Holdings.'

Barkley's eyes floated in pink pools. He wheezed, and his words were gurgles. 'I don't know what you want.'

Bud had Pike by the arm. 'Let go. Jesus, you want the police?'

Pike stepped back. Barkley clutched at his throat, then coughed and spit on the floor. 'Why did you do that? Why are you so mad?'

Pike wondered if Barkley was insane.

Cole stepped up beside him. 'How about I do the talking? Stentorum Real Holdings is a company owned by Mr Barkley. Stentorum is trying to buy the building where we found the Kings' bodies. It's the building where Larkin had her accident with the Kings and Khali Vahnich.'

Barkley was still rubbing his throat. 'What are you talking about? I own Stentorum, yeah, but I don't know what you're talking about.'

Pike read his eyes and his mouth, and listened to the timbre of Barkley's voice, gauging its rise and fall against his shifting focus and the nervous movement of his hands. He decided Barkley was telling the truth.

Pike said, 'Did you know Alex Meesh was a lie?'

Barkley flushed. His eye contact faltered, he glanced away, then his eyes rolled up and to the left. Pike saw he was ashamed of himself.

'We thought it was the only way.'

Bud stepped between them, but faced Conner Barkley. 'You knew about Vahnich? Jesus, Conner.'

Cole said, 'What about the property? I spoke with the executor of the trust. She has an option-to-buy agreement with Stentorum Real Holdings.'

'I don't pay attention to those things. I have people for that.'

Pike said, 'Kline.'

Barkley passed his hands over his head again, pushing the lank hair from his face. 'Gordon left. He's gone. I'll show you—'

Barkley led them down the hall to Gordon Kline's office. A crowd of people were going through his files and computer.

He said, 'We think he left last night. Some things are missing—'

Bud said, 'Money?'

'We think so, yes. There were discrepancies.'

Cole went to Kline's desk, where people were working at his computer. 'Could he have used Stentorum to buy the property without your knowing?'

'Of course he could. I let Gordon take care of these things. I trusted him.'

Cole spoke loud to the room. 'Who has his phone log? C'mon, you people must log the calls. Is someone checking it?'

Two women sitting on a couch looked as if they didn't know whether to answer, but Cole was with Mr Barkley, so the older one raised her hand.

'We have it.'

Cole went over. 'Any day three weeks ago, doesn't matter which. These logs include his cell and personal?'

'Yes, sir.'

The woman flipped through the pages until she found the right dates. Cole followed his finger down one page, flipped to another, and looked up.

'It's the same number we got off Luis's phone. Vahnich.'

Pike moved closer to Barkley and lowered his voice. 'Was it Kline who suggested you lie to Larkin about Vahnich?'

Barkley nodded, then realised why Pike had asked. 'Was Gordon telling Vahnich how to find her?'

Bud looked sick now, almost as sick as Barkley. 'That sonofabitch. He was probably trying to buy himself time. Maybe blaming you for holding up the deal.'

Barkley suddenly turned away and threw up. Most everyone in the room glanced over, but only one person moved to help. A well-dressed young man with spectacles went to a bar and hurried back with a napkin.

Barkley said, 'I'm sorry.'

Pike thought he looked sorry, and Pike felt sorry for him.

'Vahnich put a hundred and twenty million dollars into an investment with the Kings, sixty from a drug cartel in Ecuador and sixty from his own sources. That means terrorists, Conner. It's likely the Kings brokered the deal and thought they were coming to you for the balance.'

'Nobody came to me. I don't know anything about this.'

'Came to your company, and your company was Kline.'

Cole said, 'They needed two hundred million for the purchase. Kline probably figured he could steal the balance from you, or use your company's position to raise what he needed, but not as an investor with the Kings. He needed to buy the properties through your company in order to hide what he was doing. So the Kings gave him the one-twenty, but he couldn't raise the rest. Maybe Vahnich got scared because it was taking so long and wanted his money back. Kline probably blamed you—'

Barkley listened to him like a dog waiting to be kicked. Everyone else in the room was listening, too.

'My lawyers have advised me to call the police and the banking commission. We have to get some forensic accountants in here.'

Pike said, 'You have a bigger problem than what Kline took. Vahnich still wants his money.'

Barkley took a gulp of air when he realised what this meant, and coloured again. 'Is Larkin all right?'

'She's fine.'

'Does she know—' He wavered again, then got it out. 'Does she know I lied to her?'

'Yes.'

'I want to see her. I want to be with her right now.'

PIKE ROLLED WITH BUD and her father, and Cole trailed them, alone. Bud drove, with Pike on the passenger side and Conner Barkley in the rear. Barkley spent most of their drive on the phone, filling in his managers and attorneys. Pike filled in Bud on everything he had learned from Chen about the men from Ecuador and their possible connection to the street gang MS-13. Bud put in a call to a friend of his who worked the LAPD Gang Unit, and asked him to find out whether anyone named Carlos showed on the roster of the Los Angeles MS-13 clique.

Riding with Bud at the wheel held a strange familiarity Pike did not enjoy, as if he had been forced back to a place he made peace with leaving.

Bud said, 'Been a long time, Officer Pike.'

Pike glanced over and knew Bud was feeling it, too. Bud seemed warmed by it, but nothing felt the same about those days for Pike.

Pike directed them up the winding streets to the little house. The two youngest Armenian cousins were washing their BMW. They looked over when the Hummer parked behind the Lexus.

Conner Barkley finally closed his phone. 'This is where you've been staying? Larkin must have hated it.'

Pike got out without answering, waited for Cole to limp up, then went to the house. Pike rapped hard on the door to warn her.

'It's me.'

He pushed open the door. 'Larkin.'

The house was still in that same way he knew it was empty.

Cole, Bud and Barkley clumped up onto the porch.

Barkley said, 'Larkin, are you here?'

Pike glanced at Cole, then they separated, Cole going to the kitchen while Pike checked her room and the bath. Her things were untouched, no signs of a struggle—it was two nights ago all over again. Larkin was gone.

Pike was already heading to the door when a young voice called from outside—'Yo, bro! Bro!'

One of the cousins was on the front lawn. He was shading his eyes from the sun, but Pike knew he had seen something, and knew it was bad.

'Everything right over here, yo? Mona, she OK?'

'She isn't here. You see where she went?'

Cole, Bud and Barkley clustered behind Pike on the porch.

The boy said, 'Off with some cats. Wasn't that stalker dude, was it?'

Pike said, 'Someone picked her up?'

'She seemed cool with it, yo? Else we woulda said somethin'.'

Cole worked to relax the boy. 'You didn't do anything wrong. Say what happened.'

'She didn't act like anything was wrong. They just got in the car.'

'How long ago?'

'Half-hour, maybe, somethin' like that. We were just soapin' up.'

Bud stepped in closer. Pike could see he was tense.

'You get a clear look at these people? What about your friend?'

'Thas my cousin, Garo. Yeah, we both saw. Coupla Latin cats and a white dude. One of those big-ass American cars all chopped down with the low seats. It was sweet. Midnight black, chrome dubs—'

Pike said, 'You get the tag?'

'Sorry, bro.'

Pike unfolded the Interpol photo of Khali Vahnich.

The boy nodded. 'Thas him, yo. That the stalker dude?'

Cole made a soft hiss. 'Jesus Christ. How did he find her?'

Pike felt as if he had failed. He thought back to the dance club. Maybe it had happened then. Maybe she'd been recognised and he had missed the tail.

Barkley called from the porch. 'Does he know where she is or not? Can someone tell me, please?'

Pike closed his eyes. He had kept her safe for five days, but now he had lost her. Larkin Conner Barkley was gone.

Something touched his back. He opened his eyes and saw Cole.

'We'll find her.'

That's when Pike's cellphone buzzed. He checked the number, but didn't recognise it. He answered anyway. The timing was too damnably perfect for it to be anyone else.

'I want the money.'

Pike had heard the soft accent before. It was Khali Vahnich.

PIKE KEPT HIS VOICE EVEN. His heart rate gave a bump, but he did not want Khali Vahnich to know he was scared. 'My friend is alive and unharmed?'

'For a while. Then we will see. To whom am I speaking?'

Pike motioned to Cole it was Vahnich, then hurried back to the house. He wanted a pen to make notes. Confusion and mistakes would kill her as quickly as panic.

Pike said, 'Put her on.'

Inside, he went directly to the papers and pens spread over the dining table. He copied the incoming call number.

Vahnich sounded offended. 'She is fine. I will only kill her if I do not get the money.'

'This conversation ends unless I know she's alive.'

Cole and Barkley had followed him inside, Barkley hearing enough to realise what was happening. He stomped forward as if he wanted the phone.

'Is this about Larkin? Is she dead?'

Pike motioned for silence. Cole clamped a hand over Barkley's mouth.

'Put her on, Vahnich. Put her on or go away.'

Pike focused on the call. He covered his free ear and listened for background noise but heard nothing suggesting Vahnich's location. Then Larkin came on the line.

She sounded fine. 'Joe?'

'I'm coming.'

'I'm OK—'

Pike heard a thump as if the phone had been dropped. Larkin shrieked, but the shriek cut off. Vahnich came back on the line.

'Are you pleased to hear her living? Is this what you wanted?'

Pike hesitated. Keeping his voice level was more difficult this time.

'Yes. We only talk if she's alive.'

'To whom am I speaking?'

'Her bodyguard.'

'Let me speak with her father.'

'You'll speak only to me. Everything goes through me.'

'No more of this, then. Her father will transfer the money, and we can be done. I will give you the account number and access codes.'

'Wait—listen—Kline took your money. He transferred the money out of the country. We don't know where he is.'

'This is not my problem.'

The front door opened, and Bud burst in. Cole immediately motioned him silent. Bud nodded, but went to the table and began to scratch a note.

Pike watched it all, but stayed with Vahnich. 'This was Kline's deal. Barkley had nothing to do with this.'

'This money, it is not mine. Dangerous people entrusted it to me, and they look to me for its return. They do not care where it comes from.'

Vahnich had made a mistake. That was the problem with talking. He had been talking a lot, trying to persuade, which meant he did not feel he could command. Pike had been wrong—Vahnich and his hit teams had never been trying to kill the girl; they had been trying to kidnap her so she could be used as leverage. The people who fronted the money wanted it back, and Vahnich was trying to save his own life. Vahnich's fear could be used to buy Larkin time or manipulate him into another mistake.

Bud turned with his note and held it for Pike to see. *SHE CALLED HIM. USED NEIGHBOUR PHONE.*

The list of call numbers was still on the table. Larkin had found the calls between Vahnich and Kline, and had called him.

'Why did she call you, Vahnich?' Pike was sure he already knew.

'She wants to help him, but she helps me instead. These young girls are foolish, are they not?'

Pike didn't answer. He was staring at Conner Barkley.

'Her father loves her, Vahnich. He worships her. We can work this out—'

Bud's cellphone chimed, but he turned away fast, cupping his mouth. Pike continued. 'Let's get together so we can work out the transfer. Tell me where we can meet you.'

Vahnich laughed. 'Will you bring the money in cash? In trucks? Please. He will transfer the money. When the money is safe, I will release her.'

'He's not stupid, Vahnich. He won't transfer the money until he has his daughter.'

'Then neither of us will have what we want, and we will both be sad.'

Pike wanted to buy as much time as possible. If Vahnich wouldn't meet, they would have to find him. 'I'll talk to him. He wants her back safe. I don't know how long it will take to—'

Vahnich cut him off, 'Copy these numbers and read them back to me.' He began rattling off a string of numbers.

Pike copied them, then read them back. They were transfer and account numbers.

Vahnich said, 'Good. These numbers you have are correct. He will have the money in this account in two hours or I will cut off her hand—'

Pike said, 'Vahnich—'

'No money thirty minutes after that, I cut off her head. We need not speak again.'

The line went dead.

Cole and Conner Barkley were watching him. Bud was on his phone in the background, scribbling notes on a pad. Pike lowered his phone.

'She's alive for now, but he won't meet with us. He wants the hundred and twenty million. We have two hours.'

Barkley dropped onto the couch and his face clenched into a frustrated knot. 'Did she actually call this man? She *gave* herself to him?'

'She did it for you. She probably thought she could work out some kind of deal or convince him not to kill you.'

Barkley shoved himself from the couch, as if taking command of the situation. 'All right, I'll pay him. I can't move that amount of funds in two hours, but I'll pay him. Get him back on the line.'

Cole said, 'Money isn't the answer. Paying him isn't smart, Mr Barkley. As soon as he has the money he'll kill her.'

'He wants money, I have money—what else can we do?'

'Find him.'

Bud finished his call and rejoined them. 'Got something here—the MS-13 connection might have paid off. The book shows two veteranos named Carlos—one is incarcerated, but the other runs with a clique in LA that's been bringing in South American dope for years—'

Cole said, 'Sounds like our guy.'

'One Carlos Maroto—he lives dead-centre in a *Mara*-controlled neighbourhood. Finding him won't be easy. Getting him to cooperate will be even worse.'

Pike knew Bud was right. Time was short, and finding a gangbanger in his own barrio would be difficult. Gang membership ran in families, and could span entire neighbourhoods. In a world where pride and family were everything, Latin gangbangers would not roll on their friends.

Speed was life.

Pike said, 'It might happen if the right person asked.'

Cole's eyebrows went up when he realised what Pike was thinking.

'Frank Garcia. Frank could make this happen.'

Pike checked the time. 'I'll call him from the car.'

Cole and Bud headed for the door. Pike stopped to look at Barkley.

'I'll call you when we know.'

Barkley shoved to his feet. 'I'm coming with you.'

'Mr Barkley, this is—'

Barkley turned a deep red. 'She's my daughter, and I want to be there. This is what fathers do.'

THE DIRECTIONS led them to a narrow street on the border between Boyle Heights and City Terrace, in East LA. Stucco houses with flat roofs lined the street like matching shoe boxes, separated by driveways one car wide; most with yards the size of postage stamps. American cars lined the kerbs and more than one yard sported a deflating swimming pool, wilted and lifeless in the nuclear heat.

Bud let the big Hummer idle down the street. Pike was riding shotgun. Cole and Barkley had the back.

Bud said, 'You see him? I don't see him.'

Pike knew Bud was nervous.

'He'll come. He said wait in the car until he gets here.'

'I'm not getting out whether he's here or not, these friggin' punks.'

Bud eased on the brakes, stopping outside a small home identical to all the others except for an American flag hanging from the eaves. A yellow ribbon was pinned to the flag, bleached by the sun. More than one of the homes they passed were hung with similar ribbons.

Hard-looking young guys were standing in small groups as if they were impervious to the heat. Most wore white T-shirts and baggy jeans and were heavily tattooed. They eyed the Hummer with studied indifference.

Bud read their gang affiliations by their ink. 'Look at these guys— Florencia 13, Latin Kings, Sureños, 18th Street—Jesus, 18th Street and Mara friggin' kill each other on sight.'

Barkley said, 'Are they gangbangers?'

Cole said, 'Pretend you're watching TV. You'll be fine.'

A black Lincoln limousine appeared at the far end of the street and slowly rolled towards them. Its appearance rippled through the young gangbangers, who got out of their cars, craning to see.

Barkley leaned forward again. 'Is he the head gangbanger?'

Cole laughed.

Pike thought that was funny, too. He thought if he lived through this, he would tell Frank, and Frank would also laugh.

Bud twisted towards Barkley to explain. 'You eat Monsterito tortillas?'

'Oh, sure, that's my favourite.'

Pike thought this was a helluva thing to be talking about now.

Bud turned forward again to keep an eye on Frank's limo. 'The little drawing they have on the package, the Latin guy with the bushy moustache? That's Mr Garcia forty years ago. These kids out here—Frank used to be one of them. That was before he went to work making tortillas for his aunt. Used to make 'em in her kitchen, that whole family recipe thing. Turned those tortillas into a food empire worth, what—?'

Bud glanced at Pike, but Pike ignored him.

Cole said, 'Five, six hundred mil.'

Bud turned to Barkley again. 'Thing is, he never forgot where he came from. He's paid a lot of bills down here. He gives back. There are men in prison—Frank's been supporting their families for years. You think those boys wouldn't do anything for him? He's rich now, and he's old, but they all know he was one of them, and didn't turn his back when he made it.'

Frank's limo stopped, nose to nose with the Hummer. The front doors opened and two nicely dressed young men popped out, one Frank's bodyguard, the other his assistant. Pike knew them both.

Barkley said, 'How do you know him, Pike?'

Bud said, 'Joe almost married his daughter.'

Pike pushed open the door and got out, wanting to get away from Bud's story. Pike had met the Garcias when he was a young patrol officer. Years later, when Karen Garcia was murdered, Pike and Cole found her killer.

Pike waited as Frank emerged from the car. Frank Garcia looked a hundred years old. His dark skin had the crusty texture of bark, and his hair was silver. He was frail, but he could walk a bit if someone steadied his arm.

A craggy smiled cracked his face when he saw Pike, and he clutched Joe's arm. 'Hello, my heart.'

Pike returned his embrace, then stepped away. 'Carlos inside?'

'Abbot spoke with the people who could make it so. He will not know why he is here. I thought that best. So Vahnich could not be warned.'

Frank Garcia was a sharp old man, and so was his attorney and right-hand man, Abbot Montoya.

The bodyguard and the driver took the old man's arms and the four of them crept up the walk, moving at an old man's pace. The front door opened, revealing a burly man in his middle-forties. He was short, but wide, with a weightlifter's chest and thin legs. His face was round, and pocked so badly he looked like a pineapple; his arms were covered with gang tats and scars. He studied Pike, then looked at the old man and held his door wider.

'Welcome to my home, sir. I'm Aldo Saenz. My mother was married to Mr Montoya's cousin.'

Frank shook his hand warmly. 'Thank you, Mr Saenz. You do me an honour today.'

Pike followed Frank into a small living room, with furniture that had seen much use but was clean and orderly. This was a family home, with photographs of children and adults surrounding a crucifix on the wall, including one of a young man in a Marine Corps dress uniform.

Pike counted six men in the room. Their eyes hit Pike the instant he entered, and two of the men appeared nervous.

Saenz gestured impatiently. 'Chair. C'mon.'

One of the men hustled a chair from the dining room for Frank.

Frank said, 'Please sit. Don't let an old man keep you on your feet. I must introduce myself—Frank Garcia. And may I introduce my friend—' Frank waved Pike closer and gripped his arm. 'When I lost my daughter—when she was murdered—this man found the animal who took her. And now, now he is my heart. This man is a son to me. To help him is to help me. I wish you all to know this. Now, may we speak with Mr Maroto?'

Saenz pointed at one of the men. Maroto was a younger man, maybe in his early thirties, and now he tensed. Powerful people had ordered him to be here; people who might end his life without hesitation.

Frank said, 'Carlos Maroto of *Mara Salvatrucha*?'

Maroto's eyes flicked around the room. He was afraid, but Pike could see he was preparing himself to fight if he had to fight.

Maroto said, 'I am.'

Frank once more clutched Pike's arm. 'This man, the son of my heart, he is going to ask something of you. Here, in front of the other members of our home. Let me say I understand these are sensitive issues, that business arrangements of long standing between individuals and groups might be involved. What we ask, we do not ask lightly.' The old man released Pike's arm and made a little wave. 'Ask.'

Pike looked at Maroto. 'Where can I find Khali Vahnich?'

Maroto narrowed his eyes to show he was hard, and slowly shook his head. 'No idea. Who's that?'

Pike took out the page with Vahnich's picture and held it out. Maroto did not take it, which told Pike Maroto knew him.

'Your crew is in business with Esteban Barone. Barone asked you to take care of this man. You're helping a friend. I get that.'

Maroto was angry and feeling on the spot. 'Yeah, that's right. What is this? We don't know this fuck. For all we know, he's a cop.'

Aldo Saenz crossed his big arms, and Pike could see he was trying to control himself. 'You are here as my guest. I treat you with respect, but do not insult Mr Garcia in my home.'

'I meant no disrespect to Mr Garcia, but my clique has a long-standing and profitable business with Esteban Barone. He asks a favour, we do it.'

Pike said, 'Khali Vahnich is Barone's friend, but that isn't all he is.' He passed the Interpol sheet to Saenz.

He watched Saenz reach the bottom of the page, then saw him frown.

'What does this mean? Terrorist watch list? What is this?'

Frank clutched Pike's arm again and pulled himself to his feet. 'It means he is my enemy. He feeds the people who want to kill us, and arms their lunatics, and now—right now while we are standing here in this house—he is in Los Angeles—our *barrio*!'

Saenz was motionless except for the rise and fall of his massive chest. He passed the sheet to the nearest man, then stared at Maroto.

Maroto grew pale. 'Barone said help the guy, we helped. You think we know something like this?'

The man with the sheet passed it to the next man, and he to the next. Saenz was staring at the picture of the young Marine, and Pike knew Frank Garcia had chosen this house well.

Saenz cleared his throat, then looked at Frank. 'If you could give us a moment, *padrón*. I mean no disrespect. Just a moment.'

The bodyguard and the driver helped Frank up, and Pike followed them out. They were only halfway to his car when Saenz caught up and told them where to find Vahnich.

THEY WERE USING a small house on a low-rise in the elbow where the Glendale Freeway met the LA River. Orange orchards had once stretched as far as anyone could see, and a few withered orange trees still peeked between the older homes.

Pike said, 'Right at the next street, then up the hill.'

Maroto told them the house sat at the end of a long drive, hidden from the street by scrub oak and olive trees. Vahnich didn't live in the house, but had wanted a place to meet up with the men from Ecuador.

Larkin's father leaned forward, trying to see. 'What if she isn't here? What if he took her somewhere else?'

Cole said, 'Then Maroto is gonna have a bad night. That's why Saenz and those guys kept him—to make sure he didn't lie.'

Bud slowed. 'Coming up. Look to the left.'

The drive curved away from the street, following the roll of the hill.

Cole said, 'Saw a blue car, but that's it. He could have an army in there.'

Pike didn't mind. If you couldn't see them, they couldn't see you.

Bud kept rolling. 'Let's call the police. We gotta bring in LAPD.'

Pike turned to watch the drive, see if anyone came out to look.

'Let's make sure she's here.'

'What are you going to do?'

'I'm just going to look. Wait up the street. I'll call.'

Pike trotted up the neighbouring drive. The homes on this part of the street stepped up the gentle rise, each house a few feet above the one below. Pike followed a low retaining wall alongside the house. He stopped long enough to make sure the back yard was empty, then crossed the yard between three ancient orange trees and stepped over the edge.

Pike side-hilled the slope through more trees until he was below Vahnich's house, then worked his way up. He saw a ranch-style house in need of paint, set on a yard littered with rotten oranges. The drive curved up to a carport at the front of the house. The blue car Cole glimpsed was blocking the low-rider described by the Armenian cousins.

Two men stood at the front of the low-rider, a liquid black 1962 Bel Air. The hood was up, and both men were lost in the joys of the engine.

From the way the house was cut into the slope, Pike knew a retaining wall and walkway would run along the opposite side. He was pretty sure he would find windows, and then he might find Larkin.

Pike started through the fruit trees towards the near end of the house, but as soon as his sight line changed, he saw her through the sliding glass doors at the back of the house. Larkin was sitting on the floor in an empty room, facing the sliding doors. A man walked past her moving from left to right, heading for the front of the house. He wasn't Vahnich. Pike thought it through. At least six men were present—the five remaining Ecuadorians, plus Vahnich.

Pike felt an enormous sense of relief now he had found her. She was sitting with her knees together and her hands behind her back. He couldn't tell if she was tied, but she didn't seem uncomfortable or injured. Her head was up, her eyes open. The choppy black hair made her look tough and good to go. She was saying something to whoever she was looking at. Pike decided she was angry, which made his mouth twitch. He settled back, thinking, You are one damn fine young woman.

Pike opened his phone to dial Vahnich, and Vahnich answered.

'Yes?'

'He'll transfer the money. He's setting it up now.'

'This is a wise man. He has made the right choice.'

'I'm supposed to make sure you didn't cut off her hand or hurt her. He wants to be sure. Put her on for a second.'

Vahnich didn't object.

A man entered from the right, squatted beside the girl and held a phone to her head. It was Vahnich, and now Pike knew Larkin was tied.

Her voice came to his ear. 'Joe? He says to tell you he hasn't hurt me.'

'I won't let him hurt you.'

Vahnich came to the glass with the phone, looking out towards the Verdugo Mountains. Pike could have killed him, but three other men were still inside with the girl.

Vahnich said, 'She is well, you see? I will honour our agreement.'

'His business guy says it's going to take another few minutes to compile this much money for transfer. They have it spread all over hell and back. I'll call you again. At that time, her father will want to hear her voice personally. Just to be sure. Then they'll hit the button.'

'I understand. I have no problem with that.'

A reasonable terrorist. Polite and considerate.

Pike ended the call, then dialled Cole. Vahnich turned away from the sliding doors and exited to the left.

Cole answered.

Pike said, 'She's here. Two men are out front by the cars. The girl is inside in what looks like a family room or den at the back. At least three more men are inside, but I can't say where.'

'You see Vahnich in the house?'

'That's affirm.'

'Bud says he's calling the police.'

'Whatever. Where are you?'

'We're across the street.'

'How about you come up to watch the front? Bud can stand by—'

A big man Pike hadn't seen before came from the front of the house and pulled the girl to her feet. He shoved her towards the back.

'They're moving her. I'm going to see what's up.'

Pike closed the phone, then made his way back across the slope to the far side of the yard, then up again, and to the walkway behind the house. He edged to the window, listened, then took out his gun.

He raised up enough to peek in the corner of the window. Larkin, the big man and Vahnich were in an empty bedroom. Larkin was back on the floor with the big man standing nearby. Vahnich had a laptop open. He was getting ready for Pike's call. He had the girl ready to speak to her father, and his computer to confirm the transfer. After the transfer was confirmed, Vahnich would kill her. Then they would drive to LAX and immediately leave the country.

Pike continued on to the carport. As he got closer, he heard the two men. They had closed the hood, but were still by the car, talking.

He drifted back a bit, then phoned Cole again, whispering.

'Where are you?'

'Front of the house, holly downhill from the drive. How about you?'

Holly bushes lined the property directly across from Pike.

He said, 'You see the two men by the Bel Air?'

'Twenty feet in front of me.'

'Vahnich plus one with Larkin, plus these two are four. Can you locate the missing two from your side?'

'Stand by—'

The two men by the Bel Air suddenly straightened and looked up the drive. Pike couldn't see what they were looking at. He raised up to see for himself just as he heard Cole's reaction.

Cole said, 'Oh, shit.'

Conner Barkley stalked down the drive.

THE MEN LOOKED CONFUSED. They probably thought Barkley was a neighbour, but Pike knew their confusion wouldn't last.

Pike ran through the carport. He covered the distance silently, and fast, knowing it would go bad. Barkley looked at him, and both men turned to see what he was looking at. Pike hit the nearest man with his gun, but the second man lurched sideways, barking out a shout—

Something behind Pike exploded and another man shouted as Cole pushed through the hedges. The two missing men were in the front door, the first man firing again when Cole shot him in the chest; the man behind him shoved the door closed on his dying friend. Pike knew he would run to the back of the house.

Bud Flynn appeared at the bottom of the drive; Cole moved on the second man in a two-hand stance—only now the second man was on his knees with his hands up.

Cole said, 'Go—'

Pike ran back the way he had come. Vahnich could shoot it out in a hostage situation, or run. Vahnich didn't know how many men were on him, whether he was surrounded, or whether the police were involved, but if he stayed he would be trapped. Running was the best of the bad choices, so they would run—out the back and into the neighbourhood, steal a car, and pray.

Pike ran hard for the end of the house, and heard more shots. One shot would have been an execution, but multiple shots gave him hope. They were shooting at the front door to stall off a breach; this meant they were going to run.

Pike believed Khali Vahnich wouldn't kill Larkin until they were outside the house. Vahnich didn't know what he would be facing, and might need her as a shield. If the way was clear, he might kill her just before he went over the fence. To punish her father.

Pike took cover in the orange trees beyond the house just as the window came up. The big man climbed out first. Then they pushed Larkin through; she landed with a sharp gasp. Vahnich landed on top of her, and then the final man came out, a short guy with a bandanna tied round his head.

Pike fingered his gun and waited for something clear.

When Cole came round the far side of the house, the bandanna saw him, popped off one shot, and Cole fired back. The bandanna went down with a high, keening whine, but fired again. Cole dropped for cover as the sliding glass doors flew open, and Bud Flynn came out, gun up and ready.

He shouted, 'Police!'

The bandanna swung towards Bud, and Pike shot him in the head.

Vahnich and the big man saw Pike, and Vahnich jerked the girl in front of them for a shield as they scuttled backwards towards the slope. The big man fired at Flynn, then Cole, but the shots were wild and pointless.

Bud was behind a heavy clay pot, shouting. 'Drop your weapons *now*!'

Conner Barkley came through the doors. He did not look for cover. Maybe he didn't know that's what you were supposed to do. He stormed past Bud into the yard, and stopped—out in the open.

He shouted. 'You let her go! *Let my daughter go!*'

The big man shifted out from behind the girl to fire. Pike shot him before he could fire, and he fell like a sack.

Bud was still screaming. 'Drop you weapon, goddammit! Put it down!'

And Barkley was screaming, too: 'You let her go. Let *GO*!'

Pike stepped out from behind the orange tree. Vahnich caught the movement, and peeked from behind the girl's head. His gun was pressed hard into her neck. Pike moved into the open and lined up on Vahnich's eye. He found the rhythm of Vahnich's fear. The eye moved, the gun moved; the eye and the gun became one.

Pike said, 'Dead man.'

The first kiss of sirens wafted up the hill. Pike didn't look at Larkin because she might see his fear. He only saw Vahnich's eye, and the eye looking back.

Vahnich dropped his gun. It fell, but nothing else moved.

'I dropped it. I'm giving up. I surrender.'

Bud shouted the instructions Pike had heard a hundred times. 'Raise your hands above your head. Lace your fingers on your head!'

Vahnich raised his hands. He laced his fingers on his head. The girl still had not moved, and neither had Pike.

Pike said, 'Larkin. Go to your dad.'

She started towards Pike.

'Go to your father.'

She ran to her father.

Bud had come out from behind the pot. Cole was covering the men they had shot. Pike crabbed sideways across the yard until he was between Vahnich and the girl, his gun never leaving the eye.

Behind him, Bud said, 'Joe. Son, the police are coming.'

Pike pulled the trigger. The gun made a loud pop which sounded hollow in the open air. The body fell. He walked over to secure their weapons. He checked the bodies. All three were dead.

Bud was staring at him as if he had drained of life. Conner Barkley was holding his daughter.

Pike went to the girl. Conner watched him coming, and Pike saw he was crying. Billionaire tears looked like everyone else's.

Pike placed his hand on Larkin's back and whispered. 'I won't let them hurt you. I won't let anyone hurt you.'

She turned to him then, and hugged him. She buried her face against his chest, and Pike rested his chin on her head. Bud was watching him. Bud looked sad, and disappointed.

Pike said, 'I still hate bullies. Live with it.'

He was holding the girl when the police arrived.

OCEAN AVENUE was lit with smoky gold light that time of morning, there at the edge of the sea. Pike ran along the crown of the street, enjoying the peace and the rhythm of his body. It was three fifty-nine. The coyotes did not pace him; he was the only beast in the city.

She turned onto Ocean at San Vicente, and roared towards him through the darkness. He recognised her new car so he stayed on the centre line.

Larkin zoomed past, swung round and idled up alongside him. She had gotten a pearl-white Aston convertible. The top was down. She had kept the short hair, but had gone back to red. She grinned the lip-curling smile. Pike was glad her confidence was back.

'Only a lunatic runs this early.'

'Only a lunatic driving this early would find me.'

'I asked your boy, Cole. Since you won't return my calls any more.'

'Uh-huh.'

Pike had stopped returning her calls. They had talked often in the weeks following the incident, but Pike didn't know what more he could say.

She said, 'Can you talk while you run?'

'Sure.'

She took a moment to get it together, then told him what she came to say.

'I'm not going to bother you any more. Now, just because I'm not calling you doesn't mean you can't call me if you change your mind. You can call whenever you want but I get it you want me to stop, so I'm going to stop.'

'OK.'

The old flash of anger darkened her eyes. 'My friend, that was *way* too easy. The least you could do is pretend.'

'Not with you.'

The car idled along beside him.

After a bit, she said, 'Do you believe in angels?'

'No.'

'I do. That's why I go driving like this. I look for angels. They only come out at night.'

That was something else Pike didn't know how to answer, so he said nothing.

She looked up at him. 'I'm not going to call any more because that's what you want; not because I want to stop. You probably think you're too old for me. You probably think I'm too young. I'll bet you hate rich people.'

'Pick one.'

Larkin smiled again, and Pike was glad to see it. He loved her in-your-face smile. But then her smile faded and eyes filled, and he didn't like that.

She said, 'You probably think I'll get over it, but I won't. I love you. I love you so damn much. I would do anything for you.'

'I know you would.'

'I'd even stop calling.'

The Aston Martin roared away, its engine screaming with pain.

Pike watched her taillights flare. She turned east on San Vicente, and raced towards the city.

Pike said, 'I love you.'

He ran alone in the darkness, wishing the coyotes would join him.

JON STONE GAZED OUT over the azure gulf and dreamed of ships at sea. Sailing ships of the late 1700s; not these silicon-chip water-rockets any geek could sail, but wooden ships built by hands and sweat.

The dude's house had put him in the mood. A neo-plantation tropical palace overlooking the Gulf of Thailand—the beautiful chaos of the jungle giving way to an immaculate white beach and the blue-on-blue sweep of ocean and sky.

Jon Stone was thinking about the ships when a single, muffled *wump* from the far side of the house broke the silence.

He sighed, knowing his time here was short.

He checked his watch, then started back through the house.

A staff of four usually worked at the house. A cook, a butler, a maid and a full-time gardener. Jon had patterned their movements for three weeks, and arranged events so none of them would show up today.

No visitors, no employees, no witnesses.

Gordon Kline had been calling himself George Perkins when Jon's boy caught the scent. Told the locals he retired after selling off thirty-two McDonald's franchises up in Alberta. Cats down in town were used to stories like that from rich Europeans and Norteamericanos, most of them perverts come down to scarf the Thai boy toys, and that's what they figured for the man who was calling himself George Perkins. Only Perkins had been keeping a way more dangerous secret than paedophilia.

Stone took the long way back to Kline's office. Sixty-inch plasmas in every room, a beaten copper bar that had to be twenty feet long, a temperature-controlled triple-glazed wine room the size of Stone's bedroom; this monster salt-water aquarium drifting with neon fish. A hundred and twenty million could buy damn near anything, but not everything.

Dude's body was face-down on a beautiful leather couch, an arm and a leg dangling over the side. Blood was still pooling on the floor from a single round in the side of the neck.

Stone said, 'All set, Mr Katz?'

'Almost.'

Pike was using a passport that identified him as Richard Katz of Milwaukee, Wisconsin. Jon's own passport showed the name Jon Jordan, also of Milwaukee. Business partners on holiday together, let the locals think what they want.

Pike was behind the dude's desk, adding a laptop to a cardboard box already filled with computer CDs, papers and a couple of hard drives. Account information about where he had stashed the Vahnich money.

Stone looked at the body and lifted his pistol, aiming at what was left of the head.

Pike, over his shoulder, said, 'Stop.'

'Piece of shit. You should have let me have him.'

Stone lowered his gun, frustrated. Jon would have skinned the sonofabitch alive, an American doing business with terrorists. Jon Stone had been a soldier, a mercenary, a private military contract broker, and even an assassin, but he was also a patriot.

Pike came round the desk with the box.

Jon said, 'Got everything?'

Pike grunted. What passed for a yes.

He studied the room to make sure he hadn't missed anything.

'Pitman might be able to do something with the hard drives.'

Stone glanced at Pike's gun, which Pike had tossed onto the floor by the couch. It would be easy, he thought. Spend the rest of his life in this fine, fine house. Wouldn't be right, but it was fun to think about. Jon had made a fortune off Pike's contract anyway, and Pike hadn't taken a dime. Wouldn't. Though he made Jon help him find Kline. For free. That part of it sucked.

Pike said, 'Hold this.'

Pike pushed the box into Stone's hands, then went back to the desk. Pike took from his pocket a snapshot of the girl. Larkin Conner Barkley. He propped the snapshot against the dude's humidor so she was facing the body. Pike was a strange cat.

Pike said, 'OK. We're done.'

They drove back to the airport, turned in their rental and headed to the terminal, all the computer stuff now packed in their bags.

Stone said, 'I'm gonna grab a smoke. Wanna hang with me?'

'Meet you at the gate.'

Stone lit up as Pike disappeared into the terminal. He waited a few moments, then strolled to the end of the building and sat back to enjoy the moment. The sun was pure and bright in the very best way, and the air so clean Jon Stone wanted to stay there for ever.

Stone had one of those cellphones you get to call home when you travel abroad. He dialled a US number, then waited for the man to answer.

Stone said, 'Over and out. We're coming home.'

'Thank God. He's all right?'

'He did what he had to do, like you knew he would. That boy's a bulldog.'

'I didn't have any choice.'

'I know, I know.'

Jon thought, Jesus, shut up already! The sonofabitch had been apologising for months like he felt guilty for turning Pike loose. Jon suspected the man knew what Pike would do and how he would do it from the beginning.

'Listen, I gotta get goin'—'

'He's a good man.'

'Yeah, he is, Mr Flynn. That's why he's Pike.'

'You boys get home safe.'

Stone turned off the phone. He finished his cigarette, enjoying the clean sky and sensual air until they called for his flight, then he went inside to find Joe Pike at the gate.

ROBERT CRAIS

Robert Crais is living the American Dream. As a worldwide best-selling, multi-award-winning novelist, and creator of one of crime fiction's most popular detective duos, he has it all, including a home in the Santa Monica Mountains of Los Angeles, the city where dreams are made.

His story began in Baton Rouge, Louisiana, where he grew up within a blue-collar family in which three uncles and two cousins were police officers. The expectation was that he would train as a mechanical engineer when he left school. But, at fifteen, he bought a secondhand, paperback copy of *The Little Sister* by Raymond Chandler, and it changed his life. He knew then he wanted to write, and began to devour the writing of the likes of Dashiell Hammett, Ernest Hemingway, Robert B. Parker and John Steinbeck. He dropped out of his university course to attend a writer's workshop—'a literary boot camp', as he describes it—before heading to Hollywood in the early seventies, armed with only his newly acquired skill and plenty of ambition.

After years of amateur film-making and selling short stories, a breakthrough came when he was accepted onto a scriptwriting team for some of US television's most iconic police shows, including *Quincy*, *Cagney and Lacey* and *LA Law*. Before long, he picked up an Emmy nomination for his work on *Hill Street Blues*. 'Television had an enormous impact on my novels. There are many lessons I learned that I still carry with me, such as characterisation, the importance of dialogue and how to drive a story forward.'

What Crais didn't like about scriptwriting was the lack of freedom to create exactly what he wanted. 'It was always someone else's characters, always a collaborative effort.' In film and television, he explains, 'the writer is never truly responsible for what you see. The fact is, there're a lot of fingers in that pie. And when it comes out, there are good things in it and things that are not so good things in it.' So, Crais walked away from his lucrative job to pursue his goal. 'For me, writing is about freedom and novels were always the dream. Books are my Disneyland, my personal amusement park. I get to design whatever I want.' His first two attempts were, he candidly admits, awful, and they remain unpublished, but the death of his father in 1985 triggered an idea for his debut, *The Monkey's Raincoat*, and it proved the catalyst that propelled him to fame.

In the novel, a woman walks into Elvis's office in search of her missing husband. She is so dependant on her spouse that she struggles to handle everyday life—an all-too-real situation for Crais. 'My parents were married for fifty years and had a traditional marriage. My mother had never paid any bills and hadn't even used a credit card.' The plot allowed Crais to explore some very personal issues and he began to imbue his work with deeper emotional authenticity. 'Novel writing is about human beings and what lies beneath their surface. Every one of my books has that subtext.'

Despite warnings from Crais's own agent that the era of the traditional white, male detective was over, *The Monkey's Raincoat* won the Anthony and Macavity awards and was nominated for an Edgar. Over the next decade, Crais's fanbase grew, skyrocketing in 1999 when *LA Requiem* made the best-seller lists.

The Watchman marks the eleventh outing for Crais's detective duo, Elvis Cole and Joe Pike and, recently, he has explored both characters in greater depth. 'I think they reflect what's going on with me and the world as I see it. I'm showing sides of Joe Pike I've never revealed—what it's like being Pike from the inside. This is one seriously dangerous dude. A complex man, and a cat you definitely don't want on your case.'

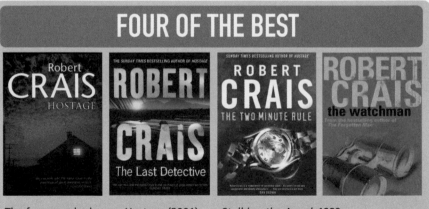

FOUR OF THE BEST

The four novels above—*Hostage* (2001), *The Last Detective* (2003), *The Two Minute Rule* (2006) and *The Watchman* (2007)—have all appeared in Select Editions because we feel that they represent the very best of Crais's books to date. Below is a list of his other works, which you may also enjoy:

The Monkey's Raincoat, 1987

Stalking the Angel, 1989
Lullaby Town, 1992
Free Fall, 1993
Voodoo River, 1995
Sunset Express, 1996
Indigo Slam, 1997
LA Requiem, 1999
Demolition Angel, 2000
The Forgotten Man, 2005

An Irish Country Doctor

Patrick Taylor

The proud owner of a brand spanking new medical degree and not much else, Barry Laverty, MD, jumps at the offer of a position in Dr Fingal O'Reilly's rural Ulster practice. But when he meets his new employer and sees O'Reilly's unconventional methods in action, young Laverty is taken aback. The man is either a charlatan—or the best teacher he could ever hope for . . .

You Can't Get There from Here

Barry Laverty—*Dr* Barry Laverty—his houseman's year just finished, ink barely dry on his degree, pulled his beat-up Volkswagen Beetle to the side of the road and peered at a map. Six Road Ends was clearly marked. He stared through the car's insect-splattered windscreen at the maze of narrow country roads that ran one into the other just up ahead. Somewhere at the end of one of those blackthorn-hedged byways lay the village of Ballybucklebo. But which road should he take? And, he reminded himself, there was more to that question than simple geography.

Most of his graduating classmates from the medical school of the Queen's University of Belfast had clear plans for their careers. But he hadn't a clue. General practice? Specialise? And if so, which speciality? Barry shrugged. He was twenty-four, single, no responsibilities. He knew he had all the time in the world to think about his medical future, but his immediate prospects might not be bright if he were late for his five o'clock appointment, and though finding a direction for his life might be important, his most pressing need was to earn enough to pay off the loan on the car.

He scowled at the map and retraced the road he had travelled from Belfast, but the Six Road Ends lay near the margin of the paper. No Ballybucklebo in sight. What to do? He looked up, and as he did he glimpsed himself in the rearview mirror. Blue eyes looked back at him from a clean-shaven oval face. His tie was askew. No matter how carefully he tied the thing, the knot always managed to wander off under one collar tip. He did not want to look scruffy. He tugged the tie back into place, then tried to smooth down the cowlick on the crown of his fair hair, but up it popped. He shrugged. It would just have to stay that way. At least his hair was cut short, not like the style affected by that new musical group, the Beatles.

Perhaps, he thought, there would be a signpost at the junction. He got out of the vehicle, and the springs creaked. Brunhilde, as he called his car, was protesting about the weight of his worldly goods: two suitcases, one with his meagre wardrobe, the other crammed with medical texts; a doctor's medical bag tucked under the bonnet; and a fly rod, creel and hip waders lying in the back seat. He leaned against the car door, conscious that his five-foot-eight, slightly built frame gave him barely enough height to peer over Brunhilde's domed roof. Even standing on tiptoe he could see no evidence of a signpost. Perhaps it was hidden behind the hedges.

He walked to the junction and looked around to find a grave deficiency of signposts. Maybe Ballybucklebo is like Brigadoon, he thought, and only appears for one day every hundred years. He walked back to the car in the warmth of the Ulster afternoon, breathing in the gorse's perfume from the fields at either side of the road. He heard the liquid notes of a blackbird hiding in the fuchsia that grew wild in the hedgerow, the flowers drooping purple and scarlet in the summer air. Somewhere a cow lowed in basso counterpoint to the blackbird's treble.

Barry savoured the moment. He might be unclear about what his future held, but one thing was certain. Nothing could ever persuade him that there was anywhere he would choose to live other than here in Northern Ireland.

As he approached the car, he thought, I'll just have to pick a road and . . . He was pleasantly surprised to see a figure mounted on a bicycle crest the low hill and pedal sedately along the road.

'Excuse me.' Barry stepped into the path of the oncoming cyclist. The cyclist wobbled, braked and stood, one foot on the ground and the other on a pedal. 'Good afternoon,' Barry said. He was addressing a gangly youth, innocent face half hidden under a Paddy hat, but not hidden well enough to disguise a set of buckteeth that would be the envy of every hare in the Six Counties. 'I wonder if you could help me? I'm looking for Ballybucklebo.'

'Ballybucklebo?' The cyclist lifted his hat and scratched his ginger hair.

'Can you tell me how to get there?'

'Ballybucklebo?' He pursed his lips. 'Boys-a-boys, thon's a grand wee place, so it is.'

Barry tried not to let his growing exasperation show. 'I'm sure it is, but I have to get there by five.'

'Five? Today, like?' The youth fumbled in the fob pocket of his waistcoat, and produced a pocket watch. 'Five? You've no much time left.'

'I know that. If you could just—'

'Och, aye.' He pointed straight ahead. 'Take that road. Follow your nose till you come to Willy John McCoubrey's red barn.'

'Red barn. Right.'

'Now you *don't* turn there.'

'Oh.'

'Not at all. Keep right on. You'll see a black and white cow in a field— unless Willy John has her in the red barn for milking. Now go past her, and take the road to your right.' As he spoke, the youth pointed to the left.

Barry felt a mite confused. 'First *right* past the black and white cow?'

'That's her,' he said, continuing to point left. 'From there, it's only a wee doddle. Mind you'—he started to mount his machine—'if I'd been you, I wouldn't have tried to get to Ballybucklebo from here in the first place.'

Barry looked sharply at his companion. The youth's face showed not the least suggestion that he had been anything other than serious.

'Thank you,' said Barry, stifling his desire to laugh. 'Thank you very much. Oh, and by the way, you wouldn't happen to know the doctor there?'

The youth's eyebrows shot upwards. His eyes widened and he let go a long low whistle before he said, 'Himself? Dr O'Reilly? By God, I do, sir. In soul, I do.' With that, he mounted and pedalled furiously away.

Barry climbed into Brunhilde and wondered why his adviser had suddenly taken flight at the mere mention of Dr O'Reilly. Well, he thought, if Willy John's cow was in the right field, he'd soon find out. His appointment at five was with none other than Dr Fingal Flahertie O'Reilly.

BARRY READ the lines on a brass plate screwed to the wall beside the green-painted front door of a three-storey house:

Dr F. F. O'Reilly, M.B., B.Ch., B.A.O.
Physician and Surgeon
Hours: Monday to Friday, 9 a.m. to noon.

By the grace of Willy John McCoubrey's black and white cow, he had arrived with five minutes to spare. He stepped back and looked around. On either side of the doorway, bow windows arced from grey, pebbledashed walls. To his right, through the glass, the furniture of a dining room was clearly visible. So, Barry thought, like many country general practitioners,

Dr O'Reilly must run his practice from home. And if the man's voice, raised and hectoring, that Barry could hear coming from behind the drawn curtains of the left-hand window was anything to go by, the doctor was in.

'You're an eejit, Seamus Galvin. A born-again, blethering, bejesusly bollocks of a buck eejit. What are you?'

Barry could not hear the reply. Somewhere inside, a door banged against a wall. He took a step back and glanced over his shoulder at a gravel walkway leading from the front gate, rosebushes flanking the path. He sensed movement and swung back to face a large man—huge in fact—standing, legs astraddle, in the open doorway. The ogre's bent nose was alabaster, the rest of his face puce, presumably, Barry thought, because it must be tiring carrying a smaller man by the collar of his jacket and the seat of his moleskin trousers. As the small man wriggled and made high-pitched squeaks, he waved his left foot, which Barry noticed was quite bare.

The large man swung the smaller one to and fro, then released his grip. Barry gaped as the little victim's upward flight and keening were both cut short by a rapid descent into the nearest rosebush. 'Buck eejit,' the giant roared and hurled a shoe and a sock after the ejectee. 'The next time, Seamus Galvin, you dirty little bugger, you come here after hours on my half day and want me to look at your sore ankle, wash your bloody feet!'

Barry turned away, ready to beat a retreat, but the path was blocked by the departing Galvin, clutching his footwear, hobbling towards the gate and muttering, 'Yes, Dr O'Reilly sir. I will, Dr O'Reilly sir.'

Barry thought of the cyclist who had fled at the mere mention of Dr O'Reilly. Good Lord, if what Barry had witnessed was an example of the man's bedside manner . . .

'And what the hell do *you* want, standing there, both legs the same length and a face as long as a Lurgan spade?'

Barry swung to face his interrogator. 'Dr O'Reilly?'

'No. The archangel bloody Gabriel. Can you not read the plate?'

'I'm Laverty.'

'Laverty? Well, bugger off. I'm not buying any.'

'I'm Dr Laverty. I answered your advertisement in the *British Medical Journal*. I was to have an interview about the assistant's position.' I will not let this bully intimidate me, he thought.

'*That* Laverty. Jesus, man, why on earth didn't you say so?' O'Reilly offered a hand the size of a soup plate.

Barry felt his knuckles grind together, but he refused to flinch as he met

Dr O'Reilly's gaze. He was staring into a pair of deep-set brown eyes under bushy eyebrows. He noted deep laughter lines round the eyes and saw that the pallor had left O'Reilly's nose, a large bent proboscis with a definite list to port. It had now assumed the plum colour of its surrounding cheeks.

'Come in, Laverty.' O'Reilly stepped aside. 'Door on your left.'

Barry went into the room with the drawn curtains. An open roll-top desk stood against one green wall. Piles of prescription pads, papers and patients' records lay in disarray on the desktop. Above, O'Reilly's framed diploma dangled from a nail. Barry stole a peep: *Trinity College, Dublin, 1936.* In front of the desk were a swivel chair and a plain wooden chair.

'Have a pew.' O'Reilly lowered his bulk into the swivel seat and pushed a pair of half-moon spectacles onto his nose. 'So you want to be my assistant?'

Barry had thought he did, but after the ejection of Seamus Galvin he wasn't so sure. He sat, and settled his bag on his lap. 'Well, I—'

'Course you do,' said O'Reilly, pulling a briar pipe from his jacket pocket. He held a lighted match over the bowl. 'Golden opportunity.'

Barry noticed that he kept sliding forward on his seat. He had to brace his feet firmly on the carpet and keep shoving his backside upwards.

O'Reilly wagged his index finger. 'You'll love it. Might even be a partnership in it for you. Course you'll have to do as I tell you for a while until you get to know the ropes.'

Barry hitched himself back up his seat. 'Does that mean I'll have to hurl patients into the rosebushes?'

'What?' A hint of pallor returned to the big man's nose. Was that a sign of temper? Barry wondered.

'I said, "Does that mean—?"'

'I heard you the first time, boy. Now, listen, have you any experience with country patients?'

'Not ex—'

'Thought not,' said O'Reilly, emitting a puff of tobacco smoke like the blast from the funnels of RMS *Queen Mary* when she blew her boilers. 'You'll have a lot to learn. Lesson number one. Never, never, never'—with each 'never' he poked at Barry with the stem of his pipe—'*never* let the customers get the upper hand. If you do, they'll run you ragged.'

'Don't you think dumping a man bodily into your garden is a little—?'

'I used to . . . until I met Seamus Galvin. If you take the job and get to know that skiver as well as I do . . .' O'Reilly shook his head.

Barry stood and massaged the back of his leg.

O'Reilly began to laugh in great throaty rumbles. 'Leg stiff?'

'Yes. Something's wrong with this chair.'

O'Reilly's chuckles grew deeper. 'No, there's not. I fixed it.'

'Fixed it?'

'Some of the weary, walking wounded in Ballybucklebo seem to think when they get in here to see me it's my job to listen to their lamentations till the cows come home. A single-handed country GP doesn't have that sort of time. That's why I advertised for an assistant. There's too much bloody work in this place.' O'Reilly had stopped laughing. His brown-eyed gaze was fixed on Barry's eyes as he said softly, 'Take the job, boy. I need the help.'

Barry hesitated. Did he really want to work for this big, coarse man? He saw O'Reilly's florid cheeks, the cauliflower ears that must have been acquired in the boxing ring, and a shock of black hair like a badly stooked hayrick, and decided to play for time. 'What have you done to this chair?'

O'Reilly's grin could only be described as demonic. 'I sawed an inch off the front legs. Not very comfortable, is it? Don't want to stay long, do you?'

'No,' said Barry, thinking, I'm not sure I want to stay here at all.

'Neither do the customers. They come in and go out like a fiddler's elbow.'

How could a responsible physician ever take a proper history if his practice ran like a human conveyor belt? Barry asked himself.

He rose. 'I'm not sure I do want to work here . . .'

O'Reilly's laugh boomed. 'Don't take yourself so seriously, son.'

Barry felt the flush begin under his collar. 'Dr O'Reilly, I—'

'Laverty, there are some *really* sick people here who *do* need us, you know.' O'Reilly was no longer laughing.

Barry heard the 'us' and was surprised to find that it pleased him.

'I need help.'

'Well, I—'

'Great,' said O'Reilly, putting another match to his pipe, rising and marching to the door. 'Come on, you've seen the surgery. I'll show you the rest of the shop.' He vanished into the hall, leaving Barry little choice but to follow, then flung open a door. 'Waiting room.'

Barry saw a large room, wallpapered with roses. Wooden chairs were arranged round the walls. O'Reilly pointed to a door in the far wall. 'Patients let themselves in here; we come down from the surgery, take whoever's next back with us, deal with them, and show them out the front door.'

'On their feet, I hope.' Barry watched O'Reilly's nose. No pallor.

The big man chuckled. 'You're no dozer, are you, Laverty?'

Barry kept his counsel as O'Reilly continued. 'It's a good system . . . stops the buggers swapping symptoms, or demanding the same medicine as the last customer. Right . . .' He headed for the staircase. 'Come on.'

Barry followed, up a flight of stairs to a broad landing. Framed photographs of a warship hung on the walls.

'Sitting room's in there.' O'Reilly indicated a pair of panelled doors.

Barry nodded, but looked more closely at the pictures of the battleship. 'Excuse me, Dr O'Reilly, is that HMS *Warspite*?'

O'Reilly's foot paused. 'How'd you know that?'

'My dad served in her.'

'Holy thundering Mother of Jesus. Are you Tom Laverty's boy?'

'Yes.'

'I'll be damned.'

So, thought Barry, will I. His father had talked about a certain Surgeon Commander O'Reilly who had been welterweight boxing champion of the Mediterranean Fleet—that would account for O'Reilly's ears and nose. In his dad's opinion, O'Reilly had been the finest medical officer afloat.

'I'll be damned. Laverty's boy.' O'Reilly held out his hand. His handshake was firm, not crushing. 'You're the man for the job. Thirty-five pounds a week, every other Saturday off, room and board all in.'

'Thirty-five pounds?'

'I'll show you your room.'

'WHAT'LL IT BE?' O'Reilly stood at a sideboard that bore glass decanters.

'Small sherry, please.'

Barry sat in a big armchair. O'Reilly's upstairs sitting room was comfortably furnished. Three watercolours of game birds adorned the wall over a wide fireplace. Two walls were hidden by floor-to-ceiling bookcases. From Barry's quick appraisal of the titles—from Plato's *Republic*, Caesar's *De Bello Gallica* and A. A Milne's *Winnie-the-Pooh* to the collected works of W. Somerset Maugham, Graham Greene and John Steinbeck, and Leslie Charteris's *The Saint* books—O'Reilly's reading tastes were wide-ranging. His record collection, stacked haphazardly beside a gramophone, was equally eclectic. Beethoven's symphonies were jumbled in with old 78s by Bix Beiderbecke and Jelly Roll Morton, along with the Beatles' most recent LP.

'Here you are.' O'Reilly handed Barry a glass, sat heavily in another armchair and propped his stoutly booted feet on a coffee table. Then he lifted his own glass, which Barry thought could have done service as a fire bucket if it hadn't been filled to the brim with Irish whiskey.

My God, Barry thought, looking more closely at O'Reilly's ruddy cheeks; don't tell me he's a raging drunk.

O'Reilly, clearly oblivious to Barry's scrutiny, nodded to the picture window. 'Would you look at that?'

Barry looked past the moss-grown, lopsided steeple of a church across the road from O'Reilly's house, down over the rooftops of the terrace cottages of Ballybucklebo's main street, and out over the sand dunes of the foreshore to where Belfast Lough, cobalt and white-capped, separated County Down from the distant Antrim Hills, hazy against a sky as blue as cornflowers.

'It's lovely, Dr O'Reilly.'

'Fingal, my boy. Fingal. For Oscar.' O'Reilly's smile was avuncular.

'Oscar, er, Fingal?'

'No. Not Oscar Fingal. Wilde.'

'Oscar Fingal Wilde, Fingal?' Barry knew he was getting lost.

'Oscar . . . Fingal . . . O'Flahertie . . . Wills . . . Wilde. I was named for him. For Oscar Wilde. My father was a classical scholar, and if you think I got a mouthful, you should meet my brother, Lars Porsena O'Reilly.'

'Good Lord. Macaulay?'

'The very fella. *Lays of Ancient Rome.*' O'Reilly took a deep drink. 'Us country GPs aren't all utterly unlettered.'

Barry felt a blush start. His first impressions of the big man sitting opposite might not have been entirely accurate. He sipped his sherry.

'So, Laverty,' O'Reilly said, clearly ignoring Barry's discomfort. 'What's it to be? Do you want the job?'

Before Barry could answer, a bell jangled from somewhere below.

'Bugger,' said O'Reilly, 'another customer. Come on.'

He rose. Barry followed. O'Reilly opened the front door.

Seamus Galvin stood on the doorstep. In each hand he carried a live lobster. 'Good evening, Doctor sir,' he said, thrusting the beasts at O'Reilly. 'I've washed me foot, so I have.'

'Have you, by God?' said O'Reilly sternly, passing the squirming creatures to Barry. 'Come in and I'll take a look at your hind leg.'

'Thank you, Doctor sir, thank you very much.' Galvin hesitated. 'And who's this young gentleman?' he asked.

Barry was so busy avoiding the crustaceans' clattering claws he nearly missed O'Reilly's reply. 'This is Dr Laverty. He's my new assistant. I'll be showing him the ropes tomorrow.'

Morning Has Broken

Barry woke to the jangling of his alarm clock. His attic room had just enough space for a bed, a bedside table and a wardrobe. Last night he'd unpacked, put his few clothes away and propped his fishing rod in a corner near the dormer window.

He rose, drew the curtains then headed for the bathroom. As he shaved, he thought about last night. O'Reilly had strapped Seamus Galvin's ankle, put the lobsters in the kitchen sink, taken Barry back up to the sitting room and poured more drinks. He'd explained that for the first month they'd work together so Barry could get to know the patients, the running of the practice and the geography of Ballybucklebo and the surrounding countryside.

Somehow the evening had slipped by. Despite a steady intake of Old Bushmills Irish whiskey, O'Reilly had given no sign of ill effects. After two sherries, Barry had been grateful to be shown to his quarters in the attic and wished a very good night.

He rinsed his razor and looked in the mirror. Just a tad of red in the whites of his eyes. Had the sherry affected his judgment so much? Certainly he had no recollection of actually agreeing to take the job, but it seemed that once O'Reilly made up his mind, lesser mortals had no choice but to go along. Well, in for a penny . . . He dried his face, went back to his garret and dressed. Best trousers, best shoes, clean shirt . . .

'Move yourself, Laverty. We haven't got all day,' O'Reilly roared up the stairwell.

Barry knotted his Queen's University tie, slipped on a sports jacket and headed for the stairs.

'EAT UP HOWEVER little much is in it, Dr Laverty dear.'

Barry looked up from his plate of Ulster mixed grill—bacon, sausages, black pudding, fried eggs, tomatoes, lamb chop and fried soda bread—into the happy face of Mrs Kincaid. He saw silver hair in a chignon, black eyes like polished jets set between roseate cheeks, a smiling mouth above three chins.

'I'll do my best.'

'Good lad. You'll be having this for breakfast a lot,' she said, setting a plate in front of O'Reilly. 'Himself here is a grand man for the pan, so.'

Barry heard the soft Cork lilt of her voice, with the habit Cork folk had of adding 'so' at the end of a sentence.

Mrs Kincaid left. O'Reilly muttered something through a mouthful of black pudding.

'I beg your pardon?'

O'Reilly swallowed. 'I forgot to warn you about Kinky. She's a powerful woman. Been with me for years. Housekeeper, cook and Cerberus.'

'She guards the gates of Hades?'

'Like the three-headed dog himself. The customers have to get up very early in the morning to put one past Kinky. You'll see. Now, get stuck into your grub. We've to be in the surgery in fifteen minutes.'

Mrs Kincaid reappeared. 'Tea, Doctor?' She poured his tea and gave him a sheet of paper.

'That's your afternoon calls for today, Doctor,' she said. 'Maggie wanted you to drop round, but I told her to come into the surgery.'

'Maggie MacCorkle?' O'Reilly sighed and dabbed at an egg stain on his tie. 'All right. Thanks, Kinky.'

'Better she comes here than you drive ten miles to her cottage.' Mrs Kincaid cocked her head and studied the mess on O'Reilly's tie. 'And take off the grubby thing, and I'll wash it for you, so.'

To Barry's surprise, O'Reilly meekly undid the knot and handed the tie to Mrs Kincaid, who sniffed, turned and left, remarking, 'And don't forget to put on a clean one.'

'JESUS,' WHISPERED O'REILLY, 'would you take a look? You'd need five loaves and two small fishes to feed that bloody multitude.'

Barry stared through the gap where O'Reilly held ajar the door to the waiting room. It was standing room only. How on earth was O'Reilly going to see so many patients before noon?

O'Reilly opened the door wide. 'Morning.'

A chorus of 'Morning, Dr O'Reilly' echoed from the waiting room.

'I want you all to meet Dr Laverty,' he said. 'My new assistant. Dr Laverty has come down from the Queen's University to give me a hand.'

A voice muttered, 'He looks awful young, so he does.'

'He is, James Guiggan. The youngest doctor ever to take the first prize for learning at the university.'

Barry tried to protest that he was no such thing, but he felt O'Reilly's hand grip his forearm and heard him whisper, 'Remember lesson number one.' *Never let the customers get the upper hand* echoed in Barry's head as O'Reilly said, 'Right. How many's here for tonics?'

Several people rose.

O'Reilly counted. ' . . . five, six. I'll take you lot first. Hang on a minute.' O'Reilly turned and headed for the surgery.

Barry followed. He watched as O'Reilly produced six hypodermics, filled them with a pink fluid from a rubber-topped bottle, and laid them in a row on a towel on top of a small wheeled trolley.

'What's that, Dr O'Reilly?'

O'Reilly grinned. 'Vitamin B12.'

'B12? But that's not—'

'Jesus, man, *I* know it's not a tonic . . . there's no such thing. *You* know it's not a tonic, but'—his grin widened—'*they* don't know it's not a tonic. Now, go get 'em. All of them.'

Barry headed for the waiting room. Heavens, this was hardly the kind of medicine he'd been taught. 'Would all those for tonics please follow me?'

The six victims trooped into the surgery, where O'Reilly waited.

'Along the couch.'

Three men and three women dutifully faced the examination couch.

'Bend over.'

Three trousered and three calico-dressed backsides were presented.

Barry watched, mouth agape, as O'Reilly grabbed a syringe in one hand, a methylated spirits-reeking cotton-wool ball in the other. He dabbed the calico over the first derriere with a ball. 'Listerian antisepsis,' he intoned as he jabbed the needle home.

'Ouch,' yelped a skinny woman. The process was repeated down the line—dab, jab, 'Ouch'; dab, jab, 'Ouch'—until O'Reilly stood before his final victim, a woman of massive proportions. He dabbed and stabbed. The hypodermic flew across the room as if propelled by a giant catapult and stuck in the wall, quivering like a well-thrown dart.

O'Reilly shook his head, filled another syringe, and said, 'Jesus, Cissie, how many times have I to tell you, don't wear your stays on tonic day?'

'Sorry, Doctor, I forgo— Ouch!'

'Right,' said O'Reilly. 'Off you go. You'll all be running around like spring chickens when that stuff starts to work.'

'Thank you, Doctor sir,' said six voices in unison. The patients filed out.

O'Reilly retrieved the syringe-dart, turned to Barry, and said, 'Don't look so disapproving, boy. It'll do them no harm, and half of them will feel better. I know it's only a placebo, but we're here to make folks feel better.'

'Yes, Dr O'Reilly.' There was some truth to what the older man said.

Barry spent the morning acting as a runner between the waiting room and the surgery, and sitting on the examining couch watching as O'Reilly dealt with a procession of men with sore backs, women and their runny-nosed children, coughs, sniffles and earaches. He noticed that O'Reilly knew every patient by name and had an encyclopedic knowledge of their medical history.

At last. The waiting room was empty. O'Reilly sprawled in his chair, and Barry returned to what now was his familiar place on the couch.

'So,' asked O'Reilly, 'what do you think?'

'Not much about you injecting people through their clothes, and I won no prizes at university.' Barry glanced at O'Reilly's nose tip. No paleness.

O'Reilly produced his briar and lit it. 'Country folk are a pretty conservative lot. You're a young lad. Why should they trust you?'

Barry stiffened. 'Because I'm a doctor.'

O'Reilly guffawed. 'It's not what you call yourself, *Doctor* Laverty; it's what you do that counts here. All I did was give you a head start.'

Someone knocked on the door. O'Reilly looked over his half-moons at Barry. 'See who that is, will you?'

Barry walked stiffly to the door. Head start, he thought. As if he wasn't fully qualified. He opened the door to a woman in her sixties. Her face was weathered, her upper lip sported a fine brown moustache. Her nose curved down, her chin curved up like that of Punch in a *Punch and Judy* show.

She wore a straw hat with two wilted geraniums stuck in the hatband. Her torso was hidden under layers of different coloured woollen cardigans, and under the hem of her rusty ankle-length skirt peeped the toes of a pair of Wellington boots. When she smiled he could see that she was as toothless as an oyster. Her ebony eyes twinkled. 'Is himself in?'

Barry felt a presence at his shoulder.

'Maggie,' he heard O'Reilly say. 'Maggie MacCorkle. Come in.' O'Reilly ushered her to the patients' chair. 'This is my assistant, Dr Laverty. I'd like him to see to you today, Maggie. Nothing like a second opinion.'

Barry stared at O'Reilly, and nodded. 'Good morning, Mrs MacCorkle.'

She sniffed and smoothed her skirt. 'It's *Miss* MacCorkle, so it is.'

'Sorry. Miss MacCorkle. And what seems to be the trouble?'

'The headaches. Lord Jesus, they've always been acute, but last night they got something chronic, so they did. They were desperate.' She leaned forward and said with great solemnity, 'I near took the rickets.'

He stifled a smile. 'I see. And where exactly are they?'

'There.' She held one hand above the crown of her flowery hat.

Barry jerked back in his chair. He wondered where O'Reilly kept the necessary forms for certifying that someone was insane.

'Above your head?'

'Oh, aye. A good two inches.'

'I see.' He steepled his fingers. 'And have you been hearing voices?'

She stiffened. 'What do you mean?'

'Well, I . . .' He looked helplessly at O'Reilly.

'What Dr Laverty means is, do you have any ringing in your ears?'

'Ding-dong or brrring?' Maggie asked, turning to O'Reilly.

'You tell me,' he said.

'Ding-dong, Doctor dear. Ding-dong it is. Dingy-dingy-dong.'

'Mmm,' said O'Reilly. 'Are the pains in the middle or off to one side?'

'Over to the left, so they are.'

'That's what we call "eccentric", Maggie.'

That's what I'd call the pair of you, thought Barry.

'Eccentric? Is that bad, Doctor?'

'Not at all, said O'Reilly. 'Fix you up in no time.'

Her shoulders relaxed. She smiled up at O'Reilly, but when she turned to. Barry, her stare was as icy as the wind that sweeps the lough in winter.

O'Reilly grabbed a small bottle of vitamin pills from the desk. 'These'll do the trick.'

Maggie rose and accepted the bottle.

O'Reilly gently propelled her towards the door. 'These are special. You have to take them exactly as I tell you.' His next words were delivered with weighted solemnity: 'Exactly half an hour before the pain starts.'

'Oh, thank you, Doctor dear.' Her smile was radiant. She made a little curtsey, turned and faced Barry, but she spoke to O'Reilly. 'Mind you,' she said, 'this young Laverty fellow . . . he's a lot to learn.'

BARRY SAT BACK in his dining-room chair and pushed his lunch plate away. Certainly, he thought, O'Reilly's clinical methods might leave something to be desired, but—he burped gently—he was willing to forgive the man's eccentricities as long as Mrs Kincaid's cooking stayed at its current level.

'Home visits,' said O'Reilly from across the table. He consulted a piece of paper. 'Anyone who's too sick to come to the surgery phones Kinky in the morning, and she gives me my list.'

'The one she gave you at breakfast?'

'Aye, and she tells me to add any who call during the morning. We're lucky today: just one. At the Kennedys'.' He rose. 'Let's get moving. There's a rugby game tonight on the telly. I want to get back in time for the kickoff.'

Barry followed him into the kitchen, where Mrs Kincaid greeted them with a smile. 'Would you like them lobsters for supper, Doctor dear?'

'That would be grand, Kinky.' O'Reilly's forward progress stopped. 'Kinky, is tonight your Women's Union night?'

'Aye, so.'

'We'll have the lobsters cold. Leave them with a bit of salad and get you away early.' He charged on, ignoring Mrs Kincaid's thanks, opened the back door and ushered Barry through.

He found himself in a spacious garden. Vegetables grew in a plot by the left-hand hedge. Some apple trees were bowed over a well-kept lawn. A chestnut tree at the far end drooped branches over a fence and shaded a dog kennel.

'Arthur!' yelled O'Reilly. 'Arthur Guinness!'

A vast black labrador hurled himself from the kennel, charged over the grass and leapt at O'Reilly.

'Who's a good boy then?' O'Reilly said, thumping the dog's flank. 'I call him Arthur Guinness because he's Irish, black and has a great head on him . . . just like the stout. Arthur Guinness, meet Dr Laverty.'

'Arf,' said Arthur, immediately transferring his affections to Barry, who fought desperately to push the animal away. 'Ararf.'

'Arthur Guinness is the best bloody gundog in Ulster.'

'You shoot, Dr O'Reilly?'

'Fingal, my boy, Fingal. Yes. Arthur and I enjoy a day at the ducks, don't we, Arthur?'

'Yarf,' said Arthur as he wound his front paws round Barry's leg and started to hump like a demented pile driver.

Barry tried and failed to hold the besotted beast at bay.

'Get on with you, sir,' said O'Reilly, pointing to the kennel. 'Go home.'

Arthur Guinness gave one last thrust, disengaged himself and wandered off in the general direction of his abode.

'Affectionate animal,' said Barry as he tried to brush the mud from the leg of his best corduroy trousers.

'If he likes you,' said O'Reilly as he walked on, 'and he obviously does.' He opened the back gate. 'Garage is out here.' He crossed a lane to a dilapidated shed and swung an overhead door upwards. Barry peered inside and saw a black, long-bonnet Rover, one of a line of cars that had not been produced for at least fifteen years.

O'Reilly climbed in and started the engine. It grumbled, spluttered and backfired. Barry hopped into the passenger seat. O'Reilly put the car in gear and nosed out onto the lane. The car stank of damp dog and tobacco smoke. Barry wound down a window.

O'Reilly turned left at the first road junction and drove past his house and on along Ballybucklebo's main thoroughfare. Terraces of whitewashed, single-storey cottages, some thatched and some with slate roofs, lined the route. They came to a crossroads and halted at a red traffic light. A maypole, paint peeling, leaning to the left, stood on the far corner.

'It's fun here on Beltane—that's the old Celtic May Day,' said O'Reilly, pointing to the pole. 'Bonfires, dancing, the pursuit of young virgins . . . The locals aren't far removed from their pagan ancestors when there's the chance of a good party.' He revved the engine and gestured at the road to the right. 'Go down there, and you'll end up at the seashore; left takes you up into the Ballybucklebo Hills.'

Barry nodded. The light changed to amber. O'Reilly slipped the clutch.

'Amber,' he remarked as he roared ahead, 'is only for the tourists.' He gestured vaguely around. 'The throbbing heart of Ballybucklebo.'

Two-storey buildings now. Greengrocer, butcher, newsagent, and a larger building, outside which hung a sign: THE BLACK SWAN. Barry noticed a familiar figure, left ankle bandaged, limping towards the front door.

'Galvin,' said O'Reilly. 'That one'd drain the lough if it was Guinness.' He changed up with a grinding of gears. 'Now. You can take this road we're on to Belfast, or if you look to starboard . . . see? You can take the train.'

Barry glanced to his right to see a diesel train moving slowly along a raised embankment. Interesting, he thought. He might just do that on his day off. He'd like to visit one of his friends from medical school because—

He was hurled forward as O'Reilly braked. 'Bloody cow!'

Barry saw a black and white bovine, eyes soft, reflecting the utter vacuity behind them, ambling along the centre of the road, chewing its cud.

O'Reilly wound down his window. 'Hoosh on, cow. Hoosh. Hoosh.'

The animal emitted a single doleful moo, and budged not one inch.

'Right,' said O'Reilly. He dismounted, slammed the door and walked to face the cow. He took a horn in one hand and pulled.

To Barry's amazement the beast took two paces forward, clearly unable to withstand the force being applied to its head.

'Move your bloody self,' O'Reilly roared.

The cow flicked her ears, lowered her head and skittered to the side of the road. O'Reilly climbed into the car, slammed it into gear and took off with a screeching of rubber on tarmac.

'Jesus Murphy,' he said. 'Animals. They're one of the delights of country practice. You just have to get used to dealing with them.'

'Fine,' said Barry, unaware of how soon Dr O'Reilly's words would be shown to be true.

O'REILLY GRUNTED and then ground the gears. Barry listened to the grumbling of the engine as the rear tyres whined and spun . . . and spun.

'Bugger it,' said O'Reilly. 'We'll have to walk.' He reached over to the back seat and grabbed his black bag and a pair of Wellingtons, which he now began to change into. 'Out.'

Barry stepped out—and sank to his ankles in a ditch. He hauled each foot loose from the mud and squelched to the lane's grassy verge. Blast! His shoes and best trousers, already stained from the attentions of Arthur Guinness, were filthy. He turned and stared at a farmhouse at the end of the rutted lane. 'Is that where we're going, Fingal?'

'Aye, that's the Kennedys' place.'

'Is there some other way to get there? My shoes . . .'

'Christ! You should always bring wellies. All right, we'll cut through the fields.' Barry noticed just a hint of pallor on the tip of O'Reilly's nose. 'Get a move on. The rugby starts in half an hour.' The big man hefted his bag, pushed open a five-bar gate in the hedge and strode off.

Barry stared at the ruin of his shoes—his only pair of good shoes. He heard O'Reilly yelling, 'Is it today you were coming?'

'Bugger off,' Barry muttered as he walked to where O'Reilly stood. The grass in the pasture was knee-deep. And damp, very damp. Oh, well, he thought, at least the dew would wash off some of the mud.

'What kept you?'

'Dr O'Reilly,' Barry began. 'My shoes and my trousers are ruined. I—'

'What,' asked O'Reilly, 'do you know about pigs?'

'I fail to see what pigs have to do with my clothes.'

'Suit yourself, but there's one coming.' O'Reilly started to walk rapidly.

Barry hesitated. Coming towards them was a pink something with the dimensions of a small hippopotamus. Its eyes—he could see them now that it was closer—were red and distinctly malevolent.

Barry set off at a canter in pursuit of O'Reilly and caught up with him halfway between the gate and the end of the field. 'It *is* a pig.'

'Brilliant,' said O'Reilly 'Bloody big teeth.' His gait moved up to a fully developed trot and opened a fair gap between Barry and himself.

Barry risked a backward glance. The beast was gaining. He began to sprint. Ten yards from the far hedge, Barry passed a flagging O'Reilly. The extra helping of Mrs Kincaid's steak-and-kidney pudding must be slowing O'Reilly down, Barry thought as he cleared a low gate.

He almost collided with a small grinning man in a flat cap, who stood in the farmyard. Before Barry could begin to explain, the quiet of the afternoon was shattered by sounds of crashing and rending, and he saw O'Reilly break through the blackthorn hedge like a tank. Although O'Reilly's cheeks were scarlet, despite his recent exertions his nose tip was alabaster.

'Dermot Kennedy,' he bellowed, 'what's so bloody funny?'

Mr Kennedy was doubled over, laughing heartily. 'Thon's Gertrude,' he gasped, 'Jeannie's pet sow. She only just wanted her snout scratched.'

'Oh,' said O'Reilly.

'Right,' said Barry. 'Animals are, I believe—and please correct me if I'm misquoting you, Dr O'Reilly—"one of the delights of country practice. You just have to get used to dealing with them." '

'You can do that if you like, Doctor sir,' said Mr Kennedy, his laughter gone, 'but it's really the farmer's job. Doctors keep an eye to the sick and I'm sore worried about our Jeannie. Would you come and take a look at her, sir?'

BARRY FOLLOWED Mr Kennedy and Dr O'Reilly to the farmhouse, a single-storey building, whitewashed and thatched with straw. Smoke drifted upwards from a chimney. Black shutters flanked every window.

Barry heard Mr Kennedy say, 'Go on in, Doctors.'

He cleaned as much muck off his muddy shoes as he could on a boot scraper and went in. He found himself in a bright kitchen.

A woman stood, pouring tea into a cup patterned with daffodils. Barry took her to be in her early fifties. 'Thanks for coming, Dr O'Reilly.'

O'Reilly parked himself at a solid-looking pine table. 'It's no trouble. This is my new assistant, Dr Laverty.'

Mrs Kennedy bobbed her head to Barry. She wore an apron. Her grey-flecked dark hair was untidy, and although she smiled at him, her smile was only on her lips. Her eyes, dark circles beneath, gave away her forced humour. 'Sit down,' she said. 'I'll fetch another cup.'

Barry pulled out a chair and sat beside O'Reilly. He thanked the woman when she gave him a cup of tea, dark and stewed.

'And you say Jeannie's been off-colour since yesterday?' O'Reilly's tone, for the first time in Barry's short acquaintance with the man, had none of its usual brusqueness.

'Aye, Doctor. She'll no' eat nothing. Says her wee tummy hurts.'

'Has she boked?'

Barry smiled at O'Reilly's use of the country vernacular for 'vomited'.

'Just the once. And she's burning up, so she is,' Mrs Kennedy said softly.

'Did you not tell all this to Mrs Kincaid when you phoned, Bridget?' O'Reilly said. 'I'd have come sooner.'

'Och, Doctor dear, we know how busy you are.' Mrs Kennedy's hands twisted her apron. 'Sure, it's only a wee tummy upset, isn't it?'

'Mmm,' said O'Reilly. 'Maybe we'd better take a look at her.'

'This way, Doctor,' Mrs Kennedy said, walking to a door.

Barry walked after her into a hall and through the door of a small bedroom. Bright chintz curtains framed the window. A beam of sunlight fell on the counterpane of a child's bed, where a little girl, black hair tied up in bunches, teddy bear clutched to her flushed cheek, lay listlessly against two pillows. She stared at him with overbright, brown eyes.

'This is Dr Laverty, Jeannie,' Mrs Kennedy explained.

Barry moved to the corner of the room and watched as O'Reilly grinned and sat on the edge of the child's bed. 'So, Jeannie,' he said, 'not so good?'

She shook her head. 'My tummy's sore.'

O'Reilly laid the back of his right hand on the child's forehead. 'Hot,' he remarked. 'May I take your pulse, Jeannie?'

She gave him her right arm.

'Hundred and ten,' said O'Reilly after a while.

Barry mentally added that fact to the rest. With the twenty-four-hour history of abdominal pain, the child not wanting to eat, vomiting, a fever and a rapid pulse rate, he was already quite sure she had appendicitis.

'Can I see your teddy, Jeannie?' O'Reilly asked.

She handed him the stuffed bear.

'Now, Teddy,' said O'Reilly, laying the toy on the counterpane, 'put out your tongue and say ah.' He bent and peered at the bear's face. 'Good. Now let's have a look at your tummy.' He nodded wisely. 'Too many sweeties.'

Jeannie smiled.

'Your turn,' said O'Reilly softly, returning the bear. 'Put out your tongue.'

The child obeyed. He bent forward and sniffed.

'Have a look at this, Dr Laverty.'

Barry stepped forward. The tongue was furred, the child's breath fetid.

'Can we pull the bedclothes down, Mummy?' O'Reilly asked.

Mrs Kennedy turned back the covers.

'Jeannie, can you point to where the pain started?'

Her finger hovered over her epigastrium, where her lower ribs flared out.

'And is it there yet?'

She solemnly shook her head and pointed to her lower right side. Barry flinched. The next part of the examination would cause intense pain. Worse, the textbooks called for the doctor to examine the patient rectally.

'Right,' said O'Reilly. To Barry's surprise, O'Reilly gently pulled the bedclothes up. 'Jeannie, would you like to go for a ride to Belfast?'

The little girl looked at her mother, who nodded. Jeannie stared into O'Reilly's craggy face. 'All right,' she said. 'Can Teddy come?'

'Oh, aye,' said O'Reilly. 'Now you just lie there like a good girl. I need to have a wee word with your mummy.' He smoothed the child's hair from her forehead, then rose and headed for the door. 'Are you coming, Dr Laverty?'

Barry hesitated. This wasn't right. O'Reilly had barely examined the patient. The man was in such a hurry to get back to watch his rugby game that he was cutting corners. He'd have this out with O'Reilly later.

'Bye-bye, Jeannie,' he said as he left, and returned to the kitchen.

Mr Kennedy stood with one arm round his wife's shoulder. O'Reilly had the phone clapped to one ear. His voice echoed from the roof beams.

'What the hell do you mean, you've no beds? I've a kiddie with appendicitis here. She'll be at Sick Children's in half an hour. . . . Balls, young man. You get hold of Sir Donald Cromie . . . I don't give a bugger if it is his day off; you tell him that Dr Fingal Flahertie O'Reilly called from Ballybucklebo.' He slammed the receiver into the cradle.

'You've called the ambulance already?' Barry asked.

'We'll take her up to Belfast in my car.'

'I thought you wanted to get home to see—'

'Don't be daft. We haven't time to wait for an ambulance.'

ONCE THE KENNEDYS had been delivered to the Royal Belfast Hospital for Sick Children, and O'Reilly was satisfied that Sir Donald Cromie agreed with the diagnosis and would operate immediately, he grabbed Barry by the arm and hustled him to the car.

'Come on. If we get a move on, we'll still be able to watch the second half.'

As O'Reilly drove from the hospital grounds onto Falls Road, Barry said, 'Dr O'Reilly, I think you were very lucky to make the right diagnosis.'

'Oh?' said O'Reilly mildly, 'and why would you think that?'

'You didn't examine the child properly because you were in a hurry.'

O'Reilly stopped at a red light and turned to Barry. 'Son, the diagnosis was as clear as the nose on your face from the minute we walked into the room. You could smell her halitosis. Did you want me to prod her belly and stick a finger up her backside just because that's what the book says?'

'Well, I—'

'Well, nothing,' said O'Reilly, driving on. 'There was no need to hurt her.'

'I suppose . . .' Barry could see O'Reilly's logic. He also knew that there had been no real need for O'Reilly to take the family to Belfast. Damn it, the more Barry thought about it, the more he recognised that the older man, the experienced man, was probably right not to have inflicted unnecessary pain. Perhaps, under his rough façade, O'Reilly had a softer side.

Barry's ruminations were interrupted as the car moved past the redbrick wall of Campbell College, his old school. He had made one good friend there, Jack Mills, who was training to be a surgeon at the Royal Victoria Hospital. They had shared a study at university in their senior year, stuck together as medical students, been housemen together. Barry decided he'd give Jack a call to see if they could get together when he had his first Saturday off. He'd be interested to hear his friend's opinion of O'Reilly.

The car left the city traffic. O'Reilly slammed his foot on the accelerator and hurled the Rover at the twisting Craigantlet Hill Road. Barry tensed as the car lurched when a wheel bounced off the verge.

'Aren't we going a bit fast, Dr O'Reilly?'

'Nonsense, my boy.' O'Reilly threw the car into a turn. 'We're coming to the Straight. We'll be home in no time.'

Or upside-down in the ditch, Barry thought. He could see that the road stretched ahead to the horizon, but it followed the undulations of the hills on either side. He took a deep breath and hoped that the queasy feeling in the pit of his stomach would pass.

'Not far now,' said O'Reilly at last, slowing to turn into a lane. 'Over the Ballybucklebo Hills and home.' He glanced at his watch. 'Ten minutes to the second half.'

He drove under elms with leaf-laden boughs, past dry-stone walls bordering little fields where sheep and cattle grazed and yellow-flowered gorse bushes stood bold against green grass. The car crested a rise. Below, Barry saw Ballybucklebo. He noted the single traffic light and the road past it that O'Reilly said led to the seashore. Above the dunes and silver scutch grass, a flock of white birds wheeled and dipped, then flew out over the white-capped waters of the lough. A single freighter butted through the chop, making its way to the port of Belfast.

He wound down his window and breathed the clean country air. From overhead he heard a skylark, and from a field nearby the rattle of a corncrake; the classical music and the rock and roll of the bird world, he thought.

The car passed the first outlying cottage.

'Nearly home,' said O'Reilly.

'Home?' For you, Dr O'Reilly, Barry thought, but will it be for me?

O'Reilly stole a glance at his passenger. 'Aye,' he said quietly, 'it is.'

BARRY CHANGED OUT of his muddy trousers and shoes, then joined O'Reilly to watch the match on television. He finished the last of Mrs Kincaid's lobster salad and put the plate on a coffee table beside his armchair. The Ireland under-twenty-three rugby squad had beaten the Scots.

O'Reilly belched contentedly, stared through the bay window and said, 'She's a dab hand in the kitchen is Kinky.'

'Agreed.' The cold meal had been delicious.

'Don't know what I'd do without her.' O'Reilly wandered over to the sideboard. 'Sherry?'

'Please.'

O'Reilly poured a small sherry for Barry and a gargantuan Irish whiskey for himself. 'I'd not have the practice if it hadn't been for Kinky.'

'Oh?'

'I came here in 1938, assistant to Dr Flanagan. Crusty old bugger. I'll tell you, some of the things he did were very unorthodox, even for back then.'

'Really?' Barry hoped that his smile would go unnoticed.

'His big concern . . . he warned me about it . . . was a strange condition that he'd only ever seen in Ballybucklebo. Cold groin abscesses. He always lanced them.'

'He did surgery here, in the village?'

'GPs did before the war. Now, of course, we have to refer surgical cases to the hospital. Anyway, "Cold groin abscesses," says Flanagan to me, "when you lance them, you never get pus. Just wind or shit . . . and the patient dies about four days later." '

Barry sat bolt upright. 'He thought inguinal hernias were abscesses?'

'He did. And when he sliced into the rupture he always cut into—'

'The bowel. Good God. What did you do?'

'Tried to suggest to him that maybe he didn't have it quite right. I only ever tried to correct Dr Flanagan that once. You've no idea how cantankerous some old country GPs could be, and I needed the money. Jobs were hard to come by back then.'

'Not like today,' Barry said, holding his glass to his lips to hide his expression. 'I'm surprised you stayed.'

'I didn't. I volunteered for the navy as soon as war broke out.'

'What brought you back?'

'When the war was over I'd had enough of the navy, so I wrote to Dr Flanagan. I got a letter back from his housekeeper, Mrs Kincaid, to say that he'd died and that the practice was up for sale. I had my gratuity as an exserviceman. That, and a bank loan, bought me the house and the goodwill of the practice, and Mrs Kincaid agreed to stay on. We've been here since 1946, but I damn nearly lost the practice in the first year.'

'What happened?'

'Country folk,' he said. 'You've got to get used to them. My mistake was to try to change things too quickly. One of my first patients was a farmer with the biggest hernia you ever saw.'

Barry laughed. 'Did you lance it like Dr Flanagan?'

O'Reilly did not laugh. 'When I refused to, the man spread the word that I was a young pup who didn't know his business. The customers stopped coming.' He took a long drink. 'The mortgage payments didn't.'

'You must have been worried.'

'Worried sick. I told you I'd have gone under if Kinky hadn't saved my bacon. She's a Presbyterian, you know. She made me go to church with her. Let the locals see that I was a good Christian man.'

'That's important here?'

'Back then they liked to think that their doctor was a churchgoer. Didn't much matter if he went to church or chapel as long as he went.'

'That's a relief. I spent enough time sorting out the casualties of the Protestant–Catholic street battles when the Divis Street riots hit Belfast.'

'You'll not see any of that here,' said O'Reilly. 'Father O'Toole and the Reverend Robinson play golf together every Monday.' He hauled out his pipe. 'On the Twelfth of July—that's next Thursday—the Orange Lodge has its parade, and half the Catholics in Ballybucklebo'll be lined up, waving

Union Jacks. They've even let Seamus Galvin—mind you, he's what you'd call a lapsed Catholic—into the pipe band.' He struck a match. 'Anyway,' he said, 'I was telling you about Kinky.'

'Right.'

'Off to church the pair of us trotted. Turned a few heads when we took our pew. I'd no doubt who they were muttering about. I head someone say that I was the young doctor who didn't know his arse from his elbow. Some of them kept turning round to stare at me. Very uncomfortable.'

'I can imagine.'

'In the middle of the last hymn a big fellow in the front row let a wail out of him like a banshee, grabbed at his chest and fell over. The minister said, "I believe there's a doctor here." Kinky gave me a ferocious nudge.'

'What did you do?'

'I grabbed my stethoscope out of my bag and rushed down the aisle. Your man was blue as a bloater. No pulse, no heartbeat. He'd popped his clogs.'

'Was CPR invented back then?'

'Not at all. But I reckoned it was my one chance to make my reputation. "Someone get my bag," says I, unbuttoning your man's shirt. Kinky gave me the bag. I grabbed whatever injection was handy, filled a syringe and stuck the victim in the chest. I clapped my stethoscope on. "He's back," says I. You could have heard the gasps of the congregation all the way to Donaghadee. I waited for a couple of minutes. "He's gone." I stuck him again. More gasps. "He's back."'

'Was he?'

'Not at all. He was stiff as a stunned mullet.'

'I don't see how losing a patient in church in front of half the village saved your practice.'

'Kinky did that for me. I heard someone sniff that the demise of the recently departed just went to show what a useless doctor I was. "Just a small, little minute," says Kinky. She stared at the minister. "You have to agree, Your Reverence, that Our Saviour brought Lazarus back from the dead." The minister agreed. Then Kinky said, "And Jesus only did it once, so. Our doctor, our Dr O'Reilly, himself here, did it twice."' O'Reilly finished his drink. 'I've been run off my feet since.'

'You wily old—'

The doorbell clanged in the hall.

'See what I mean! Be a good lad, and nip down and see who that is.'

Barry opened the front door. He was confronted by a man standing on the step. He was short and sufficiently rotund to warrant being described as spherical. He wore a black three-piece suit, a bowler hat and a scowl.

'Where the hell's O'Reilly?' The visitor forced his way into the hall. 'O'Reilly, come 'ere; I want ye. Now!' he bellowed.

'Perhaps I can—'

'I've heard about you, Laverty.' The newcomer turned to face Barry, who was thinking, I'm only a day in the place. News travels fast. 'I want himself.'

Barry stiffened. 'It's *Dr* Laverty, and if you have something—'

'*Doctor*, is it? Huh!' The little man's eyes flashed. 'Do you know who I am? I'm Councillor Bishop, Worshipful Master of the Ballybucklebo Orange Lodge, so I am.'

'Good evening, Councillor,' said O'Reilly from behind the man.

Councillor Bishop spun to face O'Reilly, who towered over him. O'Reilly was smiling, but Barry recognised the telltale paleness in his bent nose.

'My finger's beelin', O'Reilly.' He thrust his right index finger under O'Reilly's nose. Barry could see the skin, red and shiny round the nail bed, the yellow pus beneath.

'Tut,' said O'Reilly, donning his half-moon spectacles.

'Well, what are you going to do about it?'

'Come into the surgery.' He led the councillor and Barry inside, then put instruments into a steel steriliser and switched it on. 'Won't be a minute.'

'Get on with it. I'm a busy man.'

'Certainly.' O'Reilly went to a cabinet, brought out a cloth-wrapped pack and placed it on the trolley beside the steriliser. 'Open it, please, Dr Laverty.'

Barry peeled off the outer layer. Inside lay sterile towels and swabs, sponge forceps, a kidney basin and a pair of surgical gloves. He heard water running as O'Reilly washed his hands, then *snap, snap* as O'Reilly donned gloves.

'Dettol and Xylocaine are on the bottom of the trolley.'

Barry retrieved the disinfectant and the local anaesthetic, relieved that O'Reilly was not going to incise the abscess without deadening the pain.

'Thank you.' O'Reilly stuffed a couple of swabs between the jaws of the forceps. 'Now, Councillor, if you'd hold your finger over this basin.'

The ringing of the steriliser's bell to indicate that the instruments were now ready almost muffled Councillor Bishop's '*Yeeeowee!*'

Yes, indeed, Barry thought, Dettol does bite. He retrieved the now sterile forceps, scalpel and hypodermic, and carried them over. 'Local?'

'Of course,' said O'Reilly, lifting the hypodermic.

Councillor Bishop stared wide-eyed at the needle.

'I'm going to freeze your finger,' said O'Reilly. He filled the syringe's barrel. 'This'll sting,' he said, pushing the needle into the skin of the web between the index and middle finger.

'*Wheee, arr, wowee,*' howled the councillor, writhing in his chair.

'I know you're in a rush, but we'll have to wait for that to work.'

'All right,' whimpered Councillor Bishop. 'Take your time.'

'How long has the finger been bothering you?' O'Reilly asked.

'Two, three days.'

'Pity you didn't come in sooner. Surgery's always open in the mornings.'

'I will next time, Doctor. Honest to God, I will.'

There was the merest upward tilt of O'Reilly's mouth as he said, 'Do.' He picked up the scalpel. 'Right. You won't feel a thing.'

He sliced into the flesh. Barry watched blood and yellow pus ooze out.

'Oh, dear,' O'Reilly remarked, 'the councillor seems to have fainted.'

Barry looked at the little round man, who lay crumpled in the chair.

'Nasty man,' said O'Reilly as he swabbed the mess away. Then he used two clean gauze squares to dress the wound. 'Thinks he's the bee's knees because he owns half the property in the village.' He pointed to his roll-top desk. 'There's a bottle of smelling salts in there. Get them, will you?'

Barry went to the desk, aware that he had seen Dr O'Reilly perform minor surgery with all the skill of one of the senior surgeons at the Royal. And somehow he had let Councillor Bishop know that while patients might have certain expectations of their physician, courtesy was a two-way street.

By the Dawn's Early Light

A telephone rang. Barry fumbled for the receiver. The night sister must want him. His hand smacked into an unfamiliar bedside table. 'Ow.' The pain brought him to wakefulness, and he remembered he wasn't in his room in the hospital staff quarters. He was in O'Reilly's attic.

The door opened and a beam of light spilled into his room. 'Up,' said O'Reilly, 'and be quiet. Don't disturb Kinky.'

'Right.' Barry knuckled his eyes, got out of bed, dressed and crept downstairs to find O'Reilly waiting in the hall.

'Come on,' said O'Reilly.

He headed for the kitchen, then out through the back garden. Arthur Guinness stuck his head out of his doghouse.

'I'm not going shooting,' O'Reilly said.

'Umph,' said Arthur, eyeing Barry's trouser leg. The dog must have decided that love at this hour was too much trouble. He retreated into his kennel, muttering something in labradorese.

Barry climbed into the Rover. 'What time is it?'

'Half one,' said O'Reilly, backing into the lane. 'Mrs Fotheringham called. Says her husband's sick, but I doubt it.' He headed for the road. 'Major Basil Fotheringham's had every illness known to man. He always takes a turn for the worse after midnight and, as far as I can tell, he's fit as a bloody flea. It's all in his mind.' He turned left at the traffic light.

'So why are we going out into the Ballybucklebo Hills at this hour?'

'Do you know about the houseman and the surgeon?' said O'Reilly. 'Surgeon comes in to make rounds in the morning. "How is everyone?" says he. "Grand," says the houseman, "except the one you were certain was neurotic, sir." "Oh," says the great man, "gone home has he?" "Not exactly, sir. He died last night." Once in a while, even the worst bloody malingerer does actually get sick.'

'Point taken.'

'Good. Now be quiet. It's not far, but I've to remember how to get there.'

Barry sat back and watched the headlights probe the blackness ahead. Now that Ballybucklebo lay behind, the dark enveloped them as tightly as a shroud. He peered up and saw the Summer Triangle: Altair, Vega and Deneb high in the northwest. Barry's dad and mum would be seeing different stars now, he thought. The Southern Cross would sparkle over their heads. Their last letter from Melbourne, where his dad was on a two-year contract as a consulting engineer, had been full of their enthusiasm for Australia.

The car braked in a driveway and Barry came back to earth.

'When we get in there I want you to agree with everything I say, understand?' said O'Reilly.

'But doctors don't always agree. Sometimes a second opinion—'

'Humour me, son. Just open the gate.'

Barry climbed out and opened the gate, waited for O'Reilly to drive through, closed the gate and crunched along a gravel driveway to a two-storey house, where O'Reilly stood, dark against the light from an open door, talking to a woman wearing a dressing gown.

'Mrs Fotheringham, my assistant, Dr Laverty,' he said.

'How do you do?' she said, in a poor imitation of the accent of an English landed lady. 'So good of you both to come. Poor Basil's not well.'

Barry heard the harsh tones of Ulster beneath her affected gentility. He followed as she led them through a hall, expensively wallpapered and hung with prints, up a deeply carpeted staircase and into a large bedroom.

'The doctors have come, dear,' Mrs Fotheringham said, stepping up to the four-poster bed and smoothing the brow of the man who lay there.

Major Fotheringham sagged against his pillows and made a mewling noise. Barry looked for any obvious evidence of fever or distress, but no sweat was visible on the patient's high forehead; there was nothing hectic about his watery blue eyes, nor any drip from his narrow nose.

'Right,' said O'Reilly, 'what seems to be the trouble this time?'

'He's very poorly, Doctor,' Mrs Fotheringham said. 'I think it's his kidneys.'

'I'd better take a look, then,' said O'Reilly. He stepped to the bed. 'Put out your tongue, Basil.'

Here we go again, Barry thought. O'Reilly had not made the remotest attempt to elicit any kind of history, and here he was barrelling ahead with the physical examination. *Agree with everything I say.* Well, we'll see.

'Mmm,' said O'Reilly, pulling down the patient's lower eyelid and peering at the inside of the lid. 'Mmm-mmm.' He grasped one wrist and made a great show of consulting his watch. 'Mmm.'

Mrs Fotheringham stared intently at every move O'Reilly made.

'Open your pyjamas please.' O'Reilly laid his left hand palm down on the patient's chest and thumped the back of his hand. 'Mmm.' He stuffed the earpieces of his stethoscope in his cauliflower ears and clapped the bell to the front of the chest. 'Big breaths.' Major Fotheringham gasped, in out, in out. 'Sit up, please.' Major Fotheringham obeyed. More thumpings; more stethoscope applications, this time to the back; more huffing; more *mmms*.

Mrs Fotheringham's little eyes widened. 'Is it serious, Doctor?'

'We'll see,' said O'Reilly. 'Lie down.' O'Reilly quickly and expertly completed a full examination of the belly. 'Mmm, *huh.* I see.'

'What is it, Doctor?' Mrs Fotheringham's voice had the same expectancy that Barry had heard in children's voices when they wanted a treat.

'You're right,' O'Reilly said. 'It *could* be his kidneys.'

And how had he arrived at that diagnosis? Barry thought. Nothing O'Reilly had done had come close to examining the organs in question.

'Then again, it might not be,' said O'Reilly, grabbing his bag. 'I think a test's in order, don't you, Dr Laverty?'

Barry met O'Reilly's gaze, swallowed, and said, 'I don't quite see—'

'Course you do.' O'Reilly's tone hardened. 'In a case like this we can't be too careful. You'd agree, Mrs Fotheringham?'

'Oh, indeed, Doctor.' She smiled at O'Reilly.

'That's settled, then.' O'Reilly glared at Barry, then rummaged in his bag and produced a bottle that Barry recognised immediately. It would contain thin cardboard strips used to detect sugar or protein in a urine sample. What the hell was O'Reilly up to?

'I'll need your help, Mrs Fotheringham.' O'Reilly handed her several of the dipsticks.

'Yes, Doctor.' Her eyes were bright, her smile barely concealed.

'I want you to . . .' He looked at his watch. 'It's two fifteen now . . . so start the test at three. Make Basil drink one pint of water.'

'A pint?' she echoed.

'The whole pint. At four give him another pint, but not until he's passed a specimen of urine. Dip one of those dipsticks in it, and put the stick on the dressing table.'

Mrs Fotheringham looked dubiously at her handful of cardboard, sniffed and said, 'Very well.'

'And,' O'Reilly continued, 'I want you to repeat the test every hour on the hour until Dr Laverty and I come back to read the results.'

'Every hour? But—'

'It's a terrible imposition, Mrs Fotheringham, but'—O'Reilly put one large hand on her shoulder—'I know I can rely on you. Should give us the answer, don't you think, Dr Laverty?'

Barry nodded. Any protest he might make would be rolled over with the force of a juggernaut. He despised himself for his lack of courage.

'Good,' said O'Reilly to Barry. He turned to Mrs Fotheringham. 'Don't bother to see us out. You're going to have a busy night.'

BARRY SAT STIFFLY in the Rover. He was angry about O'Reilly's hocus-pocus and angrier at his own inability to intervene.

'Go on,' said O'Reilly, 'spit it out.'

'Dr O'Reilly, I—'

'Think your history-taking stinks, and you're up to no good with all that buggering about with the dipsticks.' O'Reilly chuckled. 'Son, I've known the Fotheringhams for years. The man's never had a day's real illness in his life.'

'Then why didn't you just tell them to wait until the morning?'

O'Reilly shook his head. 'It's a little rule of mine. If they're worried enough to call at night, even if I'm damn sure it's nothing, I go.'

'Always?'

'Lord, aye.'

Nothing in O'Reilly's tone suggested pride to Barry. 'I see,' he acknowledged grudgingly, 'but what was all that nonsense with the test?'

'Ah,' said O'Reilly, turning into the lane at the back of his house. ' "There are more things in heaven and earth, Horatio, than are dreamt of in your philosophy." '

'You'll not put me off by quoting *Hamlet*, Dr O'Reilly.'

'No,' said O'Reilly as he braked. 'I didn't think I would, but you'll have to wait until we go back to the Fotheringhams' if you want to find out the answer. Now, be a good lad. Hop out and open the garage door.'

BARRY LISTENED to the rain clattering off the surgery's bow windows. Even at almost noon the lights were needed in the room. He stretched and ran a hand over the back of his neck. He was feeling the effects of a broken night. He watched O'Reilly usher an old man with arthritis to the door. The morning had been busy, and yet O'Reilly showed no signs of fatigue.

'Trot along and see who's next,' he instructed Barry.

Barry shook his head and went to the waiting room to discover that only one patient remained, a young woman with long auburn hair and green eyes. 'Good morning,' he said. 'Will you come through, please, Mrs er . . . ?'

'Galvin.' She stood with some difficulty, one hand on the small of her back, the other holding her swollen belly. 'I'm a bit slow getting about,' she said.

'That's all right. Take your time. Doesn't look as though it'll be long now.'

'Just a week more.' She went into the surgery. 'Morning, Doctor.'

'How are you, Maureen?' O'Reilly asked.

'Grand.' She rummaged in her handbag, produced a small urine-sample bottle and gave it to O'Reilly.

He handed it to Barry. 'Pop a dipstick into that, would you?'

Barry took the specimen over to the sink and tested the urine. He found nothing wrong.

'Can you get up on the couch, Maureen?' O'Reilly said.

She turned her back to the table and sat. 'Are you sure there's only the one in here, Dr O'Reilly? I feel like the side wall of a house.'

'It was only a week ago when I examined you,' he said, 'but if it'll make you happier, we'll get Dr Laverty to lay on a hand.'

She lay down. O'Reilly asked the routine late antenatal questions, took her blood pressure and palpated her ankles to ensure there was no swelling.

'Right, let's see your bump.'

Barry waited while O'Reilly examined her. Maureen's green eyes never left O'Reilly's face, which betrayed no expression.

'Dr Laverty?'

Barry moved to the table. He examined the belly, felt a single baby's back on her right side, the hardness of the head just above the pubic symphysis. He grasped the head between the outstretched thumb and finger of his right hand. It refused to budge when he tried to move it from side to side.

'Here,' said O'Reilly, handing Barry a foetal stethoscope.

Tup-tup-tup-tup . . . Barry listened, counted and looked at his watch. 'A hundred and forty.' He saw questioning lines appear in Maureen's forehead. 'Absolutely normal,' he said, pleased to see the furrows disappear.

'So?' said O'Reilly.

Barry trotted out the formula he'd been taught. 'A singleton, longitudinal lie, vertex presentation, right occipito-anterior, head's engaged, heart rate . . .'

'A hundred and forty,' said O'Reilly. 'The rest's right too. So are you worried now, Maureen?'

Barry looked at the woman's face. The furrows were back. She glanced from O'Reilly to Barry, then back to O'Reilly. 'Not if *you* say so, Doctor.'

'Just like Dr Laverty said, Maureen, there's one baby, just the one. Straight up and down, the back of its head is on the right—that's the most normal way—and the head's dropped. The little divil's halfway out already.'

Her forehead became smooth and she gave a contented sigh.

Barry cleared his throat. He'd baffled the woman with his jargon, but O'Reilly had gone right to the heart of the matter in plain English.

O'Reilly helped her off the couch. 'Right. Same time next week.'

'And if the waters break or the pains start, I've to phone you.'

'You'll be fine, Maureen,' O'Reilly said. 'By the way, how's Seamus?'

'His ankle's on the mend, Doctor, and he hopes you liked the lobsters. Seamus means well. He's a heart of corn, but sometimes—'

'Don't you worry about Seamus,' said O'Reilly. 'I'll take care of him.' He winked at Barry, who had a vivid mental picture of an airborne supplicant with a dirty foot. That Galvin was this young woman's husband?

'You'll not need to much longer,' she said in a whisper. 'You'll not tell no one, Doctor, but my brother—'

'The builder in California?'

'Aye. He's got a job out there for Seamus, and we've saved up for the tickets. We're going after the baby's born.'

'Wonderful,' said O'Reilly.

'Now, don't you tell. I'll be in next week.' She left.

'I'll be damned,' said O'Reilly. He sat at the desk and wrote the results in Maureen Galvin's record. 'Maybe the worthy Seamus'll have to do an honest day's work in America. I wonder where they got the money? He's a carpenter by trade, but to my knowledge he's hardly done a hand's turn here.' He looked up. 'By the way,' he asked, 'was her urine clear?'

'Yes.' Barry hesitated. 'I'm sorry I didn't explain things to her better.'

O'Reilly fished out his pipe and lit it before he said, 'Ah, but you will the next time, won't you? Now tidy up those urine-test kits. We've another test to go and read after we've had lunch.'

'NICE DAY FOR DUCKS,' O'Reilly remarked as he hurled the car round the twists and turns on the road to the Fotheringhams, refusing to make any concession to the downpour.

Barry, to distract himself from O'Reilly's driving, muttered, '"Water, water, everywhere, And all the boards did shrink; Water, water, everywhere—"'

'"Nor any drop to drink,"' O'Reilly finished. 'Coleridge, Samuel Taylor, 1772 to 1834, poet and opium addict. Water,' he continued, stopping at the gate. 'I wonder how the Fotheringhams have been getting on with it?'

Barry shut the gate behind them and scuttled after O'Reilly.

They sheltered in the porch until a bleary-eyed Mrs Fotheringham, hair in disarray, opened the door. 'Thank goodness you've come,' she said.

Major Fotheringham sat up against his pillows, black circles under his bloodshot eyes. 'It's been a hellish night,' he croaked. 'Hellish.'

'Oh, dear,' said O'Reilly. 'Well, let's see how the test went.'

Neatly arranged on the dressing table lay fourteen soggy dipsticks. Not a single stick had changed colour.

'Oh-oh,' said O'Reilly. 'Oh-oh.'

Barry was baffled. No colour change meant that nothing untoward had appeared in the patient's urine.

'What's wrong with him, Dr O'Reilly?' Mrs Fotheringham begged.

'Can I stop the test now?' the major pleaded.

'Certainly,' said O'Reilly, 'and you are to be commended, Mrs Fotheringham, on your meticulous devotion to duty.'

She simpered. 'Thank you, Doctor. But what's wrong with him?'

'What's wrong with you, my dear Major Fotheringham?' O'Reilly paused. 'I'm very much afraid it's nothing. Absolutely nothing.'

Barry saw Mrs Fotheringham's jaw drop. 'Nothing?' she whispered.

'Well,' O'Reilly allowed, 'he might be a bit waterlogged, but other than that? Not a thing. Now we'd better be running along. We've more calls to make. Of course, if you think you need me, any time, any time at all, day or night, please don't hesitate to call.'

'I THOUGHT THAT was the only call we had to make,' said Barry.

'Just a couple more,' said O'Reilly as he reversed out of the driveway. 'I don't think,' he added with a huge grin, 'that the major or his lady will call us out again for a while. Do you?'

'I doubt it.' In spite of himself Barry chuckled. 'Mind you, it's not the sort of medicine I was taught, but it seems to work.'

'Like a charm, my boy.' O'Reilly braked at a traffic light. 'Twenty years ago I'd have read the Fotheringhams the riot act for wasting my time.'

Barry glanced down. His own thoughts exactly.

'What got you into medicine anyway?' O'Reilly asked.

Barry hesitated. He was always reticent about giving the real reasons. 'When I left school, my dad said I was too dim to read physics or chemistry, would never make a living with an arts degree, wasn't a Catholic—so the priesthood was out—and I didn't look like a soldier. So, there was nothing left for me but medicine.'

O'Reilly guffawed. 'Sounds like the sort of thing Tom Laverty would say.' He turned and looked into Barry's eyes. 'But there was more to it than that, wasn't there?'

'The light's changed, Dr O'Reilly.'

'Right.' The Rover charged across the junction, tyres shrieking as O'Reilly hauled it into a right turn. He steadied on course. 'You didn't answer me.'

'Well, I—'

'Don't like talking about it, but you'd a half-notion you'd like to help people. Do something useful—'

'How the hell did you know that?'

'Didn't make many friends at school, so you hoped if you went into medicine people would like you . . .'

Barry's mind went back to his boarding-school days. He'd had no close friends apart from Jack Mills. His four years had been lonely.

'Thought so,' said O'Reilly. 'Well, most of the customers aren't going to love you. They'll say thank you if you get it right, and treat you like dirt if you don't—and you *will* make mistakes, never doubt that.'

Barry wondered how the big man could have understood so completely.

'A few will have no consideration for the fact that you're on call twenty-four hours a day, and some are bloody rude and totally demanding. You simply don't let the Bishops get on your wick. And there's a good side too. When you *do* get a diagnosis right, make a difference in somebody's life, find you *do* fit into the local scheme of things, it is all worth it.'

'You really think so?'

'I know so, boy. I bloody well know so.'

The Rover ran along the shore of the lough, where a grassy verge dotted with sea pinks was all that separated the road from jagged rocks, black in the driving rain. Obsidian-green combers pounded against the shore.

The car slowed and O'Reilly parked it. 'Come on.'

Barry climbed out. A cottage with boxes of bright pansies on the sills sat squarely beside the road. O'Reilly knocked on the front door. Barry joined him and immediately recognised the woman who opened the door.

'Come on in out of thon, Doctor,' Maggie MacCorkle said. 'It would founder you out there, so it would.' She closed the door behind them.

A single oil lamp on a small oak table lit the tiny, low-ceilinged room. Barry saw dishes stacked to dry in a plate rack beside an enamel sink. Two easy chairs flanked a fireplace. On one chair a ginger cat lay curled in a ball.

'Would you take a cup of tea in your hand, Doctor?'

'No, thanks, Maggie. We just popped in for a minute,' O'Reilly said. 'How's the headaches?' As he spoke, his gaze darted around the room.

'I couldn't have done better at Lourdes,' she said, crossing herself. 'It's a miracle, so it is. Them wee pills—'

'Good,' said O'Reilly, glancing at Barry.

'Away out of there, General.' Maggie pushed the protesting cat out of its chair. 'Sit down by the fire, Doctor.'

O'Reilly sat. 'How is the General, Maggie?' He fondled the big cat's head. It had one ear missing and its left eye was scarred shut.

Maggie's wrinkled face split into a toothless grin. 'That one would sow dissension in a deserted house.' She turned to Barry. 'Have a seat.'

He shook his head, but out of curiosity asked, 'Why do you call your cat the General, Miss MacCorkle?'

She chuckled. 'His full name is General Sir Bernard Law Montgomery. Like the man he's named for, he's an Ulsterman, and he loves a good fight.'

The General made a deep growling noise and glowered at Barry. Barry took one step back.

'Don't you worry your head about him,' she said. 'You're not big enough for him to go after.'

O'Reilly rose. 'We'll have to be getting on, Maggie.' He crossed the room to the door. 'Now, remember, if you're out of sorts, come and see me.'

'I will,' she said, 'and thanks for popping by.'

'No trouble,' said O'Reilly, 'we were on our way to see Sonny.'

Maggie cackled. 'Sonny's not well pleased with me. His spaniel came round here yesterday, but the General saw to that dog, didn't you, General?'

The cat arched his back and spat.

Maggie held the door. 'Sonny'll tell you all about it, but pay no heed to him. He's only an ould goat anyway.'

'I DIDN'T KNOW that Miss MacCorkle had asked you to call,' Barry said as he shut the car door.

'She didn't,' said O'Reilly, driving off. 'On slow days I try to visit one or two of the ones that I worry about.'

'You were looking for something back there. What was it?'

'Little things. Dishes washed, no half-filled saucepans on the stove, clean floors.' O'Reilly turned onto a narrow road. 'Maggie's a bit different, but she's independent and I need to know that she's looking after herself.'

'So you keep an eye on her. That's very decent of you.'

'Not a bit,' said O'Reilly tersely. 'There's more to this job than runny noses and hypochondriacs who drag you out of your bed.'

'I see.'

'You will,' said O'Reilly, 'at our next stop.'

'Sonny?'

'Sonny. I'll tell you about him after we've been there,' said O'Reilly. 'But if you think Maggie's a bit odd, what do you make of this?'

He pulled to the side of the road. The rain had stopped and the summer sun was making soft tendrils of steam rise from the road's wet surface. The opposite verge was cluttered with old cars. Electrical cables ran from a roofless house set back from the road, drooped over the branches of a larch tree and led to a television set. What should have been the front garden was crammed with old cars, farm machinery and a yellow caravan.

A man wearing a brown raincoat tied at the waist with baler twine left one of the rusting cars, strode over to the caravan and opened the door. Five dogs piled out, each yapping and vying for the man's attention. O'Reilly got out of the car and crossed the road. Barry followed.

'How are you, Sonny?' O'Reilly yelled.

'I'm coming.' Sonny made his way to a gate and let himself out. 'Hush now,' he called to the dogs, then strode to where Barry and O'Reilly stood. The noise died away. 'Doctor.' He offered a hand, which O'Reilly shook.

'Sonny,' said O'Reilly, 'this is Dr Laverty.'

'Pleased to meet you, Sonny.' Barry stared at the man.

He was almost as tall as O'Reilly, older, yet stood with the bearing of a regimental sergeant major. He wore a yellow souwester, from under which locks of iron-grey hair flowed to his shoulders. His eyes were pale, and his ruddy cheeks told of years of Ulster winds. And, Barry wondered, was there the faintest tinge of blue in the skin above the man's cheekbones?

'Have you any new potatoes?' O'Reilly asked.

'I have.' Sonny produced a small sack. 'Five shillings and sixpence.' He gave the sack to O'Reilly, who counted coins into a hand bent with arthritis.

'I brought you more of these,' said O'Reilly, handing over two small medicine bottles.

'How much do I owe—?' Sonny was reaching into his trouser pocket.

'Free samples from the drug company,' said O'Reilly.

'You wouldn't be having me on? I can pay, you know.'

'Not at all,' said O'Reilly. 'How are the dogs?'

'All grand, except Sandy. Silly bugger got into a fight with Maggie's cat.'

'I heard,' said O'Reilly.

'And how is the old biddy?' Barry heard tenderness as Sonny spoke.

'Rightly,' said O'Reilly.

'I'm glad to hear that.' Sonny's pale eyes softened. 'Silly old duck.'

'Aye,' said O'Reilly. 'Well, we must be getting along.'

'WHAT ON EARTH was that all about?' Barry asked.

'Pride,' said O'Reilly as he pointed the Rover homewards. 'Sonny is the most stiff-necked man I've ever met, and yet he's one of the most contented. He has a PhD, you know. He used to work for some big chemical company in Belfast, but he'd rather stay at home and live in his car.'

'In his car? But I saw a caravan.'

'For the dogs,' said O'Reilly. 'Sonny dotes on his dogs.'

'But why is he in his car? Can he not get the roof of his house repaired?'

'Yes . . . and no. You remember the worthy Councillor Bishop? He's a building contractor. Twenty years ago, Sonny hired Bishop to replace the roof. He wanted the house all done up before he got married.'

Barry remembered how Sonny had asked about Maggie MacCorkle. 'Not to Maggie?'

'To Maggie. But Bishop—and he's a man who'd wrestle a bear for a ha'penny—tried to cheat Sonny on the price of a load of slates.'

'After the old roof had been stripped?'

'Precisely. Sonny refused to pay Bishop for the work he'd done already. Bishop said Sonny could whistle for his new roof. Maggie wouldn't marry a man who literally couldn't keep a roof over her head. Sonny quit his job, moved into his car and supports himself selling vegetables and scrap iron.'

'I'll be damned. For twenty years?'

'Aye.' O'Reilly turned the Rover into his back lane.

'Sonny's not too well, is he? His cheeks are a bit blue.'

'Smart of you to notice.'

Barry smiled. 'Heart failure?'

'Only mild.'

'What did you give him?'

'Digitalis and a diuretic. They keep it pretty well in control.'

Barry frowned. 'Can you get those for free from the drug reps?'

'Ah,' said O'Reilly, 'them as ask no questions get told no lies. Now, be a good lad and open the garage door.'

Mrs Kincaid greeted them in the kitchen.

'Any calls, Kinky?' O'Reilly asked.

'Not one, but there is a shmall little matter you should see to, so.' She glanced down at Barry's trousers. 'Have you been in the bogs again so soon? You're clabber to the knee.'

'Arthur,' said Barry resignedly. 'He was pleased to see me back.'

''Tis a good thing I washed your other trousers.'

'You said there was something for me to sort out, Kinky,' said O'Reilly.

Mrs Kincaid's bright little eyes almost disappeared when she smiled and said, 'Come and see.' She led them into the surgery, and indicated a wicker basket on the examining couch. 'You'd just gone out when somebody rang the bell. I found this thing, so.'

'Good God,' said O'Reilly. He tapped on the side of the basket.

Barry watched the basket jerk for several inches along the couch, as if moved by some primal force. A low growling, harsh and brittle, filled his ears.

O'Reilly opened the lid. Barry took a step back as a white blur erupted from the container and, with an eldritch shriek, landed on O'Reilly's shoulder.

'Begod, it's a cat,' he said, reaching up and hauling it off its perch. 'Push-wush. Pushy-wushy.' He held the animal in one big hand and stroked its head with the other.

It struggled briefly, then, seemingly accepting its lot, butted its head against O'Reilly's palm. Barry heard a low rumbling. The animal was purring.

'Mmm,' said O'Reilly. 'I doubt if we'll find out who left it, and we can't just put it out.'

'Will I find it some milk, Doctor?'

'That would be grand, Kinky,' said O'Reilly, handing her the little feline. 'And could you manage a cup of tea for us while you're at it? I don't know about you, Barry, but I could use a bit of time with my feet up.'

Barry yawned.

'Tired?'

'A bit.'

'Well,' said O'Reilly, 'it's only a couple of days till your day off.'

I'm Standing in a Railway Station

Saturday, Barry's first day off, was what the locals would call 'a grand soft day'. He turned up the collar of his raincoat against the damp that was neither heavy enough to be rain nor light enough to be mist. Mrs Kincaid had said the train to Belfast would leave Ballybucklebo at ten fifteen. Half an hour to Belfast, fifteen minutes to walk into the city centre, where he intended to invest some of his first week's pay in a pair of Wellington boots, half an hour on the bus up Grosvenor Road, and he'd still be in good time to see Jack Mills in O'Kane's Bar opposite the Royal Victoria Hospital.

He heard the rattle of an approaching train. The brakes screeched. The train stopped. Barry let himself into a compartment and was pleased to see that it was unoccupied. As he sat down he wondered how often as a student he had ridden on this train from his home in Bangor further down the line to the Queen's Quay terminal in Belfast. How many times had he ridden past Ballybucklebo without even paying attention to its existence?

The train shuddered to a halt at Kinnegar Station. Two young women tumbled aboard and sat at the other end of the compartment. Barry tried to ignore them by staring out of the window, but their chatter intruded.

'Away on. Charlie Simpson does *not* fancy Eileen.' The speaker's voice was harsh, with the flat accents of Belfast.

'He's daft about her. . . .'

'That's not what I heard.'

Poor Charlie Simpson, whoever he was, daft about some girl, Barry thought. He himself had been daft about a student nurse. He pictured her green eyes, thought about the nights in the back seat of Brunhilde, the sweetness and the softness . . . and the emptiness when she had told him that she was going to marry a surgeon. Six months ago. And still it stung.

'Do you know it would serve her right to get stuck with Charlie? He's thick as two short planks, so he is.' Barry wished the young woman would shut up. She had a voice that would cut tin.

The other chuckled. Her laugh was contralto, deep and resonant. Barry glanced at her. She had black hair with a sheen. Her face was strong, with a firm chin, Slavic cheekbones and full lips. Her dark eyes had an upward tilt. A small dimple showed in her left cheek as she laughed. But for that dimple, she could have been Audrey Hepburn in *My Fair Lady.*

'Anyway, Patricia,' her friend rattled on, 'I says to Eileen . . .'

Would she never stop prattling? He glanced down and then stole another look. Patricia turned, caught him staring and held his gaze.

'Excuse me,' he said, knowing that he was blushing. 'I'm awfully sorry . . .'

She laughed again, warm and throaty. 'A cat can look at a king . . . if it doesn't think the king's a mouse.'

The train slowed and the sign for Belfast Station glided past the window. As soon as it stopped, the two women left. Barry sat back against the cushions. Why had he not had the courage to find out more about Patricia?

He left the compartment not expecting to see any sign of her and her chatty friend, but there they were up ahead, Patricia leaning on the noisy one's arm and limping slowly. Must have hurt herself playing hockey, he thought. She certainly looked the athletic type. He took a deep breath, smoothed his hair and lengthened his stride until he drew level.

'Excuse me,' he said, 'excuse me.'

Patricia stopped and faced him.

Words tumbled out. 'Look. My name's Barry Laverty. I want . . . '

'Away off and chase yourself.' The friend tugged at Patricia's sleeve.

'Will you have dinner with me tonight? Please?'

The friend glared at Barry. 'We're busy the night.'
Patricia smiled. 'That's right. We are.'
'Oh.' Barry's shoulders sagged.
'But I'm taking the ten o'clock train back to Kinnegar.'
He saw the laughter in her dark eyes, and his breath caught in his throat.

BARRY SAT in the window alcove of O'Kane's Bar, the nearest watering hole
to the Royal Victoria Hospital. At his feet a pair of Wellington boots lay in a
brown paper bag. A shadow fell over the table, and Barry turned to see Jack
Mills wearing a long white coat and his usual grin.

'Sorry I'm late.' Jack sat. 'I'd a bugger of a night on call and this morning was murder.' He pulled out a packet of cigarettes. 'I'm knackered.'

'Pint?' Barry asked, looking forward to the afternoon with his friend.

'Can't. Sorry. The registrar in Sick Kids is sick himself and they need a
hand on a surgical case in about an hour. I got the short straw, damn it.'
Jack's smile belied his words. 'I wouldn't mind a quick bite though.'

Barry swallowed his disappointment. It would be a long day before the ten
o'clock train. He imagined dark eyes and hoped the wait would be worth it.

'Grub,' said Jack. He turned and called to the barman, 'Brendan, could
you manage a steak and mushroom pie, chips and an orange squash?'

'Right, Dr Mills.' Brendan put down the glass he was polishing. 'What
about you, Dr Laverty?'

'That would be good.' Barry never ceased to be amazed by how Brendan,
owner and barman, remembered the names of the generations of students
and junior doctors who used his establishment.

'So,' Jack asked, 'how's general practice?'

'It's different. I'm working with a Dr O'Reilly in Ballybucklebo.'

'Not Fingal Flahertie O'Reilly? Man of about fifty, fifty-five?'

'That's right.'

'Good Lord. Before the war he was one of Ireland's best rugby forwards.'

'I didn't know that.' Barry was impressed.

'You, Brother Laverty, wouldn't know an Irish rugby player from a penny
bap.' He winked at Barry. 'But I'll forgive you.'

'Here y'are.' Brendan set two plates on the table.

'Dig in,' said Jack, picking up his knife and fork. 'Come on, I want to
hear about what you're up to.'

Barry did his best to describe his first week, and O'Reilly's eccentricities.

'But you are enjoying it?'

'I think so. There's an awful lot of routine stuff. But I have seen some interesting cases.' He told Jack how O'Reilly had driven the Kennedy girl to Belfast in his own car. Jack nodded when Barry mentioned that O'Reilly's knowledge of every patient seemed encyclopedic.

'Now there's a difference,' he said. 'I never get to know anybody. We're too damn busy.' He looked at his watch, stood up, reached into his pocket, and tossed a pound note on the table. 'My half. Sorry, mate, but I'd better run. Sir Donald Cromie is like the wrath of God if his assistant's late.'

'Sir Donald who?' Was he the man O'Reilly had consulted on Tuesday?

'Sir Donald Cromie, paediatric surgeon with nimble fingers and a temper like Mount Etna on a bad day. He did an appendix the other night. Now the patient's blown up a pelvic abscess. Sick as a dog.'

'You wouldn't happen to know the patient's name?'

Jack laughed. 'No. I don't even know if it's a wee boy or a wee girl. I'm off. Good to see you, mate. I'll give you a bell next time I'm free.'

Barry paid the bill and made his way down the narrow staircase. When he stepped out onto Grosvenor Road, the drizzle had stopped. He decided to walk into Belfast. He'd lots of time to kill. He walked in a world filled with the stink of car exhaust, the constant grumble of traffic, gutters clogged with soggy newspapers. Belfast, he thought, dirty old harridan of a city, and one that I don't miss one bit. There's a lot to be said for Ballybucklebo.

He stopped where Grosvenor Road met the junction of College Square and Great Victoria Street. Two cinemas sat, one on each corner. Barry looked at his watch. He'd have time to nip over to the bookshop in Donegall Square and come back to the Ritz, which was showing *The Pink Panther*, starring Peter Sellers. He wanted to buy a book of poetry by this new chap Seamus Heaney, who had an interesting way of using words to describe Ulster life. Barry would grab a quick bite after the film. That wouldn't leave him much more than an hour to kill before ten o'clock.

THE TRAIN WOULD LEAVE in five minutes. Barry took one last long look along the Queen's Quay. It was deserted. Oh, well. Barry hefted his parcel of boots, turned and made his way towards the platform.

'Barry? Barry Laverty?'

He turned and saw her limping fast towards him.

'Come on.' She grasped his arm. 'Get a move on or we'll miss the train.' Barry helped her inside and slammed the compartment door after them.

'Just made it,' she said, sitting down.

He sat opposite. 'I thought you weren't coming.'

She laughed, her dark eyes bright in the compartment's dim light. 'So your name's Barry Laverty?'

'That's right. I heard your friend call you Patricia.'

'Patricia Spence.'

He took the hand she offered, feeling the smoothness of her skin, the firmness of her grasp. He looked into her face. He never wanted to let go.

'I'll have it back, if you don't mind.'

He eased his grip, but she let her hand linger just for a moment. Now what? Damn it, why was he always at a loss for words with women?

'You're quiet,' she said. 'Cat got your tongue? Don't know what got into you, asking a complete stranger to dinner?'

'That's right.'

The train jolted through the dark night, rattling where the rails met.

'If it makes you feel any better, I don't know what got into *me*, telling you I'd be on this train.' She tossed her dark mane. 'I think it's the way your hair sticks up . . . like a little boy's, and you looked so lost.'

His hand flew to that damned tuft. He saw her smile at him.

Now or never, he told himself. 'I just had to meet you, that's all.' He swallowed. 'I've never seen anyone so lovely.' He knew he was blushing. The train clattered to halt. 'Sydenham station,' he said.

'Thank you, sir,' she said.

'For telling you the name of the station?'

'For telling me you think I'm lovely.'

'You are,' he said, grateful that no one had boarded, knowing that Kinnegar was only two more stops down the line, anxious that his time with her was running out. He wanted to hold her hand again, but he was terrified that she might dart away like a startled bird. 'You live in Kinnegar?' he asked.

'That's right. Number 9, the Esplanade. On the seafront. I love the sea.'

'I grew up in Bangor. I know what you mean about the sea. It's never the same. It's . . .' He fumbled in his pocket and pulled out Seamus Heaney's book. He riffled through the pages, and read:

> 'You might think that the sea is company,
> Exploding comfortably down on the cliffs,
> But no: when it begins, the flung spray hits
> The very windows, spits like a tame cat
> Turned savage.'

He looked into her eyes—cat's eyes—and saw them soften.

'That's beautiful,' she said gently. 'Who's the poet?'

'Chap called Seamus Heaney.'

'Never heard of him.'

'I think you will. If you like poetry.'

'And you do?' Her question was solemn, her gaze never leaving his eyes.

'Oh, yes.' He was thrown forwards as the carriage stumbled to a halt, and felt the nearness of her. He reached out and touched her hand, and she twined her fingers with his.

The train jerked. 'I get off at the next stop,' she said. 'I'm sorry.'

'I know, but . . . Patricia, I want to see you again.'

'My phone number's Kinnegar 657334.'

Kinnegar 657334. He repeated the number in his head, over and over. 'Can I phone you tomorrow?'

'I'd like that.' She leaned forward and kissed him gently, little more than a fluttering of butterfly wings. 'Bangor's not far from Kinnegar,' she said, as the train began to slow.

'I don't live in Bangor now. I'm staying in Ballybucklebo.'

'You're what?' She sat back and laughed. 'The ten o'clock doesn't stop at Ballybucklebo. You'll have to get off here and walk home.'

'What?'

'That's right, and you'd better get a move on if you don't want to go all the way to Bangor.'

The train jolted. He hustled her onto the platform and jumped down beside her.

'I'm sorry. I shouldn't have laughed,' she said.

'It's all right. At least I can walk you home.'

'Come on, then. It's not far,' she said, as the train's red rear lights vanished.

Damn it. He'd left his new Wellington boots in the compartment.

She took his hand and, boots forgotten, he walked beside her, shortening his stride to keep pace with Patricia's uneven steps.

'How'd you hurt your leg? Hockey?'

'I didn't hurt it.' He detected a hint of bitterness.

'What happened?'

'Nineteen fifty-one.'

He stopped. Dead. Turned her to face him. 'The polio epidemic?'

She nodded. 'My left leg's a bit short.' She dropped his hand. 'I suppose I won't be hearing from you now?'

He looked up and saw Orion, high, high, each star glimmering proud and strong. He knew that to him, her short leg made no difference, none in the whole wide world. 'I don't give a damn about your leg, Patricia,' he said, watching her face. I don't care at all.'

She stared at him. 'I shouldn't, Barry Laverty, I know I shouldn't, but I think I believe you.'

He saw something silver beneath her left eye, and he wanted to taste the salt of it, but something told him he mustn't rush her. 'Come on,' he said, 'let's get you home.'

Deliver Us from Evil

'Y ou look like the *Hesperus* . . . a total wreck,' O'Reilly said, peering over the top of the *Sunday Times*.

Barry yawned. 'Late night.'

'I know. I heard Arthur. He sounded happy. What kept you?'

Barry parked himself in the other armchair. 'Fate,' he said. 'Kismet.'

'Whatever it was, it's put a grin on your face.'

Barry debated whether to tell O'Reilly about Patricia, but decided that now was not the time. She was his to relish in private.

His musing was interrupted by a rhythmic rending noise.

'Stop that,' O'Reilly yelled, tossing the *Times* colour supplement in Barry's direction.

Barry ducked. 'Stop what?'

'Not you. Her. Lady Macbeth.'

The white cat that had been left on the doorstep had been so named by O'Reilly after she'd bloodied Arthur Guinness's nose and chased him back to his doghouse—twice. She was standing on her hind paws, her front claws raking and ripping at the fabric of Barry's chair.

'Stop it, madam.' O'Reilly stood over the animal, who clawed away and condescended to give him one of those feline looks that asks, 'My good man, are you by the remotest chance addressing *moi*?'

'Stop it.' O'Reilly picked the cat up and tickled her under the chin.

Barry watched as she fixed the big man with her green eyes, laid back her ears, and made a throaty sound. 'I don't think she's very happy, Fingal.'

'Nonsense. Animals dote on me. Don't you?' He went on tickling her until she struck, fangs sinking into the web of O'Reilly's hand. 'You bitch,' he roared as she sprang from his arms. He glared at his punctured hand.

'We'd better get that cleaned up,' said Barry. 'There's a thing called cat scratch disease, you know.'

'And tetanus,' O'Reilly remarked. 'And you can disabuse yourself of any notion, Dr Laverty, that you're going to stick a needle in my backside.'

'Thought never entered my head,' Barry lied, thinking of the Dettol that would have to be poured onto the raw punctures. 'Not for a minute.'

O'REILLY WAS ONCE AGAIN ensconced in his living room. 'Now, before Her Ladyship remembered she was descended from a long line of albino sabre-toothed tigers, I was trying to find out what kept you out so late last night.'

'I got on the wrong train. The ten o'clock doesn't stop at Ballybucklebo. I had to walk from Kinnegar. That's all.'

O'Reilly chuckled. 'The exercise'll do you good.' He looked straight at Barry. 'I'd hardly call getting on the wrong train "destiny".'

'Destiny?'

'"Kismet", you said. It's from the Turkish *kisma*, meaning "destiny".' O'Reilly leaned forward. 'What's her name?'

'What?'

'You've had a dreamy look all morning. You were muttering about fate. Two and two usually make four.' O'Reilly frowned. 'You're far too young to be getting involved with a woman. Medicine's a selfish enough mistress.'

'I think, Dr O'Reilly, I can be the best judge of that.'

'You'll see.' For the first time in their week's acquaintance bitterness had crept into the older man's voice.

Mrs Kincaid bustled in, carrying a tray. 'Tea,' she said, 'and a bit of toasted, buttered barmbrack, so.' She set the tray on the sideboard. 'And how's my wee princess?' She bent over Lady Macbeth and stroked the cat's head.

'Have you seen what the beast's doing to the furniture?' said O'Reilly.

'You'll just have to train her not to claw it.'

'And how do you suggest we do that?'

'Don't look at me,' said Mrs Kincaid, turning to leave, 'but Maggie MacCorkle knows as much about cats as you do about the doctoring.'

'Now there's an idea,' said O'Reilly as he poured himself a cup of tea.

Barry was only half paying attention. He'd been disturbed by O'Reilly's attitude towards women. If that was how he felt, Barry's chances of having more time to see Patricia were probably slim, but if he didn't ask . . .

'Fingal?' Barry swallowed. 'I'd like to have more time off.'

'So it *is* a girl.' O'Reilly sipped his tea. 'What's her name?'

'Patricia. Patricia Spence. All I'm asking for is a bit more free time.'

O'Reilly stared over his teacup. 'How much?'

'An hour or two the odd evening, maybe every other Sunday.'

O'Reilly put his cup on the saucer. 'I thought you wanted to be a GP. It's not Butlins Holiday Camp here.'

Barry's shoulders sagged. He looked down. He was startled to hear O'Reilly say, 'All right. Once I can trust you not to kill too many customers, I wouldn't mind a bit of time off myself. I thought we'd take alternate weekends and have a couple of week nights each off duty.'

Barry looked up. 'Do you mean that?'

'Difficult as it is for you to believe, I wasn't always fifty-six. I suppose you'd like to take this afternoon off? Go on then. I'll hold the fort.'

Barry could have hugged the big man. 'I'd really appreciate that, Fingal.'

'Go on. Phone your Patricia . . . that's her name, isn't it?'

'It is.' Barry sped to the door and took the stairs two at a time. He was just about to lift the receiver when the double ring of the phone's bell startled him. He lifted the phone.

'Hello. Dr O'Reilly's surgery.' No voice came over the line, just a whimper that swelled to a groan, then deep breathing. 'Hello? Are you there?'

'Is that Dr Laverty?'

'Yes. Who's speaking?'

'It's Maureen Galvin. My waters burst three hours ago and the pains is every five minutes. I've sent for the midwife. Can you come now?'

'Of course. Dr O'Reilly will be round right away.'

'Thank you.' The line went dead.

Barry raced back upstairs. 'Fingal, that was Maureen Galvin. Her membranes have ruptured, and she's contracting every five minutes.'

'I'd better get round there.' O'Reilly put his cup back on the tray and faced Barry. 'She doesn't live far from here.'

Patricia, Barry thought; then he said, 'I'll get my bag.'

'Good lad. I might need a bit of help.'

O'Reilly rapidly organised his equipment and together they carried the gear to the car. For once O'Reilly deflected Arthur Guinness's amorous advances by telling the dog to get into the back seat. 'We'll give him a run on the beach when the smoke and dust have died down.'

The short drive would have been pleasanter if Arthur hadn't insisted on draping his front paws over Barry's shoulders and licking the back of his neck. He was so distracted that he couldn't pay attention to where they were going, and when the car stopped he found himself in a strange part of Ballybucklebo. By the look of the narrow-fronted terraced houses that lined the street, he could have been in one of the Belfast suburbs.

'Where are we, Fingal?'

'Council estate. Cheap housing for the less fortunate. Council voted the budget and chose the building contractor. Bishop sold them the land *and* finagled the contract. He cut so many corners it's a bloody miracle that these houses aren't circular. They don't even have inside bathrooms.'

O'Reilly slammed the car door and Barry grabbed the equipment.

'Come on. Let's get at it.' The big man crossed the footpath and pounded on the front door. Barry joined him.

A slim woman wearing the blue uniform of a district midwife answered the front door. 'Dr O'Reilly.'

'Miss Hagerty, this is Dr Laverty. How's Maureen?'

'Grand, Doctor. Three-minute contractions and the foetal heart rate's fine.'

'Right.' O'Reilly charged down a narrow hall and up a steep staircase.

There was barely space for Barry in the small bedroom. Maureen Galvin lay in bed. The midwife had spread a rubber sheet under the labouring woman. O'Reilly and Miss Hagerty stood on opposite sides of the bed. The doctor finished tying the belt of a chest-high rubber apron, then he bent over and put his ear to a foetal stethoscope pressed to Maureen's belly.

'Uuunnnhhh,' she groaned. Barry watched her face contort, her upper teeth driving the colour from her lower lip. 'Uuunnnhhh.'

'Pant, Maureen. Pant. Like this.' Miss Hagerty began to puff. Short breaths through barely open lips.

'Good lass,' O'Reilly said. 'You're not quite ready to push yet.'

The contraction passed. Maureen lay back on her pillow.

'Could you open the big pack there, Dr Laverty?'

Barry set to work preparing the sterile towels, scissors, clamps, bowls and a suturing kit.

'Now, Maureen, Miss Hagerty and I are going down to the kitchen to wash our hands. Dr Laverty'll keep an eye to you.' Together they left.

Barry moved closer and hoped that O'Reilly would get a move on. He'd never been left alone with a woman in labour before.

Maureen grabbed his hand. 'Oh Jesus. It's coming, Doctor.'

Barry tore off his jacket, flung it aside and rolled up his sleeves. 'Can you bend your knees up, Maureen?'

She parted her legs and bent her knees. 'Hail, Maaaary . . . ummmh.' Maureen pushed with all her might and a circle of damp baby's hair appeared.

Barry's hands went to work unbidden as he controlled the rate of descent of the baby's head. The contraction passed.

'Are you all right, Barry?' He looked up to see O'Reilly standing at the foot of the bed, Miss Hagerty behind.

'I think so.'

'I'll get the gear ready,' said O'Reilly. 'You carry on.'

Maureen sat up now, supported by Miss Hagerty. 'Come on, big *puuush*.'

Under Barry's fingers the baby's head advanced. He let it come further, further, a little further. As it rotated, a wrinkled forehead appeared. A squashed nose came next, and in a rush a puckered rosebud of a mouth and a tiny chin. Even before the shoulders were born, the baby gave its first wail.

Barry used both hands to guide the slippery infant out of its mother, conscious of the warmth of the body, the beating of the heart.

He heard Maureen ask, 'Is it a boy or a girl?'

'It's a boy,' he said. 'He's fine.'

'Here,' said O'Reilly, reaching out with gloved hands to swathe the little one in a green sterile towel, 'we'll just pop him on Mum's tummy.'

'Thanks, Dr Laverty,' Maureen said, when the umbilical cord was cut and the placenta expelled. 'You've a quare soft hand under a duck, so you have.'

He laughed at the country description of gentleness. 'You did very well, Maureen. What are you going to call the wee lad?'

'Well, if it's all right with the pair of you, I'd like him to go by Barry Fingal Galvin.'

'That's a mouthful for such a little lad,' Barry said, grinning.

'What'll Seamus think of that?' Miss Hagerty asked.

'Seamus? He'll be happy enough. He's down at the Black Swan with his mates wetting the bairn's head.'

Miss Hagerty busied herself tidying up the mess of the delivery and then O'Reilly examined the newborn as Barry repacked the instruments.

'Right,' said O'Reilly, 'young Barry Fingal's fit as a flea.'

'Thanks again, Doctor,' said Maureen. 'He'll make a grand wee American, won't he?' Barry remembered that the Galvins intended to emigrate.

'Indeed,' said O'Reilly. 'Now, we'd better be going. Dr Laverty could use a bath and a change of shirt. He's off somewhere tonight.'

Barry nearly dropped the bag he was carrying. In the excitement of the delivery, he had completely forgotten about Patricia.

'You run on, Dr Laverty,' said Maureen. 'You did grand, so you did, and Dr O'Reilly, I don't know how you fixed it, but Seamus'll be tickled pink that it is the wee boy you promised us.'

How in hell, Barry wondered, could O'Reilly promise what the sex of an unborn baby would be? As soon as they were back in the car, he asked.

O'Reilly grinned. 'That's one of the first useful things my predecessor taught me. The first time they come in to find out if they're pregnant, you ask them what they want. Then you write down the opposite in the record.'

'I don't understand.'

'Look, say Mrs Hucklebottom comes in in her third month and tells you she wants a boy. You write "girl" in the record. Six months later if baby Hucklebottom is a bouncing boy, Mrs H. is delighted.'

'But what if she has a girl?'

'You show her the six-month-old record, with "girl" written in it. You tell Mrs H. you're very sorry, but she must have forgotten what she asked for.'

'But that's dishonest.'

'Indeed it is, but it works wonders for your reputation.'

Barry sniffed.

'Sniff away, son, but half of curing folks is getting them to have faith in their healer. If they think you're special, they're more likely to heed your advice, and anyway, unless it's something really serious, time cures most of them. The French surgeon, Ambroise Paré, had it right more than four hundred years ago. He said, "I dressed the wound, but God cured the patient."'

When O'Reilly said 'cured the patient', Barry remembered something that had been bothering him. 'Fingal, is Jeannie Kennedy home yet?'

'No. She's still in the hospital. She blew up an abscess. They opened her again yesterday, but she's on the mend now.'

So Jack *had* been going to assist in Jeannie's re-operation.

'I always phone the hospital to see how any of my lot are getting on. Sir Donald spoke to me this morning . . . when you were still asleep . . . so I was able to let the Kennedys know they mustn't be too worried.'

'Decent of you.'

'Rubbish.' The car stopped. 'I'll take Arthur for his walk. You go and get cleaned up, make your phone call, and tell your lassie you'll not be able to see her until after supper.'

'But—'

'No buts. You still have to go and tell the proud father.'

'Could you not do that?'

'I didn't deliver the wean, you did. And, son, you did it well. Now bugger off, get organised, and walk down and meet me in the Mucky Duck.'

'The what?'

'The Black Swan, known to all and sundry as the Mucky Duck.'

BARRY BATHED, changed, and gratefully gave his splattered clothes to Mrs Kincaid to be washed. Then he phoned Patricia. He mouthed a silent, 'Oh, yes,' when she said she'd be happy to be picked up at seven.

He walked with light steps to the Black Swan. He didn't want to stay there too long. It wouldn't do to show up at Patricia's the worse for drink.

The bar, loud with competing voices and hoarse laughter, was a single timber-beamed, low-ceilinged room. The place was packed. Seamus Galvin, left ankle strapped, stood swaying in the centre of the crowd. Barry peered through the throng but saw no sign of O'Reilly.

Councillor Bishop, seated at a table, beckoned with a crooked bandaged finger. The gesture reminded Barry of a patron summoning a tardy waiter. 'Laverty, tell O'Reilly it's time he had a look at my finger.'

'It's *Doctor* O'Reilly, Bishop,' Barry said smoothly, 'and you know when the surgery's open.'

'It's *Councillor* Bishop to you, you young puppy.'

Barry turned away as the door opened and O'Reilly appeared, followed by a panting, tongue-lolling, sand-covered Arthur Guinness. Barry glanced anxiously at his corduroys, his last clean pair of trousers.

'Good afternoon to this house,' O'Reilly bellowed.

Conversation died. Every eye turned. The men who sat at the table by the door rose. Without a word of thanks O'Reilly took one of the chairs.

'Under and lie down.'

Arthur obeyed, much to Barry's relief.

'Take the weight off your feet, Barry.'

Barry sat, carefully tucking his legs out of the way of the drooling dog.

'The usual, Doctor?' he heard the barman ask.

'Aye, and a pint for Dr Laverty.'

Two pints of Guinness were delivered to the table and, moments later, the barman reappeared carrying a bowl. He bent and shoved it under the table.

'Arthur likes his pint,' O'Reilly remarked, 'but he only drinks Smithwick's bitter.'

Barry heard lapping noises under the table.

'Lovely,' said O'Reilly, sinking half the contents of his glass. 'Come on, boy. Don't let yours go flat.'

Barry sipped the bitter stout, then sensed someone standing at his shoulder. He turned to see Seamus Galvin, a lopsided grin pasted to his narrow face.

'So's a boy, Doctors? S'a wee boy?'

O'Reilly nodded.

''Nother round here, Willy,' Galvin shouted to the barman. 'On me.'

'Easy, Seamus,' O'Reilly said quietly, 'you'll need your money now.'

Seamus tried to lay one index finger alongside his nose but managed to stick it into his nostril. 'Ah, sure, I'm like Paddy Maginty; I'm going to fall into a fortune.' He favoured O'Reilly with a drooping wink.

'Oh?' said O'Reilly. 'And where would that come from, Seamus?'

Seamus extracted his finger. 'Least said, soonest mended.'

As two more pints arrived, he climbed onto a chair, where he stood, swaying like a willow in a high wind. He whistled. Silence.

'Just wanna say . . . best two doctors in Ulster . . . in all of Ireland.'

'Balls,' Councillor Bishop yelled. 'O'Reilly couldn't cure a sick cat.'

Barry looked at O'Reilly, who lifted his glass to Bishop and smiled. There was enough ice in the smile, Barry thought, to put a hole in the *Titanic*.

'Are you not going to say something, Fingal?'

O'Reilly shook his head. 'Revenge,' he said, 'is a dish best eaten cold. I'll say no more today.'

Barry stared at the corpulent councillor and thought, I'd rather not be in Bishop's boots when O'Reilly makes good on that promise.

'They got me a wee boy, so they did,' Seamus Galvin roared. 'Everybody have a drink to Farry . . . Bingal . . . Gavlin.' He finished his pint to the cheers of the crowd.

Barry felt duty-bound to join in the toast. He regarded his empty glass with surprise. That stout had vanished quickly.

'A wee boy,' Galvin continued to the renewed cheers of the patrons, waved both arms over his head, hands clasped like a boxer who had just KOed his opponent. Then, with great solemnity, he fell off the chair.

'Jesus,' said O'Reilly. 'Drink. It's the curse of the land.' He turned to Barry. 'Drink up.'

Barry took a goodly swallow from his second pint, surprised by how much better than the first it tasted.

'Willy. My shout, and don't forget Arthur,' O'Reilly roared.

Barry shook his head. 'Fingal, I have to—'

'See a certain young lady tonight. You have, haven't you?'

'Yes,' said Barry, smiling.

'Well. One more won't hurt you.'

IT HAD BEEN a wonderful afternoon, Barry thought as he accompanied O'Reilly and Arthur on the short walk back to O'Reilly's house. Wonderful. He giggled as he watched Arthur weaving along the pavement. You, Arthur Guinness, Barry thought, you are drunk. At least it's dampened your ardour, and my trousers are safe. Barry stumbled and grabbed O'Reilly's arm, and it dawned on him that he was not entirely sober either. He'd better pull himself together. Nothing was going to spoil his evening.

'I wonder . . .' said O'Reilly as he opened the back gate. 'I wonder how Galvin's going to "fall into his fortune"? I'd not like to think it'll be the cash Maureen's been saving for their emigration.'

Barry might have been concerned too if Arthur Guinness had not cocked one leg and, with the accuracy of a marksman, pissed all over his trousers.

BARRY LEFT the parked Brunhilde, smoothed the tuft of hair on his crown and looked down. He was a sight. Bloody dog. With one pair of trousers still wet from the wash and his only others reeking of dog piss, he'd had to accept O'Reilly's offer of the loan of a pair. Wearing brightly checked trousers cut for a man of six foot two, even with the cuffs rolled up and the waistband cinched with a belt, he knew he looked like an escapee from a touring circus. Nor was he convinced that a short nap, Mrs Kincaid's liberal doses of black coffee and the greasy fry-up she'd made him eat had restored him to complete sobriety. If they had, he probably wouldn't be standing here outside Number 9, the Esplanade, Kinnegar, giving a fair impression of Pantaloon. He looked at the row of bell pushes, each with a hand-lettered card. *Patricia Spence. Flat 4.* He rang the bell and waited.

The door opened and Patricia came out. 'Hello, Barry Laverty.' She turned to close the door behind her, and her high ponytail danced impertinently as she turned back to him, her dark eyes wide, her dimple deep as she smiled. She was wearing a white silk blouse and a mid-calf green skirt.

His breath caught in his throat.

'What in the world?' She stared at his trousers.

'It's a long story.' He felt the heat in his cheeks. 'I'll tell you in the car.'

He held Brunhilde's door and waited until she was seated. He rushed to the driver's side, climbed in, started the engine and drove off.

'Now,' she said, 'tell me about those trousers, Mr Laverty.'

Mr Laverty. He hadn't told her last night he was a doctor, hadn't wanted her to think he was trying too hard to impress her. 'I only own two pairs. I got both of them dirty today, so I had to borrow these from a friend.'

'A stilt-walker?'

Barry laughed. 'No, but he's big.'

'So's the Atlantic Ocean, and you're drowning in those. But don't worry about it. Where are we going?'

'I thought we'd go to Strickland's Glen. Walk down to the shore.'

'You'd ask a girl with a game leg to go for a walk?'

Was she teasing him? Was she being caustic? He couldn't tell from the tone of her voice. 'Patricia,' he said, 'if you'd rather not go for a walk, say so.'

She leaned over and kissed his cheek. 'I like you, Barry Laverty.'

For the rest of the drive they chatted about tennis and pop music. She liked the Beatles but wasn't sure about the new lot, the Rolling Stones.

We're like two strange dogs, Barry thought, circling, sniffing each other out. He wished he could take the conversation to a more personal level.

'Here we are,' he said. 'Hop out.'

He led her onto a path strewn with needles from the evergreens above, the air redolent with their piney scent. Rays of sun filtered through the trees.

'Listen,' she said. 'Song thrush. You can tell his song a mile away. I love birds. My dad's an ornithologist. He taught my sister and me about them.'

'Mine taught me astronomy.'

'Bit of a stargazer, are you?'

'Yes,' he said softly, and careless of passers-by, he bent and kissed her.

'Mmm,' she said, 'nice, but we should move along if we're going to get to the shore.'

A boy of five or six ran past, stopped, pointed and yelled, 'Mammy, look at the man in clown's trousers.'

He heard Patricia's laughter, warm as butter on fresh toast.

'Come on, then, Pagliaccio.' She tugged at Barry's hand.

'Pally who?'

'A clown. In an opera. The Beatles aren't the only ones I listen to.'

'I'm not much up on opera.'

'I'll teach you. I've tons of records back in the flat. I'm taking extra courses at Queen's this summer. I want to graduate as soon as I can.'

'I see. So you're a student and you like opera. Do you like to read?'

She frowned for a moment. 'I've tried Hemingway, but he's too curt. I prefer John Steinbeck.'

'*Cannery Row*?'

'And I love *Sweet Thursday*.'

He took her hand. 'Come on. Just over this bridge,' he said, and walked onto a small wooden arch over a stream. 'Might be trout in there.'

'Or a hobbit under the bridge. I've just finished *The Lord of the Rings*.'

She knew Steinbeck, Tolkien. 'So, you're taking an arts degree?'

'No.' She stopped walking. 'Why would you say that?'

'I dunno. You certainly seem to know the kinds of authors that I'd expect an arts student to know.'

'And women should take arts or nursing? Is that it? And there's plenty of work for good secretaries? I'm twenty-one and I'm the youngest student in my class—my civil engineering class—and there are only six of us.'

'Six what? Engineers?'

'No. There are eighty-two in the class. Only six are women.'

'I still don't understand. We'd ten women in our lot at university.'

'What exactly don't you understand?' Her eyes were narrow, lips tight.

'What are you making such a fuss about? Why shouldn't a woman be an engineer or a doctor? If you want to be an engineer you ought to have the chance.' Barry did not like the way this discussion was going.

She pursed her lips and spoke, as if to herself. 'Bloody right I should. But a lot of people wouldn't agree. It's a damn sight tougher if you're a woman. Women have to fight for their rights.'

Barry moved closer. 'Fair enough. But you don't have to fight with me.'

'You're right.'

'Right as rain,' he said. Then he grinned at her.

Like a summer squall her anger passed. 'I shouldn't have yelled at you. but . . . damn it . . .' She grabbed him and kissed him hard. 'Am I forgiven?'

He would have forgiven her for not one but all of the seven deadly sins.

'To the beach, woman,' he said, with mock sternness.

'Yes, sir.' She took his hand. 'So tell me about Barry Laverty.'

'Well, apart from my unshakeable belief that women should never be admitted to faculties of engineering—'

'Just cut that out.' She was smiling. 'I'm sorry I got shirty with you.'

'I'm twenty-four, no brothers or sisters. I like to read, to fish. I used to sail, but I'm a bit busy now.' He paused before looking her right in the eye and saying, 'My dad's a mining engineer.'

'And what does the son of a mining engineer do?'

'I'm a GP. I'm an assistant to Dr O'Reilly in Ballybucklebo.'

She pointed at his ridiculous, oversized, baggy trousers and giggled. 'Well, Doctor, I hope none of your patients have seen you this evening.'

BARRY PEEPED through the double doors of the upstairs sitting room. He saw O'Reilly sprawled in his chair, his head drooped to the left. Lady Macbeth lay tucked into the angle between his neck and his right shoulder.

O'Reilly opened one eye. 'You're home.'

'Sorry, Fingal. I didn't mean to disturb you.'

'Had a good evening?'

Barry savoured his memories of the slow walk back through the moth-fluttering gloaming. Stopping to kiss her lips, her hair. The drive to Patricia's flat, her invitation in, and his polite refusal. He'd known from the minute he'd seen her that she was different, special, and sensed that if he were too hasty he would be rebuffed. Better to let things percolate.

'I presume by your dewy-eyed silence that the answer is yes.' O'Reilly scratched his belly. The cat slid down his waistcoat and curled up in his lap.

'It was wonderful.'

'Huh. Women.'

Barry glanced at the big man, expecting from his tone to see distaste written on his face, but instead saw sadness. 'You don't mean that, Fingal.'

'Don't I, by God?' O'Reilly rose and Lady Macbeth slipped to the carpet. The doctor paced to the window and stood, staring out. 'Women? Nothing but grief.' He turned, and for a second Barry thought he could see moisture in his brown eyes.

'Jesus, would you stop it?' O'Reilly swore at Lady Macbeth, who had happily returned to reducing the furniture to tatters. 'Give over.'

Barry was relieved that the animal had distracted them. Whatever was troubling O'Reilly was none of his business. 'Maybe Kinky's right. We should ask Maggie what to do about Her Ladyship.'

'It's not Maggie we need. It's a bloody exorcist. I think she's possessed.' O'Reilly yawned. 'I'm off to bed. We'll be busy for the next few days.'

'How come?'

'Thursday's the Twelfth of July, of "glorious and immortal memory". Unless someone's at death's door they'll not want to miss the parade, so anyone with blepharitis, a blister, a bunion or bursitis, will be bellyaching in the waiting room first thing tomorrow, Tuesday and Wednesday. You'll have to wait for a few days to go back and see the light of your life.'

'Well, I—'

'Don't worry,' said O'Reilly as he left, 'you can have Friday night off.'

'Thanks, Fingal,' Barry said. He sat down. It was too soon to go to bed. He'd too much to think about. Patricia. Soft, warm, delicious and with spirit. He'd phone her tomorrow and hope to hell she was free on Friday.

'Excuse me, Dr Laverty, but I've a pair of trousers dry and pressed for you, so.' He hadn't heard Mrs Kincaid coming in. 'You can get out of himself's bags now. You don't seem to fill them too well.'

'I know.' Barry hesitated. 'Mrs Kincaid, would you mind if I asked a question? It's about Dr O'Reilly.'

He saw her stiffen, her lips narrow.

'I'm a bit worried about him.'

She relaxed almost imperceptibly. 'How so?'

'He gets very upset when I mention a young woman I've started seeing. And earlier—now please don't laugh—I thought he was going to weep.'

'Did you?' Her eyes softened. 'Sometimes I wish to God he would.' She stuffed her bulk into an armchair, glanced at the closed door, lowered her voice and said, 'You'll keep what I'm going to tell you to yourself?'

'Of course.'

'He doesn't know I know. He's a very private man, so. Old Dr Flanagan told me. In 1941, April, Easter Tuesday, them Germans dropped bombs on Belfast, aye, and Bangor.' She clenched her fists. 'A young nurse was killed. They'd been married six months. He worshipped that girl, so.'

'My God.'

'Himself was away on that big ship. He didn't get told until June that she was dead.' She looked up into his face. 'It hurt him sore, Dr Laverty.'

'It still does,' Barry whispered.

'Aye, so.' She rose and stood before him. 'I think he worries that you'll get hurt like him. He's taken quite a shine to you, Doctor. I can tell.'

'Mrs Kincaid, I thank you for telling me this.'

'Not a word now, but . . .' She smiled at Barry. 'There's only you and me to look after the big buck eejit.'

'I understand.'

Mrs Kincaid stood like a guardsman, her three chins thrust out, eyes hot. 'I hope you do, for I'll not see him let down again.' She crossed the room and turned. 'It's not my place to say it, Dr Laverty, but I'd take it kindly if you'd think of staying on here. He's a good man and he needs you.'

For Marriage Is an Honourable Estate

Although Monday morning's surgery started slowly, with three men waiting for tonic injections, their departure opened the floodgates. It seemed to Barry that every case in Ballybucklebo of back strain, sniffles, cough, hay fever and hangovers following the welcoming of Barry Fingal Galvin poured through the place. Several of the hangover sufferers had also needed attention for blackened eyes and skinned knuckles.

As the last of them left, O'Reilly said with a grin, 'I just hope we don't get a rematch on the Twelfth.' He stretched. 'Are there many more today?'

'Two children and a young woman. I think that's it for the morning.'

'Get them, would you?'

Barry brought the two children from the waiting room. He had assumed, incorrectly, that the woman was their mother. The boy Barry guessed was five or six; the blonde girl was probably a year older.

'Good morning, Colin Brown. Good morning, Susan MacAfee, and what can I do for the pair of you?' O'Reilly peered over his half-moons.

'Mr Brown and I want to get married.'

'Indeed,' said O'Reilly, without a flicker of expression. 'Married? And how do you feel about it, Mr Brown?'

The little boy looked down and tugged at the front of his trousers.

'I see,' said O'Reilly. 'Well, marriage is an honourable estate not to be entered into lightly.'

'Yes, Dr O'Reilly,' said the little girl. 'We know that.'

I wonder, thought Barry, what O'Reilly's going to say when he gets to the bit about "the union of the flesh"?

'We've saved up,' said the little girl. 'A whole shilling,'

'You know,' said O'Reilly, 'maybe you're a bit young.'

Mr Brown nodded, yanked the girl's hand and whispered into her ear.

'You'll just have to wait,' she said.

'Before you see the minister?' O'Reilly asked, a smile beginning.

Mr Brown hauled so hard on her hand that she had to take a step towards him. 'I said, you'll have to wait. What . . . ?' She bent to him. 'Oh,' she said 'Dr O'Reilly, we'll have to be running along.'

'Fine,' said O'Reilly. 'So you *are* going to wait?'

'No,' she said, putting a hand on her hip and pouting at the little boy. 'Mr Brown here's just wet himself.'

'Oh, well,' said O'Reilly, 'perhaps Mrs Kincaid can help. Come on.' He rose and took the girl's hand. 'I think she's in the kitchen.' O'Reilly turned to Barry. 'Get the last one in, will you? Start taking her history.'

'Right.' Barry waited until O'Reilly and his charges had left before he surrendered to laughter. He was still chuckling when he reached the waiting room. 'Will you come with me, please?' he asked a young woman who sat all alone. Her corn-silk hair was held in place by an Alice band and her eyes were dull and red-rimmed. By the look of the shadows beneath, she must have been short of sleep. Whatever ailed her, this was no time for frivolity.

She stood. 'Dr O'Reilly?'

No one from Ballybucklebo would have mistaken him for Fingal. 'No,' he said, 'Laverty. But Dr O'Reilly'll be along in a minute.'

She said nothing, even when she was seated in the patients' chair.

'Now,' said Barry, pulling out a blank patient-record card. 'I'll just get a few details. You're not from round here, are you?'

She shook her head. 'Rasharkin.'

'County Antrim? You're a long way from home.' He glanced at her left hand. No ring. 'Miss . . . ?'

'MacAteer. Julie MacAteer.'

He entered the name. 'How old are you?'

'Twenty.' There was a catch in her voice. 'Next week.'

'And what brings you to see us?'

A single tear fell from her left eye. She opened her handbag and brought out a handkerchief.

'I'm late,' she whispered. 'Three whole weeks. And I'm always on time.'

Barry swallowed. 'Do you think you could be—?'

'I know I am.' Her eyes flashed. 'I've thrown up every morning for the last week and I'm main sore here.' She put her hand to her breast.

Barry heard O'Reilly enter. He looked over to see the big man put a finger to his lips. 'Have you told anyone?' Barry asked her.

'Who could I tell? Da would kill me, so he would.'

'Julie, you could be wrong. Hormones are funny things. It's not unusual for young women to miss a period if they're worried about something.'

'I'm not wrong. I know I'm . . . pregnant and I don't know what to do.'

'I think we should find out for sure. Did you bring a urine sample?'

She pulled a small glass bottle from her bag. 'Here.'

Barry took the bottle. 'I'll have to send it to Belfast for a test.' He saw
O'Reilly hold up a thumb. 'We'll know for sure on . . . ?'

'Friday,' said O'Reilly.

She swung round and stared at him.

'This is Julie MacAteer,' Barry said.

'It's all right, Julie. I'm Dr O'Reilly.'

She turned back to Barry and tried to smile. 'I'll just have to wait then.'

'Will you be going back to Rasharkin today?' Barry asked.

'No. I'm stopping here.'

'Where?' Barry realised he had forgotten to take her address.

She tugged at the handkerchief. 'I'm not telling.'

'But—'

'It's not important.' O'Reilly put a hand on her shoulder. 'Dr Laverty
only needs it for the records. Barry just put "local" on the card.'

'Dr O'Reilly?' She straightened her shoulders and stared up into his
face. 'If I am . . . you know . . . I can't keep it.'

'You'll not have to,' said O'Reilly. 'I promise.'

Barry sat bolt upright. He could understand why a single woman wouldn't
want to consult a physician in her own community and he'd assumed that
was why she'd travelled to Ballybucklebo. But was O'Reilly an abortionist?

'Do you mean it?' she asked.

'I do,' said O'Reilly. 'I promise.'

Good God. Barry could not believe what he was hearing. Abortions were
illegal. 'Dr O'Reilly, I won't—'

'Hold your horses, Barry. It's not what you think.'

Barry, unable to trust himself not to say something he might regret, left
the surgery. How the hell could O'Reilly tell her that everything would be
rosy when the odds were that she *was* pregnant and there wasn't a damn
thing they could do about it?

He almost bumped into Mrs Kincaid as she let the two children out
through the front door. 'Sorry,' he snapped.

The surgery door opened, and O'Reilly, holding Julie's arm, took her to
the front door. Barry saw Mrs Kincaid peer at the young woman's face and
a look of puzzlement cross her own. Then he heard O'Reilly say, 'Come
back on Friday. Try not to worry. We'll take care of it, I promise.' The door
shut. 'Kinky. Lunch,' O'Reilly said. 'We've a lot of calls this afternoon.'

Barry went into the dining room. O'Reilly came in and sat at the table.

'You promise, do you, Fingal?' Barry could barely stop his hands from trembling. 'How can you promise her? Do you do abortions here? Is that why she's come all the way from Rasharkin?'

O'Reilly folded his arms, and looked levelly at Barry, who rushed on, 'Are you one of the charlatans who take money from well-to-do ladies and make sure they can get rid of their little inconveniences?'

'At least,' said O'Reilly mildly, 'those fellows use a sterile technique.'

'And you think that sterility's justification for what they do?'

'It's better than the backstreets.'

'Christ.' Barry stood straight. 'I won't be party to it.'

'You won't have to be.'

Barry swallowed. He saw clearly that although he was now enjoying working in Ballybucklebo, he wouldn't, couldn't, stay here. He half turned, fully intending to leave, when he heard O'Reilly say clearly and distinctly, 'I don't do abortions.'

Barry spun back. 'What?'

'I said, I don't do abortions. Mind you, I'm not sure they shouldn't be legal. I'd not want to be single and up the spout, would you?'

'No.' Barry frowned. 'But if you don't . . . how could you promise Julie she'd not have to keep it?'

'I didn't say she wouldn't have to have the baby.'

'Come on, Fingal. How could a single woman go on living in a place like Rasharkin, or here in Ballybucklebo? The shame would kill her.'

'Why don't you take a deep breath, count to ten, and sit down?' An edge of command laced O'Reilly's words and Barry sat slowly. 'If she's pregnant, I'll arrange for her to go to Liverpool. There's a charity there. A home for the Piffys.'

'Piffys?'

'PFIs. Pregnant from Ireland. Piffys. The people there will look after her until the baby's born and then arrange an adoption. The folks in Rasharkin can suspect, but they can't be sure that she's had a wee bastard.'

'Oh.' Barry could not meet O'Reilly's gaze. 'Look. I'm sorry, Fingal. I shouldn't have jumped to conclusions.'

'No. You shouldn't . . . But I'll say one thing. I admire a man who has the courage to speak his mind.'

Barry looked up and saw a soft smile on O'Reilly's face.

'So we'll say no more. Mind you, it would make life a lot easier all round if the babby's daddy would make an honest woman of her.'

'I wonder why she's here. In Ballybucklebo.'

'Haven't a clue.' O'Reilly looked over Barry's head to where Mrs Kincaid stood, holding two plates of steaming food. 'What do you think, Kinky? Why would a pregnant young woman come here from Rasharkin to see me?'

'So, the wee girl's in trouble?' She set two plates on the table.

''Fraid so.' O'Reilly grabbed his knife and fork and set to.

'I'll need to ask about,' said Mrs Kincaid. 'I've seen that girl before.'

'You do that, Kinky. I want to know by Friday.'

'WHO'VE WE to visit today, Fingal?' Barry asked, as they climbed into the car.

O'Reilly consulted his list. 'Old Archie Campbell's arthritis is playing up, Katy Corrigan's bronchitis is getting worse, Mrs Mallon thinks her Jimmy's broken his ankle . . . I doubt it, but that's very handy.'

'What is?'

'The Mallons live near Maggie's place. We'll make our last call with her and see if she has any suggestions for what to do with Lady Macbeth.'

The actual consultations didn't take long. Most of the time was consumed driving from place to place, and Barry soon understood why it was important to know the geography of the area.

At their first stop O'Reilly examined Archie Campbell's twisted hands and knuckles, red and inflamed. He told the old man to keep soaking them in salt and warm water and to double his dose of aspirin.

Katy Corrigan, lying in her bed, wheezing like a broken-down carthorse, agreed to inhale the fumes of Friar's Balsam three times daily and, in no uncertain terms, assured O'Reilly that she had not the slightest intention of giving up her cigarettes.

Jimmy Mallon's ankle had made a remarkable recovery. When O'Reilly asked to see the patient, the mother said she'd have to call young Jimmy in from where he was playing soccer. Barry expected O'Reilly to blow a fuse, but the big man simply shrugged.

'You have to make allowances,' he remarked as he pulled the Rover away from the Mallons'. 'She's got eight kids and a husband who spends even more time in the Mucky Duck than Seamus Galvin. What we need is some decent contraception . . . like this pill thingy.'

'It's been available with a prescription in England for the last year.'

'It's not available here and it bloody well should be. Anyway, we've more important things to think about right now. We've to hope that Maggie has the answer to what to do with Lady Macbeth.' O'Reilly had pulled up outside Maggie MacCorkle's cottage. 'Come on.'

'Hello, Doctors dear,' said Maggie as she turned from a window box, trowel in one hand. Barry noticed that the geraniums in her hatband had been replaced with marigolds. 'Grand day.'

It was. Out past her cottage, far out on the whitecapped lough, Barry could see a fleet of yachts running down the wind. In the sunlight their multi-hued spinnakers billowed like fairies' parachutes.

'How are you, Maggie?' O'Reilly asked.

'Grand, so I am. I'm glad you dropped by. I need a wee favour.'

'All in good time, Maggie. We've come to ask advice.'

'Oh? What about?'

'Cats,' said O'Reilly. 'I've just got a new one.'

'Good. It'll be better company for you than that great lummox of an Arthur Guinness.' Maggie looked gently at the big man.

Barry wondered just how accurate Mrs Kincaid had been when she'd assured him they were the only ones to know of O'Reilly's loss.

'I'm having trouble training her.'

Maggie cackled. 'Sure, you can't train cats.'

'Oh,' said O'Reilly, looking crestfallen. 'So I'll just have to wave good-bye to my living-room suite? She's clawing like a tiger with fits.'

Maggie frowned. 'You could try doing what I did for the General. Come inside and I'll show you.' She led the way, leaving the front door open.

The General lay on a chair beside the unlit fire. Maggie went into another room and came back carrying a long two-by-two post, covered in old carpet, and attached to a flat plywood base.

'One of these might do the trick,' she said. 'It's a scratching post, so it is.'

The General opened his eye, stared at the scratching post and made a moaning sound. Then he scuttled, belly to the floor, under the table.

'The General used to rip my bits and pieces, didn't you, you bugger?' She waved the post at the cat, who put a paw over his eye and retreated.

'I see,' O'Reilly said, 'and every time he tried to scratch the furniture you showed him the post, and he learned to use it instead. Brilliant.'

'Not at all,' said Maggie. 'When he tried it, I took the post . . . and I fetched him a right good belt on the head, didn't I, General?'

Barry was aware of an orange streak that rushed past him and out through the open door.

'Maybe,' said O'Reilly, when he finally stopped laughing, 'maybe a piece of rolled-up newspaper would work?'

'Maybe.' Maggie looked thoughtful. 'It's the best I can think of.'

'Thanks, Maggie.' O'Reilly walked to the door, stopped, and said, 'I nearly forgot. What was the wee favour you wanted?'

Maggie fidgeted, cocked her head to one side. 'I sometimes take a dander up past Sonny's place. I don't go that way often, you understand?'

'Of course,' said O'Reilly.

'But I was there this morning, and I don't think the old goat's right. He usually hides in his car if he sees me coming. He just sat in his chair. "Morning, Maggie," says he, and he coughed. A great big long hack. He looked terrible blue in the face, so he did. Would you maybe take a gander at him?'

'Of course. We'll head up there right now.'

THERE WAS NO SIGN of Sonny. Nor did he appear when O'Reilly bellowed the man's name. Four of his five dogs ran barking through the scrapyard to the gate in the hedge. The spaniel stood outside a derelict car, front paws on the sill of an open rear door.

'He must be in there,' O'Reilly said, opening the gate. He brushed aside the dogs and made his way, Barry in tow, along a well-trodden path through weeds and rusting metal. He bent at the open car door.

'Are you there, Sonny?'

Barry heard a hacking cough and a feeble 'Go away.'

'It's Dr O'Reilly.' The doctor clambered through the open door.

'Ah, Jesus, Doctor, let me be.' More coughing.

O'Reilly backed out, dragging Sonny. 'It would be a hell of a sight easier if you'd cooperate,' O'Reilly panted. 'You're sick as a dog.'

He straightened up. He held Sonny in his arms, the man's legs dangling to one side, his head pillowed on O'Reilly's chest. Barry could see that Sonny's cheeks were slate grey. His nostrils flared like a scared horse's, and his neck muscles stood out like cords every time he tried to inhale. There was no need of a stethoscope to hear the damp rattling of each laboured breath.

'Come on,' O'Reilly said, 'we'll have to get him to the surgery.'

O'REILLY LAID SONNY on the examination couch. Barry helped him remove Sonny's clothes. It took several minutes to peel away the layers of old newspaper that lay under his shirt. With each rasping inhalation, the muscles between Sonny's ribs were sucked inwards, and he whimpered.

'Hurts to breathe, does it?' O'Reilly asked as he took Sonny's pulse.

'Yuh-huh.' Sonny put a hand to his ribs.

'When did it start?'

'Just after . . . (*hack*) . . . the storm . . . (*hack*) . . . got soaked.'

'Help me sit him up.'

Barry put an arm round Sonny's shoulders. He could see that the jugular veins were distended right up to the angle of Sonny's jaw, a sign that blood was backing up behind a heart that lacked the strength to pump it further.

O'Reilly percussed Sonny's back. Barry heard sullen thumps where a resonant sound should have been. Either the lungs or the pleural cavities were filling with fluid. O'Reilly stuffed his stethoscope in his ears and listened.

'You daft old bugger. Why the hell didn't you send for me?'

Sonny hacked.

Barry eased the old man's head back onto the pillow. 'Heart failure?'

'And pneumonia and pleurisy. Both sides.' O'Reilly shook his head. 'I suppose you didn't want to bother anybody. It's the hospital for you, Sonny.'

Terror filled Sonny's eyes. 'Who'll look after . . . (*hack*) . . . my dogs?'

'Your dogs'll do a damn sight better if you're around to take care of them,' O'Reilly said, 'and you won't be if we don't get you to the Royal. And quick.' He turned to Barry. 'Go and call the ambulance. The number's by the phone. We need oxygen down here as quick as we can get it.'

'Here. Get that into you.' O'Reilly gave Barry a glass of sherry, set his whiskey on the coffee table, shoved Lady Macbeth out of his chair and sat. 'What a day! I'm worried as hell about Sonny and his place.'

'Do you not think he'll make it?'

'Touch and go. Pneumonia, pleurisy and a dicky ticker? Still, he's a tough old bird and they'll do the best they can for him in the Royal. That's not what I'm concerned about.'

Barry had learned, painfully, that no doctor could care too deeply, not about any one patient—you'd crack up. He couldn't fault O'Reilly for his apparent lack of concern about the clinical outcome, but why had he mentioned Sonny's place? Barry looked at Lady Macbeth. O'Reilly had a soft spot for animals. 'You're not going to see to Sonny's dogs?' he asked.

O'Reilly shook his head. 'No. Maggie'll look after them, if we ask her. It's more than his dogs that's got Sonny scared shitless.'

'Oh?'

'Bishop.' O'Reilly spat the word. 'Sonny told me when you were phoning for the ambulance. There's some council bylaw that if a property's derelict and the owner moves away, the council can have it repossessed. Then they sell it to the highest bidder. And who do you think that is likely to be?'

'Ah, no.'

'Ah, yes. Bloody Bishop's been trying to get his hands on Sonny's place for years.' O'Reilly ground his teeth. 'I'm damned if I can see a way out, but Bishop may not hear for a day or two, and the Council offices will be closed for the Twelfth week. Maybe we can come up with something.'

'I hope so, and I hope Sonny recovers.'

'That,' said O'Reilly, 'goes without saying.' He took a deep breath. 'I said you could have Friday off. Should you give that lass of yours a call?'

'I'd like to.'

'Go on, then.'

Barry ran downstairs, dialled and waited.

'Hello, Kinnegar 657334.'

'Patricia? It's Barry. Look, I'm off on Friday. Would you like to go out for a bite?'

'I'd love to but I've got an evening seminar.'

'Damn. It's my only night off.'

'I . . . I suppose I could ask someone to let me borrow their notes.'

'Do it. We could go to my yacht club, in Bangor.' The grub's cheaper there for members, he thought.

'Super. I look forward to it. Got to run now.'

TUESDAY AND WEDNESDAY sped by. O'Reilly's phone calls to the Royal brought the news that Sonny was holding his own. Maggie had agreed to take care of his dogs. Somewhere in the village, Julie MacAteer tried not to worry about the results of her pregnancy test. Councillor Bishop's finger needed attention. And despite the long hours, Barry began to feel truly at home in his choice of career in general and in the village in particular.

Seamus Galvin came into the surgery on Tuesday morning. He sat in the patients' chair and pulled a cloth cap off his pear-shaped head.

'Morning, Seamus. How's young Barry Fingal?' Barry asked.

'Grand. Mind you, it's a good thing men can't feed wee ones. He has Maureen up half the night, so he has.'

'Huh,' said O'Reilly, 'I don't suppose *you'd* think of giving the child a bottle once in a while?'

'Not at all. You don't buy a dog and bark yourself. That's Maureen's job, so it is.'

O'Reilly looked at Barry and shook his head. 'I'd not want you to rupture yourself, Seamus . . . But that's not why you're here, is it now?'

'Ah, no, sir. It's time for you to take a wee look at my ankle.'

'Huh,' said O'Reilly, 'and I suppose you want a line?'

'Oh, indeed, sir, I do that. I'll have to go on the burroo.'

Barry understood. Seamus wanted a medical certificate so he could draw disability insurance from the Bureau of Unemployment—the 'burroo'.

'We'll see,' said O'Reilly. 'Show me your ankle.'

The ankle in question looked perfectly normal. No swelling.

'Can you bend it?' O'Reilly asked.

Galvin made a show of trying to extend his foot. 'Ah. Ooh.'

'Hmm. Right. Let's see you walk on it.'

Galvin stood and teetered across the room, hauling his allegedly wounded ankle behind him and moaning 'Ooh, ah'.

'You're one for the textbooks, Seamus,' said O'Reilly. 'You've managed to hurt the side that was fine when you showed that hoof to me first.'

Galvin hung his head.

'*Ecce Galvinus. Homo plumbum oscillandat*,' O'Reilly remarked to Barry, who understood immediately. 'Behold Galvin. The man's swinging the lead.'

'Is that *plumbum* stuff bad, sir?' Galvin hobbled back across the room.

'All depends,' said O'Reilly. 'You want me to give you a line?'

Galvin brightened. 'Yes, please, sir. For two weeks, if that's all right?'

'I might,' said O'Reilly, 'but I'd need to know about the fortune you said you'd be falling into.'

Galvin sat back in the forward-tilting chair. 'Ach, you don't, sir. Ach, no.'

'Ach, yes, Seamus, I do. Or it's no line.'

Galvin took a deep breath. 'Maureen gave me the money.'

O'Reilly's nose tip blanched. 'She what? The money for California?'

Galvin hung his head.

'You skiver. You unmitigated gobshite. Give it back to her, do you hear?'

'I can't, sir. It's spent. On ducks. Rocking ducks.'

O'Reilly's shaggy eyebrows rose. 'What the hell are you talking about?'

'I'm going to make rocking ducks. Just like rocking horses. The timber and paint's all bought. I can sell them for twice what they'll cost to make. That's why I want two weeks off, so I can finish making them and get them sold.'

'How many will you make?'

'About a hundred, sir.'

'And how many kiddies that would want a rocking duck do you think live in Ballybucklebo?'

'I don't know, sir.'

'Forty, maybe fifty. Do you reckon they'll buy them in pairs?'

'I never thought of that, sir. But it will all work out. You'll see. So you'll give me the line, Doctor sir?'

Barry was surprised when O'Reilly said, 'A promise is a promise,' and returned to the desk to scribble on a government form. Doctors were meant to be honest when supporting genuine claims for disability money.

'Here,' said O'Reilly, handing Galvin the form. 'Two weeks. But you build those damn ducks. I might know a business in Belfast that'll take the lot. And, Seamus,' O'Reilly added softly, 'get out of your bloody bed and give that wife of yours a hand. Do you hear me?'

'I do, sir. I will.' Galvin left.

'Useless bugger,' said O'Reilly. 'I told you he was a skiver.'

'So why did you give him a disability certificate?'

O'Reilly sat in the swivel chair. 'I was getting into too many fights with my patients when I wouldn't give them their lines.'

'But that's part of our job.'

'Balls. Our job's to look after them when they're sick, not behave like some bloody civil servant. What do you know about the medical referee?'

'Not much.'

'A few years ago the politicos had the bright idea that maybe an independent doctor employed by the ministry could examine anyone their local GP thought was working the system. Sometimes the referee'd pull a certificate at random and invite the customer up for a visit. Kept a lot of people honest. Let the ministry doctor be the villain.'

'That makes sense.'

'Didn't work. You were *still* the villain as soon as you told someone you were going to send them to the referee.'

'So what do you do?'

O'Reilly chuckled. 'The referee is a classmate of mine. We worked out a code.' He handed Barry a blank certificate. 'See where it says Signature of Referring Doctor? if I sign it F. F. O'Reilly, my friend knows I believe the complaint is genuine. But'—O'Reilly's chuckle became a full laugh—'if I sign it F. F. O'Reilly, M.B., B.Ch., B.A.O., the lead-swinger's up in the ministry office before the ink's dry.'

'You wily bugger.'

'The customer doesn't know I blew the whistle. No more fights in here.'

'And how, may I ask, did you sign Galvin's line?'

'Ah,' said O'Reilly, 'let's just say my recommendation was unqualified.'

'MIGHT BE a bit difficult to park the car on Main Street. They'll be getting it ready for Thursday,' said O'Reilly, finishing his lunch. 'We've to nip round to Declan Finnegan's. He lives over the grocer's. Let's walk.'

'Fine.' Barry would be glad of the exercise. He thought wistfully of his fly rod, propped up, unused in his attic.

'Is it nice in there?' O'Reilly asked.

'Where?'

'Wherever the hell you've gone off to in your head. It's not spring, but I suppose your young man's fancy is lightly turning to thoughts of love?'

'Not *quite* how Tennyson put it, and if it's any of your business, I was thinking about fishing.'

'Were you? I noticed you've a rod. I'll have a word with His Lordship. The Marquis of Ballybucklebo. Nice old bugger. He owns a beat on the Bucklebo River. He'd probably let you on his water if I asked him.'

'Would you? I'd love a day on a good trout stream.'

'I'll see to it.' O'Reilly rose. 'Come on.'

At least, Barry thought as he closed the front door, going out this way avoids running the gauntlet past the canine world's answer to Casanova.

The town was busy. Shoppers and children on their school holidays filled the narrow footpaths. A gang of men were painting the kerbstones in bands of glistening red, white and blue. The maypole had been touched up in the same Loyalist colours, and from its peak hung a large flag: the Red Hand of Ulster centred on the red cross of St George set against a white background. Union Jacks dangled from upstairs windows.

Other men struggled to erect an arch across the road. In its centre was a picture of a man mounted on a rearing white horse. One hand held the reins; the other waved a sabre over the rider's head.

'Pity,' said O'Reilly, 'that William of Orange's charger has a squint.'

Barry looked more closely. O'Reilly was right.

'Derry, Aughrim, Enniskillen and the Boyne.' O'Reilly read the names of battles that were lettered on painted scrolls on either side of the mounted man. 'In 1690 or thereabouts. Old battles that should be forgotten.'

'You said it was all sweetness and light between the Protestants and the Catholics in Ballybucklebo.'

'There's nothing overt. Not like the taunting and ranting that go on in Belfast. But I don't like it,' said O'Reilly. 'I was a boy during the Troubles. back in the 1920s. I'd hate to see the Troubles come back, and when you keep on rubbing folks' noses in it with flags and parades . . .'

'I'm sure there'll never be anything like the Troubles again. Not here.'

'I hope you're right,' said O'Reilly, 'but long memories are the curse of Ireland. The Twelfth's just a holiday to most folks, but there's a bunch of bigots keeping the old hatred alive . . . like our worthy councillor. If he can spare the time from trying to drive a decent old man off his property, he'd be happy to string up the odd Fenian from a lamppost.' The doctor sighed. 'I don't know about you, but I'm no closer to sorting out how to help Sonny, and now I have to find a way to get Maureen Galvin's money back for her.'

'I thought you knew a company in Belfast that would buy the ducks?'

'I can phone a fellow I played rugby with, but would you want to try to sell the things?' O'Reilly started to cross the road. 'Something will turn up,' he said. 'Just what the dickens do you think this is all about?'

Barry saw the ginger-haired Donal Donnelly waving at them as he forced his way across the street. He was accompanied by a grey dog.

'Dr O'Reilly, sir. Could I have a wee word?' Donal's buckteeth trembled against his long lower lip.

'Of course.'

'This here's Bluebird.' The dog raised its narrow muzzle. 'After your man Donald Campbell's speedboat.'

'Races, does she?' O'Reilly asked, examining the dog's flanks.

'She does, sir, but she hasn't won yet.'

'So if she's slow, why do you call her Bluebird?'

'Because, sir'—Donal's left upper eyelid drooped in a slow wink—'she runs on water. But on Friday at Dunmore Park she'll be running dry.'

'Will she, by God?' O'Reilly's eyes widened.

Barry was baffled. What the hell were they talking about?

'Thought you'd like to know.' Donal peered around. 'Not a word now.'

'Thanks, Donal. I might just take a trip up to Dunmore. Dr Laverty could look after the practice.'

Barry flinched. Oh, no. Friday was to be his night off.

'We'll be running on,' said Donal. 'Got to get you fit, girl.'

'Fingal,' said Barry.' You said I could have Friday night off.'

'Don't worry. We'll both get away. You just hold the fort till it's time for you to go. I don't do it very often, but if no one's baby's due and the shop seems reasonably quiet, Kinky takes the calls. Either she asks the customer to wait until the morning, or, if she thinks it is urgent, she arranges for an ambulance to take the patient up to the Royal. So you can see the light of your life, and I can have a bit of fun myself.' O'Reilly chuckled.

'You've utterly lost me.'

'I do that sometimes,' said O'Reilly, 'and I've no time to explain now. We're running behind. Come on and we'll get Declan Finnegan looked at.'

Declan Finnegan, a man in his fifties, was sorely afflicted with Parkinson's disease. The diagnosis was apparent the moment Barry walked into the small flat above the grocer's. The man's face was a mask, expressionless, immobile. Any hope he might have treasured of a cure must have been long gone.

His wife, a worried-looking woman who bore herself like a Victorian dowager, greeted O'Reilly. '*Bonjour, monsieur le docteur.*'

'*Bonjour, Madame Finnegan. Comment va-t-il aujourd'hui?*' O'Reilly replied in barely accented French.

Barry listened, his schoolboy French barely sufficient for him to follow their conversation. It would appear that the man's condition had worsened since O'Reilly's last visit. The doctor offered what little comfort he could.

'I didn't know you spoke French,' Barry said, as they walked back to the house to collect the car.

'Oh, aye,' said O'Reilly. 'Picked it up when I was in the Med on the *Warspite*. Comes in handy once in a while. Mind you, she's the only Frenchwoman in Ballybucklebo. Declan met her somewhere in Normandy in '44.' He paused. 'I just wish there was more we could do for folks like Declan.'

IN LOCAL PARLANCE, O'Reilly went through Tuesday's afternoon calls—and most of the patients who had come to the surgery on Wednesday morning—like grease through a duckling. Barry could barely keep pace. He was glad of the respite when Mrs Kincaid set his lunch plate on the table.

'Your list, Doctor. It's not too bad.' She handed O'Reilly the sheet.

'Thanks, Kinky.' O'Reilly consulted it quickly. 'Not bad at all. Any luck with finding out about Julie MacAteer?'

'I'm not getting very far. The wee girl is living somewhere here, but nobody knows where. I—' Her reply was interrupted by the jangling of the front doorbell. 'I'll see who it is, so.' She left, and when she returned her colour was high. 'It's the wee Hitler man. His exalted excellence, Councillor Bishop. He wants to be seen now. Will I tell him to wait?'

'No,' said O'Reilly, pushing his plate aside. 'Come on, Barry.'

Councillor Bishop stood in the hall. 'You took your time.'

'Ach,' said O'Reilly mildly, 'we were at our lunch. Could you not have come during surgery hours?'

'And wait for ever with the unwashed? Don't be stupid.'

Barry saw a spark deep in O'Reilly's brown eyes.

'Come into the surgery,' said O'Reilly, crossing the hall and opening the door. When the councillor was seated, he said, 'What can I do for you?'

Councillor Bishop thrust his bandaged finger under O'Reilly's nose. 'I need this better for tomorrow.'

'Right,' said O'Reilly as he went to a tray of instruments and picked up a pair of scissors and a set of fine-nosed forceps.

Bishop gave his hand to O'Reilly, who picked up the bottom end of the bandage with the forceps, slid one blade of the scissors beneath the gauze, and began to snip. When the dressing was divided from finger base to fingertip, O'Reilly gave a ferocious yank with the forceps. Barry was sure he would have heard the material as it parted from the freshly healed flesh beneath had it not been for a deafening *yeeeow*.

'Sorry about that, Councillor,' O'Reilly said. 'I could have soaked it to soften the old blood, but I know you're in a rush. Go and rinse it in the sink.'

The councillor obeyed.

'All set for the big day tomorrow?' O'Reilly enquired.

'Don't talk to me about big days. I've bigger fish to fry. Sonny's in hospital and that parcel of land—'

Barry needed to hear no more. 'I think that's the meanest thing—'

'Nobody asked you to think,' O'Reilly snapped. He shook his head.

Barry bit back his words. He felt heat in his cheeks.

Councillor Bishop turned off the tap and glowered at his fingertip. 'Doesn't look too bad,' he allowed. 'Good. I'll be off then. I've work to do.'

'Fine,' said O'Reilly as he accompanied the councillor to the surgery door. 'And how's Mrs Bishop today?'

'She's fit to be tied. That new maid of ours. The Antrim girl. She's given her notice, and where in the hell can you find good help these days?'

'I wouldn't know,' said O'Reilly, smiling at Mrs Kincaid, who was busy in the dining room. He opened the front door and let the councillor pass.

Barry stood at O'Reilly's shoulder as the fat man marched down the path. 'You were too damn civil to that man,' he muttered. 'And I thought we were going to have it out with him about Sonny's place. When I tried to say something, why did you jump all over me?'

'Arguing with men like Bishop's no use. All it does is stiffen their resolve. If we're going to sort him out, we need an argument he can't resist.'

'And what the hell could that be?' Barry was not satisfied.

'I'm beginning to wonder, but I'm starting to get an idea. I didn't know his maid came from County Antrim.' O'Reilly looked up at the sky as if seeking divine inspiration. 'Jesus, would you look at that?'

Barry stared at the sky. Ranks of cumulonimbus clouds were marching like dark-cuirassed dragoons towards the little town of Ballybucklebo.

'I think,' Barry said, 'we're in for a storm.'

'Indeed,' said O'Reilly, glowering at the distant departing back of Councillor Bishop. 'You could be right.'

Don't Rain on My Parade

O'Reilly opened the upper half of one of the sash windows in the upstairs sitting room and said, 'We'll watch from here.'

Main Street was flanked by the citizenry. Many carried tiny Union Jacks or Ulster flags. Youngsters were hoisted onto their daddies' shoulders. Stray dogs yapped. Borne on the humid air, the rattling of side drums and the distant wailing of bagpipes drifted into the room.

'That'll be the Ballybucklebo Highlanders warming up down at the maypole,' O'Reilly remarked. 'As brave a bunch of musical heroes as ever blew into a bag. Pipe major Donal Donnelly, bass drummer Seamus Galvin, and the rest.' O'Reilly chuckled. 'We could be busy when the parade's over and that lot have gone to the Field for the speeches and the hymns and a bit of good old neighbourly pope bashing. Bagpiping's a thirsty business.'

'I know,' Barry said. 'I worked in the first-aid tent last year at the Bangor Field. I put in more stitches than a shirt factory.'

'And I'll bet some of the worst offenders were members of temperance lodges,' said O'Reilly. 'But maybe we'll get lucky today and that thunderstorm will break before they get too much of a head of steam up.' He looked at his watch. 'Eleven o'clock. Should be starting soon.'

Tah-rah-rum, tah-rah-rum. The distant side drums broke into the double triple-roll that Barry knew signalled the start of a pipe band's advance.

'Here they come,' said O'Reilly. 'That'll be the worshipful master Bertie Bishop on the off-white horse at the head of them.'

Barry could see a man riding an off-white horse. Behind him tramped the members of an Orange Lodge following its banner. Next came a drum major marching in front of a kilted pipe band.

'Ballybucklebo's finest,' said O'Reilly. 'The Highlanders.'

Now Barry recognised Councillor Bishop at the head of the procession, He could see that, even for a Clydesdale, the animal was making heavy weather of carrying the councillor's weight.

At either side of the road, two boys, whom Barry guessed to be about six or seven, plodded along. Both wore miniature orange sashes. He recognised the trouser-wetting Mr Brown clutching a braided guy rope that helped steady a great square of embroidered cloth, beneath which two bowler-hatted, white-gloved, orange-sashed men held the banner's poles. The banner was fringed with golden tassels and bordered in orange. On a blue background reared the inevitable white charger and its princely rider. Immediately over the picture were the words: *Ballybucklebo Loyal Sons of William, Lodge 747*. On the left side a slogan roared, *Remember 1690. No Surrender*, and on the right, *Civil and Religious Liberty for All*.

'Bit ironic that "for all", don't you think?' O'Reilly asked.

Barry nodded.

'And look at those faces.' O'Reilly shook his head. 'Good, strong, country Ulster faces. Ruddy. Rough skinned. And every last one with the corners of his mouth turned down to twenty to four.'

'They do look dour,' Barry said.

'You should see—' O'Reilly was cut off by a series of shrill whinnies.

Barry looked to the head of the procession to see Councillor Bishop's mount rearing. The animal bucked, unseated its rider and galloped off.

O'Reilly doubled over, hands clasped to his ample belly. 'Better,' he said, laughing like a madman, 'better than a bloody pantomime.'

Barry watched the Ballybucklebo Lodge members clustering round their fallen worshipful master. 'I hope he's not hurt.'

'I think he'll be all right. He's getting up.'

'Lord, Fingal. Look.'

The councillor's mishap had brought the marchers to an untidy halt, blocking the progress of the pipers, whose front rank shambled to a standstill.

'That's Donal Donnelly,' Barry said.

'Pipe major. How do you like his uniform?' O'Reilly snorted.

Donal's saffron kilt hung from his skinny hips. It ought to have ended at knee level but instead drooped to half-calf.

'Look out, Donal!' O'Reilly bellowed uselessly.

Barry watched open-mouthed as the red-faced piper in the rank behind, his eyes closed, fingers running up and down the chanter, marched smack into Donal's skinny back. Donal's kilt slipped off. He dropped his pipes, bent, and hastily hoisted his nether garment.

'I see,' gasped O'Reilly, 'that Donal's not dressed like a true Highlander. I wonder why he's wearing his Y-fronts back to front?'

Collapsing pipes wailed as rank tangled with file. The drum section, marching at the rear of the band, had time to avoid the melee. Seamus Galvin, peering over a huge bass drum that hung from a shoulder harness, pounded out the rhythm. The woolly heads of his drumsticks flew in counter-rotating circles above his head. He never missed a beat, now striking opposite sides of the drum's skin, then crossing his hands above its circumference to deliver a whack to its left side with his right stick, its right with his left.

'Now, that's impressive. Go, Seamus.' O'Reilly did a little jig.

Then the strap securing one stick to Seamus's wrist parted. The noise of shattering glass could have come only from O'Reilly's dining-room window.

'Shite,' said O'Reilly, but his beaming grin did not fade.

As if in celestial solidarity with the ructions below, the heavens joined in. The storm broke, rain lashing the participants and the spectators.

'I'd call this a humdinger too,' said O'Reilly, closing the sash window. 'No point getting this room soaked.'

'What about downstairs?'

'Seamus Galvin's a carpenter by trade. He'll—' The front doorbell rang. 'That'll be him. He'll have it patched up in no time.' O'Reilly strolled to the sideboard. 'How about a sherry?' he asked as he filled his glass with Bushmills. 'I don't think there'll be much business for today.'

O'Reilly was almost right, but the first of the walking wounded appeared in the surgery at four o'clock, and the last had gone by five.

BY FRIDAY THE THIRTEENTH the thunderstorm had passed and bright sunlight streamed in through one dining-room window. The day before, an apologetic Seamus Galvin had patched the other with plywood.

'Big day for the pair of us,' said O'Reilly, finishing his breakfast.

'I know,' said Barry, trying not to think too hard of his evening to come with Patricia. 'You're going to the dogs.'

'I'd hardly put it that way, but yes, I want to see how Donal's Bluebird runs. And I'm meeting an old friend.'

'Not by any chance the one that might buy Seamus Galvin's ducks?'

'The very fella,' said O'Reilly. He rose. 'But the dirt has to come before the brush. How'd you like to run the surgery this morning?'

'Me? Seriously?'

'I've been watching you, son. You did a grand job with Maureen's delivery, and last night you put in some stitches just as well as I could have done.'

'Honestly?' Barry felt a flush start under his collar.

'Time for you to fly solo. Well, dual control for a start. I'll keep you company, but you do the work. I'll not interfere.'

Barry straightened his tie, smoothed his tuft of hair, rose and said, 'If you really think so, we'd better get at it.' He started towards the waiting room.

O'Reilly stopped him. 'I'll fetch the customers. Explain to them who's in charge today. And you'—O'Reilly grabbed lady Macbeth, who was trying to get into the surgery—'can bugger off. Dr Laverty will not be in need of your advice today. We'll have a word with Kinky. She was going to find out about Julie MacAteer. Julie should be in later today to get her results.' He headed for the kitchen, stuffing a protesting Lady Macbeth under his arm like a rugby football. 'I'll bring the first customer back with me.'

With each case Barry's confidence grew. True to his word, O'Reilly offered no advice unless asked, and sat quietly on the examining couch.

Just before lunchtime, O'Reilly brought in Maureen Galvin, carrying baby Barry Fingal wrapped in a blue shawl.

'Good morning, Maureen,' Barry said. 'Is everything all right?'

'Dr Laverty, I'm worried about Barry Fingal's wee willy.' Maureen laid the little lad on the table, and unpinned a bulky towelling nappy.

'What has you worried?' Barry asked.

'It's under here.' She gently retracted the foreskin. 'It doesn't look right.'

Barry bent over to get a better look at the boy's tiny penis. 'Ah,' he said, smiling. 'Nothing there to be upset about.' He could see that Maureen looked dubious. 'That's what we call a hypospadias. It's quite common.'

Maureen frowned. 'Hypo . . . ?'

'Spadias. The urethral meatus, the little hole the pee comes through, is just a little bit underneath the glans instead of in the centre. Won't make a bit of difference.' Barry glanced at O'Reilly.

The big man put a hand on her shoulder. 'Are you worried, Maureen?'

She looked into his eyes and nodded.

'You'll be a damn sight more worried in sixteen years when he's after anything in California that wears a skirt. He'll be knocking rings round him. Up and down like a whore on hinges.'

Barry flinched. There was no need to be quite so crude.

'Thank you, Dr O'Reilly,' said Maureen, who was smiling broadly. She lifted Barry Fingal. 'You'll just be a randy wee goat, won't you?'

'He will that,' said O'Reilly. 'He'll be banging away like a buck rabbit.'

Fingal! Barry thought, but then he saw Maureen's clearly satisfied expression. He felt annoyed that he hadn't understood the real nature of her concern: how the boy would be able to function sexually when he grew up. She'd been too embarrassed to blurt it out. But O'Reilly had gone right to the heart of the matter, and in a language she clearly understood.

Maureen laughed. 'That's all I need to know.'

'Good,' said O'Reilly, 'but I should have spotted it the day he was born.'

'Och, we're none of us perfect,' said Maureen. 'There's no harm done.'

'Thank you,' said O'Reilly. 'I appreciate that.'

So do I, thought Barry. It takes an honest man to admit that he can make mistakes.

'Barry Fingal and me'd better be getting on, Doctor,' said Maureen.

'Right. How's Seamus by the way?'

'He said he'll pop round later with the glass for your window, and he's dreadful sorry he broke it. He's very busy. Him and his rocking ducks.' Her green eyes sparkled. 'He says you've fixed it up for him to sell the whole lot of them to a firm in Belfast. That we're going to make a mint.'

'I hope so,' said O'Reilly, leading her to the door.

As she left, Barry heard her singing, '"California here we come . . ."'

O'Reilly closed the surgery door. 'I hope to God she's right. I'll just have to put the screws on my friend tonight, or think of something else. And we're going to have to sort out Julie MacAteer. She's next.'

'What did the test say?'

O'Reilly grunted. 'Bloody typical.' He pulled an envelope, newly arrived with the morning's post, from his jacket pocket. 'Look at that.'

Barry read the results of an Aschheim-Zondek pregnancy test, in which a patient's urine is injected into immature female mice. '"Urine toxic. The mice died." Oh, great.'

'Right, and Mrs Kincaid's no further on finding out about the mystery woman of Ballybucklebo.' He blew out his cheeks. 'I'll go and get her.'

He returned moments later and offered Julie MacAteer a seat.

She sat, knees together, hands folded. 'Am I?' she asked, her voice steady.

'We don't know. The test didn't work. I'm really very sorry,' Barry said.

'My period's not come. I know I'm pregnant,' she said flatly.

'You may be right,' Barry said, 'but let's make sure.'

O'Reilly spoke quietly. 'We'll repeat the test. But in the meantime we've made arrangements for you to go to Liverpool. Just in case.'

'Liverpool?' Julie sat back in the chair. 'In England?'

'They'll take good care of you there. No one here need know.'

'I'd have to have the baby. Give it up?' Her tears flowed.

'Yes. It'll be hard on you,' O'Reilly said. 'I know that.'

She took two deep breaths. 'I've no choice, have I?'

'I'm sorry,' O'Reilly said gently. 'Unless you can tell us who the father is?'

Julie shook her head, tossing her corn-silk hair. 'No.' She stiffened her shoulders. 'Can I bring in a specimen this afternoon?'

'Yes,' said O'Reilly. 'Give it to Mrs Kincaid when you come back.'

'All right.' Julie sniffed. 'Liverpool. Jesus, Mary, and Joseph. I just knew I'd have to go away. I've already given my notice.'

'Oh?' said O'Reilly. 'And who's your boss?'

'I'm not telling.' She stood. 'I'd better be going.'

'I'll tell Mrs Kincaid to expect you,' O'Reilly said as he opened the door.

'FOUR O'CLOCK. Time I was going,' said O'Reilly. 'I've to pick up Donal and Bluebird and drive them up to Dunmore Park; then I'll go over to the Royal. See how Sonny's getting on. You just keep an eye on the shop until it's time for you to go out yourself.'

'I'll do my best.'

'I know that,' said O'Reilly, looking Barry in the eye. 'I told you I've been watching you, son. You've the makings of a damn good GP. And you have fun tonight. You've earned it.'

'Thanks, Fingal.' Barry knew he was grinning, but why not? Praise from O'Reilly was praise indeed.

Barry sat back in his chair. O'Reilly had been right. There was a great deal of satisfaction to be gained from the routine of a busy general practice. Still, being left alone was a little unnerving. He stood up and strolled over to the window just in time to see Julie MacAteer walk down the front path. She must have brought her urine specimen. Poor lass. Why wouldn't she tell her physicians who she worked for? Something worried away at the back of Barry's consciousness. Something that somebody had said about a maid giving her notice. An Antrim girl.

He hadn't heard Mrs Kincaid come in, and he jumped when she said, 'Would you like some tea, Dr Laverty?' She set a tray on the sideboard. 'I made it for that nice MacAteer girl, the wee lamb.'

'How is she, Mrs Kincaid?'

'She puts up a brave front, so. Very private. Himself asked me to try to find out about her.' She handed him a cup. 'Milk's in it, the way you like it.'

'Thanks.' Barry took the cup. 'And what have you discovered?'

'Not much. No one in the village seems to know her. But she works somewhere here, or out in the country a ways. Her hands are soft, so she'll not be working on a farm. Maybe she's in service.'

And then Barry remembered that it was Councillor Bishop who'd said his wife was fit to be tied because their maid had given her notice.

'Mrs Kincaid?'

'Dr Laverty, I'd be very pleased if you'd call me Kinky, like himself.'

Barry felt flattered. 'All right . . . Kinky. Could Julie MacAteer be working for the Bishops?'

Kinky's small black eyes narrowed. 'Aye, so. On Monday I'll be going to the Women's Union. Mrs Bishop's a member. I will ask her, so.'

'Good,' said Barry, finishing his tea. He heard the front doorbell. It might just be my first patient, he thought. 'I'll go,' he said.

A large, familiar-looking woman stood on the step. She wore a floral-patterned dress with the dimensions of a small tent. Barry noticed her white court shoes, over the edges of which the flesh of her ankles drooped.

'Dr Laverty? Could I have a wee word?'

'Certainly, Mrs . . . ?'

'Sloan. Cissie Sloan. I'm one of the tonics.' Her voice was rasping.

'Come into the surgery.' Barry stood aside to let her squeeze past. She was the one who'd been wearing her stays when O'Reilly had tried to inject her with vitamin B12.

'What can I do for you?' He closed the door and went to the swivel chair.

She perched her bulk on the patients' chair. 'Cold in here,' she said.

Barry was surprised that she felt cold as the room was overly warm.

'I feel the cold something chronic.'

'Do you? Is that why you came?'

She shook her head. 'I've been under Dr O'Reilly for six months and he's doing me no good. I come for a second opinion. He's away, isn't he?'

'Yes.' News travelled fast in Ballybucklebo, Barry thought.

'Donal Donnelly's my nephew. Him and his dog and Dr O'Reilly's away to Belfast. So I want *you* to tell me what's wrong with me.'

'I'll try. Can you give me a few clues?'

Barry, with great patience and with growing concern that the consultation would make him late for Patricia, managed to mine a few nuggets of clinically relevant information from the slag heap of Cissie's detailed reminiscences; reminiscences delivered in a husky, drearily slow monotone.

'I first took poorly on a Thursday. No. No. I'm wrong. It was the Wednesday that Donal's other dog died. The one with the wee short tail . . . So I said to Aggie, that's Aggie Arbuckle that was . . . now she's Mehaffey. Married to Hughie, him that's Maggie MacCorkle's second cousin . . . Anyway, Dr O'Reilly says to me . . . you know what he's like . . . you'd think he was Jehovah giving out the Commandments to Moses . . . he says to me, "You're run down, Cissie. You need a tonic." And here's me taking the tonic every six weeks for six months and I'm no better—'

'Right, Mrs Sloan.' Barry finally managed to stem the tide. 'Let's see if I've got this right. You've been tired for six months and it's getting worse?'

'Aye.'

'Muscle cramps?'

'Desperate. In my legs. And you'll not believe this, Doctor. I've been putting on weight.'

'Never,' said Barry, inwardly congratulating himself for being able to keep a straight face. 'Has any of your hair fallen out?'

'How did you know that?'

Barry ignored her question but asked, 'Are you constipated?'

'Constipated? I've been like an egg-bound hen for months.'

Barry peered at her face. Her complexion was pasty yellow, and there were puffy bags beneath both eyes. 'Let me have a look at your neck.' He placed his fingers over the front of her throat. Underneath the fat he could feel a solid, rubbery mass. Barry stepped back. She was right. She wasn't simply tired. She had all the classical manifestations of an underactive thyroid gland.

'What do you think, Doctor?'

Barry coughed. He was unsure how to answer her honestly and at the same time preserve O'Reilly's professional reputation.

'I'm not sure,' he said. 'We'll need to arrange a test at the hospital.'

'Have I cancer?'

It was possible, but her thyroid gland was smooth, not hard and craggy. 'I don't think so. I think your thyroid is a bit underactive.'

'Why'd O'Reilly not do the test?'

'Um . . .' Lord. The truth was he'd probably been in a hurry and had missed the diagnosis. 'It's new. I only heard about it this year. But if the test shows what I think it will, we'll need Dr O'Reilly to prescribe your treatment. He's much more experienced than I am. Now, I'll just go and make a phone call.'

AN IRISH COUNTRY DOCTOR | 225

The laboratory was still open when Barry phoned. Yes, they'd arrange for her to have a radioactive iodine uptake test.

'Here,' he said, handing her a requisition form. 'Monday morning, ten o'clock at the Royal. Go to the information desk. They'll show you to the lab.'

'Thank you, Dr Laverty sir.' She rose and left.

'My pleasure,' he said, and he meant it. He had been worried about being left all on his own, but unless something dramatic happened between now and half past six when he would leave to pick up Patricia, he would be quite happy to feel just a little smug.

Barry took one last look in the mirror. He brushed his hair, knowing that it was a futile gesture. Before long the tuft would be sticking up again like the crown of a broken hat. He glanced down. His shoes were newly polished and his corduroys pressed. He silently thanked Mrs Kin . . . no, Kinky.

He ran downstairs. The telephone began ringing as he cleared the last stair. He hesitated. O'Reilly had said to let Kinky take care of any calls. He lifted the receiver. 'Hello?'

'I want to speak to Dr O'Reilly.'

'I'm sorry. He's in Belfast. It's Dr Laverty. Who's speaking?'

'This is Mrs Fotheringham. It's very urgent. I want you to come at once. The major's been taken ill. Very ill.'

'What seems to be the trouble?' He glanced at his watch. Six fifteen.

'It's his neck. He's got a terrible pain in his neck.'

He *is* a terrible pain in the neck. 'Could it wait until the morning?'

'I want him seen now.'

Barry knew he couldn't justify sending for an ambulance for a man with a stiff neck. 'Very well,' he said. 'I'll be right over.'

'Don't be long.' The line went dead.

Barry raised his eyes to the heavens at Kinky, who had appeared from her kitchen. 'Major Fotheringham has a stiff neck. I'll nip round there.'

'I'll telephone your wee girl. Tell her you'll be late. What's her number?'

'Kinnegar 657334.'

'You run on, Doctor, and don't you worry. I'll take care of things here.'

Mrs Fotheringham opened the door. 'Come in, Laverty. The major's in the drawing room.' Her tone was haughty.

Barry followed her, amused by her changed attitude. On the last visit she had fawned over O'Reilly; now she was treating Barry like an underling.

'Major Fotheringham,' Barry said to his patient, who lay on a long sofa between two antimacassar-covered armchairs. 'How are you?'

The major put a limp hand to the left side of his neck. 'It's my neck,' he said. 'It's awfully stiff. It started this morning.'

'Were you doing anything when the stiffness started?' he asked.

'He was carrying stepladders,' Mrs Fotheringham said.

'You've probably just strained it.' Barry laid the back of his right hand on the major's forehead. Meningitis was one serious cause of neck stiffness, but then there'd be a fever, and the major's skin was cool and dry. The pulse rate was normal. 'Look into my eyes,' he said to the major. Both pupils were the same size. No early clues of increased pressure inside the head there.

Barry put a hand on the side of the major's neck. He could feel the tension in the sternocleidomastoid, the strap of muscle that runs from the clavicle to the base of the skull. It was probably torticollis, spasm of the muscle, which was frequently a manifestation of hysteria. He could see the clock. Twenty to seven. 'You've got a wry neck, Major Fotheringham.'

He saw Mrs Fotheringham's shoulders tense, her lips purse.

'Its correct name is torticollis,' he said, and he watched her relax. That was interesting. Technical terms had confused Maureen Galvin, but in Mrs Fotheringham's case it seemed that the old adage was true: bullshite *did* baffle brains. 'We'll soon put it right.' He opened his bag and pulled out an aerosol canister of ethyl chloride. 'This is pretty cold.' He depressed the red button and a cloud of vapour hissed out onto the skin.

'Wheee.' The major flinched as a thin rime of frost formed.

'Sorry, but it makes the muscles relax.' Barry stuffed the can back into his bag. 'If it's no better in the morning or if it gets worse, give us a call.'

The fact that Mrs Fotheringham called him Dr Laverty when she said goodbye was not lost on Barry.

BARRY DRUMMED his fingers on the steering wheel. It was nearly seven. He could only hope that Patricia would understand that not only was a doctor's time not always his own, but also that people did get stuck behind tractors on country roads. As the car crept along, he thought about the recent consultation. The only thing that bothered him was a niggling worry that perhaps his examination had been a bit hurried. He hadn't made a full neurological evaluation, testing skin sensation and reflexes, but that would have taken at least half an hour and almost certainly would have shown absolutely nothing. Stiff necks could have sinister causes, but most were rare as hen's teeth.

And that bloody tractor up ahead was going at the speed of a badly dam-aged snail. Blast. He saw the tractor's driver stick out his right arm. Barry braked. The tractor swerved right, then, as if having second thoughts, turned a good 120 degrees and went into a field on the left-hand side of the road.

Barry trod on the accelerator. Brunhilde's engine's spluttered, wheezed . . . and died. Damnation. He knew he could have written his entire knowledge of the working of the internal combustion engine on a postage stamp. He turned the key, to be rewarded by a grinding of the starter motor—a grind-ing that became fainter as the battery began to expire.

Lips pursed, he climbed out. The tractor was nosing back out onto the road.

'Hello,' Barry yelled, gratified to see the Massey-Harris halt and to recog-nise the driver, who'd come in last week for some liniment for sore knees. 'Sorry to bother you, Mr O'Hara, but do you know anything about engines?'

'Aye.'

'Could you take a look at mine?'

'Aye.' He leaned into the car and Barry heard the click of a catch being released. O'Hara rolled to the front of the car and lifted the bonnet.

He sprang back. 'Boys-a-dear!' His eyes were wide, his mouth agape, then he turned and stared along the road. 'Your engine's fallen out, Doctor.'

Barry had to smile. 'The engine's in the back in a Volkswagen. Let me show you.' He walked to the back of the car and lifted the louvred engine cover.

'There's a power of architecture about thon,' O'Hara said. 'I'll just give her a wee try.' He moved to the driver's door and peered inside. 'Excuse me, Doctor, but take a look at thon gauge. Engines go better if there's a wee taste of petrol in the tank.'

'Oh, no! And I'm late.'

'I could give you a lift to Paddy Farrelly's garage.'

'Would you?'

'Aye.' He set off and Barry followed. His watch said ten past seven.

Now he was going to be much later. Would Patricia understand?

EIGHT THIRTY. Barry's trousers were stained from the tractor's muddy seat and his hands stank of petrol. The door opened. 'I'm sorry I'm late.'

She laughed. 'It's all right. Your Mrs Kincaid phoned.' She kissed his lips, a short chaste kiss like brother to sister, yet he closed his eyes and savoured the perfumed taste of her. 'So did you save a life?'

'A life? One life? I eradicated bubonic plague from the hinterland of Ballybucklebo, brought a moribund malingerer back from the brink.'

'Stop it.' She laughed. 'You are very late. It must have been important.'

'Not exactly. Some hypochondriac with a stiff neck. It didn't take long to sort him out. Then my car ran out of petrol. I had to get a lift on a tractor. That's why . . .' He gestured at his dirty trousers. 'Look, we'd better get moving. The kitchen at the club closes at nine.'

'No need. I phoned them and cancelled. I've made us a bite. Why don't you go and have a wash?'

What a girl, he thought to himself as he scrubbed his hands. Beautiful, self-possessed and able to accept and adapt to changing circumstances.

When he returned, Patricia was in the kitchen. 'You really don't mind?'

'I like cooking. It's hardly your fault you had to do your job. And it's the first time I've heard of a fellow running out of petrol on his way to a date.'

'I know. I usually arrange that for the drive home.'

'Well, you'll not be able to try that one on tonight.'

'Me? Try it on? Never.' He reached for her but she moved away.

He did not pursue her. He wandered into the sitting room. Books were neatly stacked on shelves improvised from planks laid on piles of bricks. Many were engineering texts, but he also saw works of Steinbeck, Tolkien and—what a strange title—*The Feminine Mystique* by a Betty Friedan. A table was set for two, close to a window overlooking Belfast Lough.

Patricia came in with a dish and two plates.

'Nice place you have here,' he said.

'Thank you.' She put a record on a gramophone.

Barry listened as a soprano sang in what he guessed was Italian. The notes swelled, rose and fell in cadences that touched something deep in him.

'What's that? It's beautiful.' And so was she, standing there, backlit by the light reflected from the lough's calm waters.

'Mozart,' she said. 'It's "*Voi che sapete*" from *The Marriage of Figaro*.'

'It's amazing.'

'I hope you like lasagne,' she said.

'I had one once . . . but the wheels fell off.'

'Idiot.' She chuckled. 'It's Italian cooking.'

'Oh.'

'Italian music. Italian food and Italian wine.' She handed him a corkscrew. 'Open it, would you?' She indicated a bottle of Chianti.

'All we need now are a couple of strolling mandolin players to make this a *Bella Notte*.'

'You speak Italian?'

'Not at all, but I've seen *Lady and the Tramp.*'

'Eejit.' Her laughter filled the little room. 'Women should beware of men who make them laugh. I'll have to keep an eye on you, Barry Laverty.'

And I'll keep mine on you, Patricia, he thought, seeing the curve of her breast and the slimness of her waist and not noticing her limp at all.

'THAT,' HE SAID, laying his knife and fork on a tomato-smeared plate, 'was great.' He sipped the dark red wine, tasting Tuscan sunshine. 'Great.'

'Glad you liked it.' She lifted their plates. 'I'll just be a minute. Sit where you are. These can soak in the sink.'

Barry, replete, stretched his legs in front of him.

Patricia reappeared and bent over the gramophone. 'This is my very favourite,' she said. 'Listen.'

It was a duet. Two sopranos with voices like liquid silver and molten gold, now flowing together, now parting, always in harmony.

'It's "The Flower Duet" from Delibes's *Lakme.*'

He stood and put his hands on her waist, and she leaned against him. He lifted the hair from the nape of her neck and kissed her. He heard her breathing quicken as he turned her to face him, holding her close, feeling the softness of her. He kissed her slowly, deeply, and his hand found her breast, firm through the silk. She whimpered. He fumbled with the top button. He felt her hand on his wrist as she moved away.

'Not yet, Barry. Please. Don't spoil it.' Her voice was low.

Barry swallowed. 'All right.' Had he scared her? Had he been too fast?

'I'm sorry, Barry. I want to, but . . . not yet. Not tonight.'

He stroked her hair. 'I understand.' The hell he did. He knew that she wanted him as much as he wanted her.

'Thank you.' She led him to a small sofa. 'Barry.' She hesitated. 'Barry, I think I could fall in love with you, but I'm not sure I'm ready. It's not about sex. It's about me. I want to be an engineer. I haven't time to fall in love.'

'I have.' He knew that he was in love, in love to the depths of his soul.

'You don't understand,' she said. 'I want to do a man's job in a man's world, so I have to work twice as hard. You know what it took for you to get through medical school.'

'But I still had time for a bit of fun. I had time for a girlfriend.'

'I don't . . . for a boyfriend, I mean. Not a serious one. I daren't fall behind.' She stood up, her arms folded. He could tell by the set of her jaw that arguments would be futile.

'I'd better go.' His words were more clipped than he had intended.

'Please . . . please don't be angry.'

He stood. 'Did you ever hear the words of that old song? "Dance, balle-rina, dance . . . and just ignore the chair that's empty in the second row"?'

'What are you trying to say?' A tiny edge crept into her voice.

'The dancer gave up the man who loved her for the sake of her career. She regretted it.'

'And you think I will?' She moved away from him.

'Honestly, Patricia, I don't know . . . but *I* will.'

He waited for her to say something, anything, but she had half turned to stare into the dark night.

'All right.' He walked to the door. 'Thank you for a lovely dinner.' His words were politely cold.

'Barry, I . . . I'd still like to see you again.' She moved closer to him.

To tell me that your career is more important? To hold out a hope and dash it again? 'I'll not be free again for a couple of weeks.'

'Will you phone me?'

He hesitated. No. There'd be no future in getting his hopes up.

'Please?' She kissed him and he held her.

'I'll phone,' he said and swallowed, telling himself he was being stupid. But there could never be another Patricia. Not for him.

I Fall to Pieces

'**Y**ou've a face on you like a Lurgan spade,' O'Reilly said, referring to the extra-long turf-cutting implement peculiar to that town in County Armagh. 'Bad night?'

'Not really.' Barry sipped his tea and stared out through the putty-smudged pane of glass that Seamus Galvin had installed in the dining-room window. Yes, it had been a bad nigh, but he saw no reason to confide in O'Reilly.

'Kinky said that you were busy.'

'I saw Cissie Sloan.' Barry hesitated. 'And I think you're wrong about her.' He studied O'Reilly's face.

'Is that a fact?'

'I'm sure she has hypothyroidism.' Barry quickly listed her symptoms.

'You might just be right.' O'Reilly went to the sideboard and helped himself to a kipper. 'Good lad.'

Emboldened, Barry said, 'I'm sending her for a radioactive iodine uptake on Monday.'

'Better and better.' O'Reilly tucked into the butter-dripping kipper. 'If you *are* right, it'll do wonders for your reputation.'

'What about yours?'

O'Reilly grunted. 'I'm big enough and ugly enough to look after myself. Kinky said you went to see Major Fotheringham.'

'Another false alarm. Torticollis. I gave him a squirt of ethyl chloride and told him to call us if there was no improvement.'

'Jesus,' said O'Reilly. 'One day that man *will* have something wrong and we'll miss it. He'll not have just cried wolf. Since I've known him, he's roared on as if he was being attacked by a whole bloody pack.' He chuckled. 'I always liked the wolves. *Canis lupus*, to give them their Latin name.'

'I know. You've one of their descendants, *Canis familiaris*, in your backyard.' Far too familiar, Barry thought.

'Good old Arthur,' O'Reilly said fondly. 'And by God, I'd a lot of fun with another canine last night.'

'Donal's Bluebird?'

'The darling dog excelled herself. She won in the third at twenty to one.'

Barry's fork stopped. 'And I suppose you'd backed her.'

'Wouldn't you have if you'd had inside information?'

Barry savoured a morsel of kipper, swallowed and said, 'All that business about running on water, then running dry? Fingal, would you explain?'

'Look. At the races a bunch of dogs rush round an oval track chasing an electrical hare. After a few races the bookies figure out the likelihood of any given dog winning and on that basis offer odds. When there's money involved, people will always try to fiddle the system. It's not been above some of the doggy fraternity to help their contender along a bit.'

'How?'

'Stimulant drugs. That's why all dogs that place are immediately tested.' He held a finger to his bent nose. 'But they don't test the losing animals. What do you think the odds will be after a dog has come last in half a dozen races?'

'Relatively good.'

'See, you're beginning to understand.'

'The hell I am.'

'Water,' said O'Reilly conspiratorially. 'When Donal told me the dog had been running on water, he meant that he'd kept her thirsty until immediately before each one of her previous outings. Just before the race he let her have all she wanted to drink. No dog can run when it's waterlogged.'

'So the odds go down?'

'Right. And when Donal said the dog would run dry last night . . . No water. No handicap. Great odds and not a thing to show up on a drug test.'

'But isn't that dishonest?'

'Totally, absolutely and utterly, but it keeps the bookies humble.'

'How much did you bet?'

'Twenty quid.'

Barry whistled. That's almost as much as I make in a week, he thought. He then did the arithmetic. 'But that means you won four hundred pounds.'

'Indeed,' said O'Reilly, 'but it's going to a good cause.'

The Fingal Flahertie O'Reilly Benevolent Fund, Barry thought. 'And I suppose to top it off, Sonny's better and your friend is going to buy Seamus Galvin's rocking ducks. You said you were going to see Sonny.'

'And so I did. He's off oxygen. Temperature's normal. Unfortunately my business friend doesn't want Galvin's ducks. He's probably still laughing about them. Can't say I blame him really. But I'm sure something will turn up for Seamus.' He winked at Barry. 'I asked His Lordship if you could have a day or two's fishing on his water. "Anytime," he said.'

'Thank you, Fingal.'

'I presume you'll be spending a bit of time there soon.'

'Why do you say that?'

O'Reilly pushed his plate away. 'Young fellows who've been out on dates with beautiful young women generally beam a bit the following morning. You are decidedly deficient in the beaming department. I'd guess you and Patricia didn't hit it off.'

Barry was about to tell O'Reilly to mind his own business, but when he looked at the big man he saw nothing but kindness in his eyes. 'You could say that,' he said quietly.

'I just did. You'll get over it. But it'll take time. I know.'

I know you do, Barry thought. As he wondered how to reply he heard the telephone ringing in the hall.

'If it's one of the customers, I'll go, Barry.'

'Thanks, Fingal, I—'

Mrs Kincaid burst in. 'It's Mrs Fotheringham. She says to come at once. Her husband's unconscious.'

O'REILLY HURLED the Rover along the narrow road. Barry tried to answer O'Reilly's questions and keep an eye on the road. As the car slid out of a blind corner onto a straight section, Barry noticed a cyclist in the distance.

'Tell me again. Exactly what did you find when you examined him?' O'Reilly's fists grasped the steering wheel and he stared ahead.

'Not much. Bit of spasm in the left neck muscles. His pupils were equal in size, not dilated or constricted.'

'What about his reflexes?'

Barry was temporarily distracted. As the car came within a few yards of the cyclist—Barry recognised Donal Donnelly's ginger hair—the rider's mouth opened and he hurled himself and his rusty machine into the ditch.

'Fingal, you nearly hit Donal Donnelly.'

'Nearly doesn't count. What about Fotheringham's reflexes?'

'I didn't test them. I thought Fotheringham was up to his usual tricks.'

'I'd probably have done the same.'

'Would you?'

'Probably.' O'Reilly stamped on the brakes. 'Out. Open the gate.'

Barry obeyed, waited for the car to pass, and ran up the now familiar gravel drive into the Fotheringhams' house. He caught a glimpse of O'Reilly disappearing into the upstairs bedroom and raced up the stairs.

O'Reilly sat on the side of the four-poster taking the pulse of a clearly unconscious Major Fotheringham and barking questions at his wife.

'Dr Laverty sprayed his neck, and the pain got better?'

'That's right. Basil said the spray was working, but his head had started to feel funny so he thought he'd go to bed. He was still asleep when I got up. I was going to bring his breakfast up to him, but I heard him calling for me.'

'When did he vomit?'

Barry was aware of the acrid smell. Stiff neck, headache, vomiting, coma. It couldn't be.

'I came back up, and he said he thought someone had hit him on the head.' She sniffled. 'I told him not to be silly . . . then he boked.'

Barry could see the lines in the textbook, word for word, the ones he'd memorised before his finals: 'and headache may be so abrupt in onset as to make the patient think he has been struck'. God Almighty.

O'Reilly produced a penlight and bent to examine the major's eyes. 'Right pupil's fixed,' he said.

Barry exhaled. Major Fotheringham had suffered an intracranial haemorrhage. And his stiff neck last night had been the earliest sign.

'I'm afraid your husband's had a kind of stroke.'

Mrs Fotheringham crossed her arms and rocked back and forth, all the while making little keening noises.

And if I'd not been in a rush . . . Barry's thoughts were interrupted when O'Reilly said, 'I'm sorry Dr Laverty didn't make the diagnosis last night.' Barry stiffened. 'But I doubt if anyone could have.'

'I know. He was very nice.' She forced a tiny smile.

Barry blessed the older man for his support. What O'Reilly had said would have been true if last night's examination had been thorough, if he had tested the reflexes and found them to be normal. But that hadn't happened.

'Right,' said O'Reilly. 'We'll have to get him to the Royal.'

'Is he going to die?' Mrs Fotheringham asked.

O'Reilly nodded his shaggy head. 'I'll not lie to you. He could.'

Mrs Fotheringham yelped and stuffed a fist into her mouth.

'He could live but be paralysed. But until the specialists have done a test called a lumbar puncture, and maybe take special X-rays, we'll not know what's caused it.' Maybe it's just a bleeding aneurysm, Barry thought, and heard O'Reilly echo the idea. 'If it's just a leak from a thin-walled blood vessel, they can usually operate. Some patients make a complete recovery.'

'Really?' Barry saw hope in her eyes.

'Yes. But I won't make any promises. Dr Laverty, would you phone for the ambulance?'

'I WONDER WHERE Lady Macbeth is?' O'Reilly remarked, walking directly to the sideboard in the upstairs sitting room.

Barry neither knew nor cared.

O'Reilly handed him a tumbler of Irish whiskey. 'Get that into you.'

'I'd rather have a sherry.' Or perhaps some hemlock, Barry thought.

It had been more than an hour since Major Fotheringham and his wife had been dispatched to the Royal. O'Reilly had driven back home. They had exchanged few words.

'That's a medicinal whiskey. Sit down, drink up and shut up.'

Barry sat. The whiskey was peat-flavoured, sharp on his tongue.

O'Reilly fired up his briar and lowered himself into the other armchair. He looked Barry in the eye and said, 'I'm disappointed.'

Barry flinched. 'There's no point making excuses. So I won't.'

'Excuses? What for?'

'I was in a hurry. I didn't do a complete neurological examination.'

'And if you had, what do you think it would have shown?'

'Enough so that I could have got him to a hospital before the bleeding into his head got any worse.'

'Maybe, but what did his wife say?' O'Reilly took a pull from his glass.

'What do you mean?'

'Everything blew up this morning. Hours after you were there. If he'd had a decent bleed last night, don't you think it would have been as plain as the nose on your face? But he hadn't bled and it wasn't plain.'

'I was wrong last night.'

'And that's why I'm disappointed.'

'Because I didn't do my job right?'

O'Reilly stood and loomed over Barry. 'No, you buck eejit. You knew your patient's history of malingering. You went to see him, and you didn't have to. You could have been late for your big date. Fotheringham would have been no worse off if you hadn't been conscientious enough to go last night and we'd not gone out there till this morning.'

'It's still no excuse.'

'Christ, man. Who do you think you are? Hippocrates? Listen, what makes you think you're the only physician to make mistakes? Do you think missing Cissie Sloan's buggered-up thyroid and the Galvin baby's hypospadias are the only bollocks I've ever made?'

'Well, I—'

'Of course not. And not living up to your own personal standards last night may seem like the end of the world to you. It's not. You'll make mistakes. You're beating the holy bejasus out of yourself because you think you should be infallible. That's why I'm disappointed. You should know better than that. Go easy on yourself.'

Barry looked up at the big man. The hint of a smile was at the corner of his lips as he said, 'How long have you been here?'

'Two weeks.'

'That's long enough for me. I've told you, you've the makings of a damn good GP. But you'll never last if you insist on taking everything to heart.'

'I still think I could've done a better job.'

'Yes,' said O'Reilly levelly, 'but you recognise it and that's to your credit. What happened can't be helped. Learn from it and put it behind you.'

Barry could not honestly say that he felt as if a weight had been lifted from his shoulders, but somehow the pressure seemed to be less.

A huge grin erupted on O'Reilly's face and Barry had to smile back.

'Good man, Barry.' O'Reilly finished his whiskey and looked at his watch. 'It's only two o'clock. Why don't you grab your rod and head down to His Lordship's? Nothing like a few hours in the open air, away from whatever you do for a living, to give you a chance to get your mind straightened out.'

'I'd like that, Fingal.'

'So off you go. Kinkie'll make you some sandwiches. Forget about Fotheringham. Forget about your broken heart. I'll look after the shop and, Barry, would you do me a favour?'

'Of course.'

'Take Arthur Guinness with you. He loves an afternoon by the river.'

BARRY, ROD IN HAND and hip waders buckled to his belt, let himself out through the back door. At least if the dog had a go at Barry's leg, this time he was well dressed for the occasion. 'Here, Arthur.'

The big dog lolloped from his doghouse, poised ready to mount Barry's leg, hesitated, sniffed the rubber boots and turned away with a look of disdain.

'Heel.'

Arthur looked at Barry and sat.

'Don't sit. Heel. *Heel*, you great lummox.'

To Barry's surprise the big labrador rose and stood behind Barry's left leg. He kept his muzzle there as Barry walked down the garden to the lane.

Barry opened Brunhilde's back door. 'Get in.'

'Aarff,' said Arthur, obeying immediately.

Barry shut the door, climbed in, and drove out of Ballybucklebo and along the shore road. He was just about to pass Maggie's cottage when he saw her, sitting in a deck chair surrounded by Sonny's dogs.

He braked and wound down the window. 'How are you today, Miss MacCorkle? Dr O'Reilly saw Sonny last night. He's on the mend.'

Maggie said, 'I should hope so. Then he can come and take these flea-ridden beasts away.' But she fondled a dog's head and grinned toothlessly. 'I wonder did the pneumonia cure his stubborn streak?'

'Now that I couldn't tell, Miss MacCorkle.'

'If it did, it would be a miracle. Well, thanks for dropping by.'

'My pleasure.' Barry put the Volkswagen into gear and pulled away.

He drove past a red-brick gatehouse that stood guard over two high wrought-iron gates, each bearing the crest of the Marquis of Ballybucklebo. A long drive led to the Big House. O'Reilly had said that the first fork to the right led to the river—a rutted lane that disappeared beneath huge elms.

The car jolted along until, leaving the small wood behind, Barry found himself in a meadow, where the lane petered out.

He parked and lifted his gear from the car. Arthur leapt out and began to quarter the ground ahead of Barry, running to the left, then to the right, nose to the ground, tail thrashing. Barry followed the dog through knee-high grass until he could see up ahead the waters of the Bucklebo. He lengthened his stride, clumsy in the waders.

'Heel, Arthur.' Barry did not want the dog to disturb the water. Trout, he knew, were easily scared. To his surprise Arthur obeyed instantly.

Barry stood and studied the water. The current flowed gently from his left to his right. On the far side he saw the still, dark waters of what must be a deep pool shaded by the branches of a willow. Trout would lurk there.

'Come on, Arthur.'

Barry walked slowly upstream. Something about the solitude of a river bank was soothing. Was it the gurgling of the water, the distant lowing of a herd of Aberdeen Angus grazing on the far bank, the susurration of a breeze in the willow leaves? Whatever it was, the river bank was a place for reflection, a haven where Barry could look into his thoughts and decide whether O'Reilly was right about learning from a mistake and moving on. Or whether the calamity, as Barry saw it, of Major Fotheringham was a clear indication that general practice was the wrong choice, that a speciality with little or no contact with patients might suit his temperament better.

He stopped, sensing movement on the river's surface. A series of concentric rings were spreading outwards, exactly where he had anticipated that a fish might be lying. If he was going to catch a trout, this was the time. His difficulties could wait. The mayfly were hatching.

'How did you make out?' O'Reilly asked.

Barry grinned, parked his rod, opened the creel, produced two shining brown trout and dumped them into the kitchen sink.

'Not bad,' said O'Reilly. He opened a drawer, took out a knife and handed it to Barry. 'You caught 'em. You gut 'em.'

'Fair enough.' Barry turned on the cold tap, took the first fish and expertly slit it open, dragging the guts out with the fingers of one hand.

'That was slick,' said O'Reilly. 'Ever consider a career in surgery?'

Barry shook his head. 'No, but I did think over what you said.' Barry laid the cleaned fish aside and reached for the other. 'I didn't do all I could have for Fotheringham, but you're right. I will try to put it behind me.'

'Good lad. "To err is human." '

' "To forgive, divine." ' Barry sliced into the second fish. 'Alexander Pope.'

'And you'll be pleased to hear that the Divinity must have been keeping an eye on you. Fotheringham had a small aneurysm. The surgeon reckons he got it tied off and that the major should make a reasonable recovery.'

Barry's fingers stopped moving. He turned and saw that O'Reilly was smiling. 'Honestly?'

'Honestly.' O'Reilly flapped a hand at the counter, where Lady Macbeth sat eyeing the two trout. 'Now,' he said, 'tomorrow's Sunday. No surgery. I'd like to nip up to Belfast . . . see if I can't do something about those damn rocking ducks. Think you could manage on your own?'

Barry hesitated.

'Best thing you could do. Just like falling off a horse. Most riders think it's a good idea to get back into the saddle as soon as possible.' He turned. 'I'm off upstairs. Come and have a jar when you've cleaned yourself up.'

Barry stood holding the fish, grateful to O'Reilly for his understanding. He opened the door of the fridge, took a deep breath, looked up to the ceiling and muttered a thankyou, unsure whether the thanks were for Major Fotheringham's good fortune or for his own second chance.

THE NEXT MORNING Barry stood in the recess of the bay window. The rain was lashing down, blackening the tiles of the steeple opposite and drenching the members of the congregation, most of whom were hurrying away on foot. He saw Kinky cross the road and felt the door slam as she let herself in.

He heard the phone jangle below. The ringing stopped. Kinky must have taken the call. If someone needed him, he hoped it would be a simple case. O'Reilly had left an hour ago.

'Dr Laverty?'

He walked to the door.

'There's some foreign gentleman says he has to speak with you, so.'

'Right.' Downstairs. He took the receiver. 'Dr Laverty.'

'Crikey. Is it being the great, healing sahib?' The man's muffled voice had the singsong cadence of what was known as Bombay Welsh. 'I am very much wishing to consult the man of medicine, Dr Lavatory.'

Barry laughed. 'Stop buggering about, Mills. You're not Peter Sellers.'

'But I am tinking it is a pretty damn good impression of his Mr Banerjee, isn't it? How the hell are you, mate? What are you up to today?'

'I'm on call.'

'I'm not . . . for once. I thought I'd take a trip down to see you.'

'That'd be great. Hang on.' He turned. 'Kinky, could you manage lunch for two?'

'Aye, so.'

'Come and have lunch.' Barry gave directions.

'Great. I'll see you in about an hour.' The phone went dead.

Barry said to Kinky, 'Jack Mills is an old friend of mine. He'll be here in about an hour. Look after him, will you, Kinky, if I have to go out?'

'I will, so.' She bustled off to her kitchen, pausing only to ask, 'Would you like them fishes for your lunch?'

'Yes, please.' Barry went back upstairs. He lifted the *Sunday Telegraph* from the coffee table, found the cryptic crossword puzzle and settled into the chair, welcoming Lady Macbeth when she jumped into his lap.

HE PUT THE PAPER ASIDE. Except for six down, he had managed to finish the cryptic. 'Go on, cat.' He stood and let Lady Macbeth slip to the floor. Outside, the rain had become a steady mizzle and Ballybucklebo lay grey and gloomy under its damp shroud.

He hunted through O'Reilly's record collection. Beethoven, Beatles, Glenn Miller, *Le Nozze di Figaro*—surely that was the opera Patricia'd played on Friday night? He read the track list, looking for '*Voi che* something or other'. There it was. He put the record on the turntable and swung the needle over to the right groove. The notes filled the room, bittersweet, matching his mood. Perhaps he'd phone her tonight.

'If that one would get off the cat's tail, maybe it would stop howling.'

Barry turned to see Jack Mills standing in the doorway.

'Your housekeeper let me in. Jesus, what a miserable day.' Jack shook his head, scattering droplets from his dark hair. 'Good to see you, mate.'

'And you.'

'Could you turn that thing off! Sounds like a sick cat to me.'

Barry laughed. 'You've no culture, Mills.'

'Yes, I do . . . but it's agriculture.' Jack glanced over to the sideboard. 'Any chance of a jar? That John Jameson's looks good.'

Barry poured. 'Here.'

'You not having one?'

'The customers take a dim view if you show up smelling of booze.'

Jack gazed round the room, sipping his drink. 'Looks like your boss knows how to look after himself.'

'He's a decent man. Damn good doctor.'

'That's the word at the Royal. They reckon he was pretty quick off the mark getting that aneurysm in the other morning. Another couple of hours and . . .' Jack drew one finger across his throat.

Barry pursed his lips. 'Actually it was my fault. I misdiagnosed Major Fotheringham. The bloke with the aneurysm.'

'Don't be daft.'

'No, it's true. The night before I'd seen him for a stiff neck. I never even thought that he might be bleeding into his head. He could've died.'

'I wouldn't worry about it. We can't get them right every time. In fact, I thought we were going to lose that appendix of yours.'

'Jeannie Kennedy? Would it not have bothered you?'

'If she'd died?' Jack swirled the whiskey round in his glass. 'Honestly?'

'Honestly.'

'I don't really think so. I'd have been annoyed that the surgery hadn't gone as planned, but when they're asleep under the sterile drapes you don't really think about them as people. You can't.'

'Why not?'

'It would be too damn difficult to stick the scalpel in and rummage about in their innards as if you were gutting a fish.'

Barry had a vivid mental image of last night's trout's intestines being washed down the sink. 'I don't think I'm cut out to be a surgeon.'

Jack groaned. 'That's awful. "Cut out to be a surgeon." ' His face wrinkled into a great smile, and Barry couldn't help smiling with his friend.

'THAT THERE TROUT,' said Jack in the accents of Belfast's dockland, 'was cracker, so it was. Dead-on. Bloody wheeker.'

'I take it you approve?' Barry smiled. Jack Mills hadn't changed, not since they'd met eleven years before. Solid. Dependable. Never serious for long.

'Isn't that what I just said?'

'I caught them yesterday.'

'So you do get a bit of time off?'

'A bit.'

'Have you seen that bird you were telling me about?'

Barry's smile faded. 'Patricia? I don't think she'd be too happy to hear you call her a bird. She's an engineering student.'

'Good God. What is the world coming to? The next thing you know women'll be playing rugby.'

'I doubt it. Mind you, she's pretty single-minded about her engineering. She told me on Friday night that she didn't want to get serious. Her career was too important.' He glanced over at Jack.

'And you did? Want to get serious?'

Barry nodded.

'Oh Jesus. Is it getting to you, mate?'

'A bit.'

'You poor bugger. So what are you going to do about it?'

'I'm not sure. She asked me to phone her. I thought I might tonight.'

'I wouldn't. Remember when you tried to teach me about fly-fishing? You said that trout would be scared off if we rushed up to the river bank, that we'd have to stalk them, move up quietly, take our time?'

'So I should take my time with Patricia?'

'Definitely. If she's serious and doesn't want to see you again, you'll not hear from her. If she does want to see you again, she'll call.'

'Do you really think so?'

'It worked for me with that blonde staff nurse. Remember?' Jack rose and handed Barry a now empty whiskey glass. 'Now could you find the other half of this? A bird can't fly on one wing.'

O'REILLY CLOSED the door to the packed waiting room. 'We'll have to do something. I'm not up to facing all the woes of the world this morning.'

Barry wasn't surprised. He'd gone to bed last night, after a surprisingly call-free day, before O'Reilly had returned. Nor had Barry been graced with the big man's presence at breakfast. No doubt the little red veins in the whites of his eyes, the bags underneath, bore silent testimony to the reason he'd not appeared until moments before the surgery was supposed to open.

'What can we do? Ask some of them to go home?'

O'Reilly grunted, opened the door wide and asked, 'Who's first?'

'Me, Doctor sir.' A short, cloth-capped man rose. He wore a red scarf round his throat and had a cough, dry and hacking.

'Come on then, Francis Xavier.'

'Your turn,' said O'Reilly, massaging his temple with one hand as he did so. 'I've a bit of a strong weakness today.'

Barry took the swivel chair. 'What can I do for you, Mr . . .?'

'Francis Xavier Mac Mhuireadhaigh.'

Barry looked helplessly at O'Reilly.

'Francis Xavier Murdoch,' O'Reilly translated.

'Frankie it is, sir,' said the little man, whipping off his cap to reveal a bald pate. 'Frankie it is.'

'What brought you here today?' said Barry.

'I walked. My bike's broke, so it is.'

'Why have you come to see us?' Some Ulster folk could be rather literal.

'I've a terrible wheeze in my thrapple.' Frankie coughed.

'Sore throat?' Although Barry might not speak Irish, the local dialect posed no difficulties.

'Aye. For about a sennight.'

'A week? Anything else bothering you?'

'Just my nut. I tried rubbing it with salt herrings but it was no use.'

'I don't think there's much we can do for baldness, Frankie.'

'Aye, but if a storm's lifted the thatch, it lets the cold in and that goes to your thrapple.' One knobby hand massaged his pate, the other his throat.

'Let's have a look.' Barry lifted a tongue depressor. 'Open wide. Say aah.' The man's throat was red, flecked with yellow spots.

'It's infected, Frankie.' Barry scribbled on a prescription pad. 'Penicillin. Take one four times a day for a week. Pop in in a week if you're no better.'

'I will, sir.' Frankie rose.

O'Reilly steered Frankie out of the surgery. Barry did not hear the front door closing, and when O'Reilly returned, he carefully shut the surgery door. He held a finger to his lips and grinned at Barry.

The hairs on the nape of Barry's neck twitched when O'Reilly started howling, a moan that started low and ran through two octaves. The screeching was interrupted by O'Reilly's yells of 'Jesus, Doctor, give over. Mercy. Mercy.' O'Reilly strode out of the surgery. The front door slammed, and there was no gentility in the way he closed the door to the surgery on his return.

'What—?'

'We'll just wait five minutes,' O'Reilly whispered. 'Then when you go back to the waiting room, half the ones with nothing wrong with them will have taken to their heels.' He rubbed his forehead. 'I told you I couldn't face those multitudes today.' He walked to the door. 'You'll have an easy morning of it now. I'm off for a while.'

Barry watched the big man go. Fingal Flahertie O'Reilly, he thought, there's no doubt you're different, but it's certainly not dull working here.

When he opened the door to the waiting room, only a handful of patients remained and all eyed him with looks of silent fear. He could tell that not one of them, not one, stood the remotest chance of getting the upper hand.

O'REILLY'S TEMPER had improved somewhat by the time they left to make the afternoon's home visits. Their itinerary took them high into the Ballybucklebo Hills to see a farmer who was recuperating after being crushed several weeks previously when his tractor had rolled over. Their route back down passed the Six Road Ends. Crops that had still been green when Barry sought directions from Donal Donnelly were golden now, whiskery barley bowing and shining in the afternoon sunlight.

O'Reilly slowed as the car passed Sonny's junk yard. The roofless house looked forlorn and weeds were high among the scrap metal and ageing cars.

'What we need,' he said, 'is something to make that all-around gobshite, Councillor Bertie Bishop, come to some accommodation with Sonny. Sonny'll be discharged in a few days.' O'Reilly accelerated again.

'Fingal! Look out for that cyclist.'

O'Reilly swerved. When the Rover came back on course, Barry decided to say no more until they reached their destination.

Further down the road, O'Reilly turned into a council housing estate, where two-storey terraced houses scowled at each other across streets so narrow that at three o'clock the sunlight had gone. He braked. 'You'll not have seen what I'm going to show you next. Come on.'

A woman wearing a calico apron and fluffy slippers let them in. Barry noticed that her bare shins were mottled with a network of brown lines, a sure sign of poverty. With no other heating in the winter for their draughty, damp houses, the poor huddled in front of tiny, smoky coal fires that in some mysterious way provoked the mottling on the fronts of the legs.

'How's Hughey today?' O'Reilly enquired.

'He's out in the back yard, Doctor. There's still a wee taste of sunshine there and he loves the warmth, so he does.'

Barry wondered, as they passed through a small kitchen, why the woman picked up a tin tray and a spoon.

The back yard was typical: a cramped slab of cracked concrete hemmed in by low red-brick walls. A man in a frayed cardigan and moleskin trousers stood at the far end, bent over a wooden box where impatiens bloomed, red and white and violet. He didn't turn as they approached, which surprised Barry because O'Reilly's boots clattered on the concrete.

The woman went up to the man and tapped him on the shoulder. He spun round and looked at O'Reilly.

'How's about ye, Doctor?' The man's face, leathery brown but for several white puckered scars, broke into a grin.

'How are you, Hughey?'

The man cupped a hand behind one ear. 'What?' Hughey frowned and shook his head. 'Hit the bloody tray, Doreen.'

Barry jumped when Doreen belaboured the tray with the spoon.

'I said, How are you, Hughey? Are you managing with your medicine?' O'Reilly roared at his patient.

'I'm bravely. But them eardrops aren't worth a tinker's damn.' Barry could hardly make out the man's words above the constant clanging.

'Sorry to hear that,' O'Reilly yelled. 'Maybe you'd better stop using them. Pity they didn't work.'

'Och, what can't be cured must be endured.' Hughey gave Doreen a sideways glance. 'At least I don't have to pay any heed to her craking on.'

'Away off and feel your head,' she said and pecked his cheek. 'I'll not bang this wee drum for you any more.' And mercifully she stopped. 'So is that it, Dr O'Reilly?'

'I'm afraid so, Doreen. I asked the ear doctor in Belfast, and he says he's done the best he can. It's a shame that he can do no more.'

'It is. But I still have my man, the oul' goat.' Again she started to bang away. 'The doctor says he can do no more, Hughey. Away you, back to your flowers.'

He nodded and turned back to the little blooms as the sound of clanging and the last of the sunlight died.

'He loves his wee flowers, so he does,' she said, and Barry saw the moisture in her eyes.

'I'VE NEVER SEEN ANYTHING like that,' Barry said, closing the Rover's door.

'Bloody shipyards,' said O'Reilly, driving away. 'Hughey was a riveter. Did you see the scars on his face? You can't work with red-hot metal all your life and not get a few burns.'

'But what was the business with the tin tray?'

'Have you ever heard riveters at work?'

'No.'

'I have. In Valletta Harbour in Malta during the war. They were fixing up an aircraft carrier after she'd been bombed. A thousand men with rivet guns pounding away. It's like the proverbial hammers of hell.' O'Reilly pulled the car to the side of Main Street. 'Hughey's deaf as a post—riveters' deafness.'

'But he can hear if someone hammers on a tin tray?'

'Right. Don't ask me why, but it's true. Now, that's all the calls for today, and I need a wee cure. A hair of the dog. I'll buy you a pint.'

'Fine.'

'Just one, mind. The pair of us'll have to be in top form tomorrow. Half the ones I chased away this morning will show up, and you've to see Cissie Sloan about her thyroid. Her results should be back. And we should know for sure about the wee MacAteer girl's pregnancy.'

'We might even know more than that, Fingal. Kinky thinks that Julie could be a housemaid at the Bishops'. She'll try to find out from Mrs Bishop at the Women's Union tonight.'

'Interesting,' said O'Reilly. 'You can tell me all about it in the Duck.'

All Professions Are Conspiracies Against the Laity

Barry was disappointed that he'd not had a chance to speak to Kinky the previous night after her return from the Women's Union, but he and O'Reilly had been called out to attend another confinement. He wasn't going to complain. It worked wonders for the morale to see a baby safely delivered by a grateful, healthy woman. It might not be as challenging as brain surgery, but it felt right. He headed for the dining room.

'Morning, Fingal.'

'You look like the cat that got the cream.' O'Reilly glanced up from a plate of devilled lambs' kidneys. 'Feeling pleased with yourself?'

'Well, I . . .'

'So you should. You've a knack for midwifery.'

Barry helped himself to a small portion from the sideboard.

'I know,' said O'Reilly. 'You came down here to give general practice a try. I'd not want to force you to stay.' O'Reilly's gaze was level. 'You might do better if you specialised in obstetrics and gynaecology.'

Barry wasn't sure what to say. He had wondered last night about that very possibility.

'You have to do what's right for yourself, son.'

'That's generous of you, Fingal.'

'Balls.' O'Reilly took a deep breath. 'I wanted to be an obstetrician. Bloody war came along, so like an eejit I volunteered. After it was over, I was too old to spend another four years training. I had to make a living. I'm only telling you so you'll not think I'm being—what did you say—generous?'

Silly old bugger, Barry thought, you'd die of mortification if you let anyone suspect you'd a soft side. 'Perhaps that was the wrong word. I meant you were being fair.'

O'Reilly seemed to be mollified. 'It's up to you. Now eat and shut up. I've a lot I want to think about.' He hunched over his plate, shovelled in another mouthful and chewed fiercely.

Barry sat. He too had a lot to think about. Obstetrics and gynaecology had much to recommend it. He had no doubt that he'd enjoy obstetrics. The snag was gynaecology. Days in clinics dealing with women with vaginal discharges and heavy periods. Or having to break their hearts because they cannot conceive. And then there were the cancer cases. He shuddered.

'Your kidneys are getting cold,' O'Reilly said. 'Kinky'll kill you. Shove those bloody things back in the chafing dish. Maybe she'll not notice.'

'Right.' Barry rose and was scraping his plate when Kinky strode in.

She took one look and sniffed. 'And was there something the matter with the kidneys, so?' she asked, arms folded, chins wobbling.

'Not at all,' Barry stammered. 'My eyes were bigger than my belly. I couldn't finish what I took . . . Uh, Kinky, did you get a word with Mrs Bishop last night?'

Kinky beamed. 'Aye, and you were right. The wee Rasharkin lassie is a housemaid at the Bishops'. Only a poor wee skivvy, so.'

'How long has she worked there?' O'Reilly asked.

'Three months.'

O'Reilly nodded. 'Interesting. And how does she get on with the Bishops?'

'Mrs Bishop's heartbroken that Julie's given her notice. The wee girl wouldn't give a reason for a while. Now says she has a sick sister living in Liverpool. Mrs Bishop thinks that there's no such thing.'

'What *does* she think?'

'That Bertie Bishop's always had an eye for the ladies. Mrs Bishop thinks her husband maybe pinched the wee lass's bottom once too often.'

O'Reilly eyes were wide. 'Now there's a thing.'

Barry was not quite sure what O'Reilly might be hinting at. Trying to find out who the baby's father was seemed to be more important. 'Do you happen to know, Kinky, if Julie has a boyfriend?'

Kinky frowned. 'I did ask. Mrs Bishop didn't know, but once or twice a fellow with ginger hair had come round to the servants' quarters at night. She only caught a glimpse of him.'

'Damn.'

'Don't let that bother you, Barry.' O'Reilly was rubbing his hands with, Barry thought, the enthusiasm of Ebenezer Scrooge surveying a heap of gold sovereigns. 'Thanks a million, Kinky. You're a better spy than your man James Bond. And he can't cook.'

'And you're full of blarney for a man with work to do.'

'How much work?'

'Not too much. Half a dozen of the regulars.' Kinky's brow furrowed. 'And Cissie Sloan's here and it's not her tonic day.'

Kinky was right. The waiting room was half empty. Barry whispered, 'That must have been a better performance yesterday than you thought, Fingal. They haven't all come back.'

'They will,' said O'Reilly. He threw the door open. 'Who's first?'

Barry followed O'Reilly and the first patient to the surgery. He was a tall, lugubrious-looking, middle-aged man, dressed in a black three-piece suit. His dark hair was sleek, oiled, and split by a centre parting. His cheeks, sunken beneath high cheekbones, would have given his face the characteristics of a skull had it not been for his nose. Its last two inches had blossomed into a craggy and pitted tomato. Barry recognised the condition—rhinophyma—the result of a blockage of oil glands.

'Sit down, Mr Coffin,' O'Reilly said, taking the swivel chair. 'What seems to be the trouble?'

'Ah'm no at myself.' His voice was as gloomy as his demeanour. Barry knew that Mr Coffin meant that he just felt generally unwell.

'And you've seen the two specialists I sent you to?' O'Reilly asked.

'Aye.' The word was spoken slowly, and only after much deep thought.

'Neither one could find anything wrong with you?'

'Aye.' It sounded liked 'aaaaaaaye', its pitch gradually rising.

O'Reilly asked several more questions. All were answered with polysyllabic 'aaaaaaayes'. Finally O'Reilly said, 'I think we're at a bit of a loss, Mr Coffin. Would you consider taking a wee holiday?'

The patient frowned, looked at the ceiling, took a deep breath, then, to Barry's amazement, said one word. His 'ayes' had climbed the scale. This time he slid down it in a baleful glissando, in keeping with the descent of his narrow bottom along the seat of the forward-tilting chair.

'Nooooo.'

Barry had great difficulty keeping a straight face.

'Well,' said O'Reilly, rising, 'all I can suggest is get lots of fresh air, eat a healthy diet and get plenty of sleep.'

'Aye?' Plaintive.

O'Reilly sighed. 'I suppose you could try something my grandmother used for folks that were a bit low. You collect up a few stems of St John's wort, chop it up and make a tea to drink.'

'Aye?'

'Aye,' said O'Reilly.

It's catching, Barry thought, as O'Reilly ushered Mr Coffin to the door.

'Poor old bugger,' said O'Reilly after he had closed the door. 'Bet you can't guess what he does for a living.'

Barry shook his head.

'Mr Coffin is our undertaker,' said O'Reilly.

'He's not.'

'He is, and did you see his nose? Talk about having a cross to bear. Nothing will persuade the locals that a big red nose isn't the mark of a boozer . . . and poor old Coffin is actually the head Pioneer. They're a temperance organisation. Avoid the demon drink like the plague.' O'Reilly shuddered. 'Well, who knows, maybe my granny's herbal tea will work.'

'Aye,' said Barry.

'Lord,' said O'Reilly, 'don't you start. Go and see if the post has arrived. If you're right, there *will* be something we can do for Cissie.'

Two reports in the buff envelope: Cissie's and Julie MacAteer's. Barry's pleasure when he saw that the radioactive iodine uptake test had confirmed his diagnosis was dulled by one word on the second piece of paper: 'Positive'.

He tried to smile at Julie, who sat in the waiting room. 'Just be a minute, Julie. Will you come in, Mrs Sloan?'

Cissie followed him to the surgery like a battleship in the wake of a tugboat.

'Morning, Cissie. So, Dr Laverty?' O'Reilly held out his hand. Barry handed him the pink laboratory form. O'Reilly peered at it, then gave it to Barry. 'You'll have to tell me what this newfangled stuff means.'

Was O'Reilly serious? Barry spoke to Cissie, but kept his eyes on O'Reilly's face. 'Mrs Sloan, in a nutshell, a gland in your neck isn't making enough of a little thingy it releases into your bloodstream.'

O'Reilly's face was deadpan.

'The little thingy's supposed to help you feel full of get-up-and-go, so it's no wonder you've been feeling frazzled. And it's there to help you use the food you eat. You know, when you light a fire but keep the damper closed?'

'I do,' she said. Barry glanced at her. She was leaning forward—as far as her girth would permit—looking into his face, clearly taking in every word.

'When that happens you can pile on the coal, but it won't burn very quickly. Thyroxine—that's what the little thingy's called—well, not having enough thyroxine's like having the damper shut all the time.'

She put two hands on her belly. 'And this here's like half a hundredweight of nutty slack?'

'Exactly. Like slow-burning coal.'

'I'll be damned. Just you wait till I tell my husband that I'm all clogged up with slack because me damper's shut.' Her tone was absolutely serious.

Barry looked at O'Reilly, who said, 'Do you think some thyroid extract might do the trick, Dr Laverty?'

'Indeed. Will you write the prescription?'

'I will,' said O'Reilly, scribbling away.

'I told you,' said Barry, 'Dr O'Reilly's the expert on the treatment.'

'And amn't I the lucky one having the pair of you to look after me?'

'Oh, I don't know . . .' Barry began modestly.

'This'll put that there Aggie in her box. She said you near killed that snooty Major Fotheringham.'

Barry flinched.

'Says I to her, "Nobody's perfect, Aggie."' She looked directly at O'Reilly as she delivered those oblique words of forgiveness.

He inclined his head. 'Now, Cissie . . .' He gave her instructions for using the medication.

'Well done,' said O'Reilly when she'd left. 'That was a smart diagnosis, and you're getting the hang of explaining things. And thanks for that bit of professional courtesy, letting on that I know more about the treatment.'

'There's honour among thieves,' Barry said, smiling.

'Sure, "All professions are conspiracies against the laity."'

Barry frowned. 'Who said that?'

'Fooled you that time. George Bernard Shaw in *The Doctor's Dilemma*.'

'One to you, Fingal. And speaking of dilemmas'—Barry handed Julie MacAteer's results to O'Reilly—'she's next.'

'I'M SORRY, JULIE,' O'Reilly began. 'I'm afraid it's positive.'

She squared her shoulders. 'I knew it. So that's me for Liverpool?'

'Not for a while, but yes. Before you start to show . . . unless the father—?'

'He can't.'

O'Reilly scratched his chin. 'Do you mind me asking why he can't?'

'I don't mind you asking, Doctor . . . but I'm not going to tell you.'

'Fair enough. I had to ask,' O'Reilly said. 'Now, we should start your prenatal blood work. I'll go and get the laboratory forms.' As he passed her chair he put a hand on her shoulder and squeezed gently.

'So, Dr Laverty,' she said.

Barry decided to take the bull by the horns. 'Julie, do you enjoy working for the Bishops?'

She jerked back in her chair. 'How did you know where I work?'

'It's a small village. Is Councillor Bishop the father?'

'What? That lecher?' Her cheeks reddened. 'I've better taste than that.'

O'Reilly came back but Barry ploughed on. 'If he is, we could at least make him pay for—'

'Not him.' Her lip curled.

'Who's him?' O'Reilly enquired.

'Councillor Bishop. I asked Julie if he could be the father.'

'And I told Dr Laverty . . .' A single sob interrupted her words. 'He tried to have a go at me. I'd not let him anywhere near me.'

'It's all right, Julie. Dr Laverty was only trying to help.'

'I know that.' She dashed the tears away with the back of one hand. 'But just thinking of that man gives me the creeps.' Her green eyes flashed.

'We'll say no more about it.' O'Reilly waited.

She twitched at the front of her skirt and held out her hand. 'Give me them forms. Where've I to go to for the tests? Can I get them done here?'

O'Reilly gave her the requisitions. 'If you want to keep this to yourself, maybe you'd be better to nip down to Bangor to the health clinic there.'

'I'll do that,' she said, her chin firm. 'Would tomorrow be all right?'

'Of course. We'll have the results by Friday.'

'I can't get any more time off this week. Could I come in on Monday?'

'Of course, and we'll have all the information about Liverpool.'

She forced a smile. 'I hear there's so many Paddies living there that it's really the capital of Ireland. Maybe my poor wee bastard'll find a good Irish home.' She held out her hand to O'Reilly, who hesitated.

Barry was surprised. Women didn't usually offer men a handshake.

O'Reilly smiled and shook her hand. 'You'll be all right, Julie MacAteer.'

'She took it well, Fingal,' Barry said, after she'd left. 'I hope I didn't upset her too much, asking her about Bishop, but I did think—'

'I know exactly what you thought, Barry,' O'Reilly said. 'And it's given me an idea. I'll need your help, and we'll have to bend a few rules, but . . .'

Barry's eyes widened as O'Reilly unfolded his plan. It might just work . . .

As soon as the morning surgery was finished, O'Reilly began to make telephone calls. 'Hello? Royal Victoria? Put me through to Ward Six . . . Hello? Sister Gordon? Fingal O'Reilly here . . . I'm grand. How's your bad knee? . . . Good. I'm delighted it's on the mend. How's Sonny? . . . My customer with the pneumonia and heart failure . . . I see . . . Right . . . Right . . . Another week? Fine. Now you look after yourself.' He hung up.

'Sonny's on the mend. They'll discharge him on Saturday. The almoner's been to see him and she won't let him go back to his car. She's got a bed for him in the convalescent home in Bangor, and he'll be all right there until we get things sorted out. And to do that . . .'

He consulted the telephone directory, then dialled again. 'Dr O'Reilly here. I want to speak to Councillor Bishop.' He winked at Barry. 'Nooo. I was quite precise. I didn't say I'd like to speak to him. I said'—his voice rose to a roar—'*I want to speak to him* . . . and I meant right now.' He waited.

'Councillor. Sorry to bother you.' O'Reilly's voice oozed solicitousness. 'I won't keep you a minute. It's about Sonny's property. I know you want to acquire it. Perhaps I can help.' He held up one hand, finger and thumb forming a circle. 'Not on the phone. Could you drop in about six? . . . Splendid.' O'Reilly replaced the receiver. '"I gloat!"' he roared. '"Hear me gloat!"'

'*Stalky and Co.*, Rudyard Kipling,' Barry said. 'So he's taken the bait?'

'He's risen like a trout to a mayfly. All we have to do is play him a bit . . .'

The front doorbell rang. Barry looked at O'Reilly, who said, 'Kinky knows to bring him up here. Just agree with everything I say.'

Barry heard footsteps on the stairs. Kinky showed Councillor Bishop into the upstairs sitting room. 'It's the councillor, so.' She had a look on her face as though she had found something unpleasant on the sole of her shoe.

'Come in, Councillor,' said O'Reilly, rising. 'Have a seat. Would you like a wee . . . ?' He inclined his head towards the decanters on the sideboard.

'I've no time for that. I'm here on business, so I am.'

Councillor Bishop lowered himself into O'Reilly's recently vacated chair. Barry sat opposite. O'Reilly leaned against the mantelpiece.

'So,' said the councillor, 'is the old bugger going to die?'

O'Reilly shook his head. 'Sonny? He's very much on the mend.'

'Pity.' Bishop crossed his short legs. 'Ballybucklebo would be a damn sight better off if we could see the back of him and them scruffy dogs.'

'You're probably right,' said O'Reilly, 'but I think old Sonny'll be around for a day or two yet.'

'All right. How much for Sonny's place?'

'I'm only a country GP. I've no idea.'

Bishop's eyes narrowed. He steepled his fingers. 'Two thousand pounds.'

Barry's knowledge of land values was limited, but the figure seemed low.

O'Reilly put a match to his briar. 'I'm sure that would be very fair,' he said, 'but we're not actually talking about selling Sonny's land.'

'You said you could help me get the property.'

'Not exactly,' said O'Reilly. 'I said I knew you wanted to acquire the property and that perhaps I could help. I meant I thought I could help prevent you from getting within a beagle's gowl of the place.'

Councillor Bishop's face turned scarlet. 'Listen, you stupid country quack, there's not a fuckin' thing you can do to stop me. I'll have Sonny's place, lock, stock and barrel, by the end of next week, so I will. Two thousand pounds. Take it or leave it. I don't give a shite.'

'I think we'll leave it.' O'Reilly blew a cloud of smoke towards the ceiling.

'Right.' Bishop stood. 'I'm for home.'

'I hope Mrs Bishop will be pleased to see you.'

'What are you on about?'

'And little Julie MacAteer. She's up the pipe, you know.'

Barry clenched his teeth. This bending of the rules, this breach of a patient's confidentiality, bothered him a lot.

'What's that wee guttersnipe being pregnant got to do with me?'

O'Reilly said softly, 'She says you're the daddy.'

Councillor Bishop's face went from scarlet to puce. He gobbled like a turkey that had just been informed that tomorrow was Christmas Eve. He took a deep breath, clearly pulling himself together, secure in the knowledge that indeed he was not the father. 'If she's a bun in the oven, it's no concern of mine. Mind you, I wouldn't have minded giving her a wee poke.'

'You did, Bertie. Our tests don't lie.'

'Balls. What tests?' Bishop's narrow forehead wrinkled. 'What tests?'

'You tell him, Dr Laverty.'

'You left some pus on a couple of swabs from the night Dr O'Reilly lanced your finger,' Barry intoned. 'If you take a blood sample from a pregnant woman and mix it with pus, even old, dried-up pus, from the putative father, there can be an anaphylactoid progression of the polylobed acidophilic granulocytes.' Barry knew he was spouting gibberish, but it was what O'Reilly wanted. *Blind the councillor with science*, he'd said.

'A what?'

'Pay attention,' said O'Reilly.

'An anaphylactoid progression of the acidophilic granulocytes. It's absolutely . . . pathognomonic.' Barry stumbled over the last word. It came hard to lie to a patient, or about a patient, to a third party.

' "Pathognomonic" means that it's money in the bank,' O'Reilly said helpfully. 'You're the daddy all right. I wouldn't have thought a wizened-up, miserable gobshite like you would have had it in him.'

'There's got to be some mistake. I never laid a finger on her.' Bishop fiddled with the knot of his tie. 'Your stupid test's wrong. I can prove it.'

'How?' asked O'Reilly.

'It's her word against mine.'

'Not exactly,' said Barry. 'It's your word against hers . . . and two qualified medical men . . . and some highly sophisticated science.'

'Oh Jesus.' The councillor buried his face in his hands.

'Of course, Bertie, there's an outside chance . . . what would you say it was, Dr Laverty?'

Barry hesitated. 'About . . . about one in five hundred.'

'That the test *could* be wrong,' O'Reilly said.

'Could it?' Councillor Bishop's bluster had gone completely. 'Could it?'

O'Reilly fiddled about, relighting his pipe. 'I suppose so, but we wouldn't know for at least two weeks. By then I imagine your loyal brethren down at the Orange Lodge would have had something to say. I hear they can get a bit right-wing about Orangemen who indulge in extramarital hanky-panky. Tend to ask for resignations. The town council could be a tad upset.'

Bishop made one last attempt to bluster. 'You're bluffing, so you are.'

'And then,' said O'Reilly sweetly, 'there's Mrs Bishop. She told Kinky she'd seen you having a go at Julie MacAteer.'

'Honest-to-God, I only ever tried to feel Julie's tits. Just the once.'

'Dirty old man,' said O'Reilly. His voice hardened. 'I might just believe you, Bertie Bishop, but I'll take a lot of convincing.'

Bishop looked up at O'Reilly. 'How?'

'Not much. A wee favour. That's all. You'll fix Sonny's roof, and the rest of his place . . . free of charge.'

'What?' Bishop whimpered.

'You'll settle five hundred pounds on Julie MacAteer. That's two hundred and fifty per . . . what did you call them? Tits? You'll write her a letter of reference that would get her through the Pearly Gates . . . and if you breathe a word that she's pregnant—'

'I won't. I swear to God, I won't.'

'Good,' said O'Reilly. 'Very good . . . and just one other little thing. Seamus Galvin is looking for someone to buy a clatter of rocking ducks. About four hundred quid would see him right.'

Barry chuckled inwardly. He'd completely forgotten about the Galvins.

'I'll be fucked,' Bishop muttered. 'Ruined.'

'Indeed you will be, Bertie, if you don't do exactly as I've told you.'

Bishop hung his head. 'Can I go?' he asked.

'If you must,' said O'Reilly. 'And I'm sure when the laboratory retests the sample, it'll all turn out to have been a horrible mistake. Oh, and while you're here, Bertie.' Hardened steel was in O'Reilly's voice. 'If you ever call me a quack again, if you ever forget that Dr Laverty and I worked hard for our degrees, I'll gut you like a herring.'

WEDNESDAY MORNING surgery and lunch were over. O'Reilly consulted his list. 'Great,' he announced, 'not one sick one.'

'So we can put our feet up?' Barry rose from the table. 'I'm off to have a go at today's crossword.'

'The hell you are,' said O'Reilly, shaking his head. 'We need to drop in on a few folks that we've been neglecting.'

Barry sighed. 'All right. Who do you want to go and see?'

'The Galvins. I want to hear if Bishop's kept his word. The Kennedys. See how Jeannie's doing; then we'll have a word with Maggie about Sonny.'

'That shouldn't take long.'

O'Reilly's expression clouded. 'They're the easy ones. We'll have to make a stop with Mrs Fotheringham. I'll bet she won't have a clue what's going on. The specialists at the Royal are too busy to talk to relatives. I'll phone the ward. Check up on Fotheringham's progress.'

Barry steeled himself before saying, 'Could I do that? It should be me who tries to explain things to Mrs Fotheringham.'

O'Reilly cocked his head on one side. 'You know, I hoped you'd say that.' Barry heard the satisfaction in his senior colleague's voice as O'Reilly continued, 'You'll need to get put through to Ward 21. I'll see you at the car.'

Barry spoke to one of the medical staff on the ward and was gratified to hear that Major Fotheringham's recovery was progressing as anticipated. He'd be left with some impairment but he should be able to live a fairly normal life. He'd have his stitches taken out on Friday and be discharged for outpatient follow-up and physiotherapy the following week.

'Thank you,'. Barry said, and was about to hang up, when—why not? 'Would you reconnect me with the switchboard?' he asked. He got through at once. 'Could you page Dr Mills, please?' He waited.

'Mills here.'Jack's voice was clipped. Businesslike.

'Jack? Barry.'

'It's yourself, is it? I thought Sir Donald Cromie was after my hide when my bleeper went off. I'm running a bit late. What's up?'

'I'll not keep you, but I had to phone the Royal so I thought I'd see if you were about the place.'

'I'm on my way to theatre. It's lumps and bumps this afternoon. Minor cases: warts, sebaceous cysts, the odd ingrowing toenail. Good training for young surgeons, according to Sir Donald. You still as busy as ever?'

'Not too bad.'

'Have you heard anything from that wee bird of yours yet?'

'Patricia?' Barry shook his head. The crisis with Major Fotheringham, Cissie's thyroid disease and Julie MacAteer's pregnancy had all served to drive Patricia from his thoughts—most of the time. 'No. Not a peep.'

'She blew you out last Friday. That's only five days. Give her time.'

'But if she doesn't call?'

'Then, my old son, you're just like the Christmas turkey . . . stuffed.'

'I suppose so.' Barry knew that his friend was right. It certainly looked as though Patricia had just been letting him down gently.

'Time's a great healer,' Jack said, 'and so is the produce of Mr Arthur Guinness and Sons. Any chance of getting together again?'

'I'll call you later in the week, if I'm free.'

'Do that. I've got to run.' The line went dead.

Barry hung up and smiled.

'Are you coming?' O'Reilly bawled from outside.

Barry closed the front door and trotted to the car.

'Well?' O'Reilly asked. 'How's the major?'

'On the mend.'

'Good.' O'Reilly eased the car away from the kerb.

'Isn't it grand, Dr O'Reilly?' Maureen Galvin, eyes bright, showed O'Reilly a pile of twenty-pound notes. 'Some fellow came round first thing this morning. Says your man to me, "I hear your husband's got a load of rocking ducks for sale?" "Right," says I. "I'll take the lot," says he. And would you look at that? Four hundred quid.'

'I'm delighted,' said O'Reilly.

'You never saw such things in your life,' said Maureen. 'Not one of them looked like any duck I'd ever seen. Anyway, we got our money back and a bit of a profit.' She hesitated. 'Would you do me a wee favour?' She handed him the notes. 'Would you take care of these? I'd be happier if Seamus—'

'They'll be safe as houses,' said O'Reilly, stuffing the money in his pocket.

She smiled at him, cocked her head to one side and asked, 'Would you be free on Saturday, Doctors?'

Barry had hoped for some time off. He wanted to see Patricia if she did phone, or perhaps he'd meet Jack if she didn't. He looked at O'Reilly.

'We might,' said O'Reilly.

'We're having a wee going-away party. We'd like for you both to come.'

'What do you think, Dr Laverty?'

'We'd have it here. In the afternoon,' said Maureen.

Barry could tell by the way she looked up into O'Reilly's face that the presence of her medical advisers was important. 'I don't see why not,' he said. He might still be able to get an hour or two off after the party.

'Grand,' said Maureen.

'I tell you what,' said O'Reilly. 'Could you or Seamus get your hands on the marquee the Ballybucklebo Highlanders use? Just in case it rains. There'd be a lot more room in my back garden.'

Maureen beamed. 'You wouldn't mind, sir?'

'Not at all. You never know how many'll show up at a ceilidh.'

'Seamus'll get the big tent. We'll put it up on Saturday morning.'

'Right,' said O'Reilly. 'Now, we'll need some grub. Mrs Kincaid'll take care of that. I'll get a couple of barrels of stout over from the Duck.'

'But that'll cost a fortune.'

'No,' said O'Reilly, 'Willy the barman'll have to charge the guests.'

'We'll not have time to get a permit,' Barry said. In Ulster, if anyone wanted to sell alcohol anywhere but in a registered public house they had to apply for a permit. It usually took a week or two for one to be issued.

'We'll not need one. We'll not sell drink . . . we'll sell glasses of water,' said O'Reilly with a grin. 'Grand stuff, water. You don't need a permit to sell it and there's nothing to stop you giving away a free drink with every glass sold. To be on the safe side we'll invite Constable Mulligan. If there is a law being broken and him at the hooley, he'd have to arrest himself.'

Barry laughed and his laughter woke young Barry Fingal.

'I'd better see to the wean,' said Maureen. 'Saturday it is, Doctors.'

To BARRY'S GREAT RELIEF, the lane to the Kennedys' farmhouse was dry. Jeannie was playing in the farmyard, throwing a stick for her Border collie.

'Hello, Dr O'Reilly.' She took the stick from the dog. 'Stay, Tessie.'

'How are you, Jeannie?' O'Reilly walked over from the car.

'Much better now, thank you.'

Barry followed. He could see that this was a different little girl from the one he'd met three weeks ago. She had colour in her cheeks and her eyes were bright. He thought she might have lost a little weight, but considering how sick she had been, that was to be expected.

'She's really on the mend.' Mrs Kennedy appeared in the doorway of the farmhouse, her grey hair neatly tied up in a bun. 'We were main worried about her for a while, but them doctors at Sick Children's were smashing, so they were. There was a young one, a Dr Mills. He said if you and Dr Laverty hadn't been so quick off the mark . . .' She swallowed.

'All's well that ends well,' said O'Reilly. 'Lots of fresh air, plenty to eat, and she'll be fit as a flea in no time. Ready for school in September.'

'Dermot'll be sorry he missed you, Doctor, but he's out combining.'

'A farmer's work's never done,' said O'Reilly. 'Just like a doctor's.' He walked back to the car and opened the door. 'If the three of you have nothing to do on Saturday afternoon, we're having a bit of a ta-ta-ta-ra in my back garden for Seamus and Maureen Galvin. They're off to America soon.'

'I'll ask himself,' said Bridget. 'I'll bring some barmbrack.'

'Great.' He lowered himself into the driver's seat. 'Hop in.'

Barry climbed aboard.

'We were lucky with that one,' said O'Reilly, as the car jolted down the rutted lane. 'It would have been the death of Bridget if the wee lass hadn't pulled through.'

'Mrs Kennedy must have been a fair age when Jeannie was born.'

O'Reilly pulled onto the main road and stamped on the accelerator. 'Usual story. They couldn't afford to get married until old man Kennedy died and left his son the farm. I think Bridget was forty-two then. Took her forever to get pregnant. That wee girl's the light of her life.' O'Reilly leaned on the horn and swerved across the centre line. 'Bloody bicycles. Move over.'

Barry's head swung round as he watched the unfortunate on the bike wobble, stop and hurl himself and his conveyance into the ditch. 'Have you ever hit one?' he asked.

'Not yet. They all know the car.' O'Reilly took both hands off the steering wheel to light his pipe and said, 'Fotheringhams', next stop.'

'WOULD YOU LIKE some tea and scones?' Mrs Fotheringham asked when O'Reilly and Barry were seated in the antimacassar-draped armchairs.

'No, thank you,' said O'Reilly. 'We can stay for only a minute. Dr Laverty has something to tell you.'

Barry swallowed. 'I've had a word with the hospital about the major. He's fully conscious. Weak on his left side. His speech is a bit slurred. He's never going to be quite right, I'm afraid, but the speech therapists and physiotherapists can work wonders . . . with time.'

'I see.' Her face was expressionless. 'Perhaps if he'd gone to the hospital sooner?' she asked through thin lips.

Barry glanced at O'Reilly, who was examining his fingernails. No help would be forthcoming from that quarter. Barry inhaled. 'Yes. He might be doing better if I'd recognised what was wrong when I saw him on Friday.' Barry wondered if someone at the hospital had sown these seeds of doubt in her mind. 'I didn't think it was more than a muscle spasm in his neck.'

'But you were wrong, weren't you?'

'Yes, Mrs Fotheringham. I was.'

'I'm glad you admit it, young man.'

'Ahem,' O'Reilly grumbled. 'You know, Mrs Fotheringham, I don't think I would have done any better. There wasn't a lot to go on on Friday.'

She sniffed haughtily. 'Of course you medical men always stick together. I've had time to think this over,' she said, rising, 'and I have decided that my husband and I will be seeking our medical advice elsewhere.'

'That is, of course, your choice, Mrs Fotheringham. I hear Dr Bowman in Kinnegar is very good.' O'Reilly's tone was measured.

'In that case'—she crossed the room and held the door open—'perhaps you would be good enough to transfer our records to him?'

'With pleasure.'

Barry, his head held low, walked slowly to the hall. 'I'm sorry . . .'

' "Sorry" won't give me back a healthy husband. Now . . . ?'

'Good afternoon, Mrs Fotheringham,' O'Reilly said from the front step.

Barry walked to the gate, opened it for the car, closed it and got in.

'Don't let her get to you,' said O'Reilly. 'She's upset, angry.'

'And right,' said Barry. 'I might have—'

'Don't start that again. You were spot on about Cissie Sloan; between the pair of us we sorted out Jeannie Kennedy, and we got old Sonny put to rights.' He made a screeching left turn. 'I agree you could have done better with the major, but for every Mrs Fotheringham, every Bertie Bishop, there are the Cissies, the Jeannies, the Maureen Galvins and . . . the Maggies that do make it all worth while.'

A few minutes later he pulled the car to the verge outside Maggie MacCorkle's cottage. 'Come on. Let's tell Maggie about Sonny.'

Dogs spilled out of the front door and clustered round the car. Maggie thrust her way past them and Barry noticed the fresh pansies in her hatband.

'You're just in time, Doctors dear. The kettle's boiled.'

'Great,' said O'Reilly, 'a cup of tea would hit the spot.'

'Bugger off, General Montgomery.' Maggie shooed the ginger cat off one of her chairs. 'Have a seat, Dr O'Reilly. Light your pipe.'

She bustled round her stove, warming the teapot, dumping out the boiling water, spooning in tea leaves from a tin caddy with a picture of the coronation of Elizabeth II painted on the side. She added more boiling water.

'I'm glad you came,' she said. 'I've run out of them wee pills, and I'd another of those eggycentwhat-do-you-muhcallum headaches the other night, so I had. Would you have any more tablets with you?'

O'Reilly shook his head. ''Fraid not, Maggie. Eccentric headaches can be funny things. Could you pop in tomorrow? I'd like to take another wee look at you before I give you any more pills. Just to be on the safe side.'

Barry smiled. He wasn't the only doctor in Ballybucklebo who would be taking a complaint of headaches more seriously in the future.

'I'll be round,' she said, pouring tea into three mugs. 'Milk and sugar?'

'Just milk,' Barry said, as O'Reilly nodded.

'We just popped in to let you know about Sonny,' O'Reilly said. 'He's getting out on Saturday.'

'Told you,' said Maggie. 'They'll have to shoot that one.' She sipped her tea. 'That means he can have his dogs back.'

'Not exactly,' said O'Reilly. 'He'll have to go to Bangor to convalesce until his roof's fixed.'

Maggie sat bolt upright. 'Until what?' Her eyes widened.

'His roof's fixed. Councillor Bishop told me he's had a change of heart.'

'Jesus, Mary and Joseph. That bugger Bertie Bishop?'

'It's true, Maggie,' Barry said. 'Honestly.'

'Aye,' said O'Reilly. 'I'm going up to the Royal on Saturday. I'll run him down to Bangor, but first we're having a bit of a ceilidh at my place. To send the Galvins off to America. Sonny'll be fit enough to drop in for a wee while. How'd you like to pop by and tell him about the roof?'

Barry watched as from somewhere deep under Maggie's leathery cheeks a glow rose and spread. 'Away off and chase yourself,' she said. 'Him and me barely give each other the time of day.'

'I know,' said O'Reilly, 'but the last time I saw him, Sonny said he wanted to have a wee word . . . to thank you for taking care of his dogs.'

'That would be civil of him, right enough.'

'So you'll come?'

'I'll mull it over,' she said. 'If I do, I'll bring one of my plum cakes.'

Now Is the Time for All Good Men
to Come to the Aid of the Party

O'Reilly had left for Belfast to collect Sonny. Barry yawned and rolled his shoulders. Thursday and Friday had been hectic. Droves of patients, and last night there had been a traffic accident. Two men with broken bones and minor lacerations had needed to be given morphine, splinted and sutured before being sent to the Royal. It had been four in the morning when he and O'Reilly got into their beds.

A bit of a sleep-in wouldn't have gone amiss, but he had been woken by the sounds of Seamus Galvin and his team putting up the big tent.

Barry sighed, picked up his breakfast plates and cutlery and carried them through to the kitchen. Perhaps his tiredness somehow made his disappointment more real. It seemed that Jack's advice to wait for Patricia to phone had been wrong. Not a peep from her and it was eight days now.

Kinky straightened up from the oven. 'Pop the dishes in the sink. I'll see to them, so,' she said. 'Grand day for the hooley.'

'Suppose so.' Barry put the plates down. 'I'm not in much of a party mood.'

Kinky squinted at his face. 'It's none of my business, Dr Laverty, but . . . is it that wee girl that has you sore tried?'

Barr wondered how she had seen through him so easily. 'A bit,' he admitted. 'She told me she didn't want to get too involved.'

Kinky tutted. 'Silly girl. If you don't give, you'll not get back. I know that for a fact, so.'

Barry had wondered what had happened to Mr Kincaid. 'You were married, Kinky, weren't you?'

She nodded slowly. 'I was and it was grand, so. But I lost himself. I was only eighteen. He was a Cork fisherman. He was lost at sea and I was lost on land. It was like half of myself gone.' She moved to the counter. 'But life has to go on.' She grabbed a rolling pin and with steady, strong strokes began to flatten a mound of pastry dough. 'I thought I'd see the world.' She chuckled. 'It was a brave step from Cork to County Down before the war, so I took a job with old Dr Flanagan here . . . just till I found my way again.'

'And you never left?'

'I never met another lad like my Paudeen.' She sprinkled flour onto the now flat pastry. 'After a year or two of feeling sorry for myself, I looked hard for another lad but I never did find one.'

Barry thought he felt the same about Patricia, but at least Kinky had made an effort after she had been widowed.

'Are you content here, Kinky?'

'I am. I've had a good life, so. I'll not complain, but it pains me to see a young man moping.'

'It's daft, isn't it?'

She smiled. 'Sure there *are* times the heart rules the head.' She sprinkled flour on the sheet of pastry. 'The newspaper's in the hall. Go you up to the sitting room. It'll be quieter there. I'll call you if there are any patients. And who knows? Maybe things will turn out for you after all.' Kinky's eyes narrowed. 'Do you know what "fey" means, Dr Laverty?'

'The second sight? The gift? It's only a superstition.'

'You can believe that if you please, sir, but things *are* going to be fine.'

Despite all his scientific training, Barry felt the hairs on the back of his neck prickle. 'Are you sure?'

She spooned lumps of sausage meat onto the pastry. Her big fingers deftly rolled it to enclose the filling. 'Away on upstairs and read your paper.'

He looked at her hard, but she was bent over her work. 'All right, Kinky,' he said, knowing full well that the subject was closed.

He collected the paper and went upstairs. He turned to the crossword, but his mind kept wandering to what Kinky had said.

You know, Barry Laverty, he told himself, just because O'Reilly had turned his back on women, you don't have to. Maybe you'll never ever find anyone like Patricia, but why not be like Kinky and try again?

It must have been terrible for her to have been widowed so young. The country folk believed that the sudden death of a loved one could confer the gift of second sight. Was Kinky fey? That was a hard one to answer.

The god-awful pounding in the back garden stopped. He rubbed his eyes, stretched, lay back in the chair and nodded off.

BARRY WRINKLED HIS NOSE. Something was tickling his nostrils. He was dimly aware of a gentle whiffling and a persistent rumbling. A weight was on his chest. He opened his eyes. Lady Macbeth was crouched on his chest.

He fondled the cat's head and asked, 'What time is it?' He looked at his watch. Good Lord. One forty-five. He yawned and stretched, and Lady Macbeth spring to the floor, disturbed by his movements.

Pursued by the cat, Barry trotted downstairs and into the kitchen, where Kinky was busy loading plates of sandwiches onto a tray.

'Is Dr O'Reilly back yet?' he asked.

She shook her head, then batted Barry's hand away as he tried to steal a sandwich. 'Leave you them be. They're for the guests. I've left a plate on the shelf for you, so.' She pointed to a platter of sandwiches and sausage rolls.

'Thanks, Kinky.' Barry helped himself.

She lifted the tray. 'I'd better be getting these outside.'

He held the back door open. Kinky, burdened by the tray, moved sideways into the garden. Tail high, Lady Macbeth slipped past them both.

Barry was curious to see what arrangements had been made, so he followed Kinky and her tray out into the bright sunlight. The tent stood on the left side of the back garden, close to the house. Willy the barman was ready for action behind a trestle table that occupied the greater part of the rear wall. Pint and half-pint glasses, glasses for whiskey and glasses for wine stood there in ranks. The side walls of the big tent were lined with more tables, covered with plates of sandwiches, sausage rolls, cheeses, barmbracks, a ham and a cold leg of lamb. Kinky finished depositing her burden.

She turned to Barry. 'I think there should be enough, so.'

'Enough? You could feed five thousand. You've done a wonderful job.'

Kinky smiled. 'It'll be like a flock of locusts in here in the next couple of hours, and I have to be sure no one goes hungry. I've still one plate to get.'

As she bustled away, Barry wandered out of the tent. Rows of folding deck chairs were lined up from the side of the tent to the back fence. An open space lay between the houses, tent and chairs. He noticed something at the far end of the garden, near Arthur's kennel under the chestnut tree. An irregular shape covered in a tarpaulin.

'Any idea what that is, Willy?'

The barman stopped polishing a glass. 'No idea and don't you go near it, Doc. Seamus Galvin brought it over. It's to be a surprise for Dr O'Reilly.'

'Oh,' said Barry, almost tripping over one of the guy ropes. As he struggled to regain his balance, he was jolted from behind.

'Aaarf,' said Arthur happily, wrapping his front legs round Barry's thigh.
'Gerroff, Arthur. Sit, you great lummox.'

Arthur subsided onto the grass, tongue lolling.

'That's better,' Barry said. 'Now, behave yourself.'

He turned and started to walk back to the house. From behind he heard a hissing like a pit full of vipers followed by a sudden yelp. Barry spun on his heel. Lady Macbeth, back arched, tail fluffed, pupils fully dilated despite the bright sunlight, made what must have been her second attack on Arthur Guinness's nose. Her paw, claws unsheathed, flashed forward in a rapier thrust that drew a howl from Arthur and blood from his nose. Arthur put his tail between his legs and slunk off towards his kennel.

'It's a tough old life, Arthur,' Barry said, at the same time as he heard the back gate creak. He looked up to see the guests of honour, Seamus, Maureen and Barry Fingal Galvin, who lay in the sort of perambulator that had been popular with the nannies of the Victorian upper classes.

'Good afternoon, sir.' Seamus touched the peak of his cloth cap.

'Seamus. Maureen.' Barry moved to the pram. 'And how's Barry Fingal?'

'Grand, so he is,' said Maureen, her green eyes smiling fondly into the massive vehicle. 'Growing like a weed.'

'Would you look at that?' said Seamus, taking in the contents of the marquee. 'Feast fit for a king.'

'Can I get you something, Maureen?' Barry asked.

'I'll see to it,' Seamus said, tongue tip flickering over his lips.

Maureen sat down on the nearest deck chair, steadying her hat with one hand, holding the pram's handle with the other as Barry Fingal gurgled happily. 'It's a great day for the party,' she said. 'Where's himself?'

As if her question had worked to summon Dr Fingal Flahertie O'Reilly, the big Rover pulled into the back lane and juddered to a halt. O'Reilly opened the passenger door and helped Sonny out.

Barry opened the gate. 'How are you, Sonny?' he asked, as O'Reilly guided the old man into the garden. Sonny's grey hair was neatly combed, and his weathered cheeks had lost their ominous blue tinge.

'I am very well, thank you, sir,' Sonny said.

'You'll be even better when you take the weight off your feet,' O'Reilly said, helping him to a chair beside Maureen. 'Do you know Mrs Galvin?'

'I've not had the pleasure,' Sonny said, starting to rise again.

O'Reilly put a hand on Sonny's shoulder. 'Sit down. You've not all your strength back yet.'

Barry smiled at the man's old-world gallantry.

'Afternoon, Doctor sir.' Seamus Galvin appeared, balancing a glass of lemonade on a plate piled high with sandwiches in one hand, and clutching an already half-empty pint of Guinness in the other. 'Here you are, love.' He gave the plate to Maureen. 'I never thanked you proper, Dr O'Reilly, for getting them Belfast folks to take the rocking ducks. Can I buy you a jar?'

'No,' said O'Reilly, with a huge grin, 'I've a thirst like the Sahara Desert. You can buy me two.' He headed for the tent with Seamus, paused and said to Barry, 'Would you look after Sonny?'

Barry nodded. 'Can I get you something, Sonny?'

'A bit of that ham would be much appreciated, and do you think I'd be allowed a small glass of stout?'

'Of course,' Barry said. 'I'll get them.'

By the time he'd brought Sonny his plate and glass, the garden was filling up. Groups of women arrived, all dressed in their Sunday best, and Barry had to jostle past knots of men, some of whom he recognised as members of the Ballybucklebo Highlanders.

Mr Coffin, red nose bright in the sunlight, stood deep in conversation with Constable Mulligan, who was in civilian dress.

'It was quite upsetting,' Barry heard Mr Coffin say. 'When the sexton dropped the first shovelful onto the coffin, he uncovered a skull in the pile of earth that had been excavated from the grave.' He shook his head ponderously. 'It was in a family plot, you see.'

'A skull?' Constable Mulligan asked, eyes wide.

'The sexton nudged the thing with his spade. It rolled down the pile into the grave and rattled off the mahogany coffin lid.'

'My God.' Constable Mulligan shuddered.

'Now, you'd expect old bones to shatter, but the skull just bounced twice and sat there. All the mourners peered down, and you'll never believe what the recently departed's brother said.' Barry saw just the hint of a smile on the undertaker's face. ' "I think that was a bit of Aunt Bertha that was put in here ten years ago. She's sticking the pace bravely, so she is." '

The constable gasped. 'You're pulling my leg?'

'Oh, no, it's perfectly true.' Mr Coffin managed a dry tittering noise.

My goodness, Barry thought, perhaps that stuff O'Reilly had suggested, the St John's wort tea, *had* helped to cheer up the lugubrious Coffin.

As he listened to the ever-swelling drone of voices and laughter, someone tapped him on the shoulder. He turned to see the open face of Jack Mills.

'How's about you, Barry?' Jack said.

'What the hell are you doing here?'

'Your boss was up in the Royal today. He was having a crack with Sir Donald Cromie. I was there and got introduced. Seems O'Reilly saw me play rugby for Ulster. He asked me if I was your Jack Mills and said I should come on down to the party.'

'I'm delighted,' Barry said. 'Come on, then. Let's get a drink.'

Jack lowered one shoulder and started to clear a way towards the tent. He stopped. 'Good Lord. Who is that?'

Barry had to look twice before he recognised Maggie MacCorkle. Her skirt was ankle length, but instead of being its usual black, it was scarlet. She wore layers of cardigans, each one buttoned only at the neck. All were of different colours and resembled the icing on a layered sponge cake. The ensemble was crowned by a hat of such dizzying proportions that it could have been left over from the Ascot scene in *My Fair Lady*. And as ever, there were fresh flowers in the hatband, this time orange lilies. She carried a bundle in one hand and Lady Macbeth under an arm.

'There you are, Dr Laverty,' she said. 'Here.' She thrust the squirming cat into his arms. 'Get that wee scared moggie inside. She doesn't like the crowds. This is a Ballybucklebo ta-ta-ta-ra, and it's not hardly even got started yet. So'—she waved her bundle—'I'll just go and put this plum cake on the food table.' She scanned the crowd. 'Someone said that oul' goat Sonny was here. Have you noticed him about the place?'

'He's sitting under that apple tree,' Barry said, pointing.

'Right,' said Maggie.

O'REILLY, PINT GLASS in hand, beamed at Jeannie Kennedy, who was playing on the grass with trouser-wetting Colin Brown and his bride-to-be, Susan MacAfee. 'See how your appendix abscess made out, Dr Mills?'

'I hardly recognised her,' said Jack.

'Come on,' O'Reilly said to Barry, 'I want to hear what's happening with Maggie and Sonny.' He winked and sidled across the lawn.

Barry followed. They stood behind the apple tree, unashamedly eavesdropping on Sonny and Maggie.

'I have to thank you for looking after my dogs, Miss MacCorkle.'

'It was no bother. I'll keep then till you get home, so I will.'

From where he stood, Barry noticed that neither Maggie nor Sonny would look each other in the eye.

'That would be most generous.' Sonny cleared his throat.

'Are you sure you're all right?' The concern in Maggie's voice was plain.

'Just a little tickle. A frog in my throat.'

'I hope so. No wonder you near caught your death, living in that old car.'

'It suits me, and I'll not pay that despicable man, Bishop.'

Maggie's toothless grin was as radiant as the sunlight that streamed through the tree's leaves. 'You'll not need to. Pay him, that is.'

Sonny frowned. 'Why not?'

'Because Councillor Bishop started fixing the roof yesterday.'

Sonny's eyes widened. 'I'll not pay. Not a penny.'

O'Reilly stepped forward. 'You'll not have to, Sonny. The worm has turned. Bishop came to see me a few days ago. Said he'd had a change of heart, he was sorry you were so sick, and he'd fix your roof for free.'

'I don't know what to say.' Sonny looked from O'Reilly to Maggie.

'I do,' said Maggie, leaning over and planting a great wet kiss on Sonny's forehead. 'And if you'd ask me as nicely as you did all those years ago . . . I'll say "I do" properly when the Reverend asks the question, so I will.'

Sonny took Maggie's hand in his arthritic grip and raised it to his lips.

O'Reilly turned to Barry. 'Come on.' He lowered his voice. 'I think that pair of turtledoves would like to be left alone.'

Barry nodded to Jack, and the trio made their way back towards the tent. Suddenly they heard a ferocious wailing. Barry swung round to see Seamus Galvin, bag under his arm, drones over his shoulder, cheeks puffed, foot tapping in time to the lively notes of 'The Rakes of Mallow'. Arthur Guinness sat at Seamus's feet. The dog had his head thrown back at an impossible angle. His ululations quavered and rose and fell. In the space at the house end of the lawn, men now coatless and women with their Sunday hats cast aside had formed a set and were dancing a reel.

'Jesus,' said O'Reilly, 'it's like "The Galway Races". He sang in a surprisingly melodious baritone. ' "And it's there you'll see the pipers and the fiddlers competing; the nimble-footed dancers and they trippin' on the daisies." '

As O'Reilly sang, Constable Mulligan, less nimble than the rest, managed to get his boots entangled and went down in a heap.

'Must have been a big daisy.' O'Reilly grinned. 'Who needs another pint?'

'Me,' said Jack. Barry shook his head.

'Come on then, Mills,' said O'Reilly. He glanced at the yodelling dog. 'Arthur'll be thirsty with all that singing. I'll see if Willy the barman has a can of Smithwick's.'

Barry stood and watched the dancers.

'Could I have a wee word, Doctor sir?'

Barry turned to see Donal Donnelly holding Julie MacAteer's hand.

'Julie and me wanted to say thank you to you and Dr O'Reilly.'

Barry's mouth fell open. 'Don't tell me . . .' he started.

Donal blushed to the roots of his ginger hair. 'We couldn't afford to get wed,' he said, 'and Julie wouldn't tell nobody I was the daddy.'

'So what happened to change things?'

Donal swallowed. 'I won some money on Bluebird. It wasn't enough, but then Julie got a parcel of cash for severance from Councillor Bishop.'

'I'm sure,' she said with a wry smile as she looked deeply into Barry's eyes, 'I'm sure the doctors don't know anything about that.'

'Not a thing,' Barry said. He glanced away.

'Anyroad,' said Donal, 'I've a new job now. I'm labouring on Sonny's house for the councillor.'

'So you're getting married,' Barry said. 'I'm delighted. And Dr O'Reilly will be delighted too. There he is. You should go and tell him.'

Sometimes, he thought, the ends *do* justify the means. Sonny and Maggie. Julie and Donal. Neither pair would be together if O'Reilly, with Barry's complicity, hadn't broken the rules of confidentiality. Indeed, there wouldn't be a reason for this party at all if O'Reilly hadn't forced Councillor Bishop to buy Seamus Galvin's rocking ducks.

Barry watched Donal and Julie, still hand in hand, walk over to O'Reilly, who clapped Donal on the shoulder and whose cheerful 'Bloody marvellous!' boomed over the end of the music.

He wandered back to the bar, acknowledging the greetings of partygoers. It was a pleasant feeling to know he was becoming accepted in the village. A fiddle started to play. Someone had a penny whistle. A large man rattled out the percussion on a bodhrán, the Irish drum of parchment stretched over a circular frame. Barry recognised the tune and started to hum.

'Another sherry, Doctor?' Willy asked.

'No. I'll have a pint.'

'Good man, my da,' said Willy, building the Guinness. 'One and six for your water please, sir,' he said, with a wink.

Barry paid and made his way back into the sunlight.

Seamus Galvin had taken the bodhrán from its owner and was beating out a fierce tattoo. The buzz of conversation died. 'Ladies and gentlemen,' he yelled. 'Ladies and gennlemen.' He wobbled and grinned. 'I'd like to call upon our senior medical man, Dr Fingal Flahertie O'Reilly, for a song.'

Cheers and yells of 'Go on, Doctor!' rang out. Barry looked up to see O'Reilly, hands gripping the lapels of his tweed jacket, head thrown back.

' "I'm a freeborn man of the travelling people. Got no fixed abode, with nomads I am numbered. Country lanes and byways were always my ways. Never fancied being lumbered . . ." '

Seamus Galvin was at Barry's elbow. 'You're up next, Doc.'

'Oh, no,' Barry said, trying to back away. 'Not me. I can't sing.'

'Doesn't matter. We like a good recimatation, so we do. You're a learned man. I'll bet you do "The Boy Stood on the Burning Deck".'

' ". . . Your travelling days are over." ' O'Reilly finished to a chorus of cheers.

Seamus marched Barry to the centre of the cleared space. 'Silence for our other doctor. Young Dr Barry Laverty.'

Barry looked round the circle of expectant faces. Cissie Sloan smiled at him and said, mopping her brow with a hanky, 'Warm today, Doctor.' If she was no longer feeling cold, her thyroid medication must be starting to work.

'Get on with it, Dr Laverty,' Jack yelled and raised his glass.

Someone started to sing, 'Why are we waiting? Why-hy are we waiting?'

Barry held up both hands. 'All right. All right. "The Charge of the Light Brigade",' he announced and, to his amazement, hardly stumbling at all, he recited the poem.

When he'd finished, applause swelled. Barry let himself bask in the glow, until Kinky whispered, 'Would you come, Doctor? There's someone wants to see you, so. In the surgery, sir.'

Barry grunted, and followed Kinky to the house. He walked down the hall, opened the surgery door—and stopped dead.

'Hello, Barry,' Patricia said. 'I thought you were going to phone me.'

Barry's mouth hung wide open.

'You said you'd call.' Her voice was deep, just as he remembered.

'I know,' he said, trying to collect himself. 'I thought you were being polite . . . letting me down gently.'

She shook her head, almond eyes laughing. 'No. I meant exactly what I said. I wasn't sure that I was ready to get deeply involved.'

'Oh.'

'And before you start getting any notions, I'm still not sure.'

'Then why are you here?'

'Because . . .' She limped close to him and looked into his eyes. 'There's something about you, Barry Laverty, that I think I'd like to get to know better. And it just seemed that if you wouldn't phone me, then I should come and see you.'

He took her hand. 'I'm so glad you did.' Jack had been right, he thought. 'And you picked the best day. There's a bit of a party going on.'

'I'd never have guessed,' she said with a smile, as the sounds of the pipes and a burst of applause came from the back of the house. 'Can I come?'

'In a minute.' He pulled her to him and kissed her. He was kissing her in a room that in three weeks had become as familiar to him as his old bedroom back in his parents' house in Bangor. And he might as well have been kissing her on the far side of the moon, so lost was he in her kiss.

'Now,' she said, pulling away, a little breathless. 'What about the party?'

'Come with me,' he said. Taking her hand again, he led her through to the kitchen, where Kinky was lifting yet another tray of pastries from the oven.

'Mrs Kincaid, I'd like you to meet Patricia Spence.'

'We met at the front door, so.' Kinky put the tray on the counter and shook off her oven mitts. Nice to meet you, Miss Spence. Now, I've work to do, so run along with the pair of you.'

'Right,' said Barry, heading for the back door. He looked at Kinky and saw something in her eyes, and he knew that whether it was second sight or not she'd been right all along. 'What can I get you from the bar, Patricia?' He barely noticed Lady Macbeth slip past him back out into the garden.

'Beer, please.'

'If we ever get to the front of the queue,' Barry said, watching two men who were in a heated argument up ahead of them.

O'Reilly appeared and grabbed each of the belligerent parties by a shoulder. He roared. 'You, you daft buggers, quit your argy-bargy and get the hell out of the way before all these other folks die of thirst.'

'That's Dr O'Reilly,' Barry said to Patricia.

'Is he really such an ogre?'

Barry shook his head as O'Reilly roared, 'Pint, Barry, and what's your friend having?'

'It's not your turn,' the man who would have been next in line complained.

O'Reilly fixed the complainant with a glare that Barry thought would have done justice to the mythical basilisk. The protester blushed and muttered, 'Sorry, Doctor sir. I didn't recognise yourself.'

'Rank,' O'Reilly roared, 'has its privileges. Now, Willy. Two pints, and what for your friend, Barry?'

'A beer,' Barry yelled.

O'Reilly juggled three pint glasses between his hands and drove a way through to Barry and Patricia. 'Here you are.' He gave them a glass each.

'Fingal, this is Patricia Spence.'

O'Reilly smiled at her and extended his hand. 'How do you do, Miss Spence? And what do you think of the party?'

'Very nice,' she said.

'I'll tell you,' said O'Reilly, lowering half of his pint in one swallow, 'parties are like those rockets the Americans and Russians fire into space. Once they leave the launching pad they either wobble and blow up, or roar off into the ionosphere, out into space, and head for the stars.'

'I think that's called escape velocity,' Barry offered.

'It is,' said Patricia. 'A rocket has to achieve a critical rate of speed to overcome the gravitational pull of the earth.'

'Patricia's an engineer,' Barry explained.

'Good for you,' O'Reilly remarked. 'Escape velocity? Well, the last time I saw Seamus Galvin he was definitely flying, but poor old Mr Coffin's succumbed to earth's pull. He's asleep in the vegetable patch.'

'I thought he was a Pioneer,' Barry said.

'He is, but I've a notion that Constable Mulligan has been spicing Coffin's tea up a bit. It's cheered him up, and the rest of the assorted multitude seem to be having a grand old time. Just look at them.'

Seamus Galvin and a couple of Ballybucklebo Highlanders were piping for sets of dancers. Half a dozen men, arms round each other's shoulders, were well on their way into the later verses of 'The Rocky Road to Dublin'.

'Now, Barry,' O'Reilly said, 'before Seamus drinks himself beyond redemption, I think it's time we got any formalities over and done with. It's the Galvins' going-to-America party. Someone should say a few words.'

'Right,' said Barry. 'What do you want me to do?'

'Get hold of that friend of yours, Mills. Take one of the smaller tables from the tent and cart it up to the house end of the garden.' He eyed Barry's glass. 'And give that to me. You'll be too busy to drink it.'

Barry found Jack, and they lugged one of the smaller tables to the end of the garden to make an improvised dais in front of the rows of chairs. O'Reilly appeared, holding Kinky by the arm. She and Patricia had deckchairs-of-honour beside Maureen in a chair and Barry Fingal Galvin in his pram. Jeannie Kennedy and the want-to-be-weds, Susan MacAfee and Colin Brown, found spots on the grass.

'Would the Ballybucklebo Men's Choral Society care to join us?'

O'Reilly roared. The fiddling and whistling stopped and the singers drifted across the lawn. 'Nip over and bring Seamus, will you, Barry?'

Barry skirted the apparently tireless dancers. 'Seamus.' He tugged at Seamus's sleeve. 'Seamus.'

Seamus stopped his pipes and raised a questioning eyebrow.

'Dr O'Reilly would like everybody to gather round up there.'

'Right, sir.' Seamus giggled. 'I'll see to that.'

From the corner of his eye, Barry caught a glimpse of Lady Macbeth sidling into the now empty marquee, then he made his way to where everyone stood rank upon rank, waiting expectantly. Now that the piping had stopped, all that could be heard was a gentle murmur of conversation.

O'Reilly hoisted his bulk onto the unsteady table. 'Ladies and gentlemen,' he said. 'We are here today to bid farewell to three of Ballybucklebo's more illustrious citizens. Seamus and Maureen and wee Barry Fingal are off to start a new life in the New World.'

'Will Seamus be working?' a voice enquired from the crowd.

'I will, so I will,' Seamus yelled back.

'Mother of God,' said the voice, 'miracles still do happen.'

'Now,' said O'Reilly, 'you all know I'm a man of few words—'

'And the Pope's a Presbyterian,' a man called.

'Watch it, Colin McCartney,' O'Reilly said. 'I have my eye on you.'

'How many of him do you see, Doctor sir?' someone else asked.

When the hubbub died down, O'Reilly continued. 'All right, fair play. But all I want to do is wish the Galvins a safe journey and a grand new life.' He held his glass aloft. 'To the Galvins.'

'The Galvins,' echoed the crowd.

'Come on, Seamus. Speech!' Donal Donnelly shouted.

O'Reilly beckoned to Seamus. 'Up here.' The doctor leapt from the table.

'Right.' Seamus had to be helped to climb up. 'I've said it before . . . an' I'll say it again. Best couple of doctors in Ireland. Best village in Ireland. Best country in the whole world.' Seamus swayed and his voice cracked. 'And I don't want to go to America,' he said, tears dripping.

'We're going. The week after next,' Maureen stated. 'Dr O'Reilly's holding the cash and the tickets are ordered. Me and Barry Fingal's going anyhow.'

'And I'm coming with you, love,' Seamus announced, blowing her a kiss.

'You've a job to do right now, Seamus Galvin,' Maureen said, handing her husband a parcel.

'Right. Right. Nearly forgot.' Seamus held the package over his head.

'This here's for Dr Laverty.' The crowd applauded. 'You'se folks is very lucky he came to work with Dr O'Reilly.'

'Hear, hear!' yelled Cissie Sloan.

Barry knew he was grinning fit to bust as he walked to the table.

'Here you are, Doc.' Seamus bent forward and handed Barry the gift.

Barry ripped off the paper. Inside was a burnished aluminium box. When he opened the lid he could see it was full of beautiful, hand-tied flies. A lump was in his throat and he took a deep breath before facing the crowd and saying, 'Thank you, Seamus and Maureen. Thank you all.'

He struggled to find something more appropriate to say, but his thoughts were interrupted by a sharp, deep bark and a screech. Lady Macbeth tore past in a white blur. Hot on her heels galloped Arthur Guinness, bashing into Barry's legs and knocking him arse over teakettle. He felt the dampness of his spilt drink soaking into his trousers. It wouldn't be Ballybucklebo, he thought, if that dog weren't making a mess of my trousers.

He felt O'Reilly pulling on one arm. 'Up with you, m'son.'

Barry struggled to his feet.

'One more thing,' Seamus continued. 'This here's a token of our undying esteem for Dr O'Reilly.' He jumped from the table and stood by the canvas-covered object. 'I'd like for himself to open it.'

As O'Reilly strode across the grass, Barry returned to stand by Patricia.

She was laughing as she stared at his sodden trousers. 'I think that's what I find most interesting about you, Barry. Your trousers. I've only ever seen you once in a clean pair.' She stood and kissed him. 'Could you by any chance get away tonight? I'll cook you dinner.'

He looked into her smile and saw the promise there. 'Come hell or high water,' he said. 'And I'll wear a clean pair of trousers.'

He turned when he heard Seamus say, 'You've to pull this rope here.'

'This one?' O'Reilly tugged.

The tarpaulin slithered to the ground and there, in all its splendour—three feet tall by three feet long, green head and yellow beak bright in the afternoon sunlight, brown saddle painted on its beige back—was a rocking duck.

'Holy Mother of God,' said O'Reilly, as gasps of pure amazement rose all around. 'It's a thing of beauty, Seamus.'

He crossed the grass, lifted up Jeannie and sat her in the saddle. She started to rock back and forth, laughing and fending off a line of children who were noisily demanding their turns.

'See,' said Seamus, 'I told you they'd go down a treat with the kiddies.'

'You might just be right,' said a thoughtful O'Reilly.

'Whoever bought them'll make a fortune,' Seamus added.

Barry had no difficulty understanding why there was a hint of pallor in O'Reilly's nose. He wondered if his timing might be poor, but he left Patricia and walked up to O'Reilly. 'Fingal? I don't suppose I—'

'Could have the night off?' O'Reilly stared hard at Patricia. 'Buy me a pint and I'll say yes.'

'You're on.' Barry started to head for the tent before the queue grew too long. He felt O'Reilly's hand on his arm and turned back.

'Take tomorrow off too. I can manage without you. Although I'd like you to stay here for the long haul . . . as an assistant . . . partner in a year.'

Barry looked back into the big man's brown eyes, and said, 'I'd need to think about it, Fingal. But you know I might just do that.'

'You think about it,' said O'Reilly, 'but get me a pint like a good lad . . . and a Smithwick's for Arthur.'

Barry waited his turn in the queue, glancing over to where Patricia was deep in conversation with O'Reilly. Sunlight dappled her hair.

'Ahem? Doc,' said Donal Donnelly. 'I know you must have been thinking of something important . . . but the queue's moved a bit.'

Barry shuffled ahead. Something important? Nothing was more important to him at the moment than Patricia.

'So, sir,' remarked Donal, 'I was just thinking about that day you asked me for directions to Ballybucklebo. Do you remember?'

'Yes, I do.' Indeed he remembered—the gorse, the fuschia, the blackbird, the black and white cow, how anxious he'd been about his interview.

Donal said, 'You've been here a fair while now, sir. How do you like Ballybucklebo . . . and working for himself?'

'I like it fine,' Barry said, without a moment's hesitation. He thought about the little, quiet village with its maypole, pub and thatched cottages on the shores of Belfast Lough, and of course its inhabitants: Kinky, Donal, Julie MacAteer, Jeannie Kennedy, the Galvins, Maggie and Sonny.

Barry was distracted by O'Reilly's laughter roaring through the softness of the Ulster summer evening. Dr Fingal Flahertie O'Reilly, odd as two left feet, but Barry knew that if he himself were ever ill there was no one he'd rather have to look after him.

He smiled at O'Reilly and Patricia, and murmured to himself, 'I don't think "like" is the right word. I love it here.' And Dr Barry Laverty knew it was the truth.

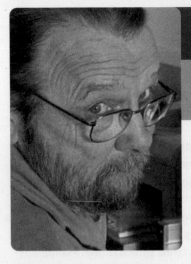

PATRICK TAYLOR

Words of wisdom: 'On life's merry-go-round you get one ticket . . . so enjoy the ride.'
Website: www.patricktaylor.ca

RD: How did your career as a doctor begin?

PT: I graduated in Belfast in 1964 and, after a year as a houseman, studied anatomy while working weekends, evenings and holidays as a supply doctor in rural practices to make ends meet. I loved general practice and applied for a job in England. Unfortunately, they were looking for someone with experience in midwifery, so I went to Glasgow to get the experience, fell in love with obstetrics, and went back to Ireland to train in obstetrics and gynaecology. I continued to make ends meet by 'moonlighting' as a rural GP—and those were the years that inspired *An Irish Country Doctor*.

RD: Many of the characters, then, are based on people you knew?

PT: Based on fact and then embellished. All of my characters are like Mrs Kincaid's recipes: a pinch of this, a teaspoonful of that, stir, and with a bit of luck you've got an interesting person derived from bits of many.

RD: Dr Fingal O'Reilly's mantra is: 'Never let the patient get the upper hand.' Did that ever happen to you?

PT: Very recently a patient thrust an internet printout of a research paper at me and asked whether I was familiar with the particular study and, if not, why not? I asked her to look closely at the author's name. My own.

RD: What was it like living in Northern Ireland during the Troubles?

PT: Bloody. Imagine being a gynaecologist, having a weekend off and returning to find not one woman on your 30-bed ward. The patients were all victims of a bomb blast.

RD: Is that why you left for Canada in 1970?

PT: Yes, we had a young daughter and didn't want her to grow up in the Troubles, which looked as if they could go on for ever. She was two when we left and thirty when they called a cease-fire.

RD: Do you miss Ireland at all?

PT: I miss the Ireland I knew, that's why I try to re-create it. It was simpler, quieter place than it is now.

RD: The scenery of Ulster comes across as idyllic in the book—and the food

sounds delicious. Do you miss those things?

PT: I do miss the scenery, particularly of a place called Strangford Lough, where as a boy I used to shoot ducks and go for peace and solace when life was too intrusive. But the scenery here in British Columbia is pretty impressive. I don't miss the delicious food because my wife, who's also from Ulster, is a superb cook.

RD: And your favourite dish is . . .?

PT: Basically, I'm a grand man for the pan. I like a full cooked breakfast with bacon, sausages, eggs, black pudding, mushrooms, barmbrack …

RD: You love sailing too. What kind do you enjoy most?

PT: Intermediate distance and offshore racing were the biggest thrill—Victoria to Maui, for example. My job was navigator, as I'm a little on the short side for deck work. My best friend, who owned the 50-foot boat had to sell her, unfortunately. But now I enjoy inshore cruising on our 26-footer and there are some wonderful waters here for that.

RD: How do you switch off from the writing to relax, now that you're retired?

PT: There's a pub on the island where I live that's small and cosy. When I finish work each day at about 3 p.m., I walk the mile and a half downhill to the pub and meet the same coterie of people, so there is always good conversation—the craic—to be had. Then I walk the mile and a half uphill back home. The exercise just about negates the beer calories and stops me getting too tall around!

MRS KINCAID'S BARMBRACK

INGREDIENTS (MAKES 2 LOAVES):

1lb (450g) sultanas	3 cups black tea	3 level tsps baking powder
1lb (450g) raisins	1lb (450g) plain flour	3 tsps mixed spice (optional)
1lb (450g) brown sugar	3 large eggs, beaten	

Preheat oven to 150°C/300°F/Gas mark 2.

METHOD:

Soak the fruit and sugar in the tea overnight. The next day, fold the flour and beaten eggs into the fruit. Finally, add the baking powder and mixed spice. Fill two greased 2lb loaf tins (or 20cm cake tins) with the mix. Level the surface and bake for 1½-1¾ hours, until firm.

To test, insert a skewer; on removal it should be clean. Cool the loaf in its tin for 10 minutes, then turn onto a wire rack. When cool, brush with melted honey to give a fine glaze. Slice and serve with butter, if liked.

COOK'S NOTE: the traditional Ulster cook uses yeast (as right), when the bread may be toasted, but this is an easier recipe. Barmbrack freezes well.

EVIL

GREG ILES

Imagine someone tells you
your spouse is plotting to kill you.
And their far-fetched theory,
outrageous at first, suddenly makes
a horrible kind of sense.
That's the situation into which
39-year-old Chris Shepard is plunged
when FBI agent Alex Morse comes
knocking at his door.

Chapter 1

Alex Morse charged through the lobby of the University Medical Center in Jackson, Mississippi, like a doctor to a code call. But she was no doctor. She was a hostage negotiator for the FBI. Twenty minutes earlier, Alex had deplaned from a flight from Charlotte, North Carolina, a flight prompted by her older sister's sudden collapse at a Little League baseball game. This year had been plagued by injury and death, and there was more to come—Alex could feel it.

When her plane had landed in Jackson, she'd called her brother-in-law again. This time he'd sobbed as he related the events of the past hour. Though still breathing on her own, Grace had lapsed into a coma and might die at any moment. Panic had filled Alex's chest, and she had sprinted down the concourse and jumped the cab queue, flashing her FBI creds and telling the driver to drive at a hundred miles an hour to the University Medical Center.

Hospitals, she thought bitterly as she waited for the elevator. She'd practically just got out of one herself. But the chain of tragedy had started with her father. Five months ago Jim Morse had died in this very hospital. Two months after that, Alex's mother, Margaret, had been diagnosed with advanced ovarian cancer. She had already outlived her prognosis, but wasn't expected to survive the week. Then came Alex's accident. And now Grace—

A bell dinged softly, and the elevator opened. A young woman in a white coat glanced up as Alex entered, looked down, then up again. Alex had endured this double take so many times since the shooting that she no longer got angry. Just depressed.

She watched the glowing numbers change above her head. After her mother's diagnosis, Alex had begun commuting regularly by plane from

Washington, DC—where she was based then—to Jackson to relieve Grace, who was struggling to teach full-time and care for their mother at night. Alex had told herself she could hack the pressure, and she did—right up until the moment she cracked. But she hadn't realised she'd cracked until she caught part of a shotgun blast in her face.

It happened during a hostage rescue operation at a bank. The shooter had fired through a plate-glass partition, and a blizzard of glass tore through her cheek and jaw, ripping away tissue and bone. The plastic surgeons had told her that, in time, the angry pink scars would fade. Alex wasn't convinced. But in the grand scheme of things, what did vanity matter? Seconds after she was shot, someone else on the hostage rescue team had paid for her mistake . . .

During the hellish days that followed the shooting, Grace had flown up to DC three times to be with Alex, despite being exhausted from caring for their mother. Tonight it was Grace fighting for her life. She'd been walking up the steps of a stadium to watch her ten-year-old son play baseball when she collapsed. A CAT scan taken forty minutes later showed a blood clot near her brain stem, the kind that too often killed people.

Alex had been swimming laps in Charlotte, where she'd been transferred as punishment duty after the shooting, when she got word from Grace's husband. Bill Fennell's voice had quavered as he had explained that while the neurological damage had initially not looked too bad—some right-side paralysis, mild dysphasia—the stroke was worsening.

Now, Alex stepped out of the elevator on the fourth floor of the UMC, and headed for a huge door marked NEUROLOGY ICU. She steeled herself for the words she was certain to hear: *I'm sorry, Alex, but you're too late.*

The ICU held a dozen glass-walled cubicles built in a U-shape around a nurses' station. In the fourth from the left, Alex saw Bill Fennell talking to a woman in a white coat, his handsome face furrowed with anxiety. Sensing Alex's presence, he looked up and froze midsentence. Alex moved towards the cubicle and he rushed over and hugged her to his chest. She'd always felt awkward embracing her brother-in-law, but tonight they both needed some kind of affirmation of family unity.

'I can't believe you made it so fast,' he said. 'She's still with us. She's regained consciousness a couple of times, and asked for you.'

Alex's heart lifted, but with hope came fresh tears.

The woman in the white coat walked out of the cubicle. She looked about fifty, and her face was kind but grave. 'I'm Meredith Andrews, Grace's neurologist,' said the woman. 'Are you the one she calls KK?'

KK was a nickname derived from Alex's middle name, Karoli. 'Yes. But please call me Alex. Alex Morse,' she said, wiping her cheeks.

'You're all she can talk about.'

'Is she conscious?'

'Not at this moment. Now, we're doing everything we can, Alex, but you should prepare yourself for the worst. Grace had a serious thrombosis when she was brought in, but she was breathing on her own. The stroke extended steadily, though, and I decided to start thrombolytic therapy to try to dissolve the clot. This can work miracles, but it can also cause haemorrhages elsewhere. I think that may be happening now. If she stops breathing, we're ready to intubate immediately. I probably should have done it already'—Dr Andrews glanced at Bill—'but I knew she was desperate to talk to you, and once she's intubated she won't be able to communicate with anyone.'

Alex winced. 'I understand,' she said. 'Can I just be with her?'

Dr Andrews nodded and led Alex into the cubicle.

Alex turned back to Bill before entering. 'Where's Jamie?'

'With my sister in Ridgeland.' Ridgeland was a suburb ten miles away.

'Don't you think he should be here?'

Bill drew a deep breath. 'No, I don't,' he said, then lowered his voice and added, 'I don't want Jamie to watch his mother die.'

'Of course not. But he should have a chance to say goodbye.'

'We don't have time for this.' He nodded into the cubicle.

Alex walked slowly to the edge of her sister's bed. The face above the hospital blanket was pale, the eyes closed. Grace Morse Fennell was thirty-five years old, but tonight she looked seventy. It's her skin, Alex realised. It's like wax. Drooping wax.

'I'll leave you with her,' Dr Andrews said.

Alex glanced at the bank of CRTs monitoring Grace's life functions. Heartbeat, oxygen saturation, blood pressure, God knew what else. A single IV line disappeared beneath a bandage on her forearm.

'You know what this has taught me?' asked the familiar bass voice.

Alex hadn't realised that Bill was still in the room. 'What?' she said.

'Money isn't really worth anything. All the money in the world won't make that blood clot go away.'

Alex nodded distantly. 'Could I be alone with her for a while?' she asked, not taking her eyes from Grace's face.

Bill's strong hand closed on her shoulder. 'I'll be back in five minutes.'

After he'd gone, Alex took Grace's hand and bent to kiss her forehead. She had never seen her sister so helpless. Grace was a dynamo. Crises that brought others' lives to a standstill hardly caused her to break stride. But this was different. This was the end, Alex knew. She wiped away a tear, then took out her cellphone and called Bill, who was standing less than thirty feet away.

'What is it?' he asked frantically. 'What's wrong?'

'Jamie should be here.'

'Alex, I told you—'

'You get him, goddamn it. This is his *mother* lying here.'

There was a long silence. Then Bill said, 'I'll call my sister.'

Alex turned and saw him standing near the nurses' station, talking to Dr Andrews. She saw him leave the neurologist and lift his cellphone. Alex leaned down to Grace's ear and tried to think of something that would reach the bottom of the dark well where her sister now dwelled.

'Sue-Sue?' she whispered, squeezing the cold hand. It was another nickname based on a middle name, a family tradition. 'Sue-Sue, it's me, KK.'

Grace's eyes remained shut.

'It's me, Sue-Sue. Wake up. I know you're playing possum. Quit faking.'

Alex felt a twitch in her hand and adrenaline surged through her.

'*Gay-Gay?*' Grace moaned. '*Iz zah wu?*'

'Yes, Gracie,' Alex said, rubbing a strand of hair out of her sister's eyes.

'*Thang Goth*,' Grace said in a guttural voice, then she began to sob. The right half of her face was paralysed, and drool ran down her chin whenever she struggled to speak. '*Wu . . . wu have tuh thave Jamie.*'

'What? I missed that.'

'*Havuh thave Jamie!*' Grace repeated, struggling to rise in the bed.

'Jamie's fine,' Alex said in a comforting voice. 'He's on his way here.'

Grace shook her head. '*Wissen! You—have—tuh—thave—Jamie.*'

'Save Jamie from what?'

'*Biw.*'

'Bill?' Alex asked, sure she must be wrong in her translation.

With painful effort, Grace nodded.

Alex blinked in astonishment. 'Why? Is Bill hurting him in some way?'

A weak nod. '*Ee wiw . . . thoon ath I'm gone.*'

Alex struggled to understand the tortured words. 'Hurt Jamie how?'

Grace shook her head. '*Biw—wiw—kiw—Jamie's—thole.*'

'Bill . . . will . . . kill . . . Jamie's . . . soul?'

Nodding, Grace gripped Alex's hand. '*Eeth a monther!*' she hissed.

'He's a monster?' Alex felt a chill. 'Is that what you said?'

Grace pulled Alex closer. '*Ee kiwd me!*'

Feeling as though ice water had been shunted into her veins, Alex drew back and looked into Grace's eyes. 'He *killed* you?'

Grace nodded once, her eyes filled with conviction.

'You don't know what you're saying, Grace.'

Grace managed a smile that said, *Oh, yes, I do.* She closed her eyes as though gathering herself for one last effort. '*You . . . onwe one . . . ooh can thop im now. Thave Jamie for me . . . Gay-Gay. Pleath.*'

Alex looked back through the glass wall. Bill was speaking to Dr Andrews, but his eyes were on Alex.

'Sue-Sue,' she whispered, 'why would Bill want to hurt you?'

'*Thum-one elth,*' Grace said. '*Wuh-man.*'

'If he wants to be with another woman, why doesn't he just divorce you?'

'*Muhn-ey . . . dum-me. Would coth Biw miw-yens . . . tuh do that.*'

Alex drew back in disbelief. She had no idea Bill was that wealthy.

Grace had closed her eyes, seemingly drained by her efforts. '*Tew . . . Mom . . .*' she said. '*Tew huh . . . I be waiting fuh hurh . . . in heaven.*' The smile animated the living half of her face again. '*If—I—make it.*'

Alex balled her free hand into a fist and held it against her mouth.

'Well, look at this, Dr Andrews!' boomed Bill Fennell. 'She looks like she's ready to get up and out of that bed.'

Grace's eyes snapped open, and she shrank away from her husband. The terror in her eyes hurt Alex's heart, and it also thrust her into full-defence mode. She stood up and blocked Bill from coming to the bedside.

'I think it's better if you don't come in,' she said.

Bill's mouth dropped open. He looked past her to Grace, who was cowering in the bed. 'What are you talking about?' he asked angrily.

'You're upsetting her, Bill,' she said. 'Go downstairs and wait for Jamie.'

'There's no way I'm leaving my wife's bedside. Not when she might—'

'What?' Alex asked, a note of challenge in her voice.

Dr Andrews stepped towards Bill and said, 'Perhaps we should give Grace and her sister some more time alone.'

'I'm Grace's husband,' Bill said irritably, 'and I'll decide who—'

'She's my *blood*,' Alex said with conviction. 'Your presence here is upsetting Grace, and that's all that matters. Isn't that right, Doctor?'

'Absolutely.' Meredith Andrews looked down at her patient. 'Grace, do you want your husband in this room?'

Grace slowly shook her head. '*I wan . . . my bay . . . be. Wan Jamie.*'

The neurologist looked up at Bill Fennell, who towered over her. 'That's good enough for me. I want you to leave the unit, Mr Fennell.'

Bill stepped close to the neurologist, his eyes sheened with anger. 'I give a lot of money to this university. A *lot* of money. And I—'

'Don't make me call security,' Dr Andrews said quietly, lifting the phone.

Bill's face went white. Alex almost felt sorry for him. And then the alarm began to sing.

'*She's coding!*' Dr Andrews shouted, but nurses were already running to the cubicle. Suddenly there was a whirlwind of motion, all directed towards sustaining the life that was fast ebbing from the body on the bed.

'You need to leave,' said a tall male nurse. 'Both of you.'

Alex backed slowly out of the ICU, watching the final act of her sister's life unfold without any hope of playing a part. As she turned away, she heard Dr Andrews say, 'I'm calling it, guys. Time of death, ten twenty-nine p.m.'

Something started to let go in her chest, but before the release, she heard a little boy say, 'Hey! Is my mom in here?'

Alex turned towards the big door that had brought her to this particular chamber of hell and saw before it a boy about four and a half feet tall. He was trying to look brave, but Alex saw fear in his wide green eyes.

'Aunt Alex?' said Jamie, finally picking her out of the uniformed crowd.

Bill's voice sounded from behind Alex. 'Hello, Son. Come over here.'

Alex looked back at her brother-in-law's stern face, and the thing that had started to let go inside her suddenly ratcheted tight. Without thought she ran to Jamie, and swept him out through the door, away from this nightmare.

Away from Bill Fennell.

Chapter 2: Five Weeks Later

Dr Chris Shepard lifted a manila folder from the file caddy at the door of Exam Room 4 and perused it. The patient was Alexandra Morse, from Charlotte, North Carolina, and her file held only the medical history form that new patients filled out on their first visit. She had not specified a complaint. Chris shrugged, and walked into the examining room.

A woman wearing a navy skirt and a cream-coloured top stood beside the examining table. Her face almost caused him to stare, but he'd seen a lot of trauma during his medical training. This woman's scars weren't actually too bad, but you figured a woman as young and attractive as her would have had plastic surgery . . .

'Hello, Dr Shepard,' the woman said in a direct tone.

'Ms Morse?' he said, remembering that the history said she was single.

She gave him a smile of acknowledgment but said nothing else.

'What can I do for you today?' he asked.

The woman remained silent, but he could feel her eyes probing him. *What's going on here?* he wondered. He studied her, trying to divine her real purpose. She had dark hair, green eyes and an oval face—not much different from those of the dozens of women he saw each day. A little better bone structure maybe, especially the cheekbones. But the real difference was the scars. And something that Chris couldn't quite nail down, something that set her apart from other women. Something in the way she stood, maybe . . .

Laying the chart on the counter behind him, he said, 'Maybe you should just tell me what your problem is. I promise, however frightening it might seem now, I've seen or heard it many times in this office, and together we can do something about it.'

'You've never heard what I'm about to tell you,' Alex Morse said with utter certainty. 'And it's not my problem, Doctor. It's yours.'

Chris frowned in confusion as the woman reached into a handbag on the chair behind her and brought out a wallet. This she flipped open and held up. He saw an ID card with a blue and white seal. Bold letters on the right side of the card read *FBI*. To the left, beside a photo of the woman standing before him, smaller letters read *Special Agent Alexandra Morse.*

'I need to tell you some things in confidence,' she said. 'It won't take much of your time. I pretended to be a patient because I don't want anyone in your life to know you've spoken to an FBI agent. Before I leave, I need you to write me a prescription for Levaquin and tell your nurse that I had a urinary-tract infection. Will you do that?'

'Sure,' he said, too surprised to make a conscious decision. 'But what's going on? Are you investigating something? Are you investigating me?'

'Not you.'

'Then who? Someone I know?'

Agent Morse's eyes didn't waver. 'I may tell you at the end of this conversation, but right now I'm going to tell you a story. Will you sit down, Doctor?'

Chris sat on the short stool he used in the examining room. 'Are you really from North Carolina? Or is that just a cover?'

'Why do you ask?'

'You talk like a Yankee, but I hear Mississippi underneath.'

Agent Morse smiled. 'You have good ears. I grew up in Jackson. But I'm based in Charlotte now.'

He was glad to have his intuition confirmed. 'Please go on with your story. Why are you here in Natchez?'

She sat on the chair where her handbag had been, regarding him coolly. 'Five weeks ago, my sister died of a brain haemorrhage at the University Medical Center in Jackson.'

'I'm sorry.'

Agent Morse nodded as though she were past it, but Chris saw the emotion in her eyes. 'Before she died, she told me something that sounded crazy. She told me she'd been murdered. By her husband.'

He wasn't sure he understood. 'What did the autopsy show?'

'A fatal blood clot on the left side of the brain, near the brain stem. No abnormal cause. No strange drugs, no poisons, nothing like that.'

'Did your sister's husband resist the autopsy?'

'No. He didn't.'

'But you still believed her? You really thought he'd killed her?'

'Not at first. I thought she must have been hallucinating. But then I remembered Grace also telling me that she thought her husband was having an affair. He's a wealthy man, and she believed he'd murdered her rather than pay the cost of a divorce. And to get custody of their son, of course.'

Chris considered this. 'I'm sure women have been killed for that reason before. Men, too, I imagine.'

'Absolutely. Anyway . . . after Grace's funeral, I told her husband I was going back to Charlotte.'

'But you didn't.'

'No.'

'Was he having an affair?'

'He was. And Grace's death didn't slow him down in the least. So I engaged the resources of the Bureau to investigate him. His personal life, his business, everything. I now know almost everything there is to know about Grace's husband—let's call him Bill. I know far more than my sister knew. For example, when I was going through Bill's records, I found that he had some rather complex connections to a lawyer who practises in Jackson. His specialty is family law.'

'Divorce?' said Chris.

'Exactly. Though he does some estate planning. Trusts, wills, et cetera.'

'Had "Bill" consulted this lawyer about divorcing your sister?'

Agent Morse shifted on her chair. 'I can't prove that,' she said. 'Not yet. There's no evidence of any relationship between Bill and this attorney until *after* my sister's death. That's when they went into business together.'

Chris wanted to ask several questions, but he suddenly remembered that he had patients waiting. 'This story is very intriguing, Agent Morse, but I can't see how it has anything to do with me.'

'You will. After I found the connection between Bill and this divorce lawyer,' she continued, 'I broadened the investigation. What I found was a web of business relationships that boggled my mind. This divorce attorney has interests in just about every business you can think of. Mostly partnerships with various wealthy individuals in Mississippi.'

'Is it strange that a rich lawyer—I'm assuming he's rich—would be into a lot of different businesses?'

'Not in and of itself. But after looking closely at these deals, I discovered that nine of the individuals that this divorce lawyer is in business with share common characteristics. Each of them was wealthy, and each had a spouse who died unexpectedly in the past five years.'

Chris tried to digest this. 'Is that unusual?' he said.

'I can show you actuarial tables if you like. It's way off the charts.'

Chris was intrigued by Morse's single-minded intensity. 'So . . . you think this divorce lawyer is helping clients to murder their spouses rather than pay them a financial settlement?'

Morse nodded. 'Or to gain sole custody of their children.'

'OK. But why are you saying this to me?'

Agent Morse looked uncomfortable. 'Because,' she said, 'one week ago, your wife drove to Jackson and spent two hours in that lawyer's office.'

Chris's mouth fell open. A wave of numbness moved slowly through his body, as though he'd been shot with a massive dose of lidocaine.

'Have you been having problems in your marriage, Doctor?'

'No,' he said, grateful to be certain of something at last. 'Look . . . if Thora went to see this lawyer, she must have had some reason other than divorce. We're not having *any* kind of marital trouble.'

'You don't think she could be having an affair?' Morse asked.

Chris stood and his face went red. 'Are you about to tell me that she is?'

'Calm down, Dr Shepard. You may not believe it, but I'm here to help you. I realise we're talking about personal matters. Intimate matters, even.

But you're forced to do the same thing in your job, aren't you? When human life is at stake, privacy goes by the board.'

She was right, of course. Chris looked away. 'What are you telling me, Agent Morse? Spell it out.'

'Your life may be in danger.'

'From my wife? You're out of your mind. I'm going to call Thora right now and get to the bottom of this.' He reached for the phone on the wall.

Morse got to her feet. 'Please don't do that, Dr Shepard. You may be the only person in a position to stop whoever is behind these murders.'

Chris let his hand fall. 'How's that?'

She took a deep breath. 'If you *have* become a target, then your wife and this attorney have no idea you're aware of their activities, and that puts you in a unique position to help us trap them.'

'You want me to get my wife jailed for attempted murder?'

Morse turned up her palms. 'Would you rather pretend none of this happened and die at thirty-six?'

He closed his eyes for a moment, trying to restrain his temper. 'You're missing the forest for the trees here. Your whole thesis is illogical.'

'Why?'

'Those men you think murdered their wives . . . they did it to keep from splitting their assets and paying out a ton of alimony, right?'

'In most cases. But at least one case was about custody of the children.'

'Again, you're miles off base. Thora and I have no children.'

'Your wife has a child. A nine-year-old son.'

He smiled. 'Sure, but she had Ben even before she married her first husband, Red Simmons. Thora would automatically get custody.'

'You've legally adopted Ben. But that brings up another important point—how your wife got her money.'

Chris sat back down and looked at Agent Morse. How much did she know about his wife? Probably only the local legend: how Thora Rayner had been working in St Catherine's Hospital when Red Simmons, a local oil man nineteen years her senior, had been carried into the ER with a myocardial infarction; how she'd become close to Red during his hospital stay, then married him six months later. Chris had known Thora as a brave and loyal wife, a woman worthy of respect. When Red died two and a half years ago, he left her an estate valued at $6.5 million, which was big money in Natchez.

'Agent Morse,' he said, 'Thora doesn't stand to gain or lose anything if we divorce. We both signed a prenuptial agreement, and each person leaves the marriage with exactly what he or she brought into it. I have money of my own. I've made some lucky investments.'

Agent Morse studied Chris in silence, then she said, 'And what happens if you die? What does your will say? Who gets your money?'

Chris's face was growing hot. 'My parents get a nice chunk. Thora gets the rest. But . . . she's worth millions of dollars,' he protested. 'What would be the point? Kill me to get an extra two million?'

Morse rubbed her chin for a few moments. 'People are murdered every day for reasons other than money,' she said. 'How well do you know your wife? Psychologically, I mean?'

'Pretty damn well.' Chris was starting to dislike Agent Morse intensely. 'You think my wife murdered her first husband, don't you?'

Morse shrugged. 'I didn't say that.'

'You might as well have. But Red had a long history of heart disease.'

'Yes, he did. But no autopsy was done,' she pointed out.

'I'm aware of that. Are you suggesting that one be done now?'

Agent Morse dismissed this idea with a flick of her hand. 'We wouldn't find anything. Whoever's behind these murders is too good for that.'

Chris looked deep into Morse's eyes. There was sincerity there, and passion. But something seemed wrong about her story.

'The first victim you told me about—if these *are* murder victims—was your sister, right? Doesn't that create some sort of conflict? Should you be investigating your own sister's death?'

'To be perfectly frank, no. But there's no one else I trust to do it right.' Morse looked at her watch. 'We don't have time to get deep into this now. I'll speak to you again soon, Dr Shepard, but I don't want you to deviate from your normal routine in any way that your wife or anyone else would notice.'

'Who else would notice?'

'The person planning to kill you.'

Chris went still. 'Are you saying someone might be following me?'

'Yes. You and I cannot be seen together in public.'

'Wait a minute. You can't tell me something like this and just walk out of here. Is the FBI giving me protection?'

'It's not like that. Nobody's trying to assassinate you with a rifle. If the past is any guide—and it almost always is—then your death will have to look natural. You should be careful in traffic. No one can protect you from that kind of hit. And you shouldn't eat or drink anything at home for a while. Nothing prepared by your wife.'

'You're kidding, right?'

'I realise that might be difficult, but we'll work it out. To tell you the truth, I think we have some time. This kind of murder takes meticulous planning.'

Chris heard a note of hysteria in his laughter. 'That's a huge comfort.'

'Does your wife have plans to be out of town anytime soon?'

He shook his head.

'Good. That's a good sign.' Morse picked up her handbag. 'You'd better write me that prescription now. For the Levaquin.'

'Oh, right.' He took a pad from his pocket and scribbled a prescription for a dozen antibiotic pills. 'You think of everything, don't you?'

'No one thinks of everything. And be glad for it. That's the way we catch most criminals. Stupid mistakes. Even the best of us make them.' She took the prescription from Chris's hand. 'I'm sorry to be the one to turn your life upside-down, Doctor I really am. I'll contact you again soon. Remember your phones may be tapped, and that includes your cellphone. And whatever you do, don't ask your wife if she's trying to kill you.'

Chris gaped after Morse as she walked towards the door.

ANDREW RUSK WAS AFRAID. He stood at the window of his law office on the sixteenth floor of the AmSouth tower and gazed out over the Jackson skyline. He lifted a tumbler of bourbon to his lips and took a long pull. Whiskey at work was an indulgence, one he'd allowed himself more and more in the past weeks, as a balm against the fear.

Refilling the tumbler, he lifted a photograph from his desk. It showed a dark-haired woman with an angular face and deep-set, confident green eyes—the kind of eyes that looked alive even on paper. That was probably what had led her to a career with the FBI.

'Special Agent Alex,' he murmured. 'Nosy *bitch.*'

He took another gulp of whiskey and walked to his desk, where his glowing flat-panel monitor showed the portal image of a Dutch website called EX NIHILO—a black hole with a shimmering event horizon. Rusk remembered a little Latin from his prep-school days: *ex nihilo* meant 'out of nothing'. For a considerable fee, EX NIHILO provided absolute anonymity in the digital domain, and Rusk would be using their very discreet services today.

All partnerships fail in the end, just like marriages, he thought, recalling his father's cynical words. Rusk hated many things about his father, senior partner of a much more venerable law firm, but one thing he could not deny: the man had been right about a great deal. Rusk moved his cursor onto a blank box and typed 3.141592654—pi to the ninth decimal place. As a boy, he'd memorised pi to the fortieth decimal place to impress his father. Immediately after his proud dinner-time recitation, dear old Dad had told him about an Indian boy who'd memorised pi to the 600th place. Typical paternal response in the Rusk home: nothing was ever good enough.

Rusk retyped his password, then clicked CONFIRM, thereby arming a digital mechanism that might now be his sole means of survival. His partner would tolerate zero risk; he had made that clear at the outset. In fact, the man was so obsessive about security that he had insisted that Andrew call him by the code name Glykon. (Rusk had Googled 'Glykon', but all he'd discovered was that it was the name of a Greek snake god.) For five years he and Glykon had experienced steady and staggering profits without a hitch, but if Glykon perceived risk, he would instantly move to eliminate it. Rusk had no illusions about that. And it meant only one thing: death.

The glue that had held their partnership together thus far was a Cold War strategy called MAD: mutually assured destruction. When each party knew that the other held the key to their destruction, trust was guaranteed. Now, for the first time in Rusk's association with Glykon, danger had reared its head. Two threats, almost simultaneously. And Rusk had concluded that for MAD to be a true deterrent each party had to *know* that a sword of Damocles hung over his head. Tacit understanding was not sufficient. EX NIHILO provided that sword. If Rusk did not log on to the website every day and authenticate his identity, then, after a grace period of ten days, EX NIHILO would forward the contents of a large digital file containing a detailed record of the partnership's activities to the FBI and the state police— enough legal dynamite to blast both men into prison for life.

The prospect of announcing the news of EX NIHILO to Glykon was what had Rusk in a state of fear. The moment that he unsheathed this 'sword', he and Glykon would become adversaries. Intellectual genius and ruthless efficiency had made Glykon the perfect collaborator; those same qualities would also make him a formidable adversary.

Rusk's fear disgusted him. The walls of his office were lined with photographs that testified to his virility: brilliant snapshots of the blond ex-college president he'd once been wearing every type of survival suit known to man. He had a stunt plane that he flew like a barnstormer, and he'd even climbed Everest last year during a hell of a storm. All this before the age of forty, yet he still felt like a boy in the presence of Glykon. And it wasn't just the age difference—it was something else, something he could not put a name to.

Rusk knew he'd made a mistake taking the Fennell case. The target's sister was an FBI agent, and her father had been a homicide cop. Rusk had planned to refuse the job, but when he'd mentioned it to Glykon, his partner had seen the FBI connection as a challenge. And when Bill Fennell had offered a fifty per cent bonus—*fifty* per cent—Rusk had caved. But now he had Special Agent Alex Morse crawling all over his life. He'd expected her to give up after a while, but she hadn't. She was tenacious.

Rusk was sure that she had broken into his office, though he hadn't reported this to the police or to Glykon. What had she discovered while she was here? The case-related data on Rusk's hard drives were encrypted, but Rusk had a feeling that Morse knew her way around computers. Probably around business records, too. His enquiries into her CV had revealed a law degree and a year working in South Florida with an FBI/DEA task force. She had also spent time as an FBI hostage negotiator, though she had proved unequal to the job. Her father's death and her mother's cancer had evidently pushed her into a zone where her judgment had abandoned her, and she'd got somebody killed. She'd almost died herself, and her butchered face bore the evidence of her brush with death.

Glykon had to know about Alex Morse.

And Morse wasn't their only problem. Right now the equivalent of a nuclear bomb was ticking beneath their partnership. 'A *client*,' Rusk muttered in disbelief, swigging from his tumbler. 'A goddamn rogue client.'

He walked over to a credenza and removed a box of aluminium foil from a drawer. Opening the long box, he tore off two squares, and laid them on a table by the northeast window of his office. There was packaging tape in the bottom drawer of his desk. He cut off several short lengths and taped the foil to the east-facing window, shiny side out. In sunlight, the squares would be visible from the elevated section of Interstate 55.

The foil was another of Glykon's ideas. Those two squares would bring about a meeting that Rusk dreaded like no other. His hand shook as he drained the bourbon. He felt as though he had summoned the devil.

CHRIS SHEPARD SWUNG the baseball bat in a fast arc, smacking a low ball at his four-foot-tall shortstop. The shortstop scooped up the ball and hummed it to the boy at first base, Chris's adopted son, Ben. The throw went wide, but Ben stretched out and sucked the ball into his glove as though by magic.

'Great catch!' Chris shouted, and Ben's eyes glowed with pride, though he maintained as stern a countenance as a nine-year-old could muster.

Chris glanced to his right. Two minutes ago, Thora's silver Mercedes had pulled onto the grassy bank behind the practice area. She didn't get out, but sat watching from behind the smoked-glass windshield. It struck him how rarely Thora came to practice any more—yet last year she had been one of the team's biggest supporters. Curiosity had brought her out today, he knew. Instead of making his evening hospital rounds early, as was his habit during the season, Chris had picked Ben up from home right after his clinic closed. Thora had been out running, so they'd missed each other. As a result, they hadn't spoken since his visit from Agent Morse.

Chris waved at the Mercedes, then started working ground balls around the infield. He'd avoided talking to Thora because he needed time to process what Morse had told him. He wished he had asked her more questions about the supposed murders. Clearly she had no forensic evidence to back up her extraordinary theory or she wouldn't need him to try to set up a trap. And yet . . . if he was honest, he couldn't deny that in the past few hours he'd been turning over certain realities about his marriage that had been bothering him on a deep level for some time.

Foremost was the baby issue. During their courtship, he and Thora had agreed that they wanted to start having children as soon as they married. But after the wedding, Thora admitted that she'd been wondering whether they should move so quickly. Chris had hidden his disappointment, but it obviously showed through, because Thora had finally stopped taking the pill. So far, however, she had not conceived.

'Alex Morse is nuts,' Chris muttered, cracking a ball towards third base. His marriage might not be in a perfect state, but the idea that his wife was planning to murder him was ludicrous. But what should he do? Call the FBI and report her? Call his lawyer? Or try to get more information? Until he knew more, he wasn't going to let his wife know anything was amiss.

Thora was standing now by the open door of her Mercedes, her blonde hair flashing in the late afternoon sun. She gave him a small wave and smiled beneath her dark sunglasses. She was wearing running clothes, which did little to conceal her lithe, muscular body.

When she had been married to Red Simmons, Thora had dressed conservatively. But after a period of mourning, at about the time she'd started seeing Chris, she had changed her style. In the beginning, Chris had approved. The new look revealed more of her beauty and signalled a new engagement with life. But lately Thora had begun wearing ultrashort shorts, see-through tops, push-up bras . . . Chris kidded her about this, but Thora continued to wear the stuff. And until today, it hadn't seemed that big a deal.

'Coach Grant,' he called to his assistant, another father. 'Let's call it a day.'

The boys cheered, and their parents started packing up ice chests and kit bags for the trek home. Ben walked beside his father to the Mercedes.

'Big Ben!' cried Thora, bending to hug her sweaty son. 'You didn't miss a catch the whole time I was here!'

Ben shrugged. 'I play first base, Mom. You can't play first and miss balls.'

Chris wished he could see Thora's eyes, but the sunglasses hid them.

She gave Ben a quick squeeze, then straightened and gave Chris her thousand-watt smile. 'You picked up Ben early today.'

'Yeah. I decided to do my rounds after practice.'

She nodded but said nothing. He wasn't sure what to say next.

Ben saved him by asking, 'Can we go to La Fiesta, Mom?'

Thora shook her head. 'We've got plenty of food at home, and it's a lot healthier than Mexican. I made chicken salad this afternoon.'

Ben rolled his eyes and wrinkled his nose.

Chris almost said, *I'll pick up something on the way home*, but that would only result in Ben begging for takeout and Thora getting irritated. 'Help me load the gear, Son. I need to get to the hospital.'

Chris and Ben tossed the two bulging canvas bags into his pick-up. Then Chris gave Ben a high five, hugged Thora lightly to his side, and climbed into the truck. 'I won't be too late,' he said through the open window.

As though in answer, Thora took off her sunglasses. Her sea-blue eyes cut through his feigned nonchalance, and her gaze held an unspoken question. He broke eye contact, gave a casual wave and drove towards town.

ALEX MORSE DROVE her rented Corolla into the parking lot of the Days Inn in Natchez, pulled up to the door of room 125 and shut off the engine. As soon as she was inside the room, she took off her shoulder holster and massaged the place where it had lain against her ribs.

Alex had checked into the room five days ago, and she'd done what she could to make it home. Her notebook computer sat humming on the desk, and beside it stood a photo of Jamie wearing his Jackson Academy basketball uniform—a gangly ten-year old with auburn hair, a freckled face and deep-set eyes that projected heartbreaking uncertainty.

Looking at the picture, she remembered how frantic Jamie had been the morning after his mother died, when Alex told him she had to take him back to his father. Running off with him after Grace's death had been an act of desperation and, in the eyes of the law, kidnapping. If Alex had kept him, Bill wouldn't have hesitated to have her arrested. Many times in the past weeks she had regretted returning Jamie, but there had been no alternative. If her efforts to prove Bill's complicity in Grace's murder failed—which without Dr Shepard's help was likely—then she would take drastic action.

On a dresser beside the desk lay several stacks of paper relating to her mother's medical care. Grace had dealt with Margaret Morse's cancer the way she dealt with every crisis: she'd declared war on it. Now, running the campaign had passed to Alex, and by Grace's standards she was doing a poor job. Instead of being at her mother's bedside, she was camped out a hundred miles southeast of Jackson, in Natchez, Mississippi, burning through her savings and risking her career in a quest to punish her sister's murderer. But she had been charged with 'saving' Jamie from his father. And the only way to do that was to prove that Fennell had murdered Grace.

Alex walked to the card table on which she kept her case materials. It was fairly primitive stuff—jotted notes, surveillance records, digital snapshots, minicassettes. But as her father had told her countless times, there was no substitute for putting your heels on the pavement. All the computers in the world couldn't nail a killer if you never left your office.

Alex kept a framed picture of her dad, as a fresh-faced patrolman, propped on the card table. Jim Morse had gone into police work after two tours with the army in Vietnam. He did well, making sergeant before anyone else in his academy class. He passed the detective's exam when he was twenty-seven and quickly got known for brilliant detective work and speaking his mind. The first trait would have assured rapid promotion had he not possessed the second in equal measure. Consequently, for most of his career, he had watched less talented men climb past him on the career ladder.

After retirement, he had opened a detective agency with a former partner—a wise old redneck named Will Kilmer. The freedom had suited both men, and they got all the referral business they could handle. Alex was certain that it was her teenage exposure to their livelier cases that had caused her to enroll in the FBI academy after law school, a choice her father had applauded, though her mother had reacted with silent reproach.

To avoid a wave of grief, Alex looked down at a jumble of snapshots of Chris and Thora Shepard. She had been following them long enough to form an impression of a typical upper-middle-class couple. Chris spent a remarkable amount of time working, while Thora alternated exercise with personal pampering. Alex felt a vague resentment as she gazed at Thora; the woman looked better after a six-mile run than most women did after two hours of prepping for a party. Chris, on the other hand, was much more down-to-earth, a dark-haired Henry Fonda type rather than a pretty boy. A little more muscular than Fonda, maybe, but with that same gravitas.

There were a few images of Chris and Ben, which she'd shot at the field where Chris coached the Little League team. Ben was only a year younger than Jamie, and his eyes held some of the same tentativeness that Jamie's did. Maybe children sense when there's something wrong at the heart of their families, she thought.

Her gaze returned to Chris Shepard. He was a good listener and quick on the uptake. She liked that. Her research had revealed that he had married his first wife, his college sweetheart, during his first year of medical school, but two years after graduation there had been a quick divorce. No kids, no fuss: nothing but 'irreconcilable differences' in the court records. But there had to be more to it than that. Otherwise, how had a good-looking, single doctor evaded marriage for so long after his divorce?

That first wife did a number on him, Alex thought. He was damaged goods for a while. That's why he went for Thora, the ice queen. There's a lot of damage in that girl, too . . .

Reluctantly, she turned her mind to finances. It cost real money to run a murder investigation, even when you were doing a lot of the legwork yourself. Most of the investigative work was being done by her father's old agency, but even with Will Kilmer giving her all the breaks he could, the fees for surveillance—which she'd contracted out to two small detective agencies—were eating her alive. On top of that, she was paying for air fares between Jackson and Charlotte, private nurses for her mother . . . there was no end to it.

Rent was her most urgent problem. For the last three years, she'd leased a condo in Washington, DC. After getting transfer orders, Alex had kept it, as a signal to her superiors that she believed in her eventual redemption. Now, on top of the condo she had a six-month lease on a place in Charlotte, an apartment she'd hardly slept in but that she had to keep on in order to maintain the fiction that she was diligently working at her FBI punishment duty.

'Shit,' she muttered, and got up and went to her computer.

She logged on to MSN and checked to see if Jamie was online, but the icon beside his screen name—Ironman QB—was red, not green. This didn't worry her. Their nightly webcam ritual normally occurred later, after Bill had gone to bed. Jamie had bought the webcam with his allowance, and it allowed him to open a video link with Alex when they were both logged on to MSN.

Leaving her screen name active, she got up from the desk, took her cell-phone from her purse and dialled her mother's house. A nurse answered.

'It's Alex. Is she awake?'

'No, she's sleeping. She's on the morphine pump again.'

Oh, God. 'How's she doing apart from the pain?'

'No change, really. Not physically. Emotionally . . . she seems down.'

Of course she is. She's dying. And she's doing it alone. 'Tell her I'll ring back later,' Alex whispered. 'Call me if there's any change.'

'I'll make sure someone does.'

'Thank you. Goodbye.'

Alex shoved her Glock into her waistband at the small of her back, flipped her shirt tail over it, then walked outside to get some air.

Beyond the parking lot stood a rectangle of oak trees. She walked towards them and sniffed the air, smelling a heavy potpourri of forest leaves, kudzu and pine needles laced with honeysuckle, azalea and sweet olive. She smelt water, too. Somewhere nearby, a creek was winding its way through the city towards the mighty river that rolled only a mile to the west. Alex had been to Natchez only three times in her life, but she knew it was different from everywhere else. The oldest city on the Mississippi, it had grown fantasti-cally wealthy before the rich Delta had even been cleared. Governed by England, France and Spain in turn, the city had absorbed the style, manners and architecture of those European powers. During the civil war, Natchez's cotton-rich leaders had surrendered the magnificent city without firing a shot, so much of its architecture had survived intact. It remained a world unto itself, seemingly immune to history, outside of time.

As she turned back towards her room, Alex wondered what had brought a man like Chris Shepard back here after medical school. She thought of him in his white coat. After five weeks of investigation, her fate—and Jamie's—lay in the doctor's hands. Alex planned to give Shepard time to think about today's meeting. She was sorry for pulling his world inside out, but she was certain, having followed Thora for several days, that the woman was leading a secret life. On some level, her husband had to know that. But would he consciously acknowledge it?

She went into her room, bolted her door and sat down at the computer. Jamie still wasn't online. Alex's throat began to tighten. She rubbed her eyes and fished an energy drink from her ice box.

'Come on, baby,' she murmured as she sat back down. 'Talk to Aunt Alex.'

Jamie's icon remained red.

CHRIS SHEPARD WALKED down the path from his house to the barn behind it, taking no joy in surroundings that had once been a source of pride. After moving to Natchez, he had used a chunk of his savings to buy a large house on the former Elgin plantation, south of town. Despite its isolation, it was only five minutes from Ben's school and less than ten minutes from both Natchez hospitals. Chris couldn't see how the location could be improved upon, but Thora had long wanted to move to Avalon, a trendy new subdivision springing up further south. Chris had finally given in, conceding that in the new neighbourhood Ben would have more friends living nearby. Now, the Avalon house was more than half finished and Thora was personally overseeing the construction. Chris rarely had time to visit the site.

A large building appeared before him in the darkness, its rustic exterior belying its real purpose. Chris had converted the barn into a video production studio to house the equipment for his 'camera hobby', as Thora called it. He unlocked the door and walked inside. This haven of blonde maple and glass elevated his mood, for here he could leave daily life behind.

Chris had got into filmmaking at college, where he'd worked on several documentaries, two of which had won awards. At medical school he had produced a documentary, shot with a hidden camera, called *A Day in the Life of a Resident*, which had almost ended his medical career before it had begun. But after a fellow student sent the tape to a national news network, it had contributed to the limiting of working hours for medical residents.

Once he was practising medicine for real, Chris had found little time for filming. But last year, after setting up partnership with Dr Tom Cage, an old-style general practitioner in Natchez, Chris had been inspired to begin work on a documentary about the decline of traditional primary-care medicine.

Tom Cage was one of those doctors who would spend a full hour listening to a patient, if a sympathetic ear was what was needed. He was seventy-three years old but still worked eighty-hour weeks. He questioned patients deeply, not only about their symptoms but also about other areas of their lives that might yield clues to their general health. He thought about his fees in terms of trying to save his patients money (thus he was not rich), and always stayed at his office until the last patient was seen.

Dr Cage's methods had come as a shock to Chris. His former partners practised defensive medicine, ordering every remotely relevant lab test but spending as little time as possible with patients, all in the name of gross income. Such practice was anathema to Tom Cage, who saw medicine as a life of service. And that, Chris believed, was worth documenting for posterity.

Chris opened the studio's refrigerator, poured a freezing shot of vodka, and drank it down. Then he sat down at his computer and began reviewing some scenes he'd filmed. As he did so, he felt a tide of emotion. Until this morning, he'd been content with his life. But now everything had changed. Alexandra Morse had released a serpent of doubt into his personal Eden.

'Goddamn it,' he murmured. 'God*damn* woman.'

'Did I mess something up?' asked a worried voice.

Chris looked over his shoulder and saw Thora. She wore a diaphanous blue nightgown and white slippers with wet blades of grass on them. He'd been so absorbed in his thoughts that he hadn't heard her enter the studio.

Thora didn't wait for a reply. 'You were pretty late getting home from the hospital,' she said diffidently. 'Did you have a lot of admissions?'

'Yeah. Most of them routine, but there's one case nobody can figure out. Don Allen consulted Tom about it, and Tom asked for my opinion.'

Thora's eyes widened. 'I can't believe Don Allen consulted with anyone.'

Chris smiled faintly. 'It killed him to do it, I could tell. But if somebody doesn't figure out what this guy has, he could die.'

'My money's on you,' Thora said, smiling. 'I know you'll figure it out. You always do.' She moved closer, then leant down and kissed Chris's forehead. 'Turn back round,' she said softly. 'Towards the monitor.'

He did so, and Thora began to rub his shoulders, working her strong hands up the sides of his neck and kneading the bunched muscles at the base of his skull. The release of tension was so sudden that he felt a mild nausea.

'You know what I was thinking?' she said.

'What?'

'We haven't tried to get me pregnant in a while.'

No remark could have surprised him more. 'You're right.'

Thora slowly spun his chair. 'Well . . . ?'

Taking his hand, she led him to the leather sofa. She slipped off her gown and lay down, pulling him with her. As he kissed her breasts she made a purring sound deep in her throat. Chris groaned, nearly overcome by her urgency, which he had not experienced in some time. But tonight she was the woman he had fallen in love with two years ago. As she whispered lewd encouragements, the interview with Alex Morse echoed in his mind. Their conversation had a surreal quality now. Had someone actually lied her way into his office, accused his wife of plotting murder? It was crazy . . .

She cried out, her nails raking his shoulder blades, and he let himself go, a white glare burning away all ambiguity.

As he came slowly back to the present, Thora strained upwards to kiss his lips, then fell back. He moved to lie on the cold leather beside her.

'You can get up if you want to,' she said. 'I'm going to stay here a minute. Let things take their natural course.'

He laughed. 'I'm fine right here.'

They lay in silence for a while. Then Thora said, 'Is everything all right?'

'Why do you ask?'

'You seemed distant today. Did something happen at work?'

God, did something happen. He forced a smile. 'Just the usual.'

Thora pulled damp hair out of her eyes. 'Oh, I forgot. I wanted to ask you something. Laura Canning is going up to the Alluvian this week. You know, that hotel in Greenwood. Up in the Delta. They have a spa up there. She asked me to go with her. If you don't want me to go, I won't, but this is Ben's last week of school, and he always asks you for help with his homework anyway. I don't have the patience.'

Chris wasn't into spas. He broke all the sweat he needed to maintaining the twenty acres of land around his house. 'When are we talking about?'

'A couple of days from now. We'd just be gone three nights. Mud packs and champagne, a little blues music, then right back home.'

Chris nodded and forced another smile, but this one took more effort. He could hear Alex Morse's voice whispering in his head: *Is your wife planning to be out of town anytime soon?*

'Chris?' Thora asked. 'Tell the truth. Do you want me to stay home?'

He recalled her face as she made love to him, the unalloyed pleasure in her blue-grey eyes. What the hell was he worried about?

'You go up to the Delta and chill out,' he said. 'Ben and I will be fine.'

Thora gave him an elfin smile, then jumped up and disappeared through a door. She reappeared a moment later, her right hand behind her back.

'What are you doing?' he asked, feeling strangely anxious.

'I've got a surprise for you.'

She brought her hand from behind her back. In it was a cardboard tube like the ones she used to carry blueprints for the new house. The prospect of discussing the Avalon house did not please Chris in the least.

'I see that frown,' Thora said, perching her perfect derriere on his knees. 'You just wait and see.'

She removed a sheet of paper from the tube, and unrolled it across her nude thighs. Chris saw what appeared to be plans for a large building behind the 7,000 square foot house that was nearing completion.

'What's that?' he asked, groaning internally. 'A private gym?'

Thora laughed. 'No. That's my housewarming present to you.' She smiled and kissed his cheek. 'A state-of-the-art video production studio.'

His face flushed. 'Thora . . . you can't be serious.'

Her smile broadened. 'Oh, I'm serious. They've already poured the foundation and run the high-tech cabling. *Very* expensive.'

This was almost too much to absorb after what Chris had endured today.

Suddenly, she tossed the plans and the tube onto the couch and hugged him tight. 'I'm not letting you slip back here every time you want to edit your videos. You're stuck with me, understand?'

He didn't. He felt as though he had swallowed some sort of hallucinogen. But then, if Alex Morse had not visited his office this morning, none of this would seem anything but a wonderful surprise.

'I finally surprised you, didn't I?' Thora said in an awestruck voice. She looked into his eyes. 'You up for a second round?'

He nodded in a daze. He felt like an astronaut cut loose from his spacecraft, drifting steadily away from everything familiar.

ALEX'S HEART LEAPT when she finally saw the little red icon on her screen turn green, indicating that Jamie had logged on to MSN. She'd been checking for the past hour, playing Solitaire while she waited.

The webcam window appeared, and an image of Jamie sitting at his desk flashed up. It was almost like being in the same room with him. Tonight Jamie was wearing an Atlanta Braves T-shirt and a yellow baseball cap.

'Hey, Aunt Alex,' he said. 'Sorry I'm late.'

She smiled genuinely for the first time all day. 'It's OK. You know I'll be here whenever you log on. What you been doing, bub?'

Jamie smiled. 'I had a baseball game.'

'How did it go?'

'I got a double.'

Alex yelped and applauded. 'That's great!'

Jamie's smile vanished. 'But I struck out twice.'

'That's OK. Even the pros strike out. What else has been going on?'

Jamie sighed like a fifty-year-old man. 'I don't know.'

'Yes, you do. Come on.'

'I think she's over here right now.'

'Missy?' Missy Hammond was Bill's mistress.

Jamie nodded.

Anger flooded through Alex. 'Why do you think that? Did you see her?'

'No.' Jamie glanced behind him, at his bedroom door. 'A little while ago I heard somebody laughing. It sounded exactly like her.'

Alex didn't know what to say. 'I'm sorry, Jamie. Let's talk about something else.'

The boy hung his head. 'That's easy for you to say. Why don't you just come get me? Dad wants to be with her, not me. I'm not sleepy at all.'

'I can't just come get you. We talked about that. But your father wants you, Jamie.' Alex wasn't sure whether this was true. 'He wants both of you.'

The boy shook his head. 'After the game, all Dad talked about was my strikeouts. And what else I did wrong. Nothing about my double.'

Alex put on a smile and nodded as though she understood. 'I think a lot of dads are like that. He's just trying to help you improve.'

'I guess. I don't like it, though.' He looked away from the screen, and Alex's heart contracted.

'Jamie? Look at me, honey. Look into the camera.'

At length, he did, and his sad eyes pierced her to the core. 'Aunt Alex?'

'Yes?'

'I miss my mom.'

Alex forced herself to repress her grief. Tears were pooling in her eyes, but they would not help Jamie. 'I know you do, baby,' she said softly. 'I miss her, too.'

She wiped her eyes, unable to shut out the memory of the night Grace died, when she'd snatched up Jamie and raced out of the hospital. She hadn't gone far, just to a nearby Pizza Hut, where she'd broken the news of Grace's death and comforted the boy as best she could. It was a tragedy of such magnitude that he simply could not process it. Alex had cradled his head to her chest, silently hoping that Grace had been out of her mind when she accused her husband of murder.

Alex now held an opened hand up to the eye of the camera. 'Be strong, little man. Things are going to get better. I'm working on it right now.'

Jamie put up his hand, too. 'Good. I better go now.'

Alex blinked back more tears. 'Same time tomorrow?'

Jamie smiled faintly. 'Same time.'

Then he was gone.

Alex got up from the desk with tears streaming down her cheeks. No matter what it took, she was going to fulfil her promise to Grace. And if the Bureau wanted to fire her for doing so, then the Bureau could go to hell.

Chapter 3

Dr Eldon Tarver walked slowly along a path in the park, his big head down, searching for feathers. In one hand he carried a Nike duffle bag, in the other an aluminium Reach-Arm device, used by most people for picking up litter from the ground. But Dr Tarver was not like most people. He was using the Reach-Arm to pick up dead birds, which he then sealed inside Ziploc bags and dropped into the duffle. He'd been out since before dawn and he'd already bagged four specimens, three sparrows and a martin, which boded well for the work he'd do later in the morning.

Dr Tarver had seen only two other humans so far, both runners. Not many people ventured into this corner of the park, and the doctor had startled both of them, not least because of his appearance.

He stood six feet three inches tall, with a barrel chest and ropy arms covered in black hair. Bald since the age of forty, Eldon Tarver wore a full grey beard, which gave him the look of a Mennonite preacher. He had preacher's eyes, too. When he was angry, those bright blue eyes burned like a prophet's, but most of the time they radiated a glacial coldness. Some women at the medical centre where he worked thought him handsome, but others called him downright ugly, because of what most people thought was a port-wine stain birthmark on his left cheek. In fact it was a severe arteriovenous anomaly, which had begun mildly in childhood but had flamed to the surface during puberty like the sign of a guilty conscience.

As the first yellow rays of sunlight spilt through the trees to the east, another runner appeared—a girl this time, a vision in blue Lycra with white wires trailing from her golden hair into an iPod strapped to her upper arm. Dr Tarver wanted to watch her, but then he noticed another bird off the path, twitching in its final death throes. It might have fallen only seconds ago.

The girl's shoes swished through the dewy grass as she left the path on the side furthest from the doctor. She tried to make it appear as though she'd done this out of courtesy, but twice her pupils flicked towards him, gauging the distance, making sure he hadn't moved closer. He smiled as the girl passed, then turned and regarded her flexing glutes with the cool appreciation of an expert anatomist.

When she'd vanished round a bend, he knelt, donned surgical gloves and withdrew a scalpel, a syringe and a culture dish from his pocket. Then he laid open the sparrow's breast with a single incision and with a long finger exposed the bird's liver. Inserting the tip of the hypodermic into the nearly black organ, he exerted a gentle back-pressure on the plunger and withdrew a barrelful of blood. Then he tossed its carcass into the underbrush.

Opening the petri dish, Dr Tarver squirted some blood onto the layer of minced chick embryo inside and rubbed it around with a sterile swab taken from his pocket. Then he closed the dish and slipped it into the duffle with the Ziploc bags and the gloves. A good morning's work. When he got back to the lab, he'd test the last bird first. He felt confident that it was a carrier.

A slow shiver in the grass where he'd tossed the sparrow raised the hair on his arms. Dr Tarver set down the Nike bag and walked towards the groove in the grass. As soon as he saw the rotting log, he knew. He closed his eyes for a moment, stilling himself. Then he reached down and lifted the log. What he saw beneath made his heart flutter: a beautiful coil of red, yellow and black.

'*Micrurus fulvius fulvius,*' he whispered.

He had uncovered an eastern coral snake, one of the shyest serpents in America, and the deadliest. With a fluid motion like that of a father stroking his child's hair, Tarver took hold of the stirring elapid behind its head and lifted it into the air. The brightly banded body coiled round his forearm— but this was not a strong snake that would try to use its muscles to whip away from him and strike. No, the coral was a refined killer. Like its relative the cobra, it injected pure neurotoxin, which shut down the central nervous system of its prey and quickly brought on paralysis and death.

Dr Tarver was not a herpetologist, but he had a long history with snakes that went back to his childhood in the Appalachian foothills of Tennessee. There, as a boy, he had watched chanting hillbillies hold dozens of rattle-snakes high in the air, believing that God had anointed them against the lethal compounds in the poison sacs behind the slitted eyes. He knew better. He had seen many of those hillbillies bitten on their hands, arms, necks and faces, and every one had suffered torments beyond their imagination.

The snake's body curled round his arm in a fluid figure eight, a symbol of infinity. His adoptive father's congregation had believed serpents to be incarnations of Satan, but the ancient Greeks had seen their skin-shedding as a process of healing and rebirth. For them snakes personified the fundamental paradox of medicinal drugs: in small doses they cured while in large ones they killed. He held the coral up to his face, feeling the intoxicating power of life and death in his hand, then slid it inside the duffle bag and zipped it shut.

DR TARVER'S JOURNEY to his laboratory took him north along Interstate 55, east of the main cluster of office buildings that surrounded Jackson's great capitol dome. To his left, the AmSouth tower jutted up from the low skyline of the capital city. His gaze moved along the sixteenth floor, to the blue-black windows of the corner office. Eldon had checked those windows almost every day for the past five years. But today was the first time that sunlight had ever flashed back from the office like a silver beacon.

The muscles of his big chest tightened, and his breathing became shallow. There had been bumps in the road before—small matters of planning, or mis-communication. But never had anything justified the use of the aluminium foil. Eldon had chosen this emergency signal because, unlike a phone or a computer or a pager, it could not be traced. No one could ever prove it was a signal. But it had to mean real trouble. Probably unwanted interest on the part of someone. But who? The police? The FBI? He had to eliminate the source of the danger. Only Andrew Rusk knew of Eldon's recent activities. And Rusk could not be trusted to keep silent under pressure.

Tarver glanced down at the Nike bag on the seat beside him. The pre-arranged meeting place was thirty miles away. Did he have time to run the birds out to his lab first? Should he risk meeting Rusk at all? What if the lawyer had been caught and, in exchange for leniency, was offering up his accomplice on a platter? Yet logic dictated Eldon should risk the meeting. No one could trap him in the place he had designated for it. There might be cops waiting at the lab though, so Eldon decided to lose the birds and the sample of the West Nile virus because the danger of capture outweighed any possible gain in research. He gripped the wheel tighter, exited I-55 at Northside Drive, then got back onto the elevated freeway, heading south.

What about the coral snake, though? He hated the idea of ditching it. A wicked smile glittered in his beard. Maybe the snake would somehow be the resolution of the problem signalled by the foil.

CHRIS, UNABLE TO SLEEP, slid out of bed early. He dressed silently, then walked out to the garage, loaded his bike onto the rack on his pick-up and drove to the north side of town. There he mounted his carbon-fibre Trek and started pedalling along the lonely grey stripe of the Natchez Trace.

Most of this stretch of the two-lane Trace was a tunnel created by the arching branches of the red oaks that lined the parkway. Through breaks in the canopy Chris saw a yellow half-moon, still high despite the slowly rising sun. He pumped his legs with a metronomic rhythm. Small animals skittered away as he passed, and every half mile or so, groups of startled deer leapt into the shelter of the trees.

A warm, steady rain began to fall. Landmarks rolled by like a film without a sound track: Loess Bluff, with its steadily eroding face of rare soil; the high bridge over Cole's Creek, from which you could see Low Water Bridge, the site of some of Chris's happiest childhood memories. After he crossed the high bridge he began to pump his thighs like a Tour de France rider, trying to work out the accumulated anxiety of the past eighteen hours. After a while, he made a 180-degree turn and headed back southwest.

As his tyres thrummed along the road, he saw another biker in the distance, approaching on the opposite side. As the distance closed, Chris saw that the rider was female. He raised his hand in greeting, then hit his brakes.

The rider was Alexandra Morse.

AGENT MORSE'S dark hair was drawn back into a soaking-wet ponytail, making her facial scars all the more prominent. He was about ready to pedal right past her when she crossed the road and stopped a yard away from him.

'Good morning, Doctor.'

'What the hell are you doing?' he asked.

'I needed to talk to you. This seemed like a good way to do it.'

'How did you know I was here?'

Morse only smiled.

Chris looked at her, taking in the soaked clothes stuck to her body and her dripping ponytail. 'And the bike?' he asked. 'You a big cyclist?'

'No. I bought it four days ago, when I found out that you were a biker and your wife was a runner.'

'You've been following Thora, too?'

Morse's smile faded. 'I've shadowed a couple of her runs. She's fast.'

'Jesus.' Chris shook his head and looked away.

A red pick-up truck whizzed past, its rider staring at them.

'Why don't we keep riding?' Morse suggested. 'We'll be less noticeable.'

'I don't intend to continue yesterday's conversation.'

She looked incredulous. 'Surely you must have some questions for me.'

Chris looked off into the trees, then turned and let some of his anger out. 'Yes, I do. My first question is, did you personally see my wife go into this divorce lawyer's office?'

'Not personally, no, but another agent followed her down to her car, then took down her licence plate.'

'Her licence plate. No chance of a mistake?'

Morse shook her head. 'He shot a picture. She was wearing a very distinctive outfit: a black dress with a white scarf and an Audrey Hepburn hat.'

Chris gritted his teeth. Thora had worn that same outfit to a party only a month ago. 'Do you have any recordings of her conversation with the lawyer? Anything that proves that they didn't talk about wills or estates, or something else legitimate.'

Agent Morse looked down at her wet shoes. 'No.'

'Agent Morse, I happen to know from my wife's recent behaviour that what you suggested yesterday is impossible.'

The FBI agent looked intrigued. 'Why don't we ride back to your truck together? I promise not to piss you off, if I can help it.'

Chris knew he could ride off, and leave Morse behind in seconds. But for some reason—maybe just the manners he'd been raised with—he simply shrugged, and started southwards at an easy pace. Morse fell in beside him.

'I'll admit I've done some thinking about what you told me,' he said. 'Especially about the medical side. For instance, I want to know more about the unexplained deaths tied to this lawyer. Was it a stroke in every case?'

'No. Only my sister's.'

'Really. What were the other causes of death?'

'Pulmonary embolism in one. Myocardial infarction in another. The other six that I've traced were all cancer.'

Chris looked sharply over at her. '*Cancer?* You're kidding, right?'

She shook her head, and water dripped off her nose. 'All blood cancers.'

'Blood cancer encompasses a whole constellation of diseases, Agent Morse. There are over thirty different types of non-Hodgkin's lymphomas alone. Were all the deaths from one type of blood cancer?'

'No. Three leukaemias, two lymphomas, one multiple myeloma.'

Chris shook his head. 'You're out of your mind. You really believe someone is murdering people by giving them different kinds of cancer?'

Morse looked at him, her eyes grim. 'I know it.'

Chris snorted. 'Even if anyone could somehow induce cancer in a victim, it could take years for that person to die, if they died at all. A lot of people survive leukaemia now. Lymphomas, too.'

'All these patients died in eighteen months or less.'

This brought him up short. 'All of them? From diagnosis to death?'

'All but one. The myeloma patient lived twenty-three months after a bone marrow transplant.'

'And all the surviving spouses were clients of the same divorce lawyer?'
Morse shook her head. 'I never said that. I said all the surviving spouses
wound up *in business* with the same divorce lawyer—*after* their spouses died.'

Chris nodded, but his mind was still on Morse's cancer theory. 'You're
talking about several different disease aetiologies. The best oncologists in
the world don't know what causes those cancers, so who do you think could
intentionally cause them?'

'Radiation causes leukaemia,' Morse said assertively. 'You don't have to
be a genius to give someone cancer.'

She's right, Chris realised. Many in Hiroshima died of leukaemia in the
aftermath of the atomic bomb, as did many 'survivors' of the Chernobyl
disaster. His mind instantly jumped to the possibility of access to gamma
radiation. In that case you'd have to consider physicians, dentists, veterinarians—hell, even some medical technologists had access to X-ray machines
or the radioactive isotopes used for radiotherapy.

'And researchers purposely cause cancer in lab animals,' Morse said.

'Of course. They do it by injecting carcinogenic chemicals into the animals. And chemicals like that are traceable. Forensically, I mean.'

She gave him a sceptical look. 'After eighteen months, all traces of the
offending carcinogen could be gone. Benzene is a good example.'

Chris knit his brow in thought. 'Benzene causes lung cancer, doesn't it?'

'Also leukaemia and multiple myeloma,' she said. 'They proved that by
testing factory workers with benzene exposure in Ohio and in China.'

She's done her homework, he thought. 'Have you done extensive toxico-
logical studies in all these suspicious deaths?'

'Almost none of them.'

This stunned him. 'Why not?'

'Several of the bodies were cremated before we became suspicious. In
the other cases, we couldn't get permission to exhume the bodies.'

'I don't buy that, Agent Morse. If the FBI wanted forensic studies, they'd
get them. What about the families? Did they suspect foul play? Is that how
you got into this case? Or was it your sister's accusation that started it all?'

'The families of several of the victims suspected foul play from the
beginning. Because most of the husbands were real bastards.'

Big surprise. 'Had all of these alleged victims filed for divorce?'

'None had.'

'None? Did the husbands file, then?'

Morse looked over at him again. 'Nobody filed.'

'So people consulted this lawyer but didn't file?'

'Exactly. We think there's probably a single consultation—maybe two. The lawyer waits for a really wealthy client who stands to lose an enormous amount of money in his divorce. Or custody of his kids. And when the lawyer senses that he has a truly desperate client—a client with intense hatred for his spouse—he makes his pitch.'

'That's a pretty elaborate theory. Can you prove any of it?'

'Not yet. This lawyer is very savvy. Paranoid, in fact.'

Chris gazed at her in disbelief. 'You can't even prove that any murders have occurred. It's all speculation. And you have to admit it's a pretty elaborate theory you've developed. It's Hollywood stuff, in fact, not real life.'

'I have my sister's word, Doctor.'

'Spoken on her deathbed, after a severe stroke.'

Morse's face became a mask of defiant determination as she rode alongside Chris. 'Doctors aren't immune to homicidal impulses, Dr Shepard. I could cite dozens of cases, all involving elaborate plans. There are four and a half thousand doctors in Mississippi. Add to that all the dentists, veterinarians, med techs, nurses—it's a massive suspect pool.'

Chris blinked against the rain. 'You've got to find the aetiology of these blood cancers,' he said. 'If it is radiation, you could start narrowing your suspect pool pretty quickly. Were there any radiation burns, or strange symptoms noted before the cancer was diagnosed?'

'No. I managed to get the medical records of two victims from angry family members. But experts had been over both of them in microscopic detail, and they hadn't turned up anything suspicious. However, I'm told that radiation could explain the variation in the cancers. You expose somebody to radiation, there's no way to predict how their cells will react.'

Chris nodded, but something bothered him. 'Your expert is right. But then, why are blood cancers the only result? Why no solid tumours? Why no melanomas? You couldn't predict that.'

'Maybe you could,' Morse suggested. 'If you were a radiation oncologist.'

'Maybe,' Chris conceded. 'And if that's true, you just shrank your suspect pool by about ten thousand people.'

Morse smiled. 'All nineteen radiation oncologists in Mississippi will come under investigation. But it's no simple matter. Because we have no way to know *when* the victims were dosed, we can't examine alibis.'

'Yeah, I see. And it's not just a doctor you're looking for, right? It's the lawyer, too. If you're right, he functions almost like the killer's agent.'

'Exactly.'

Chris laughed softly. 'How would a relationship like that get started? You can't go scouting for promising medical assassins . . .'

'I know it sounds ridiculous when you put it like that, but we're talking millions of dollars here. That's a pretty big carrot.'

Chris pedalled out in front of her so that a large truck could pass. 'A lot of what you say makes sense,' he called over the sound of the receding vehicle, 'but I still say your theory doesn't add up.'

'Why not?' Morse asked, pulling alongside again.

'The time factor. If I want to kill someone, it's because I want immediate action. I'm not going to wait months or years for them to croak, am I?'

'But you may have already waited years for your freedom. Maybe decades. Obtaining a divorce can take a very long time if the divorce is contested.' Morse started puffing hard. 'If your lawyer told you that, in the same time your divorce would take, he could save you millions of dollars, guarantee you full custody of your children—and prevent them from hating you— you'd at least *consider* what he had to say, wouldn't you?'

They were crossing the high bridge over Cole's Creek. Chris braked to a stop, climbed off, and leant his Trek against the concrete rail.

'You've got me,' he said. 'If you remove urgency from the equation, then you *could* use cancer as a weapon. If it's technically possible.'

'Thank you,' Alex said softly. She leaned her bike against the concrete and gazed at the brown water drifting lazily over the sand fifty feet below.

Chris tried to imagine Thora driving up to Jackson for a clandestine meeting with a divorce lawyer. 'I buy your logic, OK? But in my case it's irrelevant for lots of reasons. The main one is that if Thora asked me for a divorce, I'd give her one. Simple as that.'

Morse shrugged. 'I don't know the lady.'

'You're right. You don't.'

'It's beautiful down there,' Morse said after a while, gazing down the winding course of the creek. 'It's looks like virgin wilderness.'

'It's as close as you'll find. I spent a lot of time walking that creek as a boy. I found dozens of arrowheads and spear points in it. The Natchez Indians hunted along it for a thousand years before the French came.'

She smiled. 'You're lucky to have had a childhood like that.'

Chris knew she was right. Suddenly he turned and faced her. 'From the moment we met,' he said, looking into her green eyes, 'you've been digging into my personal life. I want to dig into yours for a minute.'

He could almost see the walls going up. But she nodded assent.

'Your scars,' he said. 'I can tell they're recent. How did you get them?'

She turned away and stared down at the rippling sand beneath the water. When she finally spoke, her voice told him he was hearing the truth. 'There was a man, a man I worked with at the Bureau. His name was James Broadbent. They often assigned him to protect me at hostage scenes. He . . . he was in love with me. I really cared for him, too, but he was married. Two kids. We were never intimate, but even if we had been, he would never have left his family. Never. You understand?'

Chris nodded.

Morse looked back down at the water. 'I was a good hostage negotiator, Doctor. In all the years I never lost a hostage. But last December . . .' She faltered. 'My father was killed trying to stop a robbery. Two months later, my mother was diagnosed with advanced ovarian cancer.' She shrugged. 'I sort of lost it after that. Only I didn't know it. My dad had raised me to be tough, so that's what I tried to be. "Never quit"—that's the Morse motto. Nine weeks ago, I was called to a hostage scene at a bank. Sixteen hostages inside, mostly employees. A lot of suits at the Bureau had the idea that this was a terrorist attack. The leader spoke with an Arabic accent, but it sounded fake to me. I thought I had a real chance to talk him down without anyone firing a shot. But there was a lot of pressure from above, this being Washington in a post-9/11 mindset. So an associate deputy director named Mark Dodson jerked me out of there and ordered in the Hostage Rescue Team.'

Chris saw that she was reliving the memory.

'It would mean extreme risk to the hostages and I couldn't accept that. So I marched right back through the cordon and into the bank. Some HRT snipers didn't get the word in time that I was in there, and they blew the doors and windows just as I reached the lobby.' Morse touched her scarred cheek. 'One of the robbers shot me from behind a plate-glass partition. I caught shards mostly, but what I didn't know was that James had followed me. When I was hit, he looked at me instead of up for the shooter, which was what he should have done. His feelings for me were stronger than his training. And they train us *hard,* you know?' Morse wiped away tears.

'Hey,' he said, reaching out and squeezing her arm. 'It's OK.'

She shook her head. 'No, it's not. Maybe someday it will be, but right now it's not.'

'I know one thing,' Chris said. 'In the shape you're in, you don't need to be working a murder case. You need a medical leave.'

Morse laughed strangely. 'I'm on a sort of medical leave *now.*'

As he looked down at her, everything suddenly came clear. Her deep fatigue, her obsessiveness, the thousand-yard stare of a shell-shocked soldier . . . 'You're on your own, aren't you?'

When she looked up at him, her eyes were wet with more than rain. 'Pretty much. The truth is, almost everything I've done in the last five weeks is unauthorised. They'd fire me if they knew.'

Chris whistled long and low. 'But if everything you've told me is true,' he said awkwardly, 'why *isn't* the FBI involved?'

Frustration hardened her face. 'A dozen reasons. Murder's a state crime, not a federal one. A lot of what I have is inference and supposition, not objective evidence. But how am I supposed to get evidence without resources? The FBI is the most hidebound bureaucracy imaginable. Everything is done by the book—unless it involves counterterrorism, in which case they throw the book out the window. You're my last shot at stopping these people, Doctor.'

'If you're acting alone, who saw Thora go into the lawyer's office?'

'A private detective. He used to work with my father.'

'Jesus. What does the FBI think you're doing right now?'

'They think I'm in Charlotte, working a case involving illegal aliens. They transferred me there after I was shot. I know I'm not making perfect sense about everything. but I haven't slept more than three hours a night in five weeks. It took me two weeks just to find the connection between my brother-in-law and the divorce lawyer. Then another week to get the names of his business partners. I only came up with my list of victims a week ago. There could be a dozen more. But when your wife walked into Rusk's office, that brought me to Natchez, and since then—'

'Who's Rusk?' Chris cut in. 'The divorce lawyer?'

'Yes. Andrew Rusk Jr. His father's a big attorney in Jackson.' More tears joined the raindrops on her cheeks. 'I *need* your help, Doctor. I need your medical knowledge, but most of all I need you, because you're the next victim.' Morse's eyes locked onto his. 'Do you get that?'

'Nothing you've said even remotely proves that,' Chris said quietly. 'Look, I support what you're doing, OK? I even admire you for it. But the difference is, you have personal stake in this. I don't.'

Her eyes narrowed. 'Yes, you do. You just haven't accepted it yet. Maybe you will when I tell you that your wife is cheating on you. She's screwing a surgeon right here in town. His name is Shane Lansing.'

Chris tried to keep the shock out of his face. 'Bullshit,' he whispered.

'Twice this week, Dr Lansing stopped at your new house while Thora was there. The first time he stayed inside for twenty-eight minutes. The second time it was fifty-two minutes.'

'So what? Shane lives in that neighbourhood. Thora was probably showing off the place to him. There were workmen there, right?'

Morse's reply was as blunt as a hammer. 'No workmen. Either time.'

Chris flinched.

'I know how it hurts, OK? But pride is your enemy now, Chris. You have to see things *straight*.'

'*I* should see things straight? You're the one spinning out Byzantine theories of mass murder. Cancer as a weapon, a newlywed planning to murder her husband . . . No wonder you're out on your own!'

Morse's level gaze was unrelenting. 'If I'm crazy, then tell me one thing. Why didn't you call the FBI to report me yesterday?'

For a long while he stared down at the concrete rail. 'Thora's leaving town this week. She told me last night.'

Morse's mouth dropped open. 'Where's she going?'

'Up to the Delta. A spa up in Greenwood. The Alluvian. For three nights.'

Morse made a fist and brought it to her mouth. 'My God . . . they're moving fast. You're in extreme danger. *Right now*.'

'Everything you told me is circumstantial,' he said angrily. 'There wasn't one fact in the whole goddamn pile!'

'I know it seems that way. I know you don't want to believe any of it. Denial is always the first response.'

He stared at her for a long time, then looked at his watch. 'I'm really late. I need to get back to my truck. I can't wait for you now.' He climbed onto his bike and started to leave.

Morse grabbed his elbow with surprising strength. With her other hand she removed a cellphone from her shorts. 'Take this. My cell number's programmed into it. You can speak openly on it. It's the only safe link we'll have.'

He looked at the phone suspiciously, but took it anyway.

She climbed onto her bike. 'Call me soon. We don't have much time to prepare.'

'What if I call the FBI instead?'

She shrugged. 'Then my career is over. But I won't stop. I will not stand by and let my sister be erased for someone's convenience—for his *profit*. And I'll still try to save you.'

Chris slipped his feet into his pedal clips and rode quickly away.

FOUR HOURS LATER, Alex Morse sat on a bench in the shadow of the cathedral in downtown Natchez and watched Thora Shepard walk out of the Mainstream Fitness centre. She turned right and started walking west on Main Street. Wearing sunglasses and a tailored pantsuit that cost more than Alex earned in a month, she looked fit for a magazine cover shoot. Men and women turned and stared after her as she strode past them on the sidewalk.

Alex stood up and followed Thora, who was a block ahead now. When an older man stopped Thora and engaged her in conversation, Alex turned and looked into a shop window. She had disliked Thora from the beginning, but she wasn't sure why. The daughter of a renowned Vanderbilt surgeon, born into the elite social world of Nashville, Tennessee, Thora lived with her alcoholic mother after her parents' divorce. She won a scholarship to medical school, but dropped out when she got pregnant. After Ben was born, with financial and baby-sitting help from her grandmother, she entered nursing school and after two years graduated with honours. After nine months at the VA hospital in Murfreesboro, Tennessee, she moved to St Catherine's in Natchez, where she met Red Simmons, the oil man who would become her first husband and make her a very rich widow soon after.

Alex glanced to her left. Thora hugged the older man and continued down Main Street. Alex took out her small camera and shot a picture of the man as he passed. He looked sixty, probably too old to be a paramour.

Simply following Thora through her daily routine was proving exhausting for Alex. Up at dawn for a morning run—four miles, minimum—then she would take a quick shower at home, followed by a trip to the building site in Avalon, where she would argue with the contractors for half an hour or so, then drive to the country club for a swim or a couple of sets of tennis. Afterwards, she alternated touch-ups of her hair and nails with serious weight work at Mainstream Fitness. Another shower, then lunch with a girlfriend. Afterwards, Thora often made a second trip to the building site.

The only compulsory stop of her day was at St Stephen's Prep, to pick up Ben. After taking him home to the maid, she would spend the remainder of the afternoon running errands or shopping, then stop by the Avalon site one final time before going home.

It was during these end-of-the-day stops that Dr Shane Lansing had twice stopped by for a visit. Alex had never entered the house while Lansing was inside, but if the surgeon showed up again she planned to try. If she could obtain photographic proof that Thora and Lansing were lovers, Dr Shepard would get on board with her plan.

Thora's cellphone rang. When she answered, she heard the gravelly voice of Will Kilmer.

'Got some news for you,' said the old man. 'Andrew Rusk just made one of my guys and turned rabbit. He managed to lose the tail.'

'Damn it.' Thirty yards away, Thora Shepard crossed the road and turned right. Alex followed.

Laboured breathing came down the line. Kilmer was seventy, and he had more than a touch of emphysema. 'What you want me to do now, hon?'

'Put someone out at Rusk's house, if you can. He has to go home eventually, right? Unless we really spooked him.'

'Rusk is a rich lawyer, not a CIA field agent. He'll be home. I'll send somebody out there. And if I don't have anybody free, I'll go myself.'

'You don't have to do—' Alex froze in midsentence. Thora had stopped on the sidewalk to answer a cell call. Now she was backing against the wall of a building with the phone held close to her ear.

'I've got to go,' she breached. 'Call me.'

As Alex hit END, Thora leaned out from the wall and put the phone back into her pocket, moving quickly back towards Main Street.

Straight towards Alex.

Alex darted into the nearest shop. When Thora passed the shop window, her features were set in an expression of severe concentration. Alex counted to fifteen, then followed the woman towards her Mercedes.

Something was about to happen.

Chapter 4

Andrew Rusk checked the odometer of his black Porsche Cayenne Turbo once more, then started searching the trees for the turning. He'd left the I-55 forty minutes ago, and after twenty miles he'd turned onto this narrow gravel road. Somewhere along it was the turning for the Chickamauga Hunting Camp. Rusk had been a member of the elite camp for fifteen years, and membership had proved useful in many ways beyond providing recreation in the fall.

He saw the turning at last, marked by a sign over the entrance road. He swung the wheel and stopped before the steel gate blocking his way, then punched a combination into the keypad on the post beside his vehicle. When the gate swung back, he drove slowly through.

There were more whitetail deer per acre in this area than in any other part of the United States. And they were *big*. This was deer heaven, and hunters from around the country paid premium prices for hunting leases here.

Rusk drove up to the main cabin and parked, scanning the clearing for Glykon. He saw no one. Climbing out of the Porsche, he checked the main cabin's door and found it locked. That made sense, because Glykon was not a member of the club and thus had no key. He did have the combination to the front gate, courtesy of Andrew Rusk. That was the arrangement they had made, in case of emergency, when they had planned their first joint venture here. There had been almost no face-to-face contact since.

Despite the emptiness of the clearing, Rusk was certain that his partner was already here. He would have hidden his vehicle in case any other members happened to be here—an unlikely event out of season, but you never knew. The question was, where would Glykon wait? Rusk listened to the sounds of the forest, the rustling dance of a billion spring leaves. The birds: sparrows, jays, martins. The erratic *pop-pop-pop* of a woodpecker. But nothing signalled the presence of another human.

Then Rusk smelt fire. Wood was burning—somewhere out to his left. He set off in that direction, striding through the trees, until he found himself in a small clearing. In its centre, Glykon sat tending a cast-iron skillet over a small fire. The sound and smell of sizzling meat filled the air, and hanging on a wire beside him was a freshly skinned dead fawn.

'Take a seat,' the tall man said in his deep baritone. 'I'm cooking the tenderloin. It's sinfully good, Andrew.' He speared a shaving of tenderloin with a pocketknife and held it to Rusk.

Rusk took the knife and ate the meat. 'It's good,' he said. 'Damn good.'

By killing the fawn out of season, the pathologist had broken a sacred rule of the camp, not to mention several state and federal laws. But Rusk wasn't going to mention that. He had bigger problems to deal with.

'We have a problem,' Rusk said bluntly. 'Two problems, really.'

'Don't rush things,' Glykon said. 'Sit down. Have some more venison.'

Rusk pretended to look down at the fire. He saw no rifle near Glykon, not even a handgun, only a Nike duffle bag. He'd have to keep an eye on that. 'I'd prefer to move straight to business,' he said.

'Then we should get the formalities out of the way first.'

'Formalities?'

'Take off your clothes, Andrew.'

Adrenaline blasted through Rusk's vascular system. 'Do you think I'm wearing a wire?'

Glykon smiled disarmingly. 'You said we have an emergency. Stress makes people do things they might not ordinarily do.'

'Are *you* going to strip?'

'I don't have to. You called this meeting.'

That made sense. And Rusk knew nothing substantive was going to be said unless he complied with his partner's order. Thanking God he had left his own pistol in the Porsche, he bent and untied his shoes, then took off his pants and shirt, leaving only his shorts and socks.

'OK. Get dressed,' Glykon said. 'You look like a turtle without its shell.'

Rusk pulled on his clothes, then sat down to put on his shoes. 'The last time we were here,' he said, 'you told me you hated the woods.'

Glykon chuckled softly. 'Sometimes I do.'

'What does that mean?'

'You know so little about me, Andrew. Even if I told you . . . my experience is wholly outside your frame of reference.'

He seemed to be saying, *You're from a different tribe than I am—perhaps even a different species.* And this was true.

When the pair had first met, five years ago, Glykon had come to Chickamauga as the guest of an orthopaedic surgeon from Jackson. For two days he had killed nothing, to the increasing amusement of the other members who were killing record numbers of deer that year. But all anyone talked about that weekend was the Ghost, a wise old twelve-point buck who'd managed to evade the best hunters for almost ten years. The Ghost had been sighted the previous week, and everyone was gunning for him.

On the third day—a Sunday, Rusk recalled—Glykon had marched back into camp carrying the 220-pound carcass of the Ghost across his shoulders. He upset quite a few club members by killing their near-mythical beast, but what could they say? Glykon hadn't shot the Ghost from a tree stand, the way most of them hunted, waiting in relative comfort for a deer to walk right under them. He had gone out and stalked the Ghost in the old way: the Indian way, a damned tough, three-day slog through thick underbrush.

Late that afternoon, Rusk had found himself gutting his own trophy buck outside. As though sent by fate, Glykon had walked up and offered to show him some time-saving tricks. After Rusk gave over his skinning knife, he witnessed a demonstration of manual dexterity and anatomical knowledge that left him in awe. And that part of his brain not occupied with the bloody spectacle before his eyes was turning over an idea that had been born some years ago in the dark recesses of his soul, an idea unrealised due to moral scruples and a lack of opportunity. But the more years he practised law, the more those scruples had eroded. And morality, Rusk had known even then, was not a component of his partner's personality.

'Two problems,' Glykon prompted, taking a slice of tenderloin from the skillet and dropping it into his mouth. 'That's what you said.'

'Yes. And they might be related.'

Glykon nodded. 'Does anyone know who I am, Andrew?'

'No.'

'Does anyone suspect what you are doing?'

Rusk licked his lips and tried to appear calm. 'I think I might be being followed. By an FBI agent.'

Glykon stuck out his bottom lip. 'Who is he?'

'It's a girl. Grace Fennell's sister. Her name is Alexandra Morse.'

A strange smile touched Glykon's lips. 'Ahh. Well, we knew she was a risk. Why is this girl suspicious of you?'

'Bill Fennell thinks his wife said something to her just before she died.'

Glykon's eyes bored into Rusk's with relentless intensity. 'The question, Andrew, is how does the woman even know you exist?'

'I don't know. Fennell wouldn't have told her about me. He's not stupid.'

'Has she talked to you directly?'

'No.'

'It could be she knows about you through the business connection,' Glykon said thoughtfully. 'The real-estate deal between you and Fennell.'

'Yes.'

'You should have stuck to diamonds.'

'This deal is better than diamonds, Eldon. *Way* better.'

'Not if it kills you.'

Rusk instantly noted two disturbing things: first, his partner's use of 'you', not 'us'; second, he had not said anything about prison—only death.

Glykon was watching Rusk. 'So you think the FBI is following you?'

Rusk shook his head. 'If Alex Morse is digging into her sister's death, she has to be doing it on her own time. Morse is already in deep shit with her superiors. She was almost terminated from the Bureau recently for getting a fellow agent killed. And why would the FBI investigate Grace Fennell's death? It's a state crime.'

'You're the lawyer. Look into it. What else has Morse done?'

Here goes . . . 'She may have broken into my office.'

Glykon stared without blinking. 'Are you certain of anything, Andrew? Or are you simply afraid to tell me the truth?'

'I'm not afraid,' he said, which was absurd. 'Even if she did break in, there's nothing in my office. If she got into my computer, she might be able to trace some business relationships. But everything's above-board.'

'But the *connections*—to other corpses. *Spouses* of corpses.'

'Only the earliest jobs,' Rusk said. 'The latest three years ago.'

'If you discount Grace Fennell,' Glykon reminded him.

'Right.'

Tarver dropped several more slices of raw meat into the skillet. 'I've still only heard about one threat,' he murmured.

'The second is more direct, but also more manageable.'

'Continue.'

'It's one of our former clients. William Braid, the barge company owner in Vicksburg. He's having a nervous breakdown—hallucinating, seeing his dead wife in crowds, all kinds of crazy shit. It took her so long to die, you know? He couldn't stand it. I'm afraid of what he might do. Who he might talk to.'

'Braid called you?'

'He stopped me at the golf course! Yesterday he drove by my house . . .'

Glykon's face drew taut. 'What did he tell you?'

'He's thinking of killing himself.'

'What's he waiting for? Why not just go ahead and do it?'

Rusk forced a laugh. 'I don't think he's the suicidal type. I think at the end of the day he'll lay the blame on us and go to the police.'

'You think he forgot your warning? Forgot what happened to his wife?'

'I don't think he cares any more. He's that far gone.'

'These people,' Glykon said with disgust. 'So *weak*. Where was his conscience while he was paying us to murder the old frump?'

The lawyer shrugged. 'What do you think we should do?'

'We? Is there something you can do to get us out of this?'

Rusk almost blushed. 'Well . . . I meant—'

'You meant, what am *I* going to do to save your ass.'

This is going to cost me, Rusk suddenly realised. Big-time.

Glykon stood erect and stretched his long frame. 'I'll take care of Mr Braid,' he said in an offhand voice. 'Will he be home tonight?'

'Yes. I told him I might drive over to talk to him.'

'Moron. What if he told his mistress that?'

'She left him ten days ago. Nobody talks to him now.'

'All right.'

Rusk was breathing easier. No mention of money so far.

'Two hundred and fifty thousand,' Glykon said, as if reading his mind.

Rusk crumpled inside. 'That seems like a lot,' he ventured. 'I mean, he's a threat to both of us, right?'

All humanity went out of Glykon's face. 'Braid is no threat to me. *You* are the only conceivable threat to me, Andrew. And I advise you not to make me dwell on that.'

'How do you want the money?'

'The safe way. We'll make the transfer here, sometime next week.'

Rusk nodded. A quarter of a million dollars . . . just like that. All to shut the mouth of one guilt-ridden client. He had to start screening them better. Demand was high, of course, but few people were truly suitable. It took a deep-rooted hatred and considerable fortitude to watch your spouse die in agony, knowing that you had brought about that pain.

'If the money bothers you,' Glykon said, 'think about prison for twenty-five years. Or think about sticking your hand inside that bag.' He gestured at the Nike duffle bag at his feet. 'Because I could make a strong argument for that. There's no risk to me, and it absolutely guarantees my safety.'

'It would also deprive you of future income,' Rusk said bravely, though the core of his mind was focused on the question *What's in that bag?* He'd been watching it for a while now, and was almost positive that it was moving.

'Do you want to see?' Glykon asked.

Rusk shook his head. 'We need to talk about something else.'

'What's that, Andrew?' A new watchfulness came into Glykon's eyes.

'I knew today would upset you. Especially the stuff about Morse. So I felt I had to take steps to protect myself.'

The doctor's eyelids dropped. 'What did you do?'

'Take it easy. All I did was make a simple and absolutely safe arrangement whereby if I don't do a certain thing every day, certain events will be set in motion.' Rusk heard his voice quavering, but he had to go on. 'Events which would ensure you going to prison for multiple murder.'

A strange light had come into the half-lidded eyes. 'Don't tell me that you left some sort of confession with your attorney, or in a safe-deposit box?'

'No, no, it's much more discreet than that! And much more reliable.'

'What if you happen to die accidentally?'

'You'll have a couple of days to get out of the country. And that's not so bad. We're set up like kings. You'd just be leaving a little earlier. The bottom line is: you can't kill me and stay in America. But why would you want to kill me? I'm making you more money than you could get any other way.'

'Your idea of wealth is very provincial, Andrew. The profits from my research will dwarf what we've earned. I consider our little operations piecework, like a student cutting lawns during medical school.'

This irritated Rusk, but he didn't argue. He was still looking at the bag. There was definitely something alive in it.

'I need to get back to the city,' he said.

Glykon reached down and unzipped the bag. As Rusk edged away from the fire, something black and yellow emerged from the open bag. It looked like a lizard's head. A black lizard with a yellow band across its head.

'Before you go,' Glykon said. 'Tell me about the woman. Alex Morse.'

'She was a hostage negotiator for the Bureau. The best they had, until she fucked up.'

'What was the nature of her mistake?'

'She let her emotions override her logic.'

'A common pitfall.' With an almost balletic fluidity, Glykon reached behind the black and yellow head and lifted a snake from the bag.

The narrow, brightly coloured tail was twenty inches long. Rusk stared at the alternating bands: *red, yellow, black; red, yellow, black—*

His blood pressure dropped so rapidly that he thought he might faint. It was a goddamned coral snake. A killer . . .

'Where did you get that fucking thing?' he asked in a quavering voice.

'I found him this morning. He's a shy fellow, like all his kind.'

'He came right on out of that bag when you opened it.'

The doctor smiled. 'I think he wanted to warm himself in the sun. He's cold-blooded, remember?'

Just like you . . . thought Rusk.

'Is Agent Morse married?' Glykon asked.

'Never.'

'Interesting. Children?'

'Just the nephew, Fennell's boy.'

The doctor seemed lost in thought.

'Oh, one more thing,' Rusk said. 'I've got a potential client tomorrow. This guy is a total redneck, but there's nothing provincial about his bank account. And I know for a fact that he hates his wife.'

'Greedy boy. What's the potential take?'

'We could each clear a million, I think.'

Glykon held the snake's head mere inches from his eyes. 'Really?'

'Hell, yes. It would cost him ten times that to get divorced.'

'Then do it.'

'No worries about Braid?' Rusk ventured.

The doctor shook his head. 'Forget Braid. I'll handle him. Focus on your sales presentation. That's your gift, Andrew. Sales.'

Rusk smiled in relief. 'I really need to go,' he said, backing further away from the fire. 'How will I know that Braid has been taken care of?'

Irritation flashed in Glykon's blue eyes. 'Have I ever promised anything that did not become fact?'

'No. My mistake.'

'Go away, Andrew. And remember—two hundred and fifty thousand dollars in uncut stones—not that flashy stash you use to seduce college girls.'

'Uncut white crystals,' Rusk acknowledged. 'You'll have them next week.'

Glykon was mostly a silhouette now, but Rusk saw him hold up an arm with the coral snake coiled round it. '*I will indeed*,' he called.

Rusk turned and started running.

CHRIS HAD BEEN WORKING nonstop for hours. The last face he expected to see when he walked into his private office for a break was his wife's. Thora was sitting behind his desk, typing on the keypad of her Treo smartphone. At the rustle of his white coat, she looked up and gave him a brilliant smile.

'Hey,' he said. 'What are you doing here?'

'Well, I happened to be driving past on the highway, so I turned in here to see your face and get a kiss.' She got up and came round the desk, stood on tiptoe and kissed him on the cheek. 'Sit down.'

He did. Thora moved behind him and began rubbing his shoulders. The soft scent of perfume reached him. He tried to go with it, mostly to please her, but a massage wasn't going to resolve any of his current problems.

'I had lunch with Laura Canning at Planet Thailand,' Thora was saying. 'She told me the Alluvian had a cancellation this morning. They gave us reservations for the next three nights.'

Chris leaned back and looked up at her inverted face. 'You mean you're driving up there today?'

'No, no, we'll leave tomorrow morning.'

He leaned forward again, absorbing this in silence.

'Don't worry, I'll still take Ben to school, and Mrs Johnson can take him to Cameron's birthday party, if you can't get away.'

Chris had completely forgotten the birthday party: a bowling party, like so many held by Ben's classmates.

Thora came round the chair and sat on the desk. 'You're pretty quiet,' she said, concern in her eyes.

He wished he could do something about his mood, but after Alex Morse's accusations and a morning dealing with terminally ill patients, it was tough to relax. As he looked at Thora propped against the desk, something struck him with odd force. He'd actually noticed it last night, but his starved libido had relegated it to minor importance.

'How much weight have you lost?' he asked, staring at her concave belly beneath her thin silk top.

Thora looked flustered. 'What?'

'Seriously. You look too thin.'

A little laugh. 'That's what running does to you.'

'I know. And it can be unhealthy. Let's get you weighed.'

Thora reached down and squeezed his thigh. 'You're being silly, Chris.'

'No, I'm being serious. Come down the hall,' he said, standing, 'I want to weigh you. And I want to draw some blood, too.'

'Blood?' Thora looked stunned. 'No way.'

'I'm worried about your general health, Thora. Plus, all the running you're doing could be interfering with your ability to conceive.'

Thora looked sober but said nothing.

'Come on.' He took her by the arm and walked her to the nurse's station.

Thora stepped up onto the medical scale and Chris worked the black iron balances until the bar settled into a level position.

'A hundred and eleven pounds,' he said. 'You were a hundred and twenty-six when we got married.'

'I never weighed that in my life.'

She was lying about that. 'You're five feet six, Thora. You don't need to lose fifteen pounds when your starting point is one twenty-six.'

She sighed and stepped off the scale.

Chris knew he'd never get her into the lab, so he sat her down and fastened a blood-pressure cuff round her upper arm. After he'd pumped it up, he dug into a bottom drawer and took out a syringe.

'Just sit back and be calm. I'm very good with a needle.'

She sat back and let him draw ten ccs of dark venous blood into the barrel of the syringe. 'God,' she said. 'I come in for a kiss and I get violated instead. No wonder I don't come here very much.'

Chris laughed. 'I thought you liked me violating you,' he said.

'Not today.' She got up and walked back towards his office.

When Chris got there, she was slipping her Treo into her purse. 'I've got to get ready for my trip,' she said, coming to the door. 'I'll see you back at the house, OK?' She leaned close. 'Maybe after Ben's game we can do a replay of last night.'

'Maybe so,' he said.

Thora turned and walked towards the private exit, her silk trousers swishing gracefully around her ankles.

Chris closed the door to his office and sat at his desk. As he tried to summon the concentration to examine his next patient, he distractedly opened his drawer. Lying on top of a prescription pad was the silver Motorola phone that Alex Morse had given him that morning. As he took it out he saw that its blue LCD window said 1 MISSED CALL. The phone's ringer was set to silent. He flipped open the phone and checked the time of the call. One minute ago. Strangely flustered, he speed-dialled the only number programmed into the memory.

After only half a ring, a woman said, 'It's Alex. Can you talk?'

'Yes.'

'I'm right outside your office. Thora just left. I followed her here.'

'Jesus, Alex. What are you doing?'

'I have something to show you, Chris. Something unequivocal. Meet me in the park at the end of this boulevard in five minutes. I'll be waiting on the big hill in the middle.'

The big hill? 'That's a ceremonial mound. And it's not a park. It's a historical site. The Grand Village of the Natchez Indians.'

'Fine. Whatever. Please hurry.'

FIFTEEN MINUTES LATER, Chris was jogging under a thick stand of oak trees, past a replica of an Indian hut. In the distance stood two steep mounds. The nearer was a ceremonial mound where the chief of the Natchez, the Great Sun, had once presided over the rituals of this unique tribe. Farther on stood the Temple mound. Both had been built by the sun-worshipping natives who had settled this land a thousand years before the white man came.

Chris shielded his eyes with his hand and studied the crest of the nearer mound. A small silhouette appeared against the sky. He wasn't sure if it was

Alex Morse, but he walked in that direction anyway and climbed the slope.

'It's been twenty minutes,' said the silhouette above him.

When Chris reached the crest, he recognised her. She had exchanged her biking garb for khakis and a pale yellow top.

'What do you have to show me?' he asked.

'We're pretty exposed here,' she said. 'Can we move somewhere else?'

'I guess so. St Catherine's Creek runs through this site. There's a path under those trees over there that leads down to it.'

'Fine.' She started in that direction without waiting for him.

Chris shook his head in frustration, then followed. The trees changed from oak to elm to cottonwood and thick stands of bamboo. Then they were walking on damp beige sand, and ahead was a wide, placid creek.

'That's far enough,' said Morse. 'Put your game face on, Doctor.'

Chris clenched his fists at his sides.

She opened her purse and handed him a photograph of Thora standing very close to Shane Lansing. Behind them was a sheet of black granite that Chris recognised as the face of the fireplace in their new house in Avalon. Thora's face was highly animated—seemingly by anger, but he couldn't be sure—and Lansing was listening with a submissive expression.

'I took that picture forty-five minutes ago. I shot it through a window, and printed it in my car on a portable Canon.'

Chris felt unsteady on his feet. Thora was wearing the same silk top and blue pants she had worn to his office only minutes ago. She had said nothing about the meeting.

'Did you hear what they said?' he asked.

'I couldn't get close enough without her seeing me.'

Chris walked over to a large log and sat down heavily. 'I know this looks bad,' he said, holding up the picture. 'But it doesn't *prove* they're having an affair. Maybe Lansing is confiding in Thora about something.'

Morse opened her mouth in astonishment.

'Goddamn it,' he said before she could speak. 'You're saying she got it on with Lansing, then drove straight to my office to give me a kiss?'

'Did she tell you that's why she came to your office?'

Chris looked away. 'What else did she do today?'

'The usual. She ran, she showered, she swam at the country club. Then she drove to Mainstream Fitness, and showered again there. She was walking to Planet Thailand when her phone rang. She took the call, then suddenly she turned round and went back to her car. That's when she drove out to Avalon.'

Chris looked up sharply. 'Thora didn't eat lunch at Planet Thailand?'

'No. What did she tell you?'

I had lunch with Laura Canning at Planet Thailand . . .

'Chris?'

He couldn't look at Morse.

'She lied to you, didn't she?' Alex said. 'If you still have any doubts, check her cellphone bill. You can do it online. There'll be a call from Lansing at twelve twenty-eight p.m. today. You have the picture that proves she met him immediately afterwards, and you know she lied to you about where she was during lunch. Once you put those things together—'

'I get it, OK!' Chris snapped, and walked swiftly away, dropping the photograph on the sand.

THE PITCHER UNLOADED a fastball. The batter swung hard—and missed. The ball glanced off the catcher's mitt and caromed off the backstop behind him. Ben exploded off third base, reaching full speed in five steps, but the pitcher was already dashing to cover home plate.

Coaching first base, Chris tensed and watched. Ben sprinted as far as he dared before dropping into his slide, then he was skidding down the baseline in a cloud of dust. Every voice in the bleachers fell silent, and Chris's heart rose into his throat. He thought Ben had it, but a flash of white at the centre of the dust cloud made him clench his fists in fear.

'*Out!*' screamed the umpire.

The stands erupted in a roar of fury and joy. Chris ran towards the plate, but it was no use arguing the call. He hadn't seen the play. Instinct told him that no one had, including the umpire. There was so much dust that the final act of the game had been obscured. Ben got up, his face red, and stared at the umpire with tears in his eyes. He seemed on the verge of challenging the ump, so Chris caught him by the arm and pulled him into the dugout.

'It was a good try,' Chris said, 'but it's over. Time to be a man.'

The two teams lined up, then filed past each other saying, 'Good game, good game,' and then it was over. Chris gathered his team behind the dugout, gave them an encouraging wrap-up talk in the gathering dusk, and dispersed them to their waiting parents.

'Dad?' said Ben, tugging at his arm. 'Can we stay and watch C.J.'s game?'

'No, honey,' said a female voice from behind Chris. *Thora's voice.*

'Aw, come on, Mom! Dad didn't say no.'

'OK,' Thora said in a clipped voice. 'Ask him and see what he says.'

Ben grinned and looked up at Chris. 'Can I, Dad? Can I?'

'Sure,' said Chris, 'Let's see how C.J. does against Webb Furniture.'

Ben screeched in delight and ran off towards the bleachers.

'Why did you do that?' asked Thora. 'I thought we were going to spend some time together at home. I'm leaving tomorrow.'

'By your choice.'

She looked at Chris as though he'd slapped her.

'You'll only be gone three days,' he said. 'Right?'

Thora nodded slowly but said nothing. He walked past her towards the bleachers. He thought she might call after him, but she didn't. As he walked, he tried to get a handle on his emotions.

Chris had been in a state of shock since Alex Morse had shown him the photograph. His first instinct had been to drive home and confront Thora, but by the time he passed the clinic in his car, he had calmed down enough to turn round and go inside. Most of Thora's blood tests had been completed by then, and the only abnormality he found was mild anaemia, which he often saw in distance runners.

After he'd finished the day's work, Chris had done as Morse suggested and checked the online billing records for Thora's cellphone. He'd found several numbers he didn't recognise, but none belonged to Shane Lansing. Stranger still, there had been no call at 12.28 p.m. Either Agent Morse was mistaken, or Thora had a cellphone he knew nothing about.

It was nearly dark in Natchez now but the stadium lights had turned the surrounding park into an emerald island in the night. After moping by the fence for a few minutes, Thora made her way up to him in the top bench of the bleachers, two sweating bottles of beer in her hands.

'Are you going to tell me what's wrong?' she whispered, sitting beside him.

'Nothing,' he said, staring straight ahead. 'I just don't like to lose.'

She set one of the bottles on the bench seat. 'I thought the prospect of sex would get you home early, win or lose,' she said in a low voice.

He looked at her. 'What did you do today?' he asked.

She drew back slightly. 'That's a quick transition.'

He shrugged.

'The usual things,' Thora said, looking back towards the field. 'I ran, I swam, I worked out at Mainstream. Then lunch. Then I argued with the contractors and bought a few things for my trip.'

Chris almost said, 'How did lunch go?' but instead he asked, 'What's happening with the contractors?'

Thora shrugged. 'Same old, same old. Delays on the woodwork, change orders. They want more money in advance.'

Chris nodded but said nothing, watching Ben's friend C.J score a triple.

'*Dad!*' Ben cried from two rows down. 'Did you see that?'

'Sure did. Next year maybe we can get you and C.J. on the same team.'

'Oh, yeah.' Ben high-fived a buddy, then climbed up to Chris's side.

Chris almost sighed with relief. He didn't want to talk to Thora. He wished she were leaving for the Delta tonight.

With Ben so close, Thora watched the game in silence. Chris scanned the fences and the other bleachers. He knew nearly every face he saw. That was how it was in small towns. Looking down towards home plate, he saw a man about his own age waving at him. A strange numbness came into his hands and face. The man was Shane Lansing.

Thora was waving back as though Lansing were a long-lost relation. '*Wave*, Chris,' she urged, nudging him in the side.

Fuck him, Chris thought, almost saying it aloud. He inclined his head slightly in Lansing's direction, then looked pointedly back at the game.

'What's got into you tonight?' Thora asked.

'Nothing, I told you.' Chris took out his wallet and took out two dollars. 'Hey, Ben? Run get me some popcorn.'

'Aw, Dad, there's a line! A long one.'

Chris handed him the money and gave him a push. Ben got up and walked dejectedly down the steps.

'You ever see Lansing out at Avalon?' Chris asked in a casual tone.

'I saw him today,' Thora said without hesitation.

This admission brought Chris up short. 'You did?'

'Yes. Shane stopped by the site on his way home for lunch.' For the first time, Thora looked uncomfortable. 'I've been meaning to talk to you about this. But you've been so busy lately—'

'You've been meaning to talk to me about what?'

'God, Chris. What's the matter? He asked me to work for him, that's all.'

Chris didn't know how to respond. He felt his face flushing. Nothing could have surprised him more. '*Work* for him? Doing what?'

'You can't tell anybody this, but Shane is planning to build a large out-patient surgery centre. It will compete with the local hospitals, so you can imagine the stink it will cause.'

The idea that Shane Lansing wanted to build a surgical centre didn't surprise Chris. Lansing was one of the new breed; they started building their empires the first year they could legally tack the letters *MD* after their names. But why would Lansing want Thora to work at his surgical centre?

'What does he want you to do?'

'Supervise the personnel. Nurses and technicians mostly.'

'You're a multimillionaire, for God's sake. Why would you go to work as a nursing supervisor?'

Thora laughed, her eyes twinkling. 'I didn't say I was going to take it. Though I do get pretty bored sometimes playing the yuppie housewife.'

Chris paused. 'Is that Lansing's only interest in you?' he said eventually.

Thora laughed louder this time, the sound like a handful of bells. 'What do you mean?' she asked.

'Don't be disingenuous.'

Her smile faded. 'Shane's married, baby.'

'And if he wasn't?'

'Come on now. You're not serious?'

'Shane's had three affairs that I know about in the last year.'

'That's just gossip,' she said dismissively. 'You know this town.'

'No, the gossip has it at six or seven. The three affairs I mentioned are fact. He had to pay off two of the women to make them go away.'

Two tall boys had joined Shane Lansing behind the backstop. The surgeon had four sons, all handsome, all good athletes.

'I hadn't heard that,' Thora said thoughtfully.

Chris turned his attention back to the game. Thora's revelation of a job offer had flabbergasted him. Could that be the explanation for their secret contact? If Lansing was putting together his own surgical centre, he was right to keep it a secret. The two local hospitals would do all they could to stop him. He said, 'I've got to pee,' and climbed down to the ground, choosing a route that took him past Lansing. Chris found himself reappraising the surgeon's sharp-jawed handsomeness and athletic build. He stopped and shook the man's hand.

'Heard you guys lost tonight,' Lansing said.

Chris forced down bile and nodded. 'What about y'all?'

The surgeon laughed. 'With four boys, you win some and lose some.'

'Hey, Thora told me you came by the house today.'

The remark seemed to take Lansing by surprise, but he recovered quickly. 'Yeah, the place is really coming along.'

Chris forced a smile. 'Been playing much golf lately?'

'When I can, you know me.'

'I was thinking about playing this week. You going to be in town?'

Lansing's eyes locked onto his. 'Yeah, sure. You want to play a round?'

Chris nodded. 'I'll call you.'

Lansing smiled, then turned back to the field at the sound of a hit.

Chris walked towards the restroom. Halfway there, he looked back at Thora. She was staring intently at Shane Lansing.

IT WAS 11.45 p.m. when Alex saw the little green icon on her screen, signalling Jamie's presence on the network. Relief flooded through her. Before she could type a word, an invitation for a videoconference popped up. She accepted, then watched the webcam window appear. When Jamie's face materialised, her voice caught in her throat. There were tears on his cheeks.

'What's the matter, little man?' she asked. 'What happened?'

'Missy's moving in with us.'

Alex felt a thunderclap of shock. '*What? Why do you say that?*'

'She came over to eat with us tonight. She was acting all weird, like she's my new best friend or something. Then Dad said something about how great it would be for me to have a lady around again. They both watched me really close after he said it. I'm not stupid, Aunt Alex.'

Alex almost got up and walked away from the webcam. What the hell was Bill thinking? His wife hadn't been in the ground six weeks, and he was planning to move his mistress in with his bereaved son?

'What should I do?' Jamie asked, and in that moment Alex felt the full weight of responsibility for his future. 'Can I come and live with you?'

'Maybe. I'm working on that every day. But you have to hang tight for the moment. You can't say anything about it. Not even to your dad.'

'I hate Missy,' Jamie said with real venom. 'Hate, hate, hate.'

Missy's not the problem, Alex thought. *Bill is the problem.*

'I didn't do my homework,' Jamie said uneasily. 'I told Dad I did, but I didn't. I couldn't think about it.'

'Do you think you can do it now?'

Jamie shrugged. 'Can you stay on while I do it?'

Alex needed to set off for Jackson. One of her mother's nurses had called and informed her that the oncologist was moving her mother back to the hospital because of worsening liver function. It was a two-hour drive. But how could she turn away from the confusion and fear in Jamie's eyes?

She forced herself to smile as if she had all the time in the world. 'Absolutely.'

FIVE MILES FROM Alex Morse's hotel room, Chris lay in his adopted son's bed, listening to Ben's slow, rhythmic breathing. Today had been one of the worst days of his life, and he had no wish to continue it by getting into further discussions with Thora before bed. His mind was spinning with Morse's accusations, and beneath them was an inchoate terror of having screwed up yet again. He had dated his first wife for five years before marrying her, but even after all that time he had not seen through the beautiful façade to the true woman within. He'd thought he'd known her. But he'd been wrong.

He'd dated Thora for less than a year before proposing. He'd known her longer than that, of course, mostly as the devoted wife of one of his patients. And he came to respect and desire her more than any other woman he'd met since his divorce. But now he sensed that the Thora he had come to know was only one facet of a much more complex character.

And what about Ben? In a remarkably short time, the boy had put all his trust and faith in Chris, looking to him for friendship, support and security. Not financial security—Thora could provide that on her own—but for the feeling that there was a man twice his size ready to stand between him and any danger that might come his way. It was hard to believe that Thora would put that bond at risk to have an affair with a guy like Lansing.

A vertical crack of yellow light appeared in the darkness. Then a shadow darkened the crack. Thora was at the door. Chris closed his eyes and lay still.

'Chris? Are you sleeping?' she whispered.

He didn't answer.

After several moments, Thora tiptoed in and kissed each of them on the forehead. 'Goodbye, boys,' she whispered. 'I love you.'

Then she slipped out and closed the door behind her.

Chapter 5

Alex blinked and stirred at a groan of pain. After helping Jamie to finish his homework late last night, she'd set off for Jackson and had almost run off the road twice during the drive. Since arriving at UMC, she had been hovering for hours in some purgatory between sleep and wakefulness, sitting in a hospital chair at the side of her mother's bed. Now, faint blue light was leaking round the window blinds.

Margaret Morse really belonged in intensive care, but one week ago she had signed a 'do not resuscitate' form to indicate that no extraordinary measures should be taken to save her life, should she crash. The cancer that had begun in her ovaries had spread to her liver. Yet still she clung to life.

Margaret groaned again. Alex squeezed her hand. Her mother was now taking so much morphine that periods of consciousness were less frequent than periods of sleep, and lucidity was rare.

Alex jumped at the chirp of her cellphone, which was tucked in her bag on the floor. Without letting go of her mother's hand, she stretched out her other arm and retrieved the phone. 'Hello?' she said softly.

'It's Will, darlin'. How's she doing?' Will Kilmer had stayed with Margaret until Alex arrived from Natchez.

'No better, no worse. But she slept more than I did.'

The old detective sighed angrily. 'Damn it, girl, I told you last week you need to take a break from this case. That damn Rusk isn't going anywhere. Anyhow, I've got some news that's going to wake you up. Remember William Braid, from Vicksburg?'

'Sure. The husband of victim number five.'

'Looks like he tried to off himself.'

A shiver of excitement brought Alex fully awake. 'How? When?'

'He was diabetic. Last night, or sometime between last night and this morning when his maid found him, seems he shot himself full of enough insulin to put him in a permanent coma.'

'Holy shit,' Alex breathed. 'Could it have been an accident?'

'Possible, but Braid's doctor said it's unlikely.'

'It was guilt,' Alex thought aloud. 'He couldn't handle the reality of what he'd done to his wife.'

'She died hard. Worse than most of the others,' Will said.

'We need to find out everything we can about Braid's last few days. Do you have any operatives in Vicksburg?'

'Know a guy over there who does matrimonial work. Owes me a favour.'

'Thanks, Uncle Will. I'd be dead in the water without you.'

'One more thing. I've got a guy willing to spend two nights at the Alluvian Hotel for you. His wife has always wanted to go up there and see the place. If you'll pay the cost of their room for a night, they'll pay the rest.'

Alex summoned a mental image of her last surviving bank account, then shoved it out of her mind. 'Do it. I'll pay.'

'Are you going back to Natchez today?'

'I don't have a choice. Shepard's my only chance.'

'You making any headway there?'

'He'll come around. Nobody likes to find out their whole life is a lie.'

Will sighed in agreement. 'Tell your mama I'll be by sometime today. And you look out for yourself, you hear? I got a feeling about this case. These are bad people we're messing with. And just because they've killed slow in the past don't mean they won't strike quickly if you threaten them. You hear me? You're the last child your daddy left on this earth, and I don't want you throwing your life away trying to avenge the dead.'

'I'm not doing that,' Alex whispered. 'I'm trying to save Jamie.'

'We'll do that one way or another,' Will said with certainty.

ANDREW RUSK HAD finally hooked the big one, he knew it. Carson G. Barnett, a legend in the oil business, was sitting opposite him. The man was a millionaire so many times over that he'd quit counting. He had made and lost three fortunes, but right now was in an up cycle—*way* up.

For the past hour, Barnett had been describing his marital situation. Rusk, wearing his most concerned look, had nodded at the appropriate places, but hadn't really been listening. He hadn't had to listen for quite a few years now. Because the stories were all variations on a theme. Rusk knew where the oil man was going long before he got there. *She hasn't grown at all since the day we got married. Not emotionally or psychologically or intellectually*, some would qualify. Quite a few would add, *Her ass, on the other hand, has grown like a goddamn baby elephant.*

Carson Barnett's marital problems had their own particular twist. Mrs Barnett—Luvy, Carson called her—had begun the marriage as a Baptist, but this had played no big part in her life until after the kids were born. Then Luvy's involvement in the church had increased exponentially. At the same time, her interest in all matters sexual had decreased in direct proportion. Carson had suffered this as best he could for a while and then, like any red-blooded male, he had sought relief where he could find it.

'If there ain't no food in the freezer, you go to the store,' he boomed. 'Ain't that right, Andy?'

'Yes, it is,' Rusk agreed.

The trouble started, he thought to himself, when the man—or woman—found a 'soul mate'. When love reared its ugly head, divorce soon followed. Barnett's 'soul mate' proved to be a sweet young thing who worked over at the barbecue place on Route 59.

'I love that little girl like nobody's business,' Barnett said. 'And I aim to marry her, one way or another.'

'So you want to divorce your wife,' Rusk said in a sombre tone.

'I never thought it would come to this, but by God she's drove me to it.'

Rusk nodded sagely. 'A lot of attorneys would discourage you, Mr Barnett. They'd encourage you to seek counselling.'

'Call me Carson, Andy. Please. And let me stop you right there. The only counselling Luvy would try was her pastor, and one visit was more than I could stomach. You never heard such hogwash in your life.'

Rusk smiled. 'I'm not going to discourage you, Carson. I can see that you're in love. Truly in love. And true love is a wonderful thing. But I can tell that you anticipate some trouble from Luvy with this idea of splitting up.'

'Oh, hell, yes,' Barnett said with a look of fear in his eyes. 'Luvy don't even believe in divorce, Andy. Says I don't have no grounds to divorce her, and she isn't going to give me one. She says if I try to go to court, she'll deny me as much time as she can with the children, seeing how I'm a sinner and a terrible role model for them. Course if I stay with her and try again, I'm just an all-round great guy. How about that?'

'Has Luvy said anything about the financial side of things?'

Barnett gritted his teeth. 'She claims she doesn't want any money for herself—beyond half of what I earned while I was married to her—but she wants everything she can legally get for the children, which means all future production from the wells I hit while we was married, or even prospects I mapped out while I was married to her.'

Rusk leaned forward. 'I'm afraid you can consider half those wells gone as of this moment. And a judge could also base an alimony figure on your current production numbers.'

Barnett went white. He got up and started pacing. 'You know what the price of oil's done lately? Even my old wells have tripled in value. If a judge did projections based on current production . . . Jesus, I'd owe her at least twenty million. There's the houses, the boat, the goddamn restaurant . . .'

Rusk turned away to hide his excitement. This was the client he had been waiting for, the payday that would take him into retirement at forty. Being in business with Glykon would not be necessary for much longer.

'Please take a seat, Carson,' he said softly.

Barnett sat down. He stared at Andrew Rusk like a penitent staring at a priest empowered to offer him a papal dispensation.

'A clever lawyer would tell you to forget about getting divorced.'

'What?' An animal look of suspicion.

'You can't afford it.'

'What do you mean? I'm worth fifty million bucks.'

'Twenty-five, Carson. If you're lucky. Getting divorced would cost you twenty-five million dollars and ninety per cent of your time with your kids. If Luvy takes the position you've outlined, you can expect to see them every other weekend, plus a special arrangement for holidays.'

'Boy . . . that just ain't right.'

'Morally, I couldn't agree with you more. But legally . . . I'm afraid it is right. How long were you planning on waiting to marry this girl?'

'I know it can't be right off. But we're getting pretty itchy, you know.'

Rusk could imagine the girl in question being *very* itchy to tie the knot.

'You should be prepared for a lot of anger on the part of your kids. They'll be made painfully aware that you're abandoning their mother for a younger woman, and they'll know who that woman is. Do you think Luvy will make an effort to integrate your new love into the life of the family?'

'She'll scream "harlot" every time she sees her. Luvy'll do everything she can to poison the kids against me. She's already told me she's praying I'll drop dead from a heart attack. Says it's better for the kids to think I'm dead than gone off and left them.' Barnett rose out of his chair again. 'Goddamn it, Andy. Sometimes I get so frustrated, I could just . . .'

Rusk let the silence stretch out. Now that Barnett's anger had reached critical mass, it wasn't going to cool anytime soon.

'Please sit down, Carson. I want to talk to you, man to man.'

This was a language Barnett understood. He sat down.

Rusk looked into the oil man's eyes. 'What I'm going to say may shock you. I'm guessing that a man like you has come across some unusual situations in your business. What you might call . . . *difficulties.*'

'That's for sure.'

Rusk nodded soberly. 'Some difficulties, I've found, are solvable by conventional methods. Others take some creative thinking . . .'

CHRIS TURNED HIS BICYCLE onto Maple Street and pumped hard up the long slope. Soon he would break out onto the bluff, with miles of open space to his left and the Natchez Cemetery on his right.

Tom Cage, as perceptive as ever, had noticed his partner's dazed mental state and told him to take the afternoon off. After leaving the practice, Chris had driven home, changed and, without really thinking about it, had begun a ride from Elgin to the Mississippi River. He was staring so intently over the endless miles of Louisiana cotton fields on his left that he almost slammed into a car that had turned broadside across the road.

Chris braked so hard that he nearly went over the handlebars. He was about to start screaming at the driver when she jumped out and started screaming at him. He stood with his mouth hanging open.

'Why haven't you been answering my calls?' Alex Morse shouted. She looked as though she hadn't slept for days.

'Because I already know what you're going to say.'

'You *don't* know what I'm going to say, goddamn it! Something terrible has happened! Something I couldn't have predicted in a million years.'

Chris pedalled up to her open door. 'What?'

'One of the husbands—a guy who's murdered his wife—tried to commit suicide last night. Insulin overdose.'

'Was he diabetic?'

Morse nodded.

'And he's in a coma, right?'

'How did you know?'

'I saw that a lot during my residency. People try insulin because it offers hope of a painless death. More times than not they wind up in a permanent vegetative state. Could it have been an accidental overdose?'

'I don't think so. The guy's name is William Braid, and his wife suffered terribly before she died. If I'm right, and Braid paid for her murder, then we have two possibilities. One, Braid was so consumed by guilt he couldn't live with himself. Some local gossip supports that scenario. But a couple of his friends say Braid's ego was so big he could never kill himself.'

'Go on.'

'It could be that whoever Braid hired to murder his wife—Andrew Rusk, for example—decided that an unstable, guilt-ridden client was an intolerable liability. Especially now, with me poking around.' Morse looked up and down the road. 'How hard would it be to put Braid into an insulin coma?'

'Child's play compared to giving someone cancer,' Chris said. 'You look terrible. Haven't you slept?'

Alex shook her head. 'I drove to Jackson last night to see my mother. They had to put her into UMC again last night. Her liver's going. Kidneys, too.'

'I'm sorry.'

'It's weird,' Morse said. 'Put me on a plane, and I can sleep from wheels-up to the arrival gate. But in hospitals . . . I can't do it. I did sleep in my car for a couple of hours,' she added. 'In the parking lot of your office. I was still asleep when you left the practice. I figured you might come out here. I've followed Thora when she runs out here.'

He felt a prick of guilt. 'Look, Agent Morse—'

'Would you call me Alex, for God's sake?' Exasperation coloured her face, darkening the scars round her right eye.

'OK. Alex. I've heard everything you've told me, OK? But I didn't feel like listening to any more today. That's why I didn't answer your calls.'

Her expression changed. 'What do you feel like doing?'

'Riding.'

She turned up her palms. 'Fine. Why not?' She nodded at an approaching car. 'But we should get off this road. Where were you going from here?'

'I was going to do some sprints in the cemetery, then sit on Jewish Hill and watch the river go by.'

'I can't ride with you today,' Alex said, nodding at the empty bike rack attached to her rear bumper. 'Could we just take a walk in there?'

Chris looked away. Could she walk beside him without bringing up her obsession? He doubted it. Yet, oddly enough, Alex Morse was the only person who might remotely understand what was eating him. 'We're liable to run into people who know me in there, believe it or not.'

Alex shrugged. 'If we do, tell them I'm a doctor from out of town. You and Tom Cage are thinking of bringing in a new associate.'

Chris smiled for the first time in many hours, maybe days. Then he mounted his bike and pedalled towards the nearest cemetery gate. Alex drove through the open gate and parked her Corolla on the grass. Chris chained his bike to her rack, then led her in silence down one of the narrow lanes that divided the tall and silent stones.

They walked some distance without speaking, penetrating ever deeper into the cemetery. Like much of old Natchez, it had a classical feel to it, thanks to the Greek Revival architecture favoured by the cotton planters before the Civil War. After a while, Chris decided to open the conversation.

'I've been doing a little reading in my oncology texts,' he said.

'What have you learned?'

'That we don't know what causes ninety per cent of blood cancers. We *do* know that most of them have different causes. They can tell that from the changes in various blood cells, and by other factors like tumour-suppressor genes, cellular growth factors, et cetera.'

'Was I right about radiation?'

'As far as you went, yes. You could cause a whole spectrum of cancers with radiation. But *not* undetectably. You fire gamma rays into somebody without a qualified radiation oncologist directing the beam, you're going to have severe burns, skin rotting off, vomiting around the clock.'

'But it's *possible* with enough expertise,' Alex insisted. 'Did you come up with any other options?'

'Chemicals,' said Chris, making steadily for Jewish Hill. 'But the toxins known to cause cancer are some of the most lasting on the planet. You put one nanogram of dioxin into somebody, it'll be there on the day they die. As for volatile compounds like benzene, you'd have the same problem you have with radiation. Using enough to reliably kill people would almost certainly cause acute illness. So basically, chemicals are a less reliable oncogenic murder weapon than radiation, and more likely to get you caught.'

'I'm sorry. Oncogenic?'

'Cancer-causing,' Chris clarified. 'So, if we dispense with radiation and chemicals, that leaves only one other possibility. Oncogenic viruses.'

She turned towards him. 'A professor I spoke to last week mentioned viruses, but a lot of what he said was over my head.'

'OK. Some viruses in the herpes family are known to cause cancer. And at least one retrovirus is known to be oncogenic. I was thinking of calling my old haematology professor from medical school, Peter Connolly. He's up at Sloan-Kettering now and he's done ground-breaking work on gene therapy, which actually uses viruses to carry magic bullets to tumour sites. It's one of the newest forms of cancer therapy.'

They had reached Jewish Hill at last, but Chris glanced at his watch. 'Alex, I hate to say this, but I've got to run. Ben's at a birthday party, and with Thora gone, I've got to pick him up.'

She smiled. 'It's OK. I can jog back to the car.'

They set off downhill, but Alex clearly didn't intend to squander her remaining time with him. 'I've wondered about someone simply injecting tumour cells from a sick being into a healthy one. I saw that done with mice on the Discovery Channel.'

Chris nodded. 'They can do that because the mice used for cancer research are either nude mice, which means they have no immune systems, or because they're genetic copies of each other—clones, basically. That's like injecting cells from a tumour in my body into my identical twin. But if I injected cells from my tumour into you, your immune system would recognise the foreign cells as an alien invader and wipe them out.'

'What if you beat down your victim's immune system beforehand?'

'You mean like with cyclosporine? Anti-organ-rejection drugs?'

'Or corticosteroids.' Alex had been doing her homework.

'If you compromised someone's immune system sufficiently, they'd be vulnerable to all sorts of infections. They'd be noticeably sick. Do the medical records of your victims show illnesses before their cancer diagnosis?'

'The two victim records I have access to don't show anything like that.'

Chris cut across the grass towards the Corolla, weaving between the graves. 'If you had the records of every victim, you could move this forward.'

Alex stopped beside a black granite tombstone. 'I feel so inadequate in this investigation,' she admitted. 'My knowledge stops at high-school biology. But you speak the language, you know the experts to talk to—'

'Alex—'

'Please, Chris. Will you really be able to avoid thinking about all this?'

He grabbed her hands and squeezed hard. 'Listen to me!' he said. 'I'm not sure what to do yet. I'm still trying to come to terms with everything that's happened to me. I'm working on it, OK? In my own way. I am going to call my friend at Sloan-Kettering tomorrow.'

Alex closed her eyes and exhaled with relief. 'Thank you.'

'But right now I need to pick up Ben, and I don't want to be late.'

He unlocked his bike, took it off her rack and climbed onto it.

'Promise me you'll be careful,' she implored. 'Stay away from the traffic.'

'I'll be fine. I do this all the time. Now, let me go. We'll talk later.'

'Promise?'

'Jesus.'

Alex bit her bottom lip and looked at the ground. When she raised her head, he saw that her eyes were bloodshot from lack of sleep.

'I'm out on the edge here, Chris. You are, too. Only you don't know it.'

He looked back long enough for her to see that he meant what he was going to say. 'I do know.'

Before she could say more, he kicked his right pedal forward and made for the cemetery gate.

ELDON TARVER EXITED off I-55 South and drove his white van into the low-rent commercial sprawl of south Jackson. His destination was an old, disused bakery surrounded by a razor-wire-topped fence. He pulled up to the gate, got out and unlocked a heavy padlock. Once he'd driven through, he closed the gate behind the van but didn't lock it, as he was expecting a delivery.

In this neighbourhood, he was known not as Eldon Tarver, MD, but as Noel D. Traver, DVM. He was ostensibly running a breeding facility, selling animals to research institutions around the country, but in reality that was merely a cover for what was really taking place inside the building. Dr Tarver had chosen it because of its large, hidden, underground basement.

He unlocked the front door and was just entering a large holding area, when he heard the blare of a horn behind him.

Cursing, he hurried back outside. A refrigerated truck with ice cream sundaes painted on its side was rumbling up to the delivery entrance. Eldon was eager to see what the Mexicans had brought him this time.

Luís Almodóvar, a heavyset man with a black moustache, jumped down from the cab. Luís almost always wore a smile, but today Dr Tarver saw anxiety in his eyes.

'How many do you have for me today?'

'Two, *señor.* This is what you asked for, no?'

'Yes. Open the truck.'

Luís unlocked the door at the rear of the truck, and Dr Tarver stepped up onto the bumper. A stench hit him.

'What happened?' he asked.

Luís was wringing his hands. 'The refrigerator, *señor.* He broke.'

'Jesus.' Tarver pressed his shirt over his nose. The smell of excrement was almost suffocating in the Mississippi heat. 'How long ago?'

'At Matamoros, *señor.*'

Dr Tarver shook his head in disgust and climbed into the truck. It was filled with animals of different species in cages, including at least a dozen primates. The prize cargo, two chimpanzees for which Tarver had paid $30,000 apiece on the black-market, lay lethargically in a large cage. The coat of one had several bald patches that might indicate any number of diseases. It was obvious that they had not eaten for days.

'*Goddamn idiots,*' he muttered. He turned and roared, 'Get these cages out of here!'

Luís nodded, then forced his way past Dr Tarver in the narrow aisle between the cages.

'You stupid bastard,' Eldon said to Luís's back. 'Do you know what kind of delay this causes? I have to get them back to normal weight before I can run any tests. And I can't begin to measure the effects of the stress you put them through. Stress directly impacts the primate's immune system.'

'*Sí, señor!*' Luís grunted as he struggled to lift the cage containing the chimps. Unable to manage on his own, he called the driver from the cab.

After the two Mexicans had finally got the cage into the bakery, Tarver escorted them outside and sent them on their way.

When he walked back into the shipping area, his adoptive brother Judah had loaded the cage onto a piano dolly and was moving it towards the lift platform that led to the basement. At fifty-five, with a shock of black hair and pale eyes beneath his low forehead, Judah was as wide and as hard as a tree trunk. One of four brothers in the family that had adopted Eldon as a boy, Judah had been a wilful child until his father decided to break him. Since then, he had not spoken much, but he was devoted to his adoptive brother, who had always taken care of him in the 'outside world', which was so unlike the one they had known as children in Tennessee. As the lift groaned downward, Eldon instructed Judah to delouse and bathe the chimps, then sedate them for a complete physical examination. Judah nodded silently.

When the lift hit bottom, Eldon turned the wheel that opened a security door and walked into the spotless primate lab. The west wall held the primate cages, luxurious custom-built affairs that at the moment held four chimpanzees, two dozen macaques, four marmosets, two baboons and a cottontop tamarin, all of them resting in climate-controlled comfort.

The mouse cages were stacked against the north wall. Near the east wall hung breeding bubbles of fruit flies. Beneath these stood three stacks of terrariums that seemed to contain nothing but foliage. But closer inspection revealed the scaled bodies of Dr Tarver's prize serpents.

The rest of the space was occupied by massive refrigerators used for storing cell cultures, and cutting-edge testing machines. Dr Tarver had initially tried to carry on his experiments at the UMC medical school, under cover of his legitimate work, but the levels of supervision had made it impossible, and he'd had to construct a $6 million copy of the UMC labs right here. Some of the money had come from his wife, an early believer in his talent, but after her death he'd been forced to find more creative sources of financing. Like Andrew Rusk.

Foreign governments and other bodies were ready to provide him with funds, but Dr Tarver would have no truck with them. Not that he wasn't tempted. Since chimpanzees had been put on the endangered species list, nearly all the chimps used for medical research in the United States were bred domestically, at highly regulated breeding centres. But Dr Tarver couldn't use animals from those centres for what he was doing. Wherever those primates went, government inspectors would follow.

Your Chinese, on the other hand, didn't care how many chimps were left in the wild. The animal rights fanatics could go straight to hell, for all they cared. Dr Tarver shared this view. How the hell anyone expected scientists to cure cancer or AIDS without using animals to set up testable models was beyond him. But Dr Tarver didn't stop there. Because the truth was, animal models only took you so far. When you got into neurological diseases or viral studies, it wasn't enough to experiment on a *similar* metabolism. You had to use the real thing. And the real thing meant *Homo sapiens*. Any serious medical researcher could tell you that. Only most of them wouldn't. Because research dollars were often controlled by foggy-minded liberals who hadn't a clue what science really was, and no one wanted to risk his research budget for something so politically dangerous as the truth.

Dr Tarver walked across the lab and watched his adoptive brother carefully bathe a sedated chimp. After patting Judah on the shoulder, he walked over to the metal table he used as a desk . On it lay a stack of thick file folders, each of which held a comprehensive record of a person's life: daily schedules; medical histories; copies of keys labelled to indicate what they opened—cars, houses, offices; Social Security numbers, passport numbers, PINs, and credit card numbers; and photographs. Eldon spent most of his time poring over the medical records, searching for something that might make someone a candidate for a particular approach. Dr Tarver was as meticulous in this work, as he was in all things.

Everyone was in such a hurry. Twenty-first century man had no patience, no notion of deferred gratification. When Eldon faced a problem, he handled it himself. He never let unfamiliarity stop him. When a mechanic tried to fleece him for repairing an engine, he'd ordered a maintenance manual from Ford, studied it for four days, then repaired the engine himself. This kind of thing was beyond most Americans now. And because of that, the day was coming when conventional war would not be an option against any major power. Only a special weapon would suffice.

Dr Tarver intended to be ready.

CHRIS WAS WORKING LATE editing video footage in his studio when he had the sensation that he was not alone. His first thought was that Ben had woken up. Any other night he would have put Ben to bed in the house, then come out to the studio to work. But fifty yards of darkness separated the converted barn from the house, so tonight he'd let the boy fall asleep on the sofa and, once he was dead to the world, moved him to a bed in the back room.

Now he walked down the hall to check on the boy. 'Ben?' he called softly, opening the door.

Ben lay stomach-down on the bed, fast asleep. Chris stared for a second, then rushed back to the front room and switched off the light. After listening carefully for twenty seconds, he edged up to the window and drew back the curtain. The darkness outside slowly revealed itself to be empty. Feeling a little foolish, Chris switched on the light and went back to his workstation.

He was reaching for the flywheel when a sharp knock sounded at the studio door. He jumped up and went over to it, grabbing an aluminium baseball bat that had been left propped against the wall.

'Who's there?'

'It's Alex,' said a recognisably female voice. 'Alex Morse.'

He yanked open the door. She stood there looking even more drawn than she had that afternoon. In her hand was a black automatic.

'What the hell are you doing?' he demanded. 'If I'd had a gun, I might have shot you!'

'I'm sorry for just showing up like this. I tried to call.'

'The listed number only rings in the main house. You'd better come in.'

Alex stepped inside and closed the door behind them. Chris motioned for her to sit on the sofa, then rolled his chair across the floor and sat facing her.

'Why are you carrying your gun?' he asked.

She set the pistol down on the sofa beside her. 'I'll tell you in a minute. Has Thora called you tonight?'

'Oh, yeah. She's having a great time.'

'Did she ask if you were in the house or the studio?'

'She wouldn't have to. My private line only rings out here. What are you doing here, Alex?'

'I knew that once Thora left town, someone might make a move against you. I've been watching your house for the last three hours, from the carport of the house that's for sale across the road.'

'Did you see anything?'

'When I pulled into Elgin, I passed a van coming out. A white van. Does anybody who lives back in here own a white van?'

He thought about it. 'I don't think so. But there are about sixty houses out in these woods, and we get a fair number of strangers out here. Kids parking, or nosy people just trying to check out the houses.'

This didn't mollify Alex. 'About fifteen minutes ago, another vehicle drove slowly down the road. It came as far as the last curve, then nosed into the drive of the house where I was parked. It came far enough up the hill for its lights to illuminate my car, then stopped and backed out.'

'Did they see you?'

'I don't think so. I took cover pretty quickly. But I didn't ID the vehicle.'

Chris saw genuine fear in her eyes. 'I know it looks suspicious but I've seen that kind of thing happen here before. Poachers drive out to spotlight deer. But they know there's only the one road in and out, so they're paranoid as hell. You're too tired to think straight,' he added gently. 'You told me yourself we have a margin of safety before anybody tries anything.'

'That was before William Braid and his insulin coma.'

'Alex, even if some guy drove here to kill me, once he saw you parked across the street, he'd realise the game was up.'

Alex didn't look convinced.

'I mean, he has to make it look like an illness, right? There's no way he can pull that off now. You told me yourself that someone trying to kill me would be watching me, tapping my phones, that kind of thing. If they have any sense at all they're lying low, hoping you'll get tired of chasing them.'

'I won't.'

He smiled. 'I know that. But tonight you can take a break. A short rest. I'm going to fix up a bed for you in the main house, and—'

He was interrupted by the ringtone of her cellphone.

She checked the LCD, and her face darkened. 'It's my father's old partner. He's a private detective.' She opened the phone. 'Uncle Will?'

Alex listened, her face growing taut. After a short while, she asked some questions about her mother's prognosis, then hung up.

'What is it?' Chris asked. 'It sounded like renal failure.'

She stood and lifted her gun off the sofa. 'The doctors think this is the end. Two or three hours, barring a miracle.'

'You can't drive to Jackson now. Not in this state.'

'I don't have a choice. It's my mother.'

He stood and took hold of her free hand. 'Do you think she would want you to risk your life to be there when she's not even conscious?'

Alex looked up at him with determined eyes. 'She'd do it for me.'

He saw that there was no arguing the point. 'If I didn't have Ben to worry about, I'd drive you myself.'

'You don't need to do that. You stay here with Ben. You have a gun in the house, don't you?'

He nodded.

She walked to the door. 'I'll talk to you tomorrow, OK?'

'Tonight,' he said. 'Call me when you get to Jackson. Call before that if you can't stay awake.'

'I will. But I'll be all right.'

She lingered for a moment, as though she wanted to say more, then she turned and walked away. In seconds she was swallowed by the blackness.

ALEX TURNED LEFT out of the driveway across from Chris's house and headed towards Highway 61. It was nearly a mile to the turn, with much of the narrow lane threading between high, wooded banks. Thankfully, she didn't see a single headlight on the road.

Turning north on 61, she soon passed the Days Inn. A little further on she realised that a pair of headlights was pacing her from behind. Her first thought was 'cop', because the car seemed to have come up suddenly, then remained at a uniform distance behind. But after watching the lights for a while in her rearview mirror, Alex decided they were too high off the ground for a police cruiser. More probably a pick-up or a van.

A Baptist church drifted by on her right. Then construction work narrowed the road to a single lane, where a new stretch of the Natchez Trace highway intersected Highway 61. Alex could see the Super Wal-Mart across the junction. She accelerated steadily, then whipped the Corolla across the oncoming traffic and into the Wal-Mart lot.

The vehicle behind kept on at a constant rate of speed. As it passed the turn, she saw that it was indeed a van—a white van covered with patches of mud and primer. She didn't have the angle to see the licence plate.

She parked thirty yards from the store, the nose of her Corolla pointed towards the highway. *What do I do now?* she wondered. She could call the local police, complain of harassment, and have them stop the van—if they could find it—but she didn't want to do anything that would force her to reveal her FBI credentials. So she cradled her Glock in her lap and waited. Occasional cars passed, but she saw no further sign of the van.

'That's long enough,' she said aloud. She put the car in gear and drove out to the highway, but there she turned back in the direction she'd come.

She hadn't gone more than fifty yards when an approaching vehicle made a U-turn immediately after passing her. She hadn't seen the make, but she made a quick right turn anyway, which put her on Liberty Road. If her memory served correctly, this road would take her past a few of the town's premier mansions, then into the heart of downtown.

Headlights appeared behind her, high enough to be a van. She took the first right turn she came to, this time into what appeared to be a residential estate. The headlights slowed, stopped, then rolled into the road behind her.

Alex wrenched her wheel left, sped up a low incline, then took another left into a lane that wound beneath a pitch-black canopy of trees. She idled past the broad front steps of a mansion, then accelerated and found herself at another intersection. As she pondered which way to go, the high headlights floated towards her from behind. There could be no doubt now.

She drove thirty more yards, then on impulse turned into a long driveway beside a one-storey ranch house. She shut off her engine and got out, moving quickly underneath a carport that held two sedans. She worried that the occupants of the house might wake up, but no lights came on.

The headlights glided up the road, then passed the driveway without slowing down. Alex leaned back, her heart pounding. Was she going crazy? Her left hand went to the cellphone in her pocket. Who could she call? Chris? He couldn't leave Ben. Even if he did, he wasn't trained for this kind of situation. Will Kilmer was too far away to help. Even if she called 911, she couldn't direct help to her exact position.

No headlights reappeared, and her heartbeat slowed steadily. As she stood there waiting, it occurred to her that the driver of the van might only have been ensuring that she was out of the way before attacking Chris.

She dug out her phone and dialled him.

'Hey, you doing OK?' he asked.

'No. Listen to me. The white van followed me after I left your place. I'm parked in a neighbourhood off Liberty Road, and it took off about five minutes ago. It's possible he could be headed to your place. Is your gun close by?'

'In my hand. Should I call the police?'

'It wouldn't hurt. You could just say you saw a prowler.'

'OK. What are *you* going to do?'

'Find the van.'

'Alex—'

'I'm hanging up now.'

She was reaching into her pocket for her keys when, deep in her unconscious brain, some threat sensor was triggered. There was no warning, no sound, nothing tangible to make her freeze—yet she did. Adrenaline flushed through her. It took all her self-control not to panic and run.

She crouched and moved swiftly to the inside corner of the carport, sweeping the area with her Glock, hearing only the steady thrum of air conditioners in the humid darkness. Then it came: a percussive skating sound, like a stone skipping across cement. Her pistol flew to the right, where the carport opened to the driveway. She stared so hard into the blackness that she was almost entranced—when a leather-gloved hand seized her throat.

Before she could react, another hand slammed her Glock against the carport wall. She fought with every fibre in her body, but her struggles were useless. She couldn't even see her attacker; his enormous bulk blocked out the light. She tried to scream, but no air escaped her windpipe.

Think! What can you do? What weapon do you have? One free hand—

She struck again and again where she thought a face should be, savage blows, yet they had no effect. He didn't even move to avoid them.

He was choking her to death. In seconds she would lose consciousness. She tried to gouge the invisible eye sockets with her fingernails, but her assailant simply drew back his head, putting them out of reach.

A ringing crash of metal heralded a barrage of canine fury. A huge dog had launched itself against the chain-link fence at the end of the drive and was barking thunderously. The grip at Alex's throat lessened for a moment, and the massive thigh pinning her to the wall twisted away.

With all her strength, she hammered her knee into the apex of faint light at the centre of the shadow attacking her. The dark figure gave an explosive grunt and the grip at her throat loosened, but before she could exploit the instant of uncertainty, the glove closed round her throat with redoubled force, and the hand pinning her arm slid down towards her Glock.

If he gets my gun, I'm dead . . . In desperation she thrust her left hand deep into her pocket and jerked out her car keys. Raising her hand high, she stabbed again and again. She felt the Glock tear loose from her hand, but her next blow struck something soft and yielding, and a gasp of pain gave her hope. Praying she'd hit an eye, she whirled away.

In the same instant, the carport light switched on.

What she saw disoriented her: not a face, just a huge, formless shape sitting on a massive pair of shoulders. A door flew open behind her and a man shouted a warning. The Glock flashed up to her face and blotted out the light.

'HEY, MISS? HEY! Are you OK?'

Alex blinked her eyes open and looked up at the face of a bald man wearing pyjamas. In his right hand was a pump shotgun, in his left her Glock 23.

Her right hand flew to her face. There was blood there, lots of it.

'Am I hit?' she asked. 'I heard shots.'

'You're not hit,' said the man. 'That fella fired one shot, but when I jammed my twelve-gauge through the door, he slammed this pistol into your head, then dropped it and took off running.'

'Did you see his face?'

'No, ma'am. He was wearing a T-shirt or something on his head.'

Alex breathed deeply and tried to calm down. 'Did you call the police?'

'Hell, yes! They're on their way. What was that guy trying to do to you?'

Alex rolled over slowly, then got carefully to her feet. 'Sir, I'm Special Agent Alex Morse of the FBI. My credentials are in my car.'

Pyjama Man took a step back. 'Maybe I ought to take a look at them.'

As she retrieved her purse, a laser show of blue light ricocheted off the faces of the nearby houses, then the squad car squealed to a stop.

'Over here!' called Pyjama Man. 'In the driveway!'

The homeowner's wife offered Alex a paper towel to wipe the blood from her face, and Alex had her creds out when the cops trotted up. They were amazed to find an FBI agent at the end of their call. She presented the situation as an attempted rape and practically ordered them to issue an APB for the white van. She repeatedly assured them that there was no chance of lifting fingerprints from her Glock, since her attacker had worn gloves, and in answer to their questions informed them that she was staying at the home of Dr Christopher Shepard, an old friend. The last thing she wanted was Natchez cops walking into her room at the Days Inn and discovering what even rookie patrolmen would recognise as a murder investigation. After thanking Pyjama Man repeatedly for saving her life—and leaving her cell number with the cops—Alex got into her car and drove back to Highway 61.

Her whole body was shivering from delayed stress. She pulled to the shoulder and took out her phone. Chris answered after six rings. She apologised for bothering him again, and then—before she could explain what had happened—heard a sob escape her throat.

'Where are you?' Chris asked.

'On the side of the road. In town. I think I may need stitches.'

'What happened?'

'He's here, Chris. The guy who killed Grace. He almost killed *me*.'

'I'll call Mrs Johnson and tell her I have a medical emergency. She'll come over. Can you get to my clinic?'

'Uh-huh. But take Ben to Mrs Johnson's, OK? Your house isn't safe. And bring your gun.'

'I'll be there in ten minutes.'

ALEX LAY FLAT on her back, squinting up into a blue surgical light while Chris stitched beneath her eye.

'This laceration runs through some existing scar tissue,' he said. 'I don't know what your plastic surgeon will think about my work, but I guess you don't want to broadcast this injury to the world by going to the ER.'

'Exactly. Thank you for doing this, Chris.'

'You have no idea who this guy was?' he said, tying off the last stitch.

'No. The question is, was he after me or you?'

'I think that's pretty obvious,' Chris said. 'He's probably been on your tail all day, but in your sleep-deprived state you wouldn't have noticed a herd of elephants following you. You're not still planning to drive to Jackson, are you?'

'I don't know. But I'd like you to do me one favour. Come with me to the Days Inn to get my computer? I really need it.'

Chris turned and set his instrument tray in a sink. 'If you promise to stay the night at my house, I'll go with you.'

She hesitated, then took out her cellphone and dialled Will Kilmer. After she explained the situation, Will practically ordered her to remain in Natchez.

'She's not even conscious, Alex. There's no change at all. Hell, she's just liable to fool the doctors again. She's a tough old bird.'

Alex hung up and turned to Chris. 'Your house it is. But first, my place.'

THE DAYS INN'S parking lot was silent but well lit. Alex parked the Corolla four doors down from her room, then waited for Chris to pull up beside her in his pick-up. He climbed out of his truck with his .38 in his hand.

'I really appreciate this,' she whispered, handing him her room key. 'The room's one twenty-five, right down there. I'd like you to unlock the door and turn the handle, but don't go in. I'll be right behind you, and I'm going in hard. If anything crazy happens, just get away and call the police.'

Chris stared at her in disbelief. 'You're kidding, right?'

She gave him a deadly earnest look. 'No. And no Southern heroics.'

'You don't know what you're missing.'

He eased down the side of the building, then inserted the key and turned the handle. When Alex heard the mechanism open, she crashed through the door with her Glock levelled, sweeping it from side to side.

'*Clear!*' she called, moving cautiously towards the bathroom.

Suddenly she heard a sliding sound from behind the door and froze. She waved Chris back. After he'd taken cover behind the far bed, she yelled:

'Federal Agent! Throw out your weapon and come out with your hands up!'

Nothing happened. After five seconds of silence, Alex heard the sound again. Like a shower curtain sliding along the side of a bathtub.

She cursed to herself, then charged forwards and kicked open the bathroom door.

She saw no one.

The sliding sound came again. She looked down, then leapt back in terror. A brilliantly coloured snake was writhing on the floor beneath the commode, its body twisting wildly and whipping back upon itself.

'*Chris!*' she hissed. '*What is that?*'

He jerked her out of the doorway. 'It's a goddamn coral snake. The deadliest snake in the US.'

'Are you sure?'

'Positive. See the red bands touching the yellow ones? They teach you a rhyme in the Boy Scouts: "Red over yellow, kill a fellow, red over black, venom lack." Coral snakes carry neurotoxic venom like cobras.'

He grabbed a pillow off the nearest bed and blocked the open door with it. Then he went out to his truck and came back carrying a white bucket filled with baseballs.

'What are you going to do with those?' Alex asked. 'Stone it to death?'

He held up the bucket with both hands, leant over the pillow in the doorway and smashed the bucket's base down onto the snake with all his strength, grinding it against the tile floor. Then he lifted the bucket and slammed it down again. The next time he raised it, the snake was stuck to its bottom like a bug on a windshield.

'Is it dead?' Alex asked.

Chris examined the serpent. 'Dead as a hammer.'

He carried the bucket outside and tossed it into the bed of his pick-up.

Alex gathered up her computer and her case materials, and put them in her car. When she returned she asked, 'Is the coral snake native to Mississippi? I mean, I grew up here, but I don't remember any.'

'They're native to Mississippi, all right. But not *this* part of Mississippi. You'd have to drive two hours to reach coral snake territory.'

'So there's no way it could have simply wandered—'

'No way in hell. Somebody put that snake in your room. And that answers your question once and for all.'

'What question?'

'The guy who attacked you in that carport came here for you, not me.'

Chapter 6

Eldon Tarver nosed his white van through a thicket of bushes blocking the rutted track. This was the fourth route he had tried, and this time he felt lucky. At the end of the other tracks, the sand had been soft and the river shallow. He needed a shoulder of land that would bear the van's weight right up to the river's edge, then a good ten feet of water in which to sink it. The current would do the rest, rolling the van downstream with a force guaranteed to make it disappear by morning.

He extinguished the headlights, shut off the engine and climbed out of the van, then walked slowly forward in the blackness. He had a sense that he was above the river, but how far above he could not tell. Ten steps further took him to a cliff. The dark waters of the Mississippi River swirled twenty feet below. He pulled off his blood-soaked shirt and tossed it into the current. The woman had stabbed him in the throat, but with a blunt weapon. Probably a key. Had she used a knife, he would be dead.

He jogged back to the van, opened its rear doors and set up an aluminium ramp. Then he rolled a Honda motorcycle to the ground. The machine was designed for street and off-road riding, and he'd taken it with him on every operation for the past five years. He set it on its kickstand, then unloaded a small Igloo ice chest and his duffle bag from behind the passenger seat.

Eldon kick-started the Honda to be sure he would not be stranded, then climbed into the van, put it in low gear and drove slowly towards the cliff's edge. Fifteen feet from the precipice, he leapt from the open door and rolled, paratrooper-style, onto the sandy ground. As he stood up, he heard a loud splash. He ran to the cliff's edge and stared down at the absurd spectacle of a Chevy van floating like a barge down the Mississippi River.

Part of him wanted to remain in Natchez, to finish the work he'd started. But he had more important problems to deal with first. Andrew Rusk, for example. Rusk had lied to him, he was certain of that. And it angered him.

Eldon shut out the images of revenge welling up inside and focused on survival. He had always known a day like this would come. Now that it had, he was ready. Sanctuary was less than forty miles away. There he could rest and plan his response. He strapped the Igloo and the duffle bag to the Honda, climbed onto the bike and kicked it into gear.

CHRIS MADE his morning rounds at St Catherine's as conscientiously as he could, but the events of last night would not leave him. After saying goodbye to his last patient, he took the stairs down to the first floor, heading for the ICU. There he met Michael Kaufman, Thora's ob-gyn, coming up. Chris had sent some of Thora's blood to Kaufman for analysis, to check for hormone imbalances that might be affecting her fertility.

'I'm glad I ran into you,' Mike said, pausing on the stairs. 'I found something strange in Thora's sample.'

'Really? What?'

'A high level of progesterone. She's still trying to get pregnant, right?'

'Of course. What level are we talking about? Contraceptive level?'

'More. Like morning-after pill.'

Chris felt blood rising to his cheeks. Mike Kaufman had just committed an ethical breach, and seemed to be realising it. Now they were both aware that Chris's wife was not being honest with him about an important matter. Kaufman gave Chris an embarrassed nod, then continued up the stairs.

Chris walked slowly down to the intensive care unit. Was it possible that Thora's seduction of him in the studio—her talk about trying to get pregnant—had been a charade, a cold-blooded act designed to cover up an affair?

When he passed through the big doors of the ICU, the cooler air and the humming and beeping of machinery gave him momentary respite from the burgeoning hell in his mind. Here he had no choice but to concentrate on work. A teenager with a resistant bilateral pneumonia had failed to respond to two powerful antibiotics. Last night, during evening rounds, Chris had ordered a vancomycin drip. If the boy's condition had not improved, he intended to pass the case up to a specialist he knew at UMC.

When he looked towards the glass-walled cubicles, the first thing he saw was Tom Cage. 'Tom! I didn't know you had anybody in the unit.'

'I don't,' Dr Cage replied, writing on a chart. 'I was looking in on your pneumonia case. His white count dropped significantly during the night.'

'I'll be damned!' Chris said excitedly. 'I was really starting to worry.'

Tom sighed. 'I'm seeing more and more of these atypical pneumonias, particularly in young adults.'

'Are you done with your rounds?'

'Yeah, I'm headed over to the clinic.'

'I'm right behind you.'

Chris walked into his patient's cubicle, and immediately noticed the change. There was a brightness in the boy's eyes that had not been there for at least a week, and when Chris listened to his chest with a stethoscope he heard marked improvement. Chris was laughing at a joke the boy had made when he caught sight of Shane Lansing at the nurses' counter outside.

Mike Kaufman's words replayed in his mind: *Like morning-after pill.*

Chris felt some relief at finding the surgeon in Natchez this early in the morning. Greenwood was over four hours away, and he would have to have left Thora at 4 a.m. to be here now. Still, Chris felt an irrational urge to punch the surgeon's lights out. He told his patient he'd be back to check his progress, then updated the chart and walked out to the counter.

'Morning, Chris,' said Lansing. 'Thought any more about that golf game?'

'I can't do it this afternoon.' Chris searched Lansing's eyes for signs of fatigue. 'But maybe I can get away tomorrow.'

'Just give me a call. Or leave a message with my service.'

Chris turned on his heel and walked out of the ICU. As he trudged down the hall, he almost walked into Jay Mercier, Natchez's sole haematologist who, like all small-town specialists, often found himself treating everything from poison ivy to the gout. He also served as a general-purpose, first level oncologist. Chris thought of pulling him aside and asking about whether it was remotely possible that cancer could be intentionally induced in human beings, but if he did, Mercier was certain to pepper him with questions.

'Morning, Chris,' Mercier said with a smile. 'How's that resistant pneumonia coming?'

'I think the vancomycin's going to do the trick.'

'Good. That kid was looking shaky.'

They had slowed enough to stop for a fuller conversation, but Chris forced himself to continue down the corridor. Once he rounded the corner, the exit was only a short walk away but, without quite knowing why, he stopped, leaned against the wall and waited.

Less than a minute later, Shane Lansing appeared.

Chris stepped directly in front of him, blocking his path. 'Are you fucking my wife, Shane?'

Lansing blinked. 'Hell, no. What are you talking about?'

Chris stared without speaking for a few moments. 'I think you're lying.'

The surgeon's eyes narrowed. He started to speak, then he closed his mouth and tried to sidestep Chris.

Chris caught him by the arm and slammed him against the wall. 'Don't walk away from me, you son of a bitch.'

Lansing looked stunned. 'You've lost your mind, Shepard!'

'I'll bet you've been through a lot of these scenes. Well, you're not going to skate this time. There's a kid at stake. And I know you don't really give a shit about Thora. Oh, you like fucking her, I'm sure. But the whole package doesn't interest you, does it?'

Lansing's eyes continued to betray nothing. But then, in the ensuing silence, a more frightening scenario entered Chris's mind.

'Or *does* it?' he said. 'It's the *money*. You always did love money. And Thora's got enough to make your mouth water, hasn't she?'

Lansing abandoned all pretence at innocence—or so it seemed. He was saying something, but Chris didn't hear. His reptilian brain was reacting to the fist he saw rising from the surgeon's waist. Chris was no boxer, but he had wrestled during high school. He threw himself back with the momentum of Lansing's punch, then grabbed the extended wrist and hurled the surgeon bodily over him, smacking him to the floor.

Lansing's breath exploded from his lungs. Chris flipped him onto his stomach, shoved a knee into his back, and wrenched one arm behind his back. As Lansing yelped in pain, two nurses rounded the corner.

'Move on!' Chris shouted at the gaping women. 'Leave!'

They scurried down the hall, but never took their eyes off the scene.

Chris put his mouth against Lansing's ear. 'A friend of mine almost got killed last night. So remember this: you're not the only one involved here.' He twisted Lansing's right arm until the surgeon screamed. 'You do something to hurt Ben, and it'll be a year before you operate on anybody again. Do you hear me, Shane?'

Lansing grunted.

'I thought so.' Chris got to his feet. 'Now, if you're innocent, you just call the police and press charges against me. I'll be waiting at my office.'

He walked through the glass exit doors to his pick-up. As he drove away, he saw the hospital administrator standing outside the door, staring after him.

WHEN CHRIS REACHED the clinic, he walked into his private office, buzzed the front desk, and asked his receptionist Jane to get Dr Peter Connolly of the Sloan-Kettering Cancer Center in New York on the telephone.

The phone buzzed seconds later, and Chris picked up the receiver. 'Yes?'

'I'm on the phone with his nurse. Dr Connolly is teaching right now, but she can give you his voicemail if you want to leave a message.'

'OK, yeah.'

After a click, he heard a digital voice say, 'Please leave a message.'

'Peter, this is Chris Shepard calling from Mississippi. I've got a pretty strange question, so I'm just going to lay it out and give you time to think about it. I want to know if it would be possible to induce cancer in a human being in such a way that a pathologist wouldn't detect that it had been done. I'm talking about blood cancers, and an eighteen-month time frame from diagnosis to death. I know you're busy, but I'd really appreciate it if you could get back to me when you get a chance.'

Chris hung up and buzzed Jane. 'When Connolly calls back, get me, no matter what I'm doing.'

'I will.'

'Thanks.' Chris took a deep breath, walled off the paranoid fears writhing in his brain, and walked out to face the day's patients.

ALEX JERKED ERECT in bed with her Glock in her hand and her eyes wide open. Sunlight streamed through a crack in the drapes. It took her several seconds to remember where she was: a guest room in the Shepards' house.

As she stared at her surroundings, her cellphone began to ring inside her bag. It had been ringing before, she realised. That was what had woken her. What frightened her was that her private phone—the one she was using to run her murder investigation—was lying silent on the bedside table. The one in her bag was her official phone. *Oh, God . . .*

Memories of last night's attack flashed through her mind. She had given her real name to the Natchez police: she'd had no choice. She stared at the words UNKNOWN CALLER in the message window, and allowed the call to switch to voicemail. After waiting a full minute, she dialled voicemail.

'Agent Morse,' began a familiar voice with a priggish Boston accent, 'this is Associate Deputy Director Mark Dodson in Washington.'

Alex's chest tightened.

'I'm calling to inform you that we have dispatched a Bureau jet to Jackson, Mississippi, to bring you back to Washington for an interview with the Office of Professional Responsibility . . .'

Her blood pressure went into free fall.

'. . . if you are anywhere other than Jackson, call me back immediately so that I can reroute the plane to wherever you are. Do not delay, Agent Morse. You will only make matters worse for yourself.'

She heard a click, and Dodson was gone.

'Damn it!' she cried, climbing off the bed and pulling on yesterday's clothes. If they were sending a jet, they must know everything. The extra sick leave, the classmate covering for her in Charlotte . . . they probably even knew about last night's attack. That was probably what had started the collapse of the whole house of cards. And all for nothing! Every white van checked by the police last night had been legally registered.

'Stupid, stupid, *stupid*,' she cursed. Then, fighting back tears, she dialled the main switchboard of the J. Edgar Hoover Building in Washington and asked to be connected to Associate Deputy Director Dodson's office. When she gave her name, she was immediately put through.

'Special Agent Morse?' said Dodson.

'Yes, sir.'

'Where are you at this moment?'

'Natchez, Mississippi.'

There was a longish pause. 'I see they have an airport there that can take a Lear. Be there in thirty minutes, packed and ready to go.'

'Yes, sir. May I ask why, sir?'

'You may not.'

'Yes, sir.'

'That's all.' Dodson hung up.

NEVILLE BYRD delicately adjusted the joystick in his lap, shifting the laser on the roof above him five millimetres to the right. Then he donned his goggles to check the line of the beam. *Hello.* This time he'd done it. The green beam terminated precisely at the centre of a window on the sixteenth floor of the AmSouth tower. Not only would the laser rig pick up all of Andrew Rusk's conversations by measuring the vibration of the window glass, but it would also track which keys were depressed on Rusk's computer keyboard—and in which order—by measuring changes in the electromagnetic field of the office. The optical scope alone could make out about two-thirds of Rusk's keyboard and monitor, which meant that much of what was typed would also be recorded onto digital video.

Byrd leant against the window of his room in the Marriott Hotel, across the street from the AmSouth tower. He was here at the behest of Noel D. Traver, who had given him very simple instructions then offered double his usual rates for this job. It had made the former Netscape software engineer a happy man. High-tech security work wasn't exactly a growth business in Mississippi. And this job was different.

Andy Rusk was one of the top five divorce lawyers in the city, and he had hired Neville on several previous occasions. In Neville's not-so-humble opinion, Rusk was an ageing frat boy with too much money and more ego than was good for him. Dr Traver seemed a decent guy, and was certainly a lot smarter than Rusk. Neville knew Traver was a veterinarian because he had looked him up on the Internet: *A Breed Apart, Noel D. Traver, DVM.*

Neville wondered if maybe Dr Traver was married to Rusk's secretary and was keeping an eye on her. But she was no more than thirty—and *hot*—while Dr Traver was close to sixty and had that ugly birthmark on his face.

Neville waited, confident that he would know everything there was to know about Rusk, his secretary and the old vet before the week was out.

ALEX STOOD on the edge of the little concrete apron at the Natchez airport and watched a Lear 35 taxi towards her. The side door opened and a clean-cut, stereotypical FBI agent walked down the little staircase. Blue suit, dark sunglasses. His jacket was cut a little full, but even so, she could make out the butt of his weapon beneath the cloth under his left arm.

'Special Agent Alex Morse?'

'I'm Alex Morse.'

'Special Agent Gray Williams,' he said, without offering his hand. 'Are you carrying a weapon, Agent Morse?'

'Yes.' Alex was afraid he would order her to surrender her sidearm.

'Do you have any other bags?'

'Nope.' She bent to lift her soft-sided suitcase.

'Let's get aboard then.'

Williams's tone indicated reluctance to talk to her—a sure sign that she was known to be an official leper. She tossed her suitcase through the doorway, then climbed in after it, and took a forward-facing seat. Williams sat two seats behind her. Alex could hear him talking softly on his cellphone, confirming that she was aboard and bound for Washington.

She took out her private phone, plugged it into a outlet beside her seat, and checked her voicemail. A ragged male voice came through the ether. 'Alex, this is Uncle Will.' She clicked the volume down to minimum level using the side button. 'Your mom's the same as she was last night. You did the right thing getting some rest. I'm calling because I got a report from my guy at the Alluvian Hotel. He couldn't find out which floor Thora Shepard was staying on, but his wife talked to her in the wet area a couple of times. Thora's girlfriend was with her, and everything seemed legit. But around five thirty this morning, my guy's wife happened to look out of her window and saw a guy carrying a small suitcase out to the back parking lot. He was in a big hurry. It was fast and in poor light, but she thinks it could have been Dr Lansing. She's sixty per cent sure. I'm going to check out the possibility that Lansing could be commuting back and forth to get his poontang from Mrs Shepard. You call me as soon as—'

Voicemail had cut Will off before he finished his message. There were no more messages, and Alex saw no point in calling Chris to pass on an inconclusive report. She'd already phoned him to explain what had happened.

She sat back in her seat for take-off. The roar of the engines and the shuddering airframe caused a hundred memories to assail her. How many times had she been rushed to a jet like this one and been ferried to some strange city where a man with a gun held innocent people under his power? Being the person that the Bureau counted on in those situations had engendered its own sense of power within Alex. And she had justified their faith time and time again. It had destroyed a part of her to break that faith, to forge daily reports, to ask fellow agents to cover for unauthorised absences. But there was a higher duty—the obligation to one's family. To *blood*. And no matter what it cost, she would not break that faith.

Fed up with being passive, Alex took out her cellphone and clicked into text-messaging mode. If she had to sweat out the next twenty-four hours, she wasn't going to do it alone.

ANDREW RUSK'S HEART began to race as he saw the text message outlined in blue on his cellphone:

> You're going to pay for what you did. I don't care how long it takes. You're going to ride the needle, Andy. For Grace Fennell, for Mrs Braid, for all the others. I don't care what happens to me. Nothing will stop me. Nothing.

Rusk checked the source of the message, but no number showed up. It didn't matter. He knew who had sent it. The FBI agent. His first instinct was to get up and tape two squares of aluminium foil to his northeast window, but good sense stopped him. Glykon was already upset enough about Alex Morse. This new development would only add fuel to the fire.

She's trying to provoke me, he thought. It's like throwing a rock into a thicket to try to make your prey move into your sights. That means somebody's watching to see which way I jump. Waiting for me to lead them somewhere. Does she have the backing of the FBI, or is she going it alone?

'Just stay cool,' he murmured. 'Stay cool.'

He picked up the phone and dialled the number of a detective agency.

CHRIS WAS IN an examining room checking a prostate gland when Jane called him out to take Dr Connolly's call. He hurried to his office. 'Pete? It's Chris Shepard,' he said.

'Hey, boy! The last I heard, you were playing Albert Schweitzer in the Mississippi Delta.'

'Just a phase.'

'I know better. Now, what's all this about giving people cancer on purpose? Have you switched from making documentaries to horror movies? Or did somebody get murdered down there?'

'To tell you the truth, Pete . . . I can't talk about it.'

There was a long pause. Then Connolly said, 'OK, well, I did some thinking about it during what passed for my lunch. You ready?'

'Shoot.'

'Multiple myeloma can be caused by a spectrum of chemical agents. Herbicides are particularly damaging. But you're talking about a twenty-year incubation period. Toxins could work much faster, but virtually all are detectable. The CSI guys would bust you in a hurry.'

'On TV they would. I'm finding out that the real world is different.'

'What the heck are you into, Chris? No one's going to be mixing this stuff up in his kitchen sink. Not even in an average university lab.'

'I hope you're right,' Chris replied, ignoring the question.

'Radiation is another obvious choice,' Connolly went on. 'There's no doubt you could induce leukaemia with it.'

'But could you do it undetectably?'

'Not easily. X-rays would probably cause all sorts of side effects, local and systemic, so forget that. Radiotherapy pellets could cause burns, skin tumours, maybe nausea early on. But the most interesting radiation option is in liquid form. Against some tumours, we use irradiated liquids that have very short half-lives. Twenty-four to forty-eight hours.'

Chris grabbed a pen and began writing. 'Go on.'

'Take thyroid cancer. We put radioactive iodine into the bloodstream. The iodine collects in the thyroid, kills the cancer cells, then is harmlessly excreted from the body. A sociopathic radiation oncologist could probably figure a way to induce cancer like that without leaving any trace. But listen, if I really wanted to give someone cancer without being caught, I'd explore two avenues. The first is viruses. Though you'd have to be willing to wait a while for your victim to die.'

'Up to a point, time isn't a factor in these cases,' Chris said.

'Well, then. You know that the Kaposi's sarcoma associated with HIV is the result of infection with herpes 8, and of course, the human papilloma virus is known to cause cervical cancer. Herpes 8 may also be a factor in multiple myeloma. Over the next ten years I think we're going to discover that viruses are responsible for all sorts of cancers. But remember, millions carry HPV, but only a few develop cervical cancer. It wouldn't be enough to infect someone with an oncogenic retrovirus. You'd have to solve other riddles, too: how to switch off tumour suppressor genes, how to increase cellular growth factors. It would take massive research.'

'So it's beyond the reach of present-day technology.'

'Not at all. I've already done it myself, right here in my lab.'

Connolly's words hit Chris like a body blow. '*What?*'

'It's amazing, really, but we did. In trying to understand the cause of chronic myelogenous leukaemia, my team and I attached a leukaemia-inducing gene to a retrovirus, then infected a healthy mouse with the virus. Within weeks the mouse had developed the rodent version of CML.'

'Christ, Peter! So . . . it's *possible.*'

Connolly considered this. 'I suppose if you had some higher primates to test your work on—or, God forbid, human beings—then, yes, it's possible. And if you used this technology to kill someone, the greatest pathologist in the world wouldn't realise a crime had been committed. But it would cost millions of dollars. Not to mention that they'd have to sit pretty goddamn high on the intelligence curve.'

A deep shiver went through Chris. 'You mentioned two possible avenues of exploration, didn't you?'

'Right. The second is far scarier, because it requires much less expertise. All you do is remove marrow cells from your patient as you would in a bone marrow transplant; irradiate or otherwise poison them in the lab, causing your malignancy of choice; then reinject them into the patient.'

'What would be the result?'

'A cancer factory powered by the victim's own bone marrow. Exactly the kind of thing you described to me, in fact. A spectrum of blood cancers.'

'And no one could ever prove what had been done?'

'Barring a confession, no way in hell.'

Chris analysed this scenario as rapidly as he could. 'Would you have to use marrow cells for that?'

'Hmm,' Connolly mused. 'I suppose you could use just about any kind of living cell that contained the patient's DNA, even a hair root.'

Chris had received too much information to process it efficiently without further help. 'Pete, can you tell me anything about the haematology and oncology departments at UMC now? Do you know of anyone who's working on the kind of stuff we've been talking about?'

'I don't know of any ongoing retrovirus trials there, but give Ajit Chandrekasar a call. First-rate virologist. There's another guy there . . . I used him for difficult histology. His name was . . . Tarver. Eldon Tarver.'

'I've got it.'

Chris heard a female voice in the background at Connolly's end. 'They're calling for me, buddy. Did I help you at all?'

'You scared the shit out of me.'

'Can't you tell me why you need this stuff?'

'Not yet. But if someone I know turns out to be right, I'll have some reportable cases you can write up for the journals.'

Connolly laughed. 'I'm always happy to do that. Keeps the research money flowing.'

Chris hung up and looked down at his notes. He'd been a fool to discount Alex's theories on the basis of professional prejudice. Now that he'd been shown the error of his ways, he would become a zealous convert.

After all, his life was at stake.

ALEX SAT in a low chair opposite the desk of the FBI's Associate Deputy Director, Administration, a man who had long ago revealed himself to be her enemy. Outside the Bureau's Washington headquarters, Mark Dodson was said to have been eugenically bred as a bureaucrat. By judicious use of his family's political connections, he had insinuated himself into the Bureau's halls of power with almost unprecedented speed. Dodson had taken a set against Alex early during her Washington service, she had no idea why. After the fiasco at the Federal Reserve bank, Dodson had pushed relentlessly to have her fired. He'd nearly succeeded. But Alex had turned out to be right that day. The bank robber had been a disaffected employee, not a terrorist. She'd made a terrible procedural mistake, but her instinct had been proved correct. And Dodson had never forgiven her for that.

He stared at her now across his desk with open satisfaction. 'You had a good flight, I trust?'

'Can we not play games?' Alex asked wearily. 'I'm really too tired.'

The good humour left Dodson's face. He leaned forward and spoke in a harsh voice. 'Very well, Agent Morse. Tomorrow morning at nine a.m. you will meet with three representatives of the Office of Professional Responsibility. Before the interview, you will be ordered to take a drug test. Failure to submit to that test will constitute grounds for dismissal from the Bureau. Failure to answer every question truthfully and fully will also constitute grounds for dismissal. Do you understand?'

Alex nodded once.

'You're not going to skate this time,' Dodson went on. 'I mean, what the hell were you thinking down there? As far as I can tell, you've been carrying on a one-man murder investigation in Mississippi. You've broken so many rules I don't know where to begin. Do you have any comment, Agent Morse?'

Alex shook her head.

'Is there some purpose to your silence?' Dodson asked with narrowed eyes. 'Are you attempting to communicate the fact that you despise me?'

Her eyes flashed. She hoped he could read her mind.

Dodson jabbed a forefinger at her. 'You won't look so goddamned high-and-mighty at tomorrow's meeting. You'll be living proof that even blue flamers can crash and burn.'

Alex studied her fingernails. Two had broken in last night's struggle. 'Are you finished gloating?'

Dodson leaned back in his seat. 'Lady, I'm just getting started.'

ELDON TARVER squatted beside a sandy stream, his eyes peeled for any movement. His motorcycle was parked beneath a sycamore, and his duffle bag lay beside it. Eldon had spent the last eighteen hours in the woods of Chickamauga, while forty miles away the Natchez police combed the area for a white van that was tumbling along the bottom of the Mississippi River.

Snakes liked this kind of ground, down in the cool hollows near water. They needed to drink just as people did. That was one of the secrets of handling them, knowing that they weren't so different from people. Cold-blooded, yes, but Eldon had learned young that many humans shared that trait. Snakes lived to eat, sleep and mate, just as humans did. To eat, they had to kill. And to kill, they had to hunt.

Most humans hunted, too, those who weren't so alienated from their natures that they retained nothing of their ancient selves. People hunted in different ways now: in offices, financial markets, laboratories and dark city streets. A few still carried the spirit of the true hunter within their breasts. Alex Morse was one of these. A hunter born from a hunter's loins, she was simply fulfilling her destiny, as her genes bade her to do.

Right now she was hunting *him*. Which meant Morse had a tough job ahead. Eldon knew ways of hiding that even animals did not. There had been times when he had made himself literally invisible to people passing within a foot of him. Today was a good example. He wasn't tearing across the country in a panic, as so many who had killed would now be doing. He was living quietly, close to the earth, near the sites of his attacks.

As he listened to the whisper of the creek, he let his mind drift. Before his adoptive father came to believe that Eldon had been ordained by God to handle serpents, he had flown into rages and beaten the boy without mercy. Even now, Eldon had more than a dozen burn scars on his body, souvenirs of his father's efforts to 'prove' that he had been touched by the Evil One. (Being burned by the flame constituted damning proof of sin.)

The sound of a cellphone was alien in these woods, and many creatures stopped to listen. Eldon let it ring three more times before he answered.

'Dr Traver? It's Neville Byrd.'

'Yes?'

'I think I may have him, sir. Or, rather, I think I may have the thing you were asking for. The *mechanism*.'

'Go on.'

'Andy Rusk just logged onto this Dutch website. It seems to me he's going through an authentication protocol of some kind. And if he does that tomorrow, I'd say we've found the trigger, you know? Like, if he didn't log in the next day, all hell would break loose. Or whatever you're expecting.'

Eldon found it hard to adjust to the sudden intrusion of modernity. 'Very good. Call me when . . . you're certain.'

'I'll do that, Doctor. Is there anything else?'

'No.'

The connection went dead. Eldon hit END, then walked slowly back to his motorcycle. He saw a shiver in the pine straw as he walked, a shiver that filled him with anticipation. He threw out his right foot.

A thick black snake reared up before him, exposing the milky lining of its mouth and two long fangs. A cottonmouth moccasin. The tip of its tail vibrated like a rattlesnake's, but this viper had no rattle. Still, it stood its ground more fiercely than a rattler would have done.

'*Agkistrodon piscivorus*,' Eldon murmured. 'Are you a sign, my friend?'

The cottonmouth was not brilliantly hued like the coral, but corals were rare, and the one he'd found in the park was probably dead by now. Agent Morse would almost certainly survive, even if she'd been bitten in her room at the motel. But she would have tasted the enmity that God had promised in Genesis, and she would know that her present hunt was like no other.

The cottonmouth advanced in a rush, showing that he meant business.

Eldon sidestepped the snake whose body was nearly as thick as his forearm. A snake like that could be a very persuasive tool.

'I believe you are,' he said. 'A sign of rebirth.'

As he shouldered his duffle bag and climbed aboard the Honda, his laughter echoed strangely through the trees.

CHRIS WAS SITTING at his kitchen table dictating charts when the cellphone Alex had given him began to ring. Ben was in the den playing on his Xbox, but they could see each other through the open door.

'Alex?' he said. 'How's it going up there?'

'Not so good. They don't want me talking to you, Chris. They don't want me talking to anyone associated with any of the cases.'

'They still don't believe you, then. Have they fired you?'

'Not yet. If I give up everything, stop trying to find out what happened to Grace, they probably won't fire me. They want me to go to a goddamn psychiatric hospital. They think I'm having some kind of breakdown.'

Chris had suspected the same thing for a while.

In a small voice, Alex said, 'Is that what you think?'

'Absolutely not. Listen, I spoke to my old haematology professor up at Sloan-Kettering today. He scared me to death, Alex. Murdering someone by giving them cancer *is* possible. Connolly has done it himself, to mice.' Chris quickly recounted the scenarios Connolly had outlined to him.

'My God. I wish I had talked to him a week ago,' Alex said. 'Listen, I called to let you know that I'm sending someone down to watch over you and Ben tonight.'

Chris looked across at Ben, who was still glued to the television screen, his hands flying over the game controller. 'Who?'

'Will Kilmer, my father's old partner. He's an ex-homicide detective, now private. He's about seventy, but he's tougher than he looks.'

'I'm not going to turn him away. I'm nervous as a cat here.'

There was a brief silence. Then Alex said, 'I also want you to know something else. Will has a detective staying up at the Alluvian watching Thora. I had to do it, Chris.'

Chris felt a surprising ambivalence about this. 'I understand. Has he seen anything suspicious?'

'The detective's wife thinks she may have seen Lansing leave the hotel about five thirty this morning. She's not positive, though.'

'I saw Lansing early this morning in Natchez. He couldn't have made it back here from Greenwood in that time.'

'We'll know the truth soon enough, I think. Be nice to Will, when you see him. He practically raised me, and he's doing this for free.'

'Thanks. When are you coming back?'

'I'm meeting with the people from the Office of Professional Responsibility in the morning. They'll probably ask for my badge and gun. There may be paperwork to do, but I'll get back as soon as I can. Just make sure you're alive and well when I get there.'

'OK. Don't do anything crazy in that meeting tomorrow.'

Alex laughed. 'That's what everybody tells me.'

CHRIS LAY on the sofa bed in his home theatre and listened to Ben's slow, regular breathing. Ben had asked him to open up the bed on the pretext that it was more comfortable for watching a movie, but Chris knew that with his mother gone the boy wanted to sleep down here rather than up in his room.

Thora had called from Greenwood about twenty minutes after his conversation with Alex. Her tone had been light and breezy as she gushed about the quality of the spa, and read the names of treatments to Ben, who by then was on the other extension. The experience seemed surreal to Chris, who was thinking about the morning-after pill and his scuffle with Shane Lansing, but he wasn't about to get into anything while Ben was awake, so he'd matched his tone to Thora's and ended the conversation.

He eased himself off the sofa bed and went to the kitchen to make himself a sandwich. He was taking his first bite when someone knocked at the garage door. He walked through the pantry and put his eye to the peephole. Through its bubble lens, he saw a grey-haired man wearing glasses.

'Who is it?' he called loudly.

'Will Kilmer,' said a strong male voice. 'Alex Morse sent me.'

Chris opened the door. Kilmer was about five feet ten, and in surprisingly good shape for a man his age. He wore khakis, a polo shirt and grey running shoes and was carrying a backpack. When he smiled and offered his hand, Chris shook it, getting the iron grip he expected from an ex-cop.

'I'm sorry you had to drive all the way down here, Mr Kilmer.'

'Call me Will, Doctor.' Kilmer released his hand. 'It's no problem. From what Alex told me, I'd say it's reasonable to expect you might get trouble.'

'Well, can I offer you something to eat and drink?' Chris asked.

'I don't want to put you out.'

'I was about to eat a sandwich myself. Come on.'

Chris led Kilmer through to the kitchen. While he made a second turkey-and-Swiss, the detective set his backpack on the floor and sat at the counter. Chris slid a plate across, then opened a Corona and passed it over.

Kilmer's eyes lit up. 'Thanks, Doc. It's pretty damn hot for May.'

Chris nodded and went back to his own sandwich. 'You used to work with Alex's father?' he prompted after a while.

'That's right. First at the PD, then at our detective agency. Never knew a better man in a tight spot.'

'He was killed recently?'

'Yessir. Trying to help some people in trouble, as I'd have guessed.'

'You've known Alex her whole life?'

Kilmer's eyes sparkled. 'From the day she was born. Worst tomboy I ever saw in my life. And smart?' Kilmer shook his head. 'By the time she was fourteen, she made me feel stupid. Not just me, either.'

Chris laughed. 'What about that murder theory of hers?'

Kilmer pressed his lips together and sighed. 'I'm not sure what to think. The technical side is over my head. But I worked homicide for more years than anybody ought to, and I think a lot more people have been murdered in divorce situations than anybody suspects—especially before the forensics became what they are now. I had lots of cases where I just *knew* the husband had offed his wife and made it look like an accident.' Kilmer looked abashed. 'Look, just because I think Alex may be on to something don't mean I think your wife is doing you wrong. I'm just here as a favour to Alex.'

'I understand. I've only known Alex a few days, but I can see why you like her so much.' Chris took a swallow of beer. 'But I have wondered if she hasn't gone through so much in the past few months that she's not quite in control of her emotions.'

Kilmer raised his eyebrows. 'She's been through a lot, all right. And you may not know the worst of it. I believe Alex loved that fella who got killed the day she was shot. But he was married, and she wasn't the type to break up a family. So that day was pretty rough. She lost half her face and the man she loved in about five seconds. She feels guilty that she loved him and guilty that she got him killed.' Kilmer met Chris's eyes. 'But if Alex believes you're in danger, watch out. She ain't down here to waste her time or yours.'

'Well,' Chris said, getting up and taking his plate to the sink, 'I'm going to hit the rack pretty soon. You're welcome to sleep in the house tonight. There's a guest room right off that hall over there.'

'Where's your boy?' Kilmer asked.

'He fell asleep in the TV room.' Chris pointed. 'That glow right down there. I'll be just past it in the master bedroom.'

As Chris reached up to the top of the refrigerator, where he'd stashed his .38, a sudden thought struck him. He brought down the gun and said, 'Do you have any identification on you, Will?'

Kilmer nodded, walked to his backpack and reached inside. Chris felt himself tense, but Kilmer brought out only a wallet. He showed Chris a Mississippi driver's licence. And the face on it matched.

'Look here,' Kilmer said, flipping open a plastic picture holder. 'This is Alex in her younger days, with me and Jim.'

Chris looked down at a snapshot of Alex at what looked like her high-school graduation. She was pressed between two handsome men in dark suits. Two women were in the picture also, classic Mississippi wives with wide, genuine smiles. Chris could see a hint of the woman that Alex would become.

'Ain't she something?' Kilmer said.

'Do you have kids, Will?'

The older man swallowed. 'We had a girl, a year behind Alex in school. We lost her on homecoming night the year Alex graduated. Drunk driver. After that . . . I guess Alex kind of took her place in my heart.' Kilmer closed the wallet, went back to the counter and finished off his beer.

'I'm sorry,' Chris said.

'Part of life,' Kilmer said stoically. 'You take the good with the bad. Go on to bed, Doc. And don't worry about nothing. I got you covered.'

ELDON TARVER stood in the deep moon shadow beneath the low-hanging limbs of a water oak and watched the lights go out in the house on the hill. His motorcycle lay in the underbrush back near the highway. He'd spent the day at the Chickamauga Hunting Camp in Jefferson County waiting for night to fall, and had not answered any of Andrew Rusk's calls.

When he arrived last night and found the woman here, his first thought was that he had made a mistake about the house. The wife was supposed to be out of town. But when he checked the coordinates on his pocket GPS unit, they had matched the notes that Rusk had given him. He had moved close enough to see the woman clearly and compare her to the photos in his backpack. She did not match. However, she *did* match an image deep in Eldon's mind—one he had seen in the Fennell file supplied by Rusk. The woman in the house was Special Agent Alexandra Morse, the sister of Grace Fennell. Her presence there—talking to his next target—had such profound implications that he almost panicked. But life had taught him to expect the unexpected.

He'd thought Morse would be easy prey, despite her Bureau training. She was a hostage negotiator, after all, not a tactical specialist. And the way she had played it—slipping into that driveway in an amateurish attempt to trick him—told Eldon one thing: Morse had no back-up. Yet she had fought like a demon when he moved in for the kill.

Tonight, it seemed better that she had survived. Had Alex Morse died, a hundred FBI agents would have descended on this corner of Mississippi. Now he had time to do what was necessary for a clean escape.

Eldon shouldered his backpack and walked slowly up the hill. As he neared the house, he veered right and moved round dense azaleas to the cluster of air conditioners that served the house. He had studied the blueprints provided by Rusk until he knew them inside-out. He continued circling the building, moving past the swimming pool and along a path to the storeroom, where he pulled down a collapsible stairway and climbed into the attic. From here, he could reach the attic of the main house.

Squeezing his bulky shoulders through the hatchway, he entered a forest of rafters and ceiling joists. Walking carefully on the joists, he crossed over to the air-conditioning duct he needed, then reached into the backpack for a respirator gas mask. He fitted the mask over his nose and mouth, donned a pair of goggles and pulled out a heavy gas canister. After laying a rubber mat over the duct to dampen vibration, he took a battery-powered hand drill and bored a hole in the duct. Then he laid a thin piece of rubber over the hole, lifted the cylinder and punched its sharp nozzle through both rubber and hole, creating a seal. Once he was certain of his set-up, he opened the valve on the cylinder. There was a soft hissing sound.

Within two minutes, whoever was in the house below would be unconscious. They would remain that way until long after Eldon had left. The gas in the cylinder, similar to that used in the Moscow theatre siege, had been provided by a former army officer known to Dr Tarver who now worked for a large corporation handling defence contracts.

Tarver sat absolutely still for two minutes, then moved deeper into the attic to a trap door over the closet of the master bedroom. After opening the trap door, he braced himself with both arms over the hatch and pushed down on the spring-mounted ladder that led into the closet. After descending the rungs, carrying his backpack, he paused in the closet and unpacked an aluminium Thermos. Inside were two preloaded syringes. One contained a mixture of corticosteroids to suppress the human immune system. The other contained a solution that had taken over a year to develop. It was different from those used on the other targets. And for that reason Eldon was excited, even though he knew this would be his last operation.

He walked into the master bedroom and, setting the syringes on a dresser, pulled the covers off Shepard, who was lying on his side in the bed.

Dr Tarver took a small LED flashlight from his pocket, switched it on, then got the steroid injection from the dresser. He pulled down Shepard's boxer shorts and injected the steroids between the buttocks. Dr Shepard hardly stirred. Eldon repeated the procedure with the other solution, but at the last instant Shepard's lower body flinched. Eldon depressed the plunger to the bottom of the syringe's barrel, pulled the covers over the doctor, then loaded everything back into the pack and walked quickly down the hall.

He found the boy on a sofa bed in the home theatre. To his surprise, he discovered an older man sleeping in an easy chair in the den, with three empty beer bottles beside him. Eldon did not know the man. He shot a picture of him with his cellphone, then took the stranger's wallet from his back pocket. Beside William Kilmer's feet was a backpack. When Eldon opened it, a strange numbness spread through him. Inside were a handgun, a starlight scope, a canister of pepper spray and a pair of handcuffs.

He retraced his steps back to the duct in the attic, and ten minutes later he was walking swiftly through the trees. The sense of exhilaration had vanished, to be replaced by anxiety, anger, even fear.

Tonight, everything had changed.

Chapter 7

'Have you got enough silk?' asked the nurse.

'I think so,' said Chris, tying off the last of twenty-three stitches. The lacerated forearm belonged to a fifty-year-old handyman who had come to Tom Cage's clinic to be sewn up rather than visit the ER, which would have cost four times as much and taken four times as long.

Chris set down his forceps and examined his work. As he stared, a sharp throbbing stabbed the base of his skull. He'd felt it intermittently since waking this morning and had taken three Advil, but the pain had grown worse. At first he'd thought it was a tension headache, but this pain had a relentless quality to it, and he wondered if he might be getting a migraine.

'Looks great, Mr Johnese,' he said, rubbing his neck. 'Just let Holly give you a tetanus booster, and you can be on your way.'

Johnese smiled. 'I sure appreciate it, Doc.'

As Chris left the surgery, walked into his office and shut the door. Sitting in his chair, he massaged his temples with his thumbs, then tried to work the muscles at the base of his neck. This brought no relief. He reached into his desk and popped another Advil. 'That ought to do it,' he muttered.

He'd intended to call the University Medical Center to try to speak to a couple of the doctors Pete Connolly had mentioned, but he was in no mood to do that now. He leaned back in his chair, recalling Ben's fright this morning when he'd discovered Will Kilmer asleep in the easy chair in the den. The boy had raced back to Chris's bedroom and shaken him awake. But once Chris had explained that Kilmer was a distant cousin who was passing through, the boy put it out of his mind and started getting ready for school. Kilmer had apologised profusely and quickly left the house.

On the way to school Ben had mentioned the three empty beer bottles beside 'Cousin Will's' chair. Chris hadn't seen them, but he figured that was why Kilmer had fallen asleep before reaching the guest room. *Not much of a watchdog*, he thought wryly.

'Dr Shepard?' Holly's voice intruded into his reverie. 'You've got patients waiting in all four rooms.'

Chris rubbed his eyes and sighed heavily. 'I'm on my way.'

ALEX SAT in a straight-backed wooden chair before a tribunal of stone-faced OPR officials—two men and a woman.

Almost no FBI agent got through his or her career without a few OPR reviews. Usually they resulted from minor infractions of the rules, but today's hearing was different. One of the worst offences in the eyes of the OPR was 'lack of candour', which meant deception of any kind, including lies of omission. Judged by this standard, Alex's offences were grave.

One of the male officials had recounted all the charges that Associate Deputy Director Dodson had levelled against her, then the woman had held up a copy of the threatening text message that Alex had sent to Andrew Rusk yesterday. Alex had no idea how Mark Dodson could have come into possession of that, but she knew not to ask. Now they were coming to a part of the proceedings that she could not ignore.

'Special Agent Morse,' said the woman, 'do you have anything to say on your behalf before we close this hearing?'

'No, ma'am.'

The woman frowned, then conferred quietly with her colleagues.

'Special Agent Morse,' she said eventually, 'as a result of this hearing, we are suspending you from your duties until final and formal disposition of your case. You will turn in your credentials and your weapon, and all further contact with the Bureau should be handled through your attorney.'

In silence, Alex lifted her bag off the floor, removed her FBI identity card and her Glock, walked forward and laid both on the table.

'You don't turn those in to us,' said the woman, who seemed stunned that someone could walk away so dispassionately from the agency to which they were giving their life. 'You turn them in on the first floor.'

Alex turned away and walked to the door.

'Agent Morse,' the woman called after her. 'You're not to leave Washington until this matter has been fully resolved. Agent Morse?'

Alex went out, leaving the door open. For good or ill, she was free now.

CHRIS WAS EXAMINING a man with congestive heart failure when Jane knocked at the door and told him he needed to come to the phone.

'It's the secretary at St Stephen's School, Doctor.'

Alarm hit Chris with surprising force. 'Has something happened to Ben?'

'Just a headache, but it's bad enough that he wants to come home.'

'A headache?' Chris echoed. 'I've got a headache, too.' He walked into the reception area and picked up the receiver.

'Dr Shepard? This is Annie out at St Stephen's. Ben's had a headache all morning, and I think it's bad enough that he ought to go home. Ben tells me your wife is out of town, so I called your office.'

'I'm on my way. Please keep him with you until I get there.'

Chris hung up and walked down the hall to Tom Cage's office, where the white-bearded doctor was saying goodbye to a drug rep.

'Excuse me, guys,' Chris cut in. 'Tom, I've got to pick up Ben from school. He's got a bad headache. Can you hold the fort while I'm gone?'

'No problem. Take off.'

As Chris shook Tom's hand, the drug rep said, 'Are you the guy who punched out Shane Lansing?'

Chris reddened. He and Tom had not yet spoken about this, though Tom must have heard about it. 'We had a little disagreement. Nothing major.'

The drug rep stuck out his hand. 'Well, I want to shake your hand. I hate that arrogant son of a bitch.'

This was risky talk, especially in front of two doctors, but the rep probably knew that Tom wasn't the type to talk out of school.

'I'd guess Lansing had it coming,' said Tom, giving Chris a private wink.

Chris was smiling as he darted into his office to retrieve his keys. Alex's cellphone was blinking on the desk. She'd left three voice messages in the last fifteen minutes. As he walked out to his truck, he speed-dialled her.

'Chris?' she answered.

'Yeah, what's up?'

'I'm history. Suspended. Pending final disposition of my case. But I'm basically a private citizen now, just like you.'

Shit. 'What are you going to do?'

'I'm supposed to stay here in the District. But I want to come back to Mississippi and keep working the case.'

Chris got into his truck. 'What's stopping you?'

'They're monitoring my credit cards. Probably my cellphone, too. But they don't know I have this phone.'

Chris pulled onto Jefferson Davis Boulevard, thinking quickly. 'I'll book you a flight. Do you want to fly into Baton Rouge or Jackson?'

'Jackson. There's a nonstop flight.'

'I can't pick you up,' he said. 'But I'll rent you a car.'

'Thanks, Chris. I don't know what I'd have done. Did Will show last night?'

'Yeah. We got along great.' He thought of adding, *He drank three beers and fell asleep in my den*, but Alex was having a bad enough day. 'Will sure thinks the world of you. Call me when you land, OK?'

He hung up and stepped on the gas, heading south towards St Stephen's. He couldn't remember the last time Ben had had a headache. He couldn't remember the last time he'd had one either. That kind of coincidence was almost never random.

WEARING ONLY A TOWEL round his trim waist, Andrew Rusk opened the glass door of the Racquet Club steam room and walked into a cloud of eucalyptus-scented water vapour. Behind him a club employee slapped a CLOSED FOR REPAIRS sign on the door. Rusk waved his hand through the cloud, trying to disperse enough steam to catch sight of his quarry, Carson G. Barnett.

'Rusk?' said a deep voice, low and utterly devoid of good humour.

'Yes,' he said. 'Carson?'

'I'm in the corner. Over by these goddamn rocks. Damn near burned my pecker off a second ago.'

For Rusk, the latent anger in the oil man's voice wasn't necessarily a bad sign. But first he had to get rid of the steam. He knelt by the control panel, felt for the knob and turned it back fifty per cent. When he stood up, he caught sight of Barnett's bulldog countenance floating in the whiteness. The man's jaw was clenched tight, and he glowered at Rusk through the haze.

'I been thinking about what you said,' Barnett muttered. 'I don't reckon I'm the first one who ever heard that pitch you made me.'

Rusk shook his head.

Barnett climbed onto the top bench. 'How much is it going to cost me?'

'A hell of a lot less than your net worth.'

'But still pricey I bet.'

'Oh, it'll hurt,' Rusk conceded. 'But a lot less than a divorce.'

'You know, you pitch this kind of thing to the wrong man, and he's liable to beat the shit out of you.'

'Hasn't happened yet. I'm a pretty good judge of character.'

'A good judge of bad character,' said Barnett. 'It's a damn low thing what we're talking about. But nobody can say she didn't ask for it.'

Rusk sat in silence. He wasn't thinking about Carson G. Barnett or his doomed wife. He was thinking about Glykon. He had been unable to reach him since their meeting at the hunting camp, seventy-two hours ago. Glykon had neutralised the threat from William Braid, as promised. But he must have done something to Alex Morse as well. Otherwise, why would Morse have sent the threatening text message? Rusk felt he had done right by turning over the message to the Bureau. His FBI contacts had painted a picture of Morse as a rogue agent, already in deep trouble because of the Federal Reserve bank debacle, and with powerful enemies in the Hoover Building. The Bureau represented no danger to him or Glykon. Morse was the threat. Every little straw Rusk could pile onto that particular camel's back would push her closer to breaking. Being out of contact with Glykon was disconcerting, but he could not afford to let Barnett get away. They could earn two to four times their normal fee for this job. All he had to do was close the deal.

'Mr Barnett, have you had any contact with any law-enforcement agency about this matter?'

'Hell, no.'

'All right. There's something you need to understand. No one is going to murder your wife. She will die of natural causes. Do you understand?'

There was a long silence. 'I guess I do. How fast would it happen?'

'Not fast. The likely time frame is twelve to eighteen months. If it can be sooner, it will be. But you should prepare yourself for that wait.'

Barnett was nodding slowly. 'So what next?'

'You and I will not meet again after today. One week from now, I will park a silver Chevrolet Impala in the lot of the Annandale Golf Club. In the trunk you will find a legal-sized envelope with printed instructions regarding payment. Payment in your case will be made using rough diamonds.'

Barnett was about to ask a question, but Rusk held up his hand.

'That will all be in your instructions. When you pick up the envelope, you will leave me a box containing a complete copy of your wife's medical history; copies of all the keys that have any importance in your wife's life— cars, houses, safe-deposit box, home safe, jewellery boxes; blueprints of your house; passwords to your security system and to your computers; also, a weekly schedule of your wife's activities. In short, that box should contain everything remotely related to your wife's life. Do you understand?'

Barnett was staring at him in horror as the reality finally sank in.

'This is between you and your conscience, Mr Barnett. If you have any doubts, you should express them now.' Rusk took a deep breath of wet, dense air. 'Would you like some time to think about your answer?'

Barnett was cradling his face in his hands, and his big shoulders appeared to be shaking. Rusk wondered if he had pushed too hard.

'I can't advise you, Carson. If you're unsure, we could let the box be your decision. If the box is there a week from today, I'll know we're going forward. If it's not, I'll know the opposite.'

The oil man lifted his head. 'What if you went to get the box and found the sheriff waiting by your car?' he asked.

'It would be a shame about your twins.'

Barnett came off the bench quicker than Rusk could react. The oil man slammed him against the wall and seized his throat with an iron grip.

'That's not a threat,' Rusk croaked. 'I just want you to be aware that my associates aren't the kind of people you cross.'

Twenty seconds passed before Barnett released his grasp.

'Is that a yes or a no?' Rusk asked, massaging his voice box.

'I've got to do something,' said Barnett. 'I guess this is it. I'm not going to give up the one woman in this world who can bring me some peace.'

There was nothing else to say. Rusk knew better than to offer his hand; you didn't shake hands over a deal as unholy as this. He gave Barnett a curt nod, then reached for the doorknob.

'How do I get into the car?' Barnett asked. 'The Impala.'

'I'll leave a spare key on the left front tyre of your car when I leave here.'

'You know which vehicle I'm in?'

'The red Hummer,' Rusk said, and made his way out.

ALEX SPENT the first hour of her return flight in shock, sipping vodka and reliving incidents from her truncated career. Her sense of being on the outside, of no longer being a player in critical events, was overwhelming. Somewhere over eastern Tennessee, she felt she couldn't remain disconnected any longer. Surreptitiously, she leant against the window and switched on her cellphone. This was against the law, and she had no FBI credentials to flash for special treatment. The phone connected to a network and an announcement of three voicemail messages popped up. She dialled voicemail.

The first message was from Will Kilmer, saying that his detective in Greenwood had shot a video of Thora Shepard and Shane Lansing in flagrante delicto at 4 a.m. that morning and that he was sending a captured still to her cellphone. The second message was from Chris Shepard's office: the rental car information Alex would need when she arrived in Jackson.

When she heard the third message, her heart nearly stopped. The speaker was John Kaiser, one of the top field agents in the entire FBI. Kaiser had spent several years working serial homicides for the Investigative Support Unit in Quantico, Virginia, but had returned to normal duty at his own request some years ago. Widely respected throughout the Bureau, he had spent the past few years based in New Orleans and Alex had got to know him on a hostage case. She had tried to reach him ten days ago, when she'd first realised what she might be dealing with, but she had been told that he was on an extended vacation with his wife.

'Alex, this is John,' said Kaiser. 'I'm only just now getting back to you because I've been working undercover. When I heard your messages, I couldn't believe it. You've got my cell number. Call me anytime.'

Relief welled up within Alex, enough to bring tears to her eyes. But then a terrible thought struck her: Kaiser had probably left that message before hearing that she'd been suspended. She slumped down in the seat. Of all the people in the world whose help she could have wished for, Kaiser was the man. She took several deep breaths, then called his cellphone.

'Kaiser,' he answered.

'It's Alex Morse, John.'

He didn't respond at first. Then he said, 'I heard what happened this morning. I'm sorry.'

'Not a good day, amigo.'

'Do you plan to stop working your case?'

She hesitated. 'Are you going to report anything I say today?'

'You know better than that.'

'I can't stop, John. I know I'm right, and now the doctor who's the next target believes it, too. This case is crazy. You wouldn't believe the crime signature. It's a team scenario, I think—a lawyer and a medical professional—and they're killing people by giving them cancer.'

'Cancer,' Kaiser said softly. 'Alex, are you sure?'

She closed her eyes. 'Positive.'

'What's the motive?'

'I think it's mixed between the perpetrators. But at bottom it's a divorce attorney saving rich clients millions of dollars by killing their spouses.'

There was a long silence. 'What exactly do you want me to do?'

'You're not supposed to do anything.'

Dry laughter came through the ether. 'Let's say I don't know that. What would you want me to do then?'

'Drive up to Jackson, Mississippi. It's three hours by car. I'm on a flight there now. I want you to meet this doctor. Listen to him, then listen to me. I need your brain, John. Your experience. Please tell me you'll come.'

After a long silence, Kaiser said, 'Where do you want to meet?'

Alex suggested the Cabot Lodge, which offered accommodation near the UMC. Kaiser said he could make no promises, but that he would try to be there. Then he hung up.

CHRIS AND BEN were sitting on the leather couch in Chris's examination room when Alex rang. Chris had taken 800 milligrams of ibuprofen, and his head was still pounding. Ben's headache was just as bad.

Chris touched Ben on the thigh. 'You lie down here. I'm going to turn off the lights and go in my bathroom to take this call. OK?'

Ben nodded dispiritedly, and Chris switched off the lights and stepped into his private cubicle, then put the phone to his ear.

'Chris, I need you to come to Jackson this afternoon,' Alex said urgently.

'Why?'

'To meet an FBI agent named John Kaiser. He's one of the top agents in the Bureau, a specialist in serial murder. He's going to help us.'

'Why would he help you? I thought they fired you.'

'They're going to. But Kaiser is a good friend. Will has just emailed me a photo of Thora and Shane, Chris, and when I forward it to you, you're going to want to do something. The best thing you can do is come to Jackson. You owe it to yourself, and to Ben.'

'I can't go anywhere, even if I wanted to. Ben is sick. He's got a headache. A bad one. And I've had one, too, since this morning.'

There was a pause.

'I need to go, Alex.' Chris hung up, and left the bathroom.

'Who was that?' asked Ben.

'A doctor in New York that I'm consulting on a case.'

'A lady doctor?'

Chris sometimes forgot how acute the senses of children were compared to those of adults. 'That's right. How's your head?'

'It still hurts. Can we go home now?'

'Not yet, buddy.' Chris sat beside him and squeezed his arm. 'Son, I need to bring a patient in here. Let's take you out to Jane's office. You can play games on her computer, OK?'

Ben shrugged apathetically.

Chris led him to the front office, then returned to his own. At his desk, he typed in his password and opened his email account. The newest message had been forwarded by Alex from wkilmer@argusoperations.com. The mail simply read, *I'm sorry, Doctor Shepard. Sincerely, Will Kilmer*. At the bottom a file was attached. Chris sat with his forefinger poised over the mouse, painfully certain that opening this picture would change his life for ever.

He opened it.

Though the resolution was poor, the picture showed Thora standing with her elbows on a steel balcony rail. She was stark naked. Chris's hands clenched into fists as his eyes slid to the male figure standing behind his wife, his hand on her taut abdomen. It was undoubtedly Shane Lansing.

A wave of nausea overcame Chris. He jumped up, ran into the bathroom and ejected what remained of his lunch into the toilet.

'Dr Shepard?' called a female voice. Holly, his nurse.

By the time he got back to his desk, the screen had mercifully gone black. 'Come in,' he called, knowing his face was probably red with anger.

Holly put her head round the door. 'Are you all right?' she asked.

'Yeah. I'm just feeling a little tired.'

She studied him without speaking. Then, hesitantly, she said, 'Mr Martin's been waiting in room three for a good while.'

'I'm coming!' Chris snapped.

Holly turned and left without a word.

Some morbid part of him wanted to reopen the photo, but he resisted the urge. His mind was filled with images dating to the day he had first noticed Thora Rayner on a ward in St Catherine's Hospital. How could the woman who had so devotedly cared for her dying husband so casually betray a man who loved her as Chris did? How could she throw away a father who had bonded so deeply with her son? He felt an unbearably heavy pall of grief.

The cellphone was ringing again. Alex, of course. He picked it up.

'Are you all right?' she asked. 'I know seeing that was rough.'

'Yep.'

'Lansing's been flying in and out of Greenwood from Natchez, using a charter flight service. I'm so sorry, Chris.'

'Are you?'

'Of course. All I care about in this is you and Ben.'

'That's not true. You want to nail Andrew Rusk.'

'Well, yes, but not out of some cheap sense of vengeance. It's for Grace, and for you, and for all the other people whose lives have been destroyed.'

Chris said nothing.

'There's something else,' Alex said eventually. 'Something that's scaring me. You and Ben both have headaches, right?'

'Yes.'

'Uncle Will has one, too. A bad one. It won't go away.'

A strange buzzing started in Chris's head.

'What do you think?' she prompted.

'I don't like it.'

'It seemed like too much coincidence to me, too. But I don't see what could have happened. I mean, Will was guarding you all night, right?'

'He was passed out in my easy chair all night.'

'*What?*'

'He drank three beers and went out like a light.'

'Shit.'

A sudden image of Alex's room at the Days Inn flashed into Chris's mind: the coral snake writhing in the bathroom. 'Alex, is there anything I need to know that you haven't told me?'

Another pause.

'Goddamn it, what are you holding back?'

'Well, Will has been checking into Shane Lansing's business affairs. You know Lansing has his hand in a lot of stuff, right?'

'Yeah. Truck stops with gambling, nursing homes, all kinds of shit.'

'Well, it seems he's also part owner of a radiation oncology clinic in Meridian, Mississippi. The Humanity Cancer Care Center.'

'But that means Lansing has access to—'

'I know. Caesium pellets, liquid iodine—everything.'

'But . . . you told me these crimes go back like five years. How could Lansing be a part of it? I mean, if Thora just went to see Andrew Rusk a couple of weeks ago, how could Rusk possibly have found Lansing and hired him to kill me in that time? Unless . . . Oh God. *Red Simmons.*'

'Exactly. Thora may have used Andrew Rusk three years ago, to have Red Simmons killed. If so, she first contacted Rusk at *least* three years ago. She could even have met Lansing through Rusk.'

'But Red didn't die of cancer.'

'Neither did my sister.'

Chris's thoughts were tumbling over themselves. Fear and anger were melding into a kind of dark desperation whose only outlet could be action. 'What time did you say this friend of yours would be in Jackson?'

'As soon as he can get there,' said Alex, relief suffusing her voice. 'If you leave within the hour, you'll probably get there the same time Kaiser does.'

'Good. I'll be there.'

'Thank you, Chris.'

'Don't thank me. This is survival now.'

Alex started to say something, but he hung up and put the phone in his desk drawer. After closing his email account, he walked down to Tom's end of the clinic, and found the old man sitting at his desk writing up notes.

'Hey, slugger,' Tom said in his good-humoured baritone. 'What's up?'

'I need to talk to you.'

'Sit down.'

Chris shook his head. 'Do you have an exam room open?'

Tom led the way to the nearest examination room and closed the door. He looked at his young partner with paternal concern.

'I need you to do me a favour, Tom. No questions asked.'

The older man nodded soberly. 'Name it.'

'I want you to examine me. My whole body.'

'What am I looking for? Are you having symptoms?'

'I've got a severe headache,' Chris said, 'but that's not really the problem. I have reason to suspect . . . something. I want you to go over every inch of my body with a light. Even a magnifying glass, if you need it. Look for anything abnormal. A needle mark, a bruise, a lesion, a small incision.'

Tom stared at him for a long time. Chris could almost see the questions turning inside his mind. But in the end Tom said simply, 'You'd better strip and get on the table.'

While Chris removed his clothes, Tom donned a headpiece with a light mounted on it. Chris climbed onto the examining table and lay on his back.

'OK, let's start in your mouth.'

Chris opened wide.

Tom took a tongue depressor and a small mirror and checked Chris's mouth. 'Looks clear to me.' He withdrew the instruments. 'Remember to floss after every meal.'

Chris was in no mood for levity, but Tom gave him a wry look anyway.

'OK, let's take a look at your skin.' Tom started at Chris's neck and moved slowly down his body. 'This reminds me of my internship,' he said. 'I worked several months in the Orleans Parish Prison. The cops used to have me check between suspects' toes for needle marks.'

'Same deal,' Chris said, turning onto his stomach.

He felt cold hands on his buttocks. He expected Tom to move on immediately, but he didn't.

'What do you see?'

'I'm not sure,' Tom murmured. 'Looks like maybe an injection site.'

Chris's breath died in his throat. 'Are you serious?'

'Afraid so. Looks like somebody stuck in a needle and you tried to jerk away. There's definite bruising. This is weird, Chris. Are you going to tell me what's going on?'

Chris got off the table and pulled on his pants. 'We need to check Ben, too. He has the same headache I do.'

AFTER CHECKING BEN for marks and not finding them, Chris put the boy in Holly's care and walked down the hall to the X-ray room. There he asked Nancy, their tech, to shoot an X-ray of his midsection. She looked nonplussed at the request, but wasn't about to refuse her employer. Two minutes later, Chris jammed the X-ray into the clip of a light-box. What did the needle mark mean? Had a radioactive liquid been injected into him?

'What are you looking for?' Tom asked from behind him.

'Overexposure.' Chris could hardly speak as he scanned the X-ray. He was terrified of seeing black spots, caused by radioactive emissions, over-exposing the film. But he saw nothing abnormal.

'Looks fine,' Tom said. 'Does this have to do with the needle mark?'

Chris nodded. Then he felt Tom's hand on his shoulder.

'What's going on, son? Talk to me.'

There was no hiding it any more. Chris turned to his partner and said, 'Somebody's trying to kill me, Tom.'

After a shocked silence, Tom said, 'Who?'

'Thora.'

The older man's eyes narrowed. 'Can you substantiate that?'

'No. But I'm working with an FBI agent to prove it.'

Tom nodded slowly. 'Is Shane Lansing tied up in this somehow?'

'I believe so. Did you know he part-owns a radiation oncology centre?'

As Tom shook his head, Chris saw the old doc's mind working quickly behind his wise eyes. It wouldn't take him long to connect the dots.

'Sounds to me like you need some time off,' Tom said.

Chris gratefully shook Tom's hand, then collected Ben and left the office. His headache was still going strong, but Ben's had started to subside.

Chris dropped Ben off at Mrs Johnson's house. The widow had been minding Ben since before Thora married Chris, and loved him like her own. She promised to keep Ben overnight if necessary; all Chris had to do was call.

Shortly after that, Chris skidded into the driveway of the Elgin house, his heart pounding with anger and fear. On the passenger seat beside him was a wooden case he'd borrowed from the radiologist at St Catherine's Hospital.

He charged inside with it and ran to the master bedroom.

First he tore the bedclothes off the king-size bed, exposing the mattress. Then, kneeling beside it, he opened the case. Inside was a Geiger counter. Chris switched on the machine, dreading the *click-click-click* that would indicate the presence of radioactivity, but it emitted only a faint hum. It had a carrying handle and a wand attached to it by a flexible cable. Chris moved the wand over the entire surface of the bed, but heard no clicks.

Sweating and exasperated, he stared around the room. Where would they put it? he wondered. Where would I get sufficient exposure? He picked up the Geiger counter and ran down the hall to the den, to the easy chair where Will Kilmer had spent the night in beer-induced slumber. But when he passed the wand over the seat, he heard nothing.

He realised then that he had almost been hoping for the telltale click. Why? he asked himself. Because nothing is worse than not knowing. That was his problem. He had no idea what the needle mark meant. Had someone sedated him while they irradiated him in some way? Ben and Kilmer both had headaches, too, yet Chris had found no needle mark on Ben. Had they all been sedated in some other way, while only Chris was attacked through hypodermic injection? He had no way of knowing.

Chris stared around him, his mind spinning.

He started to switch off the machine, but an almost paralysing terror stopped him. Nancy had only shot an X-ray of his trunk. What if the radiation source had been placed elsewhere? Standing there, Chris held the wand at his feet and began moving it up along each leg.

Almost unwilling to believe the silence, he kept moving up until he reached his scalp. Then he switched off the machine.

He felt like puking. Some part of him wanted to believe that it was all bullshit, that Alex Morse was as crazy as a road lizard. But Tom had found *something*. And Chris had seen Shane Lansing and Thora in that picture. And Lansing was part owner of a radiation oncology centre. And then there were the headaches: three on the same day. That couldn't be coincidence.

There was no escaping the truth: Grace Fennell's killer had struck again.

Chapter 8

Eldon Tarver sat alone in his office at the University Medical Center, studying numbers on a piece of paper in front of him. But only part of Dr Tarver's mind was occupied with the most recent data on the *in vitro* testing. On a deeper level, he was working out his next move.

He had received several false spam emails from Andrew Rusk, agreed signals for a meeting at the Annandale Golf Club. But Dr Tarver had not gone. Nor had he driven the forty-five miles to Chickamauga Hunting Camp, despite the aluminium foil glinting from the sixteenth-floor window of the AmSouth tower. He chuckled at the idea of Andrew Rusk waiting for him in the oppressive heat of Chickamauga, freaking out because he'd pitched to the new client he'd boasted about. Rusk lived for money and, even with the risk quotient rising daily, all he could think about was the next big score.

Dr Tarver knew that score would never happen. Their collaboration was over. Christopher Shepard's injection marked the end. Eldon was already shutting down the primate lab. Only one problem remained.

Rusk himself.

For five years now, Dr Tarver and the lawyer had had an escape plan, one that would allow them to leave the United States and live in safety and relative luxury for the rest of their lives. Using intelligence connections dating back to the late 1960s, Dr Tarver had worked out a deal for the two of them, a deal worthy of a greedy lawyer's fantasy. But *not* worthy of a dedicated scientist. And now Tarver had ongoing research projects to maintain, and preferred to remain in the US to do that. After all, his *in vivo* subjects resided in the US. Moreover, five years of working with Andrew Rusk had convinced him he never wanted to see the lawyer again. Rusk was an accident waiting to happen. Eldon could see him sitting at a bar, umbrella drink in his hand, bragging to some record company exec about how he had saved the rich and famous millions by snuffing their wives. No thanks.

The irony was, Eldon had always had a choice of escape routes. There had always been countries ready and willing to pay him staggering amounts to work for them. The only problem was that Eldon Tarver was a patriot. And the countries that wanted to pay for his services were the wrong ones.

He started at the sound of his cellphone. He looked down at the caller ID and answered, 'Dr Traver.'

'It's Neville Byrd, Doctor. I've got it, sir. The thing Rusk is doing to protect himself. Two days in a row, near the end of the day, he's logged on to this one website and entered a series of passwords. All at the same site.'

Dr Tarver's pulse quickened. 'Did you record his keystrokes?'

'Yes, sir. Every one.'

'Fax them to me on the number I gave you.'

'Yes, sir. I'll send the keystrokes through. But I can give you the site right now, if you want to check it out. It's called EX NIHILO. It's a Dutch site, and it exists solely to allow people to be anonymous on the Net.'

'This sounds very promising. Thank you.' Dr Tarver hung up.

Ten seconds later he was staring at the black hole that welcomed visitors to EX NIHILO. One click took him to a page that listed the company's available services. Thirty seconds later, Neville Byrd's fax came through.

'My God,' said Dr Tarver, using Rusk's passwords to retrace the lawyer's digital footsteps. It was just as he had suspected. Each day Rusk had to log onto the site, to verify his continuing existence. If he failed to do so for ten consecutive days, EX NIHILO would forward the contents of a large digital file to the state police and the FBI. Eldon tried to open the file, but the site refused to allow it. It needed a separate password. He cursed. Obviously Rusk had not accessed the file since creating it, which meant that Neville's laser system had not recorded the keystrokes of the password.

It doesn't matter, he told himself. As long as he logged on to EX NIHILO once a day—as Andrew Rusk—the system would not send out its destructible file, and he would remain safe.

He laughed. It started as a chuckle, then grew in his chest to a rolling, heaving barrel of laughter. EX NIHILO changed everything. Now Eldon could write Andrew Rusk right out of his plans. Or, he thought with a unexpected thrill, I could rewrite them with a very different ending.

From the beginning, Eldon had demanded his fee in uncut diamonds. Rusk had groused at first, but he soon realised the wisdom of this system of payment. Unlike cash, rough diamonds were immune to both fire and water. They could be buried for years. They could not be traced. Best of all, when it came time to move them, they looked like rocks. A box of rocks!

Rusk had taken his early payments in the form of inclusion in the business deals of his wealthy clients. He'd thought this was a brilliant stroke, because he paid taxes on the earnings, and that kept the IRS off his back. But as the business connections multiplied, so did his traceable connections to a list of murders. And that, Eldon was almost sure, was what had brought Special Agent Morse down on their backs.

Realising the error of his ways, Rusk too had started taking his fee in uncut diamonds, and he must have built up quite a box of rocks by now. The question was, where did he keep them? If Eldon could learn the answer, he could make the transition to his next life as a much richer man.

It was time for drastic measures. It was time to call in his markers—all of them. And that meant Edward Biddle. Eldon hadn't spoken to Biddle in over two years, not since the TransGene man had delivered the gas canisters to him. Still, the gas delivery had made one thing clear: Biddle was living up to his promise to take care of 'his people'—the former staff members of the VCP, a project begun back in the golden age when government, industry and the military worked hand in hand. Only a dedicated few at VCP understood that every scientific discovery was a double-edged sword: a scalpel could remove a patient's tumour or slit his carotid artery; a viral infection could deliver lifesaving gene therapy or cause a global holocaust. It was the responsibility of some to discover and develop those potentialities; others made decisions about how to use them. Eldon had always understood his place in this hierarchy, and Edward Biddle had valued him for that.

Dr Tarver flipped through his Rolodex and found Biddle's card. *Edward Biddle, Vice President, TransGene Corporation.* And below that: *America Leading the World.* Dr Tarver loved them for having the balls to put that right on the card in the so-called Age of Globalisation. Microbiology was the one arena in which America had kept its competitive lead. He dialled the number on Edward Biddle's card.

It rang twice, then a clipped voice answered. 'This is Biddle.'

'Eldon Tarver, General.'

An irony-laced laugh came down the line. 'And what can I do for you?'

'It's time for me to relocate.'

A brief pause. 'Do you have a destination in mind?'

'I'd like to remain in-country. But I will require a new identity.'

'I understand.' Not a moment's hesitation. A good sign. 'I've been following your research at the University of Mississippi Medical Center. I can't help but feel they're not making full use of your talents there.'

It was Tarver's turn to laugh. 'The regulations on research are pretty claustrophobic these days. For that reason, I've been carrying out some private studies for some time. Very similar to what we were doing at the VCP.'

'Is that so?' Deep interest now.

'Yes, sir. You might say I picked up where we left off. Only this time, I'm talking about *in vivo* studies.'

'Primate studies?' Biddle asked.

'*Higher* primates, sir. Exclusively.'

'I'm intrigued, Eldon. I have a feeling your work might dovetail nicely with some things our more adventurous people are doing here at TransGene. What sort of time frame do you have in mind for your relocation?'

'Two or three days, if possible. Maybe sooner.'

A brief pause. 'That's possible. You and I should speak face to face. If I flew down in the next couple of days, could we meet?'

Eldon smiled with satisfaction. 'Absolutely, sir.'

'Good. Call me later. It's good to be working with you again, Eldon.'

'You, too, sir.'

Dr Tarver hung up, removed Biddle's card from his Rolodex and put it in his pocket with the fax from Neville Byrd. His whole future in one pocket. The only threat to that future was Andrew Rusk. And by tomorrow night Rusk would be dead, and his cache of diamonds part of Eldon Tarver's portfolio.

ALEX RODE the elevator to the fifth floor of the University Medical Center, her excitement at the possibility of John Kaiser's help punctured by Chris's news that he'd probably been injected with something during the night. Since Kaiser was still an hour south of Jackson, she'd decided to visit her mother.

When the elevator doors opened, she walked down to the Oncology Wing, where she found her mother much as she had left her two days ago. Alex sat beside her, holding the limp hand, trying to fight off waves of despair. At times like this, it seemed there was no happiness in the world. She squeezed her mother's hand, then wrote a brief note for the nurses to read to her later. *Dear Mom, I was here. I love you. I hope it doesn't hurt too much. I'm close by, and I'll be back soon. I love you. Alex.*

Alex walked back to the elevator and waited for the car to come.

A bell dinged softly. She stepped into the elevator. A man in a white coat was inside and he backed into the car's right rear corner. Alex instinctively took the opposite corner—and stood facing the door.

The elevator doors were highly polished, and in the blurred reflection she saw that the big man had a beard, with a flaming birthmark above it. It must be bad, she thought, to show even in the dim reflection.

The man looked over and nodded. Instead of looking away afterwards, he continued to study her. It broke one of the unwritten laws of elevator etiquette, but Alex figured that her scars had drawn his *professional* attention.

'Shotgun?' asked the man, touching his own cheek.

She coloured deeply. He was the first one to guess right. Maybe he was a trauma surgeon. 'Yes,' she said.

'I don't mean to make you uncomfortable. I can relate to having people stare at your face.'

Alex stared back. The big, bearded man was about sixty, with a reassuring, deep voice. 'Is that a birthmark?'

He smiled. 'Not technically. It's an arteriovenous anomaly. It's not bad when you're born, but when you hit puberty it suddenly explodes into this.'

Alex started to ask a question but, as though he could read her mind, the stranger said, 'Surgery often makes it worse. I don't want to risk that.'

She nodded. He wasn't handsome, but he would have been decent-looking without that awful web of indigo and scarlet on his left cheek.

The bell dinged again.

'Miss?' The man with the birthmark was holding the door open with his elbow. 'This is the lobby.'

'Oh! I'm sorry. Thank you.'

He waited until she had cleared the doors. 'Tough night?'

'My mother is dying.'

Sympathy furrowed his brow. 'You got on at Oncology. Is it cancer?'

Alex nodded. 'Ovarian.'

He shook his head. 'A terrible disease. I'm sorry. Will you be all right?'

'Yes. I'm staying right over at the Cabot Lodge.'

He smiled. 'Good. They know how to take care of people over there.'

'Yes. Thank you, again.'

'Any time.' The man gave her a small wave, then walked away.

ELDON TARVER stood at the window of the second floor doctors' lounge and watched Special Agent Morse walk purposefully across the parking lot. He felt a near-euphoric sense of triumph.

'She doesn't know me,' he said softly. 'She looked into my face, heard my voice . . . and didn't recognise me.' The fact that his beard hid the wound she'd given him undoubtedly helped. Everything's falling my way, he thought.

And it was. First Neville Byrd had discovered the EX NIHILO site, and now Alex Morse had walked right into his hands. She'd even given him the name of her hotel! Eldon didn't believe in fate, but it was hard not to see a pattern in all this. It was time to call Biddle back.

ALEX TRUDGED through the lobby of the Cabot Lodge to check in, and saw Chris sitting in a chair against the wall to her right. His head was bent over his knees, and he was rubbing his temples.

She walked over and crouched beside him. 'Chris?'

He looked up with red-rimmed eyes. 'Hey.'

'My God. How's your headache?'

'A little better. My stomach's the problem now. I talked to Pete Connolly again, and he told me to take some strong antiviral drugs. Tom Cage already called in a prescription for them. I think that's why I'm nauseated.'

'Does Connolly think those will work?'

Chris laughed darkly. 'How can he be sure when he doesn't know what was injected into me? He thinks I should start chemotherapy as well.'

'Then why haven't you done that?'

'A lot of chemotherapy drugs are carcinogenic themselves. I'm not sure I'm desperate enough to try that.'

Alex tried to follow the logic. 'How could chemotherapy help you, if you don't have cancer yet?'

Chris looked up slowly. 'It's possible that I do.'

Alex paled. 'What?'

'Remember Pete's scariest scenario? Where someone gets hold of your cells, turns them cancerous in the lab, then injects them back into you?'

Alex nodded slowly.

'Those would be active from the moment they entered my body.'

'What do you think happened last night? Did someone steal cells in order to alter them? Or did they inject cancerous cells into you?'

Chris's eyes held only bitterness. 'I pray it's the first. But I doubt it.'

'Why?'

'Because there are easier ways to get my cells. Think about it. Who has constant access to my body?'

'Thora? But how could she take your blood without you knowing?'

'Not blood.'

Alex thought for a moment. 'Semen?'

'Exactly. How's that for cold and calculating?'

She stared at him, not knowing what to say.

'The other night,' Chris whispered, 'Thora came to my studio and made love with me. She told me she wanted to get pregnant. It was really out of character, with the way things had been, but I went with it, hoping for the best.' Chris's jaw flexed in fury. 'Three days later, I found out from a blood test one of my colleagues did that she'd taken a morning-after pill.'

Alex shook her head in disbelief. 'But surely no one could induce cancer in those cells that rapidly, not even in the lab.'

'I hope not. That's one reason I haven't taken the chemo yet.'

Alex put both arms round him and hugged tight. Chris stiffened at first, but then she felt him go limp. When his arms closed round her back, she realised he was shivering. Was it the drugs?

'Let's go upstairs,' she said. 'Have you checked in?'

He nodded.

She had arranged to meet Will Kilmer in the hotel lobby. He was bringing her an unregistered gun. Now she left a message at the desk for him.

Seconds later she and Chris were unlocking the door to a suite on the 'executive' floor. Attached to the bedroom was a little den with a sofa, two club chairs and a desk. Alex walked to the window and looked out.

'Is Kaiser in town yet?' Chris asked.

'He'll be up any minute.'

Chris checked the minibar. 'Why did you pick him?'

'Kaiser worked with the Investigative Support Unit for a long time. Before that he served in Vietnam. He's a first-class guy.'

She started at a knock on the door. She went through the bedroom and opened it, expecting Kaiser. Will stood there with a shoe box in his hands.

'Thanks,' she said, taking the box. 'What is it?'

'A Sig nine. Untraceable.'

'Thanks, Will. Has the headache gone?'

'Yes, thank God.' The old detective looked as if he'd been wrestling demons. 'I feel like I let the doc down last night.'

'Doesn't matter now. It's going to work out. You'd better get going, Will.'

Kilmer trotted down the hall to the fire stairs. Alex went back to the den. Chris was drinking bourbon. 'Room service delivers shoes?' he asked.

'Nine-millimetre shoes.' She took the box into the bedroom and stowed it on the top shelf of the closet. 'Kaiser doesn't need to know.'

Chris nodded. 'I wouldn't mind using it on a certain person.'

Who? Alex wondered. Thora? Shane Lansing? Both of them? 'Chris . . .' She touched his arm. 'I hope you're kidding. Because that would only guarantee that Ben would be raised by someone besides you.'

Chris's eyes went dead.

She changed the subject. 'What do you think caused the headaches?'

'I think we were all sedated before the attack. I'm not sure how. In the end, it doesn't really matter, does it? As long as Ben and Will aren't sick.'

Three strong knocks echoed through the room.

Chris followed Alex to the door. A tall man with deep-set eyes stood there.

'You gonna invite me in?' the newcomer asked.

Alex smiled and hugged Kaiser, who turned and held out a hand to Chris. 'Dr Shepard? Glad to meet you.'

Chris shook his hand. 'You, too.'

Alex folded her arms and looked up at Kaiser. 'It's worse than I thought, John. Chris is already in bad trouble. He was hit last night.'

Kaiser's eyes roamed over Chris, taking in the look of fatigue and desperation. 'Somebody fill me in before Dr Shepard passes out.'

JOHN KAISER stood at the window. Alex was sitting beside Chris on the bed, holding a trash can for him whenever he vomited. He'd started about twenty minutes into Alex's summary of events, and the waves were still coming.

'It's probably the drugs,' he said, clutching his cramping midsection with both arms. 'My body's not used to them, and I'm taking three at once.'

'What do you think, John? Is there anything you can do?' Alex asked.

Kaiser turned from the window. 'You need objective evidence of murder. Some kind, any kind.'

'Is there any way that you can expedite autopsies of the victims?'

'Not without an ongoing murder investigation, and the local authorities don't even believe that any crimes have occurred.'

'I know. But I was thinking, Chris may have been injected with some drug that's capable of giving people cancer. Why couldn't you classify that as a biological weapon? If you did, couldn't the Bureau investigate it?'

Kaiser pursed his lips. 'That's actually not a bad idea. But you'd have to isolate the compound from his blood.'

'Can we try that?'

'We don't know what to look for,' Chris croaked. 'A radioactive metal? A retrovirus? A toxin? Is it even traceable?'

Kaiser nodded dejectedly. 'And who's going to do that for us?'

'Pete Connolly will start testing me if I fly up to Sloan-Kettering,' Chris told them. 'Maybe he could isolate something.'

The FBI agent looked deep into his eyes. 'Do you believe your wife is capable of murder, Chris?'

'I didn't at first. But then I didn't think she was capable of cheating on me.'

'Is there *anything* you can do to help, John?' Alex asked.

'At the very least, I can pull some strings and get local surveillance on Andrew Rusk. I can't do anything that will put me on the Bureau radar, but I can get you background checks on licence plates, that kind of thing.'

'I appreciate that, John. But those are baby steps. These guys have been killing people for years, and my involvement hasn't even slowed them down.'

Kaiser's jaw muscles flexed. 'This is going to sound cold, but that's a good thing. If they went to ground now, we'd never get them. The best thing we can do right now is poke Andrew Rusk with a sharp stick. I'll do my part. I'm going to find out everything there is to know about that asshole.'

Alex's face flushed with hope.

Kaiser walked over to Chris. 'Get that chemotherapy, Doctor. There's nothing else you can do to help this investigation. Your job is to survive.'

Chris wanted to respond, but at that moment he doubled over the trash can and began to dry-heave.

As Kaiser led Alex into the other room, Chris pulled back the bed-clothes, crawled into the bed, and pulled the sheet up to his neck.

By the time Alex returned, he was asleep.

CHRIS AWOKE in the dark to the chirp of his cellphone. He blinked several times, then turned and saw a shaft of sunlight where the curtains didn't quite meet. In its faint glow, he saw Alex asleep on the other bed, wearing just a shirt. He scrabbled on the night table until he found his phone.

'Hello?' he said.

'*Chris?*' A frantic female voice. 'Where are you?'

It was Thora. 'Um . . . Jackson.'

'You left Ben with Mrs Johnson, and she had no idea where you were!'

'That's not true. She knew I might go out of town.'

'She told me that some woman named Alex called her last night about Ben sleeping over with her. Who the hell is Alex?'

Chris sat up slowly, then stood and walked into the adjoining den. 'Look, I had to drive up here to see a patient at UMC. There's nothing to freak out about. Where are you?'

'In Greenwood, where I'm supposed to be.' Thora's voice had lost none of its hysteria.

He clenched his jaw but said nothing.

'Chris? Are you there? What the hell is going on down there?'

He stood in the dark room, almost too weak to hold the phone, and fought to keep from screaming from the depths of his soul. Alex had begged him not to confront Thora, but he couldn't pretend that everything was fine.

'What about Shane Lansing? Is he where he's supposed to be?'

Now there was only silence.

'Or is he where *I'm* supposed to be?'

'What are you talking about, Chris?'

'I know you took a morning-after pill after we had sex in the studio.'

He heard a gasp.

'I've also got a nice snapshot of you and Shane on the hotel balcony. You'll be what . . . his tenth conquest this year?'

He heard a muffled scream, then a male grunt.

'Is he there now?' Chris asked, reeling. 'If he is, put him on the phone.'

No response.

'I know what you did, OK? And I may be dead in a year. But *you* . . . you and Lansing, you're dead, too. Spiritually dead. And you're going to prison!'

She was sobbing now.

'How could you do this to Ben, Thora?'

Thora wailed like a woman rending her flesh in mourning.

Chris hung up and stood shivering in the darkness. He was no longer alone. Alex was standing in the door that divided the bedroom from the den, her face confused, her bare legs outlined in the light from the window.

'What did you do?' she asked.

'I couldn't pretend any more.'

'But . . . You may have ruined everything.'

'How? You heard Kaiser: poke them with a sharp stick, he said. Well, I just poked Thora. And my guess is, she's going to poke Andrew Rusk like he's never been poked before.'

Alex raised her hand and rubbed her eyes. 'How's your stomach?'

'Better. Did you phone Mrs Johnson to ask if it was OK to keep Ben?'

'Yes, I found her number on your cell. She said he was fine.'

'Shit. Thora acted like she was in a panic. She also didn't like hearing that a woman had called. Asked me who the hell Alex was.'

Alex smiled. 'Screw her.'

'No, thanks. Never again.' He sat down on one of the club chairs.

Alex started pulling on her jeans. 'Why did you marry Thora?' she asked. 'Was it because she's beautiful?'

He thought about it for a while. 'I didn't think so at the time. But now . . . I think maybe that had more to do with it than I knew.'

Alex nodded.

'It wasn't only that, though,' he went on. 'And I still don't know why she would do this. I mean, why not just ask me for a divorce? I'd give it to her.'

'I think it's about Ben. She knows how much he loves you. She can't tell him she wants to take away his wonderful new father because she's suddenly bored. Death solves the problem. If you die, she's a noble widow, not a selfish divorcée. And noble widow is a role Thora already knows how to play.'

'That's for sure.'

'Not to mention adding a couple of mil to her bank account.'

He sighed but said nothing.

'People used to think I was beautiful,' Alex whispered, her hand rising to her scarred cheek. 'Before this.'

'You still are. You just can't see it right now. You're not the same as you were, that's all. It's like women who get chemotherapy. They're still beautiful, they're just bald. I call it the Sinéad O'Connor look.'

Alex laughed, then disappeared into the bathroom. Chris went to his bag and took his morning dose of antivirals: AZT, ritonavir, enfuvirtide and vidarabine. As he swallowed the last pill, Alex came out.

Chris sighed. 'I'm going to be bald myself soon, if I take the chemo.'

'No ifs, bud.' Alex wagged her forefinger in his face. 'You're taking it.'

'You're my doctor now?'

'You want to play Russian roulette with your life?'

'That's what chemotherapy would be under these circumstances. We don't know what was injected into me. My best chance for survival is to find out exactly what's killing me.'

Alex considered this. 'How do you plan to do that?'

'How about you and Kaiser catch the son of a bitch for me?'

'I guess you feel a lot better this morning.'

Chris picked up his pants and struggled to put them on.

'Where are you going?' Alex asked.

'Over to UMC to see the experts Peter Connolly told me about. If they're not there any more, I'll get the names of the top people in Haematology and Oncology and try to see them . . .' A wave of dizziness hit him, and he walked back to the bed. 'I think we've focused too much on Lansing. OK, he owns a radiation oncology centre. But if what was injected into me was radioactive, it would have shown up on the X-ray I had yesterday. I think it's more likely that Connolly's right—someone got hold of my blood—or semen—then altered it and reinjected it into me. If that's the case, the odds are against Lansing. He doesn't have that depth of knowledge. We're looking for experts, Alex, on genetics, oncogenic viruses. There aren't many of those in this state, and the ones we do have are right across the street.'

Alex looked up at him, excitement in her eyes. She walked to the bedside phone. 'I'm going to order some breakfast. Can you eat anything?'

'Toast and a bowl of grits. And hot tea.'

'Good call.' She smiled broadly. 'You're the only man I've spent the night with in the last ten years who ordered grits in the morning.'

'Welcome home.'

CURSING ALEX MORSE with visceral hatred, Andrew Rusk swerved off the interstate ten miles south of Jackson and pulled into the Wendy's drive-through restaurant. Two cars followed him. He was in deep shit.

'Goddammit!' he shouted.

Last night, when he received a coded spam email reply from Glykon, Rusk had been elated, and looking forward to a leisurely drive down to the hunting camp. Now it was impossible. If he led those sons of bitches in the government sedans to Chickamauga, Glykon would kill them and him without a second's hesitation.

Rusk ordered a cheeseburger and a Coke and watched one of the tail cars park in the lot a few yards away. What the hell could he do? If they were following him, they were tapping his phones as well. All thanks to Alex Morse.

When he had arrived at his office this morning, his secretary had reported twelve messages left by Thora Shepard, each one more frantic than the last. Thora wasn't so stupid as to have stated her reason for calling, but something told him that Alex Morse was involved. That, or Thora was having second thoughts about killing her husband.

He took his cheeseburger from the girl at the window and paid with a ten-dollar bill. 'Ketchup,' he said. 'I need some ketchup.'

He took a gulp of his Coke and pulled into the exit lane. One of the tails pulled up behind him. They weren't even trying to conceal themselves.

The funny thing about Thora Shepard, he thought as he turned onto I-55 North, was that they hadn't even had to kill her first husband. The poor guy had died of natural causes. Of course, Rusk had never told *her* that. Thora had made her payments as instructed, and he was happy to take her money. The irony of that woman becoming a return customer was almost too much. But Rusk didn't have time to enjoy it now. Thora was flipping out, and it could cost him dearly. He needed to make contact with Glykon, and soon. He had no idea how to do that, but as he roared north towards Jackson, he realised that he didn't have to—Glykon would do it for him. All he had to do was play it cool. Sometime soon, he'd walk round a corner or step into an elevator, and his partner would be there. Like magic. That was how the guy worked. And all the FBI agents in the world wouldn't be able to stop him.

Rusk knew it was time to cash in his chips and split the country. He only hoped he could fleece Carson Barnett before D-day.

He slowed until the dark sedan behind him had no choice but to pass. As its clean-cut driver glanced his way, he smiled like a Cheshire cat.

DR TARVER REGRETTED the look of dumb incomprehension on his adoptive brother's face, but it was exactly as he had expected. They were standing beside the primate cages, not the best place for this discussion.

'All of them?' Judah said. 'Even the chimps?'

'I'm afraid so,' said Eldon. 'Nothing can remain that would tell anyone what we've been doing here.'

'I thought what we were doing was good.'

'It is good, Judah. But people won't understand that.'

'But what if *I* kept them? Just some of them?'

'I wish you could. I really do. But that's impossible if I'm not here.'

A new fear entered Judah's eyes. 'Where are you going?'

'I don't know yet but I'm going to send for you once I get there. I tell you what, you take care of the beagles and leave the primates to me. I know how hard that would be for you.'

Judah bit his bottom lip. 'The beagles is hard, too, you know? I know every one of 'em now. Every one has a name.'

It amazed Eldon that a man as tough as Judah could be so soft when it came to animals. He put his arm round his brother's massive shoulders and led him away from the primate cages, to their little colony of beagles. It would take Judah most of the day to euthanise them all. Not that they would resist. One of the reasons beagles were used for medical research was that they were so docile.

'How are you going to do it?' Judah asked. 'The chimps, I mean?'

'I'm going to dart them with a barbiturate. After they're fully unconscious, I'll use potassium chloride. They won't feel a thing, Brother.'

Judah was biting his lip. 'Does it have to be *fire*?'

'We have to purify this place. Fire is what God used, so we shall, too.'

Judah closed his eyes, and when he opened them, Eldon saw that he had accepted this as his lot. 'OK. Where do I go when it's done?'

'I'll explain everything when I come back.'

Eldon smiled, then walked back to the primate area. He had some reading to do; explosives were not his line. Still, he was confident in his abilities. What a production it would be. An explosion, then fire—fire hot enough to melt steel—and by the time the firefighters arrived, they would find a building burning at 3,000 degrees Celsius.

Chapter 9

Chris followed Alex into the Haematology Department of UMC. Near the end of the corridor was a door with a brass nameplate that read MATTHEW PEARSON, MD, CHIEF OF HAEMATOLOGY.

Chris paused and said, 'Remember, not a word about the FBI, murder, or anything like that. One whiff of litigation or even liability, and we'll be out the door. Just follow my lead.'

Alex rolled her eyes. 'I can do that.'

He knocked at the door, then walked in. A red-haired woman looked up from a stack of papers. 'Can I help you?'

'I hope so,' Chris said. 'I'm Dr Chris Shepard from Natchez. I happen to be up here visiting a friend'—he nodded at Alex—'and I was hoping to talk to Dr Pearson about a cluster of cancer cases back home.'

'Do you have an appointment, Dr Shepard?'

'I'm afraid not. But I was talking to Dr Peter Connolly up at Sloan-Kettering, and he spoke very highly of Dr Pearson. Pete seemed to think I would have a good chance of speaking with him on short notice.'

The woman's face brightened. 'You know Dr Connolly?'

'I studied under him when I went to school here.'

'Oh, I see.' She stood up. 'Well, Dr Pearson *is* busy right now, but let me just slip in there and see if he can't get away for a minute.'

When the woman disappeared into the inner office, Alex whispered to Chris, 'Aren't you something.'

The door opened, and a smartly dressed man in his mid-forties walked out with his hand extended towards Chris. 'Dr Shepard?'

'Yes, sir,' said Chris, taking the hand firmly. 'Glad to meet you at last.'

'You, too. I see your name on a lot of records that pass through here. You send a lot of referral business our way. We appreciate it. Now, Joan said something about a cancer cluster?' Pearson prompted.

'Right. But I've forgotten my manners.' Chris turned towards Alex. 'This is Alexandra Morse. Her mother is here in your department right now.'

A sombre look came over Pearson's face. 'I'm familiar with the case. I'm sorry we have to meet under these circumstances, Ms Morse.'

'Thank you,' Alex said. 'All the staff have been wonderful.'

'Is your mother part of this cancer cluster?'

'No,' Chris said. 'Alex is just a friend. As for the cluster, I don't have statistical backing yet, but we've had several similar cases in Natchez this past year, and it's really starting to worry me.'

'What type of cancer?' asked Dr Pearson.

'All blood cancers. Leukaemias, lymphomas and a myeloma.'

Dr Pearson nodded with genuine interest. 'I'm surprised we haven't picked this up ourselves. Have the patients passed through here?'

'Some. Dr Mercier has treated several in Natchez, and some of the others have gone to M. D. Anderson. The thing is, some local doctors have wondered if there might be an environmental factor linking these cancers.'

More concerned nodding from Pearson. 'That's certainly possible. It's a very complex subject, of course. Controversial, too.'

'I've also wondered,' Chris went on, 'if there might be some other aetiological link between the cases. Radiation is one possibility. We've got two nuclear plants nearby, and two of these patients work at one of them. I've also been intrigued by the role of oncogenic viruses in cancer.'

Dr Pearson looked sceptical. 'I see.'

'I was hoping,' Chris concluded, 'that you could put me in touch with faculty members who specialise in carcinogens and oncogenic viruses. Pete Connolly gave me a couple of names. One was Ajit Chandrekasar.'

'Ajit is no longer here.'

'I see. He also mentioned an Eldon Tarver?'

Pearson nodded. 'Dr Tarver is still with us. He's done some great work and knows as much about retroviruses and oncogenic viruses as any virologist I've ever met. He'd be glad to talk to you—with sufficient notice.'

Chris let his disappointment show.

'For the environmental toxins, you'd have to go a long way to beat Dr Parminder,' Pearson continued. 'For radiation, I'd suggest Dr Colbert. I'd be happy to try to set something up. Why don't you give me your phone number, and I'll call you after I've spoken to them.'

Chris gave Pearson his cell number. 'I appreciate you taking the time to see us, Doctor. I'll tell Pete how helpful you've been.'

'Never too busy for a colleague,' said Pearson, offering his hand again.

Chris nodded, then escorted Alex through the door. As soon as it shut behind them, Alex veered to the right, towards another row of doors.

'What are you doing?' Chris whispered.

'We're going to find the guys he talked about.'

WILL KILMER, parked at the base of the AmSouth tower, was stunned to see Thora Shepard climb out of her silver Mercedes and storm into the lobby of the building. He only happened to be there because the operative tailing Rusk had reported that his target had reversed direction ten miles south of town and headed back towards Jackson. Since there had been FBI vehicles tailing Rusk, Will had decided to take over the surveillance.

The couple he had watching Thora Shepard in Greenwood had seen her checking out of the Alluvian Hotel early that morning. They, like Will, had assumed that Thora would be driving straight back to Natchez. But now here she was in Jackson, storming into Andrew Rusk's office building.

Will got out of his Ford Explorer and entered the building. He told the doorman that he was going up to the AmSouth offices on the second floor, then got into the elevator and punched 2 and 16.

As soon as the doors opened on 16, he heard a woman yelling at full volume: *'I've paid your boss one hell of a lot of money, and I'm going to talk to him one way or another.'*

Will stepped out of the elevator into an ultramodern reception area. Thora Shepard was standing with her back to him, facing an attractive blonde.

'Mrs Shepard,' said the receptionist, 'I've told you repeatedly that Mr Rusk is out of town. I haven't been able to reach him, but as soon as I do I will relay your message and the urgency of your situation.'

Thora stood with her hands on her hips, looking as if she meant to stand in that spot all day if that was what it took. Then suddenly, without warning, she whirled round and marched back towards the elevator.

'You going down, ma'am?' Will asked.

'You're damn right,' Thora snapped.

As the elevator whooshed towards the lobby, Thora cursed steadily under her breath. In the closeness of the car, Will saw that her neck was blotchy with red spots, the way his wife looked when she was about to explode in a fit of temper. There were dark circles under both eyes. He needed to talk to Alex in a hurry, but her cellphone was permanently on voicemail. Something had gone down last night, and they needed to know what it was.

When the elevator opened, Will followed Thora out to the street, adrenaline flushing through his system the way it always did when a case started to break. He felt younger than he had in years.

ALEX AND CHRIS walked down the hospital corridor to the academic offices. The first brass plate they came across said ELDON TARVER, MD. Alex knocked hard, but there was no answer. She knocked again. No response.

'Hello,' said a familiar bass voice behind them. 'I'm Dr Tarver. What can I do for you?'

Alex turned and saw the bearded man with the birthmark whom she'd met the previous day in the elevator.

Chris held out his hand and Tarver shook it. 'Dr Tarver, I'm Chris Shepard, an internist from Natchez. Pete Connolly at Sloan-Kettering recommended you to me as an expert on oncogenic viruses.'

Tarver looked surprised. 'I'm not sure I would put myself forward as that. I hold several degrees, but I'm not board-certified in virology.'

'Well, Pete seems to think you're very knowledgeable in the area.'

Dr Tarver looked at Alex. 'Hello again. And you are . . . ?'

'Nancy Jenner. I'm Dr Shepard's chief nurse.'

Dr Tarver's eyes twinkled. 'Why don't we step into my office?' he said, glancing at his watch. 'I have about five minutes before I'm due somewhere.'

He admitted them to a small office lined on three walls with bookshelves; the fourth was studded with framed photographs, including a picture of Tarver with President Nixon. Alex studied the photos while Chris put his theories and questions to the doctor.

'A cluster of cancers in Natchez, you say,' Tarver replied eventually. 'I wasn't aware of that.'

'Blood cancers, specifically,' said Chris. 'Several local doctors are starting to wonder if these cases might have a common aetiology.'

'A *viral* aetiology?'

'Well, we don't know. I was thinking radiation exposure, but we can't pin down a common source. Most of the patients work at different places and live in different parts of town.'

'Which mitigates against an environmental cause,' said Tarver.

'That's how I got onto the virus angle. I know that several cancers have been proved to have viral origins.'

'That's more true in animals than humans. I can't think of a single case in which a virus has produced a cluster of cancers.'

Alex was moving from photo to photo. The birthmark made it easy to pick out Dr Tarver, even in large group shots. As she studied the pictures, a fact she'd learned back at Quantico bubbled into her mind. Many serial murderers suffered some physical deformity that set them apart during childhood. It was crazy to suspect Tarver, of course, and yet . . . he certainly had the knowledge that their high-tech murders would require.

Chris was speaking medical jargon now, far above her level. As he droned on, a photograph caught Alex's eye. In it, Dr Tarver and a man in army uniform stood in front of a fortress-like building with a sign on its front that read VCP. The breast of Tarver's lab coat bore the same letters: VCP.

At the first pause in the conversation, Alex asked, 'What's VCP?'

'I beg your pardon?' said Dr Tarver.

'In this photo, you're wearing a coat that says VCP.'

'Oh.' Tarver smiled. 'The Veterans' Cancer Project. It was a governmentsponsored project to look into the high incidence of cancer in combat veterans. Principally from Vietnam, but also from World War Two and Korea.'

Before Alex could ask another question, Chris said, 'Do you retain blood samples from patients who've died on the oncology ward?'

Alex's pulse raced, and she turned away. Some of *her* victims had died in this very hospital. If their blood had been preserved, might it be possible to discover some common carcinogen that would prove mass murder?

'I know the pathology lab retains all specimens for ten years. We probably retain samples of blood and neoplastic cells in some cases.'

'I could give you a list of the patients we're concerned about,' Alex said.

Dr Tarver gave her an accommodating smile. 'I suppose I could pass it on to Dr Pearson for you.'

Struggling to mask her excitement, Alex walked to his desk and took a pen from a silver cup. 'May I write on this prescription pad?'

'Of course.'

She began writing a list of names.

'This may sound nuts,' Chris said, 'but I wonder if it's possible that someone might be purposely inducing cancer in human beings.'

Alex looked up from her list. Dr Tarver was staring at Chris as though he had suggested that priests might secretly be killing babies during baptisms.

'That's one of the most remarkable things I've ever heard. What makes you suggest something like that?'

'Nothing else seems to explain these cases. And all these patients were married to wealthy people who wanted to divorce them.'

Tarver looked incredulous. 'Are you suggesting that someone is *murdering* people by giving them cancer?'

'More than that. I think it's a doctor.'

Dr Tarver laughed. 'I'm sorry, but I don't know what to say to that. Do any law-enforcement authorities agree with your hypothesis?'

'Yes,' Alex said sharply. She wasn't sure why Chris had gone this route, but she wasn't about to leave him twisting in the wind. 'Dr Tarver, I'm actually a special agent of the FBI. And we are looking into these cases.'

'May I see your identification?'

Alex reached for her back pocket, then froze. She had never felt so ridiculous in her life. 'I left my ID at the hotel,' she said lamely.

'I'd like to help you, Dr Shepard,' Tarver said, 'But I must tell you, if Dr Pearson knew that this visit had anything to do with legal matters, he would be very upset. I should terminate this interview until we can continue it on an official basis.' He looked at his watch. 'Besides, I'm late for a meeting.' He gathered up some papers, then ushered them to the door. Once they were in the hall, he locked the office, said 'Good day,' then hurried to the elevators.

'I don't know why I did that,' Chris said. 'Once Pearson hears about it, I'll be *persona non grata* at this institution.'

'Not if you really refer that many patients up here. Money talks, brother. And my mother's a patient. They can't kick me out.'

Chris moved towards a bench opposite the elevators and collapsed on it.

'Are you all right?' Alex asked.

'I don't know. I need to get back to Cabot Lodge. I need the bathroom.'

'That's fine with me. I need to charge my phone.' She pressed the elevator button. 'What do you think about Tarver?'

Chris shrugged. 'Typical specialist.'

'He gives me a weird feeling.'

The bell dinged and the elevator opened.

Chris had already boarded the car when a thought struck Alex. 'You go ahead,' she said. 'I'm going back to ask Dr Pearson something.'

Chris held the door open. 'What?'

'In one of Dr Tarver's photos, he's standing in front of a building with a sign that says FREE AIDS TESTING. It looked familiar to me. I think it was a restaurant in downtown Jackson called Pullo's that my dad used to take me to when I was a kid. I want to know why they were testing for AIDS there. It doesn't make sense.'

'I'll go with you.' Chris started forward.

She gently pushed him back into the elevator. 'No. I'll be right down. Sit on a bench and wait for me.'

He sagged against the elevator wall. 'OK.'

ELDON TARVER stood behind the trunk of a large oak tree, his eyes locked on the hospital entrance. He had watched Shepard emerge into the cloud of smoke generated by the patients and nurses getting their nicotine fixes outside the entrance, then retreat back into the building. Where was Morse? Was she at this moment recounting her suspicions to Dr Pearson? The part of Eldon's brain that handled threat assessment was lit up like a small city. Yesterday he had congratulated himself on his decision to pull out early. Fate had now revealed that it was not early at all. It was very late.

The conversation with Morse and Shepard was one of the most remarkable he had ever experienced. Not only had he murdered Morse's sister, but Shepard was a walking dead man! He wondered if the doctor knew he was doomed. Of course, the cancer did not yet exist. Eldon had simply initiated a cascade of events that, left unchecked, would terminate in carcinogenesis at the cellular level. And the only man alive who could stop that lethal cascade for Chris Shepard was Eldon Tarver. But Shepard's death represented valuable research data; alive, he was useless, possibly even dangerous.

He thought back to the demeanour of Morse and Shepard in his office, and decided that the worm had not quite turned. If they had anything concrete on him—or more important, if the FBI were handling this officially—they would have played it differently. He looked back over his shoulder. Morse and Shepard had still not emerged from the hospital.

ALEX PUT ON a smile and pushed open the door of Dr Pearson's office. The receptionist was still at her post, but the door to the inner office was open.

'Hello again,' Alex said. 'I forgot to ask Dr Pearson one question.'

The receptionist sighed. 'I think it's better if you call with it.'

Alex raised her voice, trusting to Pearson's goodwill. 'It's just one question, nothing medical at all.'

Pearson poked his head out of his door. 'Hello again.'

'Yes, I was actually talking to Dr Tarver a moment ago. He invited us into his office—and he had some very interesting pictures on his wall. I grew up in Jackson, and one of them is really bugging me. It's of a long building with glass windows, and it says FREE AIDS TESTING on a banner in front. It looks like a restaurant on Jefferson Street that I used to go to as a girl.'

Pearson's eyes lit up; he was genuinely happy to be able to help. 'Yes, of course. That used to be Pullo's restaurant until Dr Tarver bought it. He wanted a site that would be easily accessible to the residents of the city, the homeless, the poor, the medically underserved.'

A fillip of excitement went through Alex. 'Easily accessible for what?'

'His clinic. It's a free clinic for the poor. Dr Tarver gives a great deal of his time to it, testing for many of the common viruses that afflict the lower socioeconomic classes: AIDS, hepatitis C, herpes, all that stuff. He treats them as well. He's won a lot of grants. Of course, the records of his work are also quite valuable in a statistical sense.'

'Oh, I see.' Alex felt as though she was nearing something important. 'I didn't realise we had something like that in Jackson.'

'We didn't for many years. But when Dr Tarver lost his wife, he decided he wanted to make something positive out of her loss.'

'Lost his wife?' Alex echoed. 'What did she die of?'

'Cervical cancer. A terrible case, I believe. Seven or eight years ago—

before my time here. But Dr Tarver inherited quite a bit of money from his wife, and he wanted to put it to good use, which he certainly did.'

Alex had run out of words, but her mind was racing.

'Is that all you wanted?' Dr Pearson asked.

'Um . . . yes. Only that Dr Shepard told me to thank you again,' Alex said with her best Southern-belle smile, then she backed out of the office.

Outside, she turned, heart pounding, and ran to the elevator. When it was too slow in coming, she took the fire stairs to the ground floor.

Chris was standing inside the hospital entrance doors. 'Hey,' he said. 'I wanted to go outside, but the smoke is so thick it could choke you.'

She took his arm. 'Chris, you're not going to believe this. That building I asked about—Dr Tarver owns it now. Pearson told me it's a free clinic for the poor. He tests people for viruses—AIDS, hepatitis, herpes—and treats them. He started the clinic in memory of his wife, who died of cervical cancer seven years ago. And guess what?'

'What?'

'He inherited a pile of money from her.'

Chris's mouth fell open.

'Doesn't that seem suspicious to you?'

'I'd say yes, except that he turned around and used the money to open a free clinic in memory of his dead wife.'

'Right, but that put him down in the inner city, where he could do God knows what under the guise of treating the poor for free. I wonder if I can discover any connection between Tarver and Andrew Rusk.'

'I think it's worth exploring.' Chris grimaced. 'But right now I need to find a bathroom and a bed. I'm feeling pretty rough.'

'I'm sorry,' Alex said, slipping an arm under his so that he could lean on her. 'Let's go to the car. I'll get Kaiser onto Dr Tarver when we get back.'

Chris nodded, then walked slowly through the doors. 'When I'm distracted,' he said, 'like upstairs, I can almost put the reality out of my head. But when I'm alone, like a minute ago . . .'

Alex pressed her cheek to his head as they walked. 'You're not alone,' remember that. You have Ben, and . . . I'll be right beside you, no matter what happens.'

He squeezed her shoulder.

'But nothing bad's going to happen,' she said forcefully. 'We're going to find these assholes, and we're going to get you cured. Right?'

His reply was a whisper. 'I hope so.'

BACK AT CABOT LODGE, Alex's cellphone began to ring as soon as she plugged it in. It was Will.

'Kid, I've been trying to reach you all morning. This thing's breaking wide open. Thora Shepard just confronted Rusk on the street below his office. She's lost her mind. Stood right in front of his car, screaming at him to call off the hit on her husband.'

'Jesus! Where are they now?'

'Up in Rusk's office, I think.'

Alex thought quickly. She had already called Kaiser about checking out Eldon Tarver, but she didn't want to wait for answers. 'Can you get someone to stay on Thora? I want you to come with me to the old Pullo's restaurant.'

'That place closed years ago.'

'I know. It's a free clinic now.'

'And you need me there because—'

'There's a small chance it could get dicey.'

'How small?'

'Ten per cent. But you never know, right? Isn't that what you taught me?'

Will chuckled. 'OK. I'll meet you in fifteen minutes. In Smith Park.'

Chris came out of the bathroom and sat on the edge of the bed. 'What happened?' he asked hoarsely.

She didn't want to lie, but she wasn't about to tell Chris that his wife was running amok on the streets of Jackson. Not in his present state. 'Will almost got into an accident,' she said.

Chris gave her a sidelong glance. 'You said, "Where are they now?"'

'I meant the people who almost hit him.' Alex pulled back the bedclothes and motioned for Chris to get under them. 'You need rest. Come on, get in.'

He looked back at her with hollow eyes, but rather than protest, he let himself fall onto the sheet and shoved his feet under the covers.

Alex leaned over and kissed him on the forehead. 'I'll be back soon.'

As she straightened up, he caught hold of her wrist with surprising force. 'Be careful, Alex. These people don't care about anybody.'

'I know.'

He jerked her wrist, hard. 'Do you?'

At last his concern penetrated the buzz of excitement in her brain. 'Yes.'

'Good.'

When Chris let go of her arm, she removed the borrowed Sig Sauer from the shoe box in the closet, slipped it into her waistband at the small of her back, and hurried into the hall.

ANDREW RUSK stopped the elevator one floor short of his office. He wasn't about to drag a hysterical Thora Shepard past his secretary.

When the doors opened, he smelt sawdust. Several walls had been knocked out on this floor, where a refurbishment was in progress.

He walked over exposed concrete to a tall window, then turned and spoke to Thora with all the pent-up frustration of the past hours. 'What the hell has gotten into you, lady? Have you lost what little mind you have?'

'*Fuck you!*' Thora shouted, shaking her forefinger in his face. 'You told me nothing could go wrong. But somehow Chris knows everything!'

'That's impossible.'

Her eyes blazed. 'You think so? He *called* me, you stupid prick. He said, "I might be dead in a year, but you're dead, too." He said I'd never see Ben again, because I'd be in prison. Does that wipe the smirk off your face?'

Rusk tried not to show how deeply her words had disturbed him.

'You have to call it off,' Thora insisted. 'That's the only option.'

'Listen, Chris can't prove anything. He's getting all this from an FBI agent who's already been fired. It's going to be OK, Thora.'

'You think I believe that? Call off whatever scumbag does this stuff for you right now! You're not going to get another cent from me anyway.'

Rusk grabbed her arms. 'Before you start making threats, you should know a couple of things. First, you can't hurt me without hurting yourself. Because the person who handles these jobs is an extremely dangerous man. If you upset him by doing something as insane as refusing to pay his fee, you will incur his wrath. Now . . . If your husband suspects the truth, I'll do what I can to stop what's been set in motion. But *you* will do nothing. If my partner had witnessed your behaviour today, you would already be dead.'

She stared wildly at him. 'What am I supposed to do?' she whimpered. 'Where can I *go*?'

'You can stay in my office for now. But you can't say one word about any of this within those walls. My office may be bugged.'

'I don't want to stay here. I want to see my son.'

'You can't. Not yet.'

'Bullshit! I haven't broken any law.'

Rusk gasped in amazement. 'You hired someone to kill your husband! *Twice!* And last time it made you a multimillionaire.'

'I consulted a divorce lawyer. No one can prove I did anything else.'

'You've already paid me a million dollars!'

Cool arrogance descended like a curtain over her eyes. 'I followed the investment advice you gave me. That put a million dollars under your control. If anyone looks at that deal, it'll look like you stole the money.'

Rusk was speechless.

'Now, I'm going back to my old life. *You* are going to make sure that nothing happens to my husband. But if something should, I will hang your ass out to dry. Are we clear?'

Rusk's mind was spinning. This delusional bitch had no clue as to the reality of the situation. 'Let me show you why you can't just go back to your old life.' He nodded to the window, then offered to escort her with his arm.

She looked contemptuously at the arm, but she did walk to the window.

'See those men down there?' he asked, stepping over a toolbox. 'There, on the corner. And on the steps across the street. See him?'

'The guy reading the newspaper?'

'Yep. FBI. The woman, too. The jogger.'

Thora's mouth opened. 'How do you know?'

'I have contacts at the Bureau.'

'But why are they here? How much do they know?'

'I don't know yet. Do you see any other likely agents?'

As Thora stood on tiptoe, he bent and lifted a claw hammer out of the toolbox. Thora turned at the movement, but by then Rusk was already swinging the hammer. It smashed into her skull and she tottered, then fell.

This spoiled bitch had threatened everything he'd worked five years to build . . . But now Glykon would cease to see him as a gutless middleman afraid to get his hands dirty. He stood over the corpse. Never had he felt such elemental power. He only wished his father were there to witness it.

WILL WAS WAITING for Alex when she arrived at Smith's Park. She got out of the Corolla, locked it and climbed into the passenger seat of his Explorer.

'What's the deal with this clinic?' Will asked.

'It's owned by a doctor from UMC. Eldon Tarver. I got a funny feeling when I talked to him. His wife died of cancer years ago, and he inherited a lot of money. He opened up this place in memory of her. He treats a lot of poor people, but I think he might be doing more. He's a cancer specialist, and this would be a perfect front for him. He could give those patients any kind of virus or toxin he wanted to, then monitor them.'

Will's eyes crinkled 'A freako, then.'

'Maybe.' Alex bit her lip. 'We're about to find out, I hope. Let's go.'

'Hey, how's Dr Shepard?'

She laid her hand on the detective's arm. 'He's sick, Will. Bad. But it's not your fault, OK?'

'Bullshit, it ain't. Sleeping at my post. They used to shoot us for that.'

'You were drugged. All three of you. Now, let go of that and get your mind on the game. I need you.'

Will rubbed his wrinkled face between both hands and sighed. 'You taking your piece in with you?'

She shook her head. 'Not this time.'

Will reached into the glove box and brought out a short-barrelled .357 magnum. 'I'm gonna be close, then.'

'That's where I like you, partner.'

THE RENOVATED PULLO'S restaurant possessed little of its former personality. Just inside the door of the clinic a receptionist sat at a scarred metal desk. To her right was a large group of chairs, several of which were occupied by emaciated men who smelt of alcohol, cigarettes and body odour.

'Can I help you?' asked the receptionist, eyeing Alex up and down. Well-dressed Caucasian women were clearly not usual visitors at the clinic.

'I was just speaking to Dr Tarver over at the medical centre. He asked me something and now I've got the answer for him.'

'Well, the doctor's not here. But let me go back and talk to somebody. He may be coming in soon.'

'Thank you. I'd appreciate it.'

The woman got up and walked down a corridor that led deeper into the building. Alex stepped closer to the desk. There were bills addressed to the Tarver Free Clinic. A magazine lay open beside the appointment book. Written on a lined pad in an almost illegible scrawl were the words *Energy bill late—Noel D. Traver, DVM.* Beneath this was a number: *09365974.* Alex was memorising it when the receptionist returned.

'He ain't coming in today,' she said, giving Alex a territorial glare and she sat down and went back to her magazine.

Alex started to ask her to take a message, then thought better of it. Turning to leave, she almost bumped into a man wearing what had to be a $2,000 business suit. 'Excuse me,' she said. 'I'm sorry.'

The newcomer had close-cropped grey hair and steel-blue eyes. His face triggered something in her mind. But what?

'Not a problem, miss,' the man said with the slightest of smiles. He stepped aside for her to pass.

Alex exited the clinic, and strode down the street towards Will's Explorer.
'Any luck?' Will asked, as she climbed in beside him.
'Nothing good.'
'You see that guy who just went in?'
'Yeah. You know him?'
'I know his type. Soldier. But check out the guy in the dark sedan.'
Alex could see a young man wearing an army uniform sitting behind the wheel of a car she had just walked past.
'He drove the sharp-dressed guy here?'
'Yep. And the car door has U.S. GOVERNMENT printed in black on it.'
'What the hell? Who are they?'
As he drove down the block to where Alex's Corolla was parked, Will said, 'They sure as shit ain't the IRS.'
She nodded. 'You ever hear of a veterinarian named Noel Traver?'
'Can't say I have. But *Traver* is pretty damn close to *Tarver*, ain't it?'
Alex pictured the notepad in her mind— 'Shit! It's an anagram. Noel *D.* Traver. There was a note on a desk in there about a late bill.'
'Now we're getting somewhere.' Will's eyes flashed. 'A cancer doctor with an alias. That make sense to you?'
Alex shook her head. 'Let's go back and see how long that government guy stays inside the clinic. Circle the block.'
'Yeah. If he's still there, maybe Tarver is inside with him.'
Will hit the gas. But the instant they turned back onto Jefferson Street, Alex saw that the dark sedan was gone.
'If I had to guess,' said Will, 'I'd say he's headed for the interstate.'

Chapter 10

'Describe her to me,' said Dr Tarver.
Edward Biddle pursed his lips and looked around the spartan office. Dr Tarver knew Biddle was wondering if this was where the 'ground-breaking' research had been done. 'About five eight,' Biddle said. 'Dark hair, pretty, scars on the right side of her face.'
Dr Tarver remained impassive, but Biddle was not deceived.
'Who is she, Eldon? Another of your obsessions?'

'She's an FBI agent. Working alone, though. No Bureau support.'

He saw the displeasure in Biddle's eyes. 'An FBI agent?'

'She's not a problem, Edward. That's an unrelated matter.'

Biddle nodded. 'Let's get down to brass tacks, then. What have you got?'

A few minutes ago, luckily, Pearson had called Tarver to give a friendly warning that Dr Shepard and a friend might show up. And now Alex Morse had put the whole deal in jeopardy. If she was so goddamned observant that she could look at a photo of this clinic for a few seconds and make the connection to Pullo's restaurant, then she would eventually realise that the army major in the VCP photo had just walked in here. And once she did, she would quickly uncover the true nature of the VCP. And that would allow her to track Eldon from his old life to his new one. He couldn't take that chance.

'You want to know what I've got, Edward?' Dr Tarver leaned back in his chair. 'I've got exactly what you were looking for all those years ago.'

'Which is?'

'The perfect weapon.'

'*Perfect* is a mighty big word, Eldon.'

Tarver smiled. 'Wasn't it you who spoke of the Holy Grail at Fort Detrick? A weapon that couldn't be perceived as a weapon? Well, here it is.' Eldon opened his desk drawer and took out a small vial filled with brown liquid.

'What is it?'

'A retrovirus.'

'Source?'

'That must remain my proprietary secret, for now.'

'Tell me what else makes it a perfect weapon.'

'First, it has a long incubation period. Ten to twelve months, with death from cancer following in an average of sixteen months.'

Biddle tilted his head to one side. He was already thinking about the larger implications. 'Eldon, the indiscriminate nature of that kind of weapon renders it unusable on a large scale. You know that.'

Tarver leaned forward. 'I've solved that problem. I've created a vaccine.'

'So we'd have to vaccinate our forces prior to using the weapon.'

'Yes, but we could do it under cover of the usual immunisation. And I can even sabotage the virus *after* infection, before oncogenesis occurs.'

Biddle's poker face finally slipped. 'You can kill the virus *after* infection?'

Dr Tarver settled back in his chair, his confidence unshakable. 'I created this virus, Edward. And I can destroy it.'

Biddle was shaking his head, but there was excitement in his eyes.

'After about three weeks,' Eldon went on, 'there's no stopping the cascade. But before that, I can short-circuit the infection.'

'So what you're telling me is—'

'I have your weapon for China.'

Biddle had the look of a man whose mind has just been accurately read.

'I know you, Edward,' Tarver said with a sly smile. 'I see what's happening in the world. I know the limits of oil reserves and strategic metals. I know the direction in which those reserves are flowing, where the heavy manufacturing is going. And I know the capabilities of Chinese nuclear submarines. I know about their missile programme. The yellow men can afford to lose half a billion people if we have to go nuclear. We can't. More important, they're *willing* to lose them. And we're not.'

Biddle's eyes were half closed. 'So you're telling me that we could set this virus loose in a slum in Shanghai, and—'

'By the time the first cases started dying, they'd have fifteen months of exponential infection. It would be in every major Chinese city. They'd see a host of different cancers, not just one. The chaos would be unimaginable.'

'It would also have crossed the oceans,' Biddle observed.

Eldon's smile vanished. 'Yes. There would be some casualties. But only for a while. With the example of AIDS, most countries would initiate crash programmes to find a vaccine. Your company could take the lead in the US.'

'And you could head it up,' said Biddle. 'Is that what you're thinking?'

'I should be part of it. And before the death toll climbs too high over here, we'll come forward with an experimental vaccine.'

Biddle wet his lips with his pale tongue. 'Nevertheless, with China's population, this wouldn't be a decisive weapon, merely a destabilising one . . .'

'You want apocalypse? I can give you that. I can lengthen the incubation period. With a five-year incubation, seventy per cent of the population over fifteen could be infected before anyone got sick.' Eldon leaned forward. 'So now you know what I'm offering, I'd like to hear how interested you are.'

'Obviously, I'm interested,' Biddle said. 'But just as obviously, there are some issues. You're ahead of your time, Eldon. You always were.'

Tarver nodded but said nothing.

'*But*,' Biddle went on, 'not nearly so far ahead as you once were. The regulatory climate is loosening up. Everyone's ramping up their primate-breeding capacity, including China. In fact, we're already doing some of our primate research there. As far as getting you a new identity is concerned, I can take care of that. If you want money, big money—'

'I want what this technology is worth.'

A look of surprise. 'That will take longer . . . Three years. Maybe five.'

Anger and bitterness rose from Tarver's gut. 'I'm fifty-nine, Edward. The world looks different than it did in 1970.'

Biddle nodded. 'You don't have to tell me. But think about this. You'll be working for a company that will give you a free hand with research.'

'Can you promise that? No one looking over my shoulder?'

'Guaranteed. My concern, old friend, is the risk of waiting even one minute to move to the next phase. I want you to come with me now. Today. I don't want anything happening to you before my people see your research data.'

Tarver drew back. 'We haven't agreed to anything yet.'

Biddle looked hard into his eyes. 'Listen to me, Eldon. The money will come. Recognition will come, too. But what's most important is what you'll be doing for your country. It's up to us to insure our nation's survival. I've bled for this country, Eldon. You have, too, in your way. But you don't resent it, do you? I think you feel the same obligation I do.'

Dr Tarver looked down at his desk. There had never been any question of refusing, of course. He had merely hoped that the more tangible symbols of appreciation would come more quickly. 'All right, Edward. I'm on board.'

Biddle's face split in an expansive smile. 'Let's talk timing.'

Eldon held up his hands. 'I need a day, Edward. One day.'

Suspicion clouded Biddle's eyes. 'What could possibly justify waiting?'

For a moment Eldon considered asking his old colleague to take care of Alex Morse for him. Biddle undoubtedly had contacts who could take her out and make it look like an accident. But if he and the TransGene board perceived Eldon Tarver as a security risk they might decide to eliminate him as soon as they possessed the virus and its documentation. No, he needed to enter his new life clean and unblemished.

'You have to trust me, Edward,' he said. 'Tomorrow I'm yours.'

Biddle looked far from satisfied, but he didn't argue further. 'Your new identity papers will take two or three days to be processed. Plus, I assume we have some logistics to take care of. What do you need to bring out besides data? Special equipment? Biologicals?'

'No machinery. I can bring the biological agents I need out in a single Pelican case, and my critical files fit in a backpack.'

'Excellent.' Biddle stared at him. 'Is there anything more I need to know?'

Tarver dodged the meaning behind the question. 'I'd like you to fly the helicopter. When I call, you come, and to wherever I say.'

Biddle scratched his chin. 'Any risk of a hot extraction?'

Eldon smiled. He loved intelligence jargon. 'I don't anticipate that.'

'All right, then.' Biddle grinned. 'Hell, I'd love to fly this mission.'

The old soldier offered his hand, and Eldon took it. 'Until tomorrow,' said the doctor as he walked Biddle to the door.

Biddle turned back, his face grave. 'Is it worth sticking around to handle unfinished business when you have an FBI agent poking around?'

Tarver regretted revealing Morse's identity. 'I'm afraid she's involved with that business.'

Biddle's cold blue eyes remained steady. 'As long as you're clean as regards our business.'

'Absolutely.'

ALEX LET HERSELF INTO the darkened hotel room at Cabot Place as quietly as she could. As she felt her way round a chair, she heard a quavering voice.

'Ah-Alex?'

'Chris? Are you OK?'

'Th-think so.'

As she felt her way along the bed, her eyes adjusted to the darkness, and she picked out Chris's eyes in the shadows. He was lying on his back with the covers pulled up to his neck. His forehead glistened with sweat.

'My God. What's going on?'

'Typical initial ruh . . . reaction to virus. Your marrow spits out a ton of immunoglobulins to d-deal with the invader . . . classic symptoms.'

Alex wanted to call 911. But Chris wasn't panicking, and he was the physician, not her.

'Don't worry,' he said weakly. 'I'll t-tell you when to panic.'

She forced a smile. 'Do you mind if I use my computer?'

He shook his head.

She bent and laid her hand on his burning shoulder, but he jerked away.

Anger and frustration surged through her. Never had she felt such impotence. Will had been unable to pursue the government car they had seen parked at Dr Tarver's clinic. John Kaiser had called but, to her dismay, most of what he'd learned about Rusk duplicated information she'd uncovered weeks ago—although he did tell her that the FBI agents tailing Rusk believed Thora Shepard was still inside the lawyer's office. She'd asked Kaiser to focus on Dr Tarver and told him about the Noel D. Traver alias.

Now she went to the hotel desk, and used her laptop to log onto the

Internet. When she tried to log into the government's data base of criminal records, she learned that her FBI access code was no longer valid. Mark Dodson had certainly been thorough. And it was a crippling blow. She'd have to go to Google, like any civilian. Cursing, she typed 'Eldon Tarver' into the search line. The name returned over a hundred hits.

As she started scrolling through, her phone rang. It was Kaiser.

'What's up?' she asked.

'Noel D. Traver has no criminal record. But when I checked into his past, I found that there's no record of him attending the vet school he claims to have graduated from. Mississippi granted him a licence based on papers he gave them from the State of Tennessee, though he's not actually practising here. He owns and operates a dog-breeding facility in south Jackson, selling dogs to medical schools for animal research.'

Alex tugged at an errant strand of hair. 'This is strange, John. Especially if he's not Noel Traver at all, but Eldon Tarver.'

'Hang on a sec.' She heard voices but could not make out words. 'Alex,' he said. 'I need to call you back.'

She hung up and went back to her computer. It struck her then that she had not tried the simplest method of finding out whether Noel D. Traver was an alias or not. She typed the name into Google, then searched IMAGES. The computer hummed and clicked, then a row of thumbnails began to load.

The first picture that popped up showed an African-American man wearing an army uniform, Captain Noel D. Traver. The second showed a square-headed man with a grey beard and a full head of hair. The caption read JACKSON BREEDER TREATS RESEARCH PUPS LIKE PETS. The picture was grainy, but Alex had no doubt: Noel D. Traver was not Eldon Tarver.

'What the hell?' she whispered.

Her cellphone rang again. It was Will.

'Dr Eldon Tarver owns a pathology lab here in Jackson,' he said. 'Jackson Pathology Associates. They do the lab testing for a lot of local doctors.'

'This guy is something.'

'You want me to ride out there and check it out?'

'Yes. Poke around and see if anything seems out of whack.'

Will chuckled. 'I know the routine.'

Alex's phone beeped, indicating a second incoming call. Kaiser's cell. 'Call me later, Will. Gotta go.' She clicked over to Kaiser's call. 'Hello?'

'I'm sorry, Alex. Things are kind of messy right now. Webb Tyler found out about my little off-duty surveillance club.'

Webb Tyler was the SAC of the Jackson field office. It was Tyler that Alex had first approached with her murder theory, and Alex assumed he'd complained about her to Mark Dodson. But she couldn't worry about that now.

'John, listen to me. I did an image search on Noel D. Traver, and I found a picture of him. And it's not Eldon Tarver.'

'Really?'

'I don't get it. Two names that are perfect anagrams couldn't be coincidence—not if one name is found on the desk of the owner of the other.'

'I agree. We're into something weird here. But changing subject, the SAC says that even if you're right, this is a homicide case so I should turn over any evidence I have to the Jackson Police Department and go back to New Orleans. And you should find a new line of work.'

'Screw Tyler. I say we check out Noel D. Traver's dog-breeding facility.'

'Tyler won't go for that. I already asked for a search warrant. No dice.'

'Jesus, what's his problem?' snapped Alex.

'Mark Dodson is his problem. Tyler knows Dodson hates your guts, and he thinks Dodson is the new director's fair-haired boy. So, Tyler's not about to help me, since I'm a disciple of the wrong acolyte.'

'I'm starting to think I'm well out of the Bureau.'

'We'll get the warrant eventually. We just have to keep piling up evidence.'

'How, without any support? Do you have any idea where Eldon Tarver is at this moment?'

'No. He lives alone, and he's not at home. He's not at the university or at his clinic, either. I'll let you know when we locate him.'

Alex grunted in dissatisfaction. 'So, where is this dog-breeding facility?'

'Don't even think about it. Not without a warrant. Call me if there's something I need to know.'

Alex hung up and dialled Will Kilmer. 'Noel D. Traver owns a dog-breeding facility in south Jackson,' she told him. 'I need you to find out where.'

'I already know.'

'I love you, old man. Give me the address.'

Will read it out. 'You planning on a visit?'

'We could ride by.'

'On my way. You stay in touch.'

'I will.'

Alex went to Chris's bed and knelt beside him. He was still shivering, but his eyes were closed now, and he was breathing regularly. She went back to the desk, packed her computer into its case, and left as quietly as she could.

WILL KILMER TOUCHED Alex's knee and said, 'That building was a bakery when I was a boy. Hell, I think it was still one till about 1985.'

Will had parked his Explorer in the bay of a defunct auto repair shop, where it commanded a good view of the dog-breeding facility owned by 'Noel D. Traver'. The building had a large parking lot surrounded by a chain-link fence topped with glittering spirals of razor wire. The only vehicle there was a panel truck parked with its rear towards the building. No one had been in or out since Alex and Will had arrived two hours ago.

The SIM card in Alex's notebook computer made a connection to the Internet, then lost it. She slammed her hand against the door in frustration. She'd been trying to get online to see if Jamie was logged on to MSN.

'I'm worried,' she said. 'I haven't talked to Jamie for forty-eight hours.'

'He'll be all right,' Will said.

Alex's cell started ringing. John Kaiser. She expelled a lungful of air in frustration, then pressed SEND. 'Hello, John.'

'Christ, Alex, I've been trying to get you for hours. Where are you?'

She grimaced, then recited her lie. 'I'm at the hotel taking care of Chris. Anything new on the background checks?'

'Shane Lansing looks clean to me. Typical surgeon. Son of a lawyer, big ladies' man. Like Rusk, he's invested in a lot of different ventures. The radiology clinic in Meridian is a legitimate concern, and though he could get access to radioactive material, he seems the least likely killer of the bunch.'

'And Tarver?'

'Eldon Tarver was born in 1946, in Oak Ridge, Tennessee, the illegitimate son of an army officer. He was dumped at the Lutheran Children's Home in Greenwood, Tennessee. At age seven he was adopted by a family from Sevierville, in the Smoky Mountains. It's commercialised now, but in the 1950s it was where the snake churches were based.'

'Snake churches?' echoed Alex, and Will's eyes swivelled towards her.

'Fundamentalist congregations that use poisonous snakes in their worship services. Drink strychnine, that kind of crap. I don't know if Tarver saw any of that, but his foster father was a lay preacher. Eldon went to the University of Tennessee on a full scholarship. That got him out of Vietnam. While I was running through rice paddies, Tarver was doing high-level graduate research in microbiology. Data's pretty scarce for that part of his life. In 1974, he went to work for a major pharmaceutical company. They fired him less than a year later. In 1976 he went to medical school. He's board-certified in multiple specialties, including pathology and haematology. He took the job at UMC in 1985, and he married a biochemistry professor there two years later. She died in 1998, of cervical cancer. You know the rest.' He hesitated. 'I think we've got a weird one, all right.'

Will grabbed Alex's knee and pointed through the windshield. Sixty yards away, a red van was nosing through the gate of the parking lot.

'Chris needs me,' Alex said, trying to make out the licence plate of the van. It was too far away and the angle was bad.

'One more thing,' said Kaiser. 'Noel Traver is a real mystery man. On paper, he didn't even exist prior to ten years ago, as far as I can tell, and his residence appears to be the same address as that dog-breeding facility.'

'I really need to run, John. Anything else?'

Kaiser laughed. 'Yeah, one thing. Just make sure you don't do something stupid, like break into Tarver's house or that breeding facility.'

Alex laughed, hoping it didn't ring hollow. 'I wish,' she said. 'Keep pushing for that search warrant.' She hung up before he could reply.

'Did you hear that?' asked Will. 'The driver just honked his horn.'

The red van had pulled up to a large aluminium door set in the side of the old bakery. As Alex stared, the door rose until it was high enough for the van to pull inside the building.

'Son of a bitch,' said Will. 'I think somebody's been in there all along.'

The overhead door stayed up but the van didn't pull inside.

In frustration, Alex grabbed her computer from the floor and took it out of hibernation yet again. This time she got an Internet connection. She checked MSN Messenger, but Jamie wasn't logged on.

'What did Kaiser tell you?' Will asked.

'Not much. Oh, he said there was a gap in the years when Tarver was in college or grad school. During Vietnam. Late Vietnam . . .' Alex murmured.

'What?'

'Something Dr Tarver said to me in his office. About a research project he worked on . . . to do with combat veterans and cancer.' She closed her eyes and saw the photograph of Tarver and the military officer again. 'VCP,' she said, scrunching her eyes tight. 'The letters were embroidered on Tarver's lab coat.'

'What are you talking about?' asked Will.

'An acronym,' she said, suddenly recalling Tarver's explanation. 'The Veterans' Cancer Project.'

Alex typed 'VCP' into the Google search field and hit ENTER. A plethora of results appeared, related only by their sharing the same acronym. Next she typed 'VCP' plus 'cancer'. The first few hits concerned a research project in

India. But the fifth started her pulse racing. The words following the acronym were Virus Cancer Program. She clicked the link, and began to read.

The VCP was a massive research effort involving some of the most distinguished scientists in the United States, all probing the possible viral origins of cancer, particularly leukaemia . . .

'My God,' Alex breathed, eyes scanning the screen.

. . . Government records confirm that tens of thousands of litres of dangerous new viruses were cultured in the bodies of living animals, and that many of these viruses were modified so as to be able to jump species barriers. In 1973, a significant part of the Virus Cancer Program was transferred to Fort Detrick, Maryland, the home of the United States biological warfare effort . . .

'This is it,' said Alex. 'Holy shit, this is it!'

'What are you yelping about?' Will asked, staring hard at her screen.

'Dr Tarver lied to me! VCP doesn't stand for Veterans' Cancer Project. It stands for Virus Cancer Program, a government project during the Vietnam era that researched links between viruses and cancer. Eldon Tarver worked for them! And he's using what he learned to kill people, and make money off Andrew Rusk and his desperate clients. We've *got* them, Will!'

'Look!' Will said, gripping her wrist. 'Son of a bitch!'

Alex looked up. The panel truck and the van had disappeared, and the big aluminium door was sliding back down to the concrete slab.

'I think Tarver is shutting everything down. I went to his office and declared myself as an FBI agent. I went to his so-called free clinic. I even gave him a list of the murder victims, for God's sake. And I asked him about the VCP picture! He *knows* I'll figure it out eventually. He's going to run, Will.' She laid her computer on the back seat and reached for the door handle.

'Wait!' cried Will, restraining her. 'If you've got him nailed with evidence, there's no point in screwing up by going in without a warrant.'

'I'm going in there. Are you coming or not?'

Will sighed, and opened the glove box to take out his .357 magnum. Then he stopped. 'Wait. The gate's open, ain't it? We're better off driving up to the front door and telling them we're lost than sneaking in there with guns.'

Alex grinned. 'I knew I brought you for a reason.'

Will pulled across the street, and as he drove through the gate of the old bakery, Alex dialled John Kaiser's cellphone.

'Hey,' said Kaiser. 'What's up?'

'I've cracked it, John! The whole case. You need to check out something called the Virus Cancer Program, a big research project in the late sixties. Tarver was part of it. There's a photo in his office of him wearing a lab coat that says VCP. When I asked him what it stood for he lied to me.'

'I'll get onto it. The SAC is still stalling on the search warrant for Tarver's house. Maybe this will tip the scales.' Kaiser hung up.

The Explorer was only twenty yards from the old bakery.

'Park in front of those casement windows,' Alex told Will.

When the car stopped, she got out and walked up to the windows. Most of the panes were blacked out, and the clear ones were too high to look through.

'Can you give me a step up?'

Will walked over, shoved his pistol into his pants, then bent at the waist and interlocked his fingers. Alex stepped onto them, caught hold of the brick sill and pulled herself up to a windowpane. She pressed her eye to the glass and saw a wall of cages. Dozens of them. And inside each one, a sleeping dog.

'You see anything yet?' Will asked.

'Dogs. A bunch of dogs asleep in cages.'

'That's what they breed here.'

'I know but . . . there's something odd about it. There must be a hundred of them. And they're *all* asleep. Maybe they drug them.'

As Alex peered into the room, the sound of a distant engine reached her, its tone rising steadily. Even before she saw the red van racing towards the fenced perimeter, her instincts kicked in.

'*Run!*' she shouted, leaping backwards off Will's hands.

'What is it?' he gasped.

'*RUN!*' Alex grabbed his arm and started dragging him away.

They were thirty feet from the building when a scorching wall of air slapped them to the ground. Alex screamed for Will, but she heard only a roar of flame.

It took her a minute to get her breath back. Then she rolled over and sat up.

Will was on his knees a few yards away, trying in vain to pull a large splinter of glass out of his back. Behind him, a vast column of black smoke climbed into the sky. All the front windows were gone and the heat emanating from the roaring building was almost unbearable. As she struggled to her feet, an inhuman shriek of terror echoed across the parking lot and a dark simian shape burst from the building, trailing smoke and fire.

Alex staggered three steps towards Will, then fell on her face.

Chapter 11

Andrew Rusk had taken two Valium, a Lorcet, and a beta blocker, yet his heart was still pounding. His head was worse.

'But I don't *understand*,' his wife Lisa said for the eighth time in as many minutes.

'Those men outside,' Rusk said, pointing to the dark patio windows of the house. 'They're FBI agents.'

'How do you know that? Maybe they're IRS or something.'

'I know because I know.'

'But I mean *Cuba*?' Lisa whined. 'It's not even American, is it?'

'*Shhh*,' Rusk hissed, squeezing her upper arm. 'You have to whisper.'

She jerked the arm away and retreated to the sofa. He knelt before her and took her hand. He had to convince her. Because they had to get out of the country, and fast. Thora Shepard's body was lying under a dust sheet in the back of his Cayenne. If the FBI agents broke into the locked garage, it was all over. But he needed Glykon's help to break free of the surveillance.

'What have you done, Andy? You said it was some kind of tax thing. How pissed off can the government be about that?'

What have I done? I killed a woman who looked a lot like you, only better. And if you keep this up, I might just kill you, too.

He glanced worriedly at the dark windows. 'You don't understand these things, Lisa. The simple truth is, we don't have a choice. We can move to Costa Rica when the heat's off. And Costa Rica is a goddamn paradise.'

She gave him a long cold stare. 'Maybe *you* don't have a choice. But *I* haven't done anything. I can stay right here until it's safe in Costa Rica. Then I can join you there.'

Rusk stared, incredulous. She sounded just like Thora Shepard! 'Baby, once we get there, you'll see how great it is. Now go and pack a suitcase.'

Lisa spoke through clenched teeth. '*I'm—not—going*. You can't make me. And if you try, I'll file for divorce.'

Rusk was stunned. She had to be bluffing. He'd written an ironclad prenup. If she divorced him, she'd get almost nothing. Except that over the past three years, he had transferred considerable assets into her name. It had made a lot of sense at the time. But now . . . now he saw himself as a sucker, like one of his pathetic clients. Before he realised what he was doing, he had slid his right hand up to her throat.

'One more inch and I'll scream,' she said evenly. 'And when those FBI guys bust in here, I'll tell them about every tax scam you ever pulled.'

Rusk stood and backed away from his wife. It doesn't matter, he told himself. To hell with her. As long as I get out of the country, it doesn't matter what she does. She can have a few million. There's plenty more for me. If only Glykon would show up. He walked towards the hall, meaning to check his email on the computer in his study, but as soon as he entered the hall he saw a massive shape silhouetted by the light spilling from the study.

'Hello, Andrew,' said Glykon. 'It's pretty crowded outside. Did you give up on me?'

Rusk couldn't see the doctor's face, but he heard the cool amusement in that voice. Nothing rattled this guy. 'Can we get out?' he asked, trying to sound calm. 'I mean, have you got something figured?'

Glykon unslung a large backpack from his shoulder and dropped it to the ground. 'Have you ever known me to not have things figured, Andrew?'

Rusk shook his head. This was true, though he couldn't remember them ever being in this kind of spot before.

'I appreciated this afternoon's email about Alexandra Morse. I'd suspected that she was acting on her own, but I had no idea that the Bureau was going to terminate her. Most convenient.'

Glykon turned towards the study. 'Call Lisa in here, Andrew. We need to get started.'

Rusk started to ask why the study, but then he realised it was because the room had no windows. He looked over his shoulder. 'Lisa? Come here.'

'You come here,' came the petulant reply.

'*Lisa.* We've got company.'

'Oh, all right. I'm coming.'

With Glykon's miraculous arrival, Rusk felt the pleasing return of male superiority. Meaning to say something witty, he turned back towards the doctor only to see the pistol rise as Glykon shot him in the chest.

ALEX STRUGGLED UP out of a dark sea into piercing white light.

'Alex?' said a deep voice.

Gradually the blur above her coalesced into the worried face of John Kaiser. 'You're in the emergency room at UMC,' he said. 'You've got a pretty serious concussion, but otherwise you seem to be all right.'

'Where's Will?' she asked, gripping the FBI agent's hand. 'Tell me he's not dead.'

'He's not. They stitched up his back and admitted him for twenty-four hours' observation. They're doing the same to you.'

She tried to sit up, but a wave of nausea rolled through her stomach. Kaiser eased her back down onto the examining table.

'I'm sorry I lied to you, John. I know you told me not to go there.'

'Stop wasting your energy. I should have known you'd go, no matter what. In your place, I probably would have gone, too.'

'What the hell happened? A bomb?'

'You tell me.'

She shook her head, trying to remember. 'All I know is, I was looking inside at dogs, lots of them, and they were all asleep. And it just seemed *wrong*. Then I heard an engine, and out of the corner of my eye I caught sight of a van racing away. Then I just *knew*, you know? I knew that somehow Noel Traver *was* Eldon Tarver, that Tarver was running away and that he had let me get that close because he meant to take me out, along with whatever evidence was in that building. Did you get the warrant for his house?' Alex asked. 'Or is the SAC still stonewalling?'

Kaiser sighed. 'Not completely. We got the warrant for Tarver's home, and there's a team there now. But so far they've found nothing.'

'Nothing tying him to Rusk?'

Kaiser shook his head. 'But the VCP stuff you uncovered is mind-blowing. That and the explosion at the breeding facility convinced Tyler to allow the search warrant. We just need to find evidence fresher than thirty years old.'

'What about Rusk? You should search his residence and his office.'

'Tyler won't budge on that. He keeps saying there's no probable cause that would allow us to investigate Rusk. But don't worry, Rusk is bottled up in his house right now, and I've got six agents covering the place.'

'No idea where Dr Tarver is?'

'None.'

'Thora Shepard?'

Kaiser looked embarrassed. 'She was in Rusk's office this afternoon, but somehow she must have slipped out without our guys seeing her.'

'What about Chris?'

'Dr Shepard is here in the hospital. He called 911 from the hotel with a high fever and dehydration, and when he got here he asked for an old med-school classmate, Dr Clarke.'

A stab of fear went through her. 'My mother's oncologist?'

'Yes. Between Dr Clarke and Tom Cage, they managed to check Chris into the oncology unit here. Just a few doors down from your mother.'

Alex could scarcely comprehend it. 'What about Chris's son? Is he OK?'

'Dr Shepard was almost delirious when he arrived, but he kept asking about the boy—and you, by the way. He finally managed to make a call. Ben's fine.'

Alex struggled to see all angles of the situation through the fog in her mind. 'Thora's got to be out of her mind with fear. And she's a major threat to Andrew Rusk and his accomplice. What if she never left that building, John? What if Rusk killed her up there?'

'I guess it's possible. Do you think they'd move that quickly?'

'Two words: William Braid.'

Kaiser grimaced. 'All right, I'll get some people searching that tower.'

'Officially?'

'No. But if we find a corpse, the case will break wide open. We can haul Rusk in and put his feet to the fire.' He squeezed her shoulder. 'I'm going now. It's time you got some rest.'

Alex snorted in contempt. 'You know I can't sleep with all this going on.'

Kaiser shook his head in exasperation, but Alex could see he was glad to see her healthy enough to argue with him.

'If you'll get them to discharge me,' she said, 'I promise I won't leave the hospital. I'll spend the night in my mother's room. That way, I can keep an eye on both her and Chris.'

Kaiser stared at her for a long time. 'Stay here,' he said finally. 'Stay right here, as in *do not move*. I'll see what I can do.'

ANDREW RUSK BLINKED awake to find himself duct-taped to the chair behind his desk. His mouth was taped shut. Lisa was sitting opposite him on the leather sofa, her slim wrists and ankles taped together, a silver rectangle of tape sealing her lips.

Glykon stood between Lisa and the desk, a maniacal light shining from his eyes, both arms held high above his head. In his hands, twisting and curling round his muscular forearms, were two thick, black snakes.

A bolt of terror shot through him when he felt the agony radiating from his sternum and saw two spots of blood on his shirt. But then he saw a shining tangle of silver wires near Glykon's feet. *Taser wires*. Now he remembered the gun coming up in the hallway . . . the nearly point-blank shot at his chest. It was a stun gun. That was how Tarver had got him into this chair. The doctor sat down and faced Rusk. The snake nearest Andrew had a diamond-shaped head and bulging poison sacs beneath its eyes. *Cottonmouth moccasin*, he thought in terror.

'I'm sure by now you've worked out exactly why I'm here, Andrew.' Rusk shook his head, but he knew all right. Glykon wanted the diamonds. 'No?' said the doctor. 'Perhaps you're a little distracted by my friends.'

He stretched out his right arm until the snake's head was within striking distance of Rusk's face. The pupil's of the moccasin's eyes were vertical ellipses, like cats' eyes. As though sensing his fear, the cottonmouth opened its huge mouth to reveal lethal two-inch fangs.

'Where are the diamonds, Andrew,' Glykon said in a voice of eminent reasonableness. 'Or perhaps your lovely bride likes serpents better than you do.' He stepped towards Lisa, huddled on the sofa, whimpering steadily.

'These are sacred creatures, Lisa,' the doctor murmured. 'I'm sure that, through your provincial eyes, you see the serpent of the Christian garden, who so easily corrupted Eve'—he bent and caressed Lisa's thighs with a scaly tail—'but that's such a *limited* view.'

The scream that burst from Lisa's diaphragm ballooned her taped-shut lips and trumpeted from her nostrils.

Laughing quietly, Glykon took two steps back, opened the mouth of a sack with his foot, then dipped and thrust one of the moccasins into the bag. Stepping on the mouth of the moving sack, he pulled it tight with a drawstring. Then, caressing the head of the remaining snake, he addressed Rusk again. 'I'm going to partly remove the tape from your lips, Andrew. You will not scream. You will not plead for your life or hers. I know the stones are here. I know your escape plan, remember? I set it up. But it's time to let go of your banana-republic dream and save yourself.'

He pulled an inch of tape from the corner of Rusk's mouth. In a parched croak, the lawyer said, 'You're going to kill me no matter what I do.'

Glykon shook his head. Then he picked up a putter that Rusk kept to practice his golf and teased the moccasin with its padded handle. 'He's a fearsome killer, *Agkistrodon piscivorus*,' said the doctor, as the snake bared its fangs and struck at the club. 'The venom is a haemotoxin, a complex mix of proteins that starts destroying blood cells and dissolving vascular walls the instant it enters your flesh. It even dissolves muscle tissue. The pain, I'm told, is beyond description. Within hours gangrene sets in, and the skin turns black. Are you sure you don't want to change your mind?'

Rusk stared back at Glykon. No matter what the doctor promised, he meant to kill them tonight. To Rusk's surprise, this knowledge freed him from much of his fear. He was willing to die in agony, but he wasn't willing to let his partner steal the fruits of five years' labour. Rusk looked steadily at his partner and said, 'The diamonds aren't here.'

What happened next blasted all his logic to hell. Glykon leaned over Lisa, rapped the snake on the snout with the golf club, then let it go. The moccasin struck in a blur, hitting Lisa in the upper chest. When the blur stopped, the snake's jaws were clenched tight round Lisa's forearm. She leapt up from the sofa and flung her bound arms around like a woman possessed. The snake let go, and its heavy body thudded against a row of books.

Glykon was on the snake in a moment. He distracted it with the flashing head of the putter, then grabbed it behind its head and held it high.

Lisa had collapsed onto the sofa and was now staring at two puncture wounds in her forearm. Her breathing grew more and more frantic.

'You see the consequences of noncooperation,' said the doctor. 'I'm going to give you one more chance, Andrew. Before I do, I shall explain something. I have no intention of killing you. That would create a host of problems for me. Your EX NIHILO mechanism, for example. Not to mention a murder investigation. But if I leave you alive, your hands are tied by your own guilt. The way it's always been. You see? You can survive this night. Your diamonds are the price of life. And what's money weighed against thirty or forty more years of life? You have plenty of time to earn more. But I don't. I must take what life offers.' Glykon came around the desk and sat only inches away from him. 'Put your trust in logic, Andrew. I'm much safer with you alive than with you dead. Now are you ready to tell me where they are?'

Rusk looked across the room to where Lisa lay shivering on the sofa, still staring at the holes in her arm. 'I'll tell you. But what about Lisa?'

'After I leave, drive her to the hospital. Tell them she was bitten while watering your lawn. Use your imagination.' Glykon reached out with his free hand and pulled Rusk's chin until they were eye to eye. 'It's time.'

'Under my bed,' Rusk whispered. 'In a flight case.'

Tarver laughed. 'You keep them under your bed?'

'I buried them like you said. But I dug them up this afternoon.'

'Good decision, Andrew.'

Glykon walked round the desk and stuffed the second cottonmouth into the sack with its mate. Then he resealed the tape over Rusk's mouth and walked out of the study.

A soft mewling rose from the other side of the desk. Rusk desperately wanted to help his wife, but the duct tape made it impossible.

A creaking floorboard announced Glykon's return. Grinning though his beard, the doctor set the heavy flight case down on Rusk's desk with a bang and pulled a small knife from his pocket. 'I'm cutting the tape on her wrists about three-quarters through,' the doctor said. 'She should be able to rip it the rest of the way in a few minutes—if you can keep her conscious.'

As Rusk struggled against the tape binding his arms, the doctor shouldered his backpack, picked up a nearby Pelican case and strode out.

Rusk flexed his jaw muscles hard, and the tape came loose. 'Lisa!' he cried. 'Can you hear me? Rip the tape off your hands. You've got to do it before you pass out. You've got to save us, baby.'

No response.

Rusk heard shifting body weight. Then he heard the blessed sound of adhesive coming loose. A low, inhuman moan filled the study.

'Lisa? Are you loose? Do your feet! Honey, can you hear me?'

Now the sound of tape coming loose was continuous.

'That's it, honey. I knew you could do it. Now get up and get me loose.'

The woman who stood up on the other side of the desk was almost unrecognisable. She looked like someone who had been dragged through the pit of hell. Her mouth hung open in mindless stupor.

'Lisa, can you hear me? I've got to get you to the hospital. There's a pocket-knife on the end table by the sofa. The one I got for a wedding present.'

A flicker of recognition in her eyes? *Yes!*

With the slow tread of a zombie, she walked to the table. She bent down. But when she came up, she was not holding the pocketknife.

'Lisa? Get the *knife,* honey. That's a golf club you're holding.'

She looked down at the putter and said softly, 'I know.'

As she walked towards the desk, Lisa lifted the putter high above her head. Then she swung it in a long arc. Strapped into the chair, Rusk could only tense as it smashed into his cranium.

ALEX LET GO of her mother's hand and quietly left the hospital room. She had sat there for the best part of an hour, talking quietly most of the time, but there'd been no response. Margaret Morse had reached the point where an ending was better than continuing, and her sedation was deep.

Alex's hospital slippers hissed along the floor as she passed the five doors that separated her mother's room from Chris's. To her surprise, she found him awake. As she leaned over his bed, she saw tears on his face.

She took his hand. 'What's the matter?'

'I just talked to Mrs Johnson. Ben's pretty upset,' Chris said. 'Thora hasn't called him, and he's picked up from my voice that something's wrong.'

Alex laid her hand on his arm. 'You need to know, Will overheard Thora telling Rusk to call off the hit on you. It's time to arrest her, Chris.'

Confusion filled his eyes. 'She tried to call it off?'

'Only because she knew you were onto her. Frankly, I think she needs to be arrested for her own protection. She's a threat to Rusk and Tarver.'

'But who would take care of Ben if Thora's arrested?'

'Mrs Johnson?' Alex suggested.

Chris shook his head. 'I'd rather Tom Cage and his wife do it. Tom will know what to do if things get crazy.'

She nodded. 'I'll call him for you. You lie back and take it easy.'

'I don't want Ben to see his mother arrested.'

'I know. And I don't think he will. But the alternative could be a lot worse.' She leant down and touched his cheek. 'I know it looks hopeless. But you're going to have a life again. You'll share it with Ben, too.'

He closed his eyes, and as she stroked his burning forehead, she was struck by the terrible possibility he might not live through the night.

JOHN KAISER CLIMBED into the back of a black Chevy Suburban parked at the edge of Andrew Rusk's property. Five agents from the Jackson field office were waiting in the Suburban—three men and two women. One of them had reported that the lawyer had not yet left for the office that morning—he was usually regular as clockwork. This had got Kaiser's attention.

'We don't have a warrant yet,' he said, 'so I'm going to go up and knock on the front door. If no one answers, I want you to spread out and check the windows. See if you can find probable cause for us to go in. Understood?'

Everyone nodded.

The Suburban rolled smoothly through the trees to the front of Rusk's home. Kaiser got out, walked up onto the porch and pressed the bell.

No one came to the door.

He rang the bell again. Another minute passed.

'OK,' he called, already filled with foreboding. 'Move out.'

All the doors of the Chevy opened simultaneously, and the agents dispersed around the house. Kaiser rang the bell again. Then he walked down the porch steps and began to circle the house.

'Around here!' shouted a female agent. 'The kitchen!'

Kaiser started running. 'What is it?'

The agent drew back from the window, her face pale. 'Looks like a female, face down on the floor. Car keys in her right hand, and a little blood beneath it. That's the only blood I see.'

Kaiser pressed his face to the glass. 'Wait five minutes, then call the state police and the sheriff's department. That sure looks like probable cause to me.'

ALEX PULLED her rented Corolla to a halt alongside the mass of law-enforcement vehicles parked outside the Rusk house. She knew Kaiser would be furious—when he'd rung to tell her the lawyer and his wife had been found dead, he'd ordered her to stay away. But after six weeks of blood, sweat and tears, she could not sit idle while others picked up the baton. Besides, she rationalised, Kaiser can't give me orders if I'm no longer an FBI agent.

She strode past a cordon of sheriff's deputies unchallenged. In less than a minute, she was in the study where what remained of Rusk was still taped to his chair. Crouched behind him were two men, one of whom was John Kaiser, and beyond them she could see the blue glow of a cutting torch. After a minute, she heard a grunt of triumph, then Kaiser stood up and turned.

'Goddamn it,' he said with genuine annoyance. 'Don't you ever listen?'

'This is my case,' she said doggedly.

'You don't have any cases! Do you get that? I'm only here myself because I told the sheriff that there might be biological weapons in this house, and that we needed to check before they do their homicide investigation.'

'What's in that safe?'

'We're about to find out. Meanwhile, look at the notepad on the desk.'

She did. Scrawled on the pad in pencil were some numbers. 'What is this?' she asked. 'It looks like GPS coordinates.'

'I think they are. And a time and date.'

She read the numbers again. 'Jesus, that's today.'

'Yep. Two p.m. I think your lawyer friend was about to bug out of town. One of our guys thinks the coordinates are on the Gulf Coast, if not actually in the Gulf of Mexico.'

The man with the torch laid some papers out on the floor, and Kaiser knelt to examine the contents of the safe.

'Anything good?' Alex asked.

'Would you call two Costa Rican passports good?'

'We have an extradition treaty with Costa Rica now.'

'Yes, but these passports aren't in the Rusks' names.'

'But they have the Rusks' photos?'

'Yep. Take a look.'

She moved forward and leaned over his shoulder. Kaiser was right. She took one of the passports and compared the smiling photo of Andrew Rusk to the bloody corpse in the chair to her left. She looked back at Kaiser, who was wading through insurance policies, wills, deeds . . .

'What else have you got?'

'Looks like a yacht to me,' Kaiser said, holding up a photograph.

Alex looked at the snapshot. 'You could sail around the world in that.'

Kaiser held up a sheet of paper and gave a low whistle. 'This piece of paper grants safe passage through Cuban territorial waters, and permission to dock at the marina in Havana. It's signed by Fidel Castro's brother, Raúl. The defence minister. The document is made out to Eldon Tarver, MD.'

Alex took the paper and read it line by line, her pulse beating faster with every word. 'This is a photocopy.'

'What it is,' Kaiser said, 'is proof that Andrew Rusk and Eldon Tarver were working together.'

Alex swallowed hard and handed the paper back to Kaiser. 'Why would Raúl Castro give Tarver permission to emigrate to Cuba?'

Kaiser looked at her. 'The Virus Cancer Program. Viral bioweapons. I'll bet the Cuban DGI offered Tarver money to come work for them. Tarver must have figured Cuba would be a good place to lie low for a while, until it was safe to transfer to Costa Rica under a different name.'

'So what do you think happened here?' Alex asked, tilting her head towards Rusk's corpse. 'Do you think Tarver did this?'

'Had to be him. Medical examiner says the wife died from a snakebite. She was bitten twice. On the forearm and on the chest, just above the heart.'

'My God.' Alex shuddered at the idea. She gazed around the room. 'Did you find that legal pad on the desk? The one with the coordinates on it?'

'No. That was found on top of the kitchen refrigerator, hidden underneath a serving tray. Also, a tech found a rectangular hole out in the garden. Looks like something had been dug up recently.'

'Cash?' she speculated.

Kaiser looked sceptical. 'I'm guessing something more durable. Gold, maybe. They found a hole in the earth at Tarver's house, too. Last night.'

'Really? These guys were pulling up stakes.'

'Sir?' said a tech who was examining the study with a powerful light. 'I've got something on the floor here. Looks like the victim tried to write something with his foot. Here in the blood.' The man leaned closer to the floor. 'It looks like . . . "A's number twenty-three".' The number sign, I mean, not the word *number.*'

'Make sure you photograph it,' Kaiser said. He took Alex by the arm and led her out of the study. 'It's too bad his wife didn't make it to the hospital. I think she was just collateral damage.'

'Why didn't she just dial 911?'

'Phone was dead. Somebody cut the wires outside.'

'With your agents watching the place?'

Kaiser nodded, then paused before the front door. 'This guy slipped right through six FBI agents. In and out without a sound. He is a formidable suspect.' Kaiser took hold of Alex's shoulders and looked deep into her eyes,. 'Listen to me. You *have* to stay out of this. At least until we figure out how we're going to handle it. This case just became a matter of national security. If Webb Tyler finds out you were here . . . let's not even go there.'

He was about to usher her out when one of the agents asked Kaiser to go with him to take a call. When Kaiser returned, he looked tense.

'That was Dodson. Webb Tyler informed him that I was taking "unauthorised measures" in a case that belonged to the Mississippi authorities. I told him about the clandestine primate lab we discovered yesterday, and how it appears Eldon Tarver was conducting genetic experiments there. That brought him up short for a moment. But then he said that the Bureau received multiple complaints from Rusk before his death that he was being persecuted by you because you blamed him for your sister's death. He also says that one Neville Byrd has been apprehended in a downtown hotel with surveillance equipment in his possession. Claimed to have been hired by one Alexandra Morse to watch the office of Andrew Rusk. At double his normal rates.'

Alex gasped in disbelief and shook her head in denial. 'I've never even heard of the guy. I swear to God.'

Kaiser stared into Alex's eyes. 'And then I read him the document we found in the safe—you are *so* goddamned lucky that was in there.'

'And you're not lucky, too? Thanks, by the way.'

Kaiser laughed. 'You don't get many paybacks like that in this life.'

'Did you tell Dodson about the GPS coordinates?'

'Had to. There's no holding back anything now. It's all going to be kicked upstairs to Director Roberts. We only won a skirmish, not the war.'

'It still feels good.'

Kaiser started to walk towards the Suburban.

'Where are we going now?' Alex asked.

'You're going back to the hospital. I'll get one of my guys to drive your car back. And don't even think about arguing. I'm going to see this guy who claims you hired him to watch Rusk.' Kaiser got into the big car. 'I'm betting Tarver hired him. To make sure his partner wasn't crossing him, you know?'

Alex nodded. As a coroner's wagon rolled by, she asked, 'Did you tell Dodson about the writing on the floor? "A's number twenty-three"?'

Kaiser said nothing.

Alex couldn't suppress her delight. 'I thought you weren't holding anything back any more?'

'Screw that precious little bastard.'

'Amen.'

A young FBI agent rapped on Kaiser's window. 'They sent me to get you, sir. They found a body in the trunk of Rusk's car.'

Kaiser put the Suburban in park. 'Stay here, Alex.'

She slammed the dashboard with her hand as Kaiser ran back to the house. Then she counted to five, got out, and sprinted after him.

Chapter 12

Alex stood outside Chris's room, wiping her eyes with Kleenex. She was trying to summon the courage to walk in and tell him that his wife was dead.

'May I help you, ma'am?' asked a passing nurse.

'No, thank you.' Alex pocketed the Kleenex and walked into the room.

When she saw him shivering in the bed, she told herself that this was the wrong time to tell him about Thora. What good could it possibly do?

'Alex?' he whispered. 'Come closer. I don't think I'm contagious.'

She walked over to his bed, took his shaking hands in hers and kissed him on the cheek. 'I know.'

He responded with a weak smile. 'Sympathy kiss?'

'Maybe.' She wanted to distract him, but she didn't know how. 'So Ben has gone to stay at Dr Cage's house?'

'Yeah. Tom's wife is great. She offered to take him soon as she heard the situation.'

'What about the chemotherapy? Have you taken any chemo drugs?'

'No. After what I've learned about the Virus Cancer Program—and Tarver's primate lab—I'm more convinced than ever that he injected me with some sort of retrovirus. No virus can induce cancer in a matter of days, so the way to attack it right now is with antiviral drugs.'

Alex squeezed his hands. 'I think you just don't want to lose your hair.'

He closed his eyes, but the ghost of a smile touched his lips.

'Are we friends, Chris?' she asked softly.

His eyes opened, questioning her without words. 'Of course we are. I owe you my life. If I live through this, that is.'

'I've got to tell you something else about Thora.'

'Oh, God,' he said wearily. 'What has she done?' Sudden fear flashed in his eyes. 'She hasn't taken Ben, has she?'

Alex shook her head. 'No. Thora's dead, Chris.'

He stared up from the pillow without changing expression.

'Somebody killed her. We're not sure who yet. Probably Rusk or Tarver.'

Chris blinked once. 'Killed her how?'

'She was beaten to death. Probably with a hammer.'

Alex saw despair in his eyes, then he rolled over to face the wall as though in denial of the news. But she knew he believed her.

'I didn't want to tell you,' she said helplessly, 'but the idea of someone else telling you was worse.'

'Ben doesn't know, does he?'

'No, no.'

'I need to see him.'

Alex had already taken care of this. 'He's on his way.' She glanced at her watch. 'He should be here any minute, actually. I called Tom Cage as soon as we—as soon as I knew. Tom went to check Ben out of school, and he promised to have him here as fast as possible.'

Chris sighed heavily, and turned back to face her. 'Thank you for doing that. Tom will know how to handle Ben. Now you've got to try to find Tarver.'

'They won't let me. They've turned me into a goddamn bystander.'

'So? You never waited for permission before. And the only way you're going to save your nephew—or me—is by nailing him. Only he can convict your brother-in-law. And only he can tell the doctors what he shot into me. Without that knowledge, I'll die before Ben grows out of Little League.'

Alex was stunned by the anger in Chris's voice and eyes. She was trying to think of a reassuring reply when her cellphone vibrated in her pocket. It was Kaiser. She pressed SEND and held the phone to her ear.

'I'm sitting with your alleged friend Neville Byrd,' he said. 'He's recanted his statements about you and admitted he was hired by Tarver.'

Alex closed her eyes in relief. 'How did you manage that?'

While Kaiser answered, Alex clicked her cellphone's speaker function, so that Chris could listen in.

'When Mr Byrd and his attorney heard the words *Patriot Act*, they became very talkative,' Kaiser said. 'But Tarver didn't hire Byrd just to keep tabs on Rusk. Rusk had set up a digital mechanism that would destroy Tarver in the event that Tarver killed him. Insurance, right? Byrd was hired to find out what that mechanism was.'

'And did he?' asked Alex.

'Yes. Rusk used a Dutch Internet service called EX NIHILO. Every day he had to log on and enter a series of passwords to verify that he was alive. If he didn't, a digital catalogue of every crime Rusk and Tarver had committed would be sent to the Bureau and the Mississippi State Police.'

'Dear God. Tell me you have that file, John.'

'I'm looking at it right now. But I can't open it because I don't have the final password. Rusk never accessed the file while Byrd was watching him. Neville's been trying to hack the password, but he hasn't been able to do it.'

'Do you have any idea what it could be?' Alex asked.

'What I'm thinking,' said Kaiser, 'is that after Dr Tarver smacked Rusk's head a few times with that putter, Rusk's last conscious thought was to get revenge on the bastard. He couldn't use the telephone, but he could move his foot enough to write in the blood on the floor.'

'A's number twenty-three!' Alex cried.

'Exactly. But what the hell does it refer to?'

'It can't be that hard,' said Alex. 'It's something Rusk thought we could figure out. What were his other passwords?'

'One was pi to the ninth decimal place. A couple were names from classical literature. One was the speed of light.'

Chris took hold of Alex's elbow and said, 'The only *A's number* I know about is Avogadro's number.'

'Who's that talking?' asked Kaiser.

'Chris,' Alex replied. 'What is Avogadro's number?' she asked the doctor.

'A constant in chemistry. It has to do with molar concentration. Every high school chemistry student has to memorise it. It's six-point-oh-two-two times ten to the twenty-third power.'

'The twenty-third power,' Alex echoed. ' "A's number twenty-three".'

'How would you type all that out?' asked Kaiser.

Chris looked at the ceiling. 'Six dot zero two two X one zero two three.'

'I heard him,' said Kaiser. 'Neville's typing it in.'

Alex waited.

'No dice,' said Kaiser, obviously deflated. 'That's not it.'

Alex closed her eyes.

'Try leaving out the decimal,' said Chris.

'All right,' said Kaiser from the phone's speaker. 'Byrd's trying it—'

Alex winced as a whoop of triumph came through the phone.

'That's it!' shouted Kaiser. 'We're in!'

Alex was squeezing the phone so tightly that her hand hurt. 'What does it say? What's in the file, John?'

'My God . . . it's a confession, all right. There's pages and pages of it.'

Alex caught Chris's hand in hers. 'Do you see Grace's name?'

'I'm looking . . . I see several of the victims you listed for me . . .' There was a pause. 'I see it,' Kaiser murmured. 'Grace Fennell.'

Alex felt tears streaming down her cheeks. The lump in her throat kept her from speaking until she managed to swallow. 'Copy that file *now*, John.'

'Neville already has,' he assured her. 'He's printing it out now.'

'What about me?' asked Chris.

'Here it is. Christopher Shepard, MD. It's all here, Alex. All the proof in the world. He says that he and Tarver murdered nineteen people.' Kaiser's voice quickened. 'Wait. I've just been handed a note. A deputy sheriff in Forrest County just spotted Andrew Rusk's powerboat. It's being towed on a trailer behind a black Dodge pick-up on Highway 49.'

'Did he see the driver?' Alex asked.

'A bald man with a grey beard and a bright birthmark on his left cheek.'

Alex's heart began to race. 'We've got him.'

'No, we don't. We know where he was fifteen minutes ago. Forrest County's on the way to the Gulf Coast, right?'

'Could be. Did you ever get the exact location for those GPS coordinates?'

'Yes,' said Kaiser. 'That location is *in* the Gulf of Mexico. Twenty-four miles south of Petit Bois Island.'

'Past the reach of the Coast Guard.' Alex looked at her watch. 'Two p.m. is less than two hours away.'

'Don't worry. I've got a chopper on standby,' Kaiser said, panting as though he were running. 'You get upstairs to the UMC helipad and I'll pick you up. We'll take six SWAT guys from Jackson and link up with some of my guys from the New Orleans office. I'll be there in ten minutes. You be waiting.'

'Don't you dare leave me behind. I don't care if the director forbids you on pain of termination. You set that chopper down on the UMC roof. Now, go!'

As she hung up, Chris was watching her, his body completely still.

'I need to go with him, Chris. I don't want to leave you alone, but—'

'I'm all right. You go get Tarver. And don't come back here until you have.'

Forcing down a rush of emotion, Alex waved goodbye and walked into the hall. She turned and ran towards the elevators. Ten steps down the hall she passed her mother's door, and slid to a stop. She darted into the room, squeezed her mother's hand and bent low beside her face.

'Mom?' she whispered. 'Jamie's going to be all right. You can go now.'

She prayed for a sign, a blinking eye or moving finger—but there was nothing. She kissed her mother's cheek, then fled the room.

ALEX LOOKED UP at the grey sky and searched for Kaiser's chopper. Feeling a vibration against her thigh, she took out her cellphone and looked at the LCD window. It read: 1 new message. When she opened the phone, she saw that the message was from Jamie. Finally! She hit READ. The message said:

Dad's packing our stuff! Says we're moving. 2DAY! Heard him talking 2 HER about Mexico. Can he take me 2 Mexico? He seems scared. I'm scared. Can u come get me? On computer. Dad wont let me call u.

Alex slammed the phone against her leg. Bill's timing was perfect, as usual. Her first reaction was to ask Kaiser to order the chopper to the Ross Barnett Reservoir to pick up Jamie, but of course she couldn't. Andrew Rusk's written confession would soon nail Bill Fennell's hide to the wall, but right this minute he had legal custody of the boy.

Alex had thought she was chasing down the man who'd murdered Grace, but now she realised that Tarver hadn't really murdered her sister. He was just the weapon. Bill Fennell was the real killer. And now, like Tarver, Bill was planning to flee the country—with Jamie in tow. That left Alex no choice. But she couldn't tell Kaiser. She might just have to commit a felony in the next half hour—a kidnapping. Kaiser couldn't be party to that.

She looked up at the sky again, then lifted the cellphone to her ear and called him. 'My mother's crashing, John,' she told him. 'All systems. She signed a DNR, so she's probably going to die soon. Can you believe it?'

'It's your call, Alex.' There was a short silence. 'Is she conscious?'

'In and out. Mostly out. But still . . . it's my mother, you know? I appreciate you getting me the chance. Just go without me. Nailing Tarver is the thing.'

'OK, Alex. I'm sorry about your mom!'

Alex ended the call and dialled Will Kilmer.

THE FBI HELICOPTER was thirty miles south of Jackson when the doubt gnawing in Kaiser's gut became intolerable. He dialled directory assistance, and got the number for the UMC. When UMC's switchboard operator came on the line, he identified himself as an FBI agent and demanded to speak to the chief nurse on the oncology floor.

'Hello?' said an irritated female voice. 'Who is this?'

'Special Agent John Kaiser of the FBI. We have a life-or-death emergency in progress, and it involves the daughter of one of your patients, Margaret Morse. Her daughter is Special Agent Alex Morse.'

'I haven't seen her since she ran out twenty minutes ago.'

'I see. Can you tell me, have you spoken to Agent Morse in the last few minutes and told her that her mother was dying?'

'No, sir. In fact, Mrs Morse seemed to be a little better this morning.'

Kaiser hung up, leaned over the pilot's helmet and spun his forefinger in a circle. 'Turn around!'

As the powerful Bell 430 banked over I-55, Kaiser dialled the Jackson field office and demanded to speak to a technical specialist.

'Yes, sir?' said a young voice.

'I need GPS coordinates on a cellphone, fast.' Kaiser read off Alex's cell number, then said, 'Call me back the instant you have them.'

'Will do, sir.'

Where the hell *was* Alex going? Kaiser wondered. Would she miss the chance of taking down the guy who killed her sister. Did she not believe that the man towing Rusk's boat towards the Gulf Coast was Tarver? Could someone have called and told her that? Had Will Kilmer discovered something at the last minute? Possibly. Then again, Alex's reason for bailing might be completely unrelated. But what could possibly be that important?

His phone was ringing. 'Hello?'

'I've got the coordinates, sir. That phone is at thirty-two degrees, twenty-five minutes and some-odd north; and ninety degrees, four minutes—'

'Just tell me where they are! Lay a map over those numbers!'

'We already did. It's Coachman's Road, near the Jackson Yacht Club. Right on the edge of the Ross Barnett Reservoir.'

'Would Rose's Bluff Drive be near there?'

'Yes, sir. Right there.'

Kaiser cut the connection. 'Her brother-in-law's house,' he muttered.

The pilot looked over at Kaiser, 'Where are we going, sir?'

Her nephew, Kaiser thought angrily. Is this some kind of custody crap? Jamie Fennell was the reason Alex had worked this case so hard and so recklessly. But . . . could Bill Fennell be helping Tarver to escape? Not if Tarver was driving down to the Gulf, he couldn't. But what if he wasn't? What if someone else had been driving that truck?

BILL FENNELL LIVED on the southwestern bank of the Ross Barnett Reservoir, fifty square miles of water that could kick up ocean-sized white-caps in a storm like the one that was on its way.

Alex and Will were roaring along Coachman's Road in a rented blue Nissan Titan that Will had substituted for his Explorer, which was recovering from the explosion at the primate lab. His .357 magnum was on the seat between them, and a shotgun lay on the back seat. Alex's borrowed Sig was in the glove box, and she had a Smith & Wesson .38 strapped to her left ankle.

'You get any more text messages?' Will asked.

'No. I just hope they haven't left yet,' she said. 'They've got to come out this way, right?'

'Not necessarily. There's half a dozen ways out of that neighbourhood.'

As the turbulent waters of the reservoir came into sight, Will turned south, heading along the spit of land that held the yacht club and the Fennell home. 'How do you want to play it?' he asked.

'We're going to ask nicely for Jamie,' said Alex. 'Then we're going to take him out of there. Bill will be arrested for murder before the day is out.' She pointed to an open wrought-iron gate fifty yards ahead. 'Slow down.'

Will did so and looked hard into her eyes. 'Before we go in, let me ask you one thing. What's the chance that we're walking into a trap?'

'That's why you're here,' she said softly. 'If I knew for sure it was just Bill, I wouldn't need anybody to help.'

Will sighed. 'That's what I figured.'

'I can go without you,' Alex said, meaning it. 'You can wait right here.'

The detective looked at her again. 'Honey, your daddy pulled me out of so many tight spots I couldn't begin to count 'em. I'm here now because he can't be. And I'm gonna do what I know he'd do. Let's go get that boy.'

He drove through the gate and round the long, sweeping drive that led to the rear of the Fennell mansion, a copy of a Louisiana plantation house with tall white columns and a wraparound porch. He parked behind a thick stand of trees a hundred yards from the house.

'This is far enough,' he said.

As Will switched off the engine, the rain that had been threatening for hours finally swept over the property in waves. Alex opened the glove box and took out the Sig, then got out into the driving rain and walked up to an oak tree. Will carried the shotgun loosely along his left leg, his pistol in his right hand. When he was beside her, they surveyed the house and grounds.

The mansion had been built facing the reservoir. In front of it, Alex knew, a pier ran far out over the reservoir, with a boathouse at the end of it.

'That's Bill's Hummer,' said Alex, pointing to a splash of yellow sticking out of the distant garage. 'He's got a pair of them. H1s.'

'I know. Used to see 'em when he dropped Jamie to go fishing with Jim.'

'I forgot you used to go with them sometimes.'

Will started marching across the open ground. 'Jamie's a good boy. Never liked his daddy much, though. Loud-mouthed prick, you ask me.'

'You know what I think,' said Alex, following closely.

They moved like shadows through the rain. When the house was twenty yards away, they halted behind some tall evergreen shrubs.

'Let's circle the house and try to get a look inside,' Will said.

They moved from behind the shrubs and started towards the right side of the house. Will pushed through the thick hedge below the porch, then climbed over the rail at the front corner of the house and waited for Alex.

Through the first window they saw only an empty room. They moved silently along the wall to the next window. Again, they saw nobody.

'Put your hands in the air,' said a commanding voice from behind them. 'I'm pointing a sawn-off twelve-gauge shotgun at your backs. Keep facing the wall, but toss your weapons back over the rail.'

'Where did he come from?' Will whispered from Alex's left.

The hedge, she realised. He was waiting behind the hedge.

Will half turned and in a tough voice said, 'Listen to me, Bill Fennell. You don't want to—'

'That's not Bill,' Alex told him.

Will looked over his shoulder, then closed his eyes and shook his head.

Alex had to admire Dr Tarver's strategy. He had sent the 'message from

Jamie', then waited behind the hedge to assess the response. Simple but brilliant. The question was, why was he here?

'Don't try to play hero, Pop,' said the doctor. 'You're past the age for it.'

Will muttered something unintelligible.

'And you, Agent Alex. You remember what it feels like to be hit with buckshot, don't you? So get those guns over the rail. *Now!*'

She could feel Will tensing beside her, like a cat preparing to spring. *Don't try it . . . you can't beat a bullet, not even buckshot—*

'Where's Jamie?' Alex asked, tossing the Sig over her shoulder.

'You'll see.'

Dear Lord, let him be alive . . .

'I love you, baby girl,' said the faintest whisper beside her.

Baby girl? That was what Will had called his daughter—

In the same motion that Will tossed his shotgun over his shoulder, he whirled away from Alex with all the speed that a seventy-year-old man could muster. He fired his pistol as he spun, trying to disorientate Tarver in order to buy Alex one last chance. Her hand was almost to the .38 in her ankle holster when the boom of the shotgun blotted out the reports of Will's pistol. When she came up with her .38, the smoking mouth of Dr Tarver's shotgun was only two feet from her eyes.

'It would be a shame to ruin the other half of your face,' he said.

Moving only her eyes, Alex glanced down to her right.

Will lay on his stomach, a dark pool spreading beneath him.

'*Aaahhhh*,' Alex moaned, her eyes stinging. 'You son of a bitch!'

'He chose his fate,' Dr Tarver said. 'Now, into the house. Go.' He pointed to the front of the house—the reservoir side.

As she walked, Alex stared along the pier, wondering if Bill's boat was in the boathouse. If she could get Jamie out of the house . . .

The front section of the wraparound porch was screened. She opened the door to the protected area, walked in, then stopped before the door that led to the main house. What nightmare lay on the other side of it?

'Go in,' Dr Tarver said.

She turned the knob and pushed open the stained cypress door.

Bill Fennell lay sprawled at the foot of the main staircase. His legs were bent at odd angles, and his mouth appeared to be frozen open. As Alex's eyes swept the room, frantically searching for Jamie, the shotgun barrel prodded her between the shoulder blades, driving her forward.

'Why did you kill him?'

'He's not dead,' said Dr Tarver. 'I sedated him.'

True or false? 'Where's Jamie?'

Tarver pointed the shotgun across the room to a corridor that led to the rear of the house. 'The laundry room.'

She braced herself for unendurable horror, then opened the slatted door.

Jamie was perched atop the washing machine, staring down at two black coils on the floor. It took Alex a moment to absorb the reality. The snakes were thick and short, with big triangular heads. *Cottonmouth moccasins*—

'Aunt Alex!' Jamie cried, his eyes flashing. 'You came!'

She forced herself to grin. 'I sure did, buddy.' She turned back to Dr Tarver and hissed, '*You sadist.*'

Tarver chuckled. 'The boy's fine. See those cases?'

He'd gestured at two large waterproof cases, one yellow, the other white. Pelicans, Alex thought. The kind of cases engineers used to haul expensive gear around the world.

'Carry them to the front of the house. Move it.'

'I'll be back, Jamie,' she promised.

Jamie nodded, but his eyes quickly returned to the snakes.

The cases were almost too heavy for Alex to lift. As she backed out with them, she saw Tarver pick up a sack and open it wide. Maybe he was going to bag the damned snakes for a while. Realising that Tarver was not following her, she dropped the cases and rushed to Bill's gun cabinet in the hallway, but it was locked tight. She was trying to break it open when Tarver walked towards her, dragging Jamie by one arm.

The boy screamed blue murder as he came. 'My aunt Alex is going to blow your head off, you big ape!'

Tarver smacked him on the side of his head, dropping him to the floor. Jamie's screaming ceased.

Where's the shotgun? Alex wondered.

Tarver walked over to a bookshelf, reached up and brought down an automatic pistol that Alex recognised as a Beretta from Bill's collection. Then he drew Alex's borrowed Sig from the small of his back.

'Why are you doing this?' she asked. 'Why didn't you just take off when you had the chance?'

Tarver gave her a tight smile. 'I'm entering a new life today. Vanishing into another identity. And I would let you live but I'm afraid you have a clue to the road I'm taking. You may not know you have it, but you do. And if I let you live, you'll eventually remember.'

With the most casual of motions, Dr Tarver half turned and shot Bill Fennell in the head with Alex's Sig.

She jumped back in shock, but she had no time to worry about Bill. Jamie was stirring. If he raised his head, he would see his father's ruined face. She lunged across the space to cover the boy with her body.

'Perfect,' said Tarver. 'How's this? You came here to rescue your nephew. Fennell resisted, so you shot him. Sadly, the boy was killed in the crossfire. I think the Bureau will want the investigation closed as quickly as possible.'

'Please,' Alex said. 'Kill me, just let him live.'

Tarver shook his head. 'He can't survive to tell your friends at the Bureau that he had two strangers as overnight guests last night.'

She blinked in bewilderment. 'Two?'

'My brother Judah and I.'

Alex pondered this. 'Is that who's driving the truck? With the boat?'

Tarver smiled. 'A little make-up can do wonders. Goodbye, Alexandra. You led us a merry chase.' He switched the Beretta to his right hand, then stepped back, settling his aim on Jamie.

Instinct told Alex to lift Jamie and run. She knew she'd accomplish nothing but it was better to die trying. At least the boy would be unconscious for the end. Forcing her arms under him, she struggled to lift his sagging weight. No shot came. Why hasn't he fired? she wondered.

Dr Tarver had cocked his head as though straining to hear something above the storm outside. Alex found herself listening, too, first in vain, but then . . . the slapping of rotor blades: a helicopter dropping over the house.

'Your plan won't work now, Doctor,' she said, summoning the calm equanimity of a hostage negotiator. 'Your being here screws it all up.'

Tarver stepped forward and slammed the Beretta into her face. She collapsed onto Jamie. Pounding footsteps receded, then returned. Tarver jerked her to her feet. As her vision returned, she saw that he was carrying a coil of rope and a roll of duct tape.

He cut a length of rope, bound Jamie's legs together, then tied him to the leg of a nearby sofa. 'Tell me who's in charge.'

'I'm the negotiator. You talk to me.'

He hit her again, this time on the bridge of the nose. A river of blood gushed over her lips and chin. Coughing blood, she dug her cellphone from her pocket and handed it over. 'Speed dial four. John Kaiser.'

Dr Tarver ripped off some duct tape and bound her wrists. Then he put her phone in his pocket and pulled his own cell out of the other. He pressed one button and waited. Alex knelt and hugged Jamie as best she could. She prayed that the SWAT agents were already dispersing across the grounds.

'Edward?' Tarver said into the phone. 'How close are you? . . . Ten minutes or less. Stay at altitude until I give you the final position . . . Right.'

Altitude? Alex thought. Does Tarver have an aircraft nearby?

Now the doctor took out Alex's cellphone, and pressed a button. 'Is this Agent Kaiser? . . . Good. These are my demands. I want an FBI Suburban with its windows spray-painted black driven to the rear door of this house in twenty minutes' time and left there. That's the side where your helicopter is. I want a Cessna Citation fully fuelled and waiting at the Madison County Airport with one pilot and its engines running. Don't attempt to block the driveway when we leave. When the back door opens, do not fire. The Fennell boy will be in front of me. Remember, twenty minutes for the Suburban.'

Tarver hung up the phone and shoved it in his pocket. Then he picked up the shotgun from behind the sofa and fired it into the floor.

Jamie cringed into Alex's chest.

Tarver took hold of Bill's corpse by the ankles and dragged it towards the back door. Alex crawled to the sofa, shoved her bound hands under it, and lifted with all her strength. 'Yank the rope loose!' she told Jamie. 'Hurry.'

She heard a grunt, like that of a shot-putter making a heroic heave. Fennell's corpse being ejected from the house. Jamie had almost got the rope loose from the sofa leg when Tarver reappeared. Jamie lay back down.

'The boy's next, Kaiser,' Tarver said into Alex's cellphone. 'You have nineteen minutes.'

Alex saw that he'd brought a bedsheet from the laundry room. Tarver shook it open, then took a pair of scissors from his back pocket and cut two holes like ghost's eyes near the centre of the cream-coloured sheet.

'What are you doing?' Jamie asked. 'Making a Halloween costume?'

Tarver laughed. 'That's right. And it'll scare the hell out of some people.'

He cut the rope that bound Jamie to the sofa leg, then cut a longer piece and tied the boy to his own body by tying them both round their waists. He left less than three feet of slack between them.

'Please don't do this, Doctor,' Alex begged. 'I'll shield you all the way out.'

She might as well have been talking to a statue. 'Put on my backpack,' Tarver said to Alex, pointing at the bag.

'That's where the snakes are,' Jamie said quietly.

'There's more than snakes in there,' Tarver said, cutting the duct tape from Alex's wrists.

She hesitated, making sure the pack was fastened, then carefully shouldered it. The pack was heavy, but to her relief she felt no movement inside.

'Get ready to carry those cases,' Tarver said, pointing to the Pelicans near the front door. 'Both of them.'

Alex suddenly realised that Tarver had made his demands only to put Kaiser and his men at the maximum tactical disadvantage. At this moment, they would be rehearsing for a scene that would never be played. Because they were on the wrong side of the house.

Dr Tarver picked up Jamie as easily as he would a sack of groceries, then pulled the king-size bedsheet over both of them. Alex could no longer tell where Dr Tarver stopped and Jamie began.

'We're going to the boathouse,' Tarver said. 'Listen to me, Alex. If you drop those cases, I'll shoot him in the head. Tell her where the gun is, Jamie.'

The sheet jerked. 'Under my chin,' answered the small voice.

'You walk ahead of us all the way. If you jump off the pier, I'll shoot him. Don't do anything crazy. Remember your grey-haired friend on the porch.'

Alex would never forget him. She picked up the heavy cases.

'Straight to the boathouse. If you slow down, Jamie's gone.'

She set off across the grass, marching into the rain. She tried to make out SWAT agents among the shrubs, but saw none. Kaiser had probably posted one or two on this side of the house. Right now, they'd be describing the strange parade: a baggage-laden woman leading a ghost towards the lake.

She was on the pier now. Barring a mistake by a nervous sniper, they would all reach the boathouse alive. Dr Tarver had already proved that he would kill without hesitation, and Kaiser wouldn't give the fire order, knowing he had a helicopter full of SWAT agents at his command.

'Open the door!' shouted Tarver.

As she pushed through the door into fetid darkness, one of his earlier phrases replayed in her mind: *Stay at altitude until I give you the final position.* Who could be coming to rescue Tarver by air?

A gleaming white Carrera speedboat rolled on the waves that crashed under the mildewed walls of the boathouse.

'Load the cases into the stern, then move up into the bow,' Dr Tarver ordered, still under the sheet with Jamie.

Alex climbed carefully into the pitching speedboat and stowed the cases back near the huge twin outboard motors. Then she unslung the backpack and walked forward to the cushioned area in the bows. A big hand shot out from beneath the sheet and jerked one of her wrists over the other.

'Hold them together!' Tarver shouted.

He whipped a long strip of duct tape round her wrists and wrapped them so tightly that she feared they would go numb.

Her cellphone rang and Tarver answered. 'Change of plan, Kaiser. I'm going for a cruise. If your chopper moves within three hundred metres of my boat, I'll kill the boy without hesitation.'

Still under the bedsheet, Dr Tarver got behind the wheel and cranked the Carrera's massive engines. The boat moved out of the boathouse into the slashing rain. It shuddered from the impact of waves against the bow, but as the engines gained power, the craft began to leap from crest to crest. They were headed for a small wooded island a few hundred yards offshore.

Alex faced the windshield and hunched over as though sheltering from the rain. She saw the Bell 430 rise above the Fennell house. It climbed and climbed, then banked and arrowed out over the lake, tracking them steadily.

Tarver gunned the throttles, and the boat swerved to starboard, circling to the far side of the little island. 'Hit the deck!' he shouted as they pulled beneath some overhanging trees.

Now Alex heard the *whup-whup-whup* of the FBI helicopter over the Carrera's idling engines. Kaiser was moving closer. She knew he would be torn between hanging back for safety's sake and fear that Dr Tarver would execute his hostages while he stood helplessly by.

'*Stay down!*' Tarver shouted.

Alex flattened herself between the boat seats. A moment later, two gunshots crashed against her ears. Terrified for Jamie, she looked up and saw Dr Tarver fire a third shot into the choppy water beside the boat.

What the hell is he doing?

Dr Tarver crouched, opened a long, narrow locker and pulled out a highpowered rifle, another weapon from her dead brother-in-law's collection.

What happened next occurred with the terrible inevitability of a nightmare. The FBI chopper dropped into sight a hundred yards from the boat. Dr Tarver smiled, then jumped up like a hunter coming out of a duck blind and fired five shots in quick succession.

Black smoke billowed from the Bell's turbines even before the final shot struck home. The helicopter began to yaw wildly in the air. Alex heard an explosion, then the chopper dropped towards the water, its rotors still spinning. It slammed nose-first into the whitecaps, but mercifully there were no more explosions. Alex stood up to look for survivors in the water, but she was thrown to the deck when the Carrera sped from beneath the trees.

Tarver was yelling into his cellphone over the roar of the engines. 'There's an island just east of the rendezvous! There's a downed chopper on one side. I'll be on the other. Stay clear of that chopper!'

Tarver hugged the perimeter of the island, and soon they were idling in its lee. The island shielded them from the wind, but the rain still stung Alex's face as she searched the dark sky.

She froze as the *whup-whup* of rotors reached her again. Was this Tarver's accomplice? Or had Kaiser summoned aerial reinforcements?

The rotor noise grew to a roar, then a group of lights flashed on high above the boat. No wonder she hadn't seen the damned thing! It was dark grey, almost indistinguishable from the sky. As she watched the chopper descend, hope died within her. Dr Tarver was talking to the pilot on his cellphone, guiding him in.

The rotor blast drove her to the deck, and static electricity crackled around the boat. Soon the grey helicopter was hovering next to the speedboat, so low that whitecaps were washing over its skids.

A huge door slid back and at Dr Tarver's signal a man in black leapt from the helicopter into the speedboat.

'Load those cases!' the doctor shouted, pointing to the Pelicans in the stern.

While the newcomer hustled to the back of the boat, Tarver slashed the rope binding him to Jamie, then wrapped the end still tied to Jamie's waist twice round his hand like a leash. With one hand he pulled the high-powered rifle out of the locker and tossed it into the hovering chopper.

The black-clad man had loaded one case and was going back for the other. Dr Tarver lifted Jamie into the crook of his arm, then planted his right foot on the gunwale of the boat and prepared to toss him into the chopper.

'Aunt Alex!' Jamie screamed, white with terror. 'Don't let them take me!'

As Jamie flailed against Tarver, Alex glanced at the chopper pilot, and her breath caught in her throat. It was the grey-haired man who had visited Tarver's clinic yesterday. In that moment, she realised he was also the army officer standing with Tarver in the VCP photograph in Tarver's office.

She saw Jamie being strapped into a seat behind the pilot, his face a mask of fear. Then the chopper dipped its nose and began to rise. Twenty feet, forty, sixty. As it rose, the pilot kept the open door facing the boat, and Alex soon saw why. Dr Tarver had picked up the rifle and was now kneeling in the door, aiming at her chest. Some distant part of her brain screamed, *Drop!* Yet her body remained frozen. If she could not fulfil her promise to Grace, what did her own fate matter?

Waiting for the muzzle flash, she saw a blur of white in front of Dr Tarver's face. The bedsheet? No, that lay discarded on the deck behind her. Then she saw Jamie beside the flapping whiteness. He'd thrown his little arms round Tarver's neck, and was jerking something tight.

A drawstring, Alex realised. *The sack!*

Tarver began flailing his arms, and the rifle flew out of the door. The doctor was swung back into the cabin, lurching into the pilot. The helicopter began to pitch wildly in the air. Seventy feet above the lake, it spun through 360 degrees and, as it did so, a Pelican case flew out.

When the helicopter came round the second time, Alex saw that Dr Tarver had seized the sack with both hands and was tearing it violently from his neck. A thick black rope hung from one of his cheeks. She shuddered as she realised it was one of the cottonmouths, attached by its two-inch fangs. Tarver ripped the snake away from his face and flung it into space. As he turned back to the interior, the chopper dipped and Jamie shot from the open door like a cannonball. Alex screamed in horror, but as Jamie fell, she realised that he was dropping in a controlled fall, feet first. He landed seventy yards from the boat.

She jumped behind the wheel, then realised that Dr Tarver had taken the key. Slamming her bound hands against the gunwale, she ran to the stern. Hope flooded through her. On the port side was an emergency trolling motor. Bill had used it to propel the boat quietly around fishing holes.

Alex looked back to the spot where Jamie had fallen. The helicopter was descending over it. Her first thought was Jamie, but then she realised they were after the fallen Pelican case, which would float even if heavily laden.

She lifted the bracket of the trolling motor so that the propeller emerged from the water and protruded just above the gunwale. She knew she could steer the boat with bound hands, but she would be useless once she reached Jamie. So she held her taped wrists over the sharp blades of the prop, and carefully sawed through the tape.

As soon as her hands were free, she lowered the prop into the water and hit the power switch. The speedboat moved forwards. Alex jumped behind the wheel and aimed the bow towards the spot where Jamie had landed.

Twenty yards away and to her right, the grey helicopter had settled just above the surface of the lake. Dr Tarver was straddling its left skid, trying desperately to pluck one of the heavy cases from the waves. She saw no sign of Jamie. As Tarver heaved the case into the belly of the chopper, a big wave sloshed inside the machine. Obviously panicked, the pilot dipped his rotors to the right, venting the water from the door and lifting the chopper above the waves. This manoeuvre dumped Dr Tarver into the lake.

The pilot ascended twenty feet and hovered, as if uncertain what to do.

As Alex slowly circled in search of Jamie, the crack of rifle fire echoed over the water. Two shots . . . five. An explosion reverberated behind her. The helicopter had risen high enough for Kaiser's snipers to get an angle on it! Alex glanced up only a moment, but it was enough to see Tarver's chopper plummeting towards the lake, black smoke pouring from its engine.

Afraid that it might crash on top of her, she steered away. As she did so, the chopper hit the waves with a strange whump, not twenty-five yards from her. Alex tried to control her fear.

'Jamie!' she shouted. '*Jamie! It's Aunt Alex!*'

Nothing. She glanced to her right. Tarver's helicopter had already sunk to its engine cowling.

'Jamie!' she screamed again.

Then she saw him. Jamie was floating face up in the heaving waves. And she could see Tarver's bald head moving fast through the water towards him. He would reach Jamie long before Alex could get there with the boat.

Instead of veering towards them, Alex continued to steer in a widening circle, which carried her out of Dr Tarver's line of sight. Instinct told her that Eldon Tarver was about to be outmatched. For six weeks she had been playing catch-up: the doctor had always been three steps ahead. But this would be different. This was a negotiation.

As the boat circled, she ran to the stern and searched for the fuel line. *There.* She yanked it loose, and gasoline ran onto the stern deck. She went back to the wheel and steered towards Tarver, who was now holding Jamie in a lifeguard's cross-chest carry. The boy appeared to be unconscious.

When Alex was thirty feet away, she ran back to the stern and switched off the trolling motor. As she did, a memory flashed into her head. She saw Bill Fennell on the Fourth of July, yanking up a seat cushion to get at some tools. She stopped, tucked her fingers under that same seat and yanked it open. In the small compartment she saw a screwdriver, a roll of electrical tape and a set of Allen keys. No knife. No flare gun. *Shit—*

'Let's talk!' shouted Tarver. 'I want to make a deal. The boat for the boy.'

Alex looked up. As the boat drifted closer to the doctor, she slid the screwdriver into her pocket.

She shook her head. 'You have a gun. I know you do.'

'I lost it in the crash.'

Alex shook her head again. 'No gun, no boat!'

Dr Tarver's right hand stopped treading water, dipped under the surface, then reappeared holding an automatic.

'Throw it away!' Alex yelled.

She saw rage in his eyes, but he threw the gun into the waves.

'Get out of the boat!' he bellowed. 'I have the key. When you're out, I'll swim to the transom and get in.'

'No!' cried Alex. 'Swim away from Jamie first.'

'He'll sink.'

She turned and snatched up a life ring. Tossing it to him, she shouted, 'Put that under his arms, then swim away.'

Seeing no alternative, Dr Tarver struggled to push Jamie's body into the life ring. As he worked, Alex saw that the dark purple mark on the left side of his face was not his deformity, but the livid swelling of a snakebite.

'All right. Swim away!' she shouted.

Reluctantly, Dr Tarver released Jamie and swam quickly towards the stern of the boat. 'Jump out!' he shouted.

Still suspicious, Alex pulled off her shoes and stripped off her jeans. She climbed onto the gunwale and dived into the cold water. As she breast-stroked towards Jamie, she sensed movement to her left. Dr Tarver had not climbed into the boat. He was kicking towards Jamie again. She started to swim freestyle, but Tarver still got there first, even though his movements appeared to be slowing. As Alex stared in disbelief, he put his big hand on top of Jamie's head and shoved him deep under the water.

'Save him now,' he snarled.

Alex couldn't see Jamie, but he didn't appear to be struggling. Dr Tarver was holding him under as easily as he might an infant. She thought of the screwdriver, but she'd never be able to overpower Tarver face-to-face . . .

Then the answer struck her. As she dived beneath the waves, her father's voice echoed in her head: *When your back's against the wall, do the unexpected.* She kicked deeper, until she was fifteen feet below the surface. Then she opened her eyes and looked up. All she could make out was a dark blur against the surface. But as she floated upwards, a tentacle swept past her eyes. She grabbed it. It was an ankle—Jamie's. She expelled all the air from her lungs and jerked the ankle straight down, then swam towards the bottom with all her strength, feeling Jamie's body come with her.

She started kicking, trying to tow him laterally, but her oxygen was disappearing fast. She had to surface. As she kicked upwards, she saw a splash above, then a black shape sweeping down towards her, trailing bubbles. Switching Jamie's ankle to her left hand, she drew the screwdriver from her pocket and waited. When the shadow reached for her, she kicked upwards and stabbed with savage force. The tool struck something, but a powerful hand seized her throat. Alex flung her arm wide and stabbed from the side. Tarver's big body thrashed, then his hand let go. Hope surged through her, urging her to a final blow. She yanked back on the handle of her weapon, but the screwdriver wouldn't pull free.

Letting go, she kicked for the grey light above. As she broke through the waves, Tarver surfaced in front of her, the screwdriver buried in his left ear. With a last wild look into Alex's eyes, he turned and began swimming awkwardly for the boat.

Alex turned in the water and started kicking towards the island. Her lungs were burning and Jamie's face was blue. She could no longer kick against the battering waves. She knew then that they might die within a few yards of the shore. An image of Grace rose into her mind, and then her mother lying unconscious in the hospital. We're the last, she thought helplessly. Jamie and me. She tried to kick, but there was nothing left.

Her mouth was full of water when she heard a male voice barking orders. *Kaiser?* She shoved Jamie higher, trying to kick with dead legs. Then a powerful arm swept round her, propelling them both towards shore. Someone dragged Jamie from her arms. She was dimly aware of someone counting chest compressions. Then she opened her eyes. John Kaiser was looking anxiously into her face.

'Jamie,' she gasped. 'Is he alive?'

As if in answer, there was a fit of coughing beside her, then a boy crying.

'Disable the boat!' shouted Kaiser, getting to his feet. 'Fire at the engine!'

'No,' Alex cried, remembering the disconnected fuel line, which, from the roar of the engines, Tarver must have reconnected. 'Stop . . . the fuel—'

'What?' called Kaiser, moving back to her.

But the rifle cracked again, and the stern of the fleeing Carrera erupted into flame. A figure leapt onto the starboard gunwale, but before it could jump clear, the speedboat blew apart.

Alex collapsed in the mud, and tried to explain about the Pelican cases, but her voice was lost in the commotion. She rolled onto her side and saw Jamie lying beside her, staring at her with wide eyes—Grace's eyes. When he held out a shivering hand, Alex pulled him to her, burying his face in her chest.

She had kept her promise at last.

Epilogue
Two Weeks Later

'Are you sure you know where you're going?' Jamie asked Alex, as they drove through a tunnel of oak trees.

'I think so. It wasn't that long ago that I was here. I stood with him on that big bridge we just went over.'

Jamie took off his seat belt, got onto his knees on the seat, and propped his elbow on the terracotta jar between them.

'Careful,' said Alex.

'Sorry.' Jamie leaned forward. 'I think I see it. Is that a road?'

'It is. Eagle eyes.'

Jamie was staring at the narrow gap in the trees. 'Man, it's dark in there.'

Alex slowed, then turned left onto deeply rutted gravel. She almost regretted coming. The washed-out road was virtually impassable without a four-wheel drive. After fifty yards it turned to sand, and she had to give up and park, unsure how she would ever get back to the Trace proper.

'Come on,' she said. 'From here we walk.'

Jamie looked surprised, but he got out. Alex lifted the clay jar off the seat, locked the door, and led Jamie along the sandy road. The air was close and muggy, and horseflies dived around their faces, thirsty for blood.

'This sucks,' said Jamie. 'I don't think there's anything down here.'

'Have a little faith, huh? You're a tough guy.'

She walked a few more yards, then stopped, listening. 'Do you hear that?'

Jamie stopped, too. 'What's that sound?'

Alex smiled. 'Water.' She broke into a trot.

Jamie ran alongside her, and a moment later they emerged from the trees into bright sunlight that flashed like diamonds from a broad, clear stream.

'Hey!' called a male voice. 'We thought you'd given up.'

Alex shielded her eyes against the sun and looked down the course of the stream. Thirty yards away, Chris and Ben Shepard sat on a fallen log facing a small campfire. The smell of cooking meat drifted on the wind.

Jamie started sprinting across the sand. Alex followed more slowly.

By the time she reached the fire, Ben and Jamie had charged into the creek and were splashing fifty yards downstream, searching for arrowheads and dinosaur bones.

Chris got up and gave her a welcoming hug. 'What's in the jar?' he asked.

She pulled off the clay lid and lifted out a bottle of chilled white wine. 'My contribution,' she said. 'Raising the tone a little bit.'

He laughed and took the bottle. 'Hope you brought a corkscrew.'

She smiled. 'Screw-off cap.'

Chris did the honours, then filled two polystyrene cups. They sat on the log a few feet apart and sipped slowly.

'How's Ben doing?' she asked at length.

Chris looked down the creek. 'He has some bad nights. He's sleeping with me for now. But overall, he's doing really well. What about Jamie?'

She smiled. 'He's much better. I think he misses Will Kilmer more than he misses his father. Will makes him think of his grandfather. My dad.'

Chris picked up a stick and poked the fire.

'How are *you* doing?' Alex asked.

'Not too bad, physically. I'm still having some strange symptoms, but Pete Connolly thinks it's a reaction to the antidote drug.'

Alex had not been privy to all the details of Dr Tarver's work. But she knew that an army doctor had treated Chris with a substance taken from one of the vials in Dr Tarver's Pelican cases. That vial represented Chris's only hope of neutralising the cancer-causing virus that Tarver had injected into him. The doctor's notes had been studied intensively by some of the best virologists in the country, and they felt confident Chris would recover, with not a trace of the virus left in his system.

Alex held up her glass in a silent toast. He touched hers, and they drank.

'What about otherwise?' Alex asked softly.

'Day by day. Tom Cage has helped me a lot.' He leaned over and refilled her cup. 'How's the custody thing coming?'

'Jamie's mine, no doubt. The judge upheld the clause in Grace's original will. I'm Jamie's godmother, and the will made it clear that if both Grace and Bill died, I should raise Jamie. So that's that.'

'Have you thought any more about where you're going to go?'

'The director offered me my old job back in Washington. But a couple of days ago, I got another offer. The SAC in New Orleans asked if I could be assigned to his office as hostage negotiator.'

Chris raised his eyebrows. 'Is John Kaiser behind that?'

She nodded. 'I think Kaiser has a lot of influence down there. Anyway, there's a lot happening in New Orleans now. Crime is really out of hand.'

'Sounds like a great place to raise a kid.'

Alex smiled ruefully. 'I know. Kaiser lives across Lake Pontchartrain, though. It's really nice over there. And it's the South, you know? I think it's time for me to come back home.'

Chris was looking steadily at her. 'I think you're right.'

She looked back at him for a while, then reached into her pocket and brought out a small plastic case.

'What's that?' he asked.

'It's the original video disk of Thora and Lansing together. I thought you might want to pay Shane Lansing back.'

Chris reached out for the disk case and dropped it into the fire.

'Lansing's a bastard,' he said. 'But he's got four kids. If he makes a hell of his own life, so be it. I won't be the one to break up his family.'

'Leave the past in the past?' Alex asked.

He nodded, his eyes on hers. 'You could try that, too, you know?'

Without warning, he raised his fingers to her face and touched the cluster of scars round her right eye. Alex flinched and started to pull back, but something steadied her, and she endured his exploring fingers.

'Thora was perfect on the outside,' Chris said. 'But inside . . . she was ugly. Selfish and cruel.' He looked into her face. 'You must know those scars don't matter.'

She smiled wistfully. 'But they do. I know, because there was a time when I didn't have them. And people treated me differently.'

He leaned forward and pressed his lips to the worst scar, a purplish ridge of tissue beneath her temple. 'Like this?'

So deeply was Alex moved that she felt driven to turn away, but Chris held her in place. 'I asked you a question,' he said.

'Maybe,' she whispered. 'Something like that.'

A scream echoed over the water. They both looked downstream. Ben and Jamie were racing towards them splashing water high above their heads. Jamie's right arm was held high, and Ben was pointing at it as they ran.

'I think they've found something,' Chris said.

'Looks like it.'

Chris let his hand fall, then took her hand in his and led her across the warm sand. 'Let's go see what it is.'

Alex wiped her eyes with her free hand and followed him into the cool, clear water.

GREG ILES

Born: Stuttgart, Germany, 1960
Home: Natchez, Mississippi
Website: www.gregiles.com

In extracts from his website and from interviews, Greg Iles expresses his thoughts about different aspects of his writing, including the turning point in his life when he decided to become a writer. Up until then, he had made a living for almost a decade as a member of the rock band Frankly Scarlet.

On becoming a published author:

Spandau Phoenix was my first novel. I wrote the first hundred pages while I was still playing in my band, as it began to come apart on the road. When the band finally imploded, I was in Mobile, Alabama, at 3 a.m. on New Year's Eve, standing at a phone booth in −28° weather. I was thirty years old, my wife was in school, and I had $9,000 to my name.

I drove home to New Orleans, shut myself in our apartment, surrounded myself with library books and started working eighteen hours a day. Literally. I gave myself one year to write and sell a novel. I did not attend writers' conferences or pay anyone to help me. I used my best buddy and fellow thriller fan as a sounding board. When I was finished, I had a manuscript almost three times the length of an average thriller today. I was consciously tying to write a best seller at the time, using as my models Jack Higgins, Frederick Forsyth and Hans Hellmut Kirst. I followed some of the 'rules' of writing and getting published, and ignored others. After a couple of nail-biting months, I had a two-book deal worth $125,000—five times my annual income at the time.

Today I feel a bit embarrassed about *Spandau Phoenix*. It is rather overwrought in its use of italics, and the most plot-driven (and least character-driven) of all my novels. That said, it is consistently ranked by the public, and particularly WWII buffs, as one of the great conspiracy thrillers out there.

On the Deep South where he lives and where most of his books are set:

I think the South always has that legacy of appearance being very different from the underlying reality; I think there's a sense in the South that there's so much hidden, so much is repressed, that anything is possible. And there's also a sense in the rest of the country that we're still a little backward; that communication is not as good, there's not as much civilisation, there's not as much law holding human impulses in check. I think a lot of that contributes to a vibe and the feeling that anything is possible.

In America, families split and people travel a thousand miles for a job, but the South is not yet like that. People live for three or four generations in the same town, even the same house. They may even bury their family in that land. It is a tie to the land that has never been broken.

On fitting into a genre:

Every book I've ever done has been a departure for me. The formula today is basically to rewrite your last book. But I just follow my nose; I write about what interests me each year. I don't put a governor on my imagination, you know what I mean? When something comes to me, I just follow it and do it.

On characterisation:

I like taking characters at the most intense moments of their lives and exploring all of that in full and then moving on.

On endings:

Ending a novel appropriately is extremely difficult. So many writers build up a huge expectation or amount of tension, and then fail to deliver on their promise. It's very easy to paint yourself into a corner. I think you have to have a good understanding of the 'subterranean' dynamics of your story even before you begin. The proper potentialities have to exist in the archetypes of your characters at the start, in order for a satisfactory catharsis or resolution to occur. Hope I don't sound like a professor.

SNAKES ALIVE!

The eastern coral snake, which appears in *True Evil*, is one of America's deadliest snakes. Native to Mississippi, it can grow up to two feet long and spends most of its life underground or in leaf piles. Its venom is a neurotoxin that disrupts neurological connections causing slurred speech, double vision, paralysis and, eventually, respiratory or cardiac failure. The snake attacks only when provoked and, to protect itself, curls the tip of its tail in order to confuse the onlooker as to where its head is. No human deaths from coral snakebites have been reported in the US since an antidote was produced in 1967.

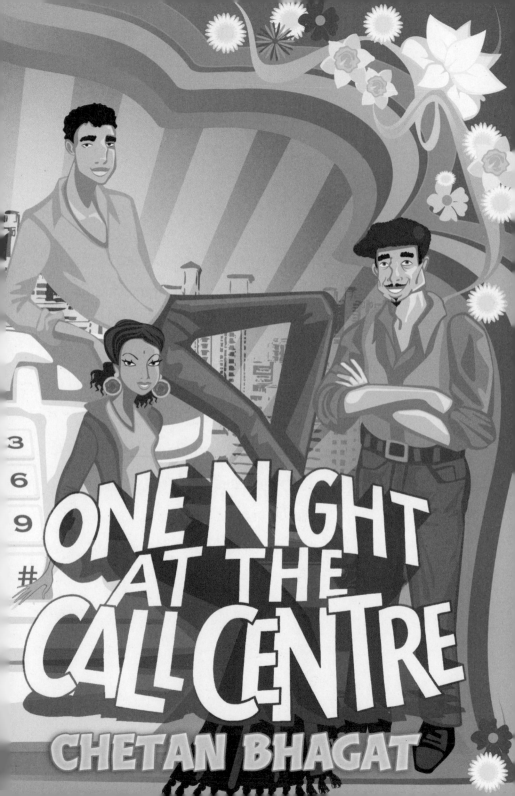

ONE NIGHT
AT THE
CALL CENTRE

CHETAN BHAGAT

It's a typical night at the call centre.
One complaining customer after another.
And, as if that wasn't bad enough, Shyam has to
sit opposite Priyanka, the girl who's just dumped
him, as well as deal with Bakshi, his insufferable
supervisor. But on this night of a
thousand calls, when life couldn't look more
uninspiring for Shyam and his friends, a unique
caller gets on the line.
And changes everything—for ever.

Prologue

The Kanpur–Delhi night train was the most memorable journey of my life. Firstly, it gave me the idea for my book. Secondly, it is not every day you sit in an empty compartment and a young, pretty girl walks in.

Yes, you see it in the movies, you hear about it from friends' friends, but it never happens to you. In most cases I shared my compartment with talkative aunties, snoring men and wailing infants. But this night was different. Firstly, my compartment was empty. Secondly, I was unable to sleep.

I had been to the Indian Institute of Technology in Kanpur to give a talk. Before leaving, I sat in the canteen chatting with the students and drank four cups of coffee, which no doubt led to my insomnia. I had no magazines or books to read and could hardly see anything out of the window in the darkness. I prepared myself for a dull and silent night.

She walked in five minutes after the train had left the station. She opened the curtains of my enclosure and looked around puzzled.

'Is this coach A4, seat 63E?' she asked.

The yellow light bulb in my compartment flickered as I looked up at her.

'Huh?' I said. It was difficult to withdraw from the gaze of her eyes.

'Actually, it is. My seat is right in front of you.' She answered her own question and heaved her heavy suitcase onto the upper berth. She sat down opposite me and sighed with relief.

'I got into the wrong coach,' she said, adjusting her countless ringlets. She was young, perhaps early to mid-twenties, and her waist-length hair had a life of its own. I couldn't yet see her face in the bad light, but I could tell one thing—she was pretty. And her eyes—once you looked into them, you couldn't turn away. I kept my gaze down.

'So, this is a pretty empty train,' she said after ten minutes.

'Yes,' I said. 'It's the new holiday special. They've just started it.' I leaned forward. 'Hi. I am Chetan, by the way, Chetan Bhagat.'

'Hi,' she said. 'Chetan . . . your name sounds familiar.'

Now this was cool. It meant she had heard of my first book. I'm rarely recognised, and never by a girl on a night train.

'You might have heard of my book, *Five Point Someone*. I'm the author.'

'Oh yes,' She paused. 'Oh yes, of course. I've read your book. About the three underperformers and the professor's daughter, right?'

'Yes. So, did you like it?'

'It was all right.'

I was taken aback. I could have done with a little more of a compliment.

'Just all right?' I said, fishing a bit too obviously.

'Well . . .' She hesitated. 'Yeah, just all right. An OK-OK type of book.'

I kept quiet. She noticed the expression of mild disappointment on my face.

'Nice to meet you, Chetan. Where are you coming from? IIT Kanpur?'

'Yes,' I said, my voice less friendly than before. 'I had to give a talk there.'

'Oh really? About what?'

'About my book—you know, the OK-OK-type one. Some people do want to hear about it,' I said, using a sweet tone to coat my sarcasm.

'Interesting,' she said, and went quiet again.

I was quiet too. I didn't want to speak to her any more.

'Is everything OK?' she asked softly.

'Yes, why?' I said.

'Nothing. You're upset about what I said about your book, aren't you?'

'Not really,' I said.

She laughed. I looked at her. Her smile was as arresting as her eyes. I knew she was laughing at me, but I wanted her to keep smiling.

'Listen. I know your book did well. You are a sort of youth writer and everything. But at one level . . .'

'What?' I said.

'At one level, you are hardly a youth writer.'

I looked at her for a few seconds. Her eyes had a soft but insistent gaze.

'I thought I wrote a book about college kids. Isn't that youth?' I said.

'Yeah, right. So you wrote a book on the Indian Institute of Technology, an elite place where few people get to go. You think that represents the youth?' she asked.

'So what are you trying to say? I had to start somewhere, so I wrote about my college experiences. And the story isn't all about IIT. It could have happened anywhere. Is that why you're trashing my book?'

'I'm not trashing it. I'm just saying it hardly represents Indian youth.'

'So what represents youth exactly?' I said.

'I don't know. You're the writer. You figure it out,' she said.

'That's not fair,' I said. I sounded like a five-year-old throwing a tantrum. She saw me grumbling to myself and smiled.

'Are you going to write another book?' she said a few seconds later.

'I'll try to.'

'What is the subject of your second novel?'

I turned to look at her carefully for the first time. Maybe it was the time of night, but she was one of the most beautiful women I had ever seen. Everything about her was perfect. I tried to concentrate on her question.

'Second novel? I haven't thought of a subject yet,' I said.

'Really? Don't you have any ideas?'

'I do. But nothing certain.'

'Inte . . . resting,' she drawled. 'Well, just bask in the success of your first book, then.'

We kept quiet for the next half an hour. I took out the contents of my overnight bag and rearranged them for no particular reason. I wondered if it even made sense to change into nightwear. I wasn't going to fall asleep.

'I might have a story idea for you,' she said, startling me.

'Huh?' I was wary of what she was going to say. 'What is it?'

'It's a story about a call centre.'

'Really?' I said. 'Call centres as in "business process outsourcing centres"?'

'Yes. Do you know anything about them?'

I thought about it. I did know about call centres, mostly from my cousins who worked in one.

'Yes, I know something,' I said. 'Some three hundred thousand people work in the industry. They help US and European companies in the sales, service and maintenance of their operations. Usually younger people work there in night shifts. Quite interesting, actually.'

'Just interesting? Have you ever thought of what they all have to face?'

'Uh, not really,' I said.

'Why? Aren't they the youth? Don't you want to write about them?' She was almost scolding me.

'Listen, let's not start arguing again.'

'I'm not arguing. I told you that I have a call-centre story for you.'

I looked at my watch. It was 12.30 a.m. A story would not be such a bad idea to kill time. 'Let's hear it, then,' I said.

'I'll tell you, but I have a condition,' she said.

Condition? 'What? That I don't tell it to anyone else?' I asked.

'No. Just the opposite. You have to promise to use it for your second book.'

'What?' I said. 'Are you kidding? I can't promise that.'

'It's up to you,' she said and turned silent.

'Can't I decide after you've told me the story?' I asked. 'If it's interesting, I may do it. But how can I decide without hearing it first?'

'No. This is not about choice. If I tell you, you have to use it,' she said. 'As if it's your own story. I'll give you the contacts of the people in the story. You can meet them, do your research, but make it your second book.'

'Well, then, I think it's better if you don't tell me,' I said.

'OK,' she said and turned quiet again. She got up to spread a bed sheet on her berth, and then arranged her pillow and blanket.

I checked my watch again. It was 1.00 a.m. and I was still wide awake. She switched off the flickering yellow light. Now the only light in the compartment was an eerie blue one; I couldn't figure out where the bulb was.

As she was sliding under her blanket, I asked, 'What is the story about? At least tell me a little bit more.'

'Will you do it then?'

I shrugged in the semi-darkness. 'Can't say. Don't tell me the story yet, just tell me what it's about.'

She sat up. Folding her legs beneath her, she began talking. 'All right,' she said, 'it's a story about six people in a call centre on one night.'

'Just one night? Like this one?' I interrupted.

'Yes, one night.'

'Are you sure that could fill a whole book? I mean, what's so special about this night?'

She heaved a sigh and took a sip from her bottle of mineral water.

'You see,' she said, 'it wasn't like any other night. It was the night of the phone call.'

'What?' I said and burst out laughing. 'So a call centre gets a phone call. That's the special part?'

She did not smile back. She waited for me to stop laughing and then continued as if I hadn't said anything. 'You see, it wasn't an ordinary phone call. It was the night . . . it was the night there was a phone call from God.'

Her words made me spring to attention. 'What?'

'You heard me. That night there was a phone call from God,' she said.

'What exactly are you talking about?'

'I'm not telling you any more. Now you know what it's about, if you want to hear the story, you know my condition.'

'It's a tough condition,' I said.

'I know. It's up to you,' she said and lay down and closed her eyes.

Six people. One night. Call centre. Call from God. The phrases kept repeating themselves in my head as another hour passed. At 2.00 a.m. she woke up to have a sip of water.

'Listen,' I said. 'Get up.'

'Huh?' she said, rubbing her eyes. 'Why?'

'Tell me the story,' I said.

'So you'll write it?'

'Yes,' I said, with a slight hesitation.

'Good,' she said, and sat up again in her cross-legged position.

For the rest of the night, she told me the story that begins below. I chose to tell the story through Shyam's eyes because, after I met him, I realised he was the most similar to me as a person. The rest of the people, and what happened that night, well, I'll let Shyam tell you.

8.31 p.m.

I was splashing my hands helplessly in the sea. I can't even swim in a pond, let alone in the Indian Ocean. While I was in the water, my boss Bakshi was in a boat next to me. He was pushing my head down in the water. I saw Priyanka drifting away in a lifeboat. I screamed as Bakshi used both his hands to keep my head submerged. Salt water was filling my mouth and nostrils when I heard loud beeps in the distance.

My nightmare ended as my cellphone alarm rang hard in my left ear and I woke up to its 'Last Christmas' ringtone. The ringtone was a gift from Shefali, my new semi-girlfriend. I squinted through a half-shut eye to see 8.32 p.m. surrounded by little bells flashing on the screen.

'Damn,' I said and jumped out of bed.

I would have loved to analyse my dream and its significance in my insignificant life, but I had to get dressed for work.

Man, the Qualis will be here in twenty minutes, I thought. Qualis was the make of car that picked us all up individually and drove us to the centre. I was still tired, but afraid of staying in bed any longer in case I was late.

By the way, I am Shyam Mehra, or Sam Marcy as they call me at my workplace, the Connexions call centre in Gurgaon. American tongues have trouble saying my real name and prefer Sam.

Anyway, I'm a call-centre agent. There are hundreds of thousands, probably millions of agents like me. But this total pain-in-the neck author chose me, of all the agents in the country. He met me and told me to help him with his second book. In fact, he pretty much wanted me to write the book for him. I declined, saying I can't even write my own CV, so there was no way I could write a whole book. I explained to him how my promotion to the position of team leader had been postponed for one year because my manager Bakshi had told me that I don't have the 'required skills set' yet. In my review, Bakshi wrote that I was 'not a go-getter'. I don't even know what 'go-getter' means, so I guess I'm definitely not one.

But this author said he didn't care. He had promised someone he'd write this story so I'd better cooperate or he would keep on pestering me. I tried my best to wriggle out of it, but he wouldn't let go. I finally relented and that's why I'm stuck with this assignment, while you are stuck with me.

Now let's get back to the story. If you remember, I had just woken up.

THERE WAS A NOISE in the living room. Some relatives were in town to attend a family wedding. My cousin was getting married to his neighbour. But I had to work, so I couldn't go to the wedding. It didn't matter, though, all marriages are the same, more or less.

I reached the bathroom still half-asleep. It was occupied.

The bathroom door was open. I saw five of my aunts scrambling to get a few square inches of the washbasin mirror. One aunt had lost the little screw of her gold earring and was flipping out.

'It's pure gold, where is it?' she screamed.

'Auntie, can I use the bathroom for five minutes? I need to get ready for the office,' I said.

'Oh, hello, Shyam. Woke up finally?' my mother's sister said. 'Office? Aren't you coming to the wedding?'

'No, I have to work. Can I have the bath—'

'Look how big Shyam has become,' my maternal aunt said. 'We need to find a girl for him soon.'

Everyone burst into giggles. It was their biggest joke of the day.

'Can I please—' I said.

'Shyam, leave the ladies alone,' one of my cousins interrupted. 'What are you doing here with the women? We are already late for the wedding.'

'But I have to go to work. I need to get dressed,' I protested.

'Use the kitchen sink,' an aunt suggested and handed me my toothbrush.

I gave them all a dirty look. Nobody noticed. I passed by the living room on my way to the kitchen. The uncles were on their second whisky and soda. One uncle said something about how it would be better if my father were still alive and around this evening.

I reached the kitchen. There was no hot water so my face froze as I washed it with cold water. Winter in Delhi is a bitch. I brushed my teeth and combed my hair. Shyam had turned into Sam and Sam's day had just begun.

I was hungry, but there was nothing to eat. They'd be getting food at the wedding, so my mother had felt there was no need to cook at home.

The Qualis's horn screamed at 8.55 p.m.

I tried to find my mother. She was in her bedroom, lost among aunties, saris and jewellery sets. I waved a goodbye to everyone, but no one acknowledged me. It wasn't surprising. My cousins are all on their way to becoming doctors or engineers. You could say I am the black sheep of my family. You see, I used to work in the website department of an ad agency before this call-centre job. However, the ad agency paid really badly, and all the people there were pseudos, more interested in office politics than websites. I left and all hell broke loose at home. That's when I became the black sheep. I saved myself by joining Connexions. With money in your wallet the world gives you some respect. Connexions was also the natural choice for me as Priyanka worked there. Of course, that reason was no longer relevant.

The Qualis's horn screamed again.

'I'm coming,' I shouted as I ran out of the house.

9.05 p.m.

'What, sahib. Late again?' the driver said as I took the front seat.

'Sorry, sorry. Shall we go to Military Uncle's first?' I panted to the driver.

'Yes,' he replied, looking at his watch.

'Can we get to the call centre by ten p.m.? I have to meet someone before their shift ends,' I said.

'Depends if your colleagues are on time,' the driver replied laconically.

Military Uncle hates it if we are late. I prepared myself for some dirty looks. His tough manner comes from his days in the Army, from which he retired a few years ago. At fifty plus he is the oldest person in the call centre. I don't know him well, but I do know that he used to live with his son and daughter-in-law before he moved out—for which read thrown out—to be on his own. His pension was meagre, and he tried to supplement it by working in the call centre. However, he hates to talk and is not a voice agent. He sits on the solitary online chat and email station. His desk is in a far corner near the fax machine. Most of his interactions with us are limited to giving us condescending 'you young people' glances.

The Qualis stopped outside his house. He was waiting at the entrance.

'You're late,' Uncle said, looking at the driver.

Without answering, the driver got out to open the Qualis's back door. Uncle climbed in and sat at the back. He gave me an it-must-be-your-fault look. I looked away. The driver took a U-turn to go to Radhika's house.

One of the unique features about my team is that we not only work together, we also share the same Qualis. Through a bit of route planning and the recruitment of an agreeable driver, we ensured that my Western Appliances Strategic Group all came and left together. There are six of us: Military Uncle, Radhika, Esha, Vroom, Priyanka and me.

The Qualis moved on to Radhika Jha, or agent Regina Jones's house. As usual, Radhika was late.

'Radhika madam is too much,' the driver said, holding the horn down.

Six minutes later Radhika came running towards us, clutching the ends of her maroon shawl in her right hand.

'Sorry, sorry sorry . . .' she said before we could say anything.

'What?' I asked her as the Qualis moved on again.

'Nothing. I was making almond milk for my mother-in-law and it took longer than I thought to crush the almonds,' she said, leaning back exhausted in her seat in the middle.

'Ask Mother-in-law to make her own milk,' I suggested.

'C'mon, Shyam,' she said, 'she's so old, it's the least I can do.'

'Yeah, right,' I shrugged. 'Just that and cooking three meals a day and household chores and working all night and . . .'

'Don't talk about it,' she said. 'Any news on the call centre? I'm nervous.'

'Nothing new from what Vroom told me. Call volumes are at an all-time low—Connexions is doomed. It's just a question of when,' I said.

'Really?' Her eyes widened.

It was true. You might have heard of those swanky, new-age call centres where everything is hunky-dory, there are plenty of clients and agents get

ONE NIGHT AT THE CALL CENTRE | 465

aromatherapy massages. Well, Connexions was not one of them. We were sustained by our one and only client, Western Computers and Appliances, and even their call flow had dwindled. Rumours that the call centre would collapse floated around every day.

The Qualis moved painfully slowly. It was a heavy wedding day in Delhi and on every street there was a procession. We edged forward as the driver dodged several fat grooms on their over-burdened horses.

'I need this job. Anuj and I need to save,' Radhika said, more to herself. Anuj was Radhika's husband. She married him three years ago after a whirlwind courtship and now lived with Anuj's ultra-traditional parents.

The driver drove to Esha Singh's (or agent Eliza Singer's) place next. She was already outside her house.

As Esha got in the smell of expensive perfume filled the vehicle. She sat next to Radhika in the middle row and removed her suede jacket.

'Mmm, nice. What is it?' Radhika said.

'You noticed.' Esha was pleased. 'Escape by Calvin Klein.' She adjusted the tassels at the end of her long, dark brown skirt.

'Oooh. Have you been shopping?' Radhika said.

'Call it a momentary lapse of reason,' Esha said.

I looked at Esha again. Her dress sense is impeccable. Her sleeveless coffee-coloured top contrasted perfectly with her skirt and she wore chunky brown earrings that looked edible and lipstick as thick as cocoa.

'The Lakmé India Fashion Week is in four months. My agent is trying to get me an assignment,' Esha said to Radhika.

Esha wants to become a model. She's hot, at least according to people at the call centre. Two months ago, some agents in the Western Computers bay conducted a stupid poll around the office. People voted for various titles, like who is hot, who is handsome and who is pretty. Esha won the title of the 'hottest chick at Connexions'. She was very dismissive of the poll results, but from that day on there's been just a tiny hint of vanity about her. Otherwise, though, she's fine. She moved to Delhi from Chandigarh a year ago, against her parents' wishes. The call-centre job gives her a regular income, but during the day she tries to get modelling assignments. She's taken part in some low-key fashion shows in West Delhi, but apart from tha,t nothing big has come her way so far.

Priyanka once told me that she thought Esha was 'too short to be a real model'. But Priyanka doesn't know crap. Esha is five-five, only two inches shorter than me (and one inch taller in her heels). I think that's pretty tall for a girl. Esha is only twenty-two, give her a chance. I think Priyanka is just jealous. Priyanka wasn't even considered for the hottest chick award. Priyanka is nice-looking, and she did get a nomination for the 'call-centre cutie award', but she didn't win. Some girl in HR won that.

We had to pick up Vroom next; his real name is Varun Malhotra (or agent Victor Mell), but everyone calls him Vroom because of his love for anything on wheels.

The Qualis turned into Vroom's road to find him beside his bike, waiting.

'What's the bike for?' I said, craning out of the window.

'I'm going on my own,' Vroom said, adjusting his leather gloves. He wore black jeans and trekking shoes that made his thin legs look extra long. His dark blue sweatshirt had the Ferrari horse logo on it.

'Are you crazy?' I said. 'It's so cold. Get in, we're late already.'

'No, I feel stressed today. I need to get it out of my system with a fast ride.' He was standing right beside me and only I could hear him.

'What happened?'

'Nothing. Dad called. He argued with Mum for two hours. Why did they separate? They can't live without screaming their guts out at each other.'

'It's OK, man. Not your problem,' I said.

Vroom's dad was a businessman who parted from his wife two years ago. He preferred his secretary to being with his family, so Vroom and his mother now lived without him.

'I couldn't sleep at all. Just lay in bed all day and now I feel sick. I need to get some energy back,' Vroom said as he straddled his bike.

'But it's freezing . . .' I began.

'What's going on, Shyam sahib?' the driver asked. I turned round. The driver looked at me with a puzzled expression and I shrugged my shoulders.

'He's going on his bike,' I told everyone.

'Come with me,' Vroom said to me. 'I'll get us there in half the time.'

'No, thanks,' I said. I wasn't leaving the cosy Qualis to get on a bike.

Vroom bent over to greet the driver. 'Hello, driver sahib,' he said.

'Vroom sahib, don't you like my Qualis?' the driver said.

'No, Driver *ji*, I'm in the mood for riding my motorbike,' Vroom said.

'Hey, Vroom. Any news on Connexions? Anything happening?' Radhika asked, adjusting her hair.

Apart from the dark circles around her eyes, you could say Radhika was pretty. She has high cheekbones and her fair skin goes well with her wispy eyebrows and soot-black eyes. She wore a plain mustard sari, as saris were all she was allowed to wear in her in-laws' house. It was different apparel from the jeans and skirts Radhika preferred before her marriage.

'No updates. Will dig for stuff today, but I think Bakshi will screw us all. Hey, Shyam, the website manual is all done by the way. I emailed it to the office,' Vroom said and started his bike.

'Cool, finally. Let's send it in today,' I said, perking up.

We left Vroom and moved to our last pick-up at Priyanka's place. It was 9.30 p.m., still an hour away from our shift. However, I was worried as Shefali finished her shift and left by 10.20.

Fortunately, Priyanka was at her pick-up point when we reached her place.

'Hi,' Priyanka said as she sat next to Esha in the middle row of seats. She carried a large, white plastic bag as well as her usual giant handbag.

'Hi,' everyone replied except me.

'I said hi, Shyam,' Priyanka said.

I pretended not to hear. Ever since we broke up, I've found it difficult to talk to her, even though I must think about her thirty times a day. I looked at her. She adjusted her dupatta round her neck. The forest-green salwar kameez she was wearing was new, I noticed. The colours suited her light brown skin. I looked at her nose and the nostrils that flared up every time she was upset. I swear tiny flames appeared in them when she got angry.

'Shyam, I said hi,' she said again.

'Hi,' I said.

'Where's Vroom?' Priyanka said.

'Vroom is riding . . . vroom,' Esha said, making a motorbike noise.

'Nice perfume, Esha. Shopping again, eh?' Priyanka said and sniffed.

'Escape, Calvin Klein,' Esha announced and struck a pose.

'Wow! Someone is going designer,' Priyanka said and both of them laughed. This is something I will never understand about her. Priyanka has bitched fifty times about Esha to me, yet when they are together they behave like long-lost sisters.

'Esha, big date coming?' Radhika said.

'No dates. I'm still so single. Suitable guys are an endangered species,' Esha said and all the girls laughed.

It wasn't that funny if you ask me. I wished Vroom was in the Qualis too. He was the only person in my team I could claim as a friend. At twenty-two he was four years younger than me but I still found it easiest to talk to him. Radhika's household talk was too alien for me, Esha's modelling trip was also beyond me and Priyanka had been a lot more than a friend until recently. Four months ago, we broke up (Priyanka's version) or she dumped me (my version). So I was trying to do what she wanted us to do—'move on'—which was why I hung out with Shefali.

Two pairs of loud beeps from my shirt pocket startled everyone.

'Who's that?' Priyanka said.

'It's my text,' I said and opened the new message.

> Where r u my eddy teddy? Come soon—curly wurly

It was Shefali. She was into cheesy nicknames. I replied to the text:

> Qualis stuck in traffic. Will b there soon

'Who's that?' Esha asked me. 'Shefali?'

'No,' I said and everybody looked at me.

'Yes, it is. It's Shefali, isn't it?' Esha and Radhika said together and laughed.

'Why does Shefali always babytalk?' I heard Esha whisper to Radhika. More titters followed.

'Whatever,' I said and looked at my watch. The Qualis was still on the NH8 road. We were ten minutes away from Connexions.

Cool, I'll meet Shefali by 10.10, I thought.

'Can we stop for a quick tea at Inderjeet? We'll still make it by ten thirty,' Priyanka said. Inderjeet dhaba on NH8 was famous among truck drivers for its all-night tea and snacks.

'Won't we be late?' Radhika crinkled her forehead.

'Of course not. Driver *ji* saved us twenty minutes in the last stretch. Come, Driver *ji*, my treat,' Priyanka said.

'Good idea. It will keep me awake,' Esha said.

The driver slowed the Qualis and parked near the Inderjeet dhaba counter.

'Hey, guys, do we have to stop? We're going to be late,' I protested.

'We won't be late. Let's treat Driver *ji* for getting us here so fast,' Priyanka said and got out of the Qualis.

'He wants to be with Shefali, dude,' Esha elbowed Radhika. They guffawed again. What's so damn funny? I wanted to ask.

'No, I just like to reach my shift a few minutes early,' I said and got out of the Qualis. Military Uncle and the driver followed us.

The driver arranged plastic chairs for us. Inderjeet's minions collected tea orders. The tea arrived in three minutes.

'So what's the gossip?' Priyanka said, cupping her hands round the glass.

'No gossip. You tell us what's happening in *your* life,' Radhika said.

'I actually do have something to tell,' Priyanka said with a sly smile.

'What?' Radhika and Esha exclaimed together.

'I'll tell you when we get to the bay. It's big,' Priyanka said.

'Tell us now,' Esha said, poking Priyanka's shoulder.

'There's no time. Someone is in a desperate hurry,' Priyanka said, glancing meaningfully at me.

I turned away.

'OK, I have something to share too. But don't tell anyone,' Esha said.

'What?' Radhika said.

'See,' Esha said and stood up. She raised her top to expose a flat midriff, on which there was a newborn ring.

'Cool, check it out,' Priyanka said, 'someone's turning hip.'

Military Uncle stared as if in a state of shock.

'Did it hurt?' Radhika said.

'Oh yes,' Esha said. 'Imagine someone stapling your tummy hard.'

Esha's statement churned my stomach.

'Shall we go?' I said, gulping down my tea.

'Let's go, girls, or Mr Conscientious will get upset.' Priyanka suppressed a smirk. I hated her.

I went to the counter to pay the bill. Vroom was watching TV.

'Hi. What are you guys doing here?' he said.

I told him about the girls' tea idea.

'I arrived twenty minutes ago, man,' Vroom said. He extinguished his cigarette and showed me the butt. 'This was my first.'

Vroom was trying to cut down to four cigarettes a night. However, with Bakshi in our life, it was impossible.

'Can you rush me to the call centre? Shefali will be leaving soon,' I said.

'Shefali. Oh, you mean Curly Wurly.' Vroom laughed.

'Shut up, man. She has to catch the Qualis after her shift. This is the only time I get with her.'

'Once you had Priyanka, and now you sink to Shefali levels,' Vroom said, and bent his elbow to rest his six-foot-two-inch frame on the dhaba counter.

'What's wrong with Shefali?' I said, shuffling from one foot to the other.

'Nothing. It's just that it's nice to have a girlfriend with half a brain. Why are you wasting your time with her?'

'I'm weaning myself off Priyanka. I'm trying to move on,' I said.

'What happened to the re-proposal plan with Priyanka?' Vroom said.

'I've told you, not until I become team leader. Which should be soon—

maybe tonight after we submit the website manual. Now can we please go?'

'Yeah, right. Some hopes you live on,' Vroom said, but moved away from the counter.

I held on tight as he zipped through NH8 at 120 kilometres an hour. I closed my eyes and prayed Shefali wouldn't be angry, and that I would get there alive.

I jumped off the bike as Vroom reached the call centre. The bike jerked forward and Vroom had to use both his legs to balance.

'Easy, man,' Vroom said in an irritated voice. 'Can you just let me park?'

'Sorry. I'm really late,' I said and ran inside.

10.18 p.m.

'I'm not talking to you,' Shefali said and started playing with one of her large silver earrings.

'Sorry, Shefali. My bay people held me up.' I stood next to her, leaning against her desk. She sat on her swivel chair and rotated it ninety degrees away from me to showcase her sulking. The dozens of work stations in her bay were empty as all the other agents had left.

'Whatever. I thought you were their team leader,' she said.

'I am not the team leader. I will be soon, but I'm not one yet,' I said.

'Why don't they make you team leader?' She fluttered her eyelashes.

'I don't know. Bakshi said he's trying, but I have to bring my leadership skills up to speed.'

'So you guys don't have a team leader.'

'No. Bakshi says we have to manage without one. I help with supervisory stuff for now. But Bakshi told me I have strong future potential.'

'Eddy Teddy?' Shefali said. I looked at her. If she stopped wearing Hello Kitty hairpins, she could be passably cute. 'Did you like my gift?'

'What gift?'

'The ringtones. I gave you six ringtones. See, you don't even remember.'

'I do. See, I put "Last Christmas" as my tone,' I said and picked up my phone to play it.

'So cute,' Shefali said. 'So cute it sounds, my Eddy Teddy.'

'Shefali, can you stop calling me that? Just call me Shyam.'

'Don't you like the name I gave you?' she said, her voice transcending from sad to tragic.

I kept quiet. You never tell women you don't like something they have done. However, they pick up on the silence.

'You can choose another name if you want. I'm not like your other girlfriends,' she said, tears appearing in her eyes. I looked at my watch. Three more minutes and time would heal everything, I thought. I took a deep breath.

'What kind of girlfriends?' I said.

'Like,' she sniffled, 'bossy girls who impose their way on you.'

'Who? What are you implying?' I said, my voice getting firmer. It was true; Priyanka could be bossy, but only if you didn't listen to her.

'Forget it. But will you give me a name if I stop crying?'

'Yes,' I said. I'd rename the rest of her family if she stopped this drama.

'OK,' she said and became normal. 'Give me a name.'

I thought hard. 'Sheffy? How about Sheffy?' I said finally.

'Nooo. I want something cuuuter,' she said. She loves to drag out words.

'I can't think of anything cute right now. I have to work. Isn't your Qualis leaving soon, too?' I said.

She looked at her watch and stood up.

'Yes, I'd better leave now. Will you think of a name by tomorrow?'

'I will, bye now.' I pecked her on the cheek and turned to go back to my bay.

'Bye bye, Eddy Teddy,' her voice followed me.

10.27 p.m.

The others were already at the desk when I got back from Shefali's bay.

Our bay's name is the Western Appliances Strategic Group or WASG. Unlike the other bay that troubleshoots for computer customers, we deal with customers of home appliances such as refrigerators, ovens and vacuum cleaners. We are called the strategic bay because we specialise in troublesome customers. These 'strategic' customers call a lot and are too stupid to figure things out—actually the latter applies to a lot of callers.

We feel special, as we aren't part of the main computers bay. The main bay has over a thousand agents and handles the huge Western Computers account. While the calls are less weird there, they miss the privacy we enjoy in WASG.

I took my seat at the long rectangular table. We have a fixed seating arrangement: I sit next to Vroom, while Priyanka is opposite me; Esha is adjacent to Priyanka and Radhika sits next to Esha. The bay is open plan so we can all see each other, and Military Uncle's chat station is in the corner of the room. At each of the other three corners there are, respectively, the rest rooms, a conference room and a stationery supplies room.

However, no one apart from Uncle was at their seat when I sat down. Everyone had gathered around Priyanka.

'What's the news? Tell us now,' Esha was saying.

'OK, OK. But on one condition. It doesn't leave WASG,' Priyanka said, sitting down. She pulled out a large plastic bag from under her seat.

'Guys,' I said, interrupting their banter.

Everyone turned to look at me. I pointed at the desk and the unmanned phones. I looked at my watch. It was 10.29 p.m. The call system routine back-up was about to finish and our calls would begin in one minute.

Everyone returned to their chairs and put on their headsets.

Calls began at 10.31 p.m. Numbers started flashing on our common switchboard as we picked up calls one after the other.

'Good afternoon, Western Appliances, Victor speaking, how may I help you?' Vroom said.

'Yes, according to my records I am speaking to Ms Smith, and you have the WAF200 dishwasher. Is that right?' Esha said.

Esha's memory impressed the caller. It was not a big deal, given that our automated system showed every caller's records. We also had details on when they'd last called us. In fact, the reason why her call had come to our desk—the Western Appliances Strategic desk—was because she was a persistent caller. This way the main bay could continue to run smoothly.

Sometimes we had customers that were oddballs even by WASG standards. I won't go into all of them, but Vroom's 10.37 p.m. call went something like this:

'Yes, Ms Paulson, of course we remember you. Happy Thanksgiving, I hope you're roasting a big turkey in our WA100 model oven,' Vroom said, reading from a script that reminded us about the American festival of the day.

I couldn't hear the customer's side of the conversation, but Ms Paulson was obviously explaining her problem with the oven.

'No, Ms Paulson, you shouldn't have unscrewed the cover,' Vroom said, as politely as possible. 'So tell me . . . yes . . . oh really?' Vroom continued, taking deep breaths. Patience did not come naturally to him.

Radhika was helping someone defrost her fridge; Esha was assisting a customer in unpacking a dishwasher. Everyone was speaking with an American accent and sounded different from the way they normally spoke. I took a break from the calls to compile the call statistics of the previous day. I didn't particularly like doing this, but Bakshi had left me little choice.

'You see, madam,' Vroom was still with Ms Paulson, 'I understand your turkey didn't fit and you didn't want to cut it, but you should not have opened up the equipment . . . I suggest you take the oven to your dealer as soon as possible,' Vroom said firmly. 'And next time, get a smaller turkey . . . and yes, a ready-made turkey would be a good idea for tonight . . . No, I don't have a dial-a-turkey number. Thank you for calling, Ms Paulson, bye.' Vroom ended the call. He banged his fist on the table.

'Everything OK?' I said, not looking up from my papers.

'Yeah. Just a psycho customer,' he mumbled.

I worked on my computer for the next ten minutes, compiling the call statistics. Bakshi had also assigned me the responsibility of checking the other agents' etiquette. Every now and then I would listen in on somebody's call. At 10.47 p.m. I connected to Esha's line.

'Yes, sir. I sound like your daughter? Oh, thank you. So what is wrong with the vacuum cleaner?' she was saying.

Esha's tone was perfect—just the right mix of politeness and firmness. Management monitored us on average call-handling times, or AHTs. As WASG got the trickier customers, our AHT benchmarks were higher at two and a half minutes per call.

'Beep!' The sound of the fax machine made me look up. I went to the machine and checked the incoming fax. It was from Bakshi.

The fax machine took three minutes to churn out the seven pages he had sent. I tore the message sheet off the machine and held the first sheet up.

From: Subhash Bakshi
Subject: Training Initiatives

Dear Shyam,
Just FYI, I have recommended your name to assist in accent training as they are short of teachers. I am sure you can spare some time for this. As always, I am trying to get you more relevant and strategic exposure.
Yours,
Subhash Bakshi
Manager, Connexions

I read the rest of the fax and gasped. Bakshi was sucking me into several hours outside my shift to teach new recruits.

'What's up?' Vroom said, coming up to me.

I passed the fax to Vroom. He read it and smirked.

'I hate accent training,' I said. 'You can't teach Delhi people to speak like Americans in a week.'

'Just as you can't train Americans to speak with a Punjabi accent,'

Vroom said and chuckled. 'Anyway, go train-train, leave your brain.'

'What will I do?' I said, beginning to walk back towards our desk.

'Go train-train, leave your brain,' Vroom said and laughed. He liked the rhyme, and repeated it several times as we walked back to the bay.

Back at my seat, Vroom's words—'train-train'—echoed in my head, bringing back memories of the National Rail Museum, where I had a date with Priyanka a year ago.

My Past Dates with Priyanka—I
National Rail Museum, Chanakyapuri: One year earlier
She arrived thirty minutes late. I had been round the whole museum twice. I went to the museum canteen and was cradling a lukewarm Coke when she finally arrived.

'OK. Don't say anything. Sorry, I'm late, I know,' she said and sat down.

I didn't say anything. I looked at her tiny nose. I wondered how it allowed in enough oxygen.

'What? Say something,' she said after five seconds.

'I thought you told me to be quiet,' I said.

'My mother needs professional help,' Priyanka said. 'She really does.'

'What happened? What was the fuel today?'

'We don't need fuel, just a spark is enough. Just as I was ready to leave to come here, she made a comment on my dress.'

'What did she say?' I asked, looking at her clothes. She wore a blue tie-dye skirt, and a T-shirt with a peace sign on it. It was typical Priyanka stuff. She wore earrings with blue beads, which matched her necklace, and she had a hint of kohl round her eyes, which I was crazy about.

'I was almost at the door when she said, "Why don't you wear the gold necklace I gave you for your last birthday?"' Priyanka said.

'And then?' She obviously wasn't wearing a gold necklace as my gaze turned to the hollow of her neck, which I felt like touching.

'And I was like, no, Mum, it won't go with my dress. Yellow metal is totally uncool, only aunties wear it. Boom, next thing we are having this big, long argument. That's what made me late. Sorry,' she said.

'You didn't have to argue. Just wear the chain in front of her and take it off later,' I said as the waiter came to take our order.

'But that's not the point. Anyway,' she said and turned to the waiter, 'get me a plate of samosas. Actually, wait, they are too fattening. I'll have popcorn. Popcorn is lighter, right?' She looked at the waiter as if he was a nutritionist.

'She'll have popcorn,' I said to the waiter.

'So, what else is happening? Have you met up with Vroom?' she said.

'I was supposed to, but he couldn't come. He had a date.'

'With who? A new girl?'

'Of course. He never sticks to one,' I said.

'I can't understand the deal with Vroom. He is the most materialistic and unemotional person I have met in my entire life,' Priyanka said.

'No he isn't,' I said, as the popcorn arrived at our table.

'Well, look at him, jeans, phones, pizzas and bikes. That's all he lives for. And this whole new-girlfriend-every-three-months thing, come on, at some point you've got to stop that, right?'

'Well, *I'm* happy to stick to the one I have,' I said.

'You are so cute,' Priyanka said. She blushed and smiled.

'Vroom has changed,' I said. 'He wasn't like this when he first joined from his previous job.'

'The one at the newspaper?'

'Yeah, journalist trainee. He started in current affairs. Do you know what one of his famous pieces was called?'

'No, what? Oh crap,' Priyanka said, looking at someone behind me.

'What happened?'

'Nothing, just don't look back. Some relatives of mine are here with their kids. Oh no,' she said, looking down at our table.

Now when someone tells you not to look at something, you always feel an incredible urge to do just that. From the corner of my eye I saw a family with two kids in the corner of the room.

'Who else do you expect to come here but kids?' I said.

'Shut up and look down. Anyway, tell me about Vroom's piece,' she said.

'Oh yeah. It was called "Why Don't Politicians Ever Commit Suicide?" The article said all kinds of people—students, housewives, businessmen, employees and even film stars—commit suicide. But politicians never do. That tells you something.'

'What?' she said, still keeping her eyes down.

'Well, his point was that suicide is a horrible thing and people do it only because they are really hurt. This means they feel something, but politicians don't. So, basically, this country is run by people who don't feel anything.'

'Wow! Can't imagine that going down well with his editor.'

'You bet it didn't. However, Vroom had sneaked it in. The editor only saw it after it was printed and all hell broke loose. Vroom somehow saved his job, but his bosses moved him to cover the society page, page three. They told him he was good-looking so he would fit in. In addition, he'd done a photography course and could take the pictures himself.'

'Cover page three as you're good-looking? That's ridiculous,' she said.

'It is ridiculous. But Vroom took his revenge. He took unflattering pictures of the glitterati—faces stuffed with food, close-ups of cellulite on thighs, drunk people throwing up all showed up in the papers the next day.'

'Oh my god.' Priyanka laughed. 'He sounds like an activist. I can't understand his switching to the call centre for money.'

'Well, according to him, there is activism in chasing money too.'

'And how does that work?'

'Well, his point is that the only reason Americans have a say in this world is because they have cash. So, the first thing we have to do is earn money.'

'Interesting,' Priyanka said and let out a sigh. 'Well, that is why we slog at night. I could have done my B.Ed. right after college, but I wanted to save some money first. I can't open my dream nursery school without cash. So until then, it's two hundred calls a night, night after night.' Priyanka rested her elbows on the table and leaned her chin on her hands. I looked at her. I think she would make the cutest nursery-school principal ever.

'Priyanka dideeee.' The five-year-old boy running towards Priyanka had a model train set and a glass of Coke precariously balanced in his hands. He tripped near our table and I lunged to save him. I succeeded, but his Coke went all over my shirt.

'Oh no,' I said even as I saw a three-year-old girl with a huge lollipop in her mouth running towards us. I moved aside from the tornado to save another collision. She landed straight on Priyanka's lap. I went to the rest room to clean my shirt.

'Shyam,' Priyanka said when I returned, 'meet my cousin, Dr Anurag.' The entire family had shifted to our table. Priyanka introduced me to everyone. Priyanka told her doctor cousin I worked at a call centre and I think he was less interested in talking to me after that. The kids ate half the popcorn and spilt the rest of it. The boy was running his model train set through popcorn fields on the table and screaming a mock siren with his sister.

'Sit, Shyam,' Priyanka said.

'No, actually I have an early shift today,' I said.

'But wait—' Priyanka said.

'No, I have to go,' I said and ran out of the museum.

10.50 p.m.

'Ouch!' Esha's scream during her call broke my train of reminiscence.

'What?' I said. I could hear loud static.

'It's a really bad line . . . Hello, yes, madam,' Esha said.

'Freaking hell,' Vroom said as he pulled off his headset from his ears.

'What's going on?' I said.

'There's shrill static coming every few seconds now. Ask Bakshi to send someone,' Vroom said, rubbing his ears.

'I'll go to his office. You guys cover the calls,' I said and looked at the time. It was 10.51 p.m. The first break was in less than an hour.

BAKSHI WAS IN his oversized office, staring at his computer with his mouth open. As I came in, he rapidly closed the windows. He was probably surfing the Internet for bikini babes or something.

'Good evening, sir,' I said.

'Oh hello, Sam. Please come in.' Bakshi called us by our Western names.

I looked at his big square face, which was unusually large for his five-foo-six-inch body. His face shone as usual. It was the first thing you noticed about Bakshi—the oil fields on his face. If you could immerse Bakshi's skin in our landscape, you'd solve India's oil problems for ever.

Bakshi was about thirty but looked forty and behaved as if he was fifty. He had worked in Connexions for three years. Before that, he did an MBA in some university in south India. He loved to talk in manager's language or 'Managese', which is another language like English and American.

'So, how are the resources doing?' Bakshi said, swivelling on his chair. He never referred to us as people; we were all 'resources'.

'Fine, sir. I wanted to discuss a problem. The phone lines aren't working properly—there's a lot of static during calls. Can you ask Systems . . .'

'Sam,' Bakshi said, pointing a pen at me. 'What did I tell you about how to approach problems?'

I thought hard, but nothing came to mind.

'I don't remember, sir—Solve them?'

'No. I said "big picture". Always start with the big picture.'

I was puzzled. What was the big picture here? There was static coming through the phones and we had to ask Systems to fix it. I could have called them myself, but Bakshi's intervention would get a faster response.

'Sir, it is a specific issue. Customers are hearing disturbance . . .'

'Sam,' Bakshi signalled me to sit down, 'what makes a good manager?'

'What?' I sat down in front of him and surreptitiously looked at my watch. It was 10.57 p.m. I hoped the call flow was moderate so the others wouldn't have a tough time when they were one down on the desk.

'Big picture,' Bakshi said. 'Focus on the big picture. Learn to identify the strategic variables, Sam.' Before I could speak, he had pulled out his pen and was drawing a diagram of a box divided into four squares.

'Maybe I can explain this to you with the help of a two-by-two matrix,' he said and bent down to write 'High' and 'Low' along the boxes.

'Sir, please,' I said, placing both my hands down to cover the sheet.

'What?' he said with irritation.

'Sir, this is really interesting, but right now my team is waiting.'

'So?' Bakshi said.

'The phones, sir. Please tell Systems they should check the WASG bay urgently,' I said, without pausing to breathe.

'Huh?' Bakshi said.

'Just call Systems, sir,' I said and stood up, 'using that.' I pointed at his telephone and rushed back to my bay.

11.00 p.m.

'Nice break, eh?' Vroom said when I returned to our bay.

'C'mon, man, I just went to Bakshi's office about the static,' I said.

'Is he sending someone?' Vroom asked as he untangled his phone wires.

'He said I should identify the strategic variables first,' I said and sat down.

'Strategic variables? What are they?' Vroom said, without looking at me.

'How the hell do I know?' I snorted. 'If I did, I'd be team leader. He also drew a diagram.'

Radhika, Esha and Priyanka were busy on calls. Every few seconds, they would turn the phone away from their ears to avoid the loud static. I wished the Systems guy would come by soon.

'What diagram?' Vroom said as he offered me some chewing gum.

'Some two-by-two matrix or something,' I said, declining Vroom's offer.

'Poor Bakshi, he's just a silly, harmless creature. Don't worry about him,' Vroom said.

'Where the hell is the Systems guy?' I called Systems myself. They hadn't yet received a call from Bakshi. 'Can you please come now . . . yes, we have an emergency . . . yes, our manager knows about it.'

'Things are bad around here,' Vroom said. 'Bad news may be coming.'

'What do you mean? Are they cutting jobs?' I asked, now a little worried and anxious as well as frustrated. It's amazing how all these nasty emotions decide to visit me together.

'I'm trying to find out,' Vroom said, clicking open a window on his screen. 'The Western Computers account is really suffering. If we lose that account, the call centre will sink.'

A visitor in our bay interrupted us. I knew he was the Systems guy as he had three pagers on his belt and two memory cards hanging round his neck.

Priyanka told him about the problem and made him listen to the static.

The Systems guy asked us to disconnect our lines for ten minutes.

Everyone removed their headsets. I saw Esha adjusting her hair. She does it at least ten times a night. Radhika took some pink wool out from her bag and started to knit. Military Uncle's system was still working, so he stayed glued to his monitor.

'What are you knitting?' Esha turned to Radhika.

'A scarf for my mother-in-law. She's very sweet, she feels cold at night.'

'She is not sweet—' Vroom began to say but Radhika interrupted him.

'Shh, Vroom. She is fine, just traditional.'

'And that sucks, right?' Vroom said.

'Not at all. In fact, I like the cosy family feeling. They're only a little bit old-fashioned,' Radhika said and smiled. I didn't think her smile was genuine, but it was none of my business.

'Yeah, right. Only a little. As in always-cover-your-head-with-your-sari types,' Vroom said.

'They make you cover your head?' Esha asked.

'They don't *make* me do anything, Esha. I am willing to follow their culture. All married women in their house do it,' Radhika said.

'Still, it is a bit weird,' Esha said doubtfully.

'Anyway, I look on it as a challenge. I love Anuj and he said he came as a package. But yeah, sometimes I miss wearing low-waisted jeans like you wore yesterday.'

I was amazed Radhika remembered what Esha had worn yesterday.

'You like those jeans?' Esha said, her eyes lighting up.

'I love them. But I guess you need the right figure for them,' Radhika said. 'Anyway, sorry to change the topic, but we're forgetting something.'

'What? Systems?' I asked, as I looked under the table where the Systems guy lurked within a jungle of tangled wires. He told me he'd need ten minutes.

'I didn't mean the static,' Radhika said as she put her knitting aside. 'Miss Priyanka has some big news for us, remember?'

'Oh yes. C'mon, Priyanka, tell us!' Esha screamed. Military Uncle looked up from his screen for a second and then went back to work.

'OK, I do have something to tell you,' Priyanka said with a sheepish grin. She brought out a box of sweets from her large plastic bag and started to carefully open the red cellophane wrapping on the box. I hate it when she's so methodical. Just rip the damn wrapping off, I thought.

'So, what's up? Ooh, milk cake, my favourite,' Radhika said, as Vroom jumped to grab the first piece.

'I'll tell you, but you guys have to swear it won't leave WASG,' Priyanka said. She offered the box to Radhika and Esha. Radhika took two pieces, while Esha broke off the tiniest piece possible with human fingers. I guess the low-cut-jeans figure comes at a price.

'Of course we won't tell anyone. Now tell us, please,' Esha said and wiped her long fingers with a tissue.

'Well, you know my mum and her obsession for a match with an expat Indian for her rebellious daughter to take her away from India?'

'Uh-uh,' Radhika nodded as she ate her milk cake.

'So these family friends of ours brought a proposal for me. It came from one of their relatives in Seattle. I would have said no as I always do. But this time I saw the photos, which were cute. I spoke to the guy on the phone and he sounded decent. He works at Microsoft and his parents are in Delhi and I met them today. They are nice people,' Priyanka said.

'And,' Esha said, her eyes opening wide and staring at Priyanka.

'I don't know, something just clicked,' Priyanka said. 'They asked for my decision up-front and I said . . . yes.'

'Waaaooooow! Oh wow!' the girls screamed at the highest pitch possible. The Systems guy trembled under the table. I told him everything was fine and asked him to continue. At least everything was fine outside. Inside I had a burning feeling, as if someone had tossed a hot coal in my stomach.

Radhika and Esha got up to hug Priyanka as if India had won the World Cup or something. People get married every day. Did these girls really have to create a scene? I looked at my computer screen and saw that Microsoft Word was open. Angrily I closed all windows with the Microsoft logo on it.

'Congratulations, Priyanka,' Vroom said, 'that's big news.'

Even Military Uncle got up and came to shake hands with Priyanka. His generation like it when young people decide to get married. Of course, he was back at his desk within twenty seconds.

'You've met the guy?' Vroom asked.

'No, he's in Seattle. But we spoke for hours on the phone, and I've seen his picture. He's cute. Do you want to see the photo?' Priyanka said.

'No, thanks,' I blurted out. Damn, I couldn't believe I'd said that. By sheer luck I hadn't said it loud enough for Priyanka to hear.

'Do you want some cake?' Priyanka asked, shunting the box towards me.

'No, thanks,' I said and slid the box back.

'I thought milk cake was your favourite.'

'Not any more. My tastes have changed,' I said. 'I'm trying to cut down.'

'Not even a small piece?' she asked and tilted her head. At one stage in my life I used to find that head-tilt cute, but today I remained adamant.

I shook my head and our eyes locked. When you've shared a relationship with someone, the first change is in how you look into each other's eyes. The gaze becomes more fixed and it's hard to pull away from it.

'Aren't you going to say anything?' Priyanka said. When girls say that, it's not really a question. It means they *want* you to say something.

'About what? The phone lines? They'll be fixed in ten minutes,' I said.

'Not that. I'm getting married, Shyam.'

'Good,' I said and turned to my screen.

'Show us the picture!' Esha screamed, as if it was Brad Pitt naked or something. Priyanka took out a photograph from her handbag and passed it round. I saw it from a distance: he looked like a regular software geek. He stood straight with his stomach pulled in—an old trick any guy with a paunch applies when he gets his picture taken. He wore glasses and had a super-neat hairstyle as if his mum combed his hair every morning. He was standing with the Statue of Liberty in the background and his forced smile made him look like a total loser, if you asked me. However, now he was hot, and girls with dimples were ready to marry him without even meeting him.

'He's so cute, like a teddy bear,' Esha said, passing the picture to Radhika.

When girls call a guy 'teddy bear', they just mean he's a nice guy but they'd never be attracted to him. Girls may say they like such guys, but teddy bears never get to sleep with anyone. Unless of course their mums hunt the neighbourhood for them.

'Are you OK?' Priyanka said to me. The others were analysing the picture.

'Yeah. Why?'

'I just expected a little more reaction. We've known each other for four years, more than anybody else on the desk.'

Radhika, Esha and Vroom turned to look at us.

'Reaction?' I said. 'I thought I said *good*.'

'That's all?' Priyanka said. Her smile had left the building.

Everyone was staring at me.

'OK,' I said, 'OK, Priyanka. This is *great* news. I am *so* happy for you. *OK?*'

'You could have used a better tone,' Priyanka muttered, and walked away quickly towards the ladies' room.

'What? Why is everyone staring at me?' I said as they all turned away.

The Systems guy finally came out from under the table.

'Fixed?' I said.

'I need signal-testing equipment,' he said, wiping sweat off his forehead. 'The problem could be external. Builders are digging all over this suburb right now, some contractor may have dug over our lines. Just take a break until I come back. Get your manager here as well,' he said and left.

I called Bakshi, but the line was busy so I left a voicemail.

Priyanka returned from the rest room and I noticed that she had washed her face. Her nose still had a drop of water on it.

'Sounds like an easy night. I hope it never gets fixed,' Radhika said.

'There's nothing better than a call-centre job when the phones aren't working,' Priyanka said and closed the box of sweets.

'So, tell us more. What's he like?' Esha said.

'Who? Ganesh?' Priyanka asked.

'His name is Ganesh? Nice,' Esha said and switched on her mobile phone. Normally agents couldn't use cellphones in the bay, but it was OK to do so when the system was down.

'Does Ganesh like to talk? Sometimes the software types are really quiet,' Radhika said.

'Oh yes, he talks a lot. In fact, I might get a call from him tonight,' Priyanka said and smiled.

'You sound *sooo* happy,' Esha said. Her 'so' lasted four seconds.

'I *am* happy. I can see what Radhika says now about getting a new family. Ganesh's mum came round today and gave me a big gold chain and hugged me and kissed me.'

'Sounds horrible,' Vroom said.

'Shut up, Vroom,' Esha said. 'Oh, Priyanka, you're so lucky.'

Vroom sensed that I wasn't exactly jumping with joy at the conversation.

'Cigarette?' he said.

I looked at my watch. It was 11.30, our usual time for taking a smoke. In any case, I preferred burning my lungs to sticking around to find out Ganesh's hobbies.

11.31 p.m.

Vroom and I went to the call-centre parking lot. He leaned against his bike and lit two cigarettes with one match. I looked at his tall, thin frame. If he weren't so skinny you'd say he was a stud. Still, a cigarette looked out of place on his boyish face. Perhaps conscious of the people who had called him Baby Face before, he always wore one-day-old stubble. He passed a lit cigarette to me. I took a puff and let it out in the cold night air.

We stayed quiet for a moment and I was thankful to Vroom for that. One thing guys do know is when to shut up.

Vroom finally spoke, starting with a neutral topic. 'I need a break. Good thing I'm going to Manali next weekend.'

'Cool, Manali is really nice,' I said.

'I'm going with my school buddies. We might ride up there on bikes. Have you been there?'

'Last year. We went by bus, though,' I said.

'Who did you go with?' Vroom said.

'Priyanka,' I said. 'It was great. We took a bus at four in the morning. Priyanka was in her anti-snob phase, so she insisted we take the ordinary slow bus and not the deluxe fast one. She wanted to enjoy the scenery slowly.'

'And then?'

'The moment the bus reached the highway, she leaned on my shoulder and fell asleep. My shoulder cramped, but apart from that it was great fun.'

'She's a silly girl,' Vroom said, letting out a big puff, his face smiling behind the smoke ring.

'She is. You should have seen her back then. She used to wear all these beads and earthy clothes she bought from Fabindia all the time. And then she'd sit with the truck drivers and drink tea.'

'Wow. I can't imagine Priyanka like that now,' Vroom said.

'Trust me, the girl has a wild side,' I said, and paused as her face came to mind. 'Anyway, it's history now. Girls change.'

'You bet. She's all set now.'

I nodded. I didn't want to talk about Priyanka any more. At least one part of me didn't. The rest of me always wanted to talk about her.

'An expat Indian catch, Microsoft and all. Not bad,' Vroom continued as he lit another cigarette. I narrowed my eyes at him.

'It's a little too fast, isn't it?' I said. 'Don't you think she's moving too quickly?'

'C'mon, man, you don't get matches like that every day. He's in freakin''

Microsoft. As good as they get. He is MS Groom 1.1—deluxe edition.'

'What's the deal with Microsoft?'

'Dude, I'm sure he packs close to a hundred grand a year.'

'What? A hundred thousand US dollars a year?'

Vroom nodded. I tried to convert one hundred thousand US dollars to rupees and divide it by twelve to get the monthly salary, but there were too many zeros and it was a tough calculation to do in my head.

'Stop calculating in rupees,' Vroom said and smiled. 'Priyanka's got a catch, I'm telling you.'

He paused and looked at me. His eyes were wet, brown and kind of like a puppy's. I could see why girls flocked to him. It was the eyes.

'I'm going to ask you a question. Will you answer it honestly?'he said.

'OK.'

'Are you upset she's getting married? I know you have feelings for her.'

'No,' I said and started laughing. 'I just find it a bit strange. But I wouldn't say I'm upset. That's too strong a word. It is not like we're together any more. No, I'm not *upset* upset.'

He waited while I continued to laugh exaggeratedly. When I'd stopped he said, 'OK, don't bullshit me. What happened to your re-proposal plans?'

I sighed. 'Well, of course I feel for her, but they're just vestigial feelings.'

'Vesti what?'

'Like vestigial organs. They serve no purpose or value. But they can give you a pain in the appendix. It's the same with my feelings for Priyanka. I'm supposed to have moved on, but obviously I haven't. Meanwhile, Mr Indian in Seattle comes and gives me a kick in the rear end,' I said.

'Talk to her. Don't tell me you're not going to,' Vroom said.

'I was planning to. I thought we'd submit the website user manual and that would make it easier for Boston to approve my promotion,' I said, referring to the company headquarters in America. 'How did I know there would be milk cake tonight? How was it? I didn't touch it.'

'The milk cake was great. Never sulk when food is at stake, dude. Anyway, listen, you still have some time. She's only just said yes.'

'I hope so. Though it's hard to compete with Mr Microsoft,' I said.

We remained silent for a few more seconds. Vroom spoke again.

'Yeah, man. Girls are strategic. They talk about love and romance but when it comes to doing the deal, they'll choose the fattest chicken,' he said.

'I guess I can only become fat, not a fat chicken,' I said.

'Yeah, you need to be fat, fresh and fluffy. That's why you shouldn't feel so upset. We're not good husband material, just accept it.'

'Thanks, Vroom, that really makes my day,' I said. I did agree with him though. It was evolution. Maybe nature wanted dimple-cheeked, software-geek, mini-Ganesh babies. They were of far more value to society than depressed, good-for-nothing junior Shyams.

'And anyway, it's the girl who always gets to choose. Men propose and women accept or, as in many cases, reject it.'

It's true. Girls go around rejecting men like it's their birthright. They have no idea how much it hurts us.

'But who knows?' Vroom said. 'Priyanka isn't like other girls, or maybe she is after all. Either way, don't give up, man. Try to get her back.'

'Speaking of getting her back, shouldn't we be heading back to the bay?' I said and looked at my watch. 'It's eleven forty-five p.m.'

AS WE RETURNED from the parking lot, we passed the Western Computers main bay. The main bay sounded like a noisy school, except the kids weren't talking to one another, but to customers.

'Still looks busy,' I said.

'Not at all. People have told me call traffic is down forty per cent. I think they'll cut a lot of staff or, worst-case scenario, cut everyone, close this poorly managed madhouse down and shift the clients to the centre based in Bangalore,' Vroom said. Bangalore was the location of the second Western Computers and Applicances call centre in India.

'Close down!' I echoed. 'Are you serious, what will happen to the hundreds of jobs here?'

'Like they care.' He shrugged his lanky shoulders. 'Shit happens in life. It could happen tonight,' Vroom said as we reached the WASG bay.

12.15 a.m.

The Systems guy was under the table again.

'No calls yet. They've asked for a senior engineer,' Priyanka said.

'It's an external fault. Some cables are damaged, I think. This area of Gurgaon is going nuts with all the building work,' the Systems guy said.

'Does Bakshi know?' I said.

'I don't know,' Priyanka said.

Vroom and I sat down at our desk.

'It's not too bad. Nice break,' Esha said as she filed her nails.

Priyanka's cellphone began to ring, startling everyone.

'Who's calling you so late?' Radhika said, still knitting her scarf.

'It's long distance, I think,' Priyanka said and smiled.

'Ooooh!' Esha squealed, like a two-year-old on a bouncy castle.

'Hi, Ganesh. I've just switched my phone on,' Priyanka said.

I couldn't hear Ganesh's response, thank god.

'Fifteen times? I can't believe you tried my number fifteen times . . . so sorry,' Priyanka said, looking idiotic with happiness.

'Yes, I'm at work. But it's really chaotic today. The systems are down . . . How come you're working on Thanksgiving? Oh, nice of the Indians to offer to work . . . Hello? . . . Hello?' Priyanka said.

'What happened?' Esha said.

'There's hardly any network,' Priyanka said, shaking her phone.

'We're in the basement. Nothing comes into this black hole,' Vroom said. He was surfing the Internet, and was on the Formula One website.

'Use the landline,' Esha said, pointing to the spare phone on our desk. Every team in Connexions had a spare independent landline at their desk for emergency use. 'Tell him to call on the landline.'

'Here?' Priyanka asked, looking to me for permission.

Normally this would be unthinkable, but our systems were down so it didn't really matter. Also, I didn't want to look like a sore loser.

I nodded and pretended to be absorbed by my computer screen. As the ad hoc team leader, I could approve personal calls and listen in on any line on the desk through my headset. However, I couldn't listen in on the independent emergency phone. Not unless I went under the table and tapped it.

Tap the landline, a faint voice echoed in my head.

'No, it's wrong,' I said.But I could still hear one side of the conversation.

'Hello . . . Ganesh, call the landline . . . yes, 22463463 and 11 for Delhi . . . Call after ten minutes, our boss might be doing his rounds soon . . . I know ten minutes is six hundred seconds, I'm sure you'll survive.' She laughed uncontrollably and hung up. When women laugh nonstop, they're flirting.

'He sounds so *cuuute*,' Esha said.

'I'm going to call Bakshi. We need to fix the systems,' I said and stood up. I couldn't bear 600-seconds-without-you survival stories.

I was walking towards Bakshi's office when I saw him coming towards me.

'Agent Sam, why aren't you at your desk?' Bakshi said.

'I was looking for you, sir,' I said.

'I'm all yours,' Bakshi said as his face broke into a smile.

Bakshi and I returned to WASG. Bakshi's heavy steps were plainly heard by everyone. Radhika hid her knitting under the table. Vroom opened his screen to an empty MS Word document.

The Systems guy came out from under the table and called his boss, the head of the IT department.

'Looks like we have technology issues here,' Bakshi said and the Systems guy nodded his head.

The head of IT arrived soon after and he and the Systems guy discussed geek stuff between themselves in so-called English. Then the IT head ranted out incomprehensible technical details to us. I understood that the system was under strain: 80 per cent of the WASG capacity was damaged, and the remaining 20 per cent could not handle the current load.

'Hmmm,' Bakshi said, 'hmmm . . . that's really bad, isn't it?'

'So, what do you want us to do?' the IT head asked.

All eyes turned to Bakshi. It was a situation Bakshi hated, where he was being asked to take a decision or recommend action.

'Hmmm,' Bakshi said. 'We really need a methodical game plan here.'

'We can shut down the WASG system tonight. Western Computers main bay is running fine anyway,' the junior IT guy suggested.

'But WASG has not lost all its capacity. Boston won't like it if we shut the bay,' the IT head said.

'Hmmm,' Bakshi said again and pressed a sweaty palm on my desk. 'Upsetting Boston isn't a good idea at this time. We're already on a slippery slope at Connexions. Let's try to be proactively oriented here.'

Vroom couldn't resist a snigger at Bakshi's jargon.

'Sir, can I make a suggestion?' I said.

'What?' Bakshi said.

'We could enlist Bangalore's help,' I said.

'Bangalore?' Bakshi and the IT head said in unison.

'Yes, sir. It's Thanksgiving and the call volume is low, so Bangalore will be running light as well. If we pass most of our calls there, it will get busier for them, but it won't overload them. Meanwhile, we can handle a limited flow here,' I said.

'That makes sense. We can easily switch the flow for a few hours. We can fix the systems here in the morning,' the junior IT guy said.

'That's fine,' I said. 'And people will start their Thanksgiving dinner in the States soon, so call volumes will fall even more.'

Everyone at the desk looked at me and nodded, thrilled at the idea of an easy shift. Bakshi, however, had fallen into silent contemplation. I would love to know what he's thinking about in these moments.

'See, the thing is,' Bakshi said and paused again, 'aren't we comparing apples to oranges here?'

'What?' Vroom looked at Bakshi with a disgusted expression.

I wondered what Bakshi was talking about. Was I the apple? Who was the orange? What fruit was Bangalore?

'I have an idea. Why don't we enlist Bangalore?' Bakshi said.

'But that's what Shyam—' the junior IT guy began, but Bakshi interrupted him. Poor junior IT guy, he isn't familiar with Bakshi's ways.

'See, it sounds unusual, but sometimes you have to think outside the box,' Bakshi said and tapped his head in self-admiration.

'Yes, sir,' I said. 'That's a great idea. We have it all sorted now.'

'Good,' the IT guys said and began playing with the computer menus.

Before the IT guys left they told us that the WASG call volume would be super-light. We were overjoyed, but kept a straight face before Bakshi.

'See, problem solved,' Bakshi said. 'That's what I'm here for.'

'Lucky us, sir,' Priyanka said.

We thought Bakshi would leave, but he had other plans.

'Shyam, as you are free tonight, can you help me with some strategic documents? It will give you some exposure.'

'What is it, sir?' I said, not happy about sacrificing my night.

'I've just printed out ten copies of monthly data sheets,' Bakshi said, holding up some documents. 'For some reason the sheets are no longer in order. There are ten page ones, then page twos and so on. Can you help fix this?'

'You haven't collated them. You can choose the option when you print,' Vroom said.

'You can choose to collate?' Bakshi asked, as if we'd told him about an option for brain transplants.

'Yes,' Vroom said. 'Anyway, it is easier to take one print-out and photocopy the rest. It comes out stapled too.'

'I need to upgrade my technical skills. Technology changes so fast,' Bakshi said. 'But, Shyam, can you help reorder and staple them this time?'

'Sure,' I said.

Bakshi placed the sheets on my table and left the room.

Priyanka looked at me with her mouth open. 'I can't believe it.' She shook her head. 'Why do you let him do that to you?'

'C'mon, Priyanka, leave Shyam alone. Bakshi runs his life,' Vroom said.

'Exactly. Because he lets him. Why can't people stand up for themselves?'

I don't know why I can't stand up for myself, but I definitely can't stand Priyanka's rhetorical questions. I tried to ignore her. However, her words had affected me. It was difficult to focus on the sheets. I stacked the first set ready to staple them when Vroom said, 'He can't take on Bakshi right now. Not at this time, Priyanka, while they're in the mood for firing people.'

'Yes, thanks, Vroom. Can someone explain the reality? I need to make a living. I don't have Mr Microsoft PowerPoint waiting for me in Seattle,' I said and pressed the stapler hard. I missed and the staple pin pierced my finger.

'Oww!' I screamed loud enough to uproot Military Uncle from his desk.

'What happened?' Priyanka said and stood up.

I lifted my finger to show the streaks of blood. A couple of drops spilt onto Bakshi's document.

The girls squealed 'eews' in rapid succession.

'Symbolism, man. Giving your lifeblood to this job,' Vroom said. 'Can someone give this guy a Band-Aid before he makes me throw up?'

'I have one,' Esha said, taking out a Band-Aid from her bag.

'It's nothing. Just a minor cut,' I said. I clenched my teeth hard.

Priyanka took out a few tissues from her bag. She held my finger and cleaned the blood around it.

'Ouch!' I screamed.

'Oh, the staple's still in there,' she said. 'We need tweezers.'

Esha had tweezers in her handbag. Girls' handbags hold enough to make a survival kit for Antarctica.

Priyanka held the tweezers and went to work on my finger with a surgeon's concentration.

'Here's the culprit,' she said as she pulled out a staple pin drenched in blood. Priyanka wiped my finger and then stuck the Band-Aid on it. Everyone returned to their seats and I went back to collating sheets.

Esha and Radhika began talking about Bakshi.

'He had no idea what IT was saying,' Radhika said.

'Yeah, but did you see his face?' Esha said. 'He looked like he was doing a CBI investigation.'

I looked at Priyanka. The letters CBI brought back memories. Even as I collated Bakshi's sheets, my mind drifted to Pandara Road.

My Past Dates with Priyanka—II
Have More Restaurant, Pandara Road: Nine months earlier
'Shyam,' Priyanka said as she tried to push me away. 'This is not the place to do these things. This is Pandara Road.'

'Oh really,' I said, refusing to move away. We were sitting at a corner table, partially hidden by a carved wooden screen. 'What's wrong with Pandara Road?' I said, continuing to kiss her.

'This is a family place,' she said, pushing me back again.

'So, families get made by doing these things.'

'Very funny. Anyway, you chose this place. I hope the food is as good as you said it was.'

'It's the best in Delhi,' I said. We were in Have More Restaurant, one of the half-dozen overpriced but excellent restaurants on Pandara Road.

'A hundred and thirty bucks for dhal!' Priyanka exclaimed as she opened the menu. It was embarrassing, especially as the waiter was already at our table to take the order.

'Just order, OK?' I said in a hushed voice.

Priyanka took five more minutes to place the order. Here is how she decides. Step one: sort all the dishes on the menu according to price. Step two: re-sort the cheaper ones based on calories.

'One naan, no butter. Yellow dhal,' she said as I glared at her.

'OK, not yellow, black dhal,' she said. 'And . . .'

'And one shahi paneer,' I said.

'You always order the same thing, black dhal and shahi paneer.'

'Yes, same girl, same food. Why bother experimenting when you already have the best?' I said.

'You are so cute,' she said, smiling. She pinched my cheeks and fed me a little vinegar-onion from the table. Hardly romantic, but I liked it.

She moved her hand away quickly when she saw a family being led to the table adjacent to us. The family consisted of a young married couple, their two little daughters and an old lady. The daughters were twins, probably four years old. The entire family had morose faces and no one said a word to each other. I wondered why they had bothered to go out when they could be grumpy for free at home.

'Anyway,' Priyanka said, 'what's the news?'

'Not much, Vroom and I are busy with the troubleshooting website.'

'Cool, how's it coming along?'

'Really well. Nothing fancy, though, the best websites are simple.'

The waiter arrived with our food.

Priyanka put micro-portions of food on her plate.

'Eat properly,' I said. 'Stop dieting all the time like Esha.'

'I'm not that hungry,' she said as I gave her human portions of food.

'Hey, did I tell you about Esha? Don't tell anyone,' she said.

I shook my head. 'You love to gossip. Don't you? Your name should be Miss Gossip FM 98.5,' I said.

'I *never* gossip,' she said. 'Oh my god, the food is so good here.'

My chest inflated with pride as if I had spent all night cooking it myself.

'Of course you love to gossip. Whenever someone starts with "don't tell anyone", that to me shows a juicy titbit of gossip is coming,' I said.

Priyanka blushed and the tip of her nose turned tomato red. She looked cute as hell. I would have kissed her right then, but the grumpy family was beginning to argue and I didn't want to spoil the sombre ambiance for them.

'OK, so maybe I gossip, but only a little bit,' Priyanka relented. 'But I read somewhere, gossip is good for you. It's a sign you're interested in people and care for them.'

'That is so lame.' I burst out laughing. 'Anyway, what about Esha? I know Vroom has the hots for her, but does she like him?'

'Shyam, that is old news. She's rejected Vroom's proposal before. The latest is that she had signed up for the Femina Miss India contest. Last week she got a rejection letter because she wasn't tall enough. She is five-five and the minimum is five-six. Radhika saw her crying in the toilet.'

'Oh wow! Miss India?'

'Come on, she's not that pretty. She should really stop this modelling thing. God, she is so thin, though. OK, I'm not eating any more.'

'Eat, stupid. Do you want to be happy or thin?' I said, pushing her plate back towards her.

'Thin.'

'Shut up, eat properly. And as for Esha, well too bad Miss India didn't work out. However, trying doesn't hurt,' I said.

'Well, she was crying. So it hurt *her*. After all, she's come to Delhi against her parents' wishes. It's not easy struggling alone,' she said.

I nodded.

We finished eating and the waiter reappeared like a genie to clear the plates.

'Dessert?' I said.

'No way. I'm too full,' Priyanka said.

'OK, one kulfi please,' I said to the waiter.

'No, order gulab jamun,' she said.

'Huh? I thought you didn't want . . . OK, one gulab jamun, please.'

The waiter went back into his magic bottle.

'How's your mum?' I said.

'The same. We haven't had a cry fest since last week's showdown, so that alone is a reason to celebrate. Maybe I will have half a gulab jamun.'

'And what happened last week?'

'Last week? Oh yes, my uncles were over for dinner. So picture this, we are all having butterscotch ice cream at the dining table. One uncle mentioned that my cousin was getting married to a cardiac surgeon.'

The waiter came and gave us the gulab jamun. I took a bite.

'Ouch, careful, these are hot,' I said. 'Anyway, what happened then?'

'So I'm eating my ice cream and my mother screams "Priyanka, make sure you marry someone well settled".'

'I'm going to be a team leader soon,' I said and fed her a slice of dessert.

'Relax, Shyam,' Priyanka said as she took a bite and patted my arm. 'It has nothing to do with you. The point is, how could she spring it on me in front of everyone? Like, why can't I just have ice cream like the others? Take my brother, nobody says anything to him while he stuffs his face.'

I laughed and signalled for the bill.

'So what did you do then?' I said.

'Nothing. I slammed my spoon down on the plate and left the room.'

'You're a major drama queen,' I said.

'Guess what she says to everyone then? "This is what I get for bringing her up and loving her so much. She doesn't care."'

I laughed as Priyanka imitated her mother. The bill arrived and my eyebrows shot up for a second as I paid the 463 rupees.

We stood up to leave and the grumpy family's voices reached us.

'What to do? Since the day this woman came to our house, our family's fortunes have been ruined,' the old woman was saying.

The daughter-in-law had tears in her eyes. She hadn't touched her food while the man was eating nonchalantly.

'Look at her now, sitting there with a stiff face. Go, go to hell now. Not only did you not bring anything, now you have dumped these two girls like two curses on me,' the mother-in-law said.

I looked at the little girls. They had identical plaits with cute pink ribbons in them. The girls were each holding one of their mother's hands and they looked really scared.

'Say something now, you silent statue,' the mother-in-law said.

'Why doesn't she say anything?' Priyanka whispered to me.

'She can't,' I said. 'When you have a bad boss, you can't say anything.'

'Who will pay for these two curses? Say something now,' the mother-in-law said as the daughter-in-law's tears came down faster and faster.

'I'll say something,' Priyanka shouted, facing the mother-in-law.

The grumpy family turned to look at us in astonishment. I looked for a deep hole to hide myself from the embarrassment.

'Who are you?' the husband asked.

'We'll worry about that later,' Priyanka said, 'but who the hell are *you*? Her husband I presume?'

'Huh? Yes, I am. Madam, this is a family matter,' he said.

'Oh really? You call this a family? Doesn't look like a family to me,' Priyanka said. 'I just see an old shrew and a loser wimp upsetting these girls. Don't you have any shame? Is this what you married her for?'

'See, she's another one,' the mother-in-law said. 'Look at the girls of today: they don't know how to talk. Look at her, eyes made up like a heroine's.'

'The young girls know how to talk and behave. It's you old people who need to be taught a lesson. These are your granddaughters and you are calling them a curse?' Priyanka said, her nose an even cuter red than before.

'Who are you, madam? What is your business here?' the husband said.

'I'll tell you who I am,' Priyanka said and fumbled in her handbag. She took out her call-centre ID card and flashed it for a nanosecond. 'Priyanka Sinha, CBI, Women's Cell.'

'What?' the husband said in half-disbelief.

'What is your number plate?' Priyanka said, talking in a flat voice.

'What? Why?' the bewildered husband asked.

She glanced at the keys on the table. 'It's a Santro, isn't it?'

'DGI 463. Why?' the husband said.

Priyanka took out her cellphone and pretended to call a number. 'Hello? Sinha here. Please retrieve records on DGI 463 . . . Yes . . . Santro . . . Thanks.'

'Madam, what is going on?' the husband said, his voice quivering.

'Three years. Harassing women is punishable by three years. A quick trial, no appeal,' Priyanka said and stared at the mother-in-law.

The old woman pulled one of the twin granddaughters onto her lap.

'What? Madam this is just a f-f-f-family affair—' the husband stammered.

'Don't say family!' Priyanka said, her voice loud.

'Madam,' the mother-in-law said, her tone now sweet, 'we are just here to have a meal. I don't even let her cook see, we just had—'

'Shut up! We have your records now. We will keep track. If you mess around, your son and you will have plenty of meals together—in jail.'

'Sorry, madam,' the husband said with folded arms. He asked for the bill and fumbled for cash. Within a minute they had paid and left.

I looked at Priyanka with my mouth open. 'CBI?' I said.

'Don't say anything,' she said, 'let's go.'

We sat in the Qualis I had borrowed from the call-centre driver.

'Stupid old witch,' Priyanka said. I started to drive. Five minutes later, Priyanka turned to me. 'OK, you can say what you want now.'

'I love you,' I said.

'What? Why this now?'

'Because I love it when you stand up for something you feel strongly about. And that you do such a horrible job of acting like a CBI inspector. I love the kohl round your eyes. I love it when your eyes light up when you have gossip for me. I love it that you say you don't want dessert and then ask me to change mine so you can have half. I love it that you believe in me and are patient about my career. Actually, you know what, Priyanka?' I said.

'What?'

'I may not be a heart surgeon, but the one little heart I have, I have given it to you.'

Priyanka laughed aloud and put her hand on her face.

'Sorry,' she said and shook her head, still laughing. 'Sorry, you were doing so well, except for the surgeon line. Now, that is seriously cheesy.'

'You know what?' I said and removed one hand from the steering wheel to tweak her nose. 'They should put you in jail for killing romantic lines.'

12.30 a.m.

'I can't believe this,' Radhika said and threw her mobile phone on her desk, breaking up my Pandara Road dream. She looked upset.

Everyone turned to look at her. She covered her face with her hands and took a couple of deep breaths.

'What's up?' Priyanka said.

'It's Anuj. Sometimes he can be so unreasonable,' Radhika said and passed her phone to Esha. On the screen was a text message. 'Read it out,' she said as she fumbled through her bag for her anti-migraine pills. 'Damn, I only have one pill left.'

'Really? OK,' Esha said and started reading the message: 'Show elders respect. Act like a daughter-in-law should. Good night.'

'What did I do wrong? I was in a hurry, that's all,' Radhika mumbled to herself as she took her pill with a sip of water.

Esha put a hand on her arm. 'What happened?' she asked softly.

'Anuj is in Kolkata. He called home and my mother-in-law told him, "Radhika made a face when I told her to crush the almonds more finely." Can you believe it? I was running to catch the Qualis and still made time to prepare her milk,' Radhika said and started to press her forehead. 'And then she told him, "I am old, if the pieces are too big they will choke my food pipe. Maybe Radhika is trying to kill me." Why would she say something so horrible?'

'And you're still knitting a scarf for her?' Vroom said.

'Trust me, being a daughter-in-law is harder than being a model,' Radhika said. 'Anyway, enough of my boring life.'

'Are you OK?' Esha said, still holding Radhika's arm.

'Yes, I'm fine. Sorry, guys, I overreacted. It's just a little miscommunication between Anuj and me.'

'Looks like your mother-in-law likes melodrama. She should meet my mother,' Priyanka said.

'Really?' Radhika said.

'Oh yes. She is the Miss Universe of melodrama. We cry together at least once a week. Though today she's on cloud nine,' Priyanka said.

My attention was diverted by a call flashing on my screen.

'I'll take it,' I said, raising my hand. 'Western Appliances, Sam speaking, how may I help you?'

It was one of my weird calls of the night. The caller was from Virginia and was having trouble defrosting his fridge. It took me four long minutes to figure out the reason. It turned out the caller was a 'big person', which is what Americans call fat people, and his fingers were too thick to turn the tiny knob which activates the defrosting mechanism. I suggested that he use a screwdriver and fortunately that solution worked after seven attempts.

'Thank you for calling Western Appliances, sir,' I said and ended the call.

'More politeness, agent Sam. Be more courteous,' I heard Bakshi's voice and felt his heavy breath on my neck.

'Sir, you again?' I said and turned round.

'Sorry, I forgot something important,' he said. 'Have you guys done the Western Computers website manual? I am finally sending the report to Boston.'

'Yes, sir. Vroom and I finished it yesterday,' I said and took out a copy from my drawer.

'Hmm,' Bakshi said as he scanned the cover sheet.

Western Computers Troubleshooting Website

User Manual and Project Details
Developed by Connexions, Delhi
Shyam Mehra and Varun Malhotra
(Sam Marcy and Victor Mell)

'Do you have a soft copy that you can email me?' Bakshi said. 'Boston wants it urgently.'

'Yes, sir,' Vroom said, 'I'll send it to you.'

'Also, did you do the collation, Sam?'

'Yes, sir,' I said and passed him the ten sets.

'Excellent. I empowered you, and you delivered the output. Actually, I have another document, the board meeting invite. Can you help?'

'What do I have to do?' I said.

'Here's a copy,' Bakshi said and gave me a five-page document. 'Can you photocopy ten copies for me, please? My secretary is off today.'

'Sir,' Vroom said, 'what's the board meeting for?'

'Nothing, just routine management issues,' Bakshi said.

'Are people going to get fired?' Vroom asked.

'Er . . .' Bakshi said, lost for words when asked something meaningful.

'There are rumours in the Western Computers main bay. We just want to know if we will be fine,' Vroom said.

Bakshi took a deep breath and said, 'I can't say much. All I can say is we are under pressure to rightsize ourselves.'

'Rightsize?' Radhika asked in genuine confusion.

'That means people are getting fired, doesn't it?' Vroom said.

Bakshi did not respond.

'Sir, we need to increase our sales force to get new clients. Firing people is not the answer,' Vroom said boldly.

Bakshi had a smirk on his face as he turned to Vroom. He put his hand on Vroom's shoulder. 'I like your excitement, Mr Victor,' he said, 'but a seasoned management has to study all underlying variables and come up with an optimal solution. It's not so simple.' He patted Vroom's shoulder and left.

Vroom waited until Bakshi was out of the room before he spoke again. 'This is insanity. Bakshi's fucked up, so they're firing innocent agents!'

'Stay calm,' I said and started assembling the sheets.

'Yes, stay calm. Like Mr Photocopy Boy here, who finds acceptance in everything,' Priyanka said.

'Excuse me,' I said, looking up. 'Are you talking about me?'

Priyanka kept quiet.

'What is your problem? I come here, make fifteen grand a month and go home. It sucks that people are being fired and I'm trying my best to save my job. Overall, yes, I accept my situation. And, Vroom, before I forget, can you email Bakshi the user manual, please?'

'I'm doing it,' Vroom said, 'though what's going on here is still wrong.'

'Don't worry. We've finished the website. We should be safe,' I said.

'I hope so. Damn, it will suck if I lose my fifteen grand a month. If I don't get my pizza three times a week I'll die,' Vroom said.

'You have pizza that often?' Esha said.

'Isn't it unhealthy?' Radhika asked. Despite her recent text, she was back to knitting her scarf. Knitting habits die hard, I guess.

'No way. Pizzas are the ultimate balanced diet. Look at the contents: grain in the crust, milk protein in the cheese, vegetables and meat as toppings. It has all the food groups. I read it on the Internet: pizza is good for you.'

Vroom got all his information off the Internet.

'Pizzas are not healthy. I gain weight really fast if I eat a lot of it,' Priyanka said, 'especially with my lifestyle. I hardly get time to exercise and on top of that I work in a confined space.'

Priyanka's last two words made my heart skip a beat. 'Confined space' means only one thing to me: that night at the 32nd Milestone disco.

My Past Dates with Priyanka—III
32nd Milestone, Gurgaon Highway: Seven months earlier

I shouldn't really call this one a date, since this time it was a group thing with Vroom and Esha joining us. Vroom picked 32nd Milestone and the girls agreed because the disco doesn't have a 'door-bitch'. According to Priyanka, a door-bitch is a hostess who stands outside the disco, screening every girl who goes in, and if you aren't wearing something cool the door-bitch will raise an eyebrow at you like you're a fifty-year-old auntie.

'Really? I've never noticed those door-girls before,' I said as we sat on stools at the bar.

'It's a girl thing. They size you up, and unless you're drop-dead gorgeous, you get that mental smirk,' Priyanka said.

'So why should you care? You *are* gorgeous,' I said. She smiled.

'Mental smirk? Girls and their coded communication. Anyway, drink, anyone?' Vroom said.

'Long Island Iced Tea, please,' Esha said, and I noticed how stunning she looked in her make-up. She wore a black fitted top and black trousers that were so tight she'd probably have to roll them down to take them off.

'Long Island? Want to get drunk quick or what?' I said.

'Come on. I need to de-stress. I ran around like mad last month chasing modelling agencies. Besides, I have to wash down last week's one thousand calls,' Esha said.

'That's right. Twelve hundred calls for me,' Vroom said. 'Let's all have Long Islands.'

'Long Island Iced Tea for me, please,' Priyanka said. She wore camel-coloured trousers and a pistachio-green sequinned kurti.

Vroom went to the bartender to collect our drinks while I scanned the disco. A remixed version of 'Dil Chahta Hai' played in the background. As it was Saturday night, the disco had more than three hundred customers. I noticed some stick-thin models on the dance floor. Their stomachs were so flat, if they swallowed a pill you'd probably see an outline of it when it landed inside. Esha's looks are similar.

Vroom came back with our drinks and we said 'cheers', trying to sound lively and happy, as people at a disco should.

'Congrats on the website, guys. I heard it's good,' Esha said, taking a sip.

'The website is cool,' Vroom said. 'The test customers love it. No more dialling. And it's so simple.'

'So, a promotion finally for Mr Shyam here,' Priyanka said. I noticed she had finished a third of her drink in just two sips.

'Now Mr Shyam's promotion is another story,' Vroom said. 'Maybe Mr Shyam would like to tell it himself.'

'Please, some other time,' I said as Priyanka looked at me expectantly.

'OK, well Bakshi said he is talking to Boston to release a headcount. But it will take a while.'

'Why can't you just be firm with him?' Priyanka said.

'Like how? How can you be firm with your own boss?' I said, irritated.

'Cool it, guys,' Vroom said. 'It's a party night and—'

A big noise interrupted our conversation. We noticed a commotion on the dance floor as the DJ turned off the music.

'What's up?' Vroom said and we all went towards the dance floor where a fight had broken out. A gang of drunken friends had accused someone of pawing one of the girls with them and grabbed his collar. Soon, Mr Accused's friends had come to his defence. The music had stopped when someone knocked one guy flat on the floor. Several others were on top of each other and bouncers finally restored peace while a stretcher emerged to carry away the knocked-out guy. Five minutes later the music resumed and the anorexic girls' brigade were back on the floor.

'That's what happens to kids with rich dads and too much money,' Vroom said.

'Come on, Vroom. I thought you said money's a good thing,' Priyanka said with the confidence that comes from drinking a Long Island Iced Tea.

'Yes, doesn't money pay for your mobile, pizzas and discos?' I asked.

'Yes, but the difference is that I've earned it. These rich kids, they don't have a clue how hard it is to make cash,' Vroom said.

'C'mon, you get good money. Significantly more than the eight grand you made as a journalist trainee,' I said.

'Yes,' Vroom said. 'We get paid well, fifteen thousand a month. That's almost twelve dollars a day. Wow, I make as much a day as a US burger boy makes in two hours. Not bad for my college degree. Not bad at all. Nearly double what I made as a journalist anyway.'

Everyone was silent for a minute. Vroom on a temper trip is unbearable.

'Stop being so depressed. Let's dance,' Esha said, tugging at Vroom's hand.

'OK, but if anyone teases you, I'm not getting into a fight,' Vroom said.

'Don't worry, no one will. There are prettier girls here,' Esha said.

'I don't think so. Anyway, let's go,' Vroom said as they went to the dance floor. The song playing was 'Sharara Sharara', one of Esha's favourites.

Priyanka and I watched them dance from our seats.

'Want to go for a walk?' Priyanka said after a few minutes.

'Sure,' I said. We held hands and walked out of 32nd Milestone. We headed to the parking lot, where the music was softer.

'It's so calm here,' Priyanka said. 'I don't like it when Vroom gets all worked up. The boy needs to control his temper.'

'He's young and confused. Don't worry, life will slap him into shape. I think he regrets moving to Connexions sometimes. Besides, he hasn't taken his dad and mum's separation so well. It shows now and then.'

'Still, he should get a grip on himself. Get a steady girlfriend maybe.'

'I think he likes Esha,' I said.

'I don't know if Esha is interested. She's really focused on her modelling.'

We reached our Qualis and I opened the door to take out a bottle.

'What's that?' she asked.

'Some Bacardi we keep handy. It's three hundred bucks for a drink inside, the cost of this whole bottle. Let's do a shot.' The bottle's lid acted as one cup, and I broke the top off a cigarette packet for another. We poured Bacardi into both and warmth travelled down from my lips to my insides.

'I'm sorry about the Bakshi comment I made inside,' she said.

'It's all right. Doesn't matter,' I said.

'I can be a bitch sometimes, but I do make it up to you. I'm a loving person, no?' she said, high from mixing her drinks.

'You're just fine,' I said and looked at her moist eyes. Her nose puckered up a bit and I could have looked at it for ever.

'Why are you looking at me like that?' she said and smiled.

'Like what?'

'The come-hither look. I see mischief in your eyes, mister,' she said playfully, grabbing both my hands.

'There's no mischief, that's just your imagination,' I said.

'We'll see,' she said and came up close. We hugged as she kissed me on my neck. 'Have you ever made love in a confined space?' she asked.

'*What?*' I said loudly, right into her ear.

'Ouch!' she said, rubbing her ear. 'Hello? You heard me right? We have the time, soft music and a desolate spot.'

'So?'

'So, step into the Qualis, my friend,' she said and opened the door. I climbed onto the back seat and she followed me.

The song changed to 'Mahi Ve' from the movie *Kaante*.

'I love this song,' she said and sat astride my lap, facing me. 'I like the lyrics. Their love is true, but fate has something else in store.'

'I never focus on the lyrics.'

'You just notice the scantily clad girls in the video,' she said and ran her fingers through my hair.

I stayed silent.

'So, you didn't answer my question—have you made love in a confined space?' she said.

'Priyanka, are you crazy or are you drunk?'

She unbuttoned the top few buttons of my shirt. 'Both,' she said.

We were quiet, apart from our breathing.

She confirmed that the windows were shut and ordered me to remove my shirt. She took off her kurti first, and then slowly unhooked her bra.

'Are you mad?' I gasped, raising my arms so she could pull my shirt over my head. She moved to kick my shirt aside and her foot landed on my left baby toe. 'Ouch!' I screamed.

'Oops, sorry,' she said in a naughty-apologetic tone. As she moved her foot away, her head hit the roof.

'Ouch,' she said. 'Sorry, this isn't as elegant as in the *Titanic* movie.'

'It's all right,' I said as I pulled her close. She started kissing me on my face, and in a few moments, I forgot I was in the company Qualis.

Twenty minutes later we collapsed in each other's arms on the back seat.

'Amazing. That was simply amazing, Ms Priyanka.'

'My pleasure, sir,' she said and winked at me. 'Can we lie here and talk for a while?'

'Sure,' I said, reaching for my clothes.

She cuddled me again after we had dressed.

'Do you love me?' she asked. Her voice was serious.

'More than anybody else on this planet,' I said, caressing her hair.

'You think I'm a caring person?' she said. She was close to tears.

'Why do you keep asking me that?' I said.

'My mother was looking at our family album today. She stopped at a picture of me when I was three: I'm sitting on a tricycle and my mother is pushing me. She saw that picture, and she said that I was so cute when I was three.'

'You're cute now,' I said and pressed her nose like a button.

'And she said I was so loving and caring then and that I wasn't so loving any more,' Priyanka said and burst into tears.

I held her tight and felt her body shake. I thought hard about what I could say. Guys can never figure out what to say in such emotional moments and always end up saying something stupid.

'Your mother is crazy . . .'

'Don't say anything about my mother. I love her. Can you just listen to me for five minutes?' Priyanka said.

'Of course. Sorry . . .' I said as her sobs grew louder. I swore to myself to stay quiet for the next five minutes. I started counting my breath to pass time. Sixteen a minute is my average; eighty breaths would mean I had listened to her for five minutes.

'We weren't always like this. My mum and I were best friends once— until class eight I think. Then as I became older, she became crazier.'

I wondered if I should point out that she had just told me not to call her mum crazy. However, I had promised myself I would keep quiet.

502 | CHETAN BHAGAT

'She had different rules for me and my brother. She would comment on everything I wore, everywhere I went, whereas my brother . . . she would never say anything to him. I tried to explain it to her, but she just became more irritating, and by the time I reached college I couldn't wait to get away.'

'Uh-huh,' I said, calculating that almost half my time must have passed.

'All through college I ignored her and did what I wanted. But at one level I felt so guilty. I tried again to connect with her after college, but she had a problem with everything: my thinking, my friends, my boyfriend.'

The last word caught my attention. I had to speak, even though only fifty-seven breaths had passed. 'Sorry, but did you say boyfriend?'

'Well, yeah. She knows I'm with you. And she has this thing about me finding someone settled.'

Settled? The word rewound and repeated itself in my head several times. *What does that mean anyway?* Just someone rich, or someone who gets predictable cash flows at the end of every month. Except parents do not say it that way because it sounds like they're trading their daughter to the highest bidder, which in some ways they are. They don't give a damn about love or feelings or crap like that. 'Show me the money and keep our daughter for the rest of your life.' That's the deal in an arranged marriage.

'I'm a loser according to your mum, aren't I?' I said.

'That's not what I said.'

'Don't you bring up Bakshi and my promotion every time we have a conversation?' I said, moving away.

'Why do you get so defensive? Anyway, if Bakshi doesn't promote you, you can look for another job.'

'I'm tired of job-hunting. There's nothing good out there. And I'm tired of rejections. Moreover, what is the point of joining another call centre? I'd just have to start as a junior agent all over again—without you, without my friends. And let me tell you this, I may not be team leader, but I am happy. I'm content. Do you realise that? I am what I am,' I said, my face beetroot-red.

'Shyam, please can you try and understand?'

'Understand what? Your mother? No, I can't. But I suspect deep down you might agree with her. Like, what am I doing with this loser?' I said.

'Stop talking nonsense,' Priyanka shouted. 'I just made love to you, for God's sake. And stop saying loser,' she said and burst into tears again.

Two brief knocks on the window disturbed our conversation. It was Vroom, and Esha was standing next to him.

'Hello? You lovebirds are inseparable, eh?' he said.

12.45 a.m.

The loud ring of the landline telephone brought me back from 32nd Milestone. Priyanka grabbed the phone. 'Hiiiii, Ganesh,' she said, her stretched tone too flirty, if you ask me. I wondered what *his* tone was like. *Get under the table. Tap the phone, Shyam,* a voice told me. I immediately scolded myself for such a horrible thought.

'Of course I knew it was you. No one else calls on this emergency line,' Priyanka said and ran her fingers through her hair. Women playing with their hair while talking to a guy is an automatic female preening gesture; I saw it once on the Discovery Channel.

'Yeah,' Priyanka said after a few seconds, 'I like cars. Which one are you planning to buy? . . . A Lexus?'

'A Lexus! The dude is buying a Lexus!' Vroom screamed.

'Ask him which model, ask him, please,' Vroom said, and Priyanka looked at him, startled. She shook her head at Vroom.

'What colour? C'mon, it's your car. How can I decide for you?' Priyanka said. Over the next five minutes Ganesh did most of the talking, while Priyanka kept saying monosyllabic yeses or the equivalent.

Tap the phone, the voice kept banging in my head. I hated myself for it, but I wanted to do it. I wondered when Priyanka would step away from the desk.

'No, no, Ganesh, it's fine, go for your meeting. I'll be here, call me later,' Priyanka said as she ended her call.

'Vroom, is the Lexus a nice car?' Priyanka said.

Vroom was already on the Net, surfing Lexus pictures. He turned his monitor to Priyanka. 'Check this out. The Lexus is one of the coolest cars. The guy must be loaded.'

Priyanka looked at Vroom's screen for a few seconds and then turned to the girls. 'He wants me to choose the colour. I don't think I should, though.'

Vroom pushed himself back in his swivel chair. 'Go for black or silver. Nothing is as cool as the classic colours. Or the dark blue mica,' he said. 'And tell him the interiors have to be dark leather.'

Meanwhile, my insides were on fire. I felt like throwing up.

I wondered when I could tap the phone. It was totally wrong, and Priyanka would kill me if she found out, but I had to do it.

I tried to set the stage so I had an excuse to get under the table.

'Why have there been no calls in the last ten minutes?' I said. 'I should check if the connections are fine.'

'Leave it alone,' Esha said. 'I'm enjoying the break.'

'Bio?' Priyanka said to Esha. It was their code word for a visit to the toilet together for a private conversation.

'Sure.' Esha sensed the need for gossip and got up from her chair.

'I'll come too,' Radhika said and stood up. She turned to me: 'The girls want a bio break, team leader.'

'You're *all* going?' I said, pretending to be reluctant, but secretly thrilled. This was my chance. 'Well, OK, since nothing much is happening right now.'

As soon as the girls were out of sight I dived under the table.

'What are you doing?' Vroom said.

'Nothing. I don't think the connections are firm,' I said.

'And what the hell do you know about the connections?' Vroom said. He bent down to look under the table. 'Tell me honestly what you're doing.'

I told him about my urge to tap the phone. He scolded me for five seconds, but then got excited by the challenge and joined me under the table.

'The girls will kill us if they find out,' Vroom said.

'They won't have a clue,' I said, connecting the wires. 'It's almost done.'

Vroom picked up the landline and we tested the arrangement. I could select an option on my computer and listen in on the landline via my headset.

'Why are you doing this?' Vroom said.

'I don't know. Don't ask me.'

'And why are the girls taking so long?'

'You know them, they have their girl talk in the toilet.'

'And you don't want to hear what they're saying? I'm sure they're discussing Mr Microsoft there.'

'Oh no,' I said, worried about what I could be missing. 'Although how would we be able to eavesdrop?'

'From the corner stall of the men's toilet,' Vroom said. 'It shares a wall with their toilet. If you press your ear against the wall, you can hear them.'

'Really?' I said, my eyes lighting up.

Vroom nodded.

'It'll be wrong, though, eavesdropping through a stall,' I said.

'Yes, it will.'

'But who cares? Let's go,' I said and Vroom and I jumped off our chairs.

Vroom and I squeezed into the corner stall of the WASG men's toilet. We pressed our ears against the wall until I could hear Radhika's voice.

'Yes, he sounds like a really nice guy,' she was saying.

'But I shouldn't tell him what colour to get, no? It's his car and it's so expensive. But do you know what he said?' Priyanka said.

'What?' Radhika said.

'He said, "No, it is *our* car," and then he said, "You have brought colour to my life, so you get to choose the colour."'

'Oh, he sounds so romantic,' Esha said.

'That is such a lame loser line. Colour to my life, my ass,' I said to Vroom.

'Shh. They'll hear us, stupid. Keep quiet,' Vroom said.

'Excuse me,' Esha said, 'but I have to change this . . . Ouch!'

'What's going on?' I said.

Vroom shrugged his shoulders.

'Esha, your wound hasn't healed for days. Just a Band-Aid isn't enough,' Priyanka said. I guessed Esha was changing the Band-Aid on her shin.

'I'm fine. As long as it heals before the Lakmé fashion week,' Esha said.

'Let's go back, girls, it is almost one a.m.,' Radhika said. 'Otherwise the boys will grumble.'

'They always grumble. Like they never have a cigarette break,' Esha said.

'But today they are extra grumbly. At least *someone* is,' Radhika said.

Vroom pointed a finger at me. Yes, the girls were talking about me.

I grumbled in lip-sync.

'You think Shyam is not taking the news well?' Priyanka said.

'You tell us. You know him better than we do,' Esha said.

'I wish I knew him now. I don't know why he sulks and acts so childishly sometimes,' Priyanka said as they left the toilet.

'Childish? Me? I am childish?' I said to Vroom. 'What the hell. Mr Microsoft says his cheesy lines and he's cute and romantic. I say nothing and I'm childish.' I banged a fist on the stall door.

'Shyam, don't behave like a kid,' Vroom said.

We came out of the stall and I jumped back as I saw Bakshi by the sink.

Through the mirror, Bakshi saw both of us. His jaw dropped.

'Hello, sir,' Vroom said and went up to the sink next to him.

'Sir, it's not what you think,' I said, pointing back at the stall.

'I'm not thinking anything. What you do in your personal lives is up to you. But why aren't you at the desk?' Bakshi said.

'Sir, we just took a short break. The call traffic is very low today,' I said.

'Did you log your break? The girls are missing from the bay as well,' Bakshi said. His face was turning from shiny pink to shiny red.

'Really? Where did the girls go?' Vroom said.

Bakshi walked to the urinal stalls. I went to the stall adjacent to him.

'Didn't you just use the toilet?' Bakshi said.

'Sir,' I said and hesitated. 'Sir, that was different, with Vroom.'

'Please. I don't want to know,' Bakshi said.

'Sir, no,' I said. 'Sir, how come you're using this rest room?' I said.

'I didn't mean to. I always use the executive toilet,' Bakshi said.

'Yes, sir,' I said and nodded my head. I had acknowledged his magnanimous gesture of peeing in the same bay as us. But why was he here?

'Anyway, I came to your desk to drop off a courier delivery for Eliza. I've left the parcel on her desk,' Bakshi said as he zipped up.

'And, Sam, can you tell the voice agents to come to my office for a team meeting later, say two thirty a.m., OK?' Bakshi said.

'What's up, sir?' Vroom said.

'Nothing. I want to share some pertinent insights with the resources,' Bakshi said. 'Anyway, thanks for the user manual, I've already sent it to Boston,' Bakshi said.

'You did?' both of us said in unison.

'Sir, if you could have copied us in on the email . . . we'd like to be kept in the loop,' Vroom said. Good one.

'Oh, didn't I? I'm so sorry. I'm not good with emails. I'll just forward it to you. But you guys man the bay now, OK?'

'Of course, sir,' I said.

'And have you finished the ad hoc task I gave you?' Bakshi said.

'What, sir?' I said, and then realised he meant the photocopying of the board meeting invite. 'Almost done, sir.'

Bakshi nodded and left us behind in the rest room.

'Is he a total moron or what? Can't cc people on an email?' Vroom said.

'Easy, man. Let's get back to the bay,' I said.

1.00 a.m.

We returned from the men's room to find the call flow had resumed. Radhika explained to a caller how to open his vacuum cleaner. Esha taught an old man to preheat an oven and dodged his telephonic your-voice-is-so-sexy pass.

Another call flashed on my screen.

'I know this guy. Can I take this call?' Vroom said.

'Who is it?' I raised my eyebrows.

'A prick called William Fox. Listen in if you want,' Vroom said.

I selected the option on my computer.

'Good afternoon, Western Appliances, Victor speaking. How may I help you today, Mr Fox?' Vroom said.

'You'd better darn well help me, smart-ass,' the man on the phone said. He sounded drunk.

'Who is he?' I whispered, but Vroom shushed me.

'Sir, if I may confirm, I am speaking to Mr William Fox?'

'You bet you are. You think just 'cos you know my name it's OK to sell me crap hoovers?'

'What is the problem with your vacuum cleaner, sir? It's a VX100?'

'It doesn't suck dust any more. It just doesn't.'

'Sir, do you remember when you last changed the dust bags?' Vroom said.

'Like fuck I remember when I changed the bags. It's just a crap machine, you dumb-ass.'

Vroom took three deep breaths and remembered the suggested line to use in such situations. 'Sir, I request you not to use that language.'

'Oh really? Then make your fucking hoover work.'

Vroom pressed a button on his phone before he spoke again. 'You son of a bitch,' he said.

'What are you doing?' I said, panicking.

'Just venting, don't worry, it's on mute,' he smirked. He pressed the button again and said, 'Sir, you need to change the dust bags when they are full.'

'Who am I speaking to?' The voice on the phone became agitated.

'Victor, sir.'

'Tell me your name. You're some kid in India, ain't ya, boy?'

'Yes, sir. I am in India.'

'So what did you have to do to get this job? Degree in nuclear physics?'

'Sir, do you need help with your cleaner or not?'

'C'mon, son, answer me. I don't need your help. Yeah, I'll change the dust bag. What about you guys? When will you change your dusty country?'

'Excuse me, sir, but I want you to stop talking like that,' Vroom said.

'Oh really, now some brown kid's telling me what to do—' William Fox's voice stopped abruptly as I cut off the call.

Vroom didn't move for a few seconds. His whole body trembled and he was breathing heavily, then he covered his face with his hands.

'You don't have to talk to those people. You know that,' I said to Vroom.

He raised his face and slowly turned to look at me. Then he banged his fist on the table. 'Damn!' he screamed and kicked hard under the table.

'What the . . .' Priyanka said. 'My call just got cut off.'

Vroom's kick had dislodged the power wires, disconnecting all our calls. He stood up and his six-foot-plus frame towered above us.

'Guys, there are two things I cannot stand,' he said and showed us two fingers. 'Racists. And Americans.'

Priyanka started laughing.

'What is there to laugh at?' I said.

'Because there is a contradiction. He doesn't like racists, but can't stand Americans,' Priyanka said.

'Why?' Vroom said, ignoring Priyanka. 'Why do some dim-witted Americans get to act superior to us? Do you know why? Not because they are smarter. Not because they are better people. But because their country is rich and ours is poor. That is the only damn reason. Because the losers who have run our country for the last fifty years couldn't do better than make India one of the poorest countries on earth.'

'Stop overreacting, Vroom. Some stupid guy calls and—' Radhika said.

'Look, you've broken the entire system.' I pointed to the blank screens.

'No more calls for now,' Priyanka said, rolling her eyes.

'Let me take a look,' I said and went under the table. I was more worried about the wires tapping the emergency phone. However, they were intact.

'Shyam, wait,' Esha said, 'we have a great excuse for not taking calls. Leave it like it is for a while.'

Everyone agreed. We decided to call Systems after twenty minutes.

'Why was Bakshi here?' Priyanka asked. 'I saw him leave the men's toilet.'

'To drop off a courier delivery for Esha,' I said. 'He told me there's a team meeting at two thirty a.m. Oh man, I still have to photocopy the invite.'

'What delivery?' Esha said. 'This?' She lifted a packet near her computer.

'Must be,' Vroom said, 'though what courier firm delivers at this time?'

Esha opened the packet and took out two bundles of hundred-rupee notes. One bundle had a small yellow Post-it Note on it. She read the Post-it and her face went pale.

'Wow, someone's rich,' Vroom said.

'Not bad. What's the money for?' Radhika said.

'It's nothing. Just a friend returning money she borrowed,' Esha said.

She dumped the packet in her drawer and took out her mobile phone. Her face was pensive, as if she was debating whether or not to make a call. I collected my sheets to go to the photocopying room.

'Want to help me?' I called out to Vroom.

'No, thanks. People I used to work with are becoming national TV reporters, but look at me. I'm taking calls from losers and being asked to help with loser jobs,' Vroom said and looked away.

1.30 a.m.

I switched on the photocopier in the supplies room and put Bakshi's stack in the document feeder. I'd just pressed the 'start' button on the agenda document when the copier creaked and groaned to a halt. 'Paper Jam: Tray 2' appeared in big, bold letters on the screen.

The copier in our supplies room is not a machine, it's a person. A person with a psychotic soul and a grumpy attitude. Whenever you copy more than two sheets, there's a paper jam. After that, the machine teases you: it gives you systematic instructions on how to unjam it—open cover, remove tray, pull lever—but if it knows so much, why doesn't it fix itself?

'Damn,' I mumbled to myself as I bent down to open the paper trays. I turned a few levers and pulled out whatever paper was in sight.

I stood up, rearranged the documents on the feeder tray and pressed 'start' again, not realising that my ID was resting on Bakshi's original document. As the machine restarted it sucked in my ID along with the paper. The ID pulled at its strap, which tightened round my neck.

'Aargh,' I said as I choked. The strap curled tighter round my neck. I screamed loudly and pulled at my ID, but the machine was stronger. I was sure it wanted to kill me. I started kicking the machine hard.

Vroom came running into the room. 'What the . . .' He appeared nonplussed. He saw A4 sheets spread all over the room, a groaning photocopier and me lying down on top of it, desperately tugging at my ID strap.

'Do something,' I said in a muffled voice.

'Like what?' he said and bent over to look at the machine. The screen was flashing 'Paper Jam' while my ID strap ran right into the machine.

Vroom looked around the supplies room and found a pair of scissors.

'Should I?' he said and smiled at me. 'I really want the others to see this.'

'Shut . . . up . . . and . . . cut,' I said.

Snap! And my breath came back.

'OK now?' Vroom asked, throwing the scissors back in the supplies tray.

I nodded as I rubbed my neck and took wheezing breaths. I rested my head on the warm, soothing glass of the photocopier, but I must have rested it too hard, or maybe my head is too heavy, because I heard a crack.

'Get off,' Vroom said and pulled me off the machine. 'You broke the glass. What is it with you, man? Having a bad office supplies day?'

'Who knows?' I said, collecting Bakshi's document. 'I really am good for nothing. I can't even do these loser jobs. I almost died. Can you imagine the headline: COPIER DECAPITATES MAN, AND DUPLICATES DOCUMENT.'

Vroom laughed and put his arm round my shoulder.

'Chill out, man. I apologise.'

'For what?' I said. Nobody has ever apologised to me in the past twenty-six years of my life.

'I'm sorry I was rude. First there are these rumours about the call centre closing down, then my old workmate Boontoo makes it to NDTV and Bakshi sends the document without copying us in. Meanwhile, some psycho caller screams curses at me. It just gets to you sometimes.'

'What gets to you?' I asked. I was trying to copy Bakshi's document again, but the photocopier had self-detected a crack in the glass. It switched itself off altogether. I think it had committed suicide.

'Life,' Vroom said, 'life gets to you. You think you're perfectly happy—you know, good salary, nice friends, life's a party—but all of a sudden, in one tiny snap, everything can crack, like the glass pane of this photocopier.'

'Vroom, you know what your problem is?'

'What?'

'You don't have real love in your life. You need to fall in love, be in love and stay in love. That's the void in your life,' I said firmly.

'You think so?' Vroom said. 'I've had girlfriends. I'll find another one soon—you know that.'

'Not those kind of girls. Someone you really care about. And I think we all know who that is.'

'Esha?' he said. 'She isn't interested. I've asked her. She has her modelling and says she has no time for a relationship. Besides, she says I don't know what love is. I care for cars and bikes more than girls.'

I laughed. 'You do.'

'That's such an unfair comparison. It's like asking women what they prefer, nice shoes or men. There's no easy answer.'

'Really? So we are benchmarked to footwear?'

'Trust me, women can ignore men for sexy shoes.'

'But do you think you love Esha?' I said.

'Can't say. But I've felt something for her for over a year now.'

'But you dated other girls last year.'

'Those girls weren't important. They were like TV channels you surf while looking for the programme you really want to see. You're with that Curly Wurly chick, even though you still have feelings for Priyanka.'

'Shefali is there to help me move on,' I said.

'Screw moving on. That girl is enough to put you off women for ever.

Maybe that will help you get over Priyanka,' Vroom said.

'Don't change the subject. We're talking about you. I think you should ask Esha again for a real relationship. Do it, man.'

Vroom looked at me for a few seconds. 'Will you help me?' he said.

'Me? You're the expert with girls,' I said.

'This one is different. The stakes are higher. Can you be around when I talk to her? Just listen to our conversation, then we can analyse it later.'

'OK, sure. So, let's do it now. We have free time. Afterwards the calls will begin and we'll be busy again,' I said.

'OK. Where do we do it?' Vroom said as he put his hand on his forehead to think. 'The dining room?'

The dining room made sense. I could be nearby, but inconspicuous.

1.45 a.m.

'Is everything OK? I heard a noise,' Esha said, as we returned.

'The photocopier died. Anyone for a snack?' I said.

'Yes, let's go. I need a walk. Come on, Priyanka,' Esha said and tried to pull Priyanka up by her upper arm.

'No, I'll stay here,' Priyanka said and smiled. 'Ganesh might call.'

A scoop of hot molten lead entered through my head and left from my toes. *Try to move on*, I reminded myself.

Radhika was about to get up when I stopped her.

'Actually, Radhika, can you stay here? If Bakshi walks by, at least he'll see some people at the desk,' I said.

Radhika sat down puzzled as we left the room.

THE DINING AREA at Connexions is a cross between a restaurant and a college hostel mess. There are three rows of long tables, with seating on both sides. The tables have a small vase every three feet. Management recently renovated the place when some overpriced consulting firm recommended that a bright dining room would be good for employee motivation. A much cheaper option would have been to just fire Bakshi, if you ask me.

Vroom took a cheese sandwich and chips—they don't serve Indian food, again for motivational reasons—on his tray and sat at one of the tables. Esha took a soda water and sat opposite Vroom. I think she eats once every three days. I took an unhealthily large slice of chocolate cake. I sat at the adjacent table, took out my phone and started typing fake text messages.

'Why isn't Shyam sitting with us?' Esha said to Vroom.

'Private texting,' Vroom said. Esha rolled her eyes and nodded.

'Actually, Esha, I wanted to tell you something,' Vroom said.

'Yeah?' Esha said to Vroom, an eyebrow rising in suspicion. The invisible female antennae were out and suggesting caution. 'Talk about what?'

'Esha,' Vroom said. 'I've been thinking about you a lot lately.'

'Really?' she said and looked sideways to see if I was eavesdropping. I made an extra effort to show that I was focusing on my cake.

'Yes, really, Esha. I may have met a lot of girls, but no one is like you. And I think rather than fool around I could do with a real relationship. So I'm asking you again, will you go out with me?'

Esha was quiet for a few minutes. 'I've told you before. I have to focus on my modelling career. I can't afford the luxury of having a boyfriend,' she said, her voice unusually cold.

'What is with you, Esha? Don't you want someone to support you?' Vroom said.

'That's right, with three different girlfriends last year I'm sure you will always be there for me,' Esha said.

'The other girls were just for fun. They meant nothing, they're like pizza or movies. They're channel surfing, you're more serious,' Vroom said.

'So what serious channel am I? The BBC?' Esha said.

'I've known you for more than a year. I thought we were friends. I just wanted to take it to the next level . . .' Vroom said.

'Please stop it,' Esha said, and covered her eyes with her hands. 'You chose the worst time to talk about this.'

'What's wrong, Esha? Can I help?' Vroom said, his voice now full of concern rather than the nervousness of romance.

She shook her head frantically.

I knew Vroom had failed miserably. Esha wasn't interested and was in a really strange mood. I finished my chocolate cake and went to the counter to get water. By the time I returned, they had left the dining room.

1.55 a.m.

I returned to the WASG bay with the taste of chocolate cake lingering in my mouth. I sat down at my desk and began surfing irrelevant websites. Radhika was giving Priyanka recommendations on the best shops in Delhi for bridal dresses, while Esha and Vroom were silent. I called IT to fix our desk. They were busy, but promised to come in ten minutes.

The spare landline's ring startled us all.

'Ganesh,' Priyanka said as she scrambled to pick up the phone. I kept a calm face while I selected the option to listen in on the call.

'Mum,' Priyanka said, 'why aren't you asleep? Who gave you this number?'

'Sleeping? No one has slept a wink today,' her mother said.

The tapped line was exceptionally clear. Her mother sounded elated, which was unusual for a woman who, according to Priyanka, had spent most of her life in self-imposed, obsessive-compulsive depression.

Priyanka's mother explained how Ganesh had just called her and given her the emergency line number. He had told her that he was 'on top of the world'.

'I'm so happy today. Look how God sent such a perfect match right to our door. And I used to worry about you so much,' Priyanka's mother said.

'That's great, Mum, but what's up?' Priyanka said. 'I'll be home in a few hours. How come you called here?'

'Can't a mother call her daughter?' Priyanka's mum said. 'Can't a mother' is one of her classic lines.

'No, Mum, I just wondered. Anyway, Ganesh and I have spoken a couple of times today.'

'And did he tell you his plans?'

'What plans?'

'He is coming to India next month. Originally he'd planned the trip so he could see girls, but now that he has made his choice, he wants to get married instead on the same trip,' Priyanka's mum announced.

'What?' Priyanka said, 'next month?' and looked around at all of us with a shocked expression. Everyone returned puzzled looks, as if they didn't know what was going on. I also pretended to look confused.

'Mum, no!' Priyanka wailed. 'How can I get married next month? That's less than five weeks away.'

'Oh, you don't have to worry about that. I am there to organise everything. You wait and see, I'll work day and night to make it a grand event.'

'Mum, I'm not worried about organising a party. I have to be *ready* to get married. I hardly know Ganesh,' Priyanka said.

'Huh? Of course you're ready for it. When the families have fixed the match and bride and groom are happy, why delay? And the boy can't keep visiting again and again. He's in an important position after all.'

Yeah, right, I thought. He was probably one of the thousands of Indian geeks coding away at Microsoft. But to his in-laws, he was Bill Gates himself.

'Mum, please. I can't go ahead with it next month. Sorry, but no. I can't marry anyone I have only known for five weeks.'

Priyanka's mother stayed silent for a while. I thought she would retaliate, but then I figured out that the silence was more effective than words.

'Mum, are you there?' Priyanka asked after ten seconds.

'Yes, I'm still here. I'll be dead soon, but unfortunately I'm still here.'

'Mum, c'mon now . . .'

'Don't even make me happy just by chance,' Priyanka's mother said. What a killer line, I thought. I almost applauded.

'Mum, please. Don't do this.'

'You know I prayed for one hour today . . . praying you stay happy . . . for ever,' Priyanka's mother said as she broke into tears. Whoever starts crying first always has an advantage in an argument. This works for Priyanka's mother, who at least has obedient tear glands, if not an obedient daughter.

'Mum, don't create a scene. I'm at work. What do you want from me? I have agreed to the boy. Now why is everyone pushing me?'

'Isn't Ganesh nice? What's the problem?' her mother said in a tragic tone that could put any Bollywood hero's mother to shame.

'Mum, I didn't say he isn't nice, I just need time.'

'You aren't distracted, are you? Are you still talking to that useless call-centre chap, what's his name? Shyam?'

I jumped.

'No, Mum. That's over. I've agreed to Ganesh, right?'

'So, why can't you agree to next month—for everyone's happiness? Can't a mother beg her daughter for this?'

There you go: can't-a-mother No. 2 for the night.

Priyanka closed her eyes to compose herself. 'Can I think about it?'

'Of course. Think about it. But think for all of us, not just yourself.'

'OK. I will. Just . . . just give me some time.'

Priyanka hung up. 'Can you believe it? She wants me to get married next month. Next month!' Priyanka said and stood up. 'They brought me up for twenty-five years, and now they can't wait more than twenty-five days to get rid of me. What is it with these people? Am I such a burden?' Priyanka repeated her conversation to Esha and Radhika.

'It doesn't matter, right? Why drag it out?' Radhika said to Priyanka.

'Yes, you get to drive the Lexus sooner, too,' Vroom said. I gave him a firm glare out of the corner of my eye.

'I'm so not ready for this. In one month I'll be someone's wife. Gosh, little kids will call me auntie,' Priyanka said.

Everyone discussed the pros and cons of Priyanka getting married in four weeks' time. Most of them felt it wasn't such a big deal once she had chosen the guy. Of course, most people didn't give a damn about me.

In the midst of the discussions the Systems guy returned to our desk. 'What happened here?' he said from under the table. 'Looks like someone ripped these wires apart.'

'I don't know,' I said. 'See if we can get some traffic again.'

Priyanka's mother and her words—'that useless call-centre chap'—resounded in my head. I remembered the time when Priyanka told me her mother's views about me. It was on one of our last dates, at Mocha Café.

My Past Dates with Priyanka—IV
Mocha Café, Greater Kailash I: Five months earlier
We promised to meet on one condition: we wouldn't fight. No blame games, no sarcastic comments and no judgmental remarks. She was late again. I fiddled with the menu and looked around. Mocha's decor had a Middle Eastern twist, with hookahs, velvet cushions and coloured-glass lamps everywhere. Many of the tables were occupied by couples, sitting with intertwined fingers, obviously deeply in love. It was perfect, like all they needed to be happy was each other. Aren't the silly delusions in the initial stage of a relationship amazing?

My life was nowhere near perfect, of course. For starters, my girlfriend, if I could still call her that, was late. Plus I could sense she was itching to dump me. Priyanka and I had ended eight of our last ten phone calls with one of us hanging up on the other.

I hadn't slept the entire day, which hadn't left me feeling too good. My job was going nowhere, with Bakshi bent on sucking every last drop of my blood. Maybe he was right—I just didn't have the strategic vision or managerial leadership or whatever you are supposed to have to do well in life. Maybe Priyanka's mum was right too, and her daughter was stuck with a loser.

These thoughts enveloped me as she came in. She had just had a haircut and her waist-length hair was now just a few inches below her shoulders. I liked her with long hair, but she never listened to me. Anyway, her hair still looked nice. She wore a white linen top and a flowing lavender skirt with lots of crinkly edges. I stared at my watch as a sign of protest.

'Sorry, Shyam,' she said as she put a giant brown bag on the table, 'that hairdresser took so long. I told him I had to leave early.'

'No big deal. A haircut has to be more important than me,' I said.

'I thought we said no sarcasm,' she said, 'and I did say sorry. We promised not to fight. Saturday is the only day I get time for a haircut.'

'I told you to keep your hair long,' I said.

'I did for a long time, but it's so hard to maintain, Shyam. I'm sorry, but you have to understand, I had the most boring hair and I couldn't do anything with it. And it's so hot in the Delhi heat.'

'Whatever,' I said dismissively, looking at the menu. 'What do you want?'

'I want my Shyam to be in a good mood,' she said and held my hand. We didn't intertwine fingers, though.

'My' Shyam. I guess I still count, I thought.

'Hmm,' I said and let out a big sigh. If she was trying to make peace, I guess I had to do my bit. 'We can have their special Maggi noodles.'

'Maggi? You've come all this way to eat Maggi?' she said, and took the menu from me. 'And check this out: ninety bucks for Maggi?' She said the last phrase so loudly that the tables and a few waiters next to us heard.

'Priyanka, we earn now. We can afford it,' I said.

'Order chocolate brownie and ice cream,' she said.

'I thought you said you'll have whatever I want,' I said.

'Yes, but Maggi?' she said and made a quirky face. Her nostrils contracted for a second. I had seen that face before, and I couldn't help but smile. I saved myself time by ordering the brownie.

The waiter brought the chocolate brownie and placed it in front of Priyanka—half a litre of chocolate sauce dripping over a blob of vanilla ice cream on top of a huge slice of rich chocolate cake. It was a heart attack served on a plate. Priyanka had two spoons and slid the dish towards me.

'Did you have a heart-to-heart with your mum?' I said.

Priyanka wiped her chocolate-lined lips with tissue. I felt like kissing her right then. However, I hesitated. When you hesitate in love, you know something is wrong.

'Me and my mum,' she said, 'are incapable of having a rational, sane conversation. I tried to talk to her about you and my plans to study further.'

'What happened?'

'In seven minutes we were crying. Can you believe it?'

'With your mother, I can. What exactly did she say?'

'She said she has never liked you because you aren't settled, and because since the day I started dating you I have changed and become an unaffectionate, cold person.'

'Unaffectionate? What the . . .' I shouted, my face turning red. 'How the hell have I changed you?'

The second comment cut me into slices. Sure, I hated the 'not settled' tag, but there was some truth to that. But how could she accuse me of turning Priyanka into a cold person?

She didn't say anything, but her face softened and I heard tiny sobs. It was so unfair, I was the one being insulted: I should be the one getting to cry.

'Listen, Priyanka, your mum is a psycho,' I said.

'No she's not. It's not *because* of you, but I *have* changed. Maybe it is because I'm older, and she confuses it with my being with you. We used to be so close, and now she doesn't like anything I do,' she said and broke down into full-on crying. I got some you-horrible-man looks from girls at other tables.

'Calm down, Priyanka. What does she want? And tell me honestly, what do you want?' I said.

Priyanka shook her head and remained silent.

'Please, talk to me,' I said.

She finally spoke. 'She wants me to show that I love her. She wants me to make her happy and marry someone she chooses for me.'

'And what do you want?' I said.

'I don't know,' she told the tablecloth.

What the hell? I thought. All I get after four years is an 'I don't know'?

'You want to dump me, don't you? I'm not good enough for your family.'

'It isn't like that, Shyam. She married my dad, who was just a government employee, because he seemed like a decent human being. But her sisters waited and married better-qualified boys, and they are richer today. Her concern for me comes from that. She is my mother. It's not as if she doesn't know what's good for me. I want someone doing well in his career too.'

'So your mother is not the only cause for the strain in our relationship. It's you as well.'

'A relationship never flounders for one reason alone, there are many issues. You don't take feedback. You're sarcastic. You don't understand my ambitions. Don't I always tell you to focus on your career?'

'Just get lost, OK,' I said. My loud voice attracted the attention of the neighbouring tables.

'Shyam, it's this attitude of yours. At home, my mother doesn't understand, and now it's you who doesn't. Why have you become like this? You've changed, Shyam, you are not the same happy person I first met.'

'Nothing has happened to *me*. It's you who finds new faults in me every day. I have a bad boss and I'm trying to manage as happily as possible. What has happened to you? You used to eat at truck drivers' dhabas, now all of a sudden you need to marry an expat cardiac surgeon to make ends meet?'

We stared at each other for two seconds.

'OK, it's my fault. That's what you want to prove, isn't it? I'm a confused, selfish, mean person, right?' she said.

I couldn't believe I had loved her and those flared nostrils for four years, and now it was difficult to say four sentences without disagreeing.

I sighed. 'I thought there was to be no arguing but that's all we've done.'

'I care for you a lot,' she said and held my hand.

'Me, too,' I said, 'but I think we need to take care of other things in our lives as well.'

We asked for the bill and made cursory conversation about the weather and the café decor. We talked a lot, but we weren't communicating at all.

'Call me in the evening if you're free,' I said as I paid and got up to leave.

It had come to this: now we had to tell each other to call. Previously, not a waking hour had passed without one of us texting or calling the other.

'OK, or I'll text you,' she said.

We had a basic hug without really touching. A kiss was out of the question.

'Sure,' I said, 'it's always nice to get your messages.'

Sarcasm. Man, will I never learn?

1.59 a.m.

Mocha Café and its coloured Arabian lights faded away from my mind as I returned to WASG's tube-lit interiors. I checked the time: it was close to 2.00 a.m. I got up to take a short walk. I went to the corner of the room where Military Uncle sat and we nodded to each other. I looked at his screen and saw pictures of animals—chimps, rhinos, hippos, lions and deer.

'Are those your customers?' I said and laughed at my own unfunny joke.

Military Uncle smiled back. He was in one of his rare good moods.

'These are pictures I took at the zoo. I scanned them to send to my grandson.'

'Cool. He likes animals?' I said and bent over to take a closer look at the chimp. It bore an uncanny resemblance to Bakshi.

'Yes, I'm sending them by email to my son. But I'm having trouble as our emails don't allow more than four-megabyte attachments.'

I decided to help Uncle. 'These are large files,' I said. 'I could try to zip them, though that won't compress images much. The other way is to make the pictures low resolution. Otherwise, you could leave a few animals out.'

He wanted to keep them high resolution, so we agreed to leave out the deer and the hippos as those weren't his grandson's favourite animals.

'Thanks so much, Shyam,' Military Uncle said, as I successfully pressed 'send' on his email. I looked at his face and there was genuine gratitude. It was hard to believe he had been booted out because he was too bossy with his daughter-in-law—a piece of gossip Radhika had once passed on to me.

'You're welcome,' I said. I noticed Vroom signal to me to come back. Hoping the topic of Priyanka's wedding was over, I returned to the desk.

'Bakshi has sent us a copy of the proposal,' Vroom said.

I opened my inbox. There was a message from Bakshi.

I opened the mail to see who had been the original recipients. It was like a *Who's Who* of Western Computers and Appliances in Boston: the sales manager, the IT manager, the operations head and several others. Bakshi had sent it to the entire directory of people in our client base.

'He's copied in everyone. Senior management in Boston in the "To" field, and India senior management in the "cc" field,' I said.

'And yet somehow he forgot to copy us in,' Vroom said.

I read out the contents of his short mail:

'Dear All,

'Attached please find the much-awaited user manual of the customer service website that has altered the parameters of customer service at Western Appliances. I have only just completed this and would love to discuss it further on my imminent trip to Boston . . .'

I let out a silent whistle.

'Boston? Why is Bakshi going to Boston?' Vroom said.

The girls heard us. 'What?' Esha said. 'What's he going to Boston for?'

'To talk about our website. Must have swung a trip for himself,' I said.

'What the hell is going on here anyway? On the one hand we're downsizing to save costs, on the other hand there's cash to send idiots like Bakshi on trips to the US?' Vroom said and threw his stress ball on the table. It hit the pen stand, spilling the contents.

'Careful,' Esha said, sounding irritated as a few pens rolled towards her. She had her mobile phone in her hand; she was still trying to call someone.

I was about to close Bakshi's message when Vroom stopped me.

'Open the document,' Vroom said, 'just open the file he sent.'

I opened the file containing our user manual. 'It's the same file we sent him. The user manual,' I said and scrolled down. As I reached the bottom of the first page, my jaw dropped, partly in horror and partly in preparation for some major cursing.

Western Computers Troubleshooting Website
User Manual and Project Details
Developed by Connexions, Delhi

Subhash Bakshi
Manager, Connexions

'Like fuck it's the same,' Vroom said, his eyes fixed on my screen. 'It says it's by Subhash Bakshi.' He tapped is finger on my monitor. 'Check this out. Mr Moron, who can't tell a computer from a piano, has created this website and this manual. Like crap he has.' Vroom banged his fists on the table.

'What is wrong with you?' Esha said. She got up and went to the conference room, desperately shaking the phone to get a connection.

'He passed off our work as his, Shyam. Do you realise that?' he said.

I stared numbly at the first page of our, or rather Bakshi's, manual. This time he had surpassed himself. My head felt dizzy and I fought to breathe.

'Six months of work on this manual alone,' I said and closed the file. 'I never thought he'd stoop this low.'

'And?' Vroom said.

'And what? I don't really know what to do. I'm in shock. And on top of all this, there's the fear he may downsize us,' I said.

'Downsize us?' Vroom said and stood up. 'We've worked on it for six months, man. And all you can say is we can't do anything as "he may downsize us"? That loser Bakshi is turning *you* into a loser. Priyanka, tell him to say something. Go to Bakshi's office and have it out with him.'

Priyanka looked up at us, and for the second time that night our eyes met. She had that look; that same gaze that used to make me feel so small. Like what was the point of even shouting at me.

She shook her head and gave a wry smile. I knew that wry smile, too, like she'd known this was coming all along. I had the urge to shake her. It's frigging easy to give those looks when you have a Lexus waiting for you, I wanted to say. But I didn't say anything. Bakshi's move had hurt me—it wasn't just the six months of toil, but that the prospects for my promotion were gone. And that meant—poof!—Priyanka was gone, too.

'Are you there, Mr Shyam?' Vroom said. 'Let's email all the recipients of this message and tell them what's going on.'

'Just cool down, Vroom. There's no need to act like a hero,' I snapped.

'Oh really? So, who should we act like? Losers? Tell us, Shyam, you should be the expert on that,' Vroom said.

Anger choked me. 'Just shut up and sit down,' I said. 'So you want to send another email to tell them about the infighting going on here? Who are they going to believe? Someone who's on his way to Boston for a meeting or some frustrated agent who claims he did all the work? Get real, Mr Malhotra. You'll get fired and that's it.' I was so caught up in the argument I didn't even notice Radhika standing next to me with a bottle of water in her hand.

'Thanks,' I said and took a few noisy sips.

'Feeling better?' Radhika said.

'I don't want to talk about this any more. This is between Bakshi and us. And I don't need the opinions of random people whose lives are just one big party.' I sat down and glared at Vroom.

He opened a notepad and drew a two-by-two matrix. 'I think I've finally figured Bakshi out. Let me explain with the help of a diagram,' Vroom said.

'I'm not in the mood for diagrams,' I said.

'Just listen,' Vroom said as he labelled the matrix.

On the horizontal axis he wrote 'good' and 'evil' next to each box. On the vertical axis, he wrote 'smart' and 'stupid'.

'OK, here is my theory about people like Bakshi,' Vroom said. 'There are four kinds of bosses in this world, based on two dimensions: a) how smart or stupid they are, and b) whether they are good or evil. With extreme good luck you get a boss who is smart *and* a good human being. However, Bakshi falls into the most dangerous category. He is stupid and he is evil,' Vroom said. 'We've underestimated him. He's like a blind snake: you feel sorry for it, but it still has a poisonous bite. He is stupid, hence the call centre is so misman-aged, but he is also evil, so he'll make sure all of us go down instead of him.'

I shook my head. 'Forget it. Destiny has put an asshole in my path.'

'Sorry to interrupt your discussion, guys,' Radhika said, 'but I hope you weren't talking about me when you mentioned people whose lives are one big party. My life is not a party, my friend. It really isn't—'

'It wasn't you, Radhika. Shyam clearly meant me,' Priyanka interrupted.

'Oh forget it,' I said. I moved from the desk, just to get away from everyone.

2.10 a.m.

As I walked away from the WASG desk, my mind was still in turmoil. I felt like chopping Bakshi up into little bits and feeding them to every street dog in Delhi. I approached the conference room to find the door was shut. I knocked and waited for a few seconds before opening the door.

Esha was sitting on one of the conference-room chairs. Her right leg was bent and resting on another chair as she examined the wound on her shin. She held a blood-tipped knife in her hand and I noticed a used Band-Aid on the table. There was fresh blood coming out of the wound on her shin.

'Are you OK?' I said, moving closer.

Esha turned to look at me with a blank expression.

'Oh, hi, Shyam,' she said in a calm tone.

'What are you doing here? And your wound is bleeding, do you want some lotion or a bandage?' I said and looked away. The sight of blood nauseates me. I don't know how doctors show up to work every day.

'No, Shyam, I like it like this. With lotion it may stop hurting,' Esha said.

'What?' I said. 'But you want to stop the pain, don't you?'

'No.' Esha smiled sadly. She pointed to the wound. 'This pain takes my mind away from the real pain. Do you know what real pain is, Shyam?'

I had no idea what she was on about, but I knew that if she didn't cover the wound up soon, I'd throw up my recently consumed chocolate cake.

'I don't know, what is it?' I said.

'Real pain is mental pain,' Esha said.

'Right,' I said, trying to sound intelligent. I sat down on a chair next to her.

'Ever felt mental pain, Shyam?'

'I don't know. I'm shallow, you see. There are lots of things I don't feel.'

'Everyone feels pain, because everyone has a dark side to their life. Something you don't like about yourself, something that makes you angry or that you fear. Do you have a dark side, Shyam?'

'Oh, let's not go there. I have so many, like half a dozen dark sides. I am a dark-sided hexagon,' I said.

'Ever felt guilt, Shyam? Real, hard, painful guilt?' she said.

'What's happened, Esha?' I said, as I finally found a position that allowed me to look at her face but avoid a view of her wound.

'Do you promise not to judge me if I tell you something?'

'Of course,' I said. 'I'm a terrible judge of people anyway.'

'I slept with someone,' she said and sighed, 'to win a modelling contract.'

'What?' I said, as it took me a second to figure out what she meant.

'Yes, my agent said this man was connected and I just had to sleep with him once to get a break in a major fashion show. Nobody forced me, I chose to do it. But ever since, I've felt this awful guilt. Every single moment. And the pain is so bad that this wound in my leg feels like a tickle,' she said and took the knife to her shin where she started scraping the skin around her wound.

'Stop it, Esha, what are you doing?' I said and snatched the knife from her. 'Are you insane? You'll get tetanus or gangrene or whatever other horrible things they show on TV in those vaccination ads.'

'This is tame. I'll tell you what's dangerous. My own brain, the delusional voice that says I have it in me to become a model. You know what the man said afterwards?'

'Which man?' I said as I shoved the knife to the other side of the table.

'The guy I slept with—a forty-year-old designer. He told my agent I was too short to be a catwalk model,' Esha said. 'Like the bastard didn't know that before he slept with me.' She began crying. I don't know what's worse, a shouting girl or a crying one. I'm awful at handling either. I placed my hands on Esha's shoulders, ready for a hug in case she needed it.

'And that son of a bitch sends some cash as compensation afterwards,' she said, sobbing. 'Give me the knife back, Shyam.'

'No, I won't. Listen, now I'm not really sure what to do in this situation, but just take it easy,' I said.

'I hate myself, Shyam. I just hate myself. And I hate my face, and the stupid mirror that shows me my face. I hate myself for believing people who told me I could be a model. Can I get my face altered?'

I don't know of any plastic surgeons who specialise in making pretty girls ugly, so I kept quiet. After ninety seconds she stopped crying and took a tissue from her bag and wiped her eyes.

'Shall we go? They must be waiting,' I said.

'Thanks for listening to me,' Esha said. Only women think there is a reason to thank people when someone listens to them.

2.20 a.m.

To my disgust, Priyanka's wedding was still the topic of discussion when Esha and I returned to the bay. Esha sat down quietly.

'I'm taking mother-in-law tips from Radhika,' Priyanka said. 'I'm so not looking forward to that part. She seems nice now, but who knows . . .'

'C'mon, you're getting so much more in return. Ganesh is such a nice guy,' Radhika said.

'I'd take three mothers-in-law for a Lexus. Bring it on, man,' Vroom said.

Radhika and Priyanka started laughing.

'I'll miss you, Vroom,' Priyanka said, still laughing, 'I really will.'

'Who else will you miss?' Vroom said and all of us fell silent.

Priyanka shifted on her seat: Vroom had put her on the spot. 'Oh, I'll miss all of you,' she said, diplomacy queen that she is when she wants to be.

'Don't wish for three mothers-in-law, Vroom. It would be like asking for three Bakshis,' said Radhika. 'Or at least it can be for some women.'

'So your mother-in-law is evil?' Vroom said.

'I never said that. But she did say those things to Anuj. What will he think?'

'Nothing. He won't think anything. He knows how lucky he is to have you,' Priyanka said firmly.

'It's hard sometimes. She isn't my mum, after all.'

'Oh, don't go there. I can get along with anyone else's mum better than my own. My mum's neurosis has made me mother-in-law proof,' Priyanka said, and everyone on the desk laughed. I didn't, though, as there's nothing funny about Priyanka's mum to me.

'Anuj will be OK now, right? Tell me: he won't hate me?' Radhika said.

'No.' Priyanka got up and went to Radhika. 'He loves you, he'll be fine.'

'D'you want to check if he's OK?' Vroom said. 'I have an idea.'

'What?' Radhika said.

'Let's play radio jockey,' Vroom said. Radhika was baffled.

'I'll call Anuj and pretend I'm calling from a radio show. Then I'll tell him he's won a prize, a large bouquet of roses and a box of Swiss chocolates which he can send to anyone he loves with a loving message. So then, we'll all get to hear the romantic lines he has for you.'

'C'mon, it will never work,' Priyanka said. 'You can't sound like a DJ.'

'Trust me, I'm a call-centre agent. I can be a convincing DJ,' Vroom said. I was curious to see how Vroom would do.

'OK,' Vroom said as he got ready. 'It's show time, folks. Take line five, everyone, and no noise. Breathe away from the mouthpiece, OK?'

Radhika gave him the number and Vroom dialled Anuj's mobile.

We glued the earpieces to our ears. The telephone rang five times then we heard someone pick up.

'Hello?' Anuj said in a sleepy voice.

'Hello there, my friend, is this 98101 46301?' Vroom said in an insanely cheerful, DJ's voice.

'Yes, who is it?' Anuj said.

'It's your lucky call for tonight. This is DJ Max calling from Radio City 98.5 FM, and you, my friend, have just won a prize.'

'Radio City? Are you trying to sell me something?' Anuj said.

'No, my friend, I'm not selling anything. I'm just offering you a small prize from our sponsor Interflora and you can request a song, too, if you want to. Man, people doubt me so much these days,' Vroom said.

'Sorry, I just wasn't sure,' Anuj said.

'Max is the name. What's yours?' Vroom said.

'Anuj.'

'Nice talking to you, Anuj. Where are you right now?'

'Kolkata.'

'Oh, the land of sweets, excellent. Anyway, Anuj, you get to send a dozen red roses, with your message, to anyone in India. This service is brought to you by Interflora, one of the world's largest flower delivery companies.'

'And I don't pay anything? Thanks, Interflora,' Anuj said.

'No, my friend, no payment at all. So do you have the name and address of your special person?'

'Yes, sure. I'd like to send it to my girlfriend, Payal.'

I think the earth shook beneath us. I looked at Vroom's face: his mouth was wide open and he was waving a hand in confusion.

'Payal?' Vroom said.

'Yes, she's my girlfriend. She lives in Delhi. She's a modern type of girl, so please make the bouquet fashionable.'

Radhika couldn't stay silent any longer.

'Payal? What did you just say, Anuj? Your girlfriend?' Radhika said.

'Who's that . . .? Radhika . . .?'

'Yes, Radhika. Your wife, Radhika.'

'What's going on here? Who is this Max guy, hey, Max?' Anuj said.

I think the Max guy just died. Vroom put his hand on his head.

'You talk to me, you asshole,' Radhika said, probably cursing for the first time since she'd got married. 'What message were you going to send this Payal?'

'Radhika, honey, listen, this is a prank. Max? Max?'

'There is no Max. It's Vroom here,' Vroom said in a blank voice.

'You bastar—' Anuj began before Radhika cut the line. She sat back down on her chair, stunned. A few seconds later she broke down in tears.

Vroom looked at Radhika. 'Damn, Radhika, I am so sorry,' he said.

Radhika didn't answer, she just cried and cried. In between, she lifted the half-knitted scarf to wipe away her tears. Something told me Radhika would never finish the scarf.

Esha held Radhika's hand. Maybe the tear bug passed through their hands because Esha started crying as well. Priyanka went to fetch some water, then Radhika cried a glassful of tears, and drank the glass of water.

'It's probably a misunderstanding,' Priyanka said. She looked at Esha, puzzled as to why she was so upset. I guessed Esha's 'real pain' was back.

Radhika rifled through her bag looking for her headache pills. She could only find an empty blister pack, cursed silently and threw it aside.

'Radhika?' Priyanka said.

'Just leave me alone for a few minutes,' Radhika said.

'Girls, I really need to talk,' Esha said as she wiped her tears away.

'What's up?' Priyanka said as she looked at Esha. They exchanged glances: Esha used the female telepathic network to ask Priyanka to come to the toilet. Priyanka tapped Radhika's shoulder and the girls stood up.

'Now where are you girls going?' Vroom said. 'Can't you talk here?'

'We have our private stuff to discuss,' Priyanka said and left the desk.

'What's up with Esha?' Vroom said to me after the girls were out of sight.

'Nothing,' I said.

'Come on, tell me, she must have told you in the conference room.'

'I can't tell you,' I said and looked at my screen. I tried to change the topic. 'Do you think Bakshi expects us to prepare for his team meeting?'

'I think Esha is feeling sorry for having said no to me,' Vroom said.

I smirked.

'Then what is it?' Vroom said. I shrugged my shoulders.

'Fine. I'll use our earlier technique. I'm going to the toilet to find out.'

'No, Vroom, no,' I said, trying to grab his shirt, but he pulled away and went to the men's room. I didn't chase after him. I didn't care if he found out. I figured he ought to know what his love interest was up to anyway.

I decided to take a walk around the room. I passed by Military Uncle's station and noticed him slouched at his desk.

'Everything OK?' I said. Military Uncle raised his head. I looked at his face: his wrinkles seemed more pronounced, making him look older.

'My son replied to the email I sent,' he said. 'I think the file was too big.'

'Really? What did he say?' I said.

Military Uncle shook his head and put it back on the desk. The message on his screen caught my eye.

Dad, You have cluttered my life enough, now stop cluttering my mailbox. I do not know what came over me that I allowed communication between you and my son. I don't want your shadow on him. Please stay away and do not send him any more emails.

'It's nothing,' Uncle said, as he closed all the windows on his screen. 'I should get back to work. What's happened? Your systems are down again?'

'A lot is down tonight, not just the systems,' I said and returned to my seat.

ONE NIGHT AT THE CALL CENTRE | 527

2.25 a.m.

'Did you know Esha's big, bad story?' Vroom whispered when he returned.

'I'd rather not discuss it. It's her private matter.'

'No wonder she won't go out with me. She needs to romp her way to the ramp, doesn't she? Bitch.'

'Mind your language,' I said, 'and where are the girls?'

'Coming back soon. Your chick was consoling Radhika when I left.'

'Priyanka is not my chick, Vroom. Will you just shut up?' I said.

'OK, I'll shut up. That is what a good call-centre agent does, right? Crap happens around him and he just smiles and says, "How can I help you?" Like someone's just slept with the one girl I care for, but it's OK, right? Pass me the next dumb customer.'

I saw the girls on their way back to the desk. 'The girls are coming. Pretend you know nothing about Esha.'

The desk was silent as the girls took their seats. The Systems guy finally showed up with new kick-proof wires and reinstalled our systems. I was relieved as calls began to trickle in. Sorting Americans' oven and fridge problems was easier than solving our life problems.

I looked over at Priyanka. 'My chick.' I smirked to myself at Vroom's comment. She was no longer my chick. She was going to marry a successful guy. But had I given up? Did I still feel for her? I shook my head at the irrelevant questions. What did it matter? I didn't deserve her and I wasn't going to have her. That was reality and, as is often the case with me, reality sucks.

The landline telephone's ring caught everyone's attention.

'This is my call. I know the system is live, but can I take it?' Priyanka said.

'Sure. The call flow is so light anyway,' Vroom said.

Priyanka's hand reached for the telephone. I casually switched the option on my screen to listen in to the conversation.

'Hello, my centre of attention,' Ganesh's voice came over the phones.

'Hi, Ganesh,' Priyanka said sedately.

'What's up, Priya? You sound serious,' Ganesh said.

'Nothing. Just having a rough day . . . sorry, night. And please call me Priyanka,' she said. Priyanka hates it when people shorten her name to Priya.

'Well, I'm having a rocking day. Everyone in the office is so excited. They keep asking me, "So when is the date?" and "Where is the honeymoon?"'

'Yeah, Ganesh, about the date,' Priyanka said, 'my mum's just called.'

'She did. Oh no. I thought I'd give you the good news myself.'

'What good news?'

'That I'm coming to India next month. Let's get married then and have our honeymoon straight from there. People say the Bahamas is amazing, but I've always wanted to go to Paris. What could be more romantic than Paris?'

'Ganesh,' Priyanka said, her voice frantic. 'Can I say something?'

'Sure. But first tell me, Paris or the Bahamas?'

'Paris. Now can I say something?' Priyanka said.

Esha and Radhika raised their eyebrows when they heard the word Paris. It wasn't difficult to guess that honeymoon planning was in progress.

'Sure. What do you want to say?' Ganesh said.

'Don't you think it's a little rushed?'

'What?'

'Our marriage. We've only talked to each other for a week. I know we've spoken quite a bit, but still.'

'You've said yes to me, right?' Ganesh said.

'Yes, but . . .'

'Then why wait? I don't get much leave here, and considering I now spend my every living moment thinking about you, I'd rather bring you over at the earliest opportunity.'

'But this is marriage, Ganesh, not just a vacation. We have to give each other time to prepare,' Priyanka said.

'But,' Ganesh said, 'you've spoken to your mother, right? You heard how happy she is about us getting married next month. My family is excited as well. Marriage is a family occasion, too, isn't it?'

'I know. Listen, maybe I'm just having a rough night. Let me sleep on it.'

'Sure. Take your time. But have you thought of a colour?'

'For what? The car?'

'Yeah, I'm going to pay the deposit tomorrow so it's here when you arrive, assuming you agree to next month,. of course.'

'I can't say. Wait, I heard dark blue mica is nice.'

'Really? I kind of like black,' Ganesh said.

'Well then, take black. Don't let me—' Priyanka said.

'No, dark blue mica it is. I'll tell the dealer it's my wife's choice.'

The words 'my wife' sizzled my insides the way they fry French fries at McDonald's. I couldn't bear to hear another man talk like this to Priyanka.

'Hey, Ganesh, it's two twenty-five a.m. here. I have to get ready for a two-thirty meeting with the boss. Can we talk later?' Priyanka said.

'Sure, I'll call you when I get home from work, OK?'

'Bye, Ganesh.' Priyanka hung up.

'I heard Paris,' Esha said as she filed her nails.

'Yes, as a honeymoon destination. And, of course, more pressure to get married next month. I don't want to, but I just might have to give in.'

'Well, if it means seeing Paris sooner rather than later . . .' Esha said and looked over at us. 'Right, guys?'

'Sure,' Vroom said. 'What do you think, Shyam?'

Stupid ass, I hate Vroom.

'Me?' I said as everyone looked round. I didn't want to come across as a sulker—or childish, my new tag for the night—so I responded.

'Might as well get it done. Then go to Paris or the Bahamas or whatever.'

Damn. I kicked myself as the words left my mouth. Priyanka looked at me and her nose twitched as she thought hard.

'What did you just say, Shyam?' Priyanka said slowly.

'Nothing,' I said. 'I just said get married and go to Paris sooner.'

'No, you also said the Bahamas. How did you know Ganesh mentioned the Bahamas?' she asked.

I kept quiet.

'Answer me, Shyam. Ganesh also suggested the Bahamas, but I didn't tell that to you guys. How did you know what he said?'

'I don't know anything. I just randomly said it,' I replied.

'Were you . . . listening to my conversation? Shyam, have you played around with the phone?' Priyanka said and got up. She lifted the landline phone and pulled it away from the table. The wire followed her. She looked down under the table and tugged at the wires again. A little wire tensed up all the way back to my seat. Damn, busted, I thought.

'Shyam!' Priyanka screamed at the top of her voice.

'Yes,' I said as calmly as possible.

'What is going on here? I cannot believe you could sink so low. This is the height of indecency,' she said.

At least I'd achieved the heights in something, I thought. Radhika and Esha looked at me. I threw up my hands, pretending to be ignorant.

Vroom stood and went up to Priyanka. He put his arm round her shoulder, 'C'mon, Priyanka, take it easy. We're all having a rough night.'

'Shut up. This is insane,' she said and turned to me. 'How could you tap into my personal calls? I could report this and get you fired.'

'Then do it,' I said, 'what are you waiting for? Get me fired. Do whatever.'

Vroom looked at Priyanka and then at me. Realising there wasn't much he could do to help, he returned to his seat.

'What the . . . he . . .' Priyanka said, anger and impending tears showing in her voice. 'Can't one expect just a little decency from our colleagues?'

I guess I was just a colleague now. An indecent colleague at that.

'Say something,' Priyanka said to me.

I stayed silent and disconnected the tapped wire. I showed her the unhooked cable and threw it on the table. Our eyes met. Even though we were silent, our eyes communicated. My eyes asked, Why are you humiliating me? Her eyes said, Why are you doing this, Shyam? I think eye-talk is more effective than word-talk. But Priyanka was in no mood to be silent.

'Why, Shyam, why? Why do you do such childish, immature things? We said we would continue to work together, and that just because we'd ended our relationship, it didn't mean we had to end our friendship. But this . . .?' she said and lifted the wire on the table, then threw it down again.

'Sorry,' I said, or rather whispered.

'What?' she said.

'Sorry,' I said, this time loud and clear. I hate it when she does this to humiliate me. If you've heard an apology, just accept it.

'Do me a huge favour. Stay out of my life, please. Will you?' Priyanka said, her voice heavy with the sarcasm she had picked up from me.

I looked up at her and nodded.

Vroom sniggered. A smile rippled over Esha and Radhika as well.

'What's so funny?' Priyanka said, her face red.

'It's OK, Priyanka. C'mon, can't you take it in a bit of good humour?' Vroom said.

'Your humour isn't funny to me at all.'

'It's two thirty, guys,' Esha said, 'time to go to Bakshi's office.'

Priyanka and I gave each other one final glare before we got up to leave.

'Is Military Uncle needed?' Esha said.

'No. Just the voice agents,' I said. I looked at Military Uncle at the end of the room. I could see he was busy at the chat helpline.

'Let's go,' Vroom said.

'You OK, Radhika?' I said.

'Yes, I'm fine. I'm surprised that I am. I think I must be in shock. My husband is cheating on me. What am I supposed to do? Scream? Cry? What?'

'Do nothing for now. Let's just go to the meeting,' Vroom said.

My brain was still fumbling with Priyanka's words. Every moment of our last date was replaying itself in my mind as I walked to Bakshi's office. We had gone to a Pizza Hut, and pizzas have never tasted the same since.

My Past Dates with Priyanka—V
Pizza Hut, Sahara Mall, Gurgaon: Four months earlier

She arrived on time that day. After all, she had a purpose. This wasn't a date: we were meeting to formally break up. She also wanted to discuss how we were to interact with each other and move forward. Pizza Hut was convenient.

'Hi,' she said. 'How are you?' She held her shirt collar and shook it for ventilation. 'I can't believe it's so hot in July.'

'It's Delhi. What else do you expect?' I said.

The waiter came and took our order. I ordered two separate small cheese and mushroom pizzas.

'I'm not good at this break-up stuff, so let's not drag this out,' I said. 'So now what? Is there a break-up line I'm supposed to say?'

She stared at me for two seconds. 'Well, I just thought we could do it in a pleasant manner. We can still be friends, right?' she said.

What is it with women wanting to be friends for ever? Why can't they make a clear decision between a boyfriend and no-friend?

'I don't think so. Both of us have enough friends.'

'See, this is what I don't like about you. That tone of voice,' she said.

'I thought we decided not to discuss each other's flaws today. I have come here to break up, not to get an analysis of my behaviour.'

She kept silent until the pizzas arrived on our table. I bit into a slice.

'Perhaps you forget that we work together. That makes it a little more complicated,' Priyanka said. 'If there's tension between us it will make it difficult to focus on work—for us and for the others,' she said.

'So what do you suggest? Should I resign?' I said.

'I didn't say that. Anyway, I'm only going to be at Connexions for another nine months. Then I will have saved enough to fund my B.Ed. If we can agree to certain terms and conditions, if we can remain friendly in the interim—'

'I can't force myself to be friendly,' I interrupted her. 'I can't fake it.'

'I'm not telling you to fake it,' she said.

'Good. Because you are past the stage of telling me what to do. Now, let's just get this over with. What are we supposed to say? I now pronounce us broken up?' I pushed my plate away. I'd completely lost my appetite.

'What? Say something,' I said. She had gone silent for ten seconds.

'I don't know what to say,' she said, her voice cracking.

'Really? No words of advice, no last-minute preaching, no moral high ground in these final moments for your good-for-nothing unsettled boyfriend? Come on, Priyanka, don't lose your chance to slam the loser.'

She collected her bag and stood up. She took out a 100 rupee note and put it on the table—her contribution for the pizza.

'OK, she leaves in silence again. Once again I get to be the prick,' I mumbled, loud enough for her to hear.

'Shyam,' she said, slinging her bag onto her shoulder. 'You know how you always say you're not good at anything? I don't think that's true, because there is something you are very good at,' she said.

'What?' I said. Perhaps she wanted to give me some last-minute praise to make me feel better, I thought.

'You are damn good at hurting people. Keep it up.'

With that, my ex-girlfriend turned round and left.

2.30 a.m.

We reached Bakshi's office at 2.30 a.m. The size of a one-bedroom flat, it's probably the largest unproductive office in the world. His desk is in one corner, and behind the desk is a shelf full of thick management books. The thought of slamming one hard on Bakshi's head had often crossed my mind.

At another corner of the room is a conference table and six chairs, and in the centre of the table is a speakerphone for multiparty calls.

Bakshi was not in his office when we got there. We sat round Bakshi's conference table.

'Where the hell is he?' Vroom said.

'Maybe he's in the toilet?' I said.

'Executive toilet, it's a different feeling,' Vroom said. He stood up. 'Hey, want to check out Bakshi's computer?' He walked over to Bakshi's desk.

'What?' I said. 'Are you crazy? He'll be here any minute.'

'Do you want to know what websites Bakshi visits?' Vroom said and opened up Internet Explorer to pull out the history of visited websites.

'Have you gone nuts? You'll get into trouble,' I said.

'OK, I've just fired a print-out,' Vroom said. He fetched the print-out from Bakshi's printer and leapt back to the conference table.

'OK, guys, check this out,' Vroom said as he held the A4 sheet in front of him. 'Timesofindia.com, rediff.com, and then we have *Harvard Business Review* website, Boston places to see, Boston real estate—'

'What's with him and Boston?' Esha said.

'He's going there on a business trip soon,' Radhika reminded her.

'There are more. Aha, here's what I was looking for: awesomeindia.com— the best porn site for Indian girls—cabaretlounge.com—a strip club in

Boston—porn-inspector.com—hello, the list goes on in this department.'

'What's with him and Boston?' I repeated Esha's words.

'Who knows?' Vroom said and laughed.

We heard Bakshi's footsteps and Vroom quickly folded up the sheet of paper. We turned quiet and opened our notebooks to fresh blank pages.

Bakshi took quick steps as he entered his office.

'Sorry, team. I had to visit the computers bay team leaders for some pertinent managerial affairs. So, how is everyone doing tonight?' Bakshi said as he took the last empty seat at his conference table.

No one responded. I nodded my head to show I was doing fine.

'Team, I've called you today to tell you about a few changes that are about to take place at Connexions. We need to rightsize people.'

'So, people are getting fired; it wasn't a rumour,' Vroom said.

Radhika's face turned white. Priyanka and Esha looked shocked.

'We never want to fire people. But we have to rightsize sometimes.'

'Why are we firing when clearly there are things we can do?' Vroom said.

'We have carefully evaluated all the plausible and feasible alternatives, I'm afraid,' Bakshi said and took out a pen. We retreated nervously. The last thing we needed was another Bakshi diagram.

'Cost-cutting is the only alternative,' Bakshi said and began to draw something. However, his pen wasn't working, despite his attempts to shake it into action. Bakshi continued to lecture us. He spoke nonstop for six minutes, going into various management philosophies. His point was that we should make the company more efficient. He just didn't have an efficient way to say it.

Vroom had promised he wouldn't mention the website to Bakshi, at least until the layoffs were over. However, this didn't stop him from taking him on.

'Sir, but cost-cutting is useless if we have no sales growth. We need more clients, not nonstop cuts until there's no company left,' Vroom said after Bakshi had finished his lecture. I guess somewhere within him was a diehard optimist who really thought Bakshi would listen to him.

'A sales force is too expensive,' Bakshi said.

'Sir, we can create a sales force. We have thousands of agents. I'm sure some of them are good at selling. We talk to customers every day, so we know what they want . . .'

'But our clients are in the US, we have to sell there.'

'So what? Why don't we send some agents to the US to try and increase our client base. Why not, guys?' Vroom said and looked at us,

I was the only one listening, but I remained quiet. Radhika was doodling on her pad. Priyanka was making a table of numbers on her notepad. Esha was digging the nib of her pen deep into hers.

'Send agents to the US? Move them to Boston?' Bakshi laughed.

'Well, a few of them, at least on a trial basis. Some of them are really smart. Who knows, they may get that one client that could save a hundred jobs. Right, Shyam?' Vroom said.

'Huh?' I said, startled to hear my name.

'Mr Victor, as a feedback-oriented manager I appreciate your input. However, I don't think it's such a good idea,' Bakshi said.

'Why not?' Vroom demanded with the innocence of a school kid.

'Because if it was such a good idea, someone would have thought of it before. Why didn't it strike me, for instance?' Bakshi said.

'Huh?' Vroom said, completely flabbergasted. I'd heard it all before so it didn't move me.

'What's the plan, sir, when do we find out who gets fir—I mean right-sized?' I said.

'Soon. We're finalising the list, but we'll let you know by this morning or tomorrow night,' Bakshi said, looking relieved that I hadn't challenged him.

'How many people will lose their job, sir? What percentage?' Radhika said, her first words in the meeting.

'Thirty to forty is the plan, as of now,' Bakshi said in a calm voice.

'That's hundreds of people,' Vroom said. As if it was a difficult calculation.

'Such is corporate life, my friend,' Bakshi said and got up, indicating that the meeting was over. 'You know what they say: it's a jungle out there.'

The girls stood up. 'Thank you, sir,' Esha said.

'You're welcome. As you know, I am an ever-approachable manager. Here or in Boston, you can contact me any time.'

We were at the door when Priyanka asked a question.

'Sir, are you going to Boston soon?'

Bakshi was back at his desk. 'Oh yes, I need to tell you, I'm transferring to Boston soon. Maybe in a month or so.'

'Transferring?' Vroom, Radhika, Esha, Priyanka and I all spoke together.

'Yes. I don't like to blow my own trumpet, but it seems they have recognised my contribution to the value-addition cycle of the company,' Bakshi said, a smug smile sliding across his shiny face. 'But details will come later. Anyway, if you don't mind, I need to make a call. I'll keep you posted.'

Bakshi signalled us to shut the door as we left. As I closed it, I felt like someone had slapped my face. We walked slowly away from his office.

2.45 a.m.

When we returned to the WASG bay after our meeting, calls were flashing on the screen, but no one attended to them. I sat at my seat and opened my email. I couldn't read anything—my mind was having a systems overload.

Vroom sat at his desk and mumbled inaudible curses. He opened the internal web page of Connexions on his computer. It had the map of the US on it. He held up a pen and tapped at a point on the US east coast.

'This is Boston,' he said and clenched his fist tight round the pen. 'This is where our boss will be while we are on the road looking for jobs.'

Everyone stayed quiet.

'I think we should start picking up a few calls,' I said.

'Like fuck we should,' Vroom said and jabbed his pen hard at the monitor. A loud ping startled everyone. Shattered glass made a nine-inch-wide spider's web pattern on Vroom's monitor, while the rest of his screen contined to work.

'What happened?' the girls said and came round to Vroom's computer.

'Damn it,' Vroom said, throwing his pen on the ground.

'Oh no. The monitor is totally gone,' Esha said. She put her hand on Vroom's shoulder. 'Are you OK?'

'Don't you dare touch me, you slut,' Vroom said, pushing her hand away.

'What?' Esha said. 'What did you just say?'

'Nothing. Just leave me alone, all right? Go and pray for your job or whatever. Bloody bitch will be a hooker soon.'

The girls stood there, stunned. Then, slowly, they walked back to their seats.

'What's wrong with him?' Priyanka asked Esha in an audible whisper.

'Maybe he's not taking my rejection so well,' Esha said to Priyanka.

'Oh really?' Vroom shouted. 'You think this is about that? Like I don't know about your escapades. Everyone knows. You thought I wouldn't find out? I wish I'd known before I proposed to a slut who'll bang for bucks.'

Esha looked at all of us, shocked, and tears appeared in her eyes. She started shaking and Radhika helped her sit down.

Priyanka went up to Vroom's seat and stared at him, her face red. Slap! She deposited a hand across Vroom's face.

'Learn how to talk to women. You say one more nasty thing and I'll screw your happiness, understand?' Priyanka said.

Vroom stared at Priyanka, his hand covering his cheek. He was too shocked to retaliate. I inserted myself between the two of them.

'Guys, can we have some peace here?' I said. 'Things are already messy. Please let's sit down and get some work done.'

'I can't work. I don't know if I'll still have a job in a few hours,' Priyanka said. 'I want him to apologise to Esha. The idiot has to watch what he says.'

Esha continued to cry as Radhika tried to console her.

'What do you care about a job? You're getting married. Women have it easy,' Vroom said.

'Don't you start that with me now,' Priyanka said. 'You think this is easy?' She pointed at Esha and Radhika. 'Radhika has found out her husband is cheating on her when she works for him and his family day and night, and Esha can't get a fair break unless she sleeps with creepy men. But they aren't breaking monitors and yelling curses, Vroom. Just because we don't make a noise doesn't mean it's easy,' she said at the top of her voice.

Radhika gave Esha a glass of water and she stopped crying.

Vroom looked at the shattered glass on his desk. 'I'm sorry,' he mumbled.

'What?' Esha said.

'I'm sorry, Esha,' Vroom said, clearing his throat. 'I said horrible and hurtful things. I was upset about something. Please forgive me.'

'It's OK, Vroom. It only hurts because there's some truth in it,' Esha said.

'I meant to say those horrible things to myself. Because,' Vroom said and banged his fists on the table, 'because the real hooker is me, not you.'

'What?' I said.

'Yes, this salary has hooked me. Every night I come here and let people fuck me,' Vroom said and picked up the telephone headset. 'And the funny thing is, I let them do it. For money, for security, I let it happen.' Vroom threw the headset on the table.

'Do you want some water?' Radhika said and handed him a glass.

Vroom took it and drank the contents in one gulp. 'Thanks,' he said. 'I needed that. I need a break, otherwise I'll go mad. I can't take this right now.'

'I need a break, too,' Priyanka said. 'It's all right, Vroom. Only a few more hours left and the shift will be over.'

'No. I want a break now. I want to go for a drive. C'mon, people, let's all go for a drive. I'll get the Qualis,' Vroom said and stood up.

'Now? It's close to three a.m.,' I said.

'Yes, now. Who gives a damn about the calls? You may not even have a job soon. Let's go.'

'Actually, if someone is going, can you please get some pills for me from the twenty-four-hour chemist?' Radhika said.

'No, all of us are going,' Vroom said.

I paused for a second. 'OK, let's go. But we have to be back soon,' I said.

'Where are we going?' Esha said. 'The new lounge bar Bed is close by.'

'No way, we're just going for a drive,' I said, but Vroom interrupted me.

'Great idea. Let's go to Bed; it's a damn cool place.'

We decided to leave individually to prevent suspicion.

'Come on, Military Uncle,' Vroom said as he went to his desk.

'Huh?' Uncle said, getting up. Normally he would have scoffed at Vroom, but I guess he was in too much pain over his son's email to give a conscious reaction.

'We're all going for a drive. The others will tell you everything. I'll get the Qualis,' Vroom said and switched off Uncle's monitor.

AT 3.00 A.M. SHARP, we were outside the main entrance of Connexions when a white Qualis drove up and stopped beside us.

'Get in,' Vroom said, reaching over to open the doors.

'It's so cold. What took you so long?' Esha said, getting in the front.

'You try shifting a sound-asleep driver to another Qualis,' Vroom said.

Radhika, Priyanka and I took the middle row, while Military Uncle sat by himself at the back. He looked slightly dazed. Maybe we all did.

Vroom started the engine and turned towards the exit gate. The highway was empty apart from a few trucks. India has a billion people, but at night, 99 per cent of them are fast asleep. Then this land belongs to a chosen few: truck drivers, late-shift workers, doctors, hotel staff and call-centre agents. We, the nocturnal, temporarily rule the roads and the country.

'Chemist first, please,' Radhika requested, massaging her head.

Vroom took a sharp right turn to a twenty-four-hour chemist. A sleep-deprived boy, no more than seventeen, manned the shop. A few medical entrance exam guides lay on the counter in front of him. He looked bored and grateful to see us.

Vroom and Radhika got out of the Qualis. I stepped out to stretch my legs as well.

Radhika walked up to the boy quickly and said, 'Three strips of Fluoxetine, and five strips each of Sertraline and Paroxetine. Urgently, please.' She began to tap on the counter anxiously, her red bangles jingling.

The boy looked at Radhika, then started rifling through the shelves. He returned with a stack of tablets and placed them on the counter. Radhika reached out to grab them, but he put his right hand on top of the pile of medicines and slid them away from her. 'This is pretty strong stuff, madam. Do you have a prescription?' he asked.

'It's three in the morning,' Radhika said in an irritated voice. 'I ran out of pills at work. Where the hell do you expect me to find a prescription?'

'Sorry, madam. It's just that sometimes young kids come here to pick up strange medicines before going to discos . . .'

'Look at me,' Radhika said, 'do I look like a teenager in the mood to party?'

Radhika did not look like a party-hard teenager to me—she looked ill, with dark circles under her eyes.

'But these are still very strong drugs, madam. What do you need them for? I mean, what's wrong with you?' the boy said.

Radhika banged her fist hard on the glass counter. The glass shook but survived the impact. 'You want to know what's wrong with me, you little punk?' she said.

'Calm down, Radhika,' I said, but she didn't hear me.

'Everything is wrong with me, you moron. My husband is shagging some bitch while I slog my guts out. Happy now?' Radhika said, her face red. She grabbed the medicines. The boy at the counter didn't protest this time.

'Water. Can I have some water?' Radhika said.

The boy ran to the back of the shop and returned with a glass of water.

Radhika tore a few pills out of her new stack. One, two, three—I think she popped in three of them. Some migraine cure this was, I thought.

'Four hundred and sixty-three rupees, madam,' the boy said, his voice sounding a little fearful.

'I am alive because of this stuff. I need it to survive, not to party,' Radhika said. She paid for the medicines and walked back to the Qualis.

Vroom and I followed a few steps behind her.

'What sort of medicine is it?' I said.

'What the hell do I know? I'm not a doctor,' Vroom said.

'Everything OK?' Esha said as we got into the Qualis. 'We heard arguing.'

'Nothing. As Bakshi would say, only a few communication issues. But now, let's get to Bed,' Vroom said as he turned the Qualis round. He pushed the Qualis to one hundred and ten.

'Slow down, Vroom,' Esha said.

'Don't use the words slow and Vroom in one sentence,' Vroom said.

'Sorry, guys,' Radhika said. 'I apologise for creating a scene back there.'

'What did you buy? Why did the chemist make such a fuss?' I said.

'Antidepressants. Chemists ask questions because they're prescription drugs, but most of the time they don't care.'

'Wow!' Vroom said. 'You mean happy drugs like Prozac and stuff?'

'Yes, Fluoxetine is Prozac. Except it's the Indian version, so it's cheaper.'

'But it's dangerous to take it without medical supervision,' Priyanka said. 'Isn't it addictive?'

'It's legal addiction. I can't live without it and, yes, it's really bad for you. But it's still better than having to deal with my life,' Radhika said.

'Leave them, Radhika, they'll harm you,' Military Uncle said.

'I have cut down, Uncle. But sometimes you need a bigger dose. Can we just talk about something else? How far is this Bed place?'

'Just two kilometres from here. Ninety seconds if I'm driving, a lot more if Shyam is,' Vroom said. I ignored his comment, as I preferred him to keep his eyes on the road.

'I heard Bed is really snooty,' Priyanka said. 'I'm not dressed up at all.' She adjusted her salwar kameez. I noticed the border of glittering stone-work on her dark green chiffon dupatta.

'Don't worry. As long as we've got cash to spend, we'll all be welcome. Plus, the DJ at Bed is my classmate from school,' Vroom said.

'All your school classmates have such funky jobs,' I said.

'Well, that's the problem: they all have rich dads. I have to work hard to match their lifestyle. If only my dad hadn't walked out on us,' Vroom said. 'Anyway, guys, welcome to Bed.' He flashed the headlights at a sign. It said 'Bed Lounge and Bar: Your Personal Space'.

3.30 a.m.

We followed Vroom towards the huge black door that was the entrance to Bed. An ultra-beefy bouncer and a skinny woman stood beside it.

'Are you a member, sir?' the underfed woman addressed Vroom. She was the hostess—or door-bitch, as Priyanka called them.

'No, we've just come for a quick drink,' Vroom said.

'I'm sorry, sir, tonight is for members only,' she replied. The bouncer looked at us with a blank, daft glare.

'How do you become a member?' I said.

'You have to fill in a form and pay the annual membership fee of fifty thousand,' the hostess said, as calmly as if she'd asked us for small change.

'What? Fifty grand for this place in the middle of nowhere?' Priyanka said and pointed her finger to the door.

'I suggest you go somewhere else then,' the hostess said. She looked at Priyanka scornfully. A fully clad female is a no-no at discos.

Vroom turned to the bouncer. 'What's the deal? Is DJ Jas inside? I know him.' The bouncer looked at us anxiously. It was obviously the most challenging question anyone had asked him in months.

'You know Jas?' the hostess said, her voice warmer now.

'School buddy of seven years. Tell him Vroom is here,' Vroom said.

'Cool. Why didn't you tell me that before, Vroom?' the hostess said and flashed him a flirtatious smile. She leaned over to release the velvet ropes.

'Can we go in now?' Esha asked the hostess in a monotone.

'Yes. Though, Vroom, next time, please tell your friends to dress up for Bed,' the hostess said and glanced meaningfully at Priyanka and Radhika.

'I could wring her tiny neck. One twist and it would snap like a chicken bone,' Priyanka said as we walked inside.

The interior design of Bed was a cross between *Star Trek* and a debauched king's harem, illuminated by ultraviolet bulbs and candles. As my eyes adjusted to the semi-darkness I noticed two rows of six beds. Only five were occupied, so I couldn't understand the big fuss at the entrance. I guess it's never easy to get people into bed. We chose a bed in the corner.

'Why is the hostess so nasty?' Esha said as she hoisted herself onto it. She took two cushions to rest her elbows on. 'Did you hear her? "Go somewhere else." Is that how you treat customers?'

'They're paid to be nasty. It gives the place attitude,' Vroom said carelessly.

'I want a job that pays me to be nasty. All they tell us in the call centre is, "Be nice, be polite, be helpful", but being mean is so much more fun,' Radhika said, reclining along one of the cushions. For someone who had just had a tough night she looked good. I wondered how Anuj could cheat on her.

Vroom went to say hi to DJ Jas and returned with twelve kamikaze shots. Military Uncle declined, and Vroom took Uncle's extra shots and drank them in quick succession.

We had barely finished when a woman came up to us with another six drinks. 'Long Island Iced Teas,' she said, 'courtesy of DJ Jas.'

'Nice. You have friends in the right places,' Radhika said as she started gulping her Long Island like it was a glass of water.

'These Long Islands are very strong,' I said after a few sips. I could feel my head spin. 'Easy, guys, our shift isn't over. We said one quick drink, so let's make our way back soon.'

'Cool it, man. Just one last drink,' Vroom said, ordering more cocktails.

'I'm feeling high,' Priyanka said. 'I'm going to miss this and you guys.'

'Yeah, right. We'll see when you move to Seattle.'

There were two flat LCD screens in front of our bed, one tuned to MTV and the other to CNN. A Bollywood number was being played on MTV, as part of its 'Youth Special' programme. The news breaking on CNN was about the US invasion of Iraq. I noticed Vroom staring at the news.

Vroom pointed to a US politician who had spoken out in support of the war. 'Look at him. He'd nuke the whole world if he could have his way.'

'No, not the whole world. I don't think they'd blow up China,' Priyanka said, sounding high. 'They need the cheap labour.'

'Then I guess they won't blow up Gurgaon either: they need the call centres,' Radhika said.

'So we're safe,' Esha said. 'Welcome to Gurgaon, the safest city on earth.' The girls started laughing and even Military Uncle smiled.

'It's not funny, girls. Our government doesn't realise this, but Americans are using us. We're sacrificing an entire generation to service their call centres,' Vroom said, convincing me that one day he could be a politician.

'C'mon, Vroom. Call centres are useful to us, too,' Esha said. 'You know how hard it is to make fifteen grand a month outside. And here we are, sitting in an air-conditioned office, talking on the phone, collecting our pay and going home. What's wrong with that?'

'An air-conditioned sweatshop is still a sweatshop,' Vroom said.

'Then why don't you leave? Why are you still here?' I said.

'Because I need the money,' Vroom said. 'And I agree the money is good. But we don't have jobs that allow us to show our potential.'

'So? What other kinds of jobs are there?' Esha said.

'Well, we should be building roads for a start. Power plants, airports, phone networks, metro trains. And if the government moves its rear end in the right direction young people in this country will find jobs. Hell, I would work day and night for that, as long as I knew that what I was doing was helping build something for my country's future. But the government doesn't believe in doing any real work, so they allow these Business Process Outsourcing places to be opened and think they have taken care of the youth. Just like stupid MTV thinks showing a demented chick dancing will turn the programme into a youth special. Do you think they really care?'

'Who?' I said. 'The government or MTV?' I got up and signalled for the check . . . in bars you always ask for the "check", never the "bill". It was 3.50 a.m. and I had had enough of Vroom's lecture. I wanted to get back to the call centre soon.

Vroom paid the bill with his credit card and we promised to split it later. The door-bitch and the bouncer gave us a puzzled look as we walked out.

4.00 a.m.

Vroom drove us away from Bed and we were soon back on the highway. Every now and then the Qualis would sway to the left or right of the road.

'Careful,' Esha said. 'You OK, Vroom?'

'I'm fine. Man, I love driving,' Vroom said dreamily.

'I can drive if you—' I said.

'I said I'm fine,' Vroom interrupted in a firm voice. 'Did you like Bed?' he said, to change the topic from his inebriated state.

'Great place,' Esha said. 'Hey, Vroom, have you got any music?'

'Of course. Let me see,' Vroom shuffled through the glove box. He took out a tape and held it up. '*Musafir Lounge*?' he asked.

'No,' Priyanka and I replied at the same time.

'Come on, guys. You two not only hate each other, you hate the same things, too?' Vroom said and smiled. He put the tape in and turned on the music. A song called 'Rabba' started playing.

I was sitting next to Priyanka. With every beat of the song, I could feel her body along my entire right side, like soft electric sparks. I had the urge to grab her hand, but restrained myself. I opened the window for some fresh air. I was worried about the next song. It was 'Mahi Ve', which would bring back memories of the 32nd Milestone parking lot.

I saw Priyanka's face change from the corner of my eye. She looked nervous. Yes, this was going to be hard.

'I love this song,' Vroom declared as it filled the Qualis.

I pressed the rewind-and-play button in the privacy of my head. Every moment of that night at 32nd Milestone replayed itself. I recalled every second of her careful, slow and amazing lovemaking. I wished Priyanka had never left me. I wished my world were a happier place.

I turned to look outside. The breeze felt cold, particularly along two lines on my cheeks. I touched my face. Damn, I couldn't believe I was crying.

'Can we please close the window? It's ruining my hair,' Esha said.

I slid the window shut and I tried to keep my eyes shut as well, but I couldn't hold back the tears. I never realised I was such a wuss.

I looked at Priyanka. Maybe it was my imagination, but her eyes seemed wet too. She turned towards me and then quickly looked away. I couldn't bear to meet her eyes right now, and I certainly couldn't look at that nose.

Vroom pulled out two tissues from the tissue box in front and swung his arm back to hand them over to us.

'What?' I said.

'I have a rearview mirror. I can see everything,' he said.

'We can all see,' Radhika and Esha said together and burst out laughing.

'You keep driving, OK?' I said. I took the tissue on the pretext of wiping my nose, then wiped my eyes. Priyanka took one and swabbed her eyes, too.

Esha reached behind her seat and rubbed Priyanka's arm.

Priyanka composed herself and changed the topic. 'How far away are we?' she said.

I looked at my watch. 'Damn, it is past four a.m. How much farther?'

'Around five kilometres from the call centre. I'm driving more slowly now. Do you want me to drive faster?'

'No,' we cried.

'We're going to be late. Bakshi will flip,' I said.

'I can take a short cut,' Vroom said. 'Next left there's an untarred road. It was made for construction projects. It cuts through some fields and saves us about two kilometres. I've used it before. Let's take it.'

After a kilometre, he took a sharp left.

'Ouch,' Esha said, 'you didn't tell us this road would be so bumpy.'

'Just a few minutes,' Vroom said. 'Actually the ground is wet today from yesterday's rain.'

We plunged on into the darkness of the unlit road, the headlights trying hard to show us the way. We passed fields and construction sites filled with cement, bricks and steel rods. In a few places there were deep holes as builders constructed the foundations for super-high-rise apartments.

'There, just one final cut through and we'll be back on the highway,' Vroom said, taking a sharp right.

Suddenly the Qualis skidded and slid down an inclined path.

'Careful,' everyone shouted, holding on to anything they could find. The Qualis went off the road into a slushy downhill patch. Vroom desperately tried to control the steering, but the wheels wouldn't grip the ground. The slope flattened out but the Qualis was still rolling forward, only slowing down when it hit a mesh of steel construction rods. Vroom braked hard, and the Qualis halted on the rods with a metallic clang, bounced twice and came to a stop.

'Damn!' Vroom said.

Everyone sat in stunned silence.

'Don't worry, guys,' Vroom said and started the ignition. The Qualis shook violently.

'Turn . . . off . . . the . . . ignition . . . Vroom . . .' I said. There was a floor of steel below us that was shaking.

Vroom's hands shook too as he turned off the engine. I think any alcohol in his body had evaporated in fear.

'Where are we?' Esha said and opened the window. She looked out and screamed, 'Oh no!'

'What?' I said and looked out again. This time I looked around more carefully. What I saw was terrifying: we had landed on a frame of exposed steel rods for reinforcing concrete that covered the foundation hole of a building. The foundation consisted of a pit that was maybe fifty feet deep, and the rods were all that supported us above it. Every time we moved, the Qualis bounced, as the rods acted as springs. I could see fear in everyone's face, including Military Uncle's.

'We're hanging above a hole, supported only by toothpicks. We're screwed,' Radhika said, summing up the situation for all of us.

'What are we going to do?' Esha said, panic in her voice.

'Whatever you do, don't move,' Vroom said.

A few minutes passed where the only sound was the heavy breathing of six people.

'Should we call for help? The police? Fire brigade? Call centre?' Esha said as she took her mobile phone out of her bag.

Vroom nodded, naked fear showing on his face.

'Damn, no reception,' Esha said. 'Does anyone have a mobile that works?'

Priyanka and Radhika's cell phones didn't work either, Military Uncle didn't have a mobile, so Vroom took out his phone.

'No network,' he said.

I took out my phone from my pocket and gave it to Esha.

'Your phone isn't working either,' Esha said, placing it on the dashboard.

'So we can't reach anyone in the world?' Radhika said.

A rod snapped under us and the Qualis tilted a few degrees to the right. I fell towards Radhika; Vroom held the steering wheel tight to keep his balance. Another rod snapped, and then another. The Qualis tilted around thirty degrees and came to a halt. All of us were too scared to scream.

'Does anyone have any ideas?' Vroom said.

I closed my eyes for a second and visualised my death. My life could end, just like this, in oblivion. I wondered when and how people would find us. Maybe labourers the next day, or even after a couple of days.

SIX IRRESPONSIBLE DRUNKEN AGENTS FOUND DEAD would be the headline.

'Try to open the door, Vroom,' Military Uncle said.

Vroom opened his door, but the Qualis wobbled so he shut it immediately.

'Can't,' Vroom said. 'Messes up the balance. And what's the point? We can't step out, we'd fall right through. Move towards the left. No weight on the right. We have to stay balanced until someone spots us in the morning.'

I checked my watch. It was only 4.14 a.m. The morning was three hours away. A lifetime. And people might turn up even later than that.

'Otherwise?' Esha said.

'Otherwise we die,' Vroom said.

We stayed quiet for a minute.

'Everyone dies one day,' I said, just to break the silence.

'Maybe it's simpler this way. End life rather than deal with it,' Vroom said.

I nodded. I was nervous and I was glad Vroom was making small talk.

'My main question is, what if no one finds us even after we die. What happens then?' Vroom said.

'The vultures will find us. I saw it on the Discovery Channel,' I said.

Beneath us there were two sharp 'pings' as another two rods snapped.

'Oh no,' Priyanka said as we heard another ping just below her. A flicker of light appeared on the dashboard. My cellphone was vibrating.

'That's my phone,' I said. It started ringing.

'How did it ring without a network?' Esha said, her voice nervous.

'Who is it?' Radhika said.

'Pick it up,' I said.

Esha lifted the phone. She looked at the screen and gasped.

'Who is it?' I said.

'Do you know someone called . . . God? It says God calling,' Esha said.

4.30 a.m.

Esha's fingers trembled as she pressed the button for speaker mode.

'Hi, everyone. Sorry to call so late,' a cheerful voice came from the phone.

'Er, who is it?' Esha said.

'It's God,' the voice said.

'God? God as in . . .' Radhika said as all of us looked at the brightly lit phone in fright.

'As in God. I noticed an unusual situation here, so I thought I'd just check on you guys.'

'Who is this? Is this a joke?' Vroom asked in a more confident voice.

'Why? Am I being funny?' the voice said.

'God doesn't normally call. Prove that you're God. Otherwise, you should get some help,' Vroom said.

'How do I prove I'm God? Do I create rain and lightning on demand? Or would you prefer a magic trick? A few special effects, maybe?' God said.

'Well, I don't know, but yeah, something like that,' Vroom said.

'So to impress you I have to break the very same laws of physics I created? I'm sorry, I'm not into that these days. And I have plenty of believers. I thought I could help, but I can hang up. See you then . . .' God said.

'No, no wait. Please help us . . . G . . . God,' Esha said and turned slightly so she could hold the cellphone between all of us.

'OK, I'll stay,' God said cheerfully. 'Tell me, how's it going? How's life?'

I'm very bad at tough, open-ended questions like that. I hate to admit the extent to which my life is screwed up.

'Well, right now we're trapped. If a few more rods break we'll all die,' I said and God interrupted me.

'Don't worry, the Qualis isn't going anywhere. Just relax.'

I let out a deep sigh. Everyone was silent.

'So back to the question, how's life going? Do you want to start Radhika?' God said.

'If you are God you must already know everything. Life is miserable,' Radhika said.

'I *do* know,' God said. 'I just want to find out how you feel about it.'

'I'll tell you how we feel. Life suc—sorry,' Vroom said, checking himself. 'It's horrible. What have we done wrong? Why are our lives in the pits, literally and figuratively? That pretty much sums it up for all of us, I think.'

We all made noises of agreement and God sighed.

'Let me ask you a question. How many phone calls do you take each day?' God said.

'A hundred, on busy days two hundred,' Vroom said.

'OK. Now do you know which is the most important call in the world?'

'No,' Vroom said and we all shook our heads.

'The inner call,' God said.

'The inner call?' everyone said in unison.

'Yes, the little voice inside that wants to talk to you, but you can only hear it when you are at peace, and even then it's hard to hear. The voice that tells you what you really want. Do you know what I mean?'

'Sort of,' Priyanka said, her eyes darting away from the phone.

'That voice is mine,' God said.

'Really?' Esha said, her mouth wide open.

'Yes. And the voice is easy to ignore, because you are distracted or busy or just too comfortable in your life. Go on, ignore it—until you get tangled in your own web of comfort. And then when you reach a point like today, where life brings you to a dead end, there is nothing ahead but a dark hole.'

'You're making sense,' I conceded, more to myself.

'I know that voice. But it isn't subtle in me. Sometimes it shouts and bites me,' Vroom said.

'And what does the voice say, Vroom?' God said.

'That I should not have taken a job just for money. There are better jobs that pay less. Jobs that give me identity, make me learn or help my country. I justified it to myself by saying money is progress, but it's not true. Progress is building something that lasts,' Vroom said, sounding as if there was a lump in his throat. He pressed his face into his hands.

Esha put her hand on Vroom's shoulder.

'Come on, guys. This is getting far too sentimental. You can do a lot better than this. You are all capable people,' God said.

It was the first time someone had used the word 'capable' to describe me.

'We can?' I said.

'Of course. Listen, let me make a deal with you. I will save your lives tonight, but in return you must give me something. Close your eyes for three minutes. Think about what you really want and what you need to change in your life to achieve it. Then once you get out of here, *act* on those changes. Do as I say, and I will help you get out of this pit. Is that a deal?'

'Deal,' I said. Everyone nodded.

We closed our eyes and took a few deep breaths. I tried to concentrate, but all I could see was commotion. Priyanka, Bakshi, my promotion and Ganesh—my mind kept jumping from one topic to another.

'So, tell me,' God said after three minutes.

We opened our eyes. Everyone's faces seemed a lot calmer.

'Let's go around the Qualis one by one. Vroom, you first,' God said.

'I want to have a life with meaning, even if it means a life without Bed or daily trips to Pizza Hut. I need to leave the call centre for good. Calling is not my calling,' Vroom said.

I thought his last line was pretty clever, but it didn't seem like the right time to appreciate verbal tricks.

Priyanka spoke after Vroom. My ears were on alert.

'I want my mother to be happy. But I cannot kill myself for it. My mother needs to realise a family is a great support to have, but ultimately, she is responsible for her own happiness. My focus should be on my own life and what I want,' Priyanka said. I wished she had said my name somewhere in her answer, but no such luck.

Military Uncle's turn came after Priyanka, and he spoke for longer than I had ever heard him speak. 'I want to be with my son and my grandson. I miss them all the time. Two years ago I was living with them, but my daughter-in-law did things I didn't like—she went to late-night parties and got a job when I wanted her to stay at home . . . I argued with them before moving out. But I was wrong. It's their life and I have no right to judge them with my outdated values. I want to visit them in the US to talk it over.'

Radhika's turn came next. She was fighting back tears as she spoke. 'I want to be myself again, just as I was before I got married. I want to divorce Anuj. I don't ever want to look at my mother-in-law's face again. To do this, I have to accept that I made a wrong decision when I married Anuj.'

Esha spoke after Radhika. 'I want my parents to love me again. I don't want to become a stupid model. I'm sure I can find a better use for my looks. Any career that makes you compromise your morals is not worth it.'

People now turned to look at me as I was the only one left to speak.

'Can I pass?' I said. I was given an even harder stare.

'OK. This will sound stupid, but I want to take a shot at my own business. I had this idea: if Vroom and I collaborate, we could set up a web design company. It may never work, because most of the things I do never work, but—'

'What else, Shyam?' God said, interrupting me.

'Uh, nothing,' I said.

'Shyam, you are not finished, you know that,' God said.

I guess you can't outsmart God and I was being forced to come to the point. I looked around and spoke again.

'And I want to be worthy of someone like Priyanka one day. Today I don't deserve her, and I accept that—'

'Shyam, I never said—' Priyanka said.

'Please, let me finish, Priyanka. It's about time people stop trampling all over me,' I said.

Priyanka went silent. I could see she was in mild shock at my firmness.

I continued. 'But one day I'd like to be worthy of someone like her, someone intelligent, witty, sensitive and fun. And yes, I want to be successful, too.'

God stayed silent.

'God? Say something now that we've poured out our deepest secrets to you,' Esha said.

'I don't really have to say anything. I'm just amazed, and delighted, at how well you have done. Knowing what you want is already a great start. Are you prepared to follow it through?'

Everyone nodded except me.

'Are you ready, Shyam?' God said.

I gave a small nod.

'Shyam, may I say something personal in front of your friends,' God said, 'because it's important for everyone else, too?'

'Sure,' I said. Yeah, use me as Exhibit 1 for 'how not to live your life'.

'There are four things a person needs for success. One, a medium amount of intelligence, and two, a bit of imagination. And all of you have those qualities,' God said. 'But the third is what Shyam has lost.'

'What's that?' I said.

'Self-confidence. The third thing you need for success is self-confidence. But Shyam has lost it. He is convinced he is good for nothing.'

I hung my head.

'You know how you became convinced?' God said.

'How?' I said.

'Because of Bakshi. A bad boss is like a disease of the soul. If you have one for long enough you will become convinced something is wrong with you. Even when you know Bakshi is the real loser, you start doubting yourself, and that is when your confidence evaporates.'

God's words shook my insides like the vibrating Qualis had a few minutes earlier. 'God, I would like to get my confidence back,' I said.

'Good. Don't be scared and you will get it back, and then there'll be no stopping you.'

I felt the blood rush to my ears. My heart was beating hard and all I wanted was to be back at the call centre. Anger surged in me when I pictured Bakshi. I wanted to get even with the man who had killed a part of me, who had put everyone's job on the line, who had ruined the call centre.

'What's the fourth ingredient for success?' Vroom said.

'The fourth ingredient is the most painful. It is something all of you still need to learn. Because it is often the most important thing,' God said.

'What?' I said.

'Failure,' God said.

'But I thought you were talking about success,' Vroom said.

'Yes, but to be really successful, you must first face failure. You have to experience it, feel it, taste it, suffer it. Only then can you shine,' God said.

'Why?' Priyanka said.

'Once you've tasted failure, you will have no more fear. You'll be able to take risks more easily, you will no longer want to snuggle in your comfort zone, you will be ready to fly. And success is about flying, not snuggling.'

'Good point,' Priyanka said.

'So, never be afraid of failure. If it comes your way, it really means I would like to give you a proper chance later,' God said.

'Cool,' Priyanka said.

'Thank you,' God said.

'If only you had given as much to India as America,' Vroom said.

'Why, don't you like India?' God said.

'Of course. Just because India is poor doesn't mean you stop loving it. It belongs to me. But even so, America has so much more,' Vroom said.

'Well, Americans may have many things, but they are not the happiest people on Earth. Any country obsessed with war can't be happy,' God said.

'True,' Radhika said.

'And many of them have serious mental issues. Issues only call-centre agents know about. And you can use them to save your call centre tonight. Yes. Consider their weak spots and you might win,' God said. 'Let me give you a clue. What exactly lies behind all this war sentiment?' God said.

'Fear. It's obvious, they are easily scared and paranoid people,' I said.

'We'll scare them into calling us. Yes, that's how to retrieve our call volume,' Vroom said, his voice excited.

'Now you're thinking. In fact, you can figure out a way to get even with Bakshi too. Not completely fair and square, but I think you deserve to be able to bend a few of the rules,' God said, and I thought I heard a chuckle.

We all smiled.

'Remember Bakshi is not your boss; your ultimate boss is me. And I am with you. So what are you afraid of?' God said.

'Excuse me, but you are not always there with us, otherwise how did we end up here?' Radhika said.

God sighed. 'I think you need to understand how my system works. You see, I have a contract with all human beings. You do your best, and every now and then I will come and give you a supporting push. But it has to start with you, otherwise how can I distinguish who most needs my help?'

'So if I listen to my inner call and promise to do my best, will you be there for me?' I said.

'Absolutely. But I have to go now. Someone else needs me,' God said.

'Wait! Help us get out of this pit first,' Esha said.

'Oh yes, of course,' God said. 'OK, Vroom, you're balancing on a few rods now. There are two tricks to get out of such a situation. One, remember the reverse gear. And two, make friends with the rods—do not fight them. Use the rods as rail tracks and they will guide you out.'

Vroom stuck his neck out of the window. 'But these steel construction rods are as thin as my fingers. How can we bunch them up?'

'Tie them,' God said.

'How?' Vroom said.

'Do I need to tell you everything?' God said.

'Dupatta. Use my dupatta,' Priyanka said.

'Here, I have this half-knitted scarf in my handbag,' Radhika said.

'I think you can take it from here. Bye now. Remember, I am inside you when you need me,' God said.

'Bye, God,' the girls said one after the other.

'Bye, everyone,' God said and disconnected the call. Silence fell.

'What . . . was . . . that?' Priyanka said.

'I don't know. Can I have the dupattas, please,' Vroom said. 'Military Uncle, can you open the rear door and tie up the rods under the wheel. Tear up the dupatta if you want to.'

Vroom and Military Uncle tied up the rods right under the wheel for the Qualis to do its ten-foot journey to firm ground.

'OK, people,' Vroom sat back on the seat, wiping his hands, 'hold tight.'

Vroom started the ignition and the Qualis vibrated as the rods below us started quivering again.

'Vroom, I am sl . . . ipping,' Esha said, trying to grip the glove-box handle.

In a nanosecond, Vroom put the Qualis in reverse and drove backwards. The Qualis shook but we didn't fall. My upper and lower jaws chattered so hard I thought a couple of teeth would break loose. In six seconds, it was all over and we were out of the pit and on the slushy mud road again.

'It's over. I think I'm alive,' Vroom said with a grin of relief. He turned round. 'Are you still there?'

4.40 a.m.

We all released our breaths together. The girls hugged, and Vroom reached out and backslapped me so hard I thought I'd broken my back. He did a U-turn and drove slowly in first gear until we reached the highway.

'We made it,' Esha said and wiped away her tears. Priyanka folded her hands and prayed a few times.

'I thought we were going to die,' Radhika said.

'What was that call?' Esha said.

'Something very strange—can we make a pact not to talk about it?' I said. Everyone nodded, as if I had said exactly what was on all their minds. It was true. The call felt so personal I didn't want to discuss it any more.

'Whatever it was, we're OK now. And we'll be back in the office soon,' Priyanka said.

'It's still only four forty. We're just two kilometres away,' Vroom said.

'I feel lucky to be alive, I don't care when we get there,' Esha said.

'I don't want to get back to find out about the layoffs. I'm leaving in any case,' Vroom said. 'Enough's enough.'

'What are you going to do?' Priyanka said.

'I don't know long-term—maybe get back into journalism. But as an immediate short-term goal, I'm going to try to save the call centre,' he said.

'Hey, d'you want to open a web design company with me?' I said.

'With you?' Vroom said, looking back at me.

'I'm leaving, too,' I said.

'Really?' Priyanka's eyes popped open. She looked at me as if a seven-year-old had just announced his decision to climb Mount Everest.

'Yes, I came close to death in that pit. I could have died there without ever having taken a risk in my life. I am tired of soft, comfortable options. It's time to face the real world, even if it's harder and more painful.'

Everyone nodded. I was taken aback; it seemed people were really listening to me for the first time.

'Plus, I've made one more promise to myself,' I said.

'What?' Vroom and Priyanka said together.

'I'm not going to work for an idiot any more, anywhere. Even if it means less money. I can't spend my life working for a moron.'

'Not bad,' Vroom said. 'Looks like Shyam has just wised up.'

'I don't know if I'm wise or not, but at least I've made a choice. We'll see what happens. For now I have a short-term goal, too.'

'Like what?' Vroom said, as he drove with utmost concentration.

'I have to take care of Bakshi. Let's teach him a lesson,' I said.

Vroom screeched the Qualis to a halt and we all fell forward.

'Now what?' I said.

'I've just had an idea for fixing Bakshi and the call centre at the same time,' Vroom said. He leaned back and whispered something in my ear.

'No way, I mean how?' I said.

'I'll tell you how when we get back. Let's meet in the WASG conference room,' he said and pressed the accelerator hard as we drove the final stretch to the centre. We entered the Connexions main gate at 4.45 a.m. Our driver was sleeping in another vehicle, so we parked quietly next to him.

'People, let's go—four forty-six,' Vroom said and jumped out of the car.

Back at our bay there was an A4-sized sheet stuck to my monitor with big bold letters scrawled on it.

'Check this out,' I said. It was Bakshi's writing.

WHERE IS EVERYONE? PLEASE CALL/REPORT TO MY OFFICE ASAP. WHERE ARE THE COPIES OF THE AGENDA FOR MY BOARD MEETING? WHAT HAPPENED TO THE PHOTOCOPIER? AND AGENT VICTOR'S MONITOR?

Vroom looked at the note and laughed. 'Whatever. He'll get his answers. But first he'll answer us. Guys, conference room first,' Vroom said.

We filed inside the conference room and Vroom bolted the door.

'Guys, sorry to sound like an MBA type, but I think for the next few hours we have a three-point agenda to consider. One, to save this call centre, and two, to teach Bakshi a lesson. Agreed?'

'What's the third point?' Radhika said.

'That's between me and Shyam. It's private. OK, listen . . .'

And that is where Vroom revealed his plan. Between laughter and intense concentration, everyone joined in to refine the plan further. At 5.10 a.m., we concluded our meeting and left the WASG conference room.

'All set?' Vroom said.

'Of course,' we said.

'Good. Step One: Bringing Bakshi out of his office,' Vroom said. 'Esha, are you ready?'

'Yes,' Esha said and winked at us.

She picked up the phone, dialled Bakshi's number and put on the voice of an older woman.

'Sir, this is Elina calling from the main bay. There's a call for you from Boston, I think,' Esha said in a dumb-but-conscientious secretarial tone.

'No, sir, I can't seem to transfer it . . . Sir, I've already tried . . . Sir, I'm a new assistant here, so I'm still not sure how the phones work . . . Sir, sorry, but can you come down, sir . . . Yes, sir,' Esha said and hung up the phone.

'Did it work?' I said.

'He's a total sucker for anything to do with Boston. He's coming right now. But he'll only be out for a few minutes, so let's rush.'

5.15 a.m.

As planned, Bakshi's office was empty when we arrived.

Vroom went straight to Bakshi's computer and opened his email.

Radhika, Priyanka, Esha and I sat at his conference table. Vroom typed furiously on Bakshi's keyboard. I knew what we were doing was wrong, but somehow it felt good. Once he'd finished, Vroom printed out several copies.

'Five copies,' he said, 'one for each of us. Fold it and keep it safe.'

I folded my copy and put it in my shirt pocket.

Bakshi came in twenty seconds later. 'I can't believe we have such outdated telephone systems.' Bakshi was talking to himself as he came into his office, then he noticed us at the conference table.

'There you all are. Where were you? And what happened to the photocopier and agent Victor's monitor?' Bakshi said.

'Sit down for a second, will you, Bakshi?' Vroom said.

'What?' Bakshi said, shocked at Vroom referring to him by his name. 'You should learn how to address seniors—'

'Whatever, Bakshi,' Vroom said and put his feet up on Bakshi's table.

'Agent Victor, what did you say and what exactly do you think you are doing?' Bakshi said, still standing.

'Ahh,' Vroom said, 'this is so much more comfortable. Why don't people always sit like this?' Vroom crossed his skinny legs on the table.

'What the hell is going on here?' Bakshi said and looked at me blankly.

Vroom pushed a print-out towards Bakshi. 'Read it,' Vroom said.

The email read as follows:

From: Subhash Bakshi
To: Esha Singh
Sent: 05.04 a.m.
Subject: Just one night

Dear Esha,
Don't be upset. My offer is very simple—just spend one night with me. You make me happy—I'll protect you from the rightsizing operation. My pleasure for your security, I think it's a fair deal. And who knows, you might even enjoy it, too. Let me know your decision soon.
Your admirer, Bakshi

Bakshi's face turned white. 'What is this?' he said, his voice shaking.

'You tell us. It's an email from your inbox,' Vroom said.

'But I didn't write it,' Bakshi said, desperately, 'I did not write this.'

'Really?' Vroom said. 'Now how can you prove you didn't write it? Can you prove to the people in the Boston office that you didn't write it?'

'What are you talking about? How is this connected to Boston?' Bakshi said, his face spouting droplets of sweat through the oilfields.

'Let's see. What if we forward Boston a copy of this email? I'm sure they love employees who do, how did you put it? "fair deals",' I said.

'I did not write it,' Bakshi said, unable to think of a better line.

'Or we could send a copy to the police,' Vroom said, 'and to some of my reporter friends. You want to be in the papers tomorrow, Bakshi?' Vroom took out his phone. 'Oh wait, maybe I could even get you on TV.'

'TV?' Bakshi said.

'Yes, imagine the headline: CALL CENTRE BOSS ASKS GIRL FOR SEXUAL FAVOURS IN EXCHANGE FOR JOB. New Delhi TV could live on that for a week. Damn, I'd make a good journalist,' Vroom said and laughed.

'But what did I do?' Bakshi said and ran to his desk. He opened his email and checked the 'Sent Items' folder.

'Who wrote this?' Bakshi said as he saw the same email on his screen.

'You didn't?' Priyanka said as if in genuine confusion.

'Mr Bakshi, I held you in such high esteem. Today my faith in my role model is shattered,' Esha said and put her hands to her face. She was good—I thought she should try for an acting career.

'I swear I didn't write this,' Bakshi said, scrambling with his keyboard.

'Then who wrote it? Santa Claus? The tooth fairy?' Vroom shouted and stood up. 'Explain it to the police, journalists and to our Boston office.'

'Hah! Look, I've deleted it,' Bakshi said with a smug smile.

'Come on, Bakshi,' Vroom said, 'it's still in your "Deleted Items" folder.'

'Oh,' Bakshi said and jerked his mouse. A few clicks later he said, 'There, it's gone.'

Vroom smiled. 'One more tip for you, Bakshi. Go to your deleted items, select the tools menu and choose the "Recover Deleted Items" option. The mail will still be there.'

Bakshi's face showed panic again as he tried to follow Vroom's instructions. He clicked his mouse over and over again.

'Oh, stop it, Bakshi. The mail is in my inbox as well. And Vroom has many print-outs,' Esha said.

'Huh?' Bakshi looked like a scared rabbit. 'You'll never get away with this. Esha, you know I didn't do it. You wear tight skirts and tops, but I only look at them from a distance. Even those jeans that show your waist, I only saw—'

'Stop right there, you sicko,' Esha said.

'You can't get away with this,' Bakshi said.

'We have five witnesses, Bakshi, and all of them will support Esha's testimony,' I said.

'Oh, and we have some other evidence as well. In Esha's drawer there is a packet full of cash, it has your fingerprints on it,' Vroom said.

Bakshi's fingers trembled as if he was getting ready to play the drums.

'We also have a print-out of your visits to porn websites,' Radhika said.

'You know it's not me, Esha. I'll be proven innocent,' Bakshi said, his voice sounding like a hapless beggar's. He looked as if he was about to cry.

'Maybe. But the amazing publicity will be enough to screw your career. Goodbye, Boston,' I said and waved my hand to indicate farewell.

Bakshi sat down. His white face had now turned red, or rather purple.

'Why are you doing this to me? I'll be leaving you for ever to go to Boston soon,' Bakshi said.

'Boston?' I said. 'You don't deserve a posting to Bhatinda. You're not just a bad boss, you're a parasite: to us, to this company, to this country. Damn you.'

'What do you want? Do you want to destroy me?' Bakshi said. 'I have a family and two kids. After a lot of effort my career is going fine. My wife wants to leave me anyway. Don't destroy me, I'm human too.'

I disagreed with Bakshi's last remark. I didn't think he was human at all.

'Destroying you is a good option,' Vroom said, 'but we have more worthwhile goals for now. I want to do a deal with you. We bury this issue and in return you do something for us.'

'What kind of thing?' Bakshi said.

'One, I want to have control of the call centre for the next two hours. I need to get on the Tannoy,' said Vroom.

'Why? Will you announce this email?' Bakshi said.

'No, you moron. It's to save jobs at the call centre. Can I use the Tannoy?'

'Yes. What else?'

'I want you to write out a resignation letter for Shyam and me. Layoffs or not, we are leaving Connexions.'

'Are you guys leaving right now?' the girls said.

'Yes. Shyam and I are going to start a small website design business. Right, Shyam?' Vroom said.

'Yes,' I said. Wow! I thought.

'Good. And this time, no one will take the credit for our websites except ourselves,' Vroom said and slapped Bakshi's face. Bakshi's face turned sixty degrees from the impact. He held his cheek but remained silent, apart from one tiny, dry sob. His facial expression had a combination of 90 per cent pain and 10 per cent shame.

'May I?' I said.

'Be my guest,' Vroom said.

Slap! I gave Bakshi's face a good slap too and it swung sixty degrees in the other direction.

'So you'll write the resignation letter, OK?' Vroom said.

'OK,' Bakshi said, rubbing his cheek. 'But Esha will delete the email, right?'

'Wait. We're not finished. Our business will require start-up capital, so we need a severance package of six months' salary,' Vroom said.

'I can't do six months. It's unprecedented for agents,' Bakshi said.

'New Delhi TV or *Times of India*, you pick,' Vroom said.

'Six months is possible. Good managers break precedents,' Bakshi said. I guess no amount of slaps could halt his jargon.

'Nice. Lastly, I want you to retract the rightsizing proposal. Ask Boston to postpone the layoffs to try a new sales-driven recovery plan for Connexions.'

'I can't do that,' Bakshi said.

Vroom lifted his mobile phone and put it in front of Bakshi's face.

'I'll make sure all of India knows your name by tomorrow,' Vroom said. 'There are agents with kids, families, responsibilities. You can't just fire them.'

'Give me half an hour. I'll set up a call with Boston,' Bakshi said.

'Good. We'll bury the email. But make sure you get the hell out of this country as fast as you can. We need a new boss, a normal, decent, inspiring human being and not a slimy, bloodsucking goofball with a fancy degree.'

Bakshi nodded while continuously wiping the sweat from his face.

'Good. Anything else? Did you have something to ask me about my monitor?' Vroom said.

'Monitor? What monitor?' Bakshi said.

5.20 a.m.

Bakshi gave Vroom the key to the broadcast room and then got straight on the phone to Boston to arrange a management meeting. I had never seen him work so efficiently.

Vroom went to the broadcast room and switched on the mikes while I went to the main computer bay to check for sound quality.

'Hello, everyone. May I have your attention, please? This is Vroom, from the strategic group.' His voice echoed through Connexions and all the agents looked up at the speakers while still talking to their customers.

'Sorry to bother you, but we have an emergency. This is about the lay-offs. Can you please disconnect all your calls,' the speaker said.

Everyone heard the word layoffs and a thousand calls ended at the same time. New calls flashed, but no one picked them up. Vroom continued:

'Idiots have been managing this place up until now and it's because of their mistakes that more than a third of you will lose your jobs tonight. It doesn't seem fair to me, does it seem fair to you?'

There was no response.

'Come on, guys, I want to hear you. Do I have your support to save your jobs and this call centre?'

The agents all looked at each other. There was a weak 'yes'.

'Louder, guys, all together. Do I have your support?' Vroom said.

'Yes!' a collective scream rocked Connexions.

Vroom continued in a firmer voice. 'Thank you. My friends, I need your support. Tell me, are you ready to work hard for the next two hours?'

'Yes!' a collective voice came back as Vroom paused to take a breath.

'Good, then listen. This call centre will survive only if we can increase our call traffic, and my plan is to *scare* the Americans into calling us. Tell them that terrorists have hit America with a new computer virus that threatens to take their country down. The only way they can stay safe is to keep calling us to report their status. We'll do it like this: pull out every customer number you have and call them. I'll send you a call script on email in the next five minutes, but until then, dig out those numbers,' Vroom said.

Noise levels rose in the main bay as hundreds of localised conversations took place simultaneously. Nobody was sure if the plan would work, but people were willing to try anything to avoid losing their jobs.

Vroom and I returned to our bay. He typed furiously on his computer and after a few minutes tapped on my shoulder.

'Check your email,' Vroom said and pointed to my screen.

I opened my inbox. Vroom had sent the same email with a script to everyone in the call centre. It explained the problem with the virus and that customers could check to see if it had affected them by carrying out a simple MS Word test. They were asked to call in every four to six hours.

Vroom grinned and winked at me as I finished reading the email.

'What's with the MS Word trick?' I said.

'Try it, open a Word file,' Vroom said.

I opened an empty Word document and typed in =rand (200,99).

As soon as I pressed Enter, 200 pages of text popped out. It was spooky, and went something like this:

The quick brown fox jumps over the lazy dog. The quick brown fox jumps over the lazy dog. The quick brown fox jumps over the lazy dog. The quick brown fox jumps over the lazy dog. The quick brown . . .

'This is unbelievable. What is it?' I asked.

'It's a bug in MS Word. Nothing is perfect. Now just wait and watch,' Vroom said.

Vroom's email reached 1,000 mailboxes and agents read it immediately. Within minutes, agents were doing a job they knew only too well: calling people to deliver a message as fast as possible. I left my seat and passed by the main bay. I picked up random sentences from the conversations.

'Hello, Mr Williams, sorry to disturb you on Thanksgiving. I am calling from Western Computers with an urgent message. America is under a virus attack,' one agent said.

'Yes, sir. According to our records your computer has been affected . . .' said another.

'Just keep calling us. Every four to six hours,' said one as she ended the call.

The more aggressive agents went a step further: 'And I want you to tell all your friends and relatives. Yes, they can call us too.'

Some customers panicked and needed reassurance: 'No problem. We will save this country. The evil forces will never succeed.'

A thousand agents, four minutes to a call—we could do 30,000 calls in two hours. If they called us every six hours, we would have over 100,000 calls a day. Even if it only lasted a week, we would hit our targets for the next two months. Hopefully, with a new manager and extra sales effort, Connexions could be on its way to recovery, and no one would lose their job.

Vroom came looking for me in the main bay and we went back to WASG. Vroom signalled me into the conference room.

'The response is amazing. We've only been calling for thirty minutes and traffic is up five times already,' Vroom said.

'Rocking, man,' I said. 'But why've you called me here?'

'We have to discuss the third private agenda.'

'What's that?' I said.

'The third agenda is for you. Don't you want Priyanka back?'

'No, Priyanka and I are over,' I said.

'Be honest, dude. You spoke to God and everything.'

I looked down. Vroom waited until I said something.

'It doesn't matter if I want her or not. Look at my competition. How am I going to succeed against Mr Perfect Match Ganesh?'

'See, that's the problem. We all think he's Mr Perfect, but nobody is perfect.'

'Yeah, right. A house, a car that costs more than ten years of my salary, freaking working for the world's top company—I don't see much imperfection in that.'

'Everyone has a flaw, dude. The trick is to find a flaw in Ganesh.'

'Well, how are we ever going to do that? And even if we find a flaw in him, what's the point? He's so good, Priyanka will still go for him,' I said.

'At least she will know she isn't making the perfect trade-off,' Vroom said.

I remained silent for two minutes. 'Yes, but how do we find Ganesh's flaw?' I said and looked at my watch. It was 5.30 a.m. 'The shift is over soon. What are you planning to do? Hire a detective in Seattle?' I said, my voice irritated.

'Don't give up, Shyam,' Vroom said and patted my shoulder.

'I'm trying to forget Priyanka, but if you search within me there is still pain. Don't make it worse, Vroom.'

'Wow, what drama. Search within me, there is pain,' Vroom laughed.

'Let's go back to the bay,' I said.

'Hey, wait a minute. You just said *search*.'

'Yes, search within me, there is still pain. Pretty cheesy, I know. Why?'

'Search. That's what we can do. Google will be our detective. Let's do a search on his name and see what comes out. There may be a few surprises.'

'What? You want to do a search for Ganesh?'

'Yes, but we need his full name. Let's find out his college as well. I think he got his Masters in computers in the US,' he said. 'Come on, let's go.'

'Where?' I said, even as I let myself get dragged along.

'To the WASG bay,' Vroom said.

Priyanka was on the phone. After she had ended a call Vroom spoke to her.

'Hey, Priyanka, quick question. My cousin also did a Masters in computers in the US. Which college did Ganesh go to?'

'Huh? Wisconsin, I think,' she said.

'Really. Let me email my cousin and ask him if it's the same one. What's Ganesh's full name by the way?'

'Ganesh Gupta,' Priyanka said as she prepared to make another call.

'Oooh. Mrs Priyanka Gupta,' Esha said, putting on a smart voice and laughing. Priyanka's new name sent ripples of pain down my rib cage.

'Cool. Keep calling,' Vroom said and went back to his seat.

As Vroom's monitor was broken, he took control of my computer. He searched for the following terms on google.com:

ganesh gupta drunk Wisconsin
ganesh gupta fines Wisconsin
ganesh gupta girlfriend

Several links popped out, but there was nothing we could make much sense or use of.

'Damn, what a boring guy. Let me try again,' Vroom said.

ganesh gupta fail
ganesh gupta party
ganesh gupta drugs

Nothing interesting emerged.

'Forget it, man. He was probably the head boy at school,' I said.

'You bet, one of those teacher's pet types,' Vroom said, letting out a frustrated breath. 'I give up. I'm sure if I type something like "ganesh gupta microsoft award" plenty of things will pop out, achiever that he is.'

More links popped out. We clicked through a few, and then we hit on one with his picture. It was Ganesh's online album.

'Damn, it is him, with his mates,' Vroom said and clicked on the link.

The link opened to a web page titled 'Microsoft Award party photos'. The party was at Ganesh's house. Ganesh had won some developer award at Microsoft and a couple of his friends had come to his house to celebrate.

'Look at the slideshow,' I said as Vroom selected the option. We looked up once to confirm the girls were still busy with their calls.

As the picture flicked onto the screen we saw a garden party full of Indian people. On the tables there was enough food to feed a small town.

'Hey, I think we've found something. Check out our man,' Vroom said. He pointed to one of the photos in which Ganesh held a beer glass.

'What's the big deal?' I said. It was hardly scandalous to hold a glass of beer. Priyanka herself could knock back ten if they were free.

'Check out Ganesh's head,' Vroom said.

'What?' I said. I looked closer and then I saw it. 'Oh no,' I said.

Ganesh had a bald spot in the middle of his head. It was the size of a Happy Meal burger and had caught the camera's flashlight.

'Unbelie—' I said.

'Shhh!' Vroom said. 'Did you see that? He has perfect hair in the Statue of Liberty picture.'

'Are all his photos in this album like this?' I said.

'Yes, sir,' Vroom said and flicked through the slideshow. One boring picture after another followed, but wherever Ganesh was, so was the shiny spot.

Vroom reclined on his chair with a proud expression. 'As I said, sir, no one is perfect. Apart from Google, of course.'

I looked at the screen and back at Vroom. 'So, now what?' I said.

'Now we invite the ladies for a viewing,' Vroom said and grinned.

'No, that's not right . . .' I said, but it was too late.

'Esha, Radhika, Priyanka. Do you want to see some more Ganesh pictures? Come here quickly,' Vroom said.

The girls dropped their phone calls. Esha and Radhika stood up.

'Where, where? Show us,' Esha said.

'What are you talking about?' Priyanka said and came over to our side.

'The power of the Internet. We found an online album. Come and see what your new house is like,' Vroom said. He kept quiet about the shiny spot so that the girls could see it for themselves.

'Nice pad,' Esha said, 'but where's Ganesh? Let me guess,' she said and touched the monitor with her finger. 'Here, this one, no. But wait, he's a baldie. Is he the elder brother?'

Priyanka looked closer. 'No, that's Ganesh,' she said, her mouth open. I could sense that the wind had been knocked out of her sails.

'But I didn't notice the bald spot in the photo you showed us, Priyanka,' Esha said. Radhika squeezed Esha's arm. Esha stopped talking.

Priyanka began flipping through the images on the screen. She didn't notice, but her hair was falling on my shoulders as she bent over. It felt nice.

But Priyanka wasn't feeling nice. She brought out the Statue of Liberty picture and we looked at it again. Ganesh had perfect hair.

'Maybe the guy is Ganesh's elder brother,' Radhika said.

'No. Ganesh doesn't have a brother. He only has one sister,' Priyanka said, her face distraught at the fact that he had deceived her like that. Such a tiny lie could lead to bigger lies.

There was silence for a few seconds.

'Well, it doesn't really matter much, eh? What's a bit of smooth skin between the true love of two souls?' Vroom said. I clamped my jaws shut to prevent a laugh escaping. 'Let's go back, people, enough fun. Don't forget to keep calling,' Vroom said.

Priyanka retraced her steps in slow motion. She went back to her seat and took out her mobile phone. She dialled a long number, probably long distance. This call was going to be fun—I only wished I could tap into it.

'Hello, Ganesh,' Priyanka said in a direct voice. 'Listen, I can't talk for long. I just want to check on something . . . yes, just one question . . . actually I was just surfing the Internet . . .' Priyanka said and got up from her seat. She moved to the corner of the room where I could no longer hear her.

I made a few calls. Priyanka returned after ten minutes and tossed her cellphone on the desk.

Esha jiggled her eyebrows up and down, as if to ask, 'What's up?'

'It *is* him in the online pictures,' Priyanka said. 'He didn't have much to say. He said his mother asked him to touch up his hair slightly in the Statue of Liberty snap as it would help in the arranged marriage market.'

'Oh no,' Esha wailed.

'He apologised several times saying he'd been against tampering with the picture, but had to agree when his mother insisted.'

'Did the apologies seem genuine?' Radhika said.

'Yes, I think so. He said he understood how I must feel and that he was ready to apologise in front of my family as well.'

'Well, then it's OK. What difference does it make? You don't really care about him being bald, do you?' Radhika said. 'Practically all men become bald in a few years anyway. It's not like you can do anything about it then.'

'That's true,' Priyanka said in a mellow voice. I could see her relenting.

'Yeah, it doesn't matter. Just make sure he wears a cap at the wedding—unless you want to touch up all the wedding pictures,' Vroom said and chuckled. Esha and I looked down to suppress our grins.

'Shut up, Vroom,' Radhika said.

'Sorry, I'm being mean. Honestly, it's no big deal, Priyanka. No one's perfect, we all know that, don't we? So, let's get back to our calls.'

6.00 a.m.

For the next half-hour we focused on making calls to save Connexions.

At 6.30 a.m. I went up to the main bay. Team leaders huddled around me as they gave me the news. The incoming calls had already shot up, even though we hadn't expected the big boost for another six hours. Some customers had called us several times an hour.

Vroom and I went to Bakshi's office with some of the senior team leaders. He had arranged an urgent video conference call with the Boston office. Bakshi supported us as we presented the new call data, insights into the call traffic and potential new sources of revenue. After a twenty-minute video discussion, Boston agreed to a two-month reprieve before deciding on layoffs. They also agreed to evaluate the possibility of sending top team leaders on a short-term sales assignment to Boston.

Reassured that Connexions was safe for now, I returned to my desk while Vroom went outside to clean the Qualis before the driver woke up. I had told Vroom I wanted to slip away—no goodbyes, no hugs and no promises to meet, especially in front of Priyanka. Vroom agreed and said he would be ready outside with his bike at 6.50 a.m.

The girls stopped their calls at 6.45 a.m. Everyone began to log out so they could be in time for the Qualis, which would be waiting at the gate at 7.00 a.m.

'I'm so excited. Radhika is moving into my place,' Esha said.

'Really?' I said.

'Yes, I am,' Radhika said. 'And Military Uncle is going to recommend a lawyer friend. I need a good, tough divorce lawyer.'

'Don't you want to try and work it out?' Priyanka said.

'We'll see. I am in no mood to compromise. And I'm not going back to his house now, for sure. My mother-in-law will be making her own breakfast.'

'And after that, I'm taking Radhika to Chandigarh for the weekend,' Esha said and smiled.

Everyone was busy making plans. I excused myself on the pretext of going to the water cooler for a drink, so I could leave the office from there.

6.47 a.m.

I reached the water cooler and bent towards the tap to take my last drink at the call centre. As I finished, I stood up to find Priyanka behind me.

'Hi,' she said. 'Leaving?'

'Oh, hi. Yes, I'm going back on Vroom's bike,' I said and wiped my mouth.

'I'll miss you,' she said. 'I'm sorry about the way things turned out.'

'Don't be sorry,' I said, shaking my fingers dry. 'It's more my fault than yours. I understand that. I acted like a loser.'

'Shyam, you know how Vroom said just because India is poor it doesn't mean you stop loving it?' Priyanka said.

'What?' I blinked at the change of topic. 'Oh yes. And I agree, it is our country after all.'

'Yes, we love India because it's ours. But do you know the other reason why we don't stop loving it?'

'Why?'

'Because it isn't completely India's fault that we are behind. Yes, some of our past leaders could have done things differently, but now we have the potential and we know it.'

'Good point,' I said. I found it strange that she should talk about nationalism at what was possibly our last moment together.

I nodded and started walking away from her. 'Anyway, I think Vroom will be waiting . . .' I said.

'I applied the same logic to something else,' she said. 'I thought, this is the same as my Shyam, who may not be successful now, but it doesn't mean he doesn't have the potential, and it sure as hell doesn't mean I've stopped loving him.'

I stood there dumbstruck. I fumbled for words and finally spoke shakily:

'You know what, Priyanka? You say such great lines that even though I've tried to hate you all night, it's impossible. And I know I should hate you and that I should move on, because I can't offer you what Mr Microsoft can—'

'Ganesh,' she interrupted me. 'Not Mr Microsoft.'

'Yes, whatever,' I kept talking, without pausing to breathe. 'I can't offer you what Ganesh can. No way could I ever buy a Lexus. Maybe a Maruti 800 one day, but that's about it.'

She smiled. 'Really? An 800? With or without AC?' she said.

'Shut up. I'm trying to say something deep and you find it funny,' I said.

She laughed again, gently. I wiped a tear from my right eye and she raised her hand to wipe the tear from my left eye.

'Anyway, it's over between us, Priyanka, and I know it. I'll get over it soon. I know, I know,' I said, talking more to myself.

She waited until I had composed myself. I bent over to splash my face with water at the cooler. 'Anyway, where's your wedding going to be? Your mum will probably blow all her cash on a big gig,' I said, straightening up.

'In some five-star hotel, I'm sure. You'll come, won't you?'

'I don't know,' I said.

'What do you mean, you don't know? It'll be so strange if you aren't there.'

'I don't want to be there and feel sad. Anyway, what's so strange if I'm not there?'

'Well, it will be a little strange if the groom isn't there at his own wedding,' Priyanka said.

I froze as I heard those words, rewinding her last sentence in my head.

'What . . . what did you just say?' I said.

She pinched my cheek and imitated me: 'What . . . what did you just say?'
I stood there speechless.

'But don't think I'm going to let you go that easily. One day I want my
800 with AC,' she said and laughed.

'What?' I said.

'You heard me. I want to marry you, Shyam,' Priyanka said.

I thought I would jump for joy, but mostly I was shocked. And even
though I wanted to hug, cry and laugh at the same time, a firm voice, like a
guard inside me, asked, What's this all about? Hell, I didn't want pity.

'What are you saying, Priyanka? That you would choose me over
Ganesh? Is this a sympathy decision?'

'My life's biggest decision can't be a sympathy decision. I've thought
about it. Ganesh is great, but . . . the whole touching up of the photo bothers
me. He's an achiever in his own right, so why did he have to lie?'

'So you're rejecting him because he's bald? My hair isn't reliable, either.'

'No. I'm not rejecting him because he's bald. Most men go bald one day,
it's horrible, I know,' she said and ruffled my hair. 'He might be fine in most
ways,' she continued, 'but the point is, he lied. And for me that's a clue as to
what sort of person he is. I don't want to spend my life with a person like
that. In fact, I don't want to spend my life with a person I don't know very
well beforehand. That's one part of my decision. The other is the big part.'

'What?' I said.

'I love you. Because you are the only person in the world I can be myself
with. And because you are the only person who knows all my flaws and still
loves me completely. I hope,' she said, with a quivering voice.

I didn't say anything.

'And even if the world says I'm cold, there is a part of me that's sentimental, irrational and romantic. Do I really care about money? Only
because people tell me I should. Hell, I prefer truck driver dhabas over five-
star hotels. Deep inside, I am just a girl who wants to be with her favourite
boy, because like you, this girl is a person who needs a lot of love.'

'Love? I need a lot of love?' I said.

'Of course you do. Everyone does. It's funny that we never say it. It's OK
to scream, "I'm starving," if you are hungry; it's OK to make a fuss and say,
"I'm so sleepy," if you are tired; but somehow we cannot say, "I need some
more love." Why can't we say it, Shyam? It's just as basic a need.'

I looked at her. Whenever she delivers these deep, philosophical lines, I
get horribly attracted to her. The guard inside reminded me to be firm.

'Priyanka?'

'Yes,' she said, sniffling.

'I love you,' I said.

'I love you, too,' Priyanka said.

'Thanks. However, Priyanka, I can't marry you. Sorry to say this, but my answer to your mind-blowing proposal is no,' I said.

'What?' Priyanka said as her eyes opened wide in disbelief. The guard inside me was in full charge.

'I can't marry you. I'm a new person tonight, and this new person needs to make a new life and find new respect for himself. You chose Ganesh, and he's fine. You have an option for a new life and you don't really need me, so maybe it's better this way,' I said.

'I still love you, Shyam, and only you. Please don't do this,' she said, coming closer to me.

'Sorry,' I said and moved three steps backwards. 'I can't. I'm not your spare wheel. I appreciate you coming back, but I think I'm ready to move on.'

She just stood there and cried. My heart felt weak, but my head was strong.

'Bye, Priyanka.' I gingerly patted her shoulder and left.

6.59 a.m.

'What the hell kept you?' Vroom said, sitting on his bike at the entrance.

'Sorry, man, Priyanka met me at the water cooler,' I said and sank onto the pillion seat.

'And?' Vroom said.

'Nothing. Just goodbye and all. Oh, and she wanted to get back together and marry me, she said. Can you believe it?'

Vroom turned to me. 'Really? What did you say?'

'I said no,' I said coolly.

'What?' Vroom said.

As we were talking, Radhika, Esha and Military Uncle came out of the main entrance into the wintry sunshine.

'Hi, you guys still here?' Radhika said.

'Shyam just said no to Priyanka. She wanted to marry him, but he said no.'

'What?' Radhika and Esha spoke in unison.

'Hey, guys, chill out. I did what I needed to do to get some respect in my life. Stop bothering me,' I said.

The Qualis arrived and the driver pressed the horn.

'We aren't bothering you—it's your life. Let's go, Esha,' Radhika said and gave me a dirty look. She turned to Esha as they walked to the Qualis.

'Where's Priyanka, madam? We are late,' the driver said.

'She's coming. She's on the phone to her mother. Ganesh's parents are going over for breakfast and her mother is making hot parathas,' Radhika said, loud enough for me to hear.

The driver started the Qualis. Priyanka came dashing out of the main entrance, avoided me and went straight to the front seat. Then the driver turned the Qualis round.

As they began to move off, Military Uncle looked out from his window and said something. I could only lip-read but I thought he said, 'You bloody idiot.'

Before I could react, the Qualis was gone.

Vroom stubbed out his cigarette.

'Oh no. I *am* a bloody idiot. I let her go,' I said.

'Uh-huh,' Vroom said as he put on his helmet.

'Is that a yes? You think I am a total idiot?'

'You are your best judge,' Vroom said, dragging the bike with his feet.

'Vroom, what have I done? If she reaches home and has parathas with Ganesh's family, it is all over. I'm such a moron,' I said.

'Stop dancing around. I have to get going,' Vroom said.

'Vroom, we have to catch the Qualis. Can you go fast enough?'

Vroom removed his helmet and laughed. 'Arc you insulting me? Do you doubt that I can catch that wreck of a Qualis? I am so hurt, man.'

'Vroom, let's go. Please,' I said and pushed his shoulders.

'No. First you apologise for doubting my driving abilities.'

'I'm sorry, boss, I'm sorry,' I said. 'Now move, Schumacher.'

Vroom kick-started his bike, and in a few seconds we had zipped out of the call centre. The main road was getting busier as the morning progressed, but Vroom still managed a top speed of ninety. On the road into the city, we dodged cars, scooters, autos, school buses and newspaper hawkers.

Four minutes later, I noticed a white Qualis at a distant traffic signal.

'It must be that one,' I pointed out.

Just as Vroom moved ahead, a herd of goats decided to cross the road and fifty of them blocked our way.

'Damn, where did they come from?' I said.

'This urban jungle of Gurgaon was a village until recently; the goats are probably asking where did *we* come from,' Vroom said.

'Shut up and do something,' I said.

'There's only one option,' Vroom said and smiled.

'Wha—' I said as Vroom lunged his bike up onto the road divider. 'Are you crazy?' I said.

'No, you're crazy to let her go,' Vroom said and started riding along the divider. The goats and drivers looked over at us in shock. Vroom dodged round the streetlights until we'd passed the herd, and once we were back on the road he accelerated to 100. One minute later our bike was level with the Qualis at a red light. I got off and tapped the front window. Priyanka looked away, so I banged the glass with my palm.

She opened the window. 'What is it? We don't want to buy anything,' Priyanka said as if I was a roadside vendor.

'I'm an idiot,' I said.

'And?' Priyanka said.

Everyone in the Qualis rolled down their windows to look at me.

'I'm a moron. I'm stupid, insane and nuts. Please, I want us to be together.'

'Oh really? What about the new man who needs respect?' Priyanka said.

'I didn't know what I was saying. What does one do with respect? I can't keep it in my pocket,' I said.

'So you want to keep me in your pocket?' Priyanka said.

'You're already in every pocket—of my life, my heart, my mind, my soul— please come back. Will you come back?' I said as the light turned yellow.

'Hmm. Let's see . . .' Priyanka said.

'Priyanka, please answer fast.'

'I don't know. Let me think. Meet me at the next red light, OK? Let's go, Driver *ji*,' she said as the light turned green. The driver took off at full speed.

'What did she say?' Vroom said as I sat on the bike.

'She'll answer at the next red light. Let's go.'

There was a mini traffic jam at the next red light, so I got off the bike and ran past a few vehicles to reach the Qualis. I tapped the window again but Priyanka wasn't there.

'Where is she?' I asked the driver, who shrugged his shoulders at me.

I looked inside the Qualis. Radhika and Esha shrugged their shoulders, too; she wasn't in there.

Someone came up from behind and hugged me. I turned round to look at Priyanka.

'I didn't know what I was saying at the water cooler,' I said.

'Shut up and hug me,' Priyanka said and opened her arms.

Our eyes met, and even though I wanted to say so much, our eyes did all the talking. I hugged her for a few seconds and then she kissed me. Our lips

locked, and every passenger in the traffic jam looked on, enjoying the spectacle. After six months apart there was a lot of pent-up feeling. Vroom and
everyone from the Qualis surrounded us and began to clap and whistle, then
all the vehicles on the road joined in, applauding with their horns. But I
couldn't see them or hear them. All I could see was Priyanka, and all I could
hear was my inner voice saying, 'Kiss her, kiss her and kiss her more.'

Well, guys, that's how that night, and my story, ends. We couldn't know
what, how or when things would happen, but that's what life's like: uncertain, screwed up at times, but still fun. However, let me tell you where we
were one month after that night. Vroom and I started our website design
company with the seed capital Bakshi had given us. We called it the Black
Sheep Web Design Company. In a month, we had only managed to get one
local order, but it helped us break even.

Esha gave up her modelling aspirations and continued to work at the call
centre, but now she works for a non-governmental organisation during the
day. Her job is to fundraise from the corporate sector and I heard she's doing
well. I guess male executives can't resist a hot woman asking for money for a
good cause. Apart from that, Vroom's asked her out for a coffee on a semi-
date—whatever that means—next week and I think she said yes.

Military Uncle got a visa for the US and went over to make amends with
his son. He hasn't come back, so things must be working out. Radhika is
fighting her divorce case with her husband and has moved in with Esha. She
is also planning to visit her own parents for a while. Anuj has apologised,
but Radhika is in no mood to relent yet.

Priyanka still works at Connexions, but in six months' time she plans to go
to college for an accelerated one-year B.Ed. We decided that marriage is at
least two years away. We meet often, but our first focus is her career. Her
mother faked three heart attacks when Priyanka said no to Ganesh, but
Priyanka yawned every single time until her mum gave up and closed the
Ganesh file.

So it looks like things are working out. As for me as a person, I still feel
the same for the most part. However, there is a difference. I used to feel I
was a good-for-nothing non-achiever. But that's not true. After all, I helped
save a lot of jobs at the call centre, I taught my boss a lesson, started my

own company, was chosen over a big-catch Indian groom from Seattle by a wonderful girl and now I've even written a whole book. This means that i) I can do whatever I really want, ii) God is always with me and iii) there is no such thing as a loser after all.

Epilogue

'Wow,' I said, 'some story that was.' She nodded, and took a sip of water from her bottle, holding it tight so it didn't spill in the moving train.

'Thank you,' I said, 'it made our night go by pretty quickly.'

I checked the time; it was close to 7 a.m. and our journey was almost over. Delhi was less than an hour away. The train was tearing through the night, and on the horizon I could see a streak of saffron light up the sky.

'So, did you like it?'

'Yes, it was fun. But it also made me think. I went through a similar phase to Shyam, at work and in my personal life. I wish I'd heard this story earlier—it might have made me do things differently.'

'There you go. It's one of those rare stories that's fun but can help you as well. And that's why I am asking you to share it. Are you ready to turn it into a book?' she said, replacing the cap on the water bottle.

'I guess. It will take some time, though,' I said.

'Of course. And I will give you all the people's details. Feel free to contact them if you want. Through which character will you tell the story?'

'Shyam. Like I said, his story's a lot like mine. I can relate to him because I had similar problems—my own dark side.'

'That's interesting,' she said. 'It's true, we all have a dark side—something we don't like, something that makes us angry and something we want to change about ourselves. The difference is how we choose to face it.'

I nodded. The train rocked in a soothing, gentle motion and we were silent until I spoke after a few minutes.

'Listen, sorry to say this, but there's one issue I think readers may have with this story.'

'What?'

'The conversation with God.'

She smiled. 'Where's the issue with that?' she said.

'Well, it's just that some people may not buy it. One has to present reality in a story. Readers always say, "Tell me what really happened." So in that context, how is God calling going to fit in?'

'Why? Don't you think that could happen?' she said, shifting in her seat. Her blanket moved, uncovering a book I hadn't noticed before.

'Well, I don't know. It obviously doesn't happen very often. I mean, things need to have a rational, scientific explanation.'

'Really? Does everything in life work that way?'

'I guess. Please try and understand,' I said. 'Calls from God don't happen often. How can I write about it?'

'OK, listen. I'm going to give you an alternative to God's phone call. A rational one, OK?' she said and put her bottle away.

'What alternative?' I said.

'Let's rewind a bit. So they drove into a pit and the Qualis was trapped, suspended by rods, right? Are you OK with that part?'

'Right. I can live with that,' I said.

'And then they felt the end was near. There was no hope in life, literally and figuratively. So let's just say that at that moment Military Uncle spoke up saying, "I noticed an unusual situation here, so I thought I'd just checkk on you guys."'

'That's exactly what God said,' I said.

'Correct. And from that point on, whatever God said, you can reword as if Military Uncle had said it—all the stuff about success, the inner call and all those other things.'

'Really? Is that what happened?' I said.

'No. I didn't say that. I just said you have the option to do that; so that everything appears more rational. Do you understand my point?'

'Yes,' I said.

'So, you choose whichever version you want in the main story. It will, after all, be your story.'

I nodded.

'But can I ask you one question?'

'Sure,' I said.

'Which of the two is a better story?'

I thought for a second.

'The one with God in it,' I said.

'Just like life. Rational or not, life is better with God in it.'

I reflected on her words for a few minutes. She became silent and I looked at her face. She looked even lovelier in the light of dawn.

'Well, it looks like we're nearly in Delhi,' she said and looked out. There were no more fields, only the houses in Delhi's border villages.

'Yeah, the trip is over,' I said. 'Thanks for everything, er, let me guess, Esha, right?' I stood up to shake her hand.

'Esha? Why did you think I was her?'

'Because you're so good-looking.'

'Thanks.' She laughed. 'But sorry, I'm not Esha.'

'So? Priyanka?' I said.

'No.'

'Don't tell me, Radhika?'

'No, I'm not Radhika, either,' she said.

'Well then, who are you?'

She just smiled.

That's when it struck me. She was a girl, she knew the full story, but she wasn't Esha, Priyanka or Radhika. Which meant that there was only one alternative left.

'So . . . that means . . . Oh my . . .' My whole body shook as I found it difficult to balance. Her face shone and our compartment was suddenly filled with bright sunlight. I looked at her and she smiled. Then I saw that the open book next to her was the English translation of a holy text. My eyes focused on a few lines on the page that lay open:

Always think of Me, become My devotee, worship Me and offer your homage unto Me. Thus you will come to Me without fail. I promise you this because you are My very dear friend.

'What?' I said as I felt my head spin. But she just smiled, raised her hand and placed it on my head.

'I just don't know what to say,' I said in the blinding light.

A sense of tiredness engulfed me and I closed my eyes.

When I opened them, the train had stopped and I knelt on the floor with my head down. The train was at Delhi station. The cacophony of porters, tea sellers and passengers rang in my ears. I slowly looked up at her seat, but she was gone.

'Sir, are you getting off on your own or do you need help?' A porter tapped my shoulder.

CHETAN BHAGAT

Born: New Delhi, April 22, 1972
Job: investment banker
Website: www.chetanbhagat.com

RD: What inspired you to write a novel in the midst of a successful, high-flying business career?

CB:While the investment banking life is exciting and challenging, it is very materially motivated. I felt there has to be more to life than my next bonus and so focused on something I love rather that what earns me the most. And that is how my first book was born. Like nature—out of love. I write fiction because I love entertaining people.

RD: Have you wanted to write for a long time?

CB: I have loved writing since my first four-line joke came out in the school magazine. I was so excited seeing my name in print, I would show the magazine to random people on buses!

RD: What inspired this particular book?

CB: It was the sudden transformation of the young Indian generation in the last ten years. Almost every middle-class person in India knows someone who works in a call centre at night. A nocturnal generation was too interesting a topic to miss.

RD: Are the characters based on particular people?

CB: Not really, though the main guy, Shyam, is based on me, in a phase of my life where I was stuck in my job and my boss was making my life miserable. It's all there in the book.

RD: I loved the character of the unpleasant Bakshi. Was he based on anyone?

CB: He was based on my stupid–evil boss in my previous job who killed my self-confidence for years. I thought maybe many other bosses are doing this to young people, so I wanted to warn my readers against these mean types.

RD: How did you set about researching the book?

CB: I visited several call centres and spent a lot of time with call-centre employees, including five of my first cousins and both my sisters-in-law. They used to tell interesting tales about their experiences. Finding out about this new industry and the people involved in it was one of the most rewarding things about writing *One Night at the Call Centre*.

RD: The book has a lot of humour. Do you find that difficult to write?

CB: It is my natural style of writing, so it was not hard. My literary talents are moderate, but the humour is my gift, I guess.

RD: What inspired you to bring God in as a character?

CB: I felt I had a message that was very important to give to the younger generation. Thus, it had to be given by an authority figure. And who better than God for some friendly advice? I have quite a spiritual bent as well, so some of it may have come from there.

RD: You say in one interview that you want your books to have a positive impact on Indian society. Could you explain a little more about that?

CB: Yes, this is a key goal. My first book is a funny look at education stress. I once heard from a kid who said that he had decided not to kill himself (because of poor grades) after reading my book, something he was planning to do otherwise. That kind of stuff shakes you up. I will always write to create some benefit for people. Hundreds have written to me that the *Call Centre* book restored their self-confidence. Having this is far more important than being internationally published or winning awards.

RD: Do you share Vroom's negative views on call centres?

CB: Yes. Call centres are good in the short-term, but the long-term effects on India's skill base may not be so positive. Of course, I am not as emotional about the issue as Vroom is.

RD: How long did it take you to write *Call Centre* and what is your writing schedule?

CB: It took me a year to write the book. Because I have a day job, I write mostly on weekends.

RD: You currently live in Hong Kong. Do you go back to India often? And do you miss it?

CB: I am in India as we speak! Yes, I come here a lot—once a month. Right now I am here in Mumbai to see the shooting of the Bollywood film based on *One Night at the Call Centre*. I miss India a lot.

RD: I read that you love cooking. What is your favourite meal?

CB: I love anything consisting of good bread and lots of dips. Lebanese and Italian antipasti are great.

RD: Could you tell us a little more about your interest in yoga?

CB: While I was going through having a bad boss I turned to yoga. It helped me a lot in terms of self-realisation and mental peace.

RD: Do you enjoy your new role as a best-selling author?

CB: Yes, God has chosen me out of nowhere and given me this gift. I don't, however, like the pressure to deliver that comes with it.

THE WATCHMAN © Robert Crais 2007
Published by Orion

AN IRISH COUNTRY DOCTOR ©2004, 2007 by Patrick Taylor
Published by Forge (USA) 2007
This book was previously published in 2004 under the title *The Apprenticeship of Doctor Laverty* by Insomniac Press, Toronto.

TRUE EVIL © 2006 by Greg Iles
Published by Hodder & Stoughton

ONE NIGHT AT THE CALL CENTRE © Chetan Bhagat 2005
Published by Transworld

The right to be identified as authors has been asserted by the following in accordance with sections 77 and 78 of the Copyright, Designs and Patents Act, 1988: Robert Crais, Patrick Taylor, Greg Iles, Chetan Bhagat.

Illustrations and Photos:
Page 4: Robert Crais © Patrik Giordino; Patrick Taylor © Sarah Taylor; page 5: Chetan Bhagat © chetanbhagat.com.
The Watchman: 6–8: image: Getty Images; illustration: Narrinder Singh @ velvet tamarind; page 142 © Patrik Giordino.
An Irish Country Doctor: 144–6: image: Getty Images; page 274 © Sarah Taylor. Page 275: Barmbrack © Anthony Blake/Anthony Blake Photo Library.
True Evil: 276–7 and page 453: © snake: Florida Images/Alamy.
One Night at the Call Centre: 454–6 : illustration: Javier Joaquain @ The Organisation; page 574 © chetanbhagat.com.
Dustjacket spine: Getty Images.

Acknowledgments: p. 187: excerpt from 'Storm on the Island' from *Poems 1965–1975* by Seamus Heaney. Copyright © 1980 by Seamus Heaney. Reprinted by permission of Farrar, Strauss and Giroux, LLC.
The Bhagvad Gita quote on page 573 is taken from www/krishna.com, copyright © The Bhaktivedanta Book Trust International, Inc. His Divine Grace A.C. Baktivedanta Swami Prabhupada, International Society for Krishna Consciousness.

Printed and bound by GGP Media GmbH, Pössneck, Germany

020-248 DJ0000-1